REAGAN'S
THIRD TERM

*How Four More Years
Saved the World and Reshaped America*

AN ALTERNATE HISTORY NOVEL

by

GIB KEARNEY

DOUGLAS & GILBERT BOOKS

"While I take inspiration from the past, like most Americans, I live for the future."

Ronald Wilson Reagan
40th President of the United States

Preface

Ronald Reagan was on record as opposing the 22nd Amendment, which limited a president to two terms.

When he left office, the Cold War was ending, congress was grid-locked, and much of what he had hoped to achieve as president remained unfinished.

But what if something unimaginable had happened during his last year in office? Perhaps an event of such magnitude that congress had no choice but to repeal the 22nd Amendment, allowing him a third term as president?

With four more years, how might Reagan have not just met the crisis at hand, but also used his mandate to remake America with the support of a united people and government?

This book answers these questions — and more.

How would President Reagan have handled actual events and crises that occurred during the first Bush presidency? Saddam Hussein's invasion of Kuwait? An environmental disaster in Alaska? Noriega's Panama, Tiananmen Square, Muammar Qaddafi and the rise of Islamic extremism?

How might he have responded to a Soviet *coup d'état* and a hot war with an expansionist USSR? A wartime economy? A radicalized Teachers Union threatening to shut down the nation's schools? Treason in the US Congress? An attack on the Pentagon?

Who would he select as his Vice President and cabinet for a third term?

What would Reagan have done on issues like abortion? Welfare reform? Guns? The war on drugs? School prayer? Two additional appointments to the Supreme Court?

And what of his legacy?

How might President Reagan have provided hope, guidance, and a new future to the GOP by personally choosing a successor who would follow in his footsteps, building coalitions, and unifying future generations of Americans in support of the conservative revolution?

And who might that person have been?

Reagan's Third Term is an invitation to dream.

In *Twelfth Night*, Shakespeare wrote that some are born great, some achieve greatness, and some have greatness thrust upon them.

All three were true for Reagan. He was a great president, who met the challenges, expanded the frontiers, renewed our faith, and left us better than before.

But what if his story had been allowed to continue?

As Ronald Reagan was fond of saying, "The best is yet to come."

This is the story of how that came to be.

Gib Kearney
Seattle, Washington

From Russia With Love

It was Valentine's Day, 1988.

Weather had been chilly that day in Washington, never rising above the mid-30s. A light wind gusted along cold streets below the clear skies of the nation's capital. Many streets were already vacant, abandoned hours before to the cold and the darkness.

Ron and Nancy had just finished dinner in their private living quarters at the White House. The meal was an old favorite: roast beef with Yorkshire pudding—prepared to perfection. Normally they would have had something less fancy, such as a chicken hash, but this was Valentine's Day—a holiday of sorts, so the first couple decided to partake of a special treat. The meal was topped off with Monkey Bread, the President's favorite. This dessert was created with a secret family recipe that had come to town with the Reagans, and would leave with them in less than a year.

Presidential duties had been typically light that Sunday, allowing the couple time to reflect on the bittersweet nature of the day. Although the Reagans had enjoyed their time in Washington, they were also anxious to return home to "the Ranch," and to the warmth and tranquility of retired life in California.

Valentine's Day always meant much to them, and their love for one another had only deepened and matured with each passing year. Hard to believe they would be celebrating their 36th anniversary in just a few weeks. This one would be their last as residents of 1600 Pennsylvania Avenue.

Nancy thought back to how they first met in 1949. Ronnie, however, was thinking ahead to their 40th anniversary, trying to remember what the official gift selection was.

"The 50th is gold—that's an easy one," he thought to himself, but the 40th? His brow furrowed as he became lost in thought, and as a result was caught somewhat off guard when his old friend and Secretary of State George Schultz entered unannounced, accompanied by CIA Director William Webster.

Reagan's mind ran through the possible reasons for the interruption: another embarrassing leak breaking in the morning papers? Some internal cabinet squabble that had one of "the boys" threatening to resign?

What could possibly be important enough to warrant such an interruption on a Sunday evening?

Feeling impatience rising, Reagan quickly reprogrammed himself. He decided to preempt the situation with some of his trademark good humor.

"Well, gentlemen," he said with a grin, "You're a bit late for dinner. But I think they might offer you some coffee and dessert if you're willing to roll up your sleeves and help out with the dishes."

The quip was answered with grim expressions.

"Mr President," said Webster, "there's been a coup in the Soviet Union."

No News Is Not Good News

Reagan's response was immediate. "Gorbachev?"

"We have no idea," replied Schultz. "This appears to have started late last night — early morning our time — and we've had no communication with those now in charge, nor word from any of our people — including the Ambassador."

"Communications have been severed," Webster added. "But we're pulling together details … bits and pieces … only now, in the last couple of hours."

The President let out an exasperated sigh. "Options?"

"We will be working through the night," Webster said. "You will have a full briefing for the cabinet meeting tomorrow at 8 o'clock. Until then, we have no options upon which we can act."

"That's where you're wrong," Reagan replied. "Our first and last option is always the same: prayer. Good night, gentlemen, and may God be with us."

As Schultz and Webster exited, Nancy put her hand on Ronnie's, and immediately he felt her strength flowing into him.

No words were spoken — or needed — as they strolled through the White House. Staff instructions were to afford them their privacy as they walked the halls and chambers, with the President stopping periodically to look upon the portraits of those who had preceded him in office. There he saw great men like Washington, Lincoln, and FDR, whose presidencies and the nation they served had been tested by war and turmoil.

Back in the residential chambers, the President prepared for bed. At the last minute, he reached for his Bible.

Nancy watched her husband read the scriptures to himself. She knew Ronnie had favorite passages, and that he frequently turned to them for guidance and strength in both good times and bad.

The President read for perhaps ten minutes, and then closed his eyes in silent prayer.

Reagan then got into bed, pulled up the covers and fell asleep almost immediately. He slept soundly, a look of calm upon his face, while Mrs Reagan tossed and turned throughout the night.

The President awoke completely refreshed, ready to take on the world — which was good, because very soon that's exactly what destiny had in store for him.

The Bear Is Back

It was a grim and gray Monday morning as the President and his team assembled to discuss the tumultuous events of the weekend, and determine how the United States should respond.

The group convened in the "Situation Room," a small space in the basement of the White House reserved for addressing critical matters of international significance. This one fit bill. The mood was somber and tense. Representatives from the military, intelligence services, state department, and the cabinet were all in attendance.

CIA Director Webster began the meeting with an overview that provided some background but very little in the way of new information:

• Gorbachev and his people were being held at an unknown location, most likely in the capital region. It was probable they would soon be separated and sent to different locations.

• Jack Matlock, the US ambassador, had been expelled and the embassy had been shut down and sealed off. Matlock and his staff were safe, and on their way back to America, following a debriefing in Germany.

• Yuri Dubinin, the Soviet Ambassador, was holed up at their embassy in Washington, not taking any calls. In fact, no Soviet representative of any stature anywhere was available for comment.

• The coup had apparently been spearheaded by former Soviet Defense Minister Sergey Sokolov, with the full support of acting Defense Minister Dmitry Yazov and the KGB.

Up until the coup, Sokolov had been serving in the Politburo. There he had a reputation as a hawk and an outspoken critic of Gorbachev. It was Sokolov who had commanded Soviet ground forces during the invasion of Afghanistan in 1979.

• Although the military was clearly in control, the new administration included a smattering of civilians—mostly politicians and businessmen—probably to suggest broader popular support.

All figures in the new regime were well known to US intelligence services. Webster provided a quick executive summary for each, systematically presented in alphabetical order:

Oleg Baklanov: Aged 55. Businessman with connections to the space program. Bright, outspoken, but cagey. Party member with vested financial interests in a state-run economy.

Vladimir Kryuchkov: Head of the KGB; aged 63. A truly ruthless character. Started his career in the diplomatic services, earning his wings helping to crush the 1956 democratic uprising in Hungary. Officially joined the KGB in 1967; was a favorite of Andropov. No doubt he was unhappy with Gorbachev's reforms. Definitely not somebody you'd want to turn your back on.

Valentin Pavlov: A 50-year-old banker from Moscow. An economist, but something of a nut case. Doesn't seem too stable, but is well connected in financial circles.

Boris Pugo: Also 50. Party boss from Latvia. An odd choice; a run-of-the-mill political hack. Not too bright, with a serious drinking problem.

Vasily Starodubtsev: 56 years old; background in agriculture. Has received various awards and citations for meeting production goals based on falsified data. A shifty character.

Gennady Yanayev: A 50-year-old career politician with connections going back to Khrushchev. Worked with all the old hardliner regimes including Brezhnev, Andropov, and Chernenko. Probably being groomed for the president's position, or as a backup if Sokolov doesn't work out.

Webster continued with his presentation:

"It seems that the coup happened fairly quickly, with only limited opposition—although there are reports of some skirmishes between the different, and possibly competing factions."

Reagan sat attentively and listened with deep concentration, nodding on occasion. When the name Sokolov was mentioned, Reagan looked puzzled. "I thought he was a goner? After that screw up with the kid from Germany."

The President was indeed correct. The previous spring, Mathias Rust, a 19-year-old from West Germany, had succeeded in flying a private plane undetected through 400 miles of Soviet air space before landing safely in the middle of Red Square.

"Apparently retired life didn't suit him," quipped Admiral William Crowe, Chairman of the Joint Chiefs of Staff. "But as we know, there are few things more dangerous than a wounded animal—especially a wounded bear."

"This bear has clawed his way back in, but he didn't do it alone," said Colin Powell. A career military man himself, Powell was currently heading the National Security Agency, having succeeded Frank Carlucci when Carlucci was promoted to Defense Secretary in November.

"This coup has deep roots in both the military and intelligence branches. It's no surprise, given Sokolov's reputation as a national hero, that he maintained connections with the old guard. Namely the hardcore conservatives who don't like Gorbachev. Never did and never will."

Webster nodded in agreement with this assessment and then took over from Powell.

"There are a lot of people like Sokolov, powerful, entrenched hardliners who feel increasingly marginalized. They see everything—*perestroika*, *glasnost*, summits, treaties—even Gorbachev's youth and vitality—as threats. It's hard to say what finally caused things to blow up, or even how long it was in the works."

"Hard to say, but not *impossible* to say," hissed Vice President George HW Bush. "I suppose this is one more thing we can pin on Bill? Still cleaning up after Mr Casey, are we?"

William Casey was an old friend of the President and had been CIA director prior to Webster officially assuming command of the agency just over a year prior. Although he had served as director for most of Reagan's two terms, Casey had been ill for some time. In his stead, Webster had been the de facto manager.

As former head of the CIA himself, Bush knew a thing or two about the spy business. Visibly incensed, he glared across the room at those he felt had been asleep at the switch. If this were not a crisis, Bush likely would have pushed for a deep and immediate house cleaning of the intelligence staff—starting with Webster.

That was not a possibility just now. Those at the table knew Reagan was loathe to fire anyone, and too wise to make major staff changes during an unfolding crisis.

As Reagan looked around the room he saw enough new faces anyway. Many had been with his administration only a short time. Not like the early days when he was surrounded by so many of his trusted old friends. Gone were Cap Weinberger, Bud McFarlane, Mike Deaver, Richard Schweiker …

But the President wasn't one to dwell on the past.

Reagan shot Bush a quick look, but said nothing. His training as an actor enabled him to communicate, with just his eyes, an expression that all those present read (and clearly understood): this was a time to meet an uncertain future with unity—not divisive squabbling. Bush got the message, submissively diverting his glance down to the stack of papers in front of him, then to his watch.

"Surprisingly, or perhaps not, many things still seem unresolved," Webster continued. "There's no evidence of a significant counter-insurgency, although some elements appear ... unresponsive. The old regime has fallen. Some players just seem to be on standby ... almost as if they are waiting to make sure this thing is a 'go' before committing. Like the left hand doesn't know what the right hand is doing."

"As a case in point," added Crowe, "the Black Sea naval forces are just frozen. Yet MIGs on the eastern frontier are buzzing about like hornets, although careful—so far—as to not cross into disputed air space."

"Likewise for the diplomatic core," said Schultz. "It seems that they were caught off guard as much as we were. Which is probably why everything has been shut down."

"Until things settle," interjected Webster, "I think it best to keep our distance and our defenses up. Nothing is more dangerous than anarchy. To what degree this occurs and how long until order returns ... this remains to be seen. But the world just became a much more dangerous place. Happy Valentine's Day—from Russia with love."

The President had not heard from his Defense Secretary yet. Reagan turned and made direct eye contact, nodding slightly as an encouragement for him to speak.

Carlucci acknowledged the prompt. "All forces are on high alert, Mr President. We are in a wait-and-see mode for now. But we're prepared to meet whatever situation presents itself—up to, and including, if warranted, a full military response."

A seasoned government veteran, Carlucci had served in various positions related to defense, intelligence, and even the diplomatic corps, as America's ambassador to Portugal during the Carter administration.

Still, Carlucci was new to the top spot in the defense department, having only taken over a few months previously from Caspar Weinberger, who had been forced to resign over the Iran-Contra affair.

Although he had never served in uniform, Carlucci seemed suited as one able to bridge the two worlds of defense and intelligence exemplified by the Cold War.

But would Carlucci still be the best choice if the Cold War turned hot?

Communicator-in-Chief

The assembled group was silent. Expressions ranged from deeply serious to those displaying traces of anxiety and fear.

All eyes were on the President as everyone looked to him for leadership in a time of great crisis and uncertainty. Reagan slowly surveyed the faces. As each met his gaze, a sense of calm filled the room.

"I think it is fair to assume that this coup will succeed," said Reagan. "We will soon find ourselves dealing with extreme hardliners again. The good news is that we know what they are about. The bad news is that what we know what they are about—and it isn't good."

No, things were not good. But at least the group knew that Ronald Reagan was a leader in the true sense of the word. As Commander-in-Chief he could be counted on to keep America safe. As the Great Communicator he would be the one to reassure and unify an anxious nation.

Word of the coup was spreading slowly with the public. It had happened on a weekend, followed by the Presidents' Day holiday. As such, Monday was a day off for many people, including most federal employees.

Still, news organizations from around the world had been badgering the White House for comments all through the night. The TV networks proved especially persistent; hoping for a scoop while attempting to drive ratings by inciting panic.

Within hours, lurid graphics depicting Soviet troops and images of exploding atomic bombs were standard backdrops on all three of the major television network newscasts. At CBS, anchor Dan Rather seemed to be in his element ratcheting up fear *and* ratings. It was a dazzling performance, unlike anything seen since Orson Welles had broken the news of a Martian invasion on Halloween night 1938.

Rather (who had been born on Halloween) was just a boy of seven at the time of the broadcast. And now, here he was, going live with his own version of a war between two different worlds—one of which just so happened to be red.

Planners at the meeting decided to release an official position statement at a press conference hosted by Press Secretary Marlin Fitzwater scheduled for one 1pm Eastern time. Later that day, the President would address the American people on television.

The press conference went well, given the anxiety caused by the lack of credible information. Sweating, red-faced and under siege, Fitzwater did his best, but what the nation needed most was to hear from its president.

All major networks carried the President's broadcast live. Many radio stations did so too. The speech began with the President seated at his desk in the Oval Office.

"My fellow Americans," Reagan calmly began, "I'm here to speak to you about recent events in the Soviet Union. As you may have heard, there has been a change in leadership that can only be described as a *coup d'état*. The government led by Secretary General Mikhail Gorbachev has been replaced by one headed by Commander Sergey Sokolov, and backed by the Soviet military.

"Though it appears to have been a bloodless coup, we do not know Secretary Gorbachev's whereabouts or condition. I ask you to join me in praying for his safety.

"It is not the policy of the United States to meddle in the internal affairs of sovereign states. However, we are justifiably concerned about any regime that uses force as a means to take control of a government. There are protocols for the legal and legitimate transfer of power that do not seem to have been observed in this instance.

"As is typically the case with a *coup d'état*, this one took place without notice and under the cover of darkness. In the hours since, there has been a self-imposed wall of silence by the Soviets, leaving the nations of the world fearful and anxious.

"Attempts to communicate with the Soviets through official diplomatic channels have been unsuccessful. So the matter is being brought before an emergency session of the United Nations Security Council. Whether the USSR will be represented at this meeting is unknown, but in the meantime, Secretary of State Schultz is actively pursuing every option available to establish a dialogue with Moscow.

"Perhaps not surprisingly, news of the coup has not yet been made public to the citizens of the USSR. As far as we can tell, life is proceeding normally in Russia, in the nations behind the Iron Curtain, and within countries aligned with the Soviets around the world.

"Naturally, our top concern is the security of America, our allies, and of the free world. This administration has continually strived to be prepared for and able to meet any situation that puts our nation at risk. Our military forces, and those of our allies, are currently on their highest level of alert.

"As your Commander-in-Chief, I assure you that the safety and security of the American people is my top priority. This change in leadership is a matter of serious concern, but for now there is no overt threat to the United States or any of our allies.

"In partnership with Secretary Gorbachev, great progress has been made on a range of issues, from arms controls to human rights. These changes have benefitted not just our two nations, but the world as a whole.

"We hope the new Soviet leadership will acknowledge the importance of these accomplishments. We expect that agreements already secured will be honored, and that the new Soviet leadership will continue to reflect the peaceful wishes of its citizens.

"I ask that you join me in remaining calm and patient. This is no time for wild speculation. America stands strong and ready; firm in our commitment to freedom and security, and dedicated to peaceful engagement with the Soviet Union.

"Thank you, and may God bless us and watch over us all."

Confusion and Panic

Nearly every TV set in America was tuned in that night. The global viewing audience was the largest in history for a speech by a US president.

The response was universal. Ronald Reagan was exactly what the world needed in a time of unparalleled crisis and uncertainty.

Unfortunately, there was no way that just one man could possibly offset the impact of such an event as the seemingly hostile military takeover of a nuclear superpower.

Everything was made worse by a lack of information from the Soviets.

Ignorance and uncertainty led to rumor and speculation, which was immediately, and irresponsibly echoed and amplified by the media. Owing to the Monday President's Day holiday, US banks and the Stock Market had been closed. Despite official calls for calm, the ripple effects began early as terrified Americans rushed stores to load up on goods.

The world economy reacted pretty much as expected: stocks plummeted and gold skyrocketed—as the precious metal jumped from around $440 an ounce to almost a $1000 by the end of the week. Meanwhile, the US Stock Market, which had been hovering around the 2000 mark, went into free-fall, dropping more than 700 points in just one day. By the time the closing bell rang on Wall Street that Friday afternoon of February 19, the Dow Jones had come to rest at just over the 1100 mark. Concerns over shortages drove the price of oil up by more than 40% in just four days, and many gas stations soon went dry.

On Tuesday morning NATO fighters scrambled to intercept two Soviet MIGS that had entered Norwegian airspace. Before the planes were brought down however, the pilots communicated their intention of defecting to the West, and were promptly escorted to a safe landing.

This was the first of many similar incidents. On a separate occasion, a lone MIG's attempt to reach Western airspace over Turkey was thwarted when a squadron of Soviets fired on it, destroying the plane and killing its crew before members could eject to safety.

It was widely rumored—though not officially confirmed—that the British had also come into possession of a Soviet Typhoon class submarine. Typhoons were nuclear-powered ballistic missile vessels capable of staying submerged for up to 120 days at a time. Whether the "Shark" had surrendered peacefully, was captured by British naval forces, or had experienced a mechanical issue prompting a rescue operation was not known.

During that first week, US intelligence sources had nothing substantive on the Soviet armed forces. Nor did non-aligned or so-called neutral nations, including those with strong diplomatic or economic ties to Moscow. The dominant theme was instead that the Soviet high command seemed to be doing little, if anything, about the rapid unraveling of the empire and its forces.

Confusion begat chaos. Provocation or accident? A deadly game of chicken, or someone seeking freedom and stability in the West? Defector or kamikaze? More than once US and NATO forces were forced to make split-second decisions to engage or stand down.

In Washington, secret plans were dusted off, modified, and readied to address every possible scenario: from a Soviet nuclear attack, to the need for martial law brought on by mass panic and civil unrest.

News of the lack of vital signs from the USSR spread quickly around the world. There were several attempts by populations held prisoner by communist regimes to use the uncertainty of the moment to break their chains and embrace liberty.

In the People's Republic of Mozambique, ordinary citizens (in conjunction with rogue elements from the military) attempted a democratic revolution, but were quickly and brutally put down by forces loyal to President Joaquim Alberto Chissano.

In Cuba, President Fidel Castro acted proactively with the imposition of martial law, curfews, and mass arrests. Troops and armed police were posted on every corner; given "shoot-to-kill" orders at any sign of an uprising.

Meanwhile, the Russians remained silent. Embassies remained shuttered; calls went to voicemail and were left unanswered.

The first real news of what was happening behind the Iron Curtain came late Thursday from Nicolae Ceaușescu, the president and communist party leader of Romania, during a phone interview with an

Italian radio station.

Ceaușescu revealed that he had recently spoken with the new Soviet leadership, stating that the transition of power had been orderly and "necessary." The Romanian dictator offered few specifics, other than to say there was no reason to worry.

"Necessary?" This seemed an odd choice of words, but Ceaușescu refused to elaborate.

Ceaușescu claimed he had no knowledge of Gorbachev's status, but did confirm that Sokolov was now fully in charge and scheduled to make a public statement to the world at noon on Saturday, February 20.

The timing of Sokolov's speech seemed directed to a European audience, as it would be Saturday night in the eastern US, but still only early afternoon in London, Paris, and Bonn.

Adding to the anticipation was the aura of complete secrecy preceding the speech. No news conferences, no press releases, and the broadcast would be closed to the media.

As the hour drew near, it was estimated that at least a quarter of the world was tuned in either by radio or television.

★ 6 ★

The Promise of a New Era

The broadcast began promptly at noon (Moscow time), opening with a montage of still images of life in the Soviet Union, while the state anthem played in the background.

The last two images — a photo of the Earth from space followed by the Soviet flag — seemed rather ominous. As the anthem drew to a close, the scene changed to that of a smiling older man, dressed in a gray suit and sitting at desk. Behind him was a dark blue velvet curtain.

All those watching the broadcast with President Reagan at the White House instantly recognized the man as Commander Sokolov. No one could recall ever having seen him in civilian clothing before. In the past, he had always been presented in full uniform, adorned with rows of badges, medals, and ribbons.

Sokolov smiled warmly. He made direct eye contact with the camera as his name and title (General Secretary of the Central Committee of the Communist Party of the Soviet Union) appeared at the bottom of the screen.

"Greetings!" (The English translation began.)

"I am here to announce the dawn of a new era for the Soviet Union and for the world.

"An era of peace and cooperation, based upon tolerance and mutual respect for the issues that unite rather than divide us.

"An era in which disagreements between nations become new opportunities for communication and understanding.

"Working together, we can rid the world of war, poverty, racism, and injustice. In doing so, we will finally realize our potential as one people, one planet." Sokolov stared straight ahead and appeared to be reading from a teleprompter. His hands were clasped together, resting upon a set of notes on the desk that likely served as a backup should Soviet technology fail him. The old man's delivery appeared rehearsed, but natural; punctuated with appropriate pauses.

"This is not a new perspective, but one that began with Sputnik and which was affirmed when the Russian cosmonaut Yuri Gagarin became the first man in space.

"For the first time in history it was possible for humanity to see the world both as it is and how it should be: a planet marked by natural cycles, not borders created by empires.

"Something changed forever that day, as evidenced by our ongoing program, dedicated to the peaceful exploration of space for the benefit of all Mankind."

Sokolov smiled, then paused. His expression returned to one of seriousness. He nodded solemnly and then continued with his speech.

"But we know it is possible for two people to look in the same direction and see very different things. Where we see an opportunity to unite and work together, others see the need to create divisions.

"We disagree with the notion that empires built on Earth have a right to extend their dominion into space.

"Instead, we believe the time has come for the peaceful to take a stand against the darker impulses of humanity spreading outward to desecrate the heavens."

Sokolov paused for effect.

"A Russian proverb I learned as child warns, that when the rich make war, it is the poor which die.

"I have spent much of my life in uniform. From fighting Hitler and the Nazis to building the Soviet Union into a counterbalance against those who now seek to encircle and threaten the planet from above.

"I know about war. I understand war. I have seen enough war for a thousand lifetimes. There is a better way.

"Preparing for war—on Earth or in the heavens—makes all of us poorer and increases the likelihood of conflict. If we don't change course, war will destroy us all.

"We therefore extend an olive branch to our adversaries. We ask that they help us build a true and permanent peace through trust and shared interests, rather than continuing with standoffs and détente, the defaults of a false diplomacy, the poisoned crops sown by the battlefields of mutual destruction.

"The Soviet Union has the power to destroy the world and all life upon it. But we choose the opposite path.

"We envision a new era of peacefully aligned nations. A new union of countries respectful of the democratic traditions of freedom of speech, and conscience, but liberated from the rigged economic systems that crush the dreams of the common man in order to enrich a small ruling minority.

"For the unaligned and still free peoples of our shared planet, we ask that you join us; not just in support of world peace, but also in a new union of global political, economic, and cultural cooperation.

"We believe it is time for the peaceful peoples of the Earth to unite. To rise up against your oppressors from that distant empire which uses force to occupy sovereign lands and sees your people as pawns in the deadly game it now intends to take into space to ensure its eternal dominion over our planet.

"This conquest must be stopped before it is too late. Working together we can do this peacefully. But it can only be achieved if we are united in brotherhood, bound by the dream of peace on Earth for all Mankind." Sokolov paused and stared straight ahead; his face expressionless. The pause seemed to go on just a little too long, and Reagan wondered if indeed something had gone awry with the teleprompter.

Apparently not. The Russian gave a slight nod, and there almost seemed to be the beginnings of a smile forming as he resumed speaking.

"The Soviet Union will soon unveil the details of a comprehensive proposal for world peace. Until then, remember that we are your friends and partners in nonviolence, striving toward a new age for our planet and all its peoples. Thank you."

The TV screen dimmed, then transitioned to a solid red screen as the official anthem began playing again. The word "PEACE" began to pop-up on the screen in various languages while the music boomed ever louder.

Mrs Reagan, who would not normally attend such meetings, was present today, and it was she who grabbed the remote and hit the MUTE button before exciting the room.

All eyes turned to the President on cue. He simply shook his head, uttering the one sentence that captured what everyone present was already thinking. It was his unique gift.

"What a load of bunk," he said, shaking his head and raising his eyebrows. "Who writes this stuff? Joe Isuzu?"

The outburst of laughter in the room was immediate, providing a much-needed break in the tension. But the levity was short-lived, as everyone acknowledged the threats woven between the lines in Sokolov's pitch.

"Yes, we are definitely dealing with a new era for the Soviets. But their end objective will be the same: divide and conquer," proclaimed the President. "After years in show business I can spot a con man a mile away, but I worry that even if others see through his pitch, they'll throw caution to the wind simply because this is what they want to hear.

"I'm sure the champagne bottles are already popping, but I'm sorry to say this is not our party. We're going to need to stay sober, to keep our wits about us, because we are the only ones able to stop them from taking the world.

"Throughout history, America has always met challenges head-on. Some say the American character was forged by adversity, and, as you know, I believe that God has endowed our nation with a special responsibility to stand when others cannot.

"There will be difficult days ahead. But I know in my heart that with God's help we will be victorious."

Reagan rose from his seat as the attendees paused to consider the magnitude of his words. Despite the uncertainty of the days that lay ahead, the group had been energized by the President's courage and vision.

Chief of Staff Baker scanned the room after a moment of silence. "Let's take five," he said. "Then it's back to work. We'll have lunches brought in ... probably our dinners, too. Ladies and gentlemen, it's going to be a long day."

A Wolf in Sheep's Clothing

The meeting reconvened with news and updates from the various attendees, starting with CIA Director Webster.

"Sokolov," began Webster, "is nothing than more than a wolf in sheep's clothing …

"He is a ruthless career military man who led the Soviet invasion of Afghanistan. In this capacity he displayed unparalleled brutality and a complete contempt for human life—whether it was for those he was fighting, innocent civilians, or even his own troops.

"Sokolov only cares about conquest and winning. This is not a man of peace.

"Three years ago he was appointed Minister of Defense for the Soviet Union, a position he held until Gorbachev canned him over the Mathias Rust scandal.

"Despite his dismissal, Sokolov, a state-designated 'Hero' has remained well-connected to the military and intelligence communities, including the acting Defense Minister and also his old pal Marshal Alexander Koldunov, whom Gorbachev had also dismissed over the Mathias Rust breach.

"Koldunov, is a World War II fighter pilot who got away with shooting down some American planes in a case of 'friendly fire' over Yugoslavia. Since being booted, Koldunov has been a fairly vocal thorn in Gorbachev's side, but apparently he's untouchable. This was partially due to his national reputation as a fellow 'Hero,' but also owing to his strong financial connections within the Soviet military-industrial complex and the KGB.

"Whether Sokolov is actually running the show remains a question for now. It's entirely possible he might just be a figurehead. What better choice than a beloved national hero, a hardened warrior who now talks peace?"

NSA Director Powell spoke next.

"We believe Sokolov was put in place by those who want war and confrontation, not peace. They are now testing a dangerous and deceitful new approach to con and conquer. They are not happy with Gorbachev's reforms or his dealings with the West. The fact that he's outgoing, gregarious, and trying to move society forward threatens those who have a vested interest in the status quo.

"It would seem they are especially concerned about Gorbachev's inability to shut us down on the Strategic Defense Initiative — even though we've offered to share the technology.

"If I were to offer up a guess, I'd propose that the roots of this coup went back to the summit in Iceland, when the President refused to abandon SDI.

"From the Soviet perspective, without the threat of their nuclear missiles, the game is over."

The Joint Chiefs nodded in support of Powell's assessment.

"The Sokolov we just saw in the broadcast is something new," Webster continued. "A creation of the KGB. They groomed him for this role and coached him on his speech. The views he expressed are completely at odds with everything he has ever said or done. But, as a propaganda tool, who better than a former man of war who has 'seen the light' and now wants to turn swords into ploughshares? We think that the Soviets want to make President Reagan look like a warmonger … to position him as the *real* threat to world peace.

"Interesting side note," concluded Webster. "Sokolov and the President are almost exactly the same age — with only a few months difference."

The group paused to consider this curious detail.

"Bottom line: Sokolov was created and put in place precisely to mirror and contrast President Reagan to the world."

"Agreed," added Powell. "As a Soviet propaganda tool, we need to take this threat very seriously.

"We believe that they are intent on creating divisions among our allies, within NATO … globally … and even within the United States," stated Powell.

"For the most part, during the transition period they have shown restraint and avoided any direct acts of provocation. But we suspect that is likely to change soon.

"With their 'peace plan' on the table, they will almost certainly try to test us. Something to force our hand … something that will require a military response designed to make us look like shoot-'em-up cowboys, and make them look like the innocent victims … martyrs.

"The Soviet objective here appears to be twofold: (1) To further isolate the United States from the rest of the free world, and (2) To incite a domestic backlash, and hopefully sway the upcoming US presidential election.

"The Soviet hardliners would much prefer to deal with a weak Democratic administration—likely led by Michael Dukakis—than with a Bush administration, which they view as an extension of the Reagan presidency.

"They regard Dukakis as someone they can bully, especially if the more left-leaning elements of his party are in control of Congress and cheering him on.

"Given the stakes, I wouldn't put it past them—in fact, I think it should be expected—that the Russians will try to tamper with, if not outright influence, the November elections in favor of the Democrats."

Reagan scowled, knowing how difficult it would be to track, much less stop the flow and influence of Soviet money.

"The Soviet plan: isolate us internationally, weaken us at home, extract huge concessions from a government willing to pay any price for peace. Then … well, I hate to even think about it, but history has shown us how the Soviets behave when they have the upper hand over a vulnerable adversary."

Powell clasped his hands. Behind aviator-style glasses, his eyes narrowed to a determined squint.

The mood was indeed somber as the three-star general's dire warning sank in. Reagan looked toward the members of the National Security Council, but no one had anything to add for now. Then it was the Defense Secretary's turn to speak.

Carlucci's presentation was extensive. It featured charts and visual aids, including poster-sized before-and-after satellite photos showing no significant change in the position of Soviet forces. He noted that US forces had been on maximum alert since the start of the coup, and that he had ordered an increase in reconnaissance missions and build-ups along borders deemed vulnerable or sensitive.

Secretary of State Schultz had been absent for much of Carlucci's presentation, but when it was his turn to speak his demeanor was deeply serious and tinged with fatigue. Bags under the Secretary's eyes suggested that he was critically short on sleep. His voice was hoarse and he appeared bordering on exhaustion.

"In the time since Sokolov's broadcast I've been consulting with our allies, and … most have given high marks to his speech.

"They believe this is the end of the Cold War."

Schultz's words were met with an audible gasp. Reagan looked incredulous. "The British?" he asked.

"They're just about the only ones who aren't buying it," answered Schultz.

"Everyone else seems to be going for it: hook, line, and sinker. Helmut Kohl and the Germans are skeptical. Most others—the French, the Spanish, the Greeks, the Turks … feel this is an idea whose time has come."

The President turned his head and looked out the window at the Washington Monument, which stood bright and clear in contrast to the dull gray skies. The room fell silent as the group waited for him to respond. When he did, his voice was calm; his message firm and resolute.

"We are in a war the likes of which we have never seen. This is a war for hearts and minds, a war between freedom and slavery, a war to define the future of this planet. It is a war between life and death.

"It will be a war with invisible and shifting borders. We will likely find ourselves going it alone. It won't be easy, but there is no other way. We have a date with destiny."

Reagan then turned to White House Press Secretary Marlin Fitzwater. "I need to take our case directly to the people," he said. "Let's plan on me going live tomorrow … Sunday at five o'clock. That'll give us time to put a speech together, and guarantee that we we're done before we get hammered in the ratings by *60 Minutes!*"

The President's humor had helped diffuse tensions once again, if only momentarily.

The United States and the Soviet Union were on a collision course. How and when it would happen was anyone's guess. Although never one to give up hope, Reagan knew he had no choice now but to prepare for the worst.

Night & Day

The President's speech had not gone well.

Reagan's delivery was firm and authoritative, but his words, hastily drafted by a team of assistants, lacked substance and nuance. Instead of conveying the need for caution and vigilance, they suggested suspicion and paranoia.

Lines from the speech were pulled out of context and provided as further evidence for those who regarded Reagan as a trigger-happy cowboy who would rather bring on Armageddon than give peace a chance. The foreign press was especially harsh. Translations were at best subjective, and commonly laced with editorial opinion presented as fact.

In short, the speech did exactly what the Soviets had hoped for: it positioned President Reagan as the true obstacle to world peace and progress.

Given the seriousness of the subject, US viewership was not as high as anticipated. Only brief clips were broadcast on the next day's news shows. In line with the media's adversarial relationship with both the President and Christianity, it was no surprise that the story they chose to cover the next day was not Reagan's speech, but rather Reverend Jimmy Swaggert's salacious confession of infidelity.

The Sunday night speech, intended as it was for an American audience, came at an hour when Europe and much of the world was still sleeping. This gave the nocturnal Soviet propagandists the time they needed to craft a response. On Monday morning, February 22, the Soviet embassies began opening right on schedule. Sokolov's picture had replaced Gorbachev's, and early public opinion polls showed that Moscow had successfully shifted attention to the dangers posed by "American hardliners."

Smiling Soviet diplomats made themselves available to the media to talk about peace and cooperation and oh, yes, trust; but they were unable to elaborate on the script sent down from Moscow, let alone deviate from it. And for the most part this worked well. The big story was the radical change in the USSR and the promise of world peace.

"Please tell us more!" was the cry.

"Gladly!" was the response.

Inquiries about Gorbachev were met with cautious language, stating only that he had been "unable to continue in his role as General Secretary."

This formulated response was a familiar one, having been used numerous times when the USSR and other totalitarian states sought to keep such details private.

Rumors (likely generated by the KGB) soon began to circulate that the reason for Gorbachev's removal was due to his reluctance to pursue a genuine peace. Rather than stand up to Reagan, he had allowed the United States to move ahead with the Strategic Defense Initiative (SDI), which would only fuel a dangerous new chapter in the arms race. Thus, Gorbachev had to be removed so that the USSR might seek a real and lasting peace.

It was a rather fanciful yarn, clearly the work of slick KGB propagandists. But even if it were true, why was Gorbachev being hidden from public view? His complete disappearance — and silencing — seemed at odds with Moscow's latest pledges of openness and tolerance.

Where was the public outcry?

One of the most famous people on the planet had just completely disappeared, as had almost all the key players in his administration, most notably Foreign Minister Eduard Shevardnadze. And no one seemed to care.

But for Reagan, Gorbachev was more than just a partner and a friend. He was also the latest victim of a system that had only gotten worse. More devious, therefore more dangerous.

Gorbachev needed to be rescued.

Charm Offensive

In the days following Sokolov's broadcast, the Soviet propaganda machine rattled along at full speed, feeding people exactly what they wanted to hear. As predicted, divisions developed between America and its allies, and within the US itself.

Everything was now open to interpretation and spin. With everyone giddy at the prospect of world peace, the lack of movement by Soviet forces was celebrated as proof of their commitment to peace and self-defense, when only recently the same troops had been seen as aggressors massing on borders in preparation for an invasion. Meanwhile, the intensive monitoring and high-alert status of the Americans was denounced as paranoid and provocative.

But the Americans had no choice. If they were to be similarly seduced into dropping their guard the world would be left defenseless. It was a difficult stance to take, but Reagan never viewed the presidency as a popularity contest. He did what he felt was right and what he had been elected to do: call things as he saw them and keep the American people safe.

Besides, Ronald Reagan understood the power of propaganda perhaps better than anyone.

In the course of his lifetime, he had seen it used by everyone from the Fascists to the Sandinistas; from Hitler to the hippies. By now the pattern was all too familiar: use lies and half-truths to grab power, then use propaganda to brainwash and maintain control.

On Thursday, February 25, the "details" Sokolov had promised during his speech were released in the form of a grand proposition unlike anything anyone could have imagined.

While most thought the Soviets would float some arms control and/ or troop reduction proposal in exchange for similar actions by NATO and a freeze on the Strategic Defense Initiative (dubbed "Star Wars" by its critics), the proposal, although presented in broad strokes, was a bid to change the entire structure of Europe, and its relationship with the United States.

The Soviet proposal would expand and transform the existing European Economic Community (EEC) from a regional trade organization to something much more expansive and comprehensive. The proposed new entity, to be called the European Union (EU) would be a political and economic coalition of nations uniting Western Europe and the USSR.

Economically, the EU would integrate all member nations into a single market. National currencies would be preserved, but these would be complemented with a common currency welcomed in all member states. By removing trade barriers, regulations, taxes, and tariffs, western capital could flow east, and eastern workers could move west to fill labor shortages.

While each member nation would retain political autonomy, certain provisions would apply across the entire European Union, if approved by a governing body—presumably to be headquartered in Moscow.

Lastly, the EU would form a united military force to be called the European Defense Organization (EDO), replacing the Warsaw Pact *and* NATO by integrating the two adversaries into a single new entity. Being a European-based defensive force, NATO's New World members—the Americans and the Canadians—would not be eligible for membership. EDO would be a private club, with membership determined by postal code.

The Soviet position was that NATO had become an obstacle to peace. By maintaining a huge threatening presence, it had forced the USSR into establishing a defensive counterbalance based on the threat of Mutually Assured Destruction (MAD). Previous attempts at arms control had been rejected by the Americans, who were now seeking to gain an irreversible advantage by militarizing space.

In support of their argument, the Soviets (in a rare reference to the former General Secretary) pointed to Gorbachev's offer to cut European nukes if Reagan would agree to drop Star Wars—which the Americans rejected, much to the dismay of the European public. The dismissal of the offer, made just two years earlier at the summit in Reykjavik, Iceland, was still very much a topic of discussion, and something which continued to affect relations and perceptions. For many this was the smoking gun: proof that the United States had no genuine interest in peace and no qualms about using European soil as a battlefield involving nuclear weapons.

But now, Gorbachev's successors were making another attempt.

It was time for the brinkmanship to end, and that could only happen if the Americans went back to where they belonged, argued the Soviets.

Under the terms and conditions of the proposed European Union, there was no longer a need for the American forces on the continent. Instead, their continued presence only contributed to tension, distrust, and the likelihood of a war starting accidentally.

The Soviets were direct: the current course was leading to poverty and environmental devastation. It was time for all Europeans to cooperate along areas of common interest, and to end the American occupation that had divided the continent since the end of World War II.

By shifting budgets and deployments from offensive to purely defensive capabilities, nations would be able to reap considerable savings to apply to other uses. Lastly, the EDO would reflect regional concerns and respect matters of sovereignty, something that did not happen under the US-dominated NATO.

Thank you, America, for helping us to defeat Hitler, but now it is time to leave Europe to the Europeans. We ask respectfully, but firmly, that you take your nuclear arsenal and hundreds of thousands of troops back across the Atlantic to where they belong.

Rallies in support of the Soviet proposal for a European Union began almost immediately, often fused with anti-American protests. Moscow made no secret of the fact that it supported these — both ideologically, and financially.

"The new USSR is open and transparent, and we have a right to confront the slick, Madison Avenue propaganda of the Americans," chided Moscow.

"Why shouldn't we apply our resources to education? To support the rights of people to assemble? To encourage the freedom of expression?" asked the Soviets. "These are European traditions which we support."

The KGB propagandists were having a field day usurping and twisting the principles of freedom, and in turn were succeeding in swaying public opinion. The message was especially well received by the French, who had been ruled by François Mitterrand's pacifistic democratic socialists since 1981.

Within days Sokolov was out on tour, drawing huge audiences

across Western Europe.

Paraded about as a kindly old gentleman, Sokolov was cheered on as a warrior who had seen both the futility of war, and the promise of peace. He spoke of bringing down walls and building bridges. And, to underscore their commitment and shared interests, the Soviets unveiled an ambitious set of European cultural exchange programs.

On March 1 1988, Sokolov addressed a cheering crowd of 250,000 in Paris as "my fellow Europeans." Holding a single red rose, the old man smiled and waved broadly to the overflow crowd. Before leaving the stage, he gave a shout of *"Vive le France! Merci!"* which, due to his heavy Russian accent, was completely incomprehensible. Still, people heard what they wanted to hear, and they were delighted.

The next night, in a government-sponsored event at Berlin's Brandenburg Gate, Sokolov told of his service during World War II to liberate Germany from the Nazis. He spoke of how the Soviet and German peoples had suffered and triumphed together in a common struggle for freedom, which, he said, "continues to this day."

Through a translator, Sokolov then seemed to imply that President Reagan had replaced Hitler as the new oppressor of the German people. This assertion was immediately challenged by Chancellor Kohl.

"If Mr Sokolov is truly a man of freedom and liberation, why is the Berlin Wall still standing?" Kohl asked, echoing Reagan's famous call to Gorbachev the previous June, demanding that the wall be torn down. Kohl continued, "We promise to welcome anyone who is not in a uniform or carrying a gun. Will he do the same?"

Made in haste during a press conference following the event, Kohl's comments were quickly picked up and twisted by the media to suggest a call for immediate German reunification based on open borders. While reunification was something that Kohl supported in principle, his attempts at clarifying conditions for migration across the fortified frontier weren't deemed nearly as newsworthy.

One of Reagan's closest allies, Kohl was a conservative who did not trust the Soviets. He supported the US presence in Germany—the largest in Europe—as a necessary deterrent to Soviet expansion. Like Reagan, he did not have a favorable opinion of Sokolov, and was not interested in a photo op where the pair could be pictured shaking hands and smiling for the camera.

Also present at the press conference, but unbeknownst to Kohl, or any of the security services, was a small man, with hard blue eyes and sandy-colored hair just visiting from East Germany. The man was not a German himself, but he worked as translator, so he spoke perfect German, with barely a trace of a Russian accent.

Like Sokolov, the man believed that he was helping liberate the German people, in this instance through his work with the East German secret police, the STASI.

A KGB agent for nearly 13 years, the thin young man watched the German Chancellor with a degree of amusement, fantasizing about snapping his fat neck while others stood by frozen and powerless. Highly-trained in martial arts, it would be so easy. Over in just a second.

"*Nyet*, that would be too quick," thought the 35-year-old Vladimir Putin as he walked from the room and out into the chilly night air of the divided city. "Reagan's dog deserves a slow death."

Kohl and British Prime Minister Margaret Thatcher were among the few European leaders willing to go on record as questioning Sokolov. When they did, the effect often backfired. For most conservative politicians were now at odds with the spell of what the press was calling "Sokolovmania."

This fissure was no more pronounced than in the United Kingdom, traditionally America's closet European ally, and home to a large American military presence.

Beginning with Sokolov's pitch and Reagan's rebuttal, Great Britain had been rocked especially hard by anti-American protests; the nation was on edge, with threats of impending strikes and calls for civil disobedience. The Soviet proposal to unify Europe and boot the yanks back across the pond resonated with the British public, already broadly supportive of a nuclear freeze. Worse yet, was the presence of the American forces, a humiliating reminder of an empire that had risen just as the sun had set upon their own.

Although Thatcher expressed her support privately, the Tory Prime Minister was advised by Scotland Yard to bide her time and avoid enflaming the situation further with any incendiary public statements. British intelligence worried that such remarks might be just the spark needed to transform rallies into full-scale riots, thus requiring a massive infusion of British troops in order to stave off anarchy in the UK.

Reagan understood completely, telling Thatcher that pitting government troops against the people is what "they do—not us.

"Even though we are being judged by different standards we must stay on the high road. Democracy is never easy, but we mustn't let them goad us into losing control.

"This would only provide them with a huge propaganda victory, which we cannot afford to give them.

"Just recently, I let myself be pushed into speaking too hastily, and look what came of it," said Reagan, sounding unusually weary. "I won't be making that mistake again. But Maggie, you know your people, and I trust you to do what's best there … you can count on me to always support you 110 percent!"

"Ron, something simply cannot be more than 100 percent!" said Thatcher, laughingly taking on the persona of a stuffy schoolteacher.

"Obviously you haven't seen the rosy financial projections being floated by the Democrats," said Reagan, chuckling. "Goodnight Maggie."

Fortunately for the President, matters were significantly less volatile in the United States. At least for the time being.

Despite his landslide victory in the last election, Reagan's domestic power and influence had been in decline due to a variety of reasons, including ongoing fallout from the Iran-Contra affair. During this, the last year of his presidency, Reagan was officially a lame duck; with both houses of Congress now controlled by the Democrats.

Reagan still scored high on the personal popularity polls, but as the leader of the free world, many Americans felt that his time had passed, and they were looking forward to the November elections—most likely to be a contest between Vice President George HW Bush and Massachusetts Governor Michael Dukakis.

How wrong they were.

Battle Lines of March

"We can realize a lasting peace and transform the East-West relationship to one of enduring co-operation."

—George HW Bush

March 1988 began on a Monday, and the morning was filled with the usual briefings and updates beginning promptly at 9am.

The President was normally joined by his second-in-command, but with the Super Tuesday primaries just over a week away, Vice President Bush was out on the campaign trail trying to "seal the deal."

Up to that point, it had been more than 150 years since a sitting Vice President had ascended to the presidency, a curse Bush was bent on breaking. Granted, the Veep had big shoes to fill. In fact, one critic went so far as to compare Bush's run for the presidency to Barney Fife's dream of replacing Andy Taylor as the sheriff of Mayberry.

A funny comparison before the Soviet coup, but now a real point of concern for an electorate that had serious reservations about a man they had already rejected once when he ran against Ronald Reagan in 1980 for the party's nomination.

If there was to be a shootout at high noon, Americans wanted Gary Cooper, not Barney Fife.

This lack of enthusiasm resulted in several upsets by Kansas Senator Bob Dole—Bush's leading opponent to represent the GOP. Dole, a centrist, forced him to move to the left. Bush's other main challenger was author, commentator, and former White House Communications Chief Pat Buchanan—a conservative who was tugging Bush to the right.

In keeping with tradition, Reagan, as a sitting president, would not weigh in with an endorsement until the people, and the party had first made their selection. Bush had been a loyal VP, and Reagan would return the favor when the time was right, if asked.

The degree to which Reagan could be of use was still being debated by the Bush campaign, which found itself in the difficult position of trying to capitalize on the best of his associations with the two-term president, while keeping a safe distance from whatever was controversial. Reagan's recent hawkishness was a real problem for candidate Bush, who feared the President might do something stupid like start a war before his time in office ran out—leaving him stuck with having to clean up the mess.

Or worse yet: get blamed for it by association, causing him to lose the election.

Meanwhile, many conservatives remained unsold on the increasingly moderate Bush, questioning his suitability as an appropriate successor to the Reagan Revolution. They cited concerns over a range of issues, from commitment to social conservatism to small government to fiscal policy. Bush's denunciation of Reaganomics as "voodoo economics" had not been forgotten, much less forgiven.

And there was just no denying that Bush lacked the personal charisma of Ronald Reagan.

While Reagan's policies were never universally popular, even his most entrenched political opponents begrudgingly admitted to liking and respecting him as a person. Nor did they ever question Reagan's sincerity—the rarest of all qualities to be found in a politician. Thus, one might disagree with Reagan but there were few who doubted his word. When Ronald Reagan took a stand people knew it was because of what he felt in his heart, and not because of what was scoring high that week with some focus group of swing voters in Burlington, Vermont.

As Super Tuesday drew closer, Bush became bogged down fighting different wars on shifting fronts: against other Republican candidates (one to his left, one to his right), the ghost of Ronald Reagan, the current Democratic frontrunner (Massachusetts Governor Michael Dukakis), and now, Sergey Sokolov, the new head of the USSR.

While Bush's targeted stump speeches always drew polite applause, the "Sokolov Show" was receiving standing ovations across Europe by those seeking salvation from a messiah of peace. Once again, Bush found himself in the shadow of yet another charismatic leader.

Although directed to the non-Soviet-dominated world, Sokolov's song of peace and love still managed to seep through tiny holes in the Iron Curtain where it was met with a mixture of skepticism and surprise. Within the USSR Sokolov was a well-known public figure, officially honored as a national hero by Brezhnev.

In the years since this designation Sokolov had become an increasingly controversial, if not an unpopular figure; blamed for the on-going debacle of the Soviet-Afghan War, now in its eighth year.

Sokolov was neither a hero nor someone deemed fit to lead.

Their true hero was Gorbachev, whose reforms had genuinely changed society for the better. *Perestroika. Glasnost.* A plan to end the war.

Gorbachev talked change and had delivered it.

So his disappearance did not suggest a promising new era to the citizens of the USSR. Instead, it looked like the end. Replacing Gorbachev with someone like Sokolov just looked more like business as usual.

As word of Sokolov's coup spread throughout the Soviet Union so did dissent. It would be hard for the new regime to roll back the hard-won freedoms all at once, especially if met with widespread public opposition.

But how?

Even under Gorbachev, large-scale public demonstrations were not permitted, unless aligned with some kind of officially-sanctioned state celebration.

One such approved event was International Women's Day. Embraced and celebrated by Vladimir Lenin, it became an official state holiday immediately following the Communist Revolution of 1917. In the years that followed, the holiday had become an important propaganda tool designed to showcase women's equality in the USSR and contrast it with the sexism of the degenerate West.

International Women's Day was officially observed on March 8, but as with most grand public events, preparations and planning usually began long before the actual day. Certainly this was the case when things began taking shape a week early in Wenceslas Square, one of the main public gathering places in the historic old town section of Prague, Czechoslovakia.

This year the crowds began to assemble earlier and the demographic was younger than it had typically been in the past for such events.

In fact, noted the state security agents monitoring the situation, the make-up of this crowd was very different from that of previous years. They cited not just the high percentage of students, but also significant numbers of union members and other well-known activists.

Photos were taken, calls were placed, and contingency plans drawn up in the event that things began to drift in the wrong direction.

The crowd in Wenceslas Square grew larger every day, and by Thursday morning the area had become a walled-off mini-city within the city. At some point, celebrants had become protestors, and access by certain visitors (such as uniformed security forces) was being denied.

These wishes were respected while Czechoslovakian authorities awaited instructions from the Kremlin.

Signs denouncing Soviet rule began to appear on Friday, followed by a directive from Moscow ordering the expulsion of all media from the area.

The Kremlin justified this action by claiming it had evidence that the protests were being orchestrated by Western agents seeking to spread disinformation and foment dissent. Weapons had been supposedly found on some of the protestors (now called terrorists and/or anarchists), along with plans to burn down the city and overthrow the government.

The Soviet authorities argued that allowing reporters to continue covering the protests only served the interests of the terrorists. By allowing them this forum, the terrorists were using the media to spread CIA propaganda and to encourage violent revolution.

Therefore, the decision had been made to shut down all news coverage for the sake of public safety. The collective of Western agents who wanted to use Wenceslas Square as their stage would still be allowed to conduct their play, but without an audience.

Due to Soviet travel restrictions, few of the "Western agents" participating in the protests had ever seen the other side of the Iron Curtain. Most of those who had been beyond the borders of the USSR had done so in uniform, serving as members of the military from World War II to the current war in Afghanistan. The fact that many chose to wear their old uniforms and medals to the protest was seen as treason.

But these were men and women of courage. Many had already met death head on and were not easily intimidated by bureaucrats with bullhorns.

So the stalemate began. Authorities gambled that without media attention the protests would begin to fade, but instead just the opposite began to happen. The cries grew louder; the chants, jeers, and calls for freedom more overt.

As the protest within the square grew, so did the response around it. Uniformed troops were brought in to clear the last of the buildings around Wenceslas Square. Using riot shields, they pushed their way through the onlookers to form a ring around the perimeter.

At nine o'clock Monday morning a series of loud speakers positioned in the buildings around the square broadcast a message informing the protestors that they would be allowed to leave freely, and without incident, if they did so by noon.

Those that chose to stay would be subject to arrest.

By the noon deadline 300 or so protestors decided to act on the offer of amnesty. All were promptly arrested and taken into custody as they attempted to leave.

Given that this was Monday, and thus truly International Women's Day, the protestors began pulling a giant statue of a woman into the center of the square.

Such sculptures of monumental heroic women were typical fare for this particular holiday, although at some point during the night, this one had been somewhat altered. A robe had replaced her worker's overalls, her upraised fist now held a torch, and around her head … well, the Soviets had no exact word for it. But they certainly recognized it: the Soviet symbol of womanhood had been transformed into a makeshift version of the Statue of Liberty!

The size of the sculpture made it visible from a great distance, whereas those pulling it along were only visible through lenses, be they cameras or rifle scopes. Both began to focus on the scene unfolding below them.

As Miss Liberty rounded the corner, it seemed her arrival was being heralded by that other popular symbol of American independence — fireworks.

But this was no celebration of independence; it was a violent repudiation of it.

Sharpshooters in the buildings above had begun firing on the edges of the crowd to block escape routes and to turn the panicking masses back upon themselves. Meanwhile, large caliber automatic weapons strafed the people in waves. Helicopters buzzed overhead, relaying information and instructions to ground troops who were in formation around the square and organized into a series of rings to stop anyone trying to flee. Blood sprayed everywhere and formed large red pools on the ground as bodies fell upon one another in heaps.

Those attempting to surrender by holding their hands up or by waving improvised white flags were downed as readily as those who raised their fists in one last act of defiance and courage.

The carnage continued for nearly an hour, resulting in the death of at least 2000 persons, including many women and children. More than 15,000 persons had been wounded, many quite seriously. Even those who thought they could escape by lying on the ground and feigning death had been injured or killed by the relentless sweeps that came from all directions.

In the end, however, the "threat" posed by these "terrorists" to the innocent Soviet people had been vanquished.

11

The Prague Massacre

Almost immediately, gruesome details and even photos of what was being called the Prague Massacre began to appear everywhere. Despite attempts at censorship, the slaughter in Wenceslas Square became the top story in most Western media.

This was unfortunate for the Soviets, but not entirely unexpected.

Back in Moscow, the propagandists took it all in stride. It would be a busy day, and they clearly had their work cut out for them.

The division in charge of formulating the official response was led by a heavyset man with twinkly eyes, bushy black eyebrows, and deep dimples; known only by his first name of Ivan.

"When life gives you rotten potatoes," laughed Ivan, "that is when you make vodka."

Ivan had been in the loop about the Prague situation from the very beginning, and was experienced at crisis management. Rather than focus on the negatives, his outlook was always positive — even when it involved grisly photos of bullet-riddled women lying on top of their children in an effort to shield them from helicopter gunfire.

"It reminded me of what the Americans did in My Lai," he grimaced. "Now that was *real* horror."

Ivan worked in broad strokes. He would set the tone and then polish the formulated responses before serving the "vodka."

"What happened in Prague was a horrible mistake, but one that only affirms the Soviet call for a new era of freedom," said Ivan to his hand-picked group of propagandists gathered together at KGB headquarters in Moscow.

"As we know, the struggle for freedom and equality is often accompanied by bloodshed. We mourn those comrades who so valiantly gave their lives to this cause. We salute our fallen heroes.

"Within the USSR there are those who fear change. During this period of great transition, some of these people still retain positions of power and authority.

"The individual who was in charge of managing the situation in Prague acted outside his authority. He had been given direct orders to maintain public safety and avoid using force except as a defensive measure against armed insurgents who were threatening violence.

"While we have recovered weapons, explosives, and other devices from those who occupied Wenceslas Square, we have no evidence that anyone in the crowd fired the first shot.

"Instead, it was … *Viktor Kulikov*, Military Commander of the Warsaw Pact who personally gave the order to open fire. Kulikov is now under arrest, and his crimes will be dealt with accordingly under Soviet law.

"We denounce his actions in the harshest of terms. There will be no clemency.

"Secretary Sokolov, has called for a moment of silence next Monday morning at nine o'clock to honor the dead," concluded Ivan.

Jaws around the table dropped at mention of Kulikov. Like Sokolov, he was also a Red Army veteran of the Great Patriotic War, a well-known figure in society, and a fellow "Hero" of the Soviet Union. The idea that a man of his stature could be implicated was unimaginable.

Ivan simply smiled and raised his bushy eyebrows. "Prague is a big deal," he said. "Someone big must take this fall.

"You, Anatoly, get your team together on writing this up … for broadcast, embassy distribution, and so forth.

Beneath a furrowed brow, Ivan's eyes sparkled. His plump right hand began to rotate, fingers snapping like a musician leading in the rhythm of a new song.

"We will never forget. *Never.* We ask that the peaceful wishes of the protesters be honored and respected by …" Ivan trailed off for just a moment while searching for the right words, then continued, "… by keeping calm and rejecting any further violence."

He was smiling again.

"Svetlana, have your people pull up some photos Kulikov looking angry and insane … Be sure to find plenty of shots of him with former Secretary Gorbachev. As you know, they were quite close. *Very, very, close,*" said Ivan, shaking his head in disapproval.

"Pavel, your job is to start working backwards … Adjusting records, purging, adding. Make all the details fit," Ivan said, tapping his watch.

"Remember, he who controls the past controls the future."

Too portly to bow, Ivan concluded the meeting with a wink and a broad upward wave.

12

The Soviet Proposal

"Make the lie big, make it simple, keep saying it, and eventually they will believe it."

—Adolf Hitler

Ivan rolled the dice and won beyond anyone's wildest dreams.

The West accepted the story of a rogue hardliner being responsible for the Prague Massacre, because that's what people wanted to believe.

In Eastern Europe news of the massacre was understood as a warning against similar protests. Although Kulikov was an established public figure — a ruthless military man who ran the Warsaw Pact with an iron fist and with a reputation as a hardliner — no one really believed the official story that he acted without direct authorization from Moscow. That's just not how things worked here.

Within days the Western media was welcomed back in, and a photo of Sokolov laying flowers on the grave of a child who had died in the massacre ran on the front page of nearly every paper in the free world.

It was for this kind of service that Ivan drove a new black Mercedes instead of a generic white Lada. It was why he had several homes, but only one name.

Emboldened by their successes abroad and by the lack of opposition at home, the Soviets set about expanding their empire during the spring of 1988. Old relationships with dependable partners were strengthened and new ones were forged. Some alliances were bought, while others were secured through more coercive means. But whatever the method, the number of red patches on the globe was rapidly increasing like a bad case of measles.

March was an especially busy month. Libya's Muammar al-Qaddafi, already tight with Moscow since the 1970s, welcomed new waves of Soviet advisors and equipment to "defend" itself from "imminent aggressive action" by Israel.

These actions were protested by the US, whose calls for a firm international response received little support in Europe lest it affect the flow of Libyan oil. Instead, America was forced to go it alone, stretching its already strained military resources by attempting to implement a naval blockade of the rogue North African state.

While successful in temporarily limiting some shipments of arms, the heavy-handed military response backfired in the court of public opinion. Reagan was criticized as a bully, and new credibility was given to Qaddafi's claim that the US was preparing for an invasion.

Almost overnight, Libya managed to transform its image from pariah to martyr. Likewise for the Soviets, who used the situation as evidence of their commitment to "stand with the oppressed and threatened of the world."

Many other nations soon followed Libya's lead, from Venezuela to Vietnam, each convinced it might become the next victim of American aggression, and finding it hard to rebuke Soviet generosity that reputedly came with no strings attached.

But the USSR had much grander plans than renewing far-flung friendships that had chilled under Gorbachev. They wanted a much bigger and much closer prize: Western Europe.

Getting control of Europe would not be possible so long as America retained its armed presence through NATO, and so the Soviets focused on an all-out public and private lobbying campaign to break the alliance.

Thus, NATO, which had been created in 1949 to curtail the complete Soviet domination of Europe, would now need to be tossed out in order to facilitate it.

Such seemed unimaginable, especially for it to happen now, under the watch of a president who had dedicated his life to fighting Soviet expansionism.

President Reagan applied everything at his disposal to fight back, beginning with an intensive counter-offensive by the state department led by Secretary Schultz. US intelligence services were directed to uncover, and expose the true intentions of the "new" USSR, while the military was to maintain its guard should the Soviets seek to test NATO's capabilities and commitment.

But it seemed a losing battle, as all across Europe, millions were turning out in support of a peaceful European Union. Each week, new details were added to the proposal, some related to policy, others to "shovel ready" projects like extending pipelines from resource rich Russia to the insatiable West.

Specifics regarding the blending of eastern and western military were to be worked out over time. But with the removal of the Americans, commitments could be scaled back significantly. According to Moscow, the European Defense Organization would be an all-volunteer force, composed proportionally of troops reflective of member populations.

As expected, Democrats and the American Left generally embraced the idea of a European Union, noting how money currently "wasted" defending Europe might be better applied to social programs in the United States, or used as foreign aid in the developing world.

The leopard had changed its spots, and it was time to celebrate with French champagne and Russian caviar.

While there were no rallies to rival those of Europe, it became widely accepted even in the US that the Soviet proposal offered a prospect for peace not found in *détente* or in the threat of Mutually Assured Destruction. For decades, these hallmarks of the Cold War policy had treated the symptoms without curing the disease. But now, thanks to Sokolov and the new Soviets, there was plan on the table for a genuine and lasting peace.

In line with the zeitgeist, some in the more progressive wing of Reagan's own party were privately dismissing him as a bit of a Neanderthal. Still loved, still revered, but a pathetic creature that had lived beyond his time and was consequently lost in a world he couldn't quite understand.

Worse yet, he seemed oblivious to the opportunities being offered to him. Here was Reagan's chance to cement his place in history as the president who had ended the Cold War. Obstinate and defiant, Reagan dug in. He prepared for war, and doubled-down on intelligence gathering so as to provide hard evidence of what he believed was the true Soviet agenda.

Most conservatives remained skeptical of the Soviets. But few were ready to make a public stand with the aging and wobbling president.

Most were instead hedging their bets on the wait-and-see ticket. Meanwhile, the public was relieved that his days in office were limited, and his powers restricted by Congress.

Please, please, please, just let this end without Reagan doing something stupid and dragging America into another war.

This being an election year, many worried that Reagan's position as an outlier would hurt the party in the November elections. As these concerns grew, so did calls from some prominent voices on the right for the President to resign and take "early retirement." GOP strategists argued "re-electing" Bush would be easier, and also cap the long-term damage Reagan was likely to inflict on the Republican Party.

Although taking over would not technically count against him serving two complete terms of his own, Bush did not support Reagan leaving office early. For one thing, he would be stuck with Reagan's entire cabinet. Worse yet, he'd be stuck with Reagan's legacy.

Better to begin with a fresh start.

In fact, the longer Reagan stayed around the better it made him look as a new kind of forward-thinking Republican. Or so he hoped.

On the campaign trail, Bush, the GOP's preferred successor had struggled to define himself for voters and his polling numbers remained flat. Advisors, led by campaign director Lee Atwater, now recommended that Bush do more to distance himself from both Reagan the man, and his policies. In short, become kinder and gentler, and write off the crazy right fringe to Buchanan, who was nearly broke and would soon be out of the race altogether.

When November came, the far right would have no choice but to pinch their noses and vote for Bush. Meanwhile, by positioning himself as a moderate best suited to moving America forward, he would have a stronger chance of attracting Independents and swing Democrats.

So, with an eye to the larger electorate, Bush moved away from Reagan, and more towards an embrace of diplomacy and cooperation, rather than distrust and confrontation with the Soviets.

The man for all seasons assured his base that he would never abandon America's commitments to freedom and European security, but then suggested that changing times required fresh and "visionary" approaches.

In a major break with official US policy, still Vice President Bush proclaimed that "Europeans must determine what is best for themselves;

it is not for us to impose solutions, but rather to support them when they support the interests of America."

And the band played on.

Austria

On a continent divided and shaped by conflict, the promise of a new beginning was hard to counter. All America could offer was more of the same: bases, missiles, domination, and the likelihood that someday, perhaps, sooner than later, someone would make a mistake and war would begin.

Whether it would just level Europe again, or be the spark that ended all life on Earth was not a risk worth taking. There was a better way forward, and it made sense: the USSR needed the West, and now had a clear incentive to change course towards a path of peace and cooperation.

Meanwhile, the US also had a clear economic imperative to maintain the status quo. The Americans loved power and needed to keep the party going in order to support a massive military industrial complex that starved children in order to feed the dogs of war.

But now, at last, Europeans would have a say in their own future, and they were looking east and to the start of a new day.

It was time to take action and step one meant getting rid of NATO and closing the chapter on the foreign military occupation of Europe.

Despite aggressive lobbying efforts, support for NATO began to unravel quickly. The first to detach were Iceland, Turkey, and Greece. Meanwhile, France, the Netherlands, and Luxembourg were moving cautiously towards exiting, while Italy and Spain were proposing national referendums.

Brussels was in a quandary over how to maintain the Cold War alliance, especially when continued NATO membership was pitting governments against the will of their citizens. The leaders of Britain and Germany were solidly with the Americans, while others engaged in games to play Moscow off Washington in a contest to see which side was willing to offer up the best deal of cash and prizes.

Reagan resented using financial incentives, seeing them as fiscally irresponsible gifts subsidized by US taxpayers. In exasperation, he denounced the proposed expenditures as a form of extortion, used by unscrupulous Europeans threatening to dump the moralistic frugality of old America for the lavish generosity of Moscow.

Again, Ivan and his fellow propagandists had a field day with Reagan's comments, noting that Americans were willing to break the bank on spending for war, but unwilling to invest a penny in peace and goodwill.

Back in North America, Canada's conservative Prime Minister Brian Mulroney could do little more than offer emotional support to his friend Ronald Reagan. Most European nations held a condescending view of Canadians, and opinions of Canada had dropped dramatically in recent years as it became more closely aligned with the United States and the Reagan administration.

Dissolving NATO presented huge financial and logistical challenges, but the issue led in nearly every public opinion poll on the continent. Not all were convinced, prompting the Soviets to offer proof of their intentions by replacing words with actions.

Although not a member of NATO (and officially neutral), Austria welcomed the Soviet invitation to serve as a model for how the benefits of greater cooperation and unification might work.

This was a somewhat surprising gesture given Austria's recent history with the Soviets, but one that had been negotiated in secret between the two former adversaries.

As with Germany, the allies — including the Soviets — had invaded Austria in 1945 from all sides and then neatly divided it into sections. Whereas the Western powers deemed Austria a victim of Nazi aggression, the Russians regarded the Austrians as willing participants in Hitler's Reich, and treated them accordingly.

Thus, they occupied a large chunk of Austria for roughly a decade, imposing harsh Soviet rule, and with it, tremendous hardship for a nation already exhausted by war. When the Soviets finally dragged their Iron Curtain back to Austria's pre-occupation borders, few were sorry to see it leave.

So why would Austria be the first to welcome the Soviets in?

The entire affair seemed suspicious, but in time it would all make sense, given the secret history of Austria's president, Kurt Waldheim. The Russians had cut deals with Nazis in the past, but this time they held all the cards.

Although Waldheim's Nazi connections had already been exposed—and presumably forgiven by the voters of Austria who elected him their president—the Russians had new, and very damaging information that would not just end his career, but most certainly result in him being charged with war crimes.

Waldheim decided to play ball, never asking the Soviets to provide proof. Which was good, as this saved the KGB the trouble of having to fabricate it.

Instead, the Soviets could focus on presenting Austria as a showcase of the new Europe; in much the same way the Nazis had created the model concentration camp Theresienstadt to illustrate their benevolence towards the Jews.

Having made Waldheim an offer he couldn't refuse, the Soviets set out to curry the favor of the public. For a nation that celebrated the arts, there came pledges of greater cultural exchanges and the return of some paintings stolen by the Nazis that had inexplicably ended up in Russia.

What sealed the deal for the Austrians was the promise to extend a natural gas pipeline that would bring jobs and lower energy costs. Delighted by the opportunity to lead Europe by example, the Austrians rolled out the welcome and shouted *"Willkommen"* to the Soviets.

Building on similar offers, the Soviets easily rolled into Greece, Turkey, and, by plane and ship, into remote little Iceland. Nothing changed immediately, other than the influx of some "defensive" troops and weapons systems, touted as needed for exercises to test how existing forces might begin the process of integration into a post-Cold War EDO.

Soviet generosity seemed genuine, with no downside. Each new partner nation received a custom list of promises of good things—and good times yet to come, in exchange for breaking free from the grip of the American Empire.

The May Day holiday happened to fall on a Sunday that year. So, when the USSR issued yet another bold pronouncement on that day, much of the West was asleep or away. High Noon in Moscow was early Sunday morning in Washington, DC.

Secretary of State Schultz waited until 6am before calling the President. When the Reagans heard the phone ring they knew it was serious, but no idea just how.

Nancy watched as her husband listened grimly for what seemed like an eternity. Finally it was the President's turn to speak.

"That's not going to happen," Reagan said with complete coolness and conviction. "Get the team together … We'll meet 8 o'clock sharp."

Reagan hung up the phone and exhaled sharply.

"The Russians want Germany."

14

Germany

April, noted the poet TS Elliot, is "the cruelest month." This certainly proved true for the President, who had to stand helplessly watching as the Soviets rapidly gained not just real estate, but hearts and minds, from Athens to the office of the Vice President.

On the world stage, the Soviets now dominated the conversation. They spoke of cooperation and hope. They contrasted a global utopia against a planet held hostage by an American Empire that sought unchallenged dominance over the heavens and the Earth.

The Soviets positioned themselves as a peaceful counterbalance. They offered protection, and an ironic new spin on the term, "solidarity" with their fellow Europeans seeking to end the American occupation of Europe.

"Join us," they cried, "and together we can achieve great things."

From ordinary citizens to elected leaders—and even royalty, Europeans danced to the tune that Sokolov, the new pied piper, played as he led the hordes to exactly where he wanted them.

Emboldened by the rate at which NATO support was dissolving, Moscow decided to strike at the direct center of the European and American alliance, by presenting a plan for the reunification of Germany.

The Soviets asserted that West Germany was an occupied nation, and that the Western allies had deceived the USSR when they divided the country up after World War II. It was now time for the massive US occupation to end, and to return Germany to the Germans.

The May Day proposal, like nearly everything else they had done so far, caught the world completely off guard. It was a bold initiative, but also reflective of the larger proposition for a united Europe.

Reunification was an emotional issue for German people, as it had divided both the former capital of Berlin and the nation as a whole. It was a symbol of defeat and humiliation, enforced by masters an ocean away.

Where Washington demanded subservience, Moscow promised liberation.

According to the Soviets, Germany had paid the price for its sins and was now entitled to become an independent member of the world community; free of foreign influence and American military occupation.

In support of this basic democratic right to self-determination, the Soviets were proposing a special referendum on unification and autonomy for the German people. If approved, the referendum would begin the formal process of uniting East and West Germany, and also lay the groundwork for the European Defense Organization, unless the Germans opted to become officially neutral. In either instance, Germany's participation in NATO would end, and the Americans would be shown the door.

The vote would be held in exactly one month's time — on June 1, and would, for the first time in decades, involve the entire German population, no matter which side of the Iron Curtain they lived on.

Shrouded in the fine print of Moscow's offer was the insinuation that Germany was under such American influence that it was impossible to have a fair vote on this issue. The Russians cited examples of American interference and intimidation at every level — starting with, but not limited to, the presence of hundreds of thousands of US troops stationed on German soil.

In other words, the Americans couldn't be trusted to play fairly. If they thought they might lose their "German colony," they'd cheat and resort to election-rigging.

This was the "American way," said the Soviets, citing "a shameful history" of tainted elections and outright fraud to "suppress" minority voters in the United States.

Not surprisingly, such claims resonated with many Europeans who held prejudicial views of the United States as a bigoted and racist nation, based on the civil rights struggles of the 1960s.

Therefore, in advance of the June vote, the Soviets announced their intention to send an undisclosed number of persons into West Germany to monitor, stabilize, and offset American influence and tampering. The "visitors" would be self-sufficient and would begin flowing across the border as early as the following week.

After all, hadn't Chancellor Kohl himself already extended the invitation?

The Russians promised to have these monitors be a multi-national group, with as many East German nationals as possible. Moscow would also assist with election costs, and intended to campaign in favor of the issue, having already signed a deal with a leading West German advertising firm.

The May Day message to America was clear: We want you out of Germany.

Raus!

15

The Co-Pilot Bails Out

"A new breeze is blowing, and a world refreshed by freedom seems reborn; for in man's heart, if not in fact, the day of the dictator is over. The totalitarian era is passing, its old ideas blown away like leaves from an ancient, lifeless tree."

— George HW Bush

Secretary Schultz's news about the Soviet plan for Germany caused Reagan to pause. But the pause was short, more akin to that which one takes when focusing on a target before pulling the trigger, than the type of confused daze that follows such a powerful and unexpected blow.

Reagan's eyes narrowed to a squint. He picked up the phone and directed Chief of Staff Howard Baker to schedule yet another 8am emergency meeting.

As had so often been the case in the past few months, the attendees represented the range of American interests, from diplomatic, to the military, to the intelligence services.

Schultz began by outlining the Soviet proposition—the details of which had been unveiled in the May Day broadcast.

Normally a proposal of such magnitude would have been presented privately, in advance of a broadcast public statement. Flagrantly spurning established diplomatic conventions suggested unprecedented Soviet arrogance and a new contempt for America.

Moscow's message was clear: this is a European issue and it is none of your business.

Despite this slap in the face, it was decided that the US should take the high road and continue to play by the rules. The process would begin with Secretary Schultz contacting the Soviets directly to convey US opposition to the proposal and privately warning them of the consequences. If unsuccessful, the diplomatic corps would begin working their allied counterparts in support of sanctions and other actions through the UN. Meanwhile, the intelligence services would continue to dig for evidence of hidden agendas and nefarious intentions.

Given the Democratic control of Congress and Reagan's imminent departure, the Soviets knew any substantive action by the US was unlikely, and Schultz was shown the door.

Frustrated and humiliated, Schultz turned to Plan B, but American efforts at diplomacy and building a coalition failed. Most nations either supported the Soviet proposition, or were reluctant to take sides.

Privately, the Soviets were more concerned about Reagan as an individual. He seemed to be something of a loose cannon; unconcerned with alienating traditional allies or even how his words and actions were hurting his party's chances in the upcoming elections.

The American president seemed to be unraveling.

The Soviets had Reagan exactly where they wanted him, and it was now time to spring the trap. They believed they held the moral high ground, and with it, the power to drive a stake through the old man's heart. Reagan would have no choice but back away—but only after causing irreparable damage to himself and the US.

It was time to turn the tables and finish him off. It was time to control the narrative with one simple question.

"How can America claim to support democracy, yet denounce the right of the German people to vote on their own future?"

Ivan smiled at the thought of the so-called "Great Communicator" being at a loss for words.

Soon, the question was on everyone's lips. If America opposed democracy, what did it support?

The fog of the Cold War seemed to be lifting, and European's were now seeing America in a very different light.

The Russian-sponsored reunification campaign was well organized and had a huge budget. Airwaves filled with commercials vacillating from heart-wrenching emotional appeals to those promoting the economic benefits of under-utilized factories and access to skilled low-wage East German laborers. In support of unification, many in the West took to wearing small red buttons emblazed with the slogan *"EINS"*—the German word for "one."

When America's UN Ambassador Vernon A Walters finally brought the matter up before the United Nations he spoke to a largely empty hall.

Undaunted, Walters gave an impassioned speech. He warned that Soviet actions threatened to upset the balance of power that had kept Europe stable, prosperous, and at peace since the end of Second World War. Losing West Germany would open new fronts on the borders of Denmark, the Netherlands, Belgium, France, Switzerland, and Austria.

"Then what?" Walters asked.

European delegations were polite, but expressionless. Applause was nonexistent, coming only as the American left the podium.

As a young man, Walters had lived in England and France, and he had traveled the continent extensively. He was fluent in four European languages and knew the Old World more intimately than any other member of the President's team.

When World War II erupted the 24-year-old New York native joined the fight to save Europe. When peace was declared, Walters went to work on the Marshall Plan to rebuild it.

But as one war ended, another began. Cooperation between the victors gave way to suspicion, and divisions in ideology split nations and closed borders. The great showdown known as the Cold War, which began in Europe, soon spread across the world, as the Russians and Americans competed for influence and territory on a global scale.

Hardened by what he saw in the years following the war, Walters became an ardent anti-communist. While stationed in Italy in 1961, he went so far as to suggest an intervention by the US military if socialists were allowed to participate in the governing of a NATO member nation. During the war, he had fought to liberate Italy from Mussolini. To see it sliding back towards totalitarianism so soon troubled him deeply.

Walters was reassigned.

Other posts soon followed, from Latin America to Asia. But in every corner of the world, he was faced with the advancing shadow of socialism.

First as a soldier, then with the CIA, and finally as a diplomat, Walters had spent his life dealing with communists. He didn't like them, didn't trust them, and if he could push a button to make them all go away he would have done it—and he made no apologies for his stance. Instead, he simply pointed to history.

And that was precisely the problem.

For the Europeans (and much of the world), Walters, like Reagan, was seen as an artifact of history. Irrelevant to the present, a threat to the future.

The Europe Walters knew no longer existed. The America Walters represented had outlived its usefulness.

At the UN, American efforts to enact sanctions were either blocked outright by the USSR, or stalled by organization's own byzantine bureaucracy.

Meanwhile Soviet "visitors" and other "goodwill ambassadors" were poring over the border into West Germany. Many in the first waves were indeed East Germans, who were welcomed by their brethren at what had once been one of the most heavily fortified borders on Earth. Exact totals were hard to come by, an odd fact given the German penchant for record keeping, but US intelligence estimated that more than 42,000 persons flowed across the increasingly porous border in just three weeks.

As promised, the visitors were largely self-sufficient.

The vast majority were organized into camps, which were really nothing more than thinly-veiled military-styled outposts. Others were housed in public facilities such as unused government buildings, schools, and vacant commercial spaces.

With funding from Moscow, they stimulated the local economy and contributed to the culture. In Munich, the goodwill ambassadors presented an art exhibit by children from Dresden, DDR (Deutsche Demokratische Republik), featuring exactly 50 tempera paintings decrying the horrors of war and the urgent need for peace (which was, in all instances, accompanied by rainbows).

Support for the Soviets was building across Europe and the promise of utopia now came complete with rainbows!

Do we need to paint you a picture? Children are the future, and it time to listen to what they wanted.

Given the grand promises and the lack of visible problems, public support in the US was rapidly tilting to favor the Soviet proposition for reunification.

Conservative opinion remained divided. While most either didn't trust the USSR or believed another enemy (likely China) would soon rise up to take its place, they did feel that the defense department could be scaled back a bit—especially if this might result in tax cuts.

Although exact figures weren't available, there was no denying that defending Germany was a costly, and until now, open-ended budget item.

For liberals, the European defense budget represented assets that could now be applied to serving the needs of the American people—and not just the military-industrial complex.

The expression "What if they gave a war and nobody showed up?" enjoyed a popular resurgence.

Democrats running for office spoke of a golden age of fully funded government assistance programs—all of which could be made possible by simply flipping the switch from guns to butter (presumably organic butter produced by free-range cattle).

People were desperate for hope and good news—and the Soviets were dishing it out.

"1999," a song released by Prince six years earlier was re-released and began to climb the charts again worldwide.

For many, Germany represented the start of an exciting new era. For others, it was the thin edge of the wedge that would lead to the Soviet domination of Europe.

As Reagan saw it, this would not end war, but make it inevitable.

The President knew he was right, and he wasn't about to give up. Instead, he would stay the course and do whatever he could to keep his nation—and the world—safe and free for as long as he had the power to do it, Lame Duck or not.

America's 40th President was determined to not go quietly. He refused to tone down his rhetoric, even though it was causing many in his own party to distance themselves from him.

Phone calls went unreturned. More than a few close friends tried to warn him of the harm he was doing to his legacy. As predicted, Reagan was now dragging down the entire GOP with less than seven months until the fall elections.

"Let him exhaust himself digging his own grave," laughed Ivan.

While never publicly taking sides, it was obvious the Soviets would prefer to deal with a Democratic administration, which now seemed likely, along with the party's control of Congress.

Despite his attempts to distance himself from Reagan, support for Vice President Bush's candidacy was in real trouble. If the election were "held tomorrow," Bush would lose to his likely Democratic challenger Governor Michael Dukakis by at least seven points.

The trajectory was clear.

But the Veep was a fighter. He would do what needed to be done.

During World War II Bush had been a pilot who, following an air battle in the Pacific, had parachuted to safety. Details of exactly what happened that day were controversial, but there was no disputing that Bush did what he needed to do in order to save himself.

And so it was on the campaign trail, when Bush did what he believed was necessary to save his political life.

In his biggest break with the President to date, Bush publically warmed to the Soviet proposals, a position which more closely aligned him with the latest opinion surveys of likely voters. He revised his stump speech to present himself as a "progressive conservative."

Reagan was a lost cause, and Bush needed to define himself as his own man—and not just the President's lap dog—a term coined by columnist George Will.

It was now or never.

Much to the chagrin of conservatives, Bush not only publicly criticized Reagan, but went so far as to compare himself to Sokolov, speaking of his own similar transformation from warrior to man of peace (and vision). Someone prepared for the "new world order."

In support of his miraculous conversion into a new kind of leader, Bush broke with tradition and announced his running mate well in advance of the Republican convention scheduled for August in New Orleans.

To everyone's surprise, Bush selected Dan Quayle, a young Senator from Indiana to be his choice as America's next Vice President. Troubling to many was the fact that Senator Quayle, with less than a dozen years of political experience, would be a heartbeat away from the presidency.

Bush's first major decision did indeed grab headlines, but the response was not favorable. The selection of Quayle had been made with no forewarning, and the big donors were not pleased.

Still the campaign team had high hopes. When Bush introduced his running mate at a rally in Gary, Indiana, it was to the tune "The Future's So Bright, I Gotta Wear Shades," which had been a minor hit two years earlier by the post-punk band Timbuk3.

Wearing matching sunglasses and high-fiving one another onstage while music blared, Bush and Quayle looked more like a third-rate Blue Brothers tribute act than the future of the Grand Old Party.

The relationship between Reagan and Bush, never strong, became considerably more strained. Even more troubling was the split taking place on Reagan's own team, with a few members, perhaps looking ahead to serving in the Bush administration, openly shifting their allegiances to the Vice President.

Whether Bush had genuinely fallen under Sokolov's spell or he was just looking to woo voters was open to debate. After a quick rise in the polls, his numbers began to fall once again.

Conservatives lambasted him as a turncoat, while centrists (and pretty much everyone else) questioned his sincerity.

Unlike Midas, who turned everything he touched into gold, Bush seemed afflicted with the opposite ability. The man could do nothing right.

In a desperate bid to appeal to the party's fiscally conservative base, the candidate urged them to "read my lips" and promised "no new taxes." But something didn't ring up right—like the uncertainty one experiences in watching a poorly dubbed foreign film. Is that really what he said? Something just seemed out of sync.

The strategy of trying to be all things to all people had backfired. Bush struggled, and instead of redefining himself, came off as the rudderless captain of a sinking ship.

Bush felt that he could still turn things around, and believed that the party would rally behind him once was he was the official nominee.

Although written off as a goodwill gesture by those still loyal to the President, a move began on Capitol Hill to repeal the 22nd Amendment which would permit him to serve a third term.

Reagan was personally touched by this act of support, but brushed away any possibility of another term with characteristic humor, telling supporters that he didn't have enough money to run again. He joked that Nancy was too much of a fiscal conservative to take out yet another mortgage on their house in California.

Despite the unpopularity of his hard stance towards the Soviets, Reagan continued polling higher than Bush. On the Democratic side, Dukakis appeared to have the nomination sewn up, although support was soft. Still, he would beat Bush — and that was all that mattered.

Unlike Bush, Dukakis stated that he would not officially announce his Vice Presidential selection until the party convention in July. This was a time-tested practice for creating suspense and mystery, which usually had more to do with indecisiveness than strategy. But this time around it seemed to have little effect. American voters had yet to express anything resembling enthusiasm for the options being offered up as their next president, and party leaders were getting nervous.

Despite the great changes taking place in the world, most voters seemed disengaged from the issues and the candidates. Reagan had represented one revolution that began eight years previous, and now the great torch of change had been passed across the Atlantic.

In France, Socialist and star-struck Sokolov supporter François Mitterrand was elected on May 8 to a seven-year term as President. Having earned the dubious distinction of being crowned the lesser of two evils, Dukakis looked forward to his November coronation and the prospect of a united Democratic Congress.

Given the absence of a direct threat and warming temperatures, Americans turned their attentions elsewhere. But as spring turned to summer, things would begin to heat up in ways no one could have forecast.

16

East is East and West is West

With no backing from the UN or the NATO allies, President Reagan was forced to take unilateral action—a diplomatic euphemism meaning "to go it alone."

Support from within his own White House team was divided for a range of reasons. Some, like Secretary of Education Lauro Cavazos, were clearly behind Vice President Bush and enthusiastic about the prospect of ending the Cold War. He saw Reagan as so brainwashed by ideology that he was unable to even grasp what the Soviets were offering.

"So be it!" thought Cavazos. Let history remember Reagan as the man who fought the Cold War and Bush as the one who won it.

Reagan personally liked Cavazos, even though he did not always see eye-to-eye with the 41-year-old Democrat. Jokingly referring to Cavazos' party affiliation as a sign of "youthful indiscretion," Reagan reminded his cabinet secretary that he himself had been a Democrat for most of his life, and that he still supported many of the party's positions.

The President was also quick to credit a Democratic president—FDR—for taking a stand against Nazi Germany and Imperialist Japan. Reagan also respected FDR's successor, and credited Truman's decision to use atomic weapons with ending World War II.

"If not for Democrats like FDR and Truman, the world would look very different today. In fact, the United States might not even exist."

Try as he might, the President's efforts to connect were unsuccessful. Descended from a proud pioneer family, Cavazos would not be "educated" on history by an actor, especially one whose final bow was now just months away.

Cavazos hailed from Texas, and he and Bush were close friends. Following his break with the President, the secretary kept a low profile, staying away from Washington as much as possible. Instead, he spent his days on the campaign trail for Bush, pitching the down, but not out, candidate to small groups of Latinos across the Southwest.

In times of turbulence, when war clouds are forming just beyond the horizon, the loss of a cabinet member like the Secretary of Education, to the Bush camp, was not something that caused Reagan to lose sleep.

Of a much greater concern was the apparent defection of Defense Secretary Frank Carlucci.

Troubling, but not totally unexpected. Carlucci was a relatively young man with a promising political future. He was also an opportunist who had worked for both Republican and Democratic administrations.

While never directly confrontational, Reagan sensed a shift in Carlucci that troubled him. Initially, the President wondered whether Carlucci had the experience to handle Defense in a square off with the Soviets, having only been in the position for less than six months. Now he questioned whether Carlucci's heart was really in the fight.

Meanwhile, stalwarts like Secretary of State George Schultz remained solidly alongside the President, as did former Defense Secretary Caspar Weinberger. Although run out of office due to the Iran-Contra affair, "Cap" remained in regular contact with Reagan as an unofficial advisor. Like the President, Weinberger regarded the Soviet proposition as little more than a sugar-coated poison pill.

"I've dealt with these people face to face," Weinberger said. "Take a look at who is running the show now. It's not Gorbachev's moderates. It's the worst of the worst." The man who had served the longest tenure as Defense Secretary in US history was not one to mince words.

Strengthened by the support of trusted advisors and old friends, Reagan stunned the world when he announced that the US would not accept the legitimacy of the Soviet-sponsored German referendum.

The current West German government had been elected by the people, Reagan argued, and it was up to that government to determine what was best for the nation — not the Russians. In a democracy, the people elect a government and it is that government which has the authority to act on behalf of its citizens.

"Obviously, it should come as no surprise that the Soviets don't understand what a democracy is and have no interest in learning," Reagan said. "In their sales pitch for a European Union, they claim they will respect individual member state protocols and political institutions. If this is the evidence for that, then it's time to say *nein*."

Later that night he took to the airwaves with a speech from the Oval Office. The President mocked the idea of reshaping borders by mob rule, and denounced the plan to flood West Germany with "election monitors" as a "Trojan Horse."

"Mr Sokolov," inquired the President, "would you be willing to permit American and NATO troops to roll across your borders, set up an election asking citizens whether they wanted to be free of communism, and then have us stay on to impose our solution with force?

"Well, would you?"

The world watched anxiously as Reagan looked directly into the camera and issued his ultimatum. Even those who disagreed with his position had to acknowledge the validity of his argument.

Fair is fair, right?

In addition to never accepting the referendum, Reagan wanted the recent waves of eastern migrants to leave West Germany by the middle of June, or they would be "politely ushered out." Beginning immediately, the Americans would be "assisting" West Germany with border security, and no further breaches would be tolerated.

The President's tone was firm and stern. And, although not expressed directly, it was clear that the US Commander-in-Chief was drawing a line in the sand, and would not hesitate from using force to defend it.

Reagan's stance was not entirely unexpected. The Russians knew they'd been on a roll. And they knew that every winning streak must, if not end, then at least have a short pause.

So be it.

Moscow had succeeded in stirring up German dissent and further positioning the Americans as aggressors, fearful, and threatened by change. A distant foreign empire that regarded West Germany as their property.

The brinkmanship of the two superpowers had an immediate impact on the world economy, but the confrontation was short-lived. Within 48 hours, the Soviets announced there would be a delay in implementing the "Reunification" referendum, and a suspension of any further influx of citizens from the east.

While backing away from a direct physical confrontation, the Soviets persisted in their support for a unified and autonomous Germany.

Reagan's tough stance was a PR coup for the Soviets, creating new divisions between Europeans and their governments, and within the various member states of NATO. But for now, the existing borders would remain in place.

Sokolov's old friend Alexander Koldunov, now serving as Minister of Foreign Affairs, attacked Reagan's "strong-arm tactics" in both the press and in a speech at the United Nations. In addition, Koldunov denounced the US-backed deportations, stating that the fate of those already in West Germany should be decided by the Germans not the Americans, and that the US had no business tearing families apart and expelling people, who, "unlike the American military, had a legitimate and historical claim to be in Germany."

On the surface, the battle over Germany appeared to be a draw. But there was no contesting that it was Moscow, and not Washington, that was winning the war for the hearts and minds in Europe—and in America.

17

From Bad to Worse

When Ronald Reagan ran for the presidency in 1980 he campaigned on the promise of a better future, and over the course of two terms in office things steadily improved. But most importantly, he had restored a sense of pride and optimism to the American people.

In his last year in office, however, much of that had eroded. The nation was skidding towards war, the economy was on the rocks, and where once there had been hope, now there was uncertainty, doubt, and fear.

If Reagan were to run for re-election, he would not be able to gamble it all on asking voters to choose him based on the simple question "Are you better off today than you were four years ago?"

If he did, he would most certainly lose.

Not surprisingly, the Democrats (led by Dukakis) were using this question to chip away at Republicans. They welcomed peace with the Soviet Union, and were happy to have Moscow define the terms.

Ending Reagan's standoff would fix the economy, and allow them to shower voters with gifts.

It was a hard argument to fight, and for the most part, American voters were buying it. Many Republicans, including George HW Bush, their presumptive candidate for president, had warmed to it.

Bush regarded himself as a visionary with cross-party appeal.

"I'm a conservative, but I'm not a nut about it. I'm a progressive-conservative. A forward-thinking progressive, that just so happens to be conservative at heart. Like sweet and sour sauce. A little bit sweet, a little bit sour!"

The coalition Bush envisioned was a fantasy. Instead, his silly pandering only served to alienate the party's conservative base, while doing little to attract Democrats.

Rather than accept personal responsibility, the Bush campaign put the blame on Reagan. Where Bush sought to build bridges, Reagan was burning them by being excessively hawkish and uncompromising. In the words of the campaign's marketing director, Reagan was "tarnishing the

Republican brand," and thus taking the party, and its chosen successor, down with him.

The President seemed to be fighting a losing battle on all fronts, and the pressure was on to tone it down — and if not exactly embrace peace with the Soviets, at least bury the hatchet. Get behind Bush — now.

The party had a plan, and it was depending on Reagan to fall in line and follow the script.

While a lesser man would have accepted the situation — especially given the small amount of time remaining to him in office — Reagan would choose a different path. He would not surrender to the Soviets in exchange for an easy peace. He would not go quietly in order to "stop embarrassing Bush" or to "cause further damage to the GOP."

He would not be blackmailed into submission.

Sustained by family, faith in God, and an unshakeable commitment to freedom, Reagan was prepared to take a stand and fight for what he believed in, and what he knew to be right.

For now, Ronald Reagan was still the President, and he would do as he saw best, and that meant pursuing peace through strength — not weakness. When his time came to leave office he would do it just as he had entered it: with his head held high, committed to the principles he believed in.

No excuses. No apologies. No surrender.

Within days, Reagan's toughness paid off. Following his direct challenge to the German reunification plan, Moscow backed down and the June 1 referendum was officially pulled from the table.

Tensions in Germany de-escalated quickly. The border between east and west was reinstated, and, with support from the Americans, the flow thinned to a trickle.

As the Bundestag debated how best to deal with the thousands of "visitors" already in the country, the Soviets made a new dramatic offer to further the goodwill, announcing that they were retargeting all missiles currently aimed at West Germany — save for the US military bases — of which there were many.

But for now West German towns and cities were no longer targeted. All for the spirit of peace.

Once again, the Soviets were controlling the story, and thus perceptions. Would the Americans and NATO respond accordingly to remove East German cities and civilian targets?

No comment.

News of the retargeting pledge was met with widespread elation. Across West Germany, rallies in support of the voided reunification referendum continued—at least partially sponsored by the Soviets. While generally peaceful, most rallies included burning an effigy of the American president, prompting Reagan to quip that he wished he had bought stock in the company that made the rubber masks of him when he had his chance.

But the damage had already been done.

For the first time in history, a majority of Germans polled now felt it was time for the US to end, or at least significantly scale back its presence in "their" country.

While elections were still some time off, Chancellor Kohl's conservatives were quickly losing ground to the far-left *Grüne Partei* (Green Party), which made unification with the east and joining Moscow's European Union cornerstones of its platform.

A similar sentiment was sweeping the continent, where, from Scandinavia to Sicily support for the European Union was leading in most opinion polls. In nations (such as Austria) where a "try some, buy some" version was already in existence, the results appeared favorable, and served as an important propaganda tool for the benefits of aligning with Moscow.

Despite its long flirtatious relationship with communism, losing Greece—the birthplace of democracy—hit President Reagan especially hard. He tried to laugh it off, noting it was "the same country that gave us Michael Dukakis." More troubling than the speed at which the Greeks had turned, was the bellicosity that now tainted their relationship with the Americans. They wanted the US out ASAP, and were even threatening to hold hostage NATO equipment until "looted ancient treasures" currently held by US museums were returned.

Greece was not alone. The second week of June went especially bad, with both Italy and Spain officially requesting that the US submit a plan to remove all military personnel and equipment from their soil within a year.

Even Great Britain, America's staunchest ally, seemed to be slipping away. Support for continued membership in NATO was now in the low twenties, and it was pretty much a given that Thatcher and her fellow Tories would be resoundingly routed at the next possible opportunity.

If there was a high point in European opposition, it had only symbolic value, when the Netherlands defeated the USSR on June 25 to win the European Football Championship 88, 2-0 in a true, David vs Goliath upset.

But the good times were to be short-lived, and whatever joy the soccer win brought was quickly displaced when later that evening a bomb exploded in a West Berlin nightclub, killing 51 Americans, including 38 US troops.

On the Paris metro, a US soldier had his throat slit; in Norway, ambassador Robert Stuart's residence was set on fire; in Northern Ireland, someone attempted to mail "More-regret" Thatcher a bomb, c/o 10 Downing Street, listing "Ronnie Raygun, Fascist Republik of Amerika" as the sender.

In response to rampant anti-Americanism, US tourism in Europe plummeted, with travelers reporting harassment, and even assaults, simply because of their nationality. Many tried to pass themselves off as Canadians, but were quickly outted when unable to answer even the most basic questions about America's neighbor to the north.

Each week seemed to bring more bad news, and July did not begin well for American interests.

First, the Soviets gained another huge PR victory with the completion of a major bridge linking Istanbul, Turkey with the continent of Europe. The bridge was at least partially paid for by Moscow, and was held up to the world as a symbol of what was possible when nations cooperated peacefully. Or more specifically, when NATO nations aligned with the USSR.

As a link between Europe and Asia, Turkey held tremendous strategic value to both sides. To the north was the Black Sea, Ukraine and Russia, to the west Greece. Turkey also shared borders with such Soviet states as Bulgaria and Georgia, as well as Russia's ally Syria to the south.

By the time the span across the Bosphorus opened for business, Turkey was already home to thousands of Soviet "bridge builders," who were warmly welcomed by the general population and the government.

Long played as a pawn between American and Soviet interests, secular Turkey became especially important to the United States following the Islamic Revolution in neighboring Iran. The West, and the US in particular, had worked hard to establish ties with the Turks, so to see Turkey gobbled up so easily was not a welcome sight.

But the opening of the bridge in Turkey would not be that day's top story.

Instead, that distinction would go to a horrific mistake made by the United States military, which accidentally shot down a civilian Iranian air liner, resulting in the deaths of 290 persons.

Iran Air Flight 655 was *en route* from Tehran to Dubai when it was blown apart while still in Iranian air space by missiles fired by the *USS Vincennes*. Under the command of William C. Rogers III, the ship, a recently commissioned guided-missile cruiser was just part of a larger operation trying to monitor and defend US and Western interests in the region.

While not directly linked to the Soviets, Iran had been a consistent problem for the US, its neighbors, and much of the civilized world.

Since 1979 the Ayatollah Khomeini had ruled Iran, who seized power following the Islamic Revolution that overthrew the Shah.

In actions supported by Khomeini, student radicals attacked the US embassy in Tehran and held 52 Americans hostage for 444 days.

Fearing a direct confrontation with the new no-nonsense president, the hostages were freed on the exact day of Reagan's inauguration. However, in the years that followed, the Iranians, either directly, or through proxy groups and organizations, became major sponsors of terrorism.

Chief among these groups was Hezbollah, which the United States believed was, through its surrogate Islamic Jihad, responsible for the 1983 Beirut barracks attack that killed nearly 300 American and French troops.

And now, in addition to all the old problems—from Iran to Lebanon—the Soviets were presenting unforeseen challenges; winning new friends (as with Turkey), while solidifying old relationships with the Syrian dictator Hafez al-Assad, and rogue aggressor states like Libya.

The Middle East was of critical strategic importance: home to the world's oil fields—the lifeblood of the West, as well as Israel, America's closest friend in the region.

Eventually, something had to give—and it did.

For months, US forces had been on maximum alert and stretched to their breaking point. With little, declining, unreliable, or no support from allies, the United States had been forced to take on far more than its share. As former Secretary of State Henry Kissinger once noted, "No country can act wisely simultaneously in every part of the globe at every moment in time."

The tragedy of Iran Air Flight 655 was that it was genuinely an accident, caused by a weary crew of sailors who, while attempting to do good, made a terrible error out of confusion and haste.

The incident was perhaps inevitable, as was the subsequent exploitation of it by Soviet propagandists.

For many, this was the final straw, positioning the United States as either incompetent or trigger-happy; take your pick. Might the US next accidentally fire off a nuclear missile?

If so, then what?

Something needed to be done, and the Soviets had just the solution.

18

The Soviets Prepare to Fight

"Americans are the great Satan ... the wounded snake."

— Ayatollah Ruhollah Khomeini

The US knew the Soviets would seek to exploit the tragedy of the downed Iranian airliner, but the degree to which they did caught everyone off guard.

On the very next day, which coincided with America's July 4 Independence Day holiday, General Secretary Sokolov again stepped on to the world stage.

The speech was scheduled for a live broadcast at 6pm that night (Moscow time), which corresponded to late morning in Washington, DC.

This year, the fourth fell on a Monday, making for a true three-day weekend in the US. Being a holiday, few were following the news; instead, most Americans were focused on family, food, and fireworks.

Meanwhile, it was business as usual for the President and his team. Ever since the February coup, intelligence gathering had been spotty at best, which meant that the Americans had no advance knowledge of what the Soviets planned to talk about that night. But, given the hype that had preceded it ("a message concerning the future of the world"), it was decided Reagan and his inner circle should tune in for the live broadcast.

Sokolov's speech, broadcast internationally (as a radio address only) opened on a somber note, touching on the events of the previous day and offering Moscow's condolences, and pledge of assistance, to the Iranian people.

The Soviet leader stated that he personally mourned the loss of the innocent lives—including women and children. He then demanded that "those responsible be brought to justice."

"Whether this slaughter of innocent civilians in Iran's own air space was intentional or truly an accident is not known, but, as the old Russian proverb warns: if you walk around with a hammer, after a while everything starts looking like a nail."

Sokolov called for an independent investigation (led by Moscow), noting that the United States had yet to assume responsibility, offer an apology, or even condolences.

"Steps must be taken to make sure something like this never happens again. Never," Sokolov said.

The issue thus framed, the Soviet leader transitioned to the real reason for his broadcast, and as he did, it became apparent that what he had to say had been planned out long in advance.

Speaking as an "independent voice, which cannot be bullied into silence by the Americans," Sokolov stated that the US had no right to use its military powers without consequence. The US was an aggressive international pariah, involved in one conflict after another, responsible for coups, and guilty of propping up right-wing dictatorships.

The American Empire was built on force, and, as the Iranian incident illustrated, a threat to innocent people everywhere.

"We are all Iranians today," Sokolov noted gravely.

"It is time for the civilized people of the world to stand as one, not just in solidarity with our Persian brothers, but in opposition to a nation that behaves with impunity, without conscience or remorse. A nation that rejects peace, on Earth, and in the heavens above.

"A line must be drawn. Space does not belong to the American Empire. The world does not wish to be held hostage by a militaristic empire that controls the high ground. If the Americans are allowed to achieve this there will be no going back: they will be unstoppable.

"But time is running out. We must start now. Only by acting together as one, might we hope to succeed.

"Therefore, the Soviet Union is prepared to step up and lead, by taking the following steps:

"First, we will immediately assist those nations seeking to improve their defensive capabilities.

"Next, we will also look at instituting regime change in nations where

America uses puppet governments to oppress the will of the people.

"This will be a global initiative, *and it will include Europe*," said Sokolov, pausing to let the impact of this statement sink in.

"We will begin on the continent that is our home—not theirs. This is where American foreign dominance is concentrated, and where it must be challenged first."

Challenged?

Reagan shot Schultz an inquisitive glance. As a term, this was a rather provocative choice. Was this a translation error, lacking nuance—or were the Soviets threatening to take on the US over Europe?

Sokolov continued speaking.

"Our plan for Europe is to begin by retargeting all Soviet weapons currently directed at European targets—save for US military outposts. This proposal expands upon the one we already have in place for Germany, but now it is our mission to make all of Europe a nuclear-free zone.

"Europeans have made it clear: They do not want these weapons on their soil, and so it is time for the Americans to leave and to take their arsenals of death with them. It is only when this forced occupation ends that the dream of a continent free of intervention, defined by peace and cooperation, can become a reality.

"If we can dismantle their empire on Earth, we can stop it from conquering space.

"Thus, we, as citizens of a new united Europe, are giving notice to our American friends: we want you to leave, and to do it peacefully by the end of this year. We are no longer your prisoners, but are from this day, July 4, 1988, free and independent!

"We do not wish to be antagonistic; this is a peace initiative. We seek to liberate without violence, and ask that the Americans behave civilly and not resort to any further aggressive actions. However, should force be required, we are prepared to respond defensively and decisively in support of the people's liberation.

"Our objective is simple: to stop the Americans from starting another war on a continent that has already suffered far too much. Therefore, we will secure these operations, neutralize the weapons, and supervise the exodus of the occupying troops."

And so began World War III.

★ 19 ★
Not On My Watch

Secretary Sokolov's speech wrapped up by promising that details of the European Independence Plan would soon be unveiled, and that the Soviets would begin immediately working with their allies and the American "occupiers" to facilitate its peaceful implementation.

"May the dream of peace soon be a reality. Thank you," Sokolov concluded, as the Soviet anthem began to play out the broadcast.

The White House audience was stunned. Had Sokolov really just announced a plan to have Soviet forces roll across Western Europe and forcibly eject the Americans?

All eyes were on the President.

"Not on my watch," said the President. "We don't want war, but God has endowed our nation with special responsibilities, from which we must not waver."

Reagan smiled, and gave that familiar tilt of his head.

"We're the good guys, remember? Good guys stand and fight, and in the end, good always triumphs."

That simple assurance, radiating confidence without bravado, strength grounded by calm conviction, was exactly what the group needed to hear from their Commander-in-Chief.

Vice President Bush was not present at the meeting; instead, he was in Maine to spend the holiday with his family, and to prepare for the Republican Party convention, scheduled for the following month at the Superdome in New Orleans.

Given what had just transpired, it was probably best that Bush, who had chosen to align with Sokolov was not there. Nor were many of his major supporters on the cabinet, other than Treasury Secretary James Baker. But, unlike Cavazos, Baker was not one to confront the President. Instead, he kept his opinions to himself and did his job.

Baker looked at the President and nodded.

Reagan held his gaze, and again, communicated what needed to be done: it would be Baker's job to deal with Bush, and deal with the corner he had painted himself into by cozying up to the Soviets. Reagan had no time for that, or for his VP's political aspirations right now.

As if on cue, the room became a flurry of activity as members broke into groups, scheduled meetings, and drew up plans.

Being a holiday, Sokolov's speech had little immediate impact on the American public, but given its significance, and potential for sensationalism, it was the top story the following morning.

Included in the coverage was a statement issued by the White House denouncing the Soviet plan and calling for calm. Secretary of State Schultz was pursuing diplomacy, and the matter was scheduled for an emergency session at the UN. Meanwhile, NATO forces were put on their highest state of alert.

It was also announced that the President would address the nation at noon that day.

Reagan's speech was short, but direct. He emphasized that the American presence was in Europe at the request of the host countries, "nations whose democratically-elected governments asked for America's help in stopping the advance of totalitarianism that accompanied the expansion of the Soviet empire at the end of the Second World War."

Resolute and forceful, Reagan continued with his denunciation of the Soviet proposal, citing the lessons of post-war history.

"The only reason they have not conquered all of Europe so far is that they were stopped by a force equal to their own, something only the United States can provide.

"As those enslaved behind the Iron Curtain know all too well, once lost, it is hard, perhaps impossible, to regain freedom if held captive by an evil empire that uses force to maintain control.

"Moscow's record is the same everywhere, including their most recent conquest: Afghanistan. A formerly free and independent nation whose brutal, illegal invasion and occupation was personally directed by Commander Sergei Sokolov—the same man who now wants to finish in Europe what his predecessor Joseph Stalin couldn't."

Reagan concluded by stating that the United States would stand with, and defend its European partners against any and all Soviet aggression.

"Freedom is never more than one generation away from extinction. We didn't pass it to our children in the bloodstream. It must be fought for, protected, and handed on for them to do the same.

"Freedom comes with a cost, one that at times must be paid for in blood. This is not something I take lightly, nor anything I welcome. But our nation must not shy from our responsibility, commitments, or principles."

As a man who had witnessed firsthand the events that led up to World War II, Reagan warned of the dangers of indecisiveness and appeasement. "History teaches us that it is always better to meet the challenge head on, as the best defense, is a good offense."

The President paused momentarily while the impact of what he was alluding to sank in, namely the hint that the United States might be considering a first-strike option against the Soviets should they attempt an invasion.

"May God bless us all as we rise to meet our destiny."

20

Hey Now, What's That Sound?

The threat of a direct military confrontation between the US and the USSR over Europe created worldwide panic: stock markets collapsed, oil, gold, and other commodities surged.

People stockpiled food, guns, and when the store shelves emptied, they rioted.

Those who had been postponing marriage tied the knot; ex-smokers, ex-drinkers, and dieters lost their will power. Suicides spiked, as some decided to choose their own time and method of saying farewell, rather than be incinerated in a mushroom cloud, or die slowly from radiation poisoning and famine.

Across the world, millions, then tens of millions, then hundreds of millions turned out for peace rallies. Never had the danger of war seemed so high, and the consequences so great as when the two superpowers squared off, neither willing to blink.

Reagan's consistency, once discredited as stubbornness, was now seen as reassuring. So long as he remained president, the Soviets would not be permitted to roll into sovereign states for the purpose of establishing a regime aligned with Moscow. If they tried, they would encounter the Americans there to stop them.

The Commander-in-Chief's resolve seemed to catch the Soviets off guard, and once again they found themselves on the defensive. Issuing a series of "clarifications," Moscow said its intentions were being misconstrued. Often, one statement seemed to contradict another, suggestive of policy being developed by a committee with dissenting points of view along with just plain old ineptitude.

During the crisis, support for Reagan's leadership grew at home and abroad, while declining even further for Bush, his would-be successor. For most of his campaign, the VP had been under the Soviet spell and he was now paying the price for it politically, especially with conservative Republicans who had abandoned him in droves. Bush's fawning over Sokolov was not easily forgotten, nor forgiven, and his pitch to be "the only one who could broker a peace deal" rang hollow, even to those who believed that such a deal might still be possible.

"A new world order," Bush's catchphrase for a utopian future based on partnering with the Soviets, quickly became a punch line for satirists.

Bob Dole, Bush's main primary rival wasn't faring much better. Having largely avoided committing one way or the other regarding the Soviets, the Senator from Kansas had done little to define himself as a leader.

With the party convention fast approaching, the GOP was in deep trouble.

Although Dukakis had been even more trusting of Moscow, he had not been hurt to the same degree politically. Many on the left still believed that peace was possible, and that their candidate was the one best suited to achieving it. In response, the campaign quickly issued a new commercial in which Dukakis assured voters he would never launch a first strike, or start a war in Europe that would spread to America.

Polling numbers also showed a growing support for Dukakis from Libertarians and other non-interventionist voters. Many Americans simply did not feel that Europe was worth fighting over.

Let the Russians have it. Hell, let them take whatever they want — just keep us out of it.

Surveys of voters showed great dissatisfaction with both leading presidential options, and no third party candidate appeared ready to ride in and save the day. In a national poll released on July 11 (ten days before the opening of the Democratic Convention in Atlanta), Dukakis was now ahead of Bush by 21 points.

Affairs at home, and all around the world were mired in confusion, fear, and uncertainty. Would it be peace or war?

Following a threat by North Korea, (a solid ally of the USSR), the summer Olympics scheduled for Seoul, South Korea were cancelled, and plans for the annual summer recess by Congress were suspended.

But, for the most part, the first three weeks of July remained quiet, with no direct military clashes between the superpowers. Since May, the USSR had been amassing forces along European borders and coastal waters. The US had attempted something similar, but with lackluster backing by other NATO members and a Congress controlled by Democrats, the advantage was definitely with the Soviets. Now, the US was scrambling to catch up, as the doomsday clock counted down the minutes.

With so much of the world's focus on Europe, it came as a great surprise when, in the early morning hours of Sunday, July 25, a squadron of Soviet MIGs entered US airspace near Alaska.

Fighters from Elmendorf Air Force Base (located near Anchorage) engaged, resulting in the downing of two Soviet planes. But this victory came with a price: the loss of six US aircraft, along with nine crewmembers.

By direct order of the President, the US hit back, first against a Soviet destroyer in nearby waters, followed by the downing of a Russian reconnaissance plane heading towards the Aleutian Islands. Then, for good measure, Reagan ordered the sinking of a Russian minesweeper (harbored in a Venezuelan port for repairs), followed by a hit on a Sverdlov-class cruiser off the coastal waters of Norway (the ship was seriously damaged, but did not sink).

A line of tanks that had just rolled across Greece's northern border with Bulgaria was completely destroyed, as was a military transport heading towards Iceland.

And so it began.

The speed and the ferocity of the US response was shocking, especially to the Soviets, who claimed the intrusion of their aircraft into US airspace was accidental, and not intended to be provocative.

President Reagan took personal responsibility for both the Soviet incursion into American airspace, and for what was denounced as an overly aggressive response that spread the conflict to other theaters, including Latin America and across the expanse of the European continent.

The Soviets demanded an apology, and spoke of reparations — poisoned bait which Reagan had no intention of taking. Instead of contrition, the President expressed courage and determination.

Reagan's message was clear: "We did not start this conflict, nor do we welcome it. However, any strike on the United States or against one of our allies will be dealt with in a way to discourage, when possible, or disable, when necessary, any further aggressive action by those who mean us harm."

Reverend Jesse Jackson, who had challenged Dukakis from the party's far left fringe in the primaries, flew to Moscow to engage in his own unique brand of shuttle diplomacy and showmanship. Seeking to "mediate and facilitate," many regarded Jackson's efforts as nothing more than an audition for the job of Secretary of State, in what now seemed an inevitable Dukakis administration.

Over the course of his three-day visit, Jackson spent most of his time in the company of KGB agents that were being passed off as reporters and photographers. Meetings with government officials (including Sokolov) were nothing more than photo ops.

No major peace deal was struck, and like Jane Fonda before him, the Reverend returned to America empty-handed, but inspired.

Despite safety concerns (given proximity to the new "front line"), President Reagan insisted on travelling to Alaska to attend a memorial service to pay his respects to the fallen. Rather than slip in using anonymous military transport, he chose to fly in on Air Force One.

The memorial service was private, and when the President left the ceremony, he appeared to have tears in his eyes. No transcript of his words was made public, and those in attendance described it only as a private ceremony, in which the President's unrehearsed and unscripted comments did much to assuage the grief felt by surviving family, friends, and fellow warriors.

Even though the Soviet incursion was by no means justification for a nuclear strike, speculation in the press was rampant as to when and where the President might call upon America's vast arsenal. When grilled by reporters, Reagan refused to either rule out this option, or provide a detailed explanation of what might prompt such a response.

Those who knew Reagan felt he would only use such weapons as a last resort, believing that such would likely destroy all life on the planet. Still, Reagan was a mystery to the Soviets; a man of peace, but also one who clearly evoked that defining character of the American identity, namely that it was better to die on one's feet than to live on one's knees.

Diplomatic efforts continued, but with little success. As a formality, several European nations went on record at the UN as stating they did not welcome an invasion/liberation by the Soviets. For the most part, European leaders avoided making any statements or taking any actions that might further enflame the situation.

Privately, most nations supported Reagan's words and actions following the Alaskan incident. He had done exactly as he said he would do. He didn't start it, but he had finished it — and true to his word, he had protected the United States. Support for his actions was especially high in the US, where the President's approval rating was continuing to climb.

Elsewhere, public support wasn't with the American President. Many Europeans viewed his actions as unjustified and completely out of proportion. The consensus was that Reagan was spoiling for a war, and would not hesitate to go nuclear. Public approval ratings by the Europeans over his response to the Alaskan incursion were directly inverse to those of the Americans.

The Atlantic never seemed wider or colder.

After Reagan's hard counterpunch, the dazed Soviets returned to their corner for most of August. The US and the USSR continued to escalate and define zones globally, but were careful to avoid any overt acts of provocation.

The Soviets seemed prepared to wait things out. The US election was now just months away, and Reagan would soon be gone — replaced by someone weaker, more cautious, and more predictable. "Reasonable" people the Soviets could work with, like President Dukakis or Secretary of State Jackson.

Large street protests continued, and Europe was hit by waves of sabotage. In the London underground, a series of synchronized bombs killed nearly 200 commuters and caused the entire rail system to be shut down for almost a week. In Paris, a municipal water plant was hit by a bomb that killed two people, and Anne Frank's home in the Netherlands was fire-bombed.

Most attacks suggested the hand of the KGB, but with no fingerprints to be found, were immediately blamed on the US. According to the left-leaning media, the Americans, whether desperate to retain control, or just out of spite, were now resorting to terrorism.

Peace rallies frequently descended into riots, with anarchist mobs clashing with police, looting stores, and setting fire to buildings and cars.

On August 28, an air disaster at Germany's Ramstein Air Base killed 75 people (and injured hundreds more) when three Italian jets collided, sending one into the stands where it exploded into a ball of fire. Terrorism was immediately suspected, but such did not turn out to be the case.

These were just a few of the events rocking Europe that August, but were they related? American efforts to produce hard evidence linking them to Moscow remained unsuccessful.

Some in the administration began to suspect a conspiracy within the CIA itself, but the President refused to believe it. Bush, going behind Reagan's back, attempted to drum up support from Powell, only to discover that the NSA Director neither believed in such a conspiracy, nor was he willing to covertly challenge the President's directives.

"With all due respect sir, I take my orders from the President, not you," Powell stated, affirming both his personal loyalty to Reagan and the appropriate chain of command.

So far America had been immune to such attacks. There had been the usual "riots for peace," followed by civil unrest and minor crime waves, but for the most part the nation was at peace, and solidly behind their President.

As the calendar page turned from August to September, the lines drawn at the end of Europe's last great war seemed to be holding. Autumn was coming, and with it the weather patterns that had hindered the conquering armies of the past, from Napoleon to Hitler.

The first Monday of September was the Labor Day holiday, which had become ever more of a magnet for those on the left who were opposed to the President and his policies. Demonstrations were held across the US, including one in the nation's capital that drew upwards of 50,000 people.

A small number of World War II veterans who had fought to liberate Europe were there as well; not to glorify war, but as a reminder that some things were worth fighting for, and that if America let Europe fall, the Soviets would next come for the United States.

The Labor Day protesters reflected an odd demographic, ranging from peace-at-any-price old hippies to young Libertarians opposed to foreign intervention. As always, thugs, thieves, hooligans and opportunists came along for the ride.

A significant contingent of the crowd was angry and confrontational. Many sites (including the Lincoln Memorial) were vandalized, the park and nearby streets were strewn with garbage and debris.

Clean up was still going full swing as the workday began for most government employees. Across town, at Washington National Airport, a Boeing 737 passenger airliner took off, headed towards Chicago, before rapidly changing course and descending.

The plane crashed hard into the Pentagon, killing all on board. Hundreds more in the building and on the ground were also killed and injured.

Moments later, air force fighter jets scrambled to intercept a second passenger jet that had also deviated from its flight path and was now heading straight for the US capital.

Attempts to contact the crew were unsuccessful, as were attempts to escort it away from its presumed destination. With time running out and no other available options, the order was given to shoot the plane out of the sky.

All on board were killed instantly, but fortunately most of the fiery debris fell upon a field and away from more heavily populated areas.

This was the day when everything changed: the war had come home to American soil.

21

Rendezvous With Destiny

Given that the nation had been on high alert status for months, there wasn't much else that could be done following the incidents with the hijacked jetliners. The President resisted calls to impose martial law, but he did impose an immediate ban on all commercial air traffic in the United States as a precaution until things could be sorted out, and new safeguards put in place.

While the culprits responsible for the hijackings remained a mystery, intelligence services immediately suspected the Soviets. Not only because of the choice of the targets—the epicenter of US military command and the seat of government—but also due to the degree of sophistication required to takeover and pilot a passenger jet on such a precise flight plan. In two separate incidents. These were not random events, but part of a well-planned and synchronized strike at the heart of America.

The attacks also represented a major shift in tactics. In the past, the KGB relied on hidden bombs to do their dirty work. But now the targets weren't the planes; the planes were the bombs, and the targets could be anything, anywhere, anyone. Anytime.

How had this happened? Were crew members responsible, or had a passenger (or passengers) managed to overpower the pilots and take over the controls? Adding to the mystery was the fact that as far as US intelligence could determine, nobody on either plane had any known connections to the Soviet Union.

The crew and passengers were all, for the most part, just ordinary Americans. Could this be this the work of sleeper agents? Brainwashed Americans programmed to act when "activated" as depicted in *The Manchurian Candidate*?

The attacks offered more questions than answers, but this much was clear: This was a new kind of warfare. These were coordinated political acts involving more than one person.

But how many? And what were they planning next?

The President and his team were at work when the news of the Pentagon attack came, and all were immediately transferred to a secure underground location just minutes before the second plane was taken down.

Within minutes, Vice President Bush phoned in from Dallas, where he had been meeting with lenders he needed to inject money into his sputtering presidential bid. Bush announced that he would be suspending his campaign indefinitely, and would be returning to Washington to stand with the President.

As a very difficult day was drawing to its end, the President received a call from Bob Michel, House Minority Leader (R-IL), informing him that the move to repeal the 22nd Amendment—allowing Reagan to run for (and if elected, serve) a third term—had taken on new urgency, and would likely pass by the end of the week with broad bipartisan support.

"Our nation needs you, Mr President," said Michel. "We mustn't change horses in midstream."

For Reagan, the attack on Washington had been the final straw that had begun with the Soviet coup. Although there had been no official declaration, America was now at war—and things were escalating rapidly.

Congressman Michel, a highly-decorated army veteran was correct: any change in leadership during a time of crisis—especially wartime—opened up vulnerabilities and risk—even if the transition was to a Vice President who retained the same cabinet as his predecessor.

The surprise attack had echoes of the last Great War, and the parallels to Pearl Harbor were clear. There was no way back now. The war had been brought home, and everyone must commit to the fight.

In times like these, a nation needs a strong leader. If chosen by the people, Reagan would be honored to serve again as its president.

True to Representative Michel's word, Congress quickly repealed the 22nd Amendment. In a joint statement, Reagan announced his intention to seek a third term; Bush officially ended his campaign, and publicly endorsed the man he had hoped to succeed.

In reality, Bush had no choice but to bow out gracefully. It was obvious that if he ran he would have lost badly. And if the Democrats won, the nation itself would be lost.

If given control, the Democrats would almost certainly adhere to their non-interventionist party platform, which was a polite way of saying that they would pursue a course of appeasement—of doing nothing while the Soviets gained an irreversible advantage. Then, with the balance of power firmly on his side, Sokolov would call the tune, and America would have no choice but to dance—or be destroyed.

This was not something that Reagan was willing to let happen. He had no choice, nor did he have any reservations. If called upon by the American people, he would stay on to finish the job.

The world had changed; Reagan had not.

Peace through strength had been his lodestar from the day he first took the oath of office. He would not back down. His third term would be one of steadiness and consistency.

This is what the American people wanted and needed.

The President's decision was supported by history, which time and again illustrated the importance of maintaining continuity during periods of crisis and conflict.

It would have been hard to imagine the successful resolution of the Civil War had Abraham Lincoln left office after one term—especially if power had been transferred to the Democrats, who at the time supported slavery. But more strikingly was the case to be made for one of Reagan's original political heroes, Franklin Delano Roosevelt.

The man Reagan cast his first presidential vote for had led his nation from the depths of the Great Depression through most of World War II, providing the kind of stable leadership that America—and the world—had needed during its darkest hours.

When Roosevelt died unexpectedly in April of 1945, Harry S Truman took over, having served less than 90 days as FDR's third Vice President.

Truman completed what would have been Roosevelt's fourth term and won re-election in 1948 in a three-way race. It was during "Give 'em Hell Harry's" time in office that congress instituted term limits on the presidency, with the passage of the 22nd Amendment.

But things had changed. The world was once again in grave danger—certainly as bad as it had been during World War II under FDR—and likely worse, as this conflict now involved superpowers with vast nuclear arsenals.

There could be no turning back now. It was time for the American people to unite and rally behind a strong and experienced leader.

As Shakespeare observed centuries before in his play *Twelfth Night*, "Some are born great, some achieve greatness, some have greatness thrust upon them."

Leading his nation in a war that had the potential to destroy all life on Earth was not how Ronald Reagan had sought greatness.

Reagan was a modest man, motivated by ideas, not ego. He had entered politics simply to serve the people, and hopefully leave the country better off than when he had entered office.

But history had other plans. This was Reagan's rendezvous with destiny, and the free world was depending on him.

22

Michael Dukakis

President Reagan's announcement that he would run for a third term was met with tremendous voter enthusiasm. With his personal popularity now back at record levels, polls indicated that if the election were held in September he would likely capture more than 75% of all votes.

His decision to run for a third term came late in the political season, the result of events that no one could have anticipated, and by then, both party nominating conventions had already taken place.

Despite lackluster support from most conservatives, Bush had come to the convention in New Orleans in August with enough delegates to secure his nomination on the first ballot. He had been, for better or for worse, the GOP's official presidential candidate, at least for a short while.

But then came the direct attacks on America, from Alaska to the nation's capital.

With his presidential hopes dashed, Bush again fell in line behind the President. Behind the scenes it was a different story.

Privately, Bush disagreed with his boss' decision to seek a third term. He cited a number of factors, including Reagan's age, and what he described as "obvious cognitive decline," charges of which were not made by anyone else, or substantiated by the President's medical team, which provided him with a clean bill of health to run again.

Bush acknowledged that his personal poll numbers were down, but believed that with Reagan aggressively stumping for him he could have beaten Dukakis. But Reagan had more important things to do than to devote all his attention to saving Bush's campaign—he needed to save the free world.

When the campaign began, Bush regarded Reagan as a wealthy, but embarrassing relative that needed to be kept from public view, then quickly die and pass down the inheritance.

While Reagan did not publicly criticize Bush the candidate, or his positions, neither did he refrain from expressing his own opinions on the issues, most notably on matters of defense and relations with Sokolov and the Soviets.

Nor did Reagan respond to any of Bush's barbs.

It was no secret Reagan and Bush never worked all that well together as a team, and the rift between them had only widened during the primary season. Bush felt that he had paid his dues, and deserved to be president, but now, here he was once again, eclipsed by Reagan.

Serving another term as VP meant being reduced to playing the understudy, while Reagan stepped into the spotlight to lead the nation during a period of unprecedented challenge. Like Lincoln and FDR, Reagan's legacy would now include that of "war president."

It was not a role that Bush felt Reagan was qualified to perform.

By now, everyone was familiar with Bush's record as a pilot during World War II. He was a bona fide military man, who felt much more qualified to command an actual war. The Vice President was quick to tout his combat experience, noting that while he had been in uniform, fighting the enemy, Reagan had been in Hollywood making propaganda films.

The "only fighting Ron ever saw," mocked Bush, "was over parking spaces on the old Warner Brothers lot."

The prospect of Reagan commanding World War III while Bush continued to lead the "War On Drugs" struck him as cruel irony.

The change in Bush following the collapse of his presidential run was overt. He became even more disengaged, irritable, and was very likely suffering from depression. His eyes betrayed a hollow stare, his smile seemed forced. For once, he had little to say.

George HW Bush, was an ambitious man who now stood helpless as he watched his life's dream wither and die.

In his desperate attempt to be all things to all people, Bush had failed to be the one thing that mattered most: a man Americans could trust as their president.

From the beginning, his campaign had lacked constancy and substance. Seemingly without guiding principles, Bush let public opinion polls define his positions on the issues.

Denounced as a flip-flopper, conservative support for Bush was weak. But then came Comrade Sokolov to save the day.

The Soviet proposal to end the Cold War was quickly embraced by the Democrats and a growing number of voters across the political spectrum, including many Republicans. Sensing a rare opportunity to bury the competition, Bush, a "visionary" and "progressive conservative" switched allegiance from the warmongering Reagan to the peace-loving Sokolov.

While the move might cost him some Republican votes in the primaries, he reasoned that this would only be a temporary setback. Bush had no real competition for his party's nomination, and once secured, believed Reagan would have no choice but to endorse him. Like Reagan, most Republicans would rather see Bush elected than any Democrat. Those that didn't would just sit things out.

Thus, Bush strategized that if he could retain the core of his conservative base and attract swing Democrats (and Independents), he would easily win the election. The Reagan coalition would be a thing of the past, replaced by one built by Bush.

But then Sokolov played his hand, forcing the Texan to fold and do damage control—but by then it was too late.

The takeaway was that Bush was easily duped. As president, would he be this easily fooled by the Soviets again? Was he even able to think independently and decisively?

Another factor contributing to Bush's fall from grace stemmed from his persistent personal criticisms of Reagan and his leadership style, which he had denounced in an interview as "disengaged" and "lazy."

The White House needed someone younger, more detail oriented. Someone who could manage, and not just delegate.

As America's oldest president, Reagan had frequently made jokes about his age, making light of popular stereotypes held about older people. In what was popularly regarded as an early endorsement of the Bush campaign, Reagan had joked that "It was time for those who were around when fire was invented to pass the torch to the next generation."

But while Reagan had a gift for gentle humor, Bush's strained attempts at comedy often came off as shrill and mean-spirited.

One especially awkward attempt at humor concerned Reagan taking a few moments to pray during a recent cabinet meeting. As the President sat still with eyes closed, Bush suggested that Reagan was praying that no one would catch him napping.

While the comment was for the most part laughed off by seniors, it offended many Evangelicals, a group that Bush struggled to connect with. Many saw Bush as someone who had probably spent more time studying the script of *Elmer Gantry* than actual scriptures.

For persons of faith, prayer is an essential part of life. Reagan's embrace and openness of his Christian faith was an inspiration — and not something to be ridiculed simply for the sake of a cheap laugh.

During the primaries, the President kept to the high road and tried to ignore Bush's little nips, which he wrote off as stemming from insecurity and desperation. But privately, Reagan let it be known that he was not pleased by unnecessary personal attacks from a man he had befriended and publicly supported as his successor.

Reagan also knew a thing or two about winning elections, and felt that the comments undermined party unity, and were at odds with the so-called "Eleventh Commandment," which was to never speak ill of a fellow Republican.

The commandment, first voiced by Gaylord Parkinson (Chair of the California Republican Party), had been taken to heart by then gubernatorial candidate Reagan, who not only popularized it, but also lived by it, and would continue to do so.

If only Bush had listened.

But with Reagan's entry into the race it was a new day in America. Whatever dreams Bush once held were gone; he would not lead the GOP ticket. Ironically, he would only hurt it if once again included as Reagan's running mate.

It was now Reagan's job to do what Bush couldn't: defeat Democrat Michael Dukakis, who was now paired with his very own Texan VP running mate; Senator Lloyd Bentsen.

A decorated World War II combat veteran, Bentsen had been in politics since the 1940s. He knew how to raise money and win elections, and appealed to many swing voters, including moderate Republicans, thanks to his pro-business stance. He was also known as someone who had supported the Vietnam War, and the use of nuclear weapons against North Korea while he was in Congress.

He had also beaten Bush almost three decades earlier in a run for the US Senate.

Unlike Bush's choice of Dan Quayle, the addition of Bentsen had given the Democratic ticket a considerable boost. But, as predicted, the lead Dukakis once enjoyed evaporated the moment Reagan entered the race. Even when adjusted for the natural margin of error, all signs indicated that Michael Dukakis was in store for the biggest rout in election history—topping even those Reagan achieved over Carter in 1980, then Mondale in 1984.

Still, it came as a major surprise when just two days after Reagan announced his intention to run, that Dukakis abruptly quit his campaign. Although he cited a personal medical condition (which "Dr Reagan" diagnosed as cold feet caused by having no spine), Dukakis wasn't fooling anyone.

As someone incapable of even fooling some of the people some of the time, Dukakis was doomed. With the scoreboard reading 50-0 and just minutes to go in the game, he decided to leave on a stretcher, and make way for fellow Bay State roller Teddy Kennedy to enter the game.

But why now, and why against Reagan the Invincible? Was the Senator from Massachusetts delusional, or just seeking martyrdom?

By all measures, Senator Kennedy was a polarizing figure, dismissed by many as the unworthy heir to a modern political dynasty. Although comfortably entrenched in the Senate since 1962, Teddy was better known nationally as tabloid fodder than for his work in Congress.

Why a savvy career politician like Kennedy would accept such a suicide mission was a mystery. But for whatever reason, Teddy said "yes," warmed as much by the prospect of claiming his right to be president, as by the tumbler of fine Irish whiskey he quickly emptied in his mouth. *Sláinte!*

With little time left until Election Day, Kennedy aggressively hit the campaign trail. Full of enthusiasm, short on specifics, he instead sought to invoke the spirit of his late brother, who had also faced down the Soviets—and won—without ever firing a shot during the Cuban Missile Crisis.

Teddy spoke of JFK's glory days, riffed on familiar misty themes and phrases, hoping that voters would crown him the new King of Camelot.

On the surface, Kennedy's running mate (Bentsen) seemed a good fit—recalling the same geographic strategy exploited by JFK and Texan Lyndon Johnson. In addition, Bentsen had known JFK from his days in the Senate.

Unfortunately, Bentsen was not quite as enamored with Teddy as he had been with his older brother, going so far as to privately tell the head of the Democratic National Committee, "I served with Jack Kennedy. I knew Jack Kennedy. Jack Kennedy was a friend of mine — but Teddy is no Jack Kennedy."

Bentsen was not happy with this new shotgun wedding, but neither was he the type to quit.

On the Republican side, there was also continued tension, and so it was a relief to all involved when Bush told Reagan he would not be on the ticket for a third term. Privately, Reagan was glad when Bush dropped out, saving him the awkwardness of having to ask a man, he still considered a friend, to step aside and do what was best for the country.

With Bush out of the way, Reagan turned to the task of assembling his cabinet, and preparing for a smooth transition.

23

Forming the Dream Team

The Vice President's decision to not join him on a third run for the White House allowed Reagan to pick a new running mate, and to assemble a "Dream Team" cabinet free of Bush loyalists.

Bush's announcement was welcome news for most Republicans. Many conservatives wanted Bush—whom they regarded a quisling—dropped, as the prospect of having him "just a heartbeat away" from the presidency presented an uncomfortable scenario.

When Bush gave his announcement to the President by phone it was not entirely unexpected.

Reagan thanked him for his service, but made no effort to dissuade him. Bush would continue until his term was over, and would, at Reagan's request, keep his decision private until his replacement had been chosen.

Before speculation and lobbying could begin in earnest, Reagan offered the Vice President's spot to Ed Meese, who was currently serving as the Attorney General. With Meese, the President got someone who was not only up to speed on events and the workings of the White House, but also someone with whom Reagan had a genuine personal rapport.

In addition to shared ideologies, the two men also had a lot of working history going back to the difficult days of the late 1960s and Reagan's tenure as the governor of California. Meese, twenty years his junior, joined the administration first as a legal affairs secretary, before eventually rising to the Governor's Chief of Staff.

In the decades that followed, the two men remained close friends. Reagan regarded Meese as one of his best counsels, and as a man of character he knew he could trust and rely upon. Furthermore, Meese had military—albeit non-combat—experience, having recently retired (at the rank of Colonel) from the US Army Reserve.

Reagan's offer—and Meese's acceptance—happened quickly and with little fanfare. In a private conversation, Reagan stated that Bush was out, and asked if Meese was interested?

He was. The two shook hands, and the deal was done in less than five minutes. Ed Meese was a good man, a good friend, a good choice. Reagan would not revisit the issue.

With this critical keystone in place, the President began to revise his cabinet, and prepare for battles ahead—both foreign and domestic.

Replacing Meese as Attorney General would be Robert Bork.

The President liked, and respected Bork, who would bring to the position of Attorney General a deep intellect along with an impeccable résumé, having served as Solicitor General, Acting Attorney General (during the Nixon Administration), US Circuit Judge—and as a professor at the Yale Law School for nearly 17 years. Bork also had a well-earned reputation as a legal scholar, authoring many important opinions as well the book *The Antitrust Paradox*—the most cited volume on this particular legal topic.

Still, the choice of Bork was bound to generate controversy, as it had been less than a year since the Senate had rejected his nomination to the Supreme Court (to fill the seat being vacated by the retirement of Lewis Powell, Jr).

Although nominated to the SCOTUS by Richard Nixon, Powell had a reputation as a centrist. Fearing that any nomination by Reagan would tilt the court to the right, Senate Democrats conspired to block—in advance—any nomination put forth by the President.

Thus, Bork was just a victim of circumstance; in the wrong place at the wrong time. As a surrogate for the President, Bork was subjected to bottled-up and misdirected anger by grandstanding senators playing to liberal fringe constituencies in advance of the upcoming elections.

The nationally-televised attack on Bork—led by Senator Teddy Kennedy—was vicious, relentless, and full of inaccuracies. While Bork could contest and argue against obvious distortions, the nature of the process—essentially a job interview—required that he maintain a cool stoicism no matter how absurd things became.

Despite his professional competency and "turn the other cheek" demeanor, Bork's nomination was rejected pretty much along party lines, much to the disappointment of the President, who had hoped that something as serious as the process of selecting a Supreme Court Justice might rise above petty partisanship.

But such was not the case.

By selecting Bork as his new Attorney General, Reagan gained a brilliant legal mind, along with an opportunity to make amends for the injustice of his treatment by Senate Democrats. Secretly, Reagan hoped that by serving as Attorney General, the American people would see the true Robert Bork, and when the time came, demand their elected representatives treat a possible re-nomination to the Supreme Court with open minds and fairness.

Although satisfied with his current Chief of Staff, Reagan was relieved when Howard Baker opted to resign in order to make way for the return of Reagan's original Chief of Staff James Baker III — usually referred to as just "Jim."

The "Baker for Baker" swap was a source of amusement for the President, although there were times when the matching surnames and titles was a cause for confusion.

Whereas Howard Baker was from Tennessee, James Baker was a Texan; one of Vice President Bush's friends, and someone who worked with the VP on numerous occasions, and in varying capacities going back to the 1950s, including Bush's 1980 primary run against Reagan.

Despite Baker's record of supporting Reagan's challengers (including Ford in 1976), the President bore no hard feelings, and the two enjoyed a solid working relationship. Never far from Reagan's side, Baker was currently acting as Secretary of the Treasury (having replaced Donald Regan).

Regan, who many felt had backstabbed the President, would not be back in any capacity for the third term — especially if Mrs Reagan had any say in the matter — which she did.

Baker was competent, smooth, and hardworking, leaving many insiders surprised that Reagan had not selected him to be his running mate instead of Meese, who was regarded as much more of an ideologue with little appeal to moderates, much less Democrats.

In typical style, Baker gratefully accepted the invitation to return to his old job as "the Chief." Whether he had expected to be offered the VP spot was never a matter of discussion, and whatever resentments or disappointments he harbored, he kept them to himself. Baker's poker face was said to be second only to that of Reagan's.

Working with Baker, Reagan wanted to see Michael (Mike) Deaver as Deputy Chief of Staff—a position he had previously held until his resignation in the spring of 1985.

Reagan regarded the 50-year-old Deaver as a reliable friend and confidant, an essential part of his team, who, along with Baker and Meese constituted the "*Troika*,"—a Russian term for "threesome" that signified their deep bond.

Deaver had been with the President through thick and thin, including that terrible day in March 1981 when Reagan was nearly killed by an assassin's bullet. Although he had been unable to shield the President then, Deaver had already saved his life once before, when he performed the Heimlich maneuver on him. The rescue had taken place in 1976, as then ex-governor Reagan was on the campaign trail, making his first bid for the White House. The incident, which took place on an airplane, would have likely been fatal if it hadn't been for Deaver's quick intervention.

It was an act that Mrs Reagan would never forget, and from then on, Mike was very much in the Reagan's inner circle, loved by both almost like family.

The years following Deaver's tenure at the White House had not gone well for him. His drinking had become a problem, and in 1987 he had been convicted of perjury. (Deaver cited his struggle with alcoholism for memory lapses as the cause for his unintentionally inaccurate testimony.)

While the charges were not directly related to his time serving in the Reagan White House, a case had been made accusing him of having used his old Washington connections for personal gain. Despite support from sworn testimonies by top administration figures including Secretary Schultz, prosecutors couldn't wait to stick it to the President's old pal.

Anxious to put the matter behind him and mitigate any further damage to the President, Deaver chose not to appeal the conviction. He was fined $100,000, sentenced to 1,500 hours of community service, and in lieu of jail time, was currently serving a year's probation.

Deaver accepted his fate, and had sought out treatment to deal with alcoholism to make sure something like this would never happen again. He was now completely, and proudly, clean and sober.

In Reagan's eyes, Mike was not a bad man; he openly acknowledged his mistakes and weaknesses, then sought to make amends. Reagan believed he had paid his debt and was a changed man.

Still, having a convicted felon serving in the White House presented a number of problems — not the least of which was how the Democrats would spin it politically.

Of course, as President, Reagan had the power to wipe the slate clean with a full pardon — but Deaver resisted this. Nor did he wish to cause the President any further embarrassment.

But Reagan was undeterred: He wanted Deaver back on his team.

Reagan also understood alcoholism — the "curse of the Irish" — and how easily it could lead even the best man astray. The President's own father Jack had been an alcoholic, and had struggled against this disease that had shortened his life to just 57 years.

Growing up, Reagan's mother had referred to Jack's battle as a "sickness" — and not a defect in moral character. It was an addiction, and one that required treatment and sympathy. But it was also something that could be overcome; Reagan witnessed it firsthand with his own father.

As with Jack, the President believed that Mike deserved a second chance; he saw the younger man's story as inspirational … one of salvation and redemption.

The 50-year-old Deaver held the phone hard against his ear, running his hand through his thinning hair while the President made his case.

Reagan was a tough and persuasive negotiator, and few could resist his charm and persistence — now coupled with a sense of urgency.

Deaver wavered, and then the two old friends brokered a deal: he would accept the position of Deputy Chief of Staff — but not a presidential pardon. "After all, you saw what pardoning Nixon did to Ford's re-election chances," he chuckled.

"Maybe Jerry was a bit tipsy when he signed it …" returned Reagan.

"Still no excuse," laughed Deaver from the other end of the line.

"Okay, Mr President, I'm on board … but please, no champagne celebration."

"Agreed," said Reagan, chuckling. "We will all need to keep our wits about us. Whatever happened in the past is just that — in the past now. I respect your decision to turn down a pardon … but I want you to know that I will stand by you, Michael, you have my word.

"Returning to public service offers a fresh start; a chance for you to introduce the new Michael Deaver to America," said Reagan.

"The opportunity to serve my country, and to earn back the trust of the people is the pardon I'm seeking," said Deaver, becoming emotional.

"And so it will be, Mike. Thank you, and God bless you."

24

The Dream Team:
Diplomacy & Economics

With the *"Troika"* of Ed Meese, Jim Baker and Mike Deaver back in place, Reagan continued to assemble the rest of his Dream Team.

Given the uncertainty of what lay ahead, the President put a priority on experience and persons with whom he already had an established relationship. However, with some new vacancies, Reagan returned to the same formula that he had successfully employed since his days as governor: seeking out those who shared his views about the need to shake up the status quo and continue the Conservative Revolution.

As Reagan reviewed options for posts major and minor, he specifically sought to avoid persons who wanted positions in government simply for prestige or to use them as a revolving door for career advancements. Instead, he looked to recruit those who weren't actively seeking to serve, but whose patriotism compelled them to serve on behalf of the greater good.

Certain key figures were already on board and would continue to serve in the same capacity, such as the current Secretary of State, George Schultz.

Although now a man of diplomacy, Schultz was a decorated World War II combat veteran who had served in the Pacific Theater fighting against Japan. For his service, (which included the infamous Battle of Peleliu), Schultz, an artillery officer, had risen to the rank of Captain before being discharged when the war ended.

Prior to his military service, Schultz earned a bachelor's degree (*cum laude*) from Princeton, and after the war, returned to school, receiving his PhD in Industrial Economics from MIT, where he was recruited back to teach by his alma mater after graduating in 1949.

By the time he joined the Reagan White House, Schultz had already served two other presidents—as a senior economist on Eisenhower's Council of Economic Advisers, then in various positions during the

Nixon Administration, including Labor Secretary, Director of the Office of Management and Budget, and finally as Secretary of the Treasury.

Since taking over from Al Haig (in 1982), Schultz had become an indispensable part of Reagan's team. He knew and understood the Soviets and the Western Europeans. With the type of wisdom that can only come from experience, Schultz was the only person Reagan could imagine in the position of America's top diplomat during such unprecedented times.

Secretary Schultz accepted the President's request to continue serving without any hesitation.

Also in diplomatic service, Vernon Walters, (who had succeeded Jeanne Kirkpatrick), would stay on as the US Ambassador to the United Nations. Not only was Walters experienced and qualified, but no one else seemed willing to take on such a frustrating assignment.

Whether Walters would stay on had been a matter of speculation for some time. It was rumored that he felt that he had let down the President, and was open to making way for someone new. As his replacement, the name floated most often was Thomas Pickering, currently serving as the US Ambassador to Israel.

In addition to Israel, Pickering had performed several other diplomatic assignments, including posts to Jordan, Nigeria, and El Salvador. Still, it was with a sigh of relief when Walters agreed to "sign on for another tour of duty."

For the President, maintaining continuity in these top diplomatic positions was critical, as it is a field very dependent on personal relationships, often cultivated over long periods of time. Reagan also preferred someone like Walters with long-standing European connections, complemented by a background in the military and intelligence services.

With his core diplomatic team set, Reagan turned to economic matters.

James Baker's move to Chief of Staff would leave an opening at the Treasury Department, which the President would fill with Nicholas Brady.

A New Jersey native and Yale graduate, Brady had served the administration in several different capacities preceding his selection to lead the Treasury Department. These included being the Chairman of the President's Commission on Executive, Legislative and Judicial Salaries, as well as serving on various other commissions, including those dedicated to Strategic Forces, Central America, Security and Economic Assistance, and the Blue Ribbon Commission on Defense Management. Most recently, Brady had chaired the Presidential Task Force on Market Mechanisms.

Brady and Reagan also held closely aligned views on matters relating to funding, budgets, and taxes — issues Reagan intended to take on with renewed vigor if elected by the people to serve a third term.

Another important post relating to the economy would go to Richard (Dick) Darman, who would be asked to lead the Office of Management and Budget.

Darman, 45, was a Harvard graduate, who, like many of his other key selections, had worked for Reagan previously, including most recently as Deputy Secretary of the Treasury.

Although he came highly recommended and certainly seemed qualified for the position, Reagan privately had concerns about Darman's economic views — especially on matters relating to taxation and deficits.

Would Darman become a problem like David Stockman, who held the position at the OMB for most of Reagan's first term? Only time would tell. But for now he appeared to be the best candidate for the job, and time was running short.

Beryl Sprinkel would stay on as Chair of the Council of Economic Advisers, a position that he had held since 1985, after first serving in the Treasury Department during Reagan's first term.

A Missouri native, and another tough World War II vet (who had participated in the Battle of the Bulge), Sprinkel shared Reagan's economic philosophies, especially in areas relating to free market economies and growth stimulation.

Sprinkel had studied at, then taught at the University of Chicago, where he earned his doctorate. A protégé of the legendary economist Milton Friedman, Sprinkel had first predicted — then guided — the administration's response to the Stock Market crash of the previous year.

Given the volatility of a war economy, Reagan was pleased when Beryl "the Pearl" accepted his invitation to stay for another term.

For the position of US Trade Representative, Reagan decided to reach outside of Washington for a real wild card, picking a businessman from Kansas.

Not quite 50, Charles Koch, who along with his older brother David, successfully ran Koch Industries, a corporation they had inherited when their father died in 1967.

In Koch, Reagan found a similar distrust of big government and bureaucracy. Koch was a true outsider, and not someone who ever envisioned himself going to work for "the enemy."

While initially—and adamantly—opposed to leaving the Midwest for the nation's capital, Reagan leaned on Koch's sense of patriotism, and the opportunity to join the revolution from within. Eventually Koch gave in and joined the team, just as Reagan was about to move on to his second choice.

Koch was well known in conservative circles for his pro-business, anti-regulatory positions. But most importantly, Koch, a graduate of the Massachusetts Institute of Technology, came with real world experience managing a large, and highly successful, business empire.

No one knew what the future held for the economy.

Would the threat of war continue to create panic and further downturns? Would the US need to borrow or ration—or both? What would be required to stimulate the economy during wartime—and beyond? How far could the deficit grow until it caused inflation?

America was entering uncharted territory, but no matter what the future held, Reagan had confidence in his new economic team as bringing together America's best and most competent.

25

The Dream Team: Defense & Intelligence

For a president entrusted with keeping his nation safe, matters of defense are a top concern. This was never more critical than during that fall of 1988, as the United States found itself on the brink of World War III.

Currently serving as Secretary of Defense was Frank Carlucci, who, with backing from Vice President Bush, had replaced Reagan's old friend, and original Secretary, Caspar Weinberger.

Like Schultz, Weinberger had also served in the Pacific Theater during World War II. Enlisting in 1941 — after graduating from Harvard, the San Francisco-born Weinberger rose to the rank of Captain in the army, with some time spent working directly with General Douglas MacArthur's elite military intelligence group.

As Secretary of Defense, "Cap" earned a reputation as an able administrator and man of vision for his championing of SDI. Under his stewardship, Weinberger rebuilt the nation's defenses from the ruins left by the Carter administration into a fighting force capable of holding the Soviets in check.

When Weinberger was forced to resign over involvement in the Iran-Contra affair, Frank Carlucci, who had served two years in the navy in the 1950s, was selected by Vice President Bush to replace him.

Prior to his appointment as Deputy Director of the CIA, Carlucci had worked for both the Ford and Nixon administrations, before coming to work for Reagan in 1981, first as the Deputy Secretary of Defense — a position he held for less than a year. Four years later, Carlucci would rejoin the team, but again, for less than a year, this time as the National Security Advisor (taking over for John Poindexter — another casualty of Iran-Contra), before settling in to the top spot at the Defense Department during Thanksgiving week, 1987

But Carlucci soon became a problem for the President.

The two men never seemed to click, and Carlucci's apparent defection to the Bush camp during the campaign had created a rift between them that seemed irreparable. Although loathe to fire anyone—or make any major changes at such a critical time—Reagan desperately wanted to see someone else heading Defense.

At the top of the President's list was Colin Powell, the man who had succeeded Carlucci at the National Security Agency, and who, in this capacity, had distinguished himself by offering extremely valuable insights and recommendations ever since the beginning of the Soviet Crisis.

In contrast to Carlucci, Powell brought extensive personal military experience. He had joined the US Army in 1958, served several tours in Vietnam, and currently held the rank of Lieutenant General.

A decorated soldier, personable, and articulate—Powell had clearly been groomed for great things. Following Vietnam, he had served a White House Fellowship, and then attended the prestigious National War College.

Described by those who knew him as having a brilliant mind for military strategy, Powell also came with Weinberger's direct blessing, after having worked closely with him on such high-profile operations as the liberation of Grenada and the 1986 air strike on Libya.

Everyone knew what needed to happen. But unlike the other Bush loyalists, Carlucci had no plan to make way for Powell.

Reagan decided to first approach the issue with Bush. If Carlucci wouldn't consider resigning completely, perhaps he would be open to switching with Powell—moving back to his former position at the NSA.

Carlucci was not interested, telling the President to his face that it was "Defense, or nothing."

So Reagan fired him on the spot.

The suddenness caught everyone off guard, and Powell, who had already been approached about taking over at Defense, accepted the President's invitation.

But now the President had a critical hole at the National Security Agency, and once again (as had been the case with the return of Michael Deaver), Reagan was prepared to face controversy for his selection, turning to the man who had filled the position for two years during his first administration: Robert "Bud" McFarlane.

Prior to his posting to the top spot at the NSA, DC-born McFarlane had served in various positions in the Reagan administration, including those associated with the State Department.

During Reagan's first term, McFarlane, then just 44, had served as assistant to Secretary of State Al Haig, which had been no easy tour of duty. Fortunately, Haig had only lasted a little over a year, before being replaced by George Schultz.

However, and perhaps most significantly, McFarlane had authored much of Reagan's foreign policy platform during the 1980 campaign. Along with Weinberger, McFarlane was a leading proponent of SDI — which Reagan wanted to be given renewed emphasis if reelected.

Like Schultz, McFarlane was a former Marine, having risen to the rank of Lieutenant Colonel before officially retiring in 1979.

As with Powell, McFarlane had also attended the National War College and was a decorated Vietnam veteran. In addition to many other awards and service citations, he was a recipient of the Navy Distinguished Service Award and the Bronze Star (with Valor Device).

While at the NSA, McFarlane had also become involved in the early stages of the Iran-Contra affair. Initially a supporter of the operation designed to help support rebels fighting to overthrow the Marxist Sandinista government of Nicaragua, McFarlane's enthusiasm cooled, putting him at odds with others who still regarded the scheme as a win-win situation. McFarlane resigned in 1985.

As an outcome of the Iran-Contra investigation, McFarlane was convicted of withholding evidence, and sentenced to two years of probation.

Issuing an official pardon would be no big deal, and Reagan wasn't worried about any potential political fallout. As with Deaver, the President was prepared to go to the wall in support of those who had served him well in the past, and who could bring something exceptional to his new administration.

A deeper concern, voiced by others close to the President, was McFarlane's state of mind.

"Could he be trusted? Could he function under pressure?" they whispered and wondered.

It was a matter of public knowledge that McFarlane had been deeply troubled by how things had turned out with the Iran-Contra affair.

He had tried to facilitate the President's dreams of supporting a democratic revolution and freeing some American hostages, all the while shielding the President from any direct involvement should anything go wrong.

McFarlane's worst fears soon materialized, with Congress using the investigation as just another way to go after his boss. If Reagan couldn't be impeached, then at least he could be humiliated and put on the defense.

Although not a major player in the affair, he felt that he had let down his president and his country. Like a Samurai whose sense of honor requires him to commit *Seppuku*, McFarlane tried to take his own life February 9, 1987.

Reagan was empathetic, and dismissive of McFarlane's critics, noting that "Bud was in a dark and difficult place, but he has received the help he needed, and now he's ready to return to active duty.

"Bud and I both believe, that the best way to help one's self is through helping others.

"This man still has a lot to give, and his country needs him. I need him," said the President, "and that settles it."

And so, with his signature, Reagan pardoned McFarlane, clearing his way back to serving his country—and the President he so admired, one more time.

Lastly, there would be no change necessary at the CIA, as William Webster would be staying on, filling the spot vacated by William Casey, who had been Reagan's first, and only other CIA Director.

Although he had been medically incapacitated for some time, Reagan had refused to officially dismiss Casey from his post. Instead, the President displayed typical loyalty and compassion, confident that operations were in the hands of a competent successor, while the clock ran down on his old friend.

Reagan's response to Casey's illness mirrored the approach he had taken with James Brady, his first Press Secretary, who was severely wounded in the 1981 assassination attempt.

Although permanently disabled and unable to return to work, Reagan kept Brady listed as his official Press Secretary, even though the actual duties were being executed first by Larry Speakes, then by Marlin Fitzwater.

Webster understood and supported the President's loyalty in regards to Casey, and was happy to serve without the official job title.

Prior to officially taking over at the CIA in 1987, Webster had spent nearly a decade heading the FBI, having been appointed by President Carter to take over for James Adams, whose tenure as the bureau's interim director had been limited to just eight days.

Eleven years Casey's junior, Webster, 64, had also served his country during World War II. But while Casey had pursued politics and business, Webster chose the legal profession, working first as an attorney, then as a judge, before eventually rising to the US Court of Appeals for the Eighth Circuit.

Webster was a thoughtful and contemplative man, and although Reagan respected his intellect and nuanced opinions, there were many times when he longed for Casey's undiluted passion and mad Irish fury. Still, he had served the President well since the beginning of the Soviet Crisis, and so Reagan saw no need to reconsider his choice of Webster as Director of the CIA.

26

The Dream Team: Domestic

With critical, high profile positions in defense, intelligence, and state filled, the President could now turn his attention to rounding out the rest of his cabinet—namely those focused on domestic issues.

While these are often regarded as a lower priority during times of war, Reagan wanted a team that could be trusted to not just manage the home front, but comprised of people who shared his vision of what America could be, in times of war and peace.

If voters elected him to a third term, it would be not just to command a war abroad, but also to continue a revolution at home. This would be his final shot at reshaping America, and so it was critical that his new administration reflect the same core conservative values.

Reagan expected—and appreciated, differences of opinion on his domestic team. However, this time around he was hoping to move beyond the deep divisiveness that had been the result of too many appointees who had been brought aboard by George Bush.

Most of the Bush people saw the writing on the wall and were accepting of the need to move on.

For various reasons (unrelated to Bush), some members of Reagan's team would also be leaving, including William Verity, the current Secretary of Commerce.

Verity had served the administration adequately, stepping in to fill the vacancy left by Reagan's original secretary, Malcolm Baldridge, who had died in 1987 at the age of 64 after being injured in a rodeo accident.

Now in his early 70s, Verity was ready to return to private life. Reagan hated to lose such a key figure, so he opted to go for the candidate on his list with the most directly-related experience. Fortunately, William Simon, who had previously served as Secretary of the Treasury during the Nixon and Ford administrations, was available and interested.

Another plus for Simon concerned his connections to the energy industry. During the OPEC oil embargo of 1973, Simon created—and administered—the Federal Energy Administration to deal with the crisis, earning him the title of America's first "Energy Czar."

Whether impacted by actual events or just market panic, maintaining a reliable energy supply would be critical in a time of war. Since the Soviet coup in February, prices and supplies had been on a rollercoaster.

Simon not only had experience dealing with markets, but also knew what role government could—and should play in what promised to be some very difficult days ahead.

At the time of the President's call, the 60-year-old Simon was working in the private sector, at a global merchant bank he had founded, and was running with his two sons. At first Simon was hesitant to leave the family business, but he knew the company would be in good hands under the stewardship of William Jr, and Peter.

Like Reagan, Simon believed that government needed to be run more like a business, with greater efficiency and accountability in terms of how it operated, and specifically in regards to how it spent the taxpayer's money. As someone who had worked in both the public and private sectors, Simon would add valuable perspective to the cabinet.

Simon's reticence was no match for Reagan's persistence, and the President succeeded in getting the Commerce Secretary he wanted.

Another member of Reagan's current team that would not continue on for a third term was Labor Secretary Ann Dore McLaughlin, who had been on the job for less than a year.

Reagan wanted Elizabeth Dole for the position, as he had worked well with her in the past. During his first term, "Liddy" had served as a special assistant (for public liaison), then as Secretary of Transportation until just over a year ago.

Dole, like Reagan, was also a former Democrat. She had actively campaigned for the Kennedy-Johnson ticket, and had been rewarded with a job in the LBJ Administration. Unlike many other Democrats, Dole stayed on to work for Nixon following his victory in 1968, but did not officially become a Republican until the mid-1970s, a fact celebrated by Reagan as "better late than never."

Born and raised in North Carolina, Dole was exceptionally bright (a graduate of both Duke *and* Harvard); deeply committed to public service; and currently acting as president of the American Red Cross.

Dole was the spouse of Kansas Senator Bob Dole, who had just run against Bush in the 1988 primaries. Although both Doles were on the moderate end of the political scale, Reagan acknowledged her as a principled and competent administrator.

While the two did not always see eye-to-eye on every issue, Reagan valued such exchanges for both their civility, and for an opportunity to see things from a fresh perspective. Most importantly, Dole, like the President, understood the importance of compromise in order to get things done.

She would be perfect, and accepted the invitation with enthusiasm.

Samuel Pierce had been with Reagan from the beginning, serving two back-to-back terms as his Secretary of Housing and Urban Development.

Greatly respected for his innovative spirit, the former Eagle Scout and World War II veteran was a role model for many conservative black Americans. However, the fractious nature of Washington politics had taken its toll, and Pierce was ready to leave government service, thereby providing an opportunity for Jack Kemp to take over at HUD.

Currently serving as a Congressman from New York, Kemp had enjoyed a successful career playing professional football before entering politics.

A native Californian, and life-long conservative, Kemp had worked on Barry Goldwater's 1964 presidential bid and Reagan's 1966 gubernatorial campaign.

While they might at times disagree on football, Reagan and Kemp were very much aligned on economic policy issues, as both men were firm believers in the principles of low taxes, free markets, and less government regulation. Kemp was also a strong advocate of SDI, and defense of the unborn.

In fact, on most issues the two were matched. Reagan regarded Kemp as a man of vision, and the likely heir to his branch of conservatism.

On matters of race, Kemp, like Reagan, was committed to making the Republican Party more inclusive and reflective of America. If the party was to grow and thrive, it would need to diversify beyond its aging white base, and disassociate itself from those who were attempting to hijack it in order to advance racist agendas.

Kemp and Reagan saw the GOP as the party that offered

opportunity; in sharp contrast to the Democrat's system of institution-
alizing and maintaining poverty through dependence.

The President was never a big supporter of HUD, but had been unable
to get rid of it during his first two terms. Now, however, with someone
like Kemp at the helm, the agency took on greater significance as a way
for the GOP to bring its message to new audiences.

After years of neglect, many in America's underprivileged communities were unfamiliar with what the GOP had to offer. As someone with
a genuine commitment to equality, opportunity, and education, Jack
Kemp would be a perfect choice to lead HUD.

Like Bush, and Liddy Dole's husband Bob, the 53-year-old Kemp
had also briefly been in the 1988 run for the White House, before
the Soviet Crisis reshuffled the deck. Although giving up his seat in
Congress might create an opening for another Democrat to slip in,
Kemp was a team player, and ready to take the field with the Gipper.

Richard Schweiker, Reagan's Secretary of Health and Human Services
during his first term, would return to direct the agency, taking over from
Otis Bowen, who had held the position since 1985.

Although several years Reagan's junior, people age at different rates,
and at 70, Bowen was ready to retire to his home state of Indiana.

Schweiker, meanwhile, was anxious to return to public service at the
White House. First elected to the House of Representatives in 1960
(representing southeastern Pennsylvania), Schweiker was elected to the
Senate in 1968, and then reelected in 1974.

When Reagan made his first run for the White House in 1976, he
chose Schweiker as his running mate. Initially a moderate, Schweiker's
views had grown considerably more conservative over the years.
Although the two still had their differences, Schweiker was a man of
integrity that Reagan knew he could rely on, and who would bring
valuable experience to the post.

Meanwhile, Dr C Everett Coop would stay on as Surgeon General,
much to the ire of liberals due to his staunch — and very public — moral
opposition to abortion, and a denunciation of unprotected sex as a leading contributor to the spread of AIDS.

Sporting colorful bow ties and a mustache-less, Amish-style beard, Koop
was a colorful figure who called it like he saw it. Consistently at odds with
the tobacco industry, earlier that year he had issued a report stating that

nicotine had addictive properties on par with cocaine and heroin.

Reagan had grown up in a time when smoking was commonplace; its dangers not yet recognized or affirmed by science. He had been a smoker himself, and had served as a pitchman for cigarette companies. Now he had lived long enough to see the consequences.

Fortunately, he had been able to quit in time through sheer willpower. But it hadn't been easy. The President agreed with Koop's findings, and supported his efforts to curtail tobacco use.

When Koop joined the administration, smoking killed nearly 400,000 Americans a year; a grim sum that exceeded the death total attributed to drugs, alcohol, and auto accidents combined.

During his first six years as Surgeon General, smoking rates in the US had dropped dramatically. Koop's tough stance on tobacco produced impressive results — and enemies, including politicians such as the Democratic Governor of North Carolina, who called for his impeachment. In a truly bipartisan effort, Republican Senator Jesse Helms demanded that Congress place Koop under immediate investigation.

Koop was a lightening rod for many different reasons. Even rock star Frank Zappa had targeted him in his 1988 song "Promiscuous," in which the 47 year-old Zappa illustrated his gift for lyricism by rhyming "Koop" with "poop."

In addition to lambasting the good doctor, Zappa went on, (in just over two minutes) to explicitly reference various sex acts, the CIA, the AMA, a green monkey, Jesus, the Devil, Reagan, and Meese.

No other cabinet selection drew as much controversy as Dr Koop. When rumors began to circulate that the President might be open to dropping Koop from his third term "Dream Team," the first to call with a suggested replacement was Orrin Hatch, the junior Republican Senator from Utah.

"Who?" asked the President, not sure that he had heard Hatch correctly.

"*Mason*. Dr James Mason," Hatch repeated.

"Oh sure. James Mason. I know him … Captain Nemo! Nice fellow … worked on a picture with Nancy once, *East Side, West Side*, back when she was under contract to MGM. She had a small part — Barbara Stanwyck was the star. Ava Gardner, Van Heflin … Mervyn LeRoy, the director of that one, was the guy that introduced me to Nancy.

"But forgive me, Orrin, I digress …

"Well, I guess if an actor can be president, one could also be Surgeon General, right? But isn't James Mason dead?"

Before the Senator could correct the President, Reagan, having played him long enough, got down to business.

"Unless, of course you're referring to that Mormon doctor from Salt Lake City. A Harvard man, I believe? Now in Atlanta at the CDC?"

There was only silence on the other end of the line. Hatch knew he'd been had.

"Listen Orrin, I know Dr Mason, and he's a good man. But Koop isn't going anywhere. Now I'm guessing that Jesse Helms put you up this, right?"

Caught red-handed, Hatch confessed. Advocating on Mason's behalf was something he had done willingly. But Reagan was right: the impetus had indeed come from Senator Hatch, still smoldering over Koop's attempts to butt out tobacco.

Although Koop and Reagan did not always agree on every issue, the President respected his Surgeon General, admired his independence, and never waivered in his support, regardless of what Helms, Hatch, Zappa, or anyone else thought.

Californian Richard Lyng would return as Secretary of Agriculture. Although he had only been in the position since 1986 (taking over from John Block), his connection to the President went back to Reagan's days as governor, where Lyng had worked for the state department of agriculture.

Oregonian Richard Hodel, the current Interior Secretary would continue on for the third term as well. Prior to serving in this capacity, Hodel had been the Secretary of Energy — a position now held by John Herrington.

Herrington, a political newcomer whose background was in law, not science, had seemed an odd choice by many when first tapped for the position in Energy. Although he had served admirably, Herrington's decision to not return allowed the President to consider other options.

At the top of Reagan's list was James Schlesinger, a Republican who had acted as the department's first secretary during the Carter Administration.

Prior to working for Carter, Schlesinger had served in the Ford and

Nixon administrations, as CIA Director, Secretary of Defense, and as Chairman of the Atomic Energy Commission. This kind of cross-departmental experience would add important depth to the cabinet, especially during wartime.

Like many on Reagan's team, Schlesinger was unapologetically hawkish on military affairs. He did not trust the Soviets, nor did he believe that deterrence could substitute for a genuine defense.

In support of this, Schlesinger had long advocated for NATO's use of conventional forces — not just nuclear weapons — as the best strategy to counter the armies of the Warsaw Pact. Schlesinger's perspectives and insights in this area were timely, given the Soviet pledge to "liberate" European nations from the governments, which many were interpreting as a euphemism for invasion by troops from the east.

Although he had a reputation for being somewhat prickly, Reagan admired Schlesinger, and felt that he could control him.

"If not, just fire him like Ford and Carter did," quipped Meese privately when discussing how Schlesinger might fit in with the rest of the team.

"Hopefully it won't come to that, but if it does, well … I'll see to it that 'firings' are listed as part of the Vice President's official job duties, and I'll let you do it," added Reagan, enjoying a brief moment of levity in what had been a very serious, and at points, exhaustive game of chess being played with actual, living people.

Whether as an actor or as a political leader, Reagan knew how important it was to have the right chemistry between people for a group to work. As is so often the case, what seems initially promising can at times require adjustment for the greater good, especially when dealing with strong personalities brought together under very demanding conditions.

In some settings, personalities like Al Haig and Don Regan might have been fine, but when added to the mix at the Reagan White House there had been problems. The stakes were higher now, and so the President was prepared to take action sooner, rather than allow individual problems to grow and become group problems later.

Reagan's prompt firing of Carlucci evidenced this. If someone was a problem, they would be shown the door before they had the chance to infect others or behave in a manner that was less than what the job demanded.

Of lesser concern than someone like Schlesinger was Lee Thomas, currently in charge of the Environmental Protection Agency. An affable southern businessman in his mid-40s, Thomas had come on board at the start of Reagan's second term, taking over for William Ruckelshaus.

Thomas, as Reagan liked to playfully remind him, was a "graduate of that *other* USC," (referring to the University of South Carolina—and not the University of Southern California).

Reagan had a long association with the "real" USC, which had produced a number of "Kitchen Cabinet" members for his tenure as California's governor.

A competent administrator, the youthful Thomas shared Reagan's pro-business, anti-regulatory sensibility. And best of all, Thomas was agreeable to continuing on as head of the EPA.

Another Carolinian—although in this case, from *North* Carolina— was Transportation Secretary James H Burnley IV, who had been promoted from Deputy Secretary (under Elizabeth Dole) when she left the administration.

The 40-year-old Burnley brought an impressive résumé to the table, with degrees from both Harvard and Yale. While Reagan appreciated his youthful energy and intellect, the President wanted someone he felt might be better suited to the job—which he found with John Sununu.

Burnley would serve out his term, allowing Sununu to get his affairs in order and prepare for the move to Washington.

At the time, the Cuba-born Sununu was serving his third term as the governor of New Hampshire. Like Burnley, Sununu was recognized as having a brilliant intellect. Having earned a perfect score on the SAT, Sununu went on to earn three science degrees from MIT, culminating in a PhD (awarded in 1966).

So, for Reagan, Sununu brought solid conservative credentials, a deep understanding of science and engineering, along with proven administrative abilities—just the qualities Reagan was seeking from a Transportation Secretary.

No one expected Secretary of Education Lauro Cavazos to stay on, and more than one hint had been dropped about protocols regarding resignations. Cavazos' tenure had been brief, punctuated by frequent and lengthy absences.

Reagan got along well with most everyone, and at least initially he and

Cavazos seemed to bond, especially on issues related to the West and ranching. Unfortunately, the relationship became strained when Cavazos sided with the Vice President over comments supporting the Soviets that Bush had made while running for president.

During the time when it looked as if Bush might have a chance, Cavazos had also spent a considerable amount of time campaigning on his behalf.

When Bush's campaign imploded, Cavazos' appearances at the White House became even more infrequent and strained. Anxious to wrap up his cabinet selections, Reagan was delighted when he received a terse, handwritten fax from Cavazos giving exactly two weeks' notice.

A grin appeared across the President's face, who then boyishly pantomimed a football player kicking a field goal.

With Cavazos out, Reagan was now able to bring back William Bennett who had previously held the position. Although he had left on his own accord in February after serving for three years, there had been speculation that Bush had pressured him into resigning. Apparently the VP was so confident about being elected, he was looking to get an early jump on reshaping the cabinet with those more reflective of his "progressive" views — and saw Cavazos as a better fit.

Whether the 45-year-old Bennett was pushed or had jumped was unknown, but in any event, he looked forward to serving in a more unified and reenergized Reagan administration.

The Harvard-educated Bennett and Reagan were kindred spirits — especially in areas of social conservatism. Both were committed to reforming the nation's school system, unafraid of the political ramifications inherent in challenging the status quo.

In Bennett, Reagan saw a partner with the will and courage to take on the big issues that were decimating public education, whether it be a tolerance for drugs and promiscuity, or the unchecked power of the teachers union.

Before serving as Secretary of Education (for most of Reagan's second term), Bennett had chaired the National Endowment for the Humanities, where he had established a reputation as an effective administrator, and a moral voice long absent from the discussion of what types of art should be underwritten by US taxpayers.

A man of deep religious conviction, the former Democrat was

pro-life, and a supporter of school prayer—two stances that would be given new emphasis in Reagan's third term as part of the Reagan Revolution's ongoing domestic agenda.

Culturally, Bennett would be a good fit; sharing the President's work ethic and the ability to roll with the punches.

Lastly, Bennett also had a real sense of humor. When times were tough, having the ability to share a joke and laugh off disappointment was essential, and this was a thread of commonality found in most of those Reagan wanted closest to him.

As he looked forward to serving another term, the President knew there would be many different kinds of battles ahead. Some would be fought in faraway lands with guns, while others would be decided at home, by ideas, advocacy, courage, and faith.

But the election was not a done deal—and there was no way that the President would ever consider instituting martial law just to hold on to power. Instead, Reagan believed that the privilege to lead should only come at the invitation of the people, using that most fundamental of all tools in a democracy: the ballot box.

With his last team member in place, Reagan bowed his head in prayer. He asked for God's guidance and courage in the uncertain times ahead. He prayed for strength, and pledged to do his best to serve the Lord, protect his nation, and to restore hope and greatness to America.

27

Marlin the Magician
Does a Disappearing Act

With his team now firmly established, the President called a meeting with Press Secretary Marlin Fitzwater to discuss how best to announce the news.

Generally, staff changes are not made public until after an election. However, because Reagan was intending to take the country in a decidedly more conservative direction, he wanted the people to know who — and what — they were voting for in advance, so that everything would be fair, transparent — and most importantly — reflective of what the people wanted.

"Mr President, I don't think we can say that the team is completely set, at least not yet," said Fitzwater, slightly more red-faced than usual.

Reagan looked puzzled. He thought he had everything sewn up, but obviously Fitzwater knew something that he didn't.

The President tried to guess who might be wavering. "Is it …?"

But before he could finish his question, Fitzwater blurted out the answer: "It's me, Ron. I'm sorry."

The news came as a complete surprise to the President. He'd never had an easy time reading Fitzwater, but the portly Kansan seemed healthy, happy with his job, and was well liked by everyone. Nor had Fitzwater served for very long; having only taken over from Larry Speakes who left in February 1987 to pursue a career on Wall Street.

Reagan regarded Fitzwater as a real "pro," who had worked in some aspect of the public relations business for every administration since Lyndon Johnson's in the 1960s. Prior to his promotion to Press Secretary (and a salary of nearly $75,000 a year), Fitzwater had served as Vice President Bush's personal Press Secretary.

Was it an allegiance to the departing Vice President? Reagan wondered to himself. Not likely.

"Marlin, is it the money? If so, let me see what I can do. I can't promise anything, but I think we can certainly bump you up by at least an extra 25¢ an hour — even if we have to finance it by selling arms to the Iranians," joked the President, his eyebrows rising, his eyes twinkling.

Once again, Reagan's humor defused the awkwardness of the moment, as both laughed.

But now, the ball was clearly in Fitzwater's court. He shook his head and continued on, never at a loss for words.

"No, Mr President, it's not about the money at all. As you probably know, practically every newspaper man, every advertising copywriter, everyone in PR, dreams of writing a novel someday ..."

"Let me guess Marlin: It's the story of a thin man with a full head of hair who loves nothing more than a fine cigar ... Based on someone we all know and love, somewhat autobiographical?" Reagan ventured good-naturedly.

"Exactly! Although there may be a tiny bit of poetic license," added the plump and balding Fitzwater. "I have, as you know, learned a thing or two about how to tell a yarn after all these years in the PR business."

The two laughed again.

"Well, I'm sad to see you go; but I never fault a man for trying to advance himself or for following his dream. If I hadn't, I'd probably still be working as a lifeguard back in Lowell Park.

"The best of luck to you, Marlin, and thank you ..."

Reagan extended his hand and gave a firm handshake, genuinely sorry to be losing Fitzwater, and glad to know that his Press Secretary was not leaving due to some philosophical reason, or worse yet, to go pen some scathing personal memoir. Just a few months prior the President had been publicly humiliated by the publication of *For the Record: From Wall Street to Washington*, Donald Regan's salacious tell-all memoir.

While the parting with Fitzwater was amicable, his unexpected departure would leave a major gap in the President's team—and at a critical time. Granted, press secretaries do not set policy, so replacing Fitzwater wouldn't be seen as affecting the administration's agenda in a third term.

However, in support of Reagan's emphasis on transparency, details of his proposed "Third Term Dream Team" would be made public as soon as possible so as to allow voters to make an informed choice. Included in the announcement would be a mention of Fitzwater's resignation, effective as soon as a suitable replacement could be found and brought up to speed.

Reagan had big plans for the years ahead, but now who would best help to him to share this with the American people?

28

The Way Things Ought To Be

During his years as governor of California, the Reagans lived in and around the state capital of Sacramento, and decades later they still had many friends and acquaintances residing in the area.

Most were, like Ron and Nancy, staunch Republicans, who frequently felt at odds with their more liberal neighbors. Still, Sacramento was not Berkeley, or even San Francisco, and the area was home to a robust and vibrant conservative movement.

For the past few years, this community had found a voice in the broadcasts of a man whose daily radio show ran weekday mornings on KFBK, an AM station located towards the far right end of the dial.

KFBK was part of a media empire that had holdings in other formats, including newspapers and television. The station offered a range of programming options, but was largely focused on content that did well on AM, specifically news and sports. Meanwhile, its sister station on the FM side (KAER) was dedicated to an "adult contemporary" music format, built around air personalities like Bob O'Connor, who had recently relocated to California from Galesburg, a small town in northwest Illinois where Reagan had lived briefly as a boy.

Talk shows were still an evolving format in the early 1980s when KFBK offered Morton Downey Jr a spot. The southern California native had bounced around the country honing his act, until an opportunity arose to do a daily show at KFBK.

Nicknamed "The Mouth," Downey gained notoriety for his provocative nature, and outrageous on-air stunts, until one day in 1984 when he went too far—using the racial slur "Chinaman" on the air—for which he was promptly fired.

Replacing Downey would be difficult. Although polarizing, the self-styled "shock jock" had done well in the ratings and enjoyed the support of a core of die-hard followers who relished his "non PC" (politically-correct) views.

But, what's done is done. As the station door closed behind him, it opened for someone new, and Downey's departure was the opportunity that Rush Hudson Limbaugh III had been waiting for all his life.

The son of a successful attorney (and World War II fighter pilot), Limbaugh was a college dropout who had dreamed of making it big in radio. Like Downey, Limbaugh had moved about the country, working at various stations and formats, but after nearly a decade had little to show for it. Instead, Limbaugh chased one dead-end job after another, occasionally playing the hits; changing formats and shifts; hired, then fired, stung by the criticism of a station manager who told the young man he'd never make it in broadcasting.

By the end of the 1970s this prophecy seemed to be coming true. Unable to land another radio job, Limbaugh moved back to St Louis to take a position working on promotions for the Kansas City Royals baseball franchise.

But Limbaugh refused to give up on his dream, so when the opportunity came to follow his beloved Kings basketball team (relocating to Sacramento) *and* work in radio again, he didn't hesitate to make the jump.

In the true tradition of the American pioneer, Limbaugh was just the latest to head west, reinvent himself, and seek his fortune in the Golden State.

Downey's shoes were difficult to fill, but Limbaugh was nothing, if not persistent, and slowly he built a following that Downey could have only dreamed of. Perhaps most incredibly, Limbaugh, nearly 20 years Downey's junior, was doing this without a script, intuitively developing a new approach to talk radio that would be widely imitated, but never equaled.

Limbaugh was a conservative with a sense of humor — a rarity in those days, but something that came naturally to the Missouri native. His shows dealt with serious, and at times revolutionary ideas, usually presented by the host himself, in contrast to the more common practice of relying on guests and the standard interview format.

Limbaugh did his homework, and welcomed the opportunity to debate, and inform live on-air, less educated, but ideologically zealous liberal callers — especially from the nearby university town of Davis.

In the days before computers were commonplace, Limbaugh was forced to do his show prep the old fashioned way: reading books, and filtering through the mostly, and unabashedly, liberal media for nuggets of truth. Many an afternoon and evening was spent at the library doing research, or chasing down print publications at newsstands such as the one found within Tower Records. In the broadcast booth, Limbaugh was ready for battle, surrounded by scribbled notes and stacks of papers.

Not one to suffer fools gladly—either on-air or in person—Limbaugh's BS meter was legendary. Simply calling oneself a "conservative" was not enough to get a free pass. In Limbaugh's world, this term was akin to a medal that must be earned—and continually recertified—by one's deeds, not just words.

Listeners took note, and Limbaugh's broadcasts became an oasis of the airwaves for conservatives. Educational and provocative, Limbaugh used the talk radio format in a way that no one else had before to engage listeners, and for many, introduce them to the ideologies that were reshaping America.

Because his shows were informative *and* entertaining, Limbaugh became something more than just another local celebrity. He was becoming a political force with a talent for getting listeners hooked on ideas.

Ron and Nancy loved his show, and were regular listeners whenever they were back visiting in the Sacramento area. On occasion, friends would send them cassette tapes of the radio shows, especially those in which Limbaugh spoke about Reagan and his policies (which was often).

Limbaugh's support for the President never wavered, even during the darkest days following the Iran-Contra affair. Tapes of programs from that period meant a lot to the Reagans, who had been abandoned by so many other fair-weather friends as well as those in the media. In recognition of this support, Reagan went so far as to write a "fan" letter to Limbaugh.

In the letter, Reagan humorlessly referenced his own days in radio ("shortly after it was invented") and thanked Limbaugh for standing with him, empathetic of how such a position might have hurt his ratings. In closing, Reagan said he looked forward to meeting Limbaugh someday, and to the opportunity to a return the favor.

The letter underscored how standing up for one's beliefs often comes with real, and negative, repercussions. For Reagan, it was with losing voter support, for Limbaugh, listeners. But in Limbaugh, Reagan saw a man not chasing daily ratings, but focused on following his conscience; doing, and saying, what he believed was right despite the consequences.

Having this recognized in him by a man he considered to be a true hero for the ages meant a lot to the young Limbaugh. Like the President, he was something of a late bloomer in his chosen field, but once Limbaugh found his guiding star he never wavered.

From tinny-tiny car radios to high-end stereo systems in riverfront mansions, Limbaugh's voice became a rallying call for the conservative revolution — and there was nowhere to go but up.

Or, perhaps, up and *out.*

Whereas others chased trends, Limbaugh became the trend, and soon people far from KFBK's broadcast range began to take note. He was a big fish in a small pond; destined for greatness.

After roughly four years fighting in the trenches of California's central valley, Limbaugh was offered national syndication. Paralleling Reagan, Limbaugh would need to leave California in order to deliver his message to a national audience.

This was the break he had been waiting for.

Pausing only long enough to give notice and pack up the car, Limbaugh moved to Manhattan and went live in August 1988.

That year had been a tumultuous one for the country, providing him with a wealth of material spanning everything from the Soviet coup to the implosion of the Bush campaign. Throughout it all, Limbaugh stood by the President. He was among the first to call for, then to support, Reagan running for a third term.

Although he had only been in national syndication for a couple of months, Limbaugh's ratings were already through the roof, and stations across the country were scrambling to add his program into their line-ups.

Wildly popular, tremendously influential, wealthy ... Rush Limbaugh, just 37 years old was at last living the life he had always dreamed of ... until one day in October when the phone rang.

On the other end of the line was the President, although Limbaugh didn't believe it at first. Rather, he thought he was being set up for a joke, and yet the conversation unfolded naturally, not veering into the type of embarrassing come-ons and silliness that were the trademark of the celebrity prank call. Besides, Limbaugh was a radio man; his world was all about voices, and this one was just too good, even for a master impersonator like Rich Little.

It didn't take long for Limbaugh to realize he was indeed dealing with the real thing, especially when the conversation turned to the letter Reagan had written him the year before—which was something Limbaugh had never mentioned publicly.

As the two "great communicators" chatted, Reagan moved the conversation towards his reason for calling. The President talked about his proposed "Dream Team," and how Fitzwater would be unable to continue on for a third term.

Although he sensed what the President was leading up to, the offer to become Press Secretary still came as a shock, and Limbaugh responded with genuine humility.

"But sir, I don't think I'm worthy ... I'm just a lowly radio talk show host. Wouldn't you be better served by a journalist instead of an entertainer?"

"Listen Rush, that's what they used to say about me; wondering how some B-movie actor who once played second banana to a chimpanzee could ever go on to do anything else.

"But you're different. Yes, you entertain—but you also inform and educate. You get people thinking and talking about the issues—and that's exactly what I need ... that's what our country needs.

"And besides, like Fitzwater, you're also a cigar smoker. If I was to hire someone else, we'd lose at least two weeks fumigating his old office," added the President, as both men enjoyed the laugh.

"I realize you'll be giving up much Rush, and that going national with the show is important ... and that it has always been your dream.

"But once I had a similar dream, which I followed from radio to Hollywood, but then something more important came along: my country was at war; it needed me, and so I had to change direction so that I could serve my country.

"We are once again approaching war, and I need the best people I can get. Will you join us, Rush?" asked Reagan.

Limbaugh, never one to embrace dead air while broadcasting or in person answered immediately.

"Absolutely, sir. After all, do you realize how hard it is getting to find a job where a man can still enjoy a good cigar at work?"

Again, the two laughed, acknowledging the camaraderie and chemistry that suggested the beginnings of what was destined to be a great friendship.

Yes, there would be difficult days ahead, but now, with the final piece in place, Reagan felt the confidence he needed to step forward and meet his destiny.

The Campaigns

The election of 1988 would be like no other in history.

A President running for a third term was not, in and of itself, all that unusual. In fact, during Reagan's own lifetime, the country had elected FDR to four terms in the White House.

Most presidents wish to continue serving, and most run for re-election. However, in the years since the imposition of the 22nd Amendment, no sitting president had made a serious challenge to term limits, nor had any Congress felt the need to rescind them until 1988, specifically with Ronald Reagan in mind.

But this was not the way things were supposed to have gone.

For the Republicans, it had been expected that after two terms as Vice President, George Herbert Walker Bush would be the official candidate. Years of preparation had gone into readying for a Bush presidency, and now it was all for naught.

As with any national campaign, huge sums of money had been raised and spent. Slick, big-budget commercials had been produced following the tried-and-true plan of promoting one's candidate — in this instance Bush, and attacking his challenger — which early on Republicans assumed would be Michael Dukakis.

But then, just days after Reagan announced his intention to run, Dukakis quit the race, leaving the Democrats in a similar quandary: materials promoting Dukakis — and attacking Bush—were now totally useless.

On both sides, print ads and broadcast spots booked long ago had to be cancelled. Campaign t-shirts, buttons, and boxes of bumper stickers gathered dust in shuttered warehouses, destined to become collector items for political junkies who thrived on "what if" scenarios — assuming of course the world itself wasn't incinerated by nuclear war.

Luckily for the parties, the two eventual candidates for president were already well known figures.

Topping the ticket for the Democrats was Massachusetts Senator Edward Moore Kennedy, regarded by many in his party as the natural heir to the throne based on bloodline. In fact, some starry-eyed Democrats regarded the loss of Dukakis a blessing in disguise, allowing for the continuation of the Kennedy dynasty by the last surviving brother.

Unfortunately, this view was not commonly held by the majority of everyday Americans, who neither believed in the right of regal ascension, nor in the man himself.

Still, there was hope based on precedent. After all, Teddy's lucky break came when he inherited his brother's US Senate seat, which JFK vacated in order to assume the presidency.

Deemed next in line for succession was bootlegger Joe Kennedy's third eldest son, Robert. Dismissed by his father as a "runt" who had once delivered newspapers while being chauffeured in the family's Rolls Royce, Bobby's big break had come when his brother Jack appointed him Attorney General in 1961.

Lacking chemistry with Jack's successor, Bobby (now reverently referred to as "RFK") resigned after serving less than a year under Johnson and ran for the US Senate representing New York. Swept into office as part of the 1964 Democratic landslide, the runt surprised everyone when he decided to make a late run for the White House, officially entering the race in March of 1968, intent on challenging LBJ for the right to another term.

Two weeks later LBJ withdrew from the race.

At the time of Bobby's death (from an assassin's bullet following the California primary in June), he was still trailing Hubert Humphrey (LBJ's Veep and the party's preferred choice by a wide, albeit not insurmountable margin) in a three-way contest that also included Senator Eugene McCarthy.

As expected, at a fractious party convention held in Chicago, the Democrats nominated Hubert Horatio Humphrey as their man.

After losing to Richard Nixon, Humphrey retreated to the Senate, where he served out the rest of his days.

With Humphrey's 1968 loss, attention now shifted to Senator Kennedy and the 1972 race — the first in which Teddy would be legally old enough to enter.

But then, scarcely a year after Bobby's death, Teddy would shoot himself in the foot, involved in a scandal so heinous as to put aside any ambitions for national office.

But back home in Massachusetts it was a different story.

Well financed and entrenched, Teddy was perpetually reelected to the Senate, as there were no term limits in the Commonwealth to restrict him. And so it was there that he stayed, seemingly destined to a life in the shadows cast by his two older brothers.

Only once before this contest had the Senator popped his head out of the safe refuge of his home state. Sensing weakness in a sitting president, Kennedy made a run against Jimmy Carter in the 1980 primaries, but lost badly.

At the time, Carter had boasted, "If Kennedy runs, I'll whip his ass!"

And he did.

The bluebloods of Boston were stunned.

Granted, Teddy was the black sheep of the family, but still, how could any *Kennedy* possibly lose to a gap-toothed peanut farmer from Georgia who was almost universally looked upon with a mixture of pity and contempt?

Ah, politics. Sometimes voters have long memories, and sometimes short ones. Since the nation's founding, more than one undeserving rogue had been elected, owing to the people's capacity to forgive and forget—at least at the ballot box.

Still, in a profession rife with scandals and scoundrels, 1980 may have just been too soon for voters to dismiss what happened just eleven years prior as water under the bridge.

Some historical context: President Kennedy had opened the 1960s with a call for Americans to go to the moon before the decade ended, and they did; landing on the lunar surface on July 20, 1969. It was truly one of the century's defining moments, bumping all other stories off the front page for some time while the mission played out. This was fortunate timing for Teddy, as just two days earlier, he had driven his mother's Olds 88 off a bridge on Chappaquiddick Island and then fled the accident scene, leaving his passenger, 28-year-old Mary Jo Kopechne, to drown.

Just as the story was breaking, Teddy was saved by the moon landing.

But now he was back again, asking the American people to trust him with saving the world.

Party officials believed that the Chappaquiddick Incident was behind him now. The Senator had been given a two month suspended sentence, and the details of what really happened that night were secured in a secret inquest that would never see the light of day.

Time to put it in drive and get back on the road.

As expected, Kennedy's campaign focused more on connections to his brother's brief shining moments as the president, than on his decades as a Senator. There was no time to introduce Teddy the politician, or for that matter, any benefit in doing such. This was all about the Kennedy brand, something even Teddy had only been marginally successful in damaging.

Highly paid consultants were sure that what people wanted in a time of crisis was the fuzzy comfort of the past. And so, voters were treated to a campaign big on nostalgia, and short on any vision for the future.

Especially worthy of exploitation was the partnership with Texan Lloyd Bentsen, spun to offer up ghostly echoes of the 1960 JFK/LBJ ticket, and with it, the promise of getting a "do over" option for a decade that started with so much promise before descending into the tangled mess that was the 1960s.

Would the torch be passed, if not to the next generation, then at least to JFK's kid brother? Or, would the new shining knight of Camelot be once again eclipsed by the dark night of Chappaquiddick?

Surrounded by yes men, Kennedy celebrated (sometimes quite liberally) even the smallest of victories, including a prediction by a well-known tabloid psychic who saw him winning by a landslide, and then saving the world from nuclear Armageddon by enlisting the help of sword-wielding angels.

But most papers weren't as certain as this particular tabloid, and when asked for details on how he would resolve the standoff with the Soviets without relying on angels, the Senator once again played up the familiar and the familial, reminding us how his brother had stared down the Russians and peacefully resolved the Cuban missile crisis using some kind of Kennedy magic.

Where Reagan was likely to destroy the planet with nukes, Kennedy had a "secret plan" to end the conflict without firing a shot. In a campaign whose very premise was based on fantasy, the idea of a secret plan seemed somewhat plausible to those wanting desperately to believe that the way forward was backward.

Reagan, meanwhile, took just the opposite approach. As a two-term sitting president, the people were already quite familiar with him, and knew they could rely on him to keep America safe. The President avoided bravado and fear mongering about the likelihood of war, and would neither confirm nor deny whether he would resort to using nuclear weapons. When pressed for an answer, Reagan would only respond by saying that he would do "whatever was needed, but no more or no less, in order to protect America."

Instead, Reagan wanted to talk mostly about domestic policies. Many of the themes were by this point familiar, but the President wanted a mandate from the voters in order to finish a conservative revolution that had been stalled by Congress.

Included on Reagan's list was an ambitious set of economic proposals built around further reducing government size and spending; cutting taxes; reining in excessive government regulations and policies that hampered job creation; and aggressively taking on tariffs, unions, and other barriers to free trade and the development of new markets.

Although he had once headed a union himself, candidate Reagan wanted to see tighter restrictions placed on union power, especially with regard to forced membership and "Stalinesque" policies restricting dissent by members.

The President wanted a balanced budget amendment and line-item veto power, two effective tools for controlling expenses that he had used to great effect during his two terms as governor.

As he had done in California, Reagan wanted to take on welfare reform; making sure the program was adequately funded for those who needed it, while tightening eligibility, closing loopholes, and going after fraud.

If reelected, the President would push for a complete ban on abortion and only nominate Supreme Court justices who "respected life from the moment of creation." On a related note, Reagan sought easing restrictions for government partnerships with religious organizations, and supported a constitutional amendment permitting school prayer.

There would be no truce in the war on drugs. Citing the drug trade as the leading cause of crime in the nation, he pledged to build new jails, add police, and take back the streets from gangs like the Bloods and the Crips.

Lastly, Reagan intended to continue the modernization and the preparedness of the nation's defenses. This would cover a broad range of objectives, from reinforcing allies and international deployments, to renewed emphasis on SDI.

The Republican candidate's proposition was direct: Give me a mandate on November 8, and I will reshape America as you have directed.

A vote for Reagan also meant a vote for his "Dream Team"—presented as a group of like-minded conservatives who would work in tandem to protect, and revolutionize America.

In accordance with the President's directives, his cabinet selections were all announced well in advance of the election, and most were names already familiar to the public. Many, such as Secretary of State Schultz would continue on in the same capacity; others (like William Simon) were known from previous administrations, while some, such as Jack Kemp, from other governmental service. A few, like Charles Koch and Rush Limbaugh, were less known to the general public.

From the beginning of the campaign, the President emphasized the importance of a unified Congress. Simply voting the Reagan/Meese ticket was not enough. If voters were sincere about change, they must do their part, by only electing those candidates willing to pledge their support for Reagan's vision of a transformed and revitalized *conservative* America.

It was now or never. Time to end partisanship and unite.

"During my first two terms in office we accomplished much, but even modest progress has been stymied by Democrats who would rather pander to special interest groups and big donors than do what's best for the country. It is time for these people to go … To break the gridlock, so that America can move forward.

Reagan then provided a list of those who either needed to be voted in—or out—at the November election. Of those in Congress not up for re-election, Reagan asked that they back him or prepare for the wrath of voters at the 1990 midterms. In other words, fall in line with what the people want, or please get out of the way.

Included on the President's "to go" list were many prominent Democrats—and even a few Republicans.

While the public appreciated Reagan's candor, the media regarded

"The List" in a far less favorable light, and few were willing to share its contents with the public. Parallels were immediately drawn with Nixon's infamous "enemies list," and the alarm was sounded: Reagan's call for a unified government was a dangerous step towards America becoming a fascist dictatorship.

The 1988 Congressional elections offered 15 open Senate seats, and winning all would give the Republicans a solid majority in the upper chamber. Prospects for taking the House offered a similar margin; with Republican control of all three branches, the nation could finally implement the remaining components of the Reagan Revolution.

As to be expected, liberal media coverage tended to focus on the prospect of nuclear war, Reagan's age and health, as well as past personal problems of Dream Team members such as Deaver and McFarlane. Although not particularly taken with Kennedy/Bentsen, the media took particular umbrage to Reagan's request that voters reject Democratic candidates. Instead, they advocated on behalf of a Congress "enriched" by "contrasting perspectives."

Reagan just shook his head and made his pitch directly to the people, in clear, and direct language.

"If you support my platform, give me the people I need to make it happen.

"It's easy to do, but I need you to take the first step. When you go to vote, just choose the candidate with the "R" by his or her name, and I'll handle the rest."

While the Kennedy/Bentsen proposition was somewhat muddled, Reagan's proposal was simple and direct: Here's what I want to do, here's the team I put together to help me do it, and here's who I need in Congress to make it happen. 1, 2, 3, period.

The Reagan/Meese 88 campaign team was led by the President's older brother Neil—better known as "Moon"—the nickname given to him as a child by their father, who referred to Ronald as "Dutch," owing to the boy's classic Dutch haircut.

The nicknames stuck, especially for those within their inner circles—although Nancy always preferred "Ronnie." Still, when the two Reagan brothers got together, it was always Moon and Dutch.

Three years older than Dutch, Moon had also worked in radio and film before finding his calling in the world of advertising.

Most notable was Moon's tenure at McCann Erickson, the agency best remembered for the its work with Coca Cola, including the tagline "It's The Real Thing," and the classic 1971 television ad featuring a group of people on a hillside singing "I'd like to buy the world a Coke."

An active conservative, Moon had worked on several political campaigns, including Barry Goldwater's 1964 run for president. Moon had also served as a delegate to the 1980 GOP convention that nominated his brother.

Like his older brother, Dutch was also a Goldwater supporter, and made a nationally broadcast speech ("A Time for Choosing"), which many credit as igniting his own political career. Reagan's words and passion caught the attention of fellow conservatives, who, after extensive lobbying, convinced him to run for governor of California in 1966.

In the gubernatorial election, the newcomer Reagan would challenge Pat Brown, a popular Democratic incumbent, now seeking a third term.

Campaigning on behalf of Brown was Senator Teddy Kennedy, who warned voters that Reagan lacked on-the-job political experience. Reagan acknowledged the fact that he had not held office before, but was quick to remind Kennedy that the same had been true for him—as Kennedy himself had not previously held office until having been *appointed* to the Senate by the Governor of Massachusetts.

The President wanted his 1988 campaign team kept small, and made up of people he already knew and trusted. It was to be a low-budget, no frills affair that focused on his vision for the future. Most importantly, Reagan wanted the tone to be one of optimism and promise.

Playing key roles in support of Moon would be Michael Deaver (who had extensive experience in Public Relations), Treasury Secretary James Baker, and Ed Rollins, who had directed Reagan's 1984 campaign.

Rollins, whose connection to Reagan went back to his days working on Nixon's 1972 re-election bid in California, was delighted to be supporting his old friend's latest venture—especially if it didn't include George Bush.

The campaign team for Reagan's third run for the White House was by necessity a fairly lean operation due to matters of financing and deadlines. There would be no debates, and there was simply no time for billboards, slick color mailers, or red, white, and blue stitched hats.

Newspaper ads were simple: Featuring just a photo of Reagan

and Meese, they presented a bulleted list of the objectives the new administration intended to pursue if elected. Direct, free of hyperbole, and without any silly campaign slogans.

A similar bare bones message was adapted for radio and television. Both featured the President speaking directly to voters about where he wanted to take the country, if "supported by the people" with their votes. The tone was upbeat and positive, focusing on brighter days ahead, rather than exploiting fears of war and economic turmoil.

Meanwhile, the Democrats went straight to attack mode, suggesting that a vote for Reagan was a vote for nuclear war. One anti-Reagan commercial featured sensationalistic footage of nuclear tests, accompanied by audio of the President announcing, "My fellow Americans, I'm pleased to tell you today that I've signed legislation that will outlaw Russia forever. We begin bombing in five minutes."

The clip was taken from a sound check preceding a radio address Reagan had delivered in August 1984. Intended as an in-studio, private joke and not for broadcast, the recording had come back to haunt him many times over the years.

The Democrats' commercial concluded with a plea from actor Gregory Peck, best remembered for his role as Atticus Finch, in the 1962 film adaptation of *To Kill a Mockingbird*. "The stakes have never been higher," intoned Peck. "Please vote Democratic on Tuesday, November Eighth."

Another ad featured cast members from *The Day After*, a popular made-for-TV movie that depicted the lives of those impacted by a Soviet nuclear attack on the American Midwest.

It would seem the Democrats had found a theme they felt they could work with, and were mining it for all it was worth.

Reagan specifically avoided the issue, and tried to keep his campaign focused on more positive themes and actual proposals.

At a press conference, Reagan was asked point blank whether he had seen the *Day After* spots, and if so, what he thought of them.

"In America, everyone has a right to express a political opinion — even actors," Reagan said with a smile.

As soon as it was announced that Kennedy would be running, Lee Atwater contacted the Reagan/Meese campaign to offer his assistance.

Atwater, a rock and blues guitar-playing South Carolinian, was a well-known political consultant who had worked for Republicans in the past, most recently for Bush in 1988, and as co-manager (with Rollins) of Reagan's 1984 re-election campaign. Reagan knew what Atwater was capable of, but didn't feel his particular skill set was needed — or welcome — this time around.

Atwater persisted, and the Reagan/Meese team agreed to listen to his pitch for a TV commercial, which promised to be "classic Lee."

The proposed commercial (presented on storyboards) began by showing a car with a KENNEDY/BENTSEN 88 bumper sticker driving erratically, while beer cans were tossed from the driver's window. As the car swerves down a dark and winding road, it passes a sign for the Chappaquiddick Bridge. The spot would then cut to a grainy photo of Teddy looking bloated and intoxicated, over which an announcer would ask, "The road ahead is uncertain, full of twists and turns … Is this who we want in the driver's seat?

"*Is it?*"

Atwater, energized, described the closing as a freeze-frame followed by the sound of tires skidding and screeching, and an authoritative voiceover supplying the final word: "NO!"

Out of respect, Reagan paused, then slowly shook his head. "Lee, now is not a good time … the American people are already worried, upset, fearful.

"No one knows what's going to happen, but at least I have my faith to sustain me. As president, it is my job to help and support the people, to be uplifting, assuring, a force for good, and stability. To, well, like that old song goes, to *accentuate the positive*. Remember 'morning in America'?

"That's where we need to be — offering a positive alternative — not sinking to their level.

"We need to project hope and confidence, then once in, do our darndest to make it happen."

Atwater disagreed, but appreciated the President's candor, and agreed not to pursue any outside funding for any direct attacks on Kennedy. He would not be an official member of the campaign team, but promised to use his connections to benefit the President.

Of much greater value was the assistance provided by Rush Limbaugh.

While it was public knowledge that he would replace Fitzwater as Press Secretary, Limbaugh would not officially take over until January 1 — *if Reagan was reelected.*

In the meantime, Limbaugh would continue on with his daily radio show, now in national syndication.

In this capacity Limbaugh's broadcasts were integral in getting Reagan's message out. Articulate, informative, *entertaining*—Limbaugh provided an insider's take on what a third term would be about. He spelled out the changes the President wanted to make, and how these would fundamentally change the nation for the better.

Whenever possible, Limbaugh welcomed members of the proposed "Dream Team" to his show so as present agendas from a first-person perspective. In one instance, future HUD Secretary Jack Kemp was on to talk about the idea of establishing inner-city enterprise zones.

However, every issue has two sides—and conflict makes for good theater.

To rebut Kemp, Limbaugh welcomed Washington DC Mayor Marion Barry on to the show. Now serving his own third term, Barry, a Democrat and Kennedy supporter, argued on behalf of the status quo; namely a system of public assistance that asked nothing of recipients in exchange for cradle-to-grave financial support. In contrast to Kemp, Barry found even the suggestion that public housing residents stay free of illegal drugs an affront to their dignity and constitutional rights.

For liberals, Limbaugh quickly became Public Enemy #1. Complaints, sometimes accompanied by petitions, were sent daily to the FCC, station managers, and advertisers. Some threatened boycotts, others violence. Hotheaded callers jammed the lines to debate and berate, but Limbaugh kept his cool, all the while continuing to build his national audience.

Thanks to syndication, the President now listened in whenever he could, impressed by the job Limbaugh was doing, never doubting for a moment that he had made the right choice of this fellow Midwesterner to be his next Press Secretary.

30

The Election

As Election Day drew nearer all signs suggested a Republican landslide. This, however, was not a reality anyone was prepared to publicly embrace and promote.

For Republicans, projecting overconfidence might cause voters to stay home, figuring the win was a done deal, and their vote wouldn't really affect the outcome. For Democrats, any hope of an upset hinged on ignoring reality and disputing the spread as reflected by polling data.

History was full of come from behind victories—although rarely by such margins. Still, with more registered Democrats than Republicans in the US, all that needed to happen was to have every possible (living) Democrat show up and vote the ticket.

For the most part, the media played up this possibility, and the classic photo of a smiling Harry Truman holding a 1948 newspaper featuring the headline "DEWEY DEFEATS TRUMAN" was recirculated endlessly, much to the embarrassment of the *Chicago Daily Tribune*, which prided itself on accuracy in addition to a good comics section.

Other polls, such as one focusing on seniors in Boston that were "concerned" about Social Security, showed Kennedy with an impressive lead.

Promoting the possibility of a Kennedy upset was, at least in this case, seemingly not related to liberal media bias. Instead, it was driven by simple economics: keep the game running for as long as possible in order to maintain public interest and maximize revenue from advertising.

On the Sunday before the election, the *New York Times* ran a major exposé on the Kennedy/Bentsen campaign. Kennedy was portrayed as something akin to Hitler in his bunker: vacillating between optimistically delusional, then bitterly lashing out at staff he blamed for the failure of his campaign.

Oddly enough, the Senator appeared to have been sampling his own Kool-Aid, drifting into bouts of despondency over concerns that if re-elected, Reagan would blow up the planet before Christmas.

When Election Day came on November 8, the win for Reagan was even bigger than projected, as many self-identified Democrats broke with their party to vote the Republican ticket from the presidency on down.

After all the votes were tallied, Reagan had won both the popular vote and the Electoral College by one of the most lopsided margins in history. He had taken every state—save for Massachusetts, which Kennedy won by less than 600 ballots.

Normally with a win so close, a recount would be in order, but Reagan resisted this. Content with his win, the President personally intervened so as to spare his opponent any further humiliation.

"No, let the man have some dignity, we have more important things to worry about," said Reagan, expressing an empathy that those around him at times found frustrating. While many on both sides of the race regarded politics as a fight to the death game of take no prisoners, when it was over, "it was over," for Reagan. He had the mandate he needed to move the country forward; contesting Massachusetts would just be a step backward. Not worth the time or trouble.

In response to Reagan's campaign request for a unified government, Republicans also took control of both houses of Congress.

In the Senate, Lowell Weicker bounced back to defeat Democratic challenger Joe Lieberman, reflecting a trend that had voters across the country willing to the vote the GOP ticket, even in cases where it meant supporting someone from the party's more liberal wing. On the other side of the country, voters elected Maria Hustace in Hawaii, toppling Spark Matsunaga, the Democratic incumbent who once led by more than 50 percentage points.

Hustace credited her win to a broad coalition of supporters, including those in the military, students, and Democrats supportive of Reagan's call to end gridlock and restart the Revolution.

As expected, Kennedy retained his Massachusetts Senate seat, although by his smallest margin ever; narrowly edging out his challenger Joe Malone, by less than four points. His running mate Bentsen did not fare as well however, losing to Congressman Beau Boulter who previously had won three back-to-back terms in the House, including a previous upset against Jack Hightower—an institution in Texas politics since the 1950s.

A similar Republican wave had also swept the US House of Representatives, with the Democrats losing a large number of seats, including many in districts once considered untouchable.

Almost immediately, pundits began suggesting that this election signified the end of the Democratic Party. Most of the blame was pinned on Kennedy personally, rather than on party policies and practices not embraced by the majority of Americans.

For those Democrats who either didn't have to run, or who managed to retain their seats, the post-election mood was largely one of contrition and submissiveness.

Democratic survivors of the 1988 bloodbath proclaimed having "heard the voice of the people" and pledged their support for the President. Even Democratic fixtures like Senator Daniel Patrick Moynihan of New York saw the writing on the wall, having had his once sizable lead whittled down from nearly 40 points to just over eight in a matter of weeks.

Granted, Moynihan had worked for both JFK and Nixon, so there was at least a remote possibility he had seen the light — despite having actively campaigned on Teddy's behalf at the outset of the contest.

But how many other Democrats had actually converted, and how many were just jumping on the conservative bandwagon was not immediately apparent. After all, they were politicians: masters of saying one thing, while doing another.

Still, the vast majority of the Donkey Party would soon fall in step behind the President, praying that their political lives be spared at the next election.

With clear and unquestionable support from the American people, Reagan now had the mandate he needed to take on the Soviets, and transform America.

31

The Soviet Response

Although there had been a slight setback following the coup in February, US intelligence services were now starting to receive better information out of the USSR.

Despite a security clampdown, many Soviet citizens were horrified by the coup and were now willing to shift allegiances to support the West. Those willing to help Western intelligence agencies ran the gamut, including top officials in the government, the military, and even some individuals from within the KGB itself.

As suspected, the coup had been engineered by a coalition of hardliners with support from the military and the KGB. Gorbachev and his team were still alive, and presumably undergoing a process of "reeducation." No trials were presently scheduled, and all were reported to be in good health.

For the CIA, the biggest revelation came from learning that Sokolov was genuinely in command—and not just an appointed figurehead as many had assumed. However, within his administration, there were various factions, with deep divisions on nearly every possible issue. Secretary Sokolov ran the show, but his grip on power was loose.

News of Reagan's re-election and the Republican sweep caught many in the Soviet leadership by surprise, suggesting an intelligence service that was being influenced more by fanciful thinking, than by readily available hard data.

When Teddy Kennedy failed to pull off an upset as hinted at by US media, the Soviet high command seemed genuinely shocked and disappointed. Kennedy appeared much more reasonable than Reagan, and would have therefore been a better partner for negotiating a deal to withdraw the American Empire from European soil in exchange for avoiding World War III.

Teddy's weaknesses—women, booze, and the grand and gilded trappings of power—were things the Soviets understood, and knew how to manage and manipulate. Best of all, Kennedy's party represented not just the American left, but a number of bona fide communists—including some that took orders directly from Moscow.

Sokolov was growing impatient with his generals, but had been persuaded to take a wait and see approach to the election, because it at least represented a *possibility* of a regime change in America. Even if the Soviets made a major move before the November election they would have still been dealing with Reagan, so why rush things?

Besides, any provocation would have likely only cemented and broadened Reagan's support, so putting operations on hold just a while longer seemed the best strategy, even though it did push a European military campaign closer towards winter.

But what of a small provocation, to which Reagan over-reacted? Such might make him look bad, and scare the people into supporting the Democratic alternative. Unfortunately, this had been tried earlier (with the Alaska incident), and the results were, at best, a draw.

Yes, they would have the element of surprise, but in many areas they were still under-prepared. Although the Americans had come in at a disadvantage, they had ramped up quickly under Reagan who had fully assumed the role of Commander-in-Chief.

Diplomacy? Again, there were divisions within Sokolov's circle, although most supported this not as a means to a genuine peace, but as a way to buy time while mobilizing for all-out war.

Whereas Kennedy was someone the Soviets felt they could have worked with, Reagan was a mystery. On one hand, the American president expressed a commitment to ridding the world of nuclear weapons, on the other, he seemed willing to get rid of those weapons by sending them to Russia mounted on missiles.

But just as Reagan had a mission, so did Sokolov, and they were diametrically at odds and heading towards an inevitable confrontation.

It was just a matter of time—*but how much time?*

＊ 32 ＊
Squaring Off

Dreams of a global Soviet Empire had been around since the birth of the USSR, but had gained new momentum in the days following the February coup that deposed Gorbachev, and replaced his administration with a coalition of expansionist hawks and hardliners.

Spring and summer had gone quite well for the Soviets, with solid gains in both popular support and territory. The promise of a united Europe free of US domination was intoxicating, and nearly irresistible when it included making the continent a nuclear-free zone.

The Soviet campaign of stirring up dissent and turning the public against their governments really had no downside, and so it would continue. The pledge to "liberate" nations held down by pro-US "puppet" governments had not fared as well, as "liberation" suggested invasion and occupation. Despite a promise to respect Western traditions in the nations needing to be rescued, the Soviet track record of how it handled previous "liberations" in Eastern Europe undermined their creditability.

And what about the nations currently held prisoner behind the Iron Curtain? Would Moscow also assist those citizens in their struggle to make their governments reflective of the people's will?

Yes, of course—and it already had! The people of Eastern Europe actually *preferred* socialism, so nothing else was needed! Life was already perfect, and the people were happy.

Outside of Europe, the pitch for solidarity with Moscow was often accompanied by financial incentives and the exploitation of long-simmering anti-American sentiments. For decades, the Soviet propagandists had depicted America as an imperialist power bent on world domination. And now, if unchecked, the Americans wanted to extend their control into space.

The long chess game that had been played out with pawns and proxies since the end of World War II had reached a new level of intensity, as both sides struggled for influence, even in remote corners of the world with little or no strategic value.

While both superpowers were still bloodied and bruised from long foreign wars (the Soviets in Afghanistan, the US in Vietnam), public dissent in the USSR had been systematically swept under the rug. Meanwhile, in the US, many remained haunted by the ghosts of what had been both the nation's longest war, and its greatest military humiliation.

The anti-war sentiment remained a significant factor in American politics and foreign policy. Even small operations like Grenada had been denounced as the "start of another Vietnam," the folly of trigger-happy Republicans who had failed to learn the lessons of history.

While Republicans took the blame for "losing" the Vietnam War (which concluded in 1975 during the Ford Administration), US involvement actually began, and escalated, under Democratic administrations. As the war in Southeast Asia dragged on, escalation—and opposition, grew.

The first president to pay the price was Johnson. He inherited the war from Kennedy, but unable to find victory or peace, left it for Nixon to deal with.

Ironically, Hubert Humphrey, Nixon's Democratic challenger in the 1968 presidential race supported the war, a position reinforced by inclusion in the official Donkey Party platform. The other major candidate in the race, George Wallace, of the American Independent Party, also backed the war, leaving those opposed to American involvement in Vietnam with no real viable options other than to sit out the election.

Many did, casting their protest votes with stones instead of ballots.

Thus, from the first days of his administration, Nixon was fighting two wars: one in Vietnam, and one in America to maintain support for US involvement. Ultimately he failed at both.

From the outset, America was warned that losing Vietnam would result in a "domino effect" that would cause communism to spread throughout all of Southeast Asia. When this failed to pan out, the anti-interventionist, anti-war sentiments embraced by the pacifist left became the new guiding principles of the Democratic Party.

With control of Congress, the Democrats had fought President Reagan on every front, from the defense budget itself to supporting anti-communist initiatives in Latin America.

Warnings of a new domino effect on America's southern doorstep were dismissed as alarmist — the paranoid delusions of Republicans who were wrong about Southeast Asia, and who seemed bent on endless war.

Time and tide would seem to favor the Soviets for most of 1988. Sokolov was a man of peace, and in the US, the long saber-rattling reign of Ronnie Raygun was set to end in November.

Patience.

There was no need to rush things and no need to provoke the old gunslinger. By law, Ronald Reagan was ineligible to run again — and besides, he was way too old. Instead, someone with a different, less provocative worldview would assume the presidency, whether it be a cowardly Democrat like Dukakis, or someone like Bush, who just wanted to be loved.

But then, history took an unforeseen detour. Reagan rose from the ashes and once again united the nation.

The radical turn of events in the US led the Soviets to pause and review options — all of which now would need to factor in a strong response by Reagan.

But who was he really?

The Soviets benefitted from a large and active network of spies operating in America, in all branches of government, and even some within the Defense Department hierarchy itself. Most were American citizens, willing to sell out their country for envelopes of cash, as contrasted with the American spy network, which recruited Soviets primarily on ideological grounds.

Both Reagan and Sokolov received regular briefings. Sometimes these were skewed and distorted by double agents, at other times they simply failed to include a missing piece that completed the puzzle. But despite all the shortcomings, the two sides had a pretty good sense of what the other was thinking.

In a nutshell, it came down to this: Reagan was prepared to fight, and the Soviets were now split as to what their next step should be. Moving militarily on any NATO nation in Western Europe would be met by a strong counteroffensive (led by the Americans). Globally, US forces were spread thin, and many alliances were strained.

Citizen support for the Soviet proposal of a united Europe was declining, as was support for NATO and the continued American presence under Commander-in-Chief Reagan. (A draw for both sides.)

In other words, trust in both Sokolov and Reagan was eroding with the European public. At home, Sokolov was disliked, but Reagan was adored. In Europe, Reagan still fared slightly less favorably than Sokolov.

The consensus across the continent (with minor regional fluctuations), was that most now supported the idea of a demilitarized European Union. They didn't trust either the Americans or the Russians, and preferred that each empire keep its distance.

Great Britain was home to the most polarized sentiments, especially with regard to maintaining an alliance that required the stationing of US troops and missiles on British soil. The UK was also home to a significant number of spies and double agents, providing Moscow with a reliable source of information on what America's premier European ally was up to at any given moment.

For instance, the Soviets learned that Britain was prepared to use a first-strike capability, and if threatened, would act independent of American wishes. Sources within the US worried about "Iron Lady" Thatcher starting something she wouldn't be able to finish, and the prospect that she would challenge US leadership in a hot conflict.

In Canada, Brian Mulroney, a reliable US supporter, was still the Prime Minister, and his conservative party appeared destined to win re-election on November 21. However, Canadian forces were woefully unprepared to handle any Soviet incursion across the northern borders, meaning that the US would need to handle most of the responses, either independently or through NORAD.

Despite Mulroney's personal friendship with Reagan, and the historically close ties between the two countries, the degree to which Canadian forces could be relied upon was in question, with an active combat role opposed by even a slim majority within the Prime Minister's own conservative party.

Meanwhile, it was revealed that the Soviets were considering an attack on Israel by one of their regional agents so as to shift additional US forces to the Middle East. They were also courting Iran and Iraq, hoping to create a situation that would affect US energy supplies. Supposedly, Soviet arms were already flowing into Iran.

Moscow had known for some time that the US had several major defense systems in rapid development or ready for introduction, including the Stealth Bomber, and a "game changer" in the SDI program.

In a clear violation of both treaties and public pronouncements, the US learned that the Soviets had much deeper reserves than had been reported, and that the missiles aimed at Germany and other European civilian zones had not been retargeted as promised, but were ready to launch with a moment's notice.

In reality, no one knew what the other side was planning, or how events would unfold. The consensus, on both sides however was that the Soviets were now in a battle against time, and that neither side was prepared to back down.

33

Veterans Day

Given the Republican sweep, President Reagan did not lose a day in transitioning from his second to third administrations. He immediately began integrating in new team members; knowing that his selections, "pre-approved" by the voters, would also all be approved by a Republican majority Congress.

Some cabinet members and administration staff scheduled for replacement (such as Education Secretary Lauro Cavazos) were already gone. Others, like Rush Limbaugh (currently based in New York), were being merged more slowly.

Limbaugh, already working closely with Marlin Fitzwater, would relocate to Washington after the New Year, and assume the full responsibilities of Press Secretary by mid-month, although Fitzwater would stay on in a supporting role until inauguration day. (In a show of continued loyalty to James Brady, Limbaugh, like Fitzwater, would officially be listed as "acting" Press Secretary.)

Elizabeth Dole, having accepted the invitation to serve as Transportation Secretary, was already residing in DC, and would unofficially begin on December 1.

Although George HW Bush would technically remain the Vice President until inauguration day on January 20, his authority and level of direct engagement was rapidly being absorbed by Vice President-elect Ed Meese.

Given the perilous and escalating situation with the USSR, the defense and intelligence teams had been in a process of integration for some time now. Frank Carlucci was long gone; replaced by Colin Powell as the new Secretary of Defense.

The first few days after the election were busy ones, as the President was pulled in many directions—from meetings with members of Congress, to graciously accepting calls of congratulations from other world leaders who secretly wished him gone.

Surprisingly, Reagan even received a congratulatory note from

General Secretary Sokolov, who looked forward to "a new era of Soviet-US relations based on peace and partnership."

Presidential Election Day in the US is set by law, and it is always the first Tuesday following the first Monday in November. Because of how things are scheduled, Election Day can fall anywhere between the second and eighth of the month.

In 1988 that Tuesday fell on the eighth, and as such, the week would end on the eleventh — and with the Veterans Day holiday.

The holiday had always held deep significance for Reagan. But this year's Veterans Day brought additional weight, and cause for reflection, as the nation under his command prepared for war.

Most of the day's official events had been scheduled long in advance, including a speech slated for the Vietnam Veterans Memorial in Washington. Weather forecasts predicted a clear day, with temperatures in the 50s. As with any public appearance, this event would likely feature a contingent of protestors, but in light of the renewed sense of national unity, these were not likely to be much of an issue.

Of greater concern were the assassination threats.

In addition to the usual loonies, intelligence sources were concerned about a wave of reports concerning everything from the influx of well-known terrorists into DC, to chatter suggesting that Reagan was a marked man.

The symbolism of assassinating the President in the nation's capital on Veterans Day would be huge. The impact would be significant as well, elevating Bush into the presidency, and derailing what the Soviets regarded as a personality cult based on Reagan himself.

Related to this scenario was the possibility that if made president, Bush might declare martial law and suspend the election results. Under the guise of needing to maintain order, Bush would now hold the office twice denied him by the electorate.

According to the NSA, such actions would unleash a range of consequences. Protests could quickly blossom into civil war, and Bush might himself be displaced by a home-grown *coup d'état*. In the confusion and turmoil, the US would be at its most vulnerable to not just an attack, but possibly an actual invasion by a Soviet-led coalition.

President Reagan listened patiently, but refused to be manipulated by such outlandish scenarios.

"Everything involves risk. It's in my job description," stated the President, as his core of advisors looked on with expressions ranging from frustration to dismay.

Reagan was well aware of the dangers. He had confronted them many times, including most recently when he traveled to the memorial service earlier in Alaska on Air Force One. He had also been informed of KGB plans to assassinate Gorbachev while the Secretary was visiting in the US the previous year.

Despite the warnings, Reagan dug in his heels, and refused to cancel.

"How can I not go? How can I talk about service to country, sacrifice, and courage if I run whenever someone says 'Boo'?

"How can I renege on a promise to those who kept their commitment when their country called on them?

"If, God forbid, we find ourselves in another war, how could I ever call upon the citizens of this country to go fight—knowing well that many will never return alive? How can I ask our nation—and the world—to show courage if I can't?"

Reagan's remarks were met by stony silence, with many of those in attendance (such as Secret Service Director John Simpson), uncomfortably averting their eyes as the President spoke.

Simpson, who had been in charge of safety for "Rawhide" (the agency's code name for Reagan) since 1981, wondered if he should inform Mrs Reagan—knowing that she was the only one who might be able to dissuade the President.

As if he was reading Simpson's mind, Reagan addressed the issue directly: "And don't bother telling Nancy—she already knows, and she's going with me. We've written a little note which we plan to leave at the monument, and there's nothing on Earth that is going to stop us."

Reagan's tone was calm and measured.

"I've given the matter a lot of thought. I understand the dangers, and the ramifications should anything happen.

"But I've also prayed on it, and I must accept that whatever happens will be God's plan.

"I believe that I have been called for a special purpose, and that the Lord will watch over me. If this is a test of my faith, I must meet it, and show God that I am His servant, here to do His bidding."

And so it was to be.

Security for the event was exceptionally tight, and protestors numbered less than a hundred persons, including a well-behaved contingent of elderly Catholic nuns.

As with any large public event, there were a fair number of arrests made for a variety of reasons.

One would-be self-styled assassin was a 67-year-old man from Florida with a history of mental illness who sought to kill the President with a venomous snake. The snake, hidden in a special bag adorned with slogans about the Illuminati and cosmic convergences, had been dead for several days at the time of its seizure. The man believed that the snake would be reanimated at the critical moment and fly towards the stage where it would kill Reagan with a single bite.

When the snake did not fly from the open the bag as planned, the man removed it himself and began chanting as he swung it about, accidentally striking some Japanese tourists who summoned the authorities.

A second man, a Belgian national with known ties to terrorist groups, was arrested at his hotel when it was learned that he was in town. However, no weapons or other evidence could be found. The man was questioned, released, and deported — two days later.

A third man never appeared on anyone's radar. In fact, he was unknown to US authorities, despite the fact that he was a 20-year veteran of the KGB.

"Viktor" was able to move freely around town and get close to those in power, and that's just what he did — when he decided to defect to the CIA, bringing with him news that would change everything.

Across town, the ceremony at the Vietnam Veterans Memorial proceeded as planned, and after the speech, the President and Mrs Reagan left their personal handwritten note at the shrine to America's fallen warriors.

The crowd was at record numbers for such an event, and many had been visibly moved by the President's speech. Little did they realize that when the President spoke of courage and faith that these were not just words, but the code by which this man lived his life.

Leading by example, Reagan had fulfilled his promise. He had shown up, stared down death, and won.

While there would be many stormy days ahead, it was once again morning in America.

34

Thanksgiving at Camp David

On the surface, the days and weeks following Reagan's Veterans Day appearance were relatively calm and uneventful.

The Soviets tested another nuclear weapon at the Semipalatinsk Test Site (in Kazakhstan, near the border with China), then followed it with the launch of an unmanned space shuttle on the fifteenth. During this period Moscow continued to call up troops, reposition equipment, lobby allies, spew propaganda, but for the most part avoided any direct conflict with the United States.

Back in the US, the President continued to meet with American allies, including Prime Minister Thatcher (in town for a state dinner). Reagan was especially concerned over Thatcher's aggressive posturing, and her threat to go it alone.

Fortunately, Reagan's re-election and words provided Thatcher with the assurances she needed. The two had been close friends and allies from the beginning, and Thatcher knew she could trust him. As they shook hands goodnight, the President knew he could also trust her to remain part of a united front.

It had now been more than nine months since the coup, and the suspense and tension had taken a tremendous toll. Was this the quiet before the storm, or was the Soviet Union having second thoughts about taking actions that might result in a war?

According to "Viktor" (the KGB agent who had defected on Veterans Day), both scenarios were true. The Kremlin was divided, but it was also determined that there could be no turning back now. Plans would need to be adjusted, but operations must continue moving forward—although perhaps on a slightly smaller scale.

Thus, while all were apparently united in the mission to "liberate and unite" Western Europe, there were significant divisions within the Kremlin as how best to achieve this—especially in light of Reagan's re-election and a unified Congress now led by Republicans.

Since the coup, the President had rarely any time off. Congress was currently in recess, and with things relatively quiet, the Reagans decided they could take a few days away from Washington to spend Thanksgiving at their home at Camp David—otherwise known as "Aspen."

Located in Maryland's wooded Catoctin Mountain Park, Camp David had been a presidential retreat since the days of FDR. Located just over 60 miles from Washington as the crow flies, the secluded hideaway seemed a world apart from the constant turmoil and distractions of the nation's capital. The old house was quite rustic, with beamed ceilings, wood-paneled walls, and windows that looked out into the forest.

Unlike the White House, where Reagan often felt a prisoner for his own safety, Camp David was quite secure: here the President was free to walk about, swim, step outside for a breath of fresh air, and most importantly, ride horses.

Aspen had long been a favorite destination for the Reagans, and since the crisis, their home away from home—as all trips west to their ranch in California had been suspended.

Camp David not only offered quick proximity to the White House, but provided all the key parallel facilities necessary to conducting the government's business.

Despite the incredible burden on his shoulders, Reagan did not show any signs of strain or weakness, and had resisted taking any time off. Still, those around him (including Mrs Reagan and the President's personal physician) had pushed hard for him to spend at least a few days away at "the Camp."

After intense lobbying, the President agreed to spend the Thanksgiving weekend at Camp David.

What finally swayed him was learning that his son, Ron Jr, would be there. Nancy, in her own, inimitable form of shuttle diplomacy, very much wanted father and son to have some quality family time away from the spotlight, and Thanksgiving was a holiday with many positive associations for all.

As with any father and son, the relationship between the two men had experienced its fair share of ups and downs. Growing up in the shadow of a famous father is never easy, and much to the disappointment of those hoping for a political dynasty like the Kennedys, Ron Jr had no interest in following his father's footsteps into politics. Instead, from a very early age, Ron tried hard to define himself as his own person, and not just his father's son.

Like his dad, Ron Jr was bright, affable, athletic, *and* opinionated—especially when it came to politics.

Although accepted into Yale, one of the nation's most prestigious universities, Ron dropped out after just one semester to follow his dream of dancing with the Joffrey Ballet. While many questioned this career path, it was clear that Ron had inherited the "performer gene" from his parents. While most were familiar with his father's career, lesser known was the fact that Nancy had also been a star of stage, screen, and television. In fact, the Reagans met in Hollywood, and even starred together in the classic World War II drama *Hellcats of the Navy*.

Despite her successful acting career, Mrs Reagan opted to give it all up in order to be a full-time wife and stay-at-home mom.

Whereas the President was a man of deep religious conviction, Ron Jr had become an atheist at age 12. While the elder Reagan was the century's most respected conservative, his son's views were distinctly liberal on nearly every issue.

And yet, both were entertainers at heart; men with an appreciation for the arts, who loved to laugh, but who could also be moved deeply by a film, a song, or the lines of a poem. Underneath the philosophical differences, there were personalities that meshed as is only possible between a father and a son.

Reagan's brush with death resulting from the assassination attempt in 1981 brought those close to him ever more mindful of life's fragility. Usually, such an awareness of this basic and inevitable truth comes too late: divisions are taken to the grave, leaving the survivor's heart heavy with guilt and remorse until similarly summoned home.

But for father and son this was a wake-up call to let bygones be bygones. Ronnie and Ron Jr would civilly agree to disagree—even after a rigorous and impassioned exchange, often punctuated with humor, rendered at the critical moment just when it was needed to deflate tensions.

Still, things were not perfect yet, and although Ron's older sister Patti would not be attending this year, Mom and Dad were looking forward to a very special, Reagan Family Thanksgiving at the Camp.

By the time the President and Mrs Reagan arrived late Wednesday afternoon, Ron was already settled in. The family enjoyed a light dinner, and then chatted about a range of neutral topics — from recollections of family vacations, to pranks the younger Reagan was prepared to finally confess to (given the unlikelihood that his parents would send him to bed without dessert or suspend his telephone privileges now that he was 30 years old).

It was a good night, and as the President lay in bed, he thanked Nancy for giving him such a wonderful son, and for her part in arranging for him to be with them for the holiday.

"You know, there's still hope for him."

Nancy looked puzzled.

"To become a conservative!" said Reagan, smiling. "At his age I was still a liberal Democrat working for a union, so let's not be too hard on the boy. And besides, he did tell me that he had voted for me all three times — so how much more can a father reasonably expect?"

The Reagans both chuckled at this. But in his heart, this tiny bit of information — only revealed for the first time that day — had meant the world to him.

35

Finland

Although officially on a mini-vacation, the Reagans still arose at essentially the same time each day, and such was the case on Thanksgiving morning. Both were very much creatures of habit, comfortable in their established routines.

Still, there were some key differences. For instance, back in Washington, the TV was rarely turned on during the day. But this being a holiday, the old color television set at Camp David went on early to catch the Macy's Thanksgiving Day Parade.

Nancy especially enjoyed the glamour and pageantry of the event, anchored this year by the team of *Today Show* weatherman Willard Scott and actress Sandy Duncan.

Watching the parade had been a family tradition when the kids were young, but this year Ron Jr was sleeping late. The President watched casually, commenting occasionally, waiting for the appearance of Santa Claus, which would signify the end—thereby allowing him to switch the set over to football.

For a lifetime football fan, the day offered a wealth of college games, as well as the main contest between the Detroit Lions and the Minnesota Vikings.

Ron Jr finally got up just in time to see the last part of the parade, after which the family moved into the dining area to begin breakfast. But just as the food was being put on the table, the President had to step away for an emergency phone call.

The Soviets were invading Finland.

As had been the case too many times in the past, Reagan would once again have to leave his family for work, and within the hour he would find himself in a helicopter racing back to the nation's capital.

Casually dressed, the President embraced his wife and son, told them not to worry, and then switched gears from the head of the family to leader of the free world.

It was a quick return flight home. Gazing out the window at the landscape passing below him, Reagan was briefed on the still-developing situation—and the news was not good. Personally, he felt frustrated by what he knew would be the limitations, both foreign and domestic, on the options available to him. But for now, he just listened intently, keeping his notes and thoughts private.

Back in Washington, Reagan hit the ground running, and was met by nearly every member of his team, from the Press Secretary to the Joint Chiefs of Staff. Most, like the President, never strayed too far from the capital, and had rarely taken any time off since the coup.

With the President now in attendance, the meeting officially came to order, beginning with news that the invasion of Finland was still taking place, and with no apparent signs of resistance.

Wedged between NATO and the Warsaw Pact, Finland had sought to position itself as a neutral buffer. It had limited defensive capabilities and was not a member of either military alliance. As such, Western forces—whether dedicated to defense or intelligence gathering had officially been kept at bay during the Cold War.

Because of its neutrality, Finland had, like Switzerland, been the site of various meetings of the superpowers over the years. Most recently, a summit with Gorbachev (scheduled for May in the Finnish capital of Helsinki), had been scrapped as a result of Sokolov's power grab.

Since the coup, various scenarios for a Soviet expansion had been explored, and so all in attendance were already familiar with Finland's precarious position as "low hanging fruit" within the broader European community.

Unaligned, and neither truly Scandinavian nor Slavic, Finland was a sparsely populated nation surrounded by larger and much more powerful neighbors. As a consequence, it had frequently been the victim of expansionist wars and foreign occupation.

For centuries Finland had been part of Sweden, its neighbor to the west. In the early 19th century, Finland was officially incorporated as part of the Russian Empire with which it shared a long and contested eastern border.

Russian domination continued until the Empire began to collapse as a result of the 1917 revolution. Sensing opportunity, Finland declared its independence.

Freedom was to be short-lived: within a year the nation was embroiled in a bloody civil war fueled by the presence of foreign troops. Moscow made no secret of its interests, or role, in seeing Finland become another Marxist state patterned after the Russian model.

Had these forces succeeded, Finland would have almost certainly been annexed outright, or forced into becoming a puppet member of the USSR. Instead, Finland declared itself an independent republic and hoped for the best.

In the years that followed, the Soviets made two more overt attempts to conquer the Finns; in the late 1930s and then again in the early 1940s. The two countries remained officially at war until 1947, following an exchange of territories, and the payment of reparations.

The Thanksgiving invasion had come quickly; by ground forces from the east, waves of aircraft, and with naval vessels from Soviet ports just across the Gulf of Finland. Helsinki, and most of the southern part of the country had been taken quickly, while the less populated regions in the north, (and those bordering Norway and Sweden), had not been challenged.

The choice of Finland made both perfect sense and no sense.

Certainly, proximity to the Soviet frontier helped with logistics, but Finland was also a nation of questionable strategic value, already in the early throes of the hard northern winter. Still, the weather did not seem to be a factor for the Russians, who had first invaded Finland almost 49 years ago to the day, launching what came to be known as the Winter War on November 30, 1939.

Relations between the two nations had warmed in recent years, and ironically, just two years previous (in 1986), the Finns had awarded Sokolov the Order of the White Rose, one of Finland's highest honors, at a special ceremony held in Helsinki.

Evidently Sokolov felt like he deserved more, and decided to come back for the entire country.

The timing of this latest invasion — on the Thanksgiving holiday — seemed specifically planned with the Americans in mind. For the world, this was just another Thursday, but for Americans — including those stationed around the globe in diplomatic and military service — it was a day of deep national significance, and a way to maintain a connection to home.

The Soviets were gambling that America's guard might be down for the holiday, and decided to exploit the opportunity. Whether this was a stroke of genius on their part, or inspired by a Hollywood movie was uncertain. After all, the hit film *Die Hard* (starring Bruce Willis and depicting a criminal heist disguised as a terrorist attack on Christmas Eve) had opened that past summer, and was still playing in many theaters around the world.

In any event, unlike the movie, American preparedness was never in question. What was in question was how best to respond to a developing situation that presented few viable options, but significant consequences.

The consensus by US intelligence was that Finland would be used in order to advance the Soviet frontier towards Sweden—another under-prepared, non-NATO nation. Because neither was part of the Western alliance, the Soviet invasions would not technically constitute an act of war, as defined by NATO's Article 5.

If Sweden were to fall, Norway and Denmark—both NATO members—would now share direct land borders with Soviet troops. Just across the water lay Germany, already surrounded by USSR member states the DDR (GDR/East Germany), Czechoslovakia, and Moscow's new puppet in the east: Austria.

Strategically, Norway was a much bigger prize than Denmark, and its position on the North Sea made it critical to the defenses of the continent. Losing Norway would block air access to the western parts of the USSR, cede control of the northern coasts of Europe to the Soviets, and provide them with ice-free harbors. Iceland, to the west, although a NATO member, was now under heavy Soviet influence, and therefore unlikely to offer any support to the Western allies.

Moving south from Sweden into Denmark would open up Greenland to the Soviets, further tightening their noose on the North Atlantic, and positioning them right above Canada—another sitting duck.

All agreed that Sweden held the key, and that a Soviet invasion was most likely to come by air, and by crossing the Gulf of Bothnia from occupied southern Finland, rather than by the long ground journey down from the frozen north.

Until the Soviet move on Finland, Sweden had been in a relatively secure position; bordered on two sides by NATO members, and separated from Warsaw Pact nations by the Baltic Sea.

Conversely, Finland had long been an area of concern due to its porous land border with Russia, leftist governments, and with a naiveté that Washington regarded as akin to "an ostrich with its head in the sand."

Despite intensive lobbying efforts—including those made personally by President Reagan—security accords were turned down, and diplomatic warnings rebuffed. Simply put, the Finns felt confident of their ability to manage their own affairs without any outside assistance. After all, twice before they had repulsed Soviet advances, and now were protected by international treaties that legally recognized their official borders.

Whether under Soviet influence or just obstinate, Finland's Social Democrat party leader Mauno Koivisto wanted to keep the West at a distance. Although he had personally fought against the previous two Soviet invasions, he had definitely cozied up to Moscow since being elected to office, first as Prime Minister in 1979, then as President three years later.

Secretary of State Schultz, summoned away for a phone call, returned to the meeting with a grave look on his face. "I've just been on the phone with Rock Schnabel—our ambassador to Finland. He's safe, and has confirmed that the Soviet invasion is continuing—*without opposition.*"

Schultz paused. "Rock just got out of an emergency meeting with the Finns, where he was informed that prior to this move, they had signed a non-aggression pact with Moscow … apparently sometime over the summer. The gist of the deal is that the Soviets promise to leave if asked, but in the meantime, they will defend Finland from any aggressive actions by the US or NATO.

"According to Rock, the Soviets told the Finns NATO had plans to invade and occupy the southern part of Finland … as a base for an invasion of the Baltics and even Leningrad—which is just across the Gulf of Finland.

"The Soviets said such a move would result in all-out war, with Finland being ground zero.

"So, they made the Finns an offer they couldn't refuse: Let us in to block NATO and spare your nation becoming the front line in America's war of aggression. We will sign a binding treaty promising to leave as soon as the danger is over, and we pledge not to interfere with any of your internal politics.

"The Soviets also hinted that if the Finns didn't sign, the Russians might have no choice but to invade anyway, so as to provide a defensive buffer against a NATO invasion. At least with a treaty there would be no bloodshed, and life—for those in power—would continue on as normal."

President Reagan just shook his head in disbelief. He was angry at the Finns for being so gullible, and angry at himself for failing to convince them of the eminent danger they faced.

But there was plenty enough blame to go around, from the State Department, to Defense. Schultz continued with his briefing.

"The Soviets did an end run: they knew we wouldn't dare invade a non-aligned nation without provocation, and by cutting a deal they positioned themselves as welcome guests of the Finns.

"This approach is different from their pledge to 'liberate' populations held hostage by their pro-US and NATO governments. With the President's re-election, that strategy seems be on hold. The scenario here is closer to what they used with Austria, although we haven't heard any big promises of economic assistance.

"If the Finns welcomed them in then the bottom line is that our hands are tied, at least in terms of direct legal options," stated Schultz.

Reagan turned to UN Ambassador Vernon Walters who just gave an open palms up gesture seemingly affirming Schultz's assessment. The President could only imagine what might have been the response from Jeane Kirkpatrick, the fiery anticommunist who had preceded Walters at the UN.

Kirkpatrick had her strengths, but from the get-go had butted heads with the State Department over policy. Disputes began with Al Haig, the administration's first Secretary of State, and then continued on under Schultz's tenure at the post.

When Kirkpatrick resigned at the start of Reagan's second term most agreed that it was for the best. As brilliant as she was, Kirkpatrick simply wasn't worth the divisiveness she brought to the administration. In time of great crisis, the President needed team players like Walters.

Reagan nodded in acknowledgement of Walters' gesture, affirming the difficult position the US found itself in.

Acting NSA Director Bud McFarlane spoke next.

"In light of this revelation, we can assume a similar scenario could take place in Sweden. As with Finland, it is a non-aligned nation, led by a somewhat clueless, left-leaning Social Democrat government."

Secretary Schultz picked up the thread with information regarding the diplomatic side of the equation.

"Our sources in Stockholm report that Prime Minister Ingvar Carlsson has been meeting with the Soviets on a fairly regular basis, and his administration has really strengthened ties with Moscow since the spring. Mostly economic and cultural—nothing too unusual, following the Austrian model.

"One thing that is rather peculiar pertains to Carlsson's ascendency to PM. He had been Deputy Prime Minister under Olof Palme, who, as we know, was assassinated under very mysterious circumstances," noted Schultz.

CIA Director Webster added to the story.

"Although Palme's assassination occurred while Gorbachev was in power, we've long suspected that it was the work of a Yugoslavian KGB agent. Read into it what you like, but I think it fair to assume that given these connections, when Moscow rings, Mr Carlsson runs to the phone."

"Do we have any reason to suspect the Swedes may have signed a similar pact?" asked the President.

"Unknown. Our ambassador—Gregory Newell—is quite a young man—not yet 40—but he's been there since '85, and I think he's doing a great job. I trust that he'll get to the bottom of this. But for now, there seems to be much going on, literally under the ice," replied Schultz.

The Secretary continued.

"Again, our options are pretty limited if the Swedes have cut a similar deal: we can't just go into a sovereign state with guns blazing. It violates international law, and that would only play into the hands of the KGB propagandists. Keep in mind, much of the world still regards us as the bad guys … the aggressors.

"We also need to acknowledge domestic political realities as well. Yes, we won the election by a landslide, but Congress is still controlled by the Democrats until January, and many of those getting the boot are not happy. Some are outright Soviet sympathizers, who will fight us tooth and nail, whether on principle or in service to their own egos.

"I can't see how a military intervention in Finland could work—at least for now. In the meantime, the State Department will continue to work all avenues, but until the Soviets hit an actual NATO member—

activating the Collective Defense clause, or someone we have a treaty with, we're stuck between a very icy rock and a very cold hard place.

"These countries have made their choices, and these are the consequences," stated Schultz with an air of resignation.

"Unless, of course," noted McFarlane, "we can show that these agreements were coerced, made under duress."

"Which I think we will," added Webster. "Oh, and one other interesting side note: the agency has learned that Finland's Prime Minister Koivisto is leaving tomorrow for a visit to Cuba."

"For a little Finn fun in the sun?" quipped Press Secretary Fitzwater. "Can't blame him, Finnish beaches can be a tad chilly at this time of the year. Selling out your country must be exhausting, so maybe he just needs a little R & R?"

"As in *regret* and *retribution*," added Deaver.

"Actually, it's a little gift from the Soviets. Tomorrow, November 25, is the Prime Minister's 65th birthday," said Webster. "Whether he'll be back in time to celebrate Finnish Independence Day on December 6 is anyone's guess. But I think it's safe to say this year's Finnish Independence Day festivities will be fairly low key."

And so, as expected, the Soviet invasion of Finland continued unabated. Diplomatic protests in the UN by the United States failed, and in retaliation, the US mission was expelled from Finland for "aggressive meddling."

Similarly, relations with the Swedes continued to deteriorate, and by the first week of December the stream of Soviet ships sailing across the Baltic Sea from the east became a regular occurrence. There could be no denying it now: the Swedes were taking the same path that the Finns had gone down.

Now completely isolated in the northern upper corner of the continent, the Norwegians were growing increasingly uneasy.

Despite NATO's assurances, the Norwegians worried that they might be sacrificed in order to avoid an all-out war. The year had not been a good one for NATO; the alliance seemed shaky, and long-standing commitments by fellow European nations such as the French were now questionable.

To avoid a confrontation, or at least slow its progress, might some smaller nations be fed to the advancing Russian bear?

There was, after all, a history of such appeasements in Europe. During World War II, the world looked the other way as Nazi Germany fattened itself on the weak and defenseless rather than risk directly challenging Hitler. Then, in the years following the war, the Western powers, exhausted by conflict, turned their backs and let the Soviets erect an Iron Curtain to enslave the nations of Eastern Europe.

With roughly four million citizens, Norway was sparsely populated and completely unprepared to take on an adversary like the Soviet Union by itself.

Norway soon found itself surrounded on all sides, from its lightly-patrolled land borders to the waters off its immense jagged coastline, which was now teeming with Soviet vessels of all types. In the skies above, Russian aircraft buzzed right up to the border, creating a perpetual state of hyper-alert and anxiety. From space, Soviet satellites monitored not just the readying of defenses, but even details as seemingly inconsequential as which cars were parked where and at which bases. Norway was brimming with spies, saboteurs, and advance agents, all poised to strike when Moscow gave the signal.

It seemed only a matter of time, especially to an isolated population struggling through a period defined by cold, darkness, and the trappings of seasonal depression and despair.

According to the Soviet propagandists, these actions were not a prelude to an attack and invasion, but to protect against one by the West. No one was buying this story, least of all the Norwegians.

Like Finland, Norway had also fought against Nazi Germany, but unlike the Finns, the Norwegians had learned the lesson that small countries need alliances in order to protect and ensure their freedom. As an early victim of Nazi conquest, Norway's neutrality did not save it from five years of brutal occupation by Hitler's dark forces.

Under Nazi occupation, a puppet government was established in Oslo, and the Holocaust of Norway's Jewish population began. Norway had paid a heavy price, learning that neutrality works only if it doesn't conflict with the interests of those holding the power.

Still bearing the scars of war, Norway had been a reliable NATO partner since the organization's inception as a counterbalance to the Warsaw Pact.

Even though most of Norway's political parties ran pretty far to the left (by US standards), the two nations maintained a solid relationship, regardless of which government held power. Despite the recent change from a conservative government to one headed by the Social Democrats, the bond between Norway and America was never in question. In fact, Reagan had been one of the first heads of state to congratulate Gro Harlem Brundtland when she became the new Prime Minister in 1986.

Since the beginning of the Soviet crisis, the US had repeatedly emphasized its support for a free and independent Norway. In no uncertain terms, it had been made clear that Norway represented the line in the sand that could not be crossed. An attack on any member state of NATO—no matter how small or distant—would be treated as an attack on all. This was not a new position, but a foundation principle of NATO—and Moscow knew it.

But if challenged, how would NATO—or more specifically, the US, respond? Was it really willing to risk all-out war over a small, left-leaning country that most Americans couldn't even locate on a map? The Norwegians were right to worry.

In light of the developments in Finland, and concerns that Sweden was taking the same path, President Reagan insisted on personally calling the Norwegian Prime Minister to convey his assurances of iron-clad American support.

Most of the call was conducted in English, and despite the fact that he did not speak the language, President Reagan delivered a convincing rendition of a famous Norwegian proverb:

Beste lækjedommen møter sykja før ho kjem i huset.

Literally translated, it means that the best cure meets the disease before it enters the home.

The message was crystal clear, and exactly what Brundtland needed to hear from the American Commander-in-Chief. As allies, the two nations would face whatever came next with unity.

The US was ready, and it would not back down. It would stand with Norway. No ifs, ands, or buts.

36

Bears vs Vikings

As predicted, Sweden slipped into the Soviet column during the month of December.

The expansion into Sweden was met with more public opposition than had been encountered in Finland, but in the end it did little to stop the Soviet influx which came by air, land, and sea.

The Swedes were promised many of the same guarantees brokered into the deal with the Finns. Namely, that the Soviets would respect all Swedish laws and customs, and leave when asked. In exchange, the Soviets offered protection from the Americans and NATO, thus insuring their autonomy and neutrality.

As with Austria, integration into a greater European partnership (led by the Soviets) came with a string of economic enticements, including the extension of yet another pipeline to bring in cheap Russian natural gas.

While the Norwegians had North Sea oil, Sweden struggled with energy issues, and had little in the way of internal resources (save for hydroelectricity) and timber. Support for nuclear power had been declining since the 1979 incident at Three Mile Island in the United States, but then hit bottom following the Chernobyl Disaster of 1986. Outside of the USSR, Sweden was the largest recipient of nuclear fallout from the accident, the result of which was a hardening public attitude towards all things nuclear.

Thus, the promise of a reliable and affordable new source of energy was an offer the Swedes found difficult to turn down — especially during the frigid and seemingly endless Nordic winter.

Related to concerns about fallout was the public's fear of a nuclear war in Europe. Although not a direct target, the winds would most certainly bring the radioactive debris to Sweden, so the prospect of removing what was viewed as an increasingly antagonistic American presence from the continent was generally thought to be a wise and proactive proposition.

On December 5, the US space shuttle *Atlantis* launched the world's first nuclear war fighting satellite—a move that was met with great public outcry in Europe, despite the fact that just the day before the Soviets had performed a nuclear "test" at Novaya Zemlya—something which Moscow initially denied, then subsequently refused to comment on.

But in the end, it was once again the Americans who were vilified for trying to extend the arms race—and their "empire"—into space.

Sweden, once an empire itself, had more robust defensive capabilities than the Finns due to both a much larger population, and a practice of mandatory conscription for most males. The nation's forces were divided into an army, an air force, and a navy.

Although still officially proclaiming its neutrality, the government announced a series of exercises that would integrate a "Soviet presence" into the nation's defenses. In sharp contrast to the usually open and transparent nature of Swedish government, few details of the alliance were made public, with the excuse given that such was military policy and not a civilian affair, so therefore not subject to scrutiny and debate so long as no laws were being broken.

It had been more than 150 years since Sweden had been in a state of war, when during the summer of 1814 it attacked, and defeated Norway. Now, as 1988 drew to a dark conclusion, Swedish troops were once again positioned on the Norwegian border.

37

The Year That Was

New Year's Eve was a time for celebration in Moscow.

1988 had been an incredible year for the Soviets, who had not only succeeded in halting Gorbachev's systematic destruction of the USSR, but who had turned things 180 degrees by expanding their worldwide empire in ways no one had previously imagined.

Granted, there had been some costs, both financial and human — but these were minor considering what had been gained. As they say, you have to spend money to make money, and so far things were really paying off for Sokolov & Company.

Nations aligned with the Soviets for a range of reasons. In some cases, incentives were linked to shipments of weapons, supplemented by tactical support and training to prop up despotic totalitarian governments. Financial inducements, whether above board or paid in secret were welcomed, with no questions asked of the gift horse. For others, the promises were loftier and more evenly distributed: a vision of a united Europe; freedom from the threat of nuclear war; a world liberated from imperialist America.

The Soviets took special delight in having cuckolded the old and impotent Uncle Sam, luring away Iceland and Turkey from his NATO harem, while enticing the other European war brides to fantasize about life after the Cold War chastity belt had been dropped. Even old flames like Austria, which once kicked the Soviets out citing domestic abuse, were back in the fold, giggling and gasping over the proposed extension of a big gas pipeline that would keep them warm all night long.

Then of course there was the girl — or rather *girls* — next door: the virgins of Scandinavia who had resisted, (at times with force), the overtures of their would-be suitors from the east. By Christmas, Soviet ships were docking in the frigid ports of Finland and Sweden, and when weather permitted, leering over the fence at Norway and wondering if she was lonely.

Like any successful Lothario, every Soviet pitch was customized to reflect what each prospect most wanted to hear. Promises, promises, promises!

As every successful salesman knows, people will fall for even the most outrageous nonsense if it's what they *want* to believe. All that's necessary to make the sale is to repeat back what the customer says with a few embellishments, then have them sign here, here, and here.

Attempts to seduce Ireland had been rebuffed, and would probably need to wait until Great Britain could be absorbed. Still, the idea of occupying the beloved land of Reagan's ancestors held a certain wicked appeal, especially if the American president were alive to watch the Emerald Isle turn red from the comfort of a tiny prison cell.

With the change in Soviet leadership, the USSR was given a fresh start; free to post a window sign announcing that it was now under new management, all the while retaining the impressive inherited physical trappings of a superpower.

Although they spoke of world liberation, preservation of traditions, and prosperity, life for the citizens behind the Iron Curtain remained the same: one of complete domination with an economy in ruins.

Sokolov was loved abroad, but hated at home. With Reagan, the sentiment was reversed. Internationally, opinions ranged from dislike to distrust, but in the US, he had never been more popular.

A similar split existed between populations and their governments; most European political leaders supported President Reagan, albeit privately, so as to not alienate the electorate, which saw him as a greater threat to world peace than Sokolov.

Granted, much of the damage to Reagan's reputation had been done long before the Soviet coup—Moscow simply built on the worst of entrenched perceptions already held around the world.

Although the Soviet leadership didn't personally believe all their own anti-Reagan propaganda, they knew enough about him to justify genuine fear, and his re-election gave them reason to pause.

The Soviets knew Ronald Reagan to be a man of principle who did not mince words—and who was not afraid to follow up with action. Although they would never admit it, the Alaska incident was not an accident. It had been intended as a test of the American president, putting to rest the debate within the Kremlin as to how the US, and its embattled president might respond.

It was a costly lesson—but a valuable one. And besides, by turning the other cheek while the US went on a global rampage of revenge, the Soviets affirmed their status as peace-seeking martyrs.

Reagan's election to a third term had been a bit of a shock, but more for how it had happened, than as a testament of the people's solidarity with their president. Soviet support for Dukakis had failed, as did efforts by their friends in Congress to retain the 22nd Amendment. Moscow tried, but from the outset Kennedy's campaign was dead in the water. Now they would have no choice but to deal with a nuclear-armed sheriff who stood in the town square waiting for them to blink. Or would he draw first?

Reagan seemed surrounded by an impenetrable wall. Of all the world leaders, he was the most difficult to read. If the President said he would do something he usually followed through on it. But he was also prone to playing his cards close so as to not reveal his hand.

What was he thinking? What would Reagan do next? Even the KGB's top psychics were unable to penetrate this fortress.

Using more conventional sources of intelligence, Moscow had a pretty good picture of American and NATO military capabilities, but no clear sense as to whether Reagan might use the first-strike nuclear option. They suspected that he would (if pushed too far), and so deemed it best to avoid any large direct confrontations—at least for now. Instead, they would use a charm offensive to seduce Europe away, while straining US resources globally with proxy wars.

The list of options for such surrogate conflicts extended to nearly every continent, and that, when acted on, would hopefully impose death on America by a thousand cuts.

In Asia, old friendships with countries like North Korea and Vietnam were being rekindled, and partnerships with Marxist rebellions in the Philippines held great promise.

Similarly, Latin America was a land of opportunity. Established allies like Cuba and Nicaragua were well positioned as regional partners, serving as Soviet spearheads for the imposition of Marxist takeovers throughout the hemisphere, from Chile to Venezuela and Columbia in the north—and even Panama, home to the canal so vital to American economic interests. Likewise for the Caribbean, where the lessons of Grenada might be applied to new acquisitions, most notably Jamaica.

The Middle East, and in particular, Egypt—which controlled the Suez Canal—also looked promising. Losing the canal would be disastrous for the West, as would allowing the Soviet Union to position troops on the border with Israel.

Soviet antagonism towards Israel had long been a problem, and in a series of proxy wars with Washington, Moscow had repeatedly backed Arab attempts to destroy the Jewish state. For most of the Cold War, the Soviets had partnered with Israel's regional enemies, including not just Egypt and Libya, but also Syria, Iraq, Yemen, and Algeria.

In 1975, the USSR, along with its Arab allies, pushed through UN Resolution 3379, which denounced Zionism as a form of racism. Although opposed by the United States, the measure passed 72-35 (with 32 abstentions).

Cairo, still fuming after a loss to Israel in the 1973 Yom Kippur War voted "Yes."

Humiliated by a string of military defeats, Egypt eventually made peace with Israel, thanks in no small part to generous financial incentives provided by the United States. Still, it was a small price to pay as part of a larger strategy to provide for regional stability, and in the defense of a solid American ally.

Under President Anwar Sadat, relations with the West improved, displacing Soviet influence. But in the years since Sadat's death in 1981, alliances had become murkier. Wisely, Israel had never let its guard down, rightfully suspicious of any treaty more evocative of extortion than of a genuine desire for peace by the Egyptians.

Like Panama, Egypt was now ruled by a military strongman. As with the case of so many others, Hosni Mubarak's political fortunes had blossomed as a result of his predecessor's assassination.

Soon after taking over as President, Mubarak welcomed the Soviets back in to assist with Egypt's industrial development, signaling that he was open to what Moscow could do for him, and his nation, in that order.

Although a Muslim, when it came to affairs of state, it seemed that Mubarak was willing to consider an open marriage; dating Moscow while still technically married to Washington.

Mubarak had trained as a pilot in the Soviet Union and spoke fluent Russian. If Sokolov were to call him, there would be no need to compromise the privacy of their conversation by bringing in a translator.

Meanwhile, nearby Syria had been solidly in bed with the USSR since 1940s. The government of Hafez al-Assad received considerable financial support, and in return, served as an important Soviet outpost—going so far as to even provide a facility for the Soviet navy in Tartus, on its Mediterranean coast.

The Syrians had been very helpful in the past, and welcomed the opportunity to renew their vows with Moscow, especially if it involved sticking it to the Americans and the Israelis.

Sub-Saharan Africa had been especially fertile ground for the Soviets, which had established footholds in a number of nations following the demise of colonialism.

For the average person, nothing much changed when socialism displaced colonialism. The portrait of the Queen was taken down, only to be replaced by Brezhnev or Sokolov or whoever happened to be leading the Circus Russe at the time. When wall space permitted, each official portrait would be flanked by photos of Vladimir Lenin, and whichever Marxist puppet now ran the show in accordance with the rules governing the Soviet style of colonialism.

Meet the new boss—same as the old boss.

And so it played out, across the four corners of the world, as one nation after another fell under the spell cast by the Soviets.

In less than a year much of the world had been fundamentally transformed, and the momentum for change was accelerating. And yet, all was not well within the Kremlin itself.

Soviet leadership was increasingly divided, especially after Reagan's re-election. Although Sokolov remained firmly in control, he now worried about the possibility of a coup that would depose him.

Everyone was suspect, even old friends like Alexander Koldunov (now serving as Minister of Foreign Affairs), who seemed to be spending an inordinate amount of time with KGB chief (and coup collaborator) Vladimir Kryuchkov. Meanwhile, Gennady Yanayev, a slick career politician said to be the main architect of the Kremlin's charm strategy, appeared to be focused on courting the support of the military and business interests.

Unlike Reagan's assembly of the "Dream Team" cabinet where great consideration had been given to how the group would function as a unit, members of "Team Sokolov" had been recruited in secret, comprised of ambitious men already on record for their willingness to use dishonesty and force in the pursuit of power.

The likelihood that divisions would open was inevitable. While factions within Sokolov's administration seemed increasingly at odds with one another, at least publicly they expressed complete allegiance to their 77-year-old leader.

But for how long?

Qaddafi

Paralleling the relationship with so many other Cold War allies, the USSR's connections with Libya had withered under Gorbachev, but were revived following the February coup.

Libya was a powerful country in a very strategic location on the north coast of Africa, within striking distance of both Israel and Europe. Best of all, it was led by a bloodthirsty lunatic who had himself risen to power in a *coup d'etat*, and who ruled with a grandiose blend of pomp and ruthlessness that was all his own. In other words, he was a good candidate for a spot on the Soviet team.

Known to most of the world simply as Colonel Qaddafi, the flamboyant dictator's official title was "Brotherly Leader and Guide of the Revolution of Libya."

The son of a Bedouin goat herder, early on Muammar al-Qaddafi had set his sights on a bigger flock, and while still in his 20s led a military coup that allowed him to trade his dingy monastic barracks for the magnificent splendor of the deposed King's palace.

In the years that followed his grand ascension, Qaddafi remade Libya as he saw best, crafting a political system that blended socialism with Islam, financed by selling oil for the highest possible price to the non-Muslim nations of Europe. Libya had extensive oil reserves and fairly state-of-the-art production facilities, most of which had been built and operated by the British before being nationalized by Qaddafi.

Owing much to the Brotherly Leader's volatility, Libya was frequently involved in clashes with its neighbors and the West, and in particular, with the United States and Great Britain. Things became especially testy when Libya fully embraced socialism in the late 1970s, and officially changed its name to The Great Socialist People's Libyan Arab Jamahiriya, which roughly translates to "state of the masses."

To shore up support from the USSR, Qaddafi made his first trip to Moscow in 1977, where he generously gave away personally autographed copies of *The Green Book*, a short tome he had recently composed outlining his political philosophy, which was now required reading for all Libyans.

A man of letters, Qaddafi wrote short stories and poetry, all of which remained in print and accessible for those seeking to learn more about the artistic and sensitive side of this self-described creative genius. The Colonel also served as a muse to others, inspiring his citizens to celebrate him and his achievements in their own artistic creations.

Thanks to its incredible oil wealth, Libya bought many new friends and built an impressive military and far-reaching state security agency. While pleased by his unflagging devotion, Qaddafi was a bit of a concern for Moscow, which believed—and justifiably so—that he was something of a loose cannon.

These comments were never expressed publicly though—at least by the Soviets. Reagan, however, called it as he saw it, describing the Colonel as everything from a "terrorist" to a "mad dog"—and worse.

Qaddafi relished taunting the American president, but was also fearful of pushing him too far—especially after Reagan ordered the 1986 strike on Libya, from which he narrowly escaped with his life. Despite coming out on the short end of the conflict, Qaddafi declared it "a spectacular military victory over the United States," then promptly celebrated by firing off some of his Soviet-supplied missiles at a US Coast Guard Station, located on an island off the coast of Italy.

The missiles missed their target, and Qaddafi retreated to his palace, denounced the US as an aggressor ... as the world's policeman, and proclaiming there would be no peace between the two nations so long as Reagan, the "Israeli dog" was in office.

Libya was something akin to a crazy girlfriend for the Soviets. Amusing, useful, but best kept at a distance unless a special favor was needed. The relationship with the USSR emboldened Libya in many areas, and Qaddafi frequently sought out new ways to express his love and fidelity, while still maintaining a degree of independence. Libya and the USSR were, at least in his mind, equal partners.

The conflicts with Libya were nothing new, but something Reagan had inherited from the Carter administration, which had done little or nothing to address the situation. Instead, Libya, fattened by oil had been allowed to grow into a serious international threat, while Carter retaliated by installing solar panels on the roof of the White House.

Emboldened by crude fortunes and a superpower sugar daddy, Libya menaced its neighbors and regularly displayed a disregard for international law. Some actions seemed silly and ego-driven, whereas others, like the occupation of neighboring Chad were more worrisome, which the US believed was motivated by a quest for uranium that Libya needed in order to develop an atomic bomb.

While some argued that nuclear weapons at least created peace in the West due to the fear of mutually assured destruction, few believed that Qaddafi would be able to express a similar restraint if given the ability to drop the Big One. Prone to impassioned rants and fits of paranoia, the prospect of Libya possessing a bomb was not something Reagan would permit to happen.

A frequent recipient of Qaddafi's paranoid outbursts (and likely first target) was Israel, which he believed was actively planning to use its own stockpile of nuclear and chemical weapons to attack him. Although Israel officially denied possessing such weapons, there was no refuting the fact that it had both superior military capabilities, and the full support of the United States in any potential conflict.

Since the coup, the new Soviet regime had been very generous to the Libyans, supplying equipment, intelligence, and even advisors to help the Libyans defend themselves (wink, wink) against an almost certain attack by the Israelis, or the Americans, or the British, or well, whomever. For obvious reasons, the Soviets sought to keep their gifts private, stipulating that Qaddafi tone down his belligerent and threatening rhetoric, especially in regards to his new capabilities of following up his threats with action. Still, it was common knowledge that Libya was ramping up, and eventually there would be a showdown with somebody.

Unlike Libya, the US and the other Western powers (namely the UK and Italy) were forced to play by the rules, meaning that they had to wait until conditions were such that the response was irrefutably defensive. Hitting Libya simply because one suspected it was preparing to do something would only generate sympathy, risk pulling in the Soviets, further alienate other gulf states—and possibly threaten the flow of oil.

As a rogue state, Libya, however, was not bound by the same caveats, concerns, or laws. Instead, it played a different game, using rules created by a psychopath to fit his needs and whims.

In addition to the unofficial military buildup, it was an open secret that Libya was a leading sponsor of world terrorism, sewing death and mayhem from Israel to Ireland and even within NATO nations like West Germany and Italy.

When the US had clear evidence it took action, as had been the case with the 1986 air strikes in retaliation for Libya's role in a terrorist bombing of a disco in Berlin. In response, Libya's activities became ever more covert and devious. Essentially, the types of actions not reflective of national governments, but rather the sinister fantasies of a despot whose authority was beyond reproach.

Qaddafi made no secret of his hatred of America, and especially for President Reagan, whom it was rumored had a bounty on his head. According to intelligence sources, the funds were already in a secret Swiss bank account, awaiting transfer authorization by Qaddafi himself. The going price for Reagan's assassination was said to be ten million dollars, with a million dollar bonus if the President could be killed publicly, or in the presence of Mrs Reagan.

Under Qaddafi, Libya had the resources needed to do what other more reputable nations shied away from. It not only had the money, but also a pool of willing agents, which ran the gamut from genuinely evil to certifiably insane. These were Libya's best: brave men and women praised by the Colonel as kindred spirits and fellow warriors.

While always a staple on the menu, terrorism became Chef Qaddafi's house specialty after the Soviet coup: just his little way of saying thank you to his new friends back in Moscow, and therapy for exercising his own frustrated demons.

And now here it was—December!

Qaddafi looked at his calendar: December 18—Christmas was just a week away. As a Muslim, the day meant nothing to him. Nor did it mean anything to his atheistic friends at the Kremlin, who would instead likely be celebrating the birth of their savior, Joseph Stalin.

Yes, thought Colonel Qaddafi, he must place a call to Moscow and pay tribute to the great man who had done so much in the creation of the expansionist USSR. Especially now, given that the Soviet Union was once again strong and growing.

Yes, yes, yes … Qaddafi felt he really should do something nice to honor Stalin … something to avenge the air attack by the Americans from two years ago … something for … *Christmas!*

Knowing enough about the holiday, Qaddafi was familiar with the practice of rewarding the good with presents, and punishing the bad by putting a lump of coal in their stockings. How he would love to play Santa and give every American and Brit a lump of coal—but such was simply not possible, even for a man as great as himself.

So instead he decided on the next best thing. He called his team together, explained his holiday vision, and entrusted them to deliver a special Christmas package.

But in the true spirit of giving, Qaddafi wanted his gift to be anonymous. While he would have preferred that the present be delivered exactly on Christmas day, the logistics of getting things to work out precisely around the holidays—especially if it involved air travel—made this impossible.

Disguised as a simple tape recorder, Qaddafi's agents had their package loaded onto a Boeing 747 that was scheduled to fly from Frankfurt, West Germany, to its final destination in Detroit, with stops scheduled for London and New York City.

Unwrapped, and with no gift tag, the package sat in darkness in the hull of the airplane. Christened *Clipper Maid of the Seas,* the craft would forever be remembered by its other name, and for its horrific destiny.

At just after 7pm on the evening of December 21, 1988, Pam Am Flight 103 was blown to pieces in the skies above Lockerbie, Scotland, killing all on board.

★ 39 ★

A New Year Begins

New Year's Day 1989 fell on a Sunday, and it was a typically cold one in Washington, DC. Despite it being a holiday—and a Sunday, President Reagan would work at least a partial day.

Rather than celebrate the night before, Reagan had insisted on keeping a clear head and getting to bed at pretty much the usual time. Whereas in other years he might have been criticized for being a no-fun stick-in-the-mud, he was now admired for his discipline and sacrifice.

After a light breakfast of cereal, toast, and coffee, the President met with his advisors for updates. Although the new administration had not been officially sworn in, Vice President Bush (reportedly suffering from exhaustion) was nowhere to be seen, his duties already assumed by Vice President-elect Meese.

Fortunately, there had been no major actions taken by the Soviets overnight. If such had been the case, the President would have been awakened, and called upon to determine how the US should respond.

Given the move made by the Soviets the previous Thanksgiving, holidays were now seen as fair game. Luckily, things had been relatively quiet since, with nothing major on Christmas or Hanukkah, and the only significant incident being the downing of Pan Am Flight 103.

The US suspected that the bombing had been the work of Libyans, a consensus shared by German and British intelligence. The *modus operandi* certainly matched, as did Colonel Qaddafi's pattern of vacillating between large-scale public provocations (such as territorial disputes in international waters), to using bombs to kill innocent civilians—which in this case included 189 American men, women, and children.

Since the beginning of his first term, Reagan had played a cat-and-mouse game with Qaddafi. In particular, skirmishes over the Gulf of Sidra (ominously referred to as "The Line of Death" by Qaddafi), were an ongoing flashpoint, and one which usually ended badly for the Libyans.

With Gorbachev in office, there had been little support for Libya's provocations with the Americans over claims to the gulf, but with the change in Soviet leadership, it now appeared unlikely that Moscow would intervene against an ally in support of international law. In fact, just the opposite seemed true, suggesting that the region could soon turn into a recurring hot spot for armed conflict.

The strategy made sense: the Soviets would be able to divert American resources into a surrogate war, while (at least publicly) keeping their hands clean and free to move other chess pieces.

Nor did the USSR need Libya's oil—it had plenty. Instead, Libya's mission was to run interference, to distract the Americans, and mess with oil supplies. If Qaddafi went down as a consequence, well, so be it. *Next!*

In addition to inflicting at least some physical harm on the Americans, the Soviets would also be able to exploit the Libyan situation as part of their propaganda campaign depicting the US as a bully. Even if the Libyans threw the first punch, the battle would seem lopsided, and Qaddafi would most certainly play the martyr card for all it was worth—which in that region, was considerable.

Thus, any military action taken by the United States would only serve to enhance Moscow's offer of "defensive" assistance, and the urgent necessity of alignment.

And so, by the middle of the first week of January 1989, history repeated itself, as Libya decided to engage the US over the Gulf of Sidra and its claim of exclusive rights to international waters.

On Wednesday, January 4, using two Soviet-made MiG-23 Floggers, Libya once again went on the attack, and, once again, came out with the short end of the stick in the skies above the Mediterranean.

Although President Reagan had not personally issued a specific shoot-to-kill order, his policy of not running from a fight if attacked was clearly understood by all—including the Libyans. Their proclivity to continue testing both American resolve and military superiority was a cause for concern, suggesting that Qaddafi had grown even more irrational.

According to CIA Director Webster, Colonel Qaddafi displayed the dangerous traits of a psychopath, from his delusions of grandeur, to impulsiveness, to a complete lack of remorse and empathy. Profilers noted his willingness to take up suicidal missions for the sake of martyrdom and glory, and his compulsion to inflict pain on America, regardless of the cost to his own people.

Following the skirmish with the Americans, Libya made no effort to search for the missing pilots—which as far as they knew, may have parachuted to safety. Instead, the Colonel unleashed new waves of threats, which, much to the delight of the Soviets, resulted in forcing a further diversion of American forces to monitor the increasingly volatile and dangerous situation.

What was next for Colonel Cuckoo? No one knew. But more clashes seemed inevitable.

For years, the US was aware that Libya was producing chemical weapons—and yet was powerless to stop it.

At a plant known as the Rabta Industrial Complex Libya secretly manufactured such deadly agents as mustard gas, sarin, and phosgene gas in flagrant violation of international law and treaties. Libya was known to have used chemical weapons at least once (against its neighbor Chad), and was busy building huge stockpiles to be used however, and whenever, Qaddafi gave the order.

Advancements on the chemical weapons program had slowed under Gorbachev—at least to the degree that direct technical assistance by the Soviets had been suspended. Also lacking was any kind of sophisticated delivery system.

Undaunted, Colonel Qaddafi pushed ahead, aided and abetted by those willing to do his dirty work for cash. Progress had been slow, but now, with the addition of "defensive" Soviet missile technology, Libya's chemical weapons program became a much more ominous threat.

Hamstrung by international law that prohibited the US from taking out the plants militarily, and stymied by a succession of Democratic congresses that had restricted America's ability to strike covertly, Reagan weighed the available options, which were few.

Although the election had reduced the Democrats to minority party status, they still controlled both Houses until later that month. While most of those who retained their seats promised to respect the wishes of the President's electoral mandate, there was not currently sufficient support in Congress to take on Libya—especially if it provoked the Soviets. With the lessons of the Iran-Contra still fresh, illegal covert action was not an option—something the President had made very clear to any potentially rogue elements within his administration.

Reagan stood solemnly at the window looking out on the city, watching as snowflakes drifted lazily down to Earth.

As the sheriff, he could not shoot until the bad guy drew first. But bad guys did not play by the rules, and although tempting, Reagan knew that such a violation would only lower him to their level.

No, he must stick to the high road, and put his trust in God.

Their time will come.

That evening, instead of reading the usual doom and gloom of the afternoon papers, the President decided to watch one of his favorite movies, the classic Western, *High Noon.*

He slept well, and awoke refreshed, ready once again to take on the world — or at least a sizable chunk of it.

40

Inauguration

President Ronald Wilson Reagan's inauguration was set for January 20, 1989.

Unlike his second inauguration, this time the weather in Washington was conducive to a large outdoor ceremony and parade. Under mostly cloudy skies, temperatures would likely rise to about 50 degrees, with only a slight breeze being forecast.

Despite serious concerns for his safety, the President-elect was adamant about having the event held outside, at the west front of the US Capitol, where he had taken his first oath of office exactly eight years to the day. From here, Reagan could look out across the great panorama of monuments dedicated to those who had served before him: to his side the elegant dome of the Jefferson Memorial, ahead, the towering column of the Washington Monument, beyond it, the grave solemnity of the Lincoln Memorial.

Matters of history and tradition were very much on his mind, given that this day would mark the 200th anniversary of when George Washington was sworn in to become America's first president on January 20, 1789.

In recognition of this, Reagan would take the oath of office using two Bibles; one of which had belonged to George Washington, and the second, his personal family Bible.

This particular Bible was one of Reagan's most cherished possessions; given to him by his mother, and also the one which had been used for both of his previous swearing-in ceremonies. In keeping with tradition, the Reagan Bible was once again opened to II Chronicles 7:14

"If my people, which are called by my name, shall humble themselves, and pray, and seek my face, and turn from their wicked ways; then will I hear from heaven, and will forgive their sin, and will heal their land."

Standing at the podium, President Reagan looked out across the wide open expanse, to the monuments of the republic, and to a sea of people that had called upon him to lead them once again.

The President began to speak:

Mr Chief Justice, Vice President Meese, Vice President Bush, Senator Dole, Congressman Michel, Senator Mitchell, Speaker Wright, my family, friends, and fellow citizens.

I stand before you today, humbled by history, and by the support of the American people who have honored me with the opportunity to serve this great nation for another term as their president.

This is not something any of us ever imagined, but it would seem that God had other plans. Therefore, I ask that you join me in a moment of silent prayer, so that we might ask for God's guidance and strength as we set forth to do His work.

Amen.

It was eight years ago to the day that I first took the oath of this office, and with it came a mandate to reshape America. Four years later I was returned to office to continue with this transformation. Unfortunately, the will of the nation was subverted by one town's gridlock; stymied by the petty bickering of politicians more concerned about pleasing special interest groups than the interests of the American people they had been elected to serve.

Things will be different now.

I ran for this office with a request that you also vote for candidates — regardless of party — that would support our shared vision for America, and you responded. Republicans now control both houses of Congress, joined by a contingent of Democrats who have pledged to put aside partisan politics and heed the wishes of the people.

As for those holdouts that would still rather listen to lobbyists than the people, we have a plan waiting in the wings — and it's called the midterm elections.

In the meantime, we now have the votes needed to begin implementing the changes that I campaigned on, and in turn, to finally complete the revolution that began eight years ago.

We the people have spoken, and the message is clear.

For starters, I will continue to reduce the size, scope, and interference of government. As government contracts, liberty expands, and freedom flourishes.

Government must be made accountable to fulfill its mission to serve the people, not rule over them.

Scaling back government also means fewer tax dollars are needed to support it, allowing us to leave that money with its rightful owners: the American people. Limiting taxes provides an opportunity to simplify the entire system and close loopholes. The current tax code is broken and unfair; designed to benefit a select few, while deceiving the average person into overpaying. We need to return simplicity, fairness, and balance to this system — and while we're at it, we need to reduce the size, power, and authority of the IRS itself. I will also advocate cutting business and corporate taxes. When a business turns a profit it uses this money — *the money it has earned* — to expand operations, markets, and payrolls. People who live in the real world understand economics in a practical, hands-on sense — so let's get government off their backs and let them do what they do best.

And while we're at, let's remove the layers of unnecessary regulations that waste money, restrict, and/or constrict growth and curtail prosperity. Over-regulation, fees, fines, and taxation simply to support a bloated government bureaucracy benefits no one — and so now we are going to regulate the government regulators.

But let me be clear: certain regulations are needed, necessary — *and beneficial*. But things have gone too far in favor of governmental agencies that are unreasonable and unaccountable, and it is time to restore balance and some basic common sense to the system.

Under this administration, there will be no sacred cows.

I am also willing to take on any entity that seeks unfair advantage or exploits its authority, be it foreign nations and matters of trade, or unions that reign with regal impunity.

But our revolution is not just about reduction; it is also about expansion, especially with regard to those rights and freedoms granted to us by God and the Founding Fathers.

I believe in freedom of speech, and that this freedom includes prayer. Americans have constitutional rights that extend to all, including school children. Therefore, I will work to see that this right is respected and upheld, by means of a constitutional amendment guaranteeing the right to school prayer.

Organized prayer in public schools is supported by the vast majority of Americans. It is a traditional value in this country, and the world over. School prayer was just a part of normal life for millions of Americans until the Supreme Court took it away in 1962.

As Patrick Henry, one of our Founding Fathers so wisely noted, "It is when people forget God that tyrants forge their chains."

School prayer is not the imposition of any religion, but rather a part of our heritage and what defines us as Americans, *and it will return during this administration.*

As a nation so blessed by God, we must not deny the most basic of blessings—that of life itself—to the innocent unborn.

The American people want an end to the barbaric practice of abortion, and this administration will actively pursue a pro-life agenda, including an all-out constitutional ban.

With our great nation's blessings come great responsibilities; domestic and foreign.

After years of progress towards peace, we now find ourselves confronted by unparalleled Soviet aggression.

The evil empire is back, led by an illegal government that seized power in a military coup. Gone—and still missing without an explanation is Secretary Gorbachev—replaced by the military commander who led the brutal Soviet invasion and occupation of Afghanistan.

Under Mr Sokolov's direction, the Soviets have pursued the global expansion of their empire, most notably in Europe where they have exploited fear and distrust in an attempt to erode sovereign boundaries and alliances. Using lies and coercion, the Soviets have slithered over the top of the Iron Curtain, and into neighboring nations, held back only by the presence of NATO, which is doing exactly what it was intended to do; stop the advance of Soviet totalitarianism.

Russia is a large and powerful nation, and its conquest of Europe at the end of the Second World War was only halted by the presence of American and allied troops. The nations of Eastern Europe that they occupied at the end of the war all remain under their control to this day.

And this is why the Kremlin is so adamant about having us leave: without an American presence, there would be no military capable of repulsing a Soviet invasion, and the free nations of Western Europe—like those to the east—would be lost forever.

In fact, the Soviets themselves openly acknowledge and embrace a policy known as the Brezhnev Doctrine, which to paraphrase, states that once a country has fallen into communist darkness, it can never be allowed to see the light of freedom.

This is not just policy, but reality.

In the decades since falling under Soviet domination there have been no free and open elections in Eastern Europe. In every instance, every challenge to Soviet rule has been violently crushed: in Hungary in 1956, in Czechoslovakia in 1968, and again just last year, in Wenceslas Square.

But the Soviets won't stop with Europe. They believe in a worldwide empire, covering all continents and nations. In pursuit of this goal they will use every tool at their disposal, from blackmail, bribery, threats, terrorism, and assassination, to direct occupation by military force.

And yes, that dream of a Soviet world empire includes the United States.

But you know what? That is not going to happen. I was not elected to this office to preside over the surrender of the free world, and so I hope they are listening, when I state, in the most direct way possible: *your days are numbered*.

Every lesson of history shows us the risk, and result, of appeasement. If forced to make a choice between surrendering or fighting, we will fight. We will not retreat; we will not sacrifice our friends and allies, and then hope that the Soviets won't come for us next; because they will.

Alexander Hamilton said, "A nation which can prefer disgrace to danger is prepared for a master, and deserves one."

We are a free people, and we will remain free. We have been blessed by God with greatness, and great responsibility.

We are the Americans, and we will rise to meet any challenge, any threat, and with it, our destiny.

I've said it before and I'll say it again—America's best days are yet to come. Our proudest moments are yet to be. Our most glorious achievements are just ahead.

God bless you and America. Thank you.

41

The Budget

The period between Ronald Reagan being sworn into office and the due date to provide a budget proposal to Congress was less than two weeks.

Because the budget must be submitted by the first Monday in February, the deadline came as no surprise, and work on it had been going on for months.

The core objectives had long been in place, and had been a centerpiece of the campaign. If elected, and supported by a united Congress, the White House wanted to cut taxes and trim, or at least freeze, most spending—save for defense—which would see a significant increase.

Still, based on constantly changing variables covering everything from the US economy to moves by the Soviets, exact details continued to be fine-tuned until the last possible moment.

It was an imperfect process that brought together many different agencies and individuals from within the government, who often came with competing interests. Before being passed on to Congress, the nuts and bolts of the proposal would need to be worked out by the Office of Management and Budget (OMB), now headed by Richard Darman.

Although the Harvard-educated North Carolinian had served him admirably in the past, the President had some lingering concerns about Darman's personal commitment to fiscal conservatism, especially with regard to matters of taxation versus the deficit.

Reagan saw tax reduction as the key to stimulating growth, even if it meant temporarily adding to the deficit. In contrast, Darman feared a growing deficit would lead to higher interest rates and inflation—which would hinder growth. While both were in agreement about the end objective of growing the economy, each held a different view as to how to best achieve this.

Fine.

Darman was entitled to his opinion, but it was the President, not the Budget Director who set policy. Darman, given his orders, would once again fall in line, applying his talents as directed.

During Reagan's first term, Darman had been central to the success of the initial package of tax and spending cuts. During the second term, he once again focused on overhauls to the tax system.

In addition, Darman's work on rescuing Social Security (in 1983) had earned him the trust of congressional Democrats as a person they could work with. A short stint in the Carter administration added to his credibility as a pragmatist and someone open to hearing both sides of an issue. Although now a minority in Congress, the ability to get Democratic support for the budget would certainly streamline matters—which is what the President wanted. And Darman was, if nothing else, a smart and savvy dealmaker.

Because Reagan had campaigned on economic issues, it was generally assumed that things would be much easier this time around. With the GOP sweep in November, the voters had sent a clear message: it was time to fully embrace Reaganomics.

For the remaining Democrats in Congress, supporting the budget would be a matter of political survival, as most were already at risk of being voted out at the midterm elections because of party affiliation. Fighting the President's budget would be political suicide.

Based upon the twin pillars of frugality and shrinking the size (and thereby the reach) of government, Reagan's budget would cut or cap spending in most areas, directing the federal government to focus on those responsibilities that were specifically its bailiwick, such as national defense.

Despite Reagan's fiscally conservative intentions, the consequence of the showdown with the Soviets would require a huge jump in the defense spending, pushing the total budget upwards to nearly $2 trillion dollars. This would make it the largest budget in US history, and would, at least for the immediate future, cause the deficit to skyrocket.

Darman was mortified.

Personally, Reagan also abhorred deficits, and when appropriate, said he would support a constitutional amendment requiring a balanced budget—like the kind he adhered to for two terms as governor. But for now this simply wasn't practical. This was wartime, and his responsibility as Commander-in-Chief was to keep the nation safe at any cost.

Although the OMB had been tasked with working out the specifics, the grand vision had come directly from Reagan himself, reflecting not just matters of ideology, but an approach supported by many leading economists as sound fiscal policy.

Reagan understood economics in a way that no other president before him had. During his first two terms, attempts to implement Reaganomics had been continuously hampered by Congress; unwilling to challenge the status quo of tax and spend.

And yet, even small applications of Dr Reagan's Economic Cure-All had delivered results, pulling the country out of recession while simultaneously pushing down interest rates and inflation. But now, with Democratic opposition marginalized, the country would begin receiving larger dosages—and those on the left were terrified.

What if Reaganomics actually worked? What if the President had been right all along?

Not surprisingly, but oftentimes overlooked or omitted, was the fact Ronald Reagan had a degree in Economics. This was not an honorary degree presented in exchange for making a speech to the alumni, but something the President had earned the old fashioned way: by attending and passing classes. This achievement was all the more exceptional, given that it came at a time—during the Great Depression—when barely seven percent of his generation even attended college.

Graduating with a degree in Economics today is difficult; in those days, extraordinary.

This was a bitter pill for Reagan's critics to swallow. In a field like politics that was dominated by lawyers, Reagan was one of the few economists, and he knew what he was talking about.

Before Reagan, the prevailing approach to managing the economy (under both Democratic and Republican administrations) was based on theories developed in the 1930s during the Great Depression by John Maynard Keynes. In a break with these outdated ideas, Reagan took his inspiration from a more contemporary school of thought that developed in the 1970s, commonly referred to as supply-side economics.

This approach was backed by many leading economists such as Arthur Laffer, Robert Mundell, and Jude Wanniski, along with a growing number of conservative politicians, including former Congressman, and now HUD Secretary Jack Kemp. Despite its innovative approach, the roots of supply-side theory went as far back as Adam Smith, and even included Alexander Hamilton, America's first Treasury Secretary.

But as president, Reagan could only propose a budget; the final authority over spending was the domain of Congress. Without even a line-item veto, Reagan had often been forced to sign off on a budget he disagreed with—or risk a government shutdown and all the repercussions that come with it.

Year after year the budgets were a compromise: Just enough to suppress the symptoms, but not enough to cure the disease.

Because members of Congress serve a specific geographic region, re-elections often hinge on "bringing home the bacon" for their constituents—which was then paid for out of the national budget. Too many in Congress had a pet program that was of little or no benefit to the nation as a whole—which put them at odds with the President, who was entrusted with putting the nation's interests first.

When spending exceeded revenue, Congress borrowed money to cover it, adding to the deficit. Not only would this money have to be paid back, but the actual amount due was snowballing as a result of compounding interest.

Additionally, Congress had an undeniable problem with efficiency and accountability. Over the years, spending to prop up programs based on failed social experiments of the 1960s had exploded, without producing any measurable benefits, much less addressing the root causes for the problems.

As Reagan was quick to point out, "The liberals had their turn at bat, and they struck out."

In contrast, the President believed that a strong and growing economy was the key to addressing most of society's challenges. It also promised quicker results and would grow the economy in accordance with real world conditions, not skewed by the theories and biases of a distant government bureaucracy.

Leaving more money in the pockets of everyday Americans also increased their sense of freedom and prosperity, which the President believed would raise the national mood; critical during wartime. While the percentage of per dollar share taken in by taxes would be smaller, the actual *number* of persons paying in would grow.

In many ways, this supply-side strategy echoed the time-tested practice employed by successful businesses that cut prices to increase sales. Although lower prices mean smaller margins per unit, the number of units sold increases exponentially, raising overall profits.

As the President framed it, "It was better to earn $5 in nickels from a hundred people, than $1 from ten who each paid a dime."

Though members of the President's economic team such as Darman and Commerce Secretary Simon presented the argument in more formal terms, it was once again Reagan's ability to take a complex subject and present it as a simple metaphor that earned him the title of the Great Communicator.

Not given as much public emphasis was the President's plan to increase the deficit. While much of the defense spending was directed towards conventional expenditures such as adding troops, a sizable portion would also go towards the highly controversial Strategic Defense Initiative—derided as "Star Wars" by its critics.

Reagan, however, had faith in the program, and had seen many promising results, which for reasons of national security, could not be shared with the public.

In the President's opinion, the program's lack of success to date was related to insufficient funding.

"We planted seeds, but didn't provide enough water. So not much grew from it, and that which did seemed small and bent—and not much like the picture on the packet.

"So if that's all you see, then yes, I suppose it looks like a failure. But for the people who understand the science, well, they see the potential of this, and that's why, even under Gorbachev, the Soviets wanted us to kill it off," Reagan said.

"They want it gone, because it would remove their power to hold the world hostage to their threats of nuclear war. SDI puts the sword of Damocles back in the sheath."

The President knew that no budget would please everyone; it was simply a roadmap. Those on the left would complain about the cuts, those on the right about the deficit.

Reagan understood that in politics, and in life, compromises were usually necessary. But again, his perspective was that of the long-view, not swayed by those on the fringes unbound by the hard realities of governing a nation, much less a nation at war and in an economic slump.

No matter what approach he took he would be criticized, so Reagan just did what he knew to be best, and pushed ahead of his critics on all sides of every issue, because this is what leaders do.

It can be lonely at the top, but as Reagan liked to point out, it's also the only place where one can truly see the Big Picture.

* 42 *

Nuclear Fallout

President Reagan's inaugural address was celebrated by America's revitalized conservative majority. With the man they elected by the largest majority in history came the voice of a nation: optimistic, courageous, and committed to a vision that crossed generations, demographics, regions, and even party affiliations.

It was the voice of a united America.

During the campaign, Reagan ran on a simple platform, and asked that voters only elect those congressional candidates—be they Republican or Democrat—that would support the reforms needed to move the country forward.

Feeling the winds of change, a number of Democrats broke with their party and got behind the President's platform. Not surprisingly, many were denounced as traitors, and did not receive funding from the party or special interest donors and lobbyists.

But eventually, things worked out as Reagan intended; the Congress became more unified, and more functional.

Critical to this transformation was the role played by Rush Limbaugh.

While it was public knowledge that he was slated to become Reagan's new Press Secretary, during the campaign Limbaugh continued on with his nationally-broadcast radio show, which kept voters informed as to where candidates stood on the issues, and which could be counted on to stand with the President.

For many, the conversion was genuine, and they welcomed the opportunity to appear on Limbaugh's show to display contrition for past sins, and to celebrate having at last seen the light. Others, like a two-term liberal Democratic Congressman from Alabama running for re-election seemed suspect—and was quickly smoked out by Limbaugh as a charlatan trying to salvage his political career.

Thanks to Limbaugh, the imposter was outted, then routed, by his Republican challenger.

Not surprisingly, there was little or no effort by the mainstream liberal media to educate voters on where the candidates stood in terms of supporting the Reagan Revolution. So instead, much of the burden fell upon Limbaugh, which was not an easy task in the days when media was much more fragmented and dependent upon expensive and slow-moving pre-internet methods of communication.

Limbaugh did what he could, affirming the potential the President had seen in him. Monday through Friday, he delivered the news and information listeners could not get elsewhere; whether it concerned details of the President's policy proposals, or which candidates could be counted on to support America's conservative revolution.

In areas where his broadcasts were unavailable, Limbaugh encouraged listeners to write the local newspapers to inform readers of where the candidates stood, and who had received Reagan's endorsement. When liberal editors refused to publish such letters, conservatives took to marching with signs, canvassing door-to-door, setting up phone trees, and employing the techniques of a grassroots movement.

Limbaugh's efforts were assisted by a number of other prominent conservatives, including such established voices as William F Buckley, Jr, Grover Norquist, the Reverend Jerry Falwell, and even the recently retired Senator (and Reagan mentor), Barry Goldwater, all of whom contributed their own money, time, and connections to facilitate the revolution.

For conservatives, there was a true sense of urgency. They knew the elections of 1988 would be do-or-die for the Reagan Revolution, and that without congressional support, the movement would again be stalled.

And so the people responded; turning out in record numbers, and delivering majorities both in terms of the popular vote, and with the Electoral College.

Although he had the majority he needed, support in Congress was not at 100%. A few left-leaning Democrats had been elected by traditionally liberal districts, and others would continue on, simply because their seats were not among those in contest during this particular election cycle.

No one knew how many of the remaining traditional Democrats would be willing to work with the majority, or how many would seek to delay progress and express contempt for the will of the voters. Many were just simply too beholden to special interests and the failed policies of the past to change; and so it would be up to voters to peacefully retire them at the next election. In the meantime, the President would continue to reach out, make overtures, compromise where appropriate, and lead with grace, reflective of his mandate.

In any nation as large and diverse as the United States, there will inevitably be dissent and opposition. While some had philosophical differences with his policies, others simply hated the man himself.

The topic that generated the most attention for those on the left concerned Reagan's comments on defense, which they read as suggesting that he was prepared to use nuclear weapons—possibly as a first strike—in what seemed to be an inevitable war looming with the Soviet Union.

The issue of a nuclear war had been the central theme in their political campaign against Reagan, who had refused to rule out the possibility of using such weapons. Even the *New Yorker* magazine weighed in with an election week cover depicting Reagan as a shriveled-up poker-playing cowboy in an Old West saloon, his hand on his unbuttoned holster. But instead of a pistol, the old cowboy's holster held a nuclear missile.

Opponents believed that once unleashed there would be no stopping an all-out nuclear war, and with it, the end to all life on Earth. Reagan was vilified as a deeply religious old man who had lived a full life, and due to his faith, had no fear of dying.

Granted, there was some truth in this. However, for those who knew the President, they understood that being at peace with one's self and inevitable mortality did not mean that he would ever consider imposing something similar on others. In other words, not fearing death does not, in and of itself, make one suicidal or cavalier about causing harm to others.

The President simply had too much respect for all life to behave in a capricious or self-serving manner.

Reagan was a man of peace, but also a leader who understood that peace is achieved in different ways. However, peace is never won through weakness and a lack of resolve.

Reagan was the voice of the free world. If his words were enough to cause the Soviets to rethink their plans, well, all the better for everyone. At the very least, a line had been drawn.

If pressed, the President refused to clarify his remarks on the use of nuclear weapons, stating calmly that "any and all options" would remain open. Nonetheless, the media continued to hound him on the topic, asserting that he "owed" the American people a definitive answer as to where, when, and how—and also because the topic drove up ratings and sold newspapers.

In lieu of an official State of the Union address, the President opted for a press conference, which was scheduled for Wednesday, February 1. Almost immediately, the issue of when he would use nukes came up.

Reagan tried to dodge the issue. At first he attempted humor, "Oh come on, they have TVs in Russia … You don't expect me to just give away the game plan, do you?"

Unfortunately, the attempt to deflect questioning on a confidential state secret was met with jeers. Recognizing a hot button topic, the same line of questioning was picked up again, and despite Limbaugh's attempt to return order and civility, the conference descended into something that looked like feeding time at the zoo's monkey house.

The President began to lose patience. Standing in front of bright lights and bombarded with shouting from all directions, Reagan was taken aback when a reporter he did not recognize broke ranks and shouted in his face, "How far are you willing to go with this *Mister* Reagan?"

The President looked the reporter directly in the eye, and fired off a one-sentence reply before abruptly ending the conference.

"Just you wait and see."

Reagan's response became a lightning rod for protesters, with demonstrations and riots breaking out in a number of cities almost immediately. Several college campuses were shut down, and a Buddhist monk set fire to himself in front of the White House while being filmed by crews from all three major TV networks—who did nothing to help.

In the House, a move to impeach the President was bandied about, but such seemed unlikely to gain traction, given the small number of supporters.

In the Senate, however, it was a different matter …

⋆ 43 ⋆

The Groundhog's Shadow

February 1989 was off to a rocky start.

The President's comments about standing up to the Soviets, and the implication that he would not rule out the use of nuclear weapons had sparked another wave of worldwide protests, threatening many of the governments still publicly aligned with the US.

Everything from the exact meaning of Reagan's remarks to his state of mind was a matter for discussion — and exploitation — by Soviet propagandists, who twisted each and every word to sow the seeds of fear and dissent.

In Europe, the war of words was especially pronounced in the United Kingdom, given the shared language and a conservative government headed by Reagan's close friend, and ally, Margaret Thatcher.

Unlike Reagan, who was attempting to restore calm and quell anxiety, Thatcher took a more incendiary stance. Where Reagan had courted ambiguity, Thatcher defiantly stated that she would not hesitate from using Britain's nuclear arsenal to strike first.

Thatcher's remark was the spark that set Britain on fire. Within hours, protestors took to the streets demanding her immediate resignation. Within days, the UK was engulfed by civil disobedience and rioting, forcing the Iron Lady to bring out the troops to impose a state of order that was at best tenuous.

Events reached a tipping point when British activists (likely with Soviet support) succeeded in breaching security at Her Majesty's Naval Base Clyde on Friday, January 27.

Located roughly 25 miles from Glasgow, Scotland, the base at Faslane was known to be the home of Britain's nuclear deterrent, and had been a frequent site of protests in the past.

While previous demonstrations had run the gamut from silent vigil to angry shouting mobs, none had seriously attempted, much less succeeded, in forcing their way into sensitive and restricted areas.

But this time things were different, in terms of ferocity, tactics, and sheer numbers. Ministry of Defense forces entrusted with protecting the base and its treasures (including a fleet of nuclear submarines armed with Trident missiles), were quickly overwhelmed and forced to retreat.

Rather than lose complete control, Thatcher issued a shoot-to-kill order. British forces retook the base, resulting in the deaths of 316 persons.

Official demands that the Iron Lady step down were met with contempt, putting the US in a very awkward position. So once again, Thatcher personally took control of the situation; dissolving Parliament and instituting martial law.

Anarchy in the UK was, for the most part, brought under control, although Britain now looked more like the war zone of Northern Ireland than the jolly old land of bowler hats, double decker buses, and Mary Poppins.

As much as it pained him personally, the President was forced to authorize a number of contingency plans should the situation in the UK deteriorate any further. These included the evacuation of American civilians, and securing US bases, embassies, and other related facilities. Also approved was a top-secret plan for a US-led occupational government—should the situation collapse into civil war, and where no legitimate British authority was able to maintain order and adequately secure the nation's considerable military resources.

Reagan called Thatcher to lend his personal support, but the strain in their conversation was obvious. He did not bother to mention that Princess Diana, who was currently in the United States on behalf of her charitable work, was also involved in discussions with his administration to develop plans for establishing a foreign base for the Royal Family should Britain collapse or fall into Soviet hands.

Protests in the United States were usually more subdued, although some did descend into all-out riots, complete with murder, arson, and looting. Local police quickly put down most, but in a few cities (such as Baltimore and Seattle) National Guard troops had to be deployed.

The President did his best to restore calm, while the KGB actively stirred the pot. Although most US media outlets officially resisted running their paid advertising, Moscow's propaganda still managed to get through, disguised as editorials and other ploys.

In Europe, the Soviets fanned dissent and continued with their strategy of separating citizens from their governments (and thus NATO). An outdoor nuclear-freeze concert drew 150,000 chilly protestors in Antwerp, while an event to peacefully link the two Germanys failed miserably.

Billed as "Joining Hands For Peace," the stunt began by having two German children, one on each side of the border, join hands. Each child was then connected to another set of hands, with the goal being to create a human chain that would link the populations across Eastern and Western Europe.

Regrettably, the event had to be cancelled due to an outbreak of the flu that seems to have originated in the east.

44

Prayers, Prime Ministers,
& Presidents

Despite the demanding state of world affairs, Reagan was also committed to various other public, non-governmental duties — most of which he was happy to perform.

One of these was the National Prayer Breakfast, always held on the first Thursday in February, and something the President had faithfully attended every year that he had been in office.

This year the event would be held at the International Crystal Ballroom, located in the Washington Hilton, but Reagan had been advised to cancel due to credible threats and difficulty securing the venue. Ironically, this was the same location where John Hinckley Jr had nearly assassinated Reagan just months into his first term.

Reagan laughed off the coincidence; noting that lighting never strikes twice in the same location. In his heart, he felt a deeper sense of calm, believing that his survival that day had been the result of Divine Intervention. Reagan believed that God had spared him because He still had plans for him, and therefore would protect him so long as the President continued to serve the Lord.

Buoyed by his faith and sense of purpose, Reagan no longer feared the unknown. He was adamant about attending — and in the end he prevailed.

This year was especially important, as the President wanted to talk about his proposal for a constitutional amendment in support of school prayer, which had been a cornerstone of his campaign. It was a subject very close to Reagan's heart, but also one that generated controversy even within the religious community due to concerns about the separation of church and state.

Reagan understood this, noting that prayer would be voluntary, and not favoring any particular religion. While deeply Christian himself, the President respected all faiths, as well as the basic freedom that allowed people to pray only if such was their choice. The President regarded prayer as a form of free speech, subject to protection under the Constitution.

"George Washington believed that religion, morality, and brotherhood were the pillars of society. He said you couldn't have morality without religion. And yet today we're told that to protect the First Amendment, we must expel God, the source of all knowledge, from our children's classrooms.

"Well, pardon me, but the First Amendment was not written to protect the American people from religion; the First Amendment was written to protect the American people from government tyranny.

"In 1962 the Supreme Court in the New York prayer case banned the compulsory saying of prayers. In 1963 the Court banned the reading of the Bible in our public schools. From that point on, the courts pushed the meaning of the ruling ever outward, so that now our children are not even allowed voluntary prayer—which restricts their rights of free speech.

"The time has come for Congress to give a majority of American families what they want for their children—a Constitutional Amendment making it unequivocally clear that children can hold voluntary prayer in their schools."

The President argued his case passionately, and the audience was very supportive, frequently breaking into applause. Often taken for granted or ignored by previous administrations, the faith-based community knew it had a genuine ally in Ronald Reagan.

Reagan's stance on matters of faith had been consistent, and with his re-election, overwhelmingly validated by voters supportive of a return to traditional American values.

While the event went off with few hitches, the Secret Service did find a loaded pistol hidden in the kitchen, but was unable to determine ownership, other than discovering that it had been reported stolen from a security guard two weeks earlier.

Reagan, the oldest president in US history had turned 78 just the day before, on Monday, February 6. The Reagans had observed the event with a small ceremony held the weekend previous, but the President was not in a very celebratory mood given the ongoing crisis and instability in Great Britain.

Prime Minister Margaret Thatcher, once his closest ally, had now become his biggest headache due to her inflammatory comments and heavy-handed approach to dealing with domestic unrest. According to the CIA, Thatcher was in imminent danger of being toppled from power, but seemingly oblivious to the threat.

Meanwhile, one of Britain's former colonies was already bubbling under, thanks to a February 10 election victory by Jamaica's socialists. The election marked the return of Prime Minister Michael Manley, who had previously led the country for most of the 1970s, a period during which he spurned the UK in favor of closer ties to the USSR.

Manley, a well-to-do member of the island nation's elite white minority was first elected to public office in 1969—following in the footsteps of his father, who had been Prime Minister just 14 years earlier.

Within three years of entering politics, Manley the son was elected Prime Minister and soon set about implementing new controls on the population. Under the guise of addressing societal violence, he spearheaded a number of policies such as the Suppression of Crime Act, which gave the police and military (under his control) greater authority to seal off and disarm communities he regarded as threatening.

With no constitutional provision that guaranteed the right of the people keep and bear arms, the citizens of Jamaica were powerless against the government's seizures. Manley succeeded in disarming the population, ensuring that any future uprising would be one that pitted the people's rocks and sticks against the government grenades and guns.

Voted out of office in 1980, Manley's return nearly a decade later seemed suspicious—especially given the lopsided margin not reflected by any of the independent polls that suggested something contrary to a landslide win for the socialists.

Located to the south of Cuba, Jamaica had been a growing concern for the United States for some time, viewed as part of a larger Soviet strategy to expand its presence deeper into the Caribbean. Although secondary to their efforts in Europe, the Soviets were anxious to add territory wherever, and whenever, possible. Adding to a rising red tide in the Caribbean would also demand attention from the United States, already distracted by Marxist activity in Nicaragua, El Salvador, Honduras, and most notably, Cuba.

Manley, leader of the People's National Party, was a close friend of

Cuba's Fidel Castro, and although he had toned down some of his fiery political rhetoric, intelligence sources indicated a pronounced drift towards a deeper, and more formal alignment with Moscow.

As Defense Secretary Colin Powell—whose parents had emigrated from Jamaica—was quick to point out, Prime Minister Manley, now on his fifth wife, was quick to change beds when it suited him.

Although it had been scheduled long in advance, news that the US had conducted a nuclear test in Nevada on that same Friday as the Jamaican elections did not help to put the world at ease. Instead, it was spun as Reagan readying his arsenal in preparation for Armageddon.

Every day added new weight to the President's shoulders. But fortunately, he had his family, his faith, and the ability to find strength in many sources, especially in history, and in the trials faced by those who held office before him during periods of great uncertainty and challenge.

One of those figures was Abraham Lincoln, America's 16th president, a man who had presided over two incredible and defining moments in America's history: the emancipation of the slaves (and thus the beginning of Civil Rights and the nation's strive for equality), and also its darkest moment: when it was split by a civil war that challenged the very notion of a nation composed of "united" states.

This year, Lincoln's birthday, February 12, would fall on a Sunday. It was not an official US holiday, but it was a day that held deep personnel meaning for Reagan—especially now.

Being a Sunday, the President's day wasn't as tightly scheduled, allowing him some personal time to reflect on Lincoln and his legacy. Like Reagan, Lincoln had been a revolutionary figure who had given life and form to the Grand Old Party, the torch of leadership which now rested in the hands of Ronald Wilson Reagan, America's 40th president.

But Reagan's hands also had access to the "button," and with it, a power that Lincoln could never have imagined.

Weak men pray for power, believing that they can manage their temptations, while morally strong men pray to be better servants. And so, on that Sunday, President Reagan lowered his head in prayer and asked God for strength and guidance.

He would need it, as very soon Reagan would be forced to confront a threat hauntingly reminiscent to that which had nearly ended Lincoln's presidency.

45

With Friends Like These

It was Valentine's Day—and also the one-year anniversary of the Soviet coup.

Last year, the collision of these two events had taken place on a Sunday, but in 1989, February 14th fell on a Tuesday, so it was just another regular "day at the office" for the President and his team.

Since returning for a third term, Reagan had been working hard to capitalize on his mandate, and to make good on his promises to the American people.

Two areas topped his agenda. The first naturally concerned matters of defense. While some initiatives were public, many others could not be disclosed, given the state of world affairs and the imminent threat of a hot war with the Soviets, or a military conflict with one of their surrogates such as Libya, Cuba, or North Korea.

Secondly, the President was also keen on advancing new economic initiatives to help the economy, including a major proposal to simplify and add fairness to the tax system.

Financial insecurity stemming from the actions of the USSR was an ongoing problem, especially for the nations of Western Europe. (This situation was, of course, exploited by Soviet propagandists who continued to tout the prosperity and stability that would follow with the formation of the European Union.)

Moscow promised that by merging east and west, labor and capital "would be free to flow across borders ... creating prosperity, enabled by cooperation, driven by competition." Resources currently dedicated to defending against a non-existent enemy could then be applied towards other, non-military purposes, described as the "Peace Dividend."

A united, peaceful Europe would be the envy of the world.

Neil "Moon" Reagan, the President's older brother and a former advertising man, found Moscow's pitch especially amusing. "For a bunch of communists, they certainly know a thing or two about branding and marketing," he noted. "Makes you wonder what they might have done if they had the Ford Pinto account!"

Despite this bit of levity at Soviet marketing savvy, no one contested the seductiveness of a pitch that promised hope to desperate and frightened people. Governments were frequently turned out of office by challengers with big promises, which, if successful, would allow for Soviet expansion free of military conflict with the Americans.

As a result of the nature of interlinked world markets, the economic situation in the United States was not much better than what Europe was experiencing. Unemployment and interest rates were up, gas and home heating oil prices were through the roof. Home sales, construction, stocks, and manufacturing were all down, and there were shortages of many basic goods.

The administration regarded economics and defense as directly linked, but despite the urgency to act on financial matters, Reagan's day was often sidetracked by "putting out fires"; addressing one situation after another that ran the gamut from annoying distraction to that of a full-blown, drop-everything-emergency.

This day was no different.

Last Friday's loss of Jamaica did not bode well for containing the Soviet expansion in the Caribbean, and US intelligence sources had already tracked the arrival of a team of Russian advisors that had covertly landed in Kingston over the weekend.

But a matter of greater concern centered on news coming out of El Salvador, one of America's leading allies in the war against the advance of communism in Central America.

El Salvador had a long and turbulent past. Since the 1970s, the government had been embroiled in a civil war against the leftist Farabundo Marti Liberation Front (FMLN), which in 1980 had merged with the Salvadoran Communist Party. By combining resources, rebel forces soon became a serious threat to toppling the democratically-elected government.

Under the Carter administration, the US stood idly by and watched as communism spread unchecked throughout the region, with well-organized guerilla armies slipping across borders, challenging elected governments, and terrorizing civilian populations.

It was only a matter of time until El Salvador fell.

Soon after taking office in 1981, the Reagan administration issued a

White Paper detailing connections between the Salvadoran rebels and neighboring Marxist states, citing evidence that Cuba and Nicaragua were both providing arms and training to the guerillas.

In response, the US began actively supporting the Salvadoran government. Defeating the rebels proved difficult, and the Salvadorans, in desperation, adopted evermore brutal and heavy-handed tactics, which strained relations with Washington and further undermined bipartisan support.

Democrats in Congress pushed to curtail US aid, and by 1986 President Jose Napoléon Duarte was forced to seek a negotiated settlement with the FMLN. It was a messy situation, and no one was happy.

War tends to bring out the worst in people. While the crimes of the Marxist rebels were well documented, Congress demanded that Salvadoran government forces adhere to a different standard no matter how dire the situation became.

There would be no fighting fire with fire or taking an eye for an eye. Government forces needed to play by the rules if they were to continue receiving assistance from the Americans.

At the time, the White House had few available options.

Reagan did not have the right to depose the current elected government if it did not comply with guidelines — even if eliminating support ensured the imposition of another permanent Marxist state in Latin America.

Making matters worse was the fact that President Duarte, in power since 1984, was now gravely ill with cancer, leading many to fear that his imminent passing would result in a military coup. Still, the Salvadorans had a plan in place for the transition of power to another civilian government, and with it, a pledge to do a better job of curtailing both military excesses and right-wing junta violence.

Even in the new Republican Congress, additional aid would likely be tied to curtailing violence against civilians. Without US assistance, the Salvadoran government would most likely soon fall, so it made sense that protocols of conduct be observed.

Or at least, that was the hope.

The President was visibly angered to learn about an event that had taken place just the day before, when Salvadoran army troops had attacked a hospital, where they raped and murdered patients.

Reagan stared out into space for a moment, considering how the US should respond.

Scowling, he looked down at his watch, noting the day had just begun. "Okay, what's next?" he asked.

NSA Director Bud McFarlane leaned in close to Reagan and said something just barely audible, but the expression on the President's face was now one of complete shock.

Reagan stood up and addressed the group in attendance, asking that only McFarlane and CIA Director Webster remain behind.

"What do you mean, a coup?" asked the President.

46

The Coup

"What do you mean, a *coup?*" repeated the President.

McFarlane paused for a moment, his expression gravely serious.

"As you know, ours is a divided country. More united than it has been in years, but still there are deep divisions, exacerbated by the election.

"On the left, there's a fringe that has become much more … *agitated* since the election. They are keyed-up by the standoff with the Soviets, and are certain that a full-scale all-out war is coming. They believe that you intend to use nuclear weapons in the very near future, and that you won't hesitate to strike first, even if that leads to Mutually Assured Destruction.

"For some, this has induced a state of near panic. They worry that if you are not removed from office—by whatever means is necessary— that you will soon end all life on Earth."

The President's expression tightened as he slowly shook his head in disagreement. He exhaled hard in exasperation.

McFarlane continued.

"Publicly, we saw some movement in the House of Representatives to initiate impeachment proceedings, but that was mostly for show … a few old windbags who had 'taken down Nixon' looking to do one more lap before they get voted out at the midterms … Plus a few firebrands from safe Democratic districts playing to their base. But again, this is just Kabuki Theater—it has no chance of going anywhere, and they know it.

"In the Senate, however, we have a different problem," McFarlane said.

The President looked perplexed.

"Senator Kennedy," added CIA Director Webster, "is actively leading an effort to topple this administration in what can only be described as a coup."

"That's ridiculous," Reagan exclaimed, shaking his head. "Yes, Teddy and I are on opposite sides of nearly every issue politically, but I would never question his love for this country or his respect for the protocols of government. A coup? No, never," stammered the President.

"Even before the election, the Senator was not ... *fully balanced*," continued McFarlane. "We had reports of increasingly volatile and unpredictable behavior—things that if made public, would have likely ended his political career.

"Sadly, he is surrounded by enablers. No one in the inner circle is willing to confront him, and so things have just been spinning out of control. The drinking has been especially bad—he's been on one long binge since at least mid-October.

"Not surprisingly, the drinking seems to be leading to a lot of, shall we say, 'bad choices' by the Senator. But beyond that, there seems to be something deeply wrong with him psychologically ... Some truly delusional thinking that goes beyond the booze.

"For instance, he believes that you rigged the election in order to hang on to power."

The President just shook his head at the absurdity of it all.

"Apparently, this is why he agreed to run for the presidency when Dukakis dropped out. He believed you were planning some kind of coup; anything to stay in office."

"Teddy knew he'd lose—but thought there'd be a mass rebellion when people discovered you stole the election. He thought they'd rally around him as the legitimate winner."

McFarlane looked the President straight in the eye.

"In recent weeks he's backed off on the election conspiracy allegations. He probably still believes it, but it likely wasn't getting the reaction he hoped for, so he's moved on to other things.

"What's really driving him now is the belief that you intend to start a nuclear war with the Soviet Union which will destroy the planet. Therefore, in Senator Kennedy's mind, this is now a life or death battle—*for all humanity.*

"Again, he believes you will do anything to hold on to power—so the normal processes to remove you from office are doomed to failure. This is why a *coup d'état*—which he will lead, is necessary, justified, urgent. Imperative. The world is depending on him to stop you from unleashing nuclear Armageddon."

Reagan looked distressed. "He needs medical help. Now."

"Agreed. But there's a bit more to the story, Mr President," added Webster.

Again, McFarlane picked up the thread.

"Senator Kennedy has been working his contacts steadily, often by phone, after hours once the top is off the bottle. But even when he's reasonably sober he's been trying to make his case; often in secret meetings with others throughout the government."

"Paranoid, delusional, at times obviously intoxicated—but nonetheless, he has picked up a few supporters. In the Senate, he seems to be working that old Kennedy charm, and now has a number of otherwise sane people behind him. He can be very persuasive," said McFarlane.

"Such as … who?" asked the President.

"All Democrats so far. Senators Cranston of California, Heflin of Alabama, Inouye of Hawaii, Metzenbaum of Ohio. Definitely Pell from Rhode Island … Nebraska's Exon seems to be leaning that way, but he's a bit of a player, so we're not 100% sure about him. Same for Simon of Illinois. There are a few more, but again, it's hard to gauge how many are just willing to nod along in exchange for something they need, and how many are truly ready to rush the White House carrying rifles," stated McFarlane.

McFarlane's image of a group of red-faced old senators in battle formation brought a fleeting smile to the President, who was still in a state of shock.

"Well, as the kids like to say, 'You and what army?'"

"I'm getting to that," replied McFarlane. "A sizable portion of military commanders began their careers under President Kennedy; he was their first Commander-in-Chief, and a genuine military hero in his own right. Granted, their allegiance is to the country, first and foremost, and not any one particular man, but the Kennedy name still resonates. At the very least it opens doors for the Senator.

"That aside, the soldier's allegiance to country could be exploited, if they believed you were genuinely intending to do something that threatened the nation."

"Such as launching a first-strike nuclear war," said Webster. "As we know, history is full of such examples of a military turning on a civilian government. That said, I don't think that we are anywhere near that point, nor do I think we will reach it."

"But no evidence of any foreign involvement?" asked the President.

"Extremely unlikely, but I wouldn't rule it out entirely," said

McFarlane. "In particular, a few House members seem to have some connections to the extreme left wing, and to organizations that have been infiltrated by communists. But this is something the FBI can help with … to connect the dots. Moscow's money is everywhere, and in this town, money buys influence."

It was a lot to take in, but Reagan continued standing, his hands on his hips, a look of determination on his face.

"Recommendations?" asked the President.

McFarlane and Webster exchanged glances, as McFarlane took the lead.

"First, that we take this matter extremely seriously, and put in place additional security measures and precautions.

Reagan nodded, clearly understanding the implication.

"Agreed. Next?"

"We'd like your authorization to bring in other people; specifically Defense Secretary Powell, Attorney General Bork, and FBI Director Sessions. Surgeon General Koop, so that we can get a medical perspective … a psychological profile. Obviously Vice President Meese. The NSC.

"Each member would be granted authority to assemble his own team to monitor and investigate, and each would report directly to me. All would be sworn to absolute secrecy.

"We are also asking authorization for the security agencies to do some deeper and more expansive investigations of our own, including surveillance, and related covert operations."

"On Kennedy—and the other senators?" inquired Reagan.

"Yes. On any and all that we think might be involved. We need a full and complete picture of what's happening, from top to bottom. For now, his contacts seem limited to the Senate, but we think it prudent to widen the scope to include the House as well," said McFarlane.

"We need to know what's what simply for reasons of national security before anything can happen as far as legal procedures. That's also why we need the Attorney General in on this as soon as possible.

"The country really hasn't seen anything like this since the Civil War, when a group of, yes, Democratic senators, was brought up for supporting the Confederacy."

"The charge of treason is pretty serious," added Webster, "unless of course you're a US Senator, in which case the laws you write don't really apply to you. They always see to that."

Reagan, tight-lipped, just shook his head in disgust.

"If found guilty, someone like Cranston would likely be expelled, but there wouldn't be any jail time.

"I'm just speculating, but I think the best bet might be to just hit these guys with the evidence and give them the option of resigning, so that they could walk away with their honor—and pensions—intact. As I said, I don't think most of them are seriously behind this, but if they've crossed the line and violated the oath of office they need to go down.

"Kennedy will likely be a bigger problem though, and I'm not sure how we will need to address that if he doesn't want to leave quietly. Right now he's only a danger to himself.

"He's well-known, well-loved, and already seen as a victim; some kind of valiant heroic martyr. The fact that he might not be right in the head would likely make any prospect of a real trial nearly impossible.

"Best case scenario is that we can involve those close to him to help with an intervention. Get him out of office, and into a medical treatment program. Then, once his head is screwed on again, hopefully he'll accept that the fact that he needs to get out of politics and do something else with his life."

Reagan nodded in agreement. "But the military—that's a different matter. We can't have that. I need to know that our forces are united."

"Absolutely," confirmed Webster. "There is a mechanism in place to address this, and it will be applied firmly."

"Yes ... Absolutely," echoed the President. His tone was firm, but tinged with sadness.

"The death penalty is an option for treason, but most will likely just do prison time at some place like Leavenworth—which is not exactly Club Med. I seriously doubt if support for a coup is very strong, but we cannot show any weakness. These cases will be tried in military court, and I think we can trust them to handle things appropriately," concluded Webster.

As the conversation paused the President's expression became somber.

"It's just a very sad situation, for all involved," Reagan said wistfully. "I always held out hope that somehow we, as a couple of Irishmen, might be able to put politics aside and get to know one another on a personal level, like I was able to do, at least a wee bit with Tip O'Neill.

"Tip and Teddy are, or were, friends, so maybe he can help."

"I think so," said Webster, "as O'Neill was one of the people who first alerted us about Kennedy."

"What about the other Senator? Kerry?" Reagan inquired.

"Pretty much useless. Obviously the same for Dukakis," McFarlane answered. "But we'll review all options."

McFarlane paused, then looked the president directly in the eye, before concluding with a warning.

"If our actions are discovered … *leaked* … there will likely be huge consequences. We are, after all, proposing that the executive branch authorize spying on elected members of Congress … specifically on members of the opposition party. That, in and of itself, would have major political repercussions.

"If word gets out — and even if the charges turn out to be nothing — rumors about the possibility of a coup attempt involving the military will rattle not just Americans, but the world — and you can imagine how the Soviet propagandists will run with that."

Reagan nodded, fully understanding the consequences.

"Based on what I've heard, I don't think we have any other options. I assume full responsibility. We don't have any time to waste. Gentlemen, I authorize you to begin … and thank you."

The rest of the President's day was spent trying to work on a range of issues — including El Salvador, and yet the news of a domestic coup, and Senator Kennedy's illness, had visibly affected him. Although engaged and able to make important decisions, those closest to him noted an undercurrent of melancholy.

It was a trying day, but the President had no choice but to internalize his pain. He worked a full day before returning to his quarters at the White House, and then on to a special Valentine's Day dinner with Mrs Reagan.

This had been one of the most trying days of his presidency, but some-how Reagan, with support from his wife, was able to tap into that deep and legendary reserve of personal strength.

Ronald Reagan was an optimist at heart, and a man who genuinely believed that good would always triumph over bad.

And so it would be — but not without a few sharp bumps.

47

Downfall

The team assigned to investigating the Kennedy-led coup quickly went to work and did a thorough job.

As suspected, Reagan's presidency had never been genuinely threatened. Still, there had been actions taken that would bring significant consequences. Conspiring against the President of the United States is serious business; this was not some trivial matter that could just be brushed under the rug and forgotten.

Like rats on a sinking ship, the conspirators quickly turned on one another. Some hoped for leniency, others testified simply out of spite.

Although no one had taken seriously Kennedy's assertion that Reagan had rigged the election, most believed that the President was indeed an imminent danger to the world, and therefore any method of removing him from office (short of assassination) was justified.

In the words of Senator Cranston, "A suicidal psychopath like Ronald Reagan should not have his finger on the button."

In accordance with McFarlane's initial hunch, there was no real support by members of the US military for a coup. Most officers had immediately reported Senator Kennedy's overtures, which in some instances, were not overtly specific, but more akin to a priest asking an altar boy if he ever thought about kissing other boys. In other words, an awkward conversation, endured out of politeness and the insecurity that comes from directly challenging one whose status, if not behavior, demanded at least a modicum of respect and courtesy.

Still, a few boys in uniform had drifted too far, and as such would be dealt with in accordance to military law, which was very specific about protocols and punishments.

On the civilian side, the administration of justice was much more complicated.

The investigation, largely managed by the FBI, revealed that a group of Democratic senators, led by Kennedy, was indeed involved in a conspiracy to depose President Reagan. These actions went well behind the constitutional guarantees of free speech, and were deemed by Attorney General Bork to constitute genuine acts of treason suitable for prosecution under the law.

Degrees of complicity ranged from minor to deeply troubling, but when faced by the evidence, all members of the treasonous Group of Seven opted to resign, so that "they might spend more time with family," rather than dig in and fight the charges.

While not the optimum solution, and in many ways hard to justify, the option of quick resignations spared the country what would have been a long and painful ordeal. And so it came to pass that the cadre of treasonous senators, with the exception of their leader, agreed to bow out quietly and disappear; effective March 31.

When confronted with the case against him, the senior Senator from Massachusetts laughed it off, vowing that he would not be blackmailed into resigning by a government that had no legitimate legal authority. Instead, he announced his intention to fight the accusations in the court of the US Senate.

Crazy as he was, Kennedy knew the law — and of his right to be tried by his peers in the United States Senate. He had no intention of going quietly, and instead vowed to turn the tables on Reagan, and put him on trial, while the hearings were televised live to the world.

Kennedy's response was not entirely unexpected, prompting the government to set about with a Plan B, which would involve an intervention by those close to the Senator who might either hold influence, or if needed, support his removal from office due to medical reasons.

Whatever course was to be taken, Reagan was adamant about minimizing any further embarrassment to Kennedy as a person, and to his legacy. Although he had been the direct target of Kennedy's attack, Reagan understood that these were the actions of a man who was not well, and who needed to be treated with compassion, not vengeance.

The other senators had been opportunists, and when offered a GET OUT OF JAIL card and $200 (or a pension for life), they happily took it and headed off to write their memoirs, practice law, or teach.

Despite conspiracy rumblings on the left, the departure of seven Democratic senators did not necessarily mean the automatic addition of seven new Republican replacements.

Each state has its own method of replacing a Senator. For some, it might be by special election—in which case the seat would indeed most likely be picked up by the GOP. In other states, a temporary replacement could be appointed, although it might come with the caveat that the replacement be from the same party.

For the Democrats, losing seven big names meant a major loss of face, influence, and fundraising. Not surprisingly, none of the Group of Seven decided to show up for the last day of March, which just so happened to be a Friday.

Friday is, for some, the unofficial start of the weekend, and so the party started early that day for Senator Kennedy. (Or maybe it began the night before? Details are hazy.) In any event, Teddy took the floor late in the afternoon on that last day of March and began to address the Senate—and the world.

Although his speech was slurred (which he attributed to having a bad cold), Teddy had been in a similar condition many times before and knew how to work around it. He was an experienced orator, comfortable with speaking passionately and extemporaneously on a range of topics that were important to him.

This was his first time addressing the full Senate since the election, and things seemed a bit off from the get-go, which began with the overly dramatic proclamation that "We are doomed! All of us ... doomed!"

The pained ferocity of the opening remark created quite a stir in the chambers, as those in attendance exchanged puzzled glances and began to confer amongst themselves.

Kennedy paused, arms raised upwards.

In addition to the usual mix of politicians and staff, Kennedy's every move was now being monitored by others from the government, whose job it was to babysit the Senator and make sure that things did not go too far. In this condition, Kennedy was not just a danger to himself, but to the nation, should he suddenly decide to burst out with some classified information he had been privy to as a long-standing member of the US Senate.

Lowering his arms, the Senator launched into a disjointed and angry diatribe that quickly crossed the line into ranting and delusional paranoia. It was an awkward and embarrassing spectacle, and the consensus was that it needed to be stopped.

Kennedy spotted figures in the distance moving towards him, and like the captain of a sinking ship who positions himself on the last tiny patch still above water, he climbed upon his chair and raised an angry fist at the sky.

With a defiant shake of his fist, Teddy collapsed, falling quickly to the ground where he was immediately surrounded by his peers and medical personnel.

Unconscious, the Senator was taken to the hospital and provided with the best possible emergency care. Although his condition was stabilized, he did not regain consciousness for some time.

When he awoke the next morning, it was April Fool's Day, and Teddy Kennedy's political career was now officially over.

It had been a difficult week for the President. That night, before turning in he once again turned to the Bible for solace and guidance.

It was close to midnight when he slid into bed and pulled up the covers. As he drifted off to sleep, his last conscious thoughts turned to the scripture he had been reading, and specifically to a passage from Hebrews:

"For I will be merciful to their unrighteousness, and their sins and their iniquities will I remember no more."

48

Panama Red

With the threat of a home-grown *coup d'état* now behind him, the President was able to take his eye off the rearview mirror and focus exclusively on the road ahead.

While there had been no major movements by the Soviets in Europe, they had continued to establish and enhance alliances elsewhere.

In support of this objective, it was announced that Sokolov would be making an official state visit to Cuba in early April to meet with President Fidel Castro. This would be the first meeting between the two leaders, intended to underscore the importance of a partnership that was central to the expansion of communism in the Americas.

While the United States (under Reagan) had successfully repulsed one Marxist coup in Grenada in 1983, Havana had continued to support insurgencies and foment political instability in the years since. Under Castro, the Cubans had not only meddled in the Caribbean, but throughout Latin America and even across the Atlantic to Africa.

As with other Soviet satellites, Moscow's support for Cuba had dipped under Gorbachev, then rebounded with Sokolov. Unlike Qaddafi, the Soviets regarded Castro as a reasonable and dependable partner, and in recognition of this association, had significantly boosted direct assistance, trusting him to use the influx of money, arms, and other forms of support, as he deemed best.

But now they wanted something in return.

Sokolov got right down to business: Recent events had created an opening in the region where one had not existed previously, and he was here to make a case for … *Panama*.

Although once considered a reliable US ally, relations with Panama under the leadership of General Manuel Noriega (aka "Maximum Leader of National Liberation") had soured, and become increasingly contentious. As a result, Noriega made it known to the Soviets that he was open to switching sides—and bringing the canal with him— so long as he could retain political power and maintain his personally-lucrative "business" empire.

"No problem, mi amigo," came the response from Moscow. *"Bienvenido a casa"*—or literally, "Welcome home."

Blocking access to the Panama Canal would be a stunning blow to the Americans, and the final step in a process that had begun when Jimmy Carter, after less than a year in office, handed over ownership to the Panamanians—making good on a promise initially given by Gerald Ford.

The spring of 1989 presented a rare window of opportunity. Elections were scheduled for the following month, compelling Sokolov and Castro to develop a plan in the event that Noriega lost—which now seemed rather likely. In addition, the KGB had learned that even if Noriega won, his days were likely numbered, either from a domestic coup or via an invasion by the US to shut down his nefarious cartel.

Both leaders agreed that a US invasion would be a major setback, but were in disagreement on how to address dealing with Panama, if it involved a regime headed by General Noriega—whether he won the election legitimately or not.

Castro was blunt. He had dealt with Noriega in the past and did not like him. He regarded him as a dishonest opportunist, and not someone who could be trusted.

"Noriega is *their* friend—already on the CIA payroll. Let them deal with him. All he wants is more money; he is only trying to play us in a bidding war against the Americans. He is a devil who only cares about himself."

Although he acknowledged Panama's strategic importance, Castro worried that imposition of a Marxist state—headed by a man neither true to the cause of socialist liberation nor supported by his people— was a dangerous proposition. This is not what Sokolov wanted to hear, nor was it appropriately respectful of the elder Russian. "No Comrade! We must begin our support of Panama—and General Noriega—*now*, before the election.

"I have spoken with him, and he knows that he cannot win this election … and that the Americans want someone else.

"So instead, he has agreed to declare himself a Marxist, suspend elections, and if necessary, impose martial law. He still commands the military, and they will follow him no matter what. They are loyal, and will fight to the death for him.

"As part of the Worldwide Peoples Revolution, he can then call out to his socialist brothers for help in pushing back a US invasion," Sokolov said, the old commander's eyes flashing with enthusiasm.

Castro paused to consider Sokolov's plan.

"But he is *not* a Marxist — *he is a fascist* … a criminal … a bully," said Castro, gesturing hard with his hands in exasperation.

"Si. But in Russia, we have a saying: 'My enemy's enemy is my friend.' And so we must support our … *amigo*. But yes, we should also plan on replacing him as soon as possible."

Castro flicked an ash from his cigar. "In Cuba, we also have an expression: 'With friends such as these, who needs enemies?'"

Sokolov was not amused. Plus, he knew this to actually be an old *Russian* expression.

Castro sighed and looked out at the setting sun.

Back in Moscow, the KGB was already at work writing Noriega's speeches and supplying him with talking points.

Although General Noriega would not officially declare his conversion to socialism until May 1 — May Day — he did turn up the anti-American, anti-imperialist, anti-capitalism rhetoric, much to the delight of his new benefactors.

To hold up their part of the bargain, Russian rubles began flowing into Noriega's personal bank accounts, while the Cuban advisers set about reinforcing the Panamanian Defense Forces.

While it had been assumed by the Russians that Noriega had complete control and loyalty, most of those in the military and intelligence services despised him and were plotting his downfall. They were also supplying the US with details of his growing connections with the Cubans, along with hard evidence of his illegal activities.

At last, the United States had the information it needed to justify taking action. It was clear that Noriega's move towards socialism was nothing more than a ploy to hang on to power, so that he could continue to run a global criminal empire, shielded by the protections afforded a sovereign state.

Here, supplied by his own officers, was proof of drug trafficking, money laundering, arms dealing, and a host of other serious offenses.

This was the final straw for President Reagan, who was now resolved to capture Noriega and bring him to justice — even if it required military action to confront the presence of Cuban and Soviet troops.

When actual Cuban military troops began to show up in the final days of April it came as no surprise to US intelligence. On Monday, May first, Comrade Noriega held a coming out party to announce his conversion to socialism.

Dressed in full military garb, Noriega stood at a podium, on a stage adorned with red balloons. Flanked by politely applauding Cubans, Noriega explained that he was only heeding "the will of the people."

Unfortunately, "the people" Noriega was referring to did not represent the vast majority of Panamanians. Jaws dropped, and for a moment there seemed to be a collective national gasp. Almost immediately "the people" mobilized into massive public demonstrations demanding his immediate resignation.

Undaunted, Noriega began to work on the anti-imperialist speech just faxed to him from Moscow. He made notes in the margins and added personal flourishes. He found it difficult to concentrate, given the shouts of "the people" who now filled the streets around him.

Should he begin the speech with a story from his boyhood, or open with a denunciation of the United States as Moscow recommended? He felt exhausted. Thank God for "Bolivian Marching Powder!"

Castro had been right: Troops sent out by Noriega to put down the protestors did not always follow orders. Large numbers of soldiers simply abandoned their posts, rather than risk their lives to support a failing dictator's inevitable date with destiny.

By midweek most of the country was paralyzed by strikes. Despite Noriega's imposition of martial law, looters and rioters brought life in the capital to a standstill, and traffic through the canal was suspended.

Home to 35,000 Americans, Panama also had a sizable US military presence which had been on high alert for some time. As the nation descended further into chaos, many terrified US civilians (including retirees) were given safe sanctuary at the bases.

On Thursday, Guillermo Endara, Noriega's main political opponent, received sanctuary from the Americans, after having just narrowly escaped an assassination attempt by a government death squad.

By Friday, May 5, large numbers of Cuban troops were arriving to reinforce Comrade Noriega, who apparently could no longer rely on his own security forces to maintain order or even ensure his personal safety.

After a very tough weekend spent getting high and firing people, General Noriega announced on Monday morning that the elections scheduled for later that week would be suspended until some semblance of order could be restored.

But like someone shouting in a hurricane, very few heard this message. Or rather, very few Panamanians did.

Meanwhile, Noriega's desperation came through loud and clear from Havana to Washington. Reagan and Castro, usually on opposite sides of nearly every issue, both shook their heads in disgust; as each determined that something needed to happen immediately to preserve their own national interests.

Things were playing out just as Castro predicted they would, and he knew that a US invasion was now imminent. Meanwhile, Reagan signed off on the plans to make it happen.

Comrade Noriega had good reason to fear the Americans now, and begged Castro to get him out of the country. He hadn't slept in two days, and was convinced that many in his administration had been replaced by American look-alikes who were using telepathy on him.

Castro hung up the phone, and gave the order that his people — the Cubans — abandon Panama immediately. The last Cubans (along with a few Russians) left Panama on Wednesday, May 10, and as they set sail east, they saw the sky darkening with a flock American military helicopters approaching from the north.

The US invasion and occupation took place with no resistance. On Sunday morning, Noriega was discovered dressed as a priest and hiding in the basement of a Chinese restaurant in Panama City. On his person was more than $75,000 in US currency.

Father Noriega was placed under citizen arrest and then nearly lynched, before being turned over to the Americans, who took responsibility for his safety until he could be brought to trial.

A special election was set up, and Guillermo Endara, a longtime friend and supporter of the United States, became the new president of Panama.

Sokolov was furious, and blamed Castro for the loss. But within the Kremlin, those who understood the difference between strategy and brute force put the blame on Sokolov.

Castro was more philosophical: acknowledging that while all

socialist countries had a common root, its application to governments and regions would naturally differ. Just as there existed a schism between the Russians and Chinese, it was natural to expect that socialism in the Americas might chart a different course than what was appropriate for Europe or in Africa.

In other words, thought Castro, the New World is *mine*.

＊ 49 ＊

Red is the Color of Money

"He will win who knows when to fight and when not to fight."

— Sun Tzu
The Art of War

The Reagan Budget—presented back in February—sailed through Congress with few modifications, and was already having a positive impact on the economy.

Implementing Reaganomics to this degree was a bold gamble, and came with the warning that a few things would likely get worse before the overall picture improved. Further complicating matters was its implementation during a time of crisis, when many of the old rules of economics might not apply.

A significant catalyst for problems stemmed from volatility in the energy market, which was, for the most part, beyond America's control. This rippled through the economy, and was felt in everything from gas shortages to demands to open up the nation's Strategic Petroleum Reserves.

Uncertainty and inflation undermined investment, and even given optimum circumstances, economic growth resulting from tax cuts would take time. Owing to inflation, many people shifted towards acquiring hard assets like gold coins, rather than keeping large sums of cash in the banks.

The lack of assets in US banks created a problem for the government, which would need to borrow not just to fund its core commitments, but to also to cover increased spending on defense. Simply printing more money would only devalue the currency (and fuel inflation), so instead the US was forced to look overseas for alternate lenders.

Most other Western nations such as the UK were in a similar predicament, and were unable to fill the gap. Luckily, America's credit rating was such that those with money were happy to make it available when Uncle Sam inquired about a loan.

But there were limits to what even old friends like Japan could provide. With traditional sources unable to meet the need, the US looked to new options, including China, or more accurately, the People's Republic of China—the biggest communist nation on the planet.

Largely insulated from the economic turbulence plaguing the West, China's economy had been growing rapidly in recent years, and relations with the United States were mostly positive. Improving financial ties was regarded as not just good economic policy, but supportive of international stability and harmony.

Stronger economic ties between the US and China also helped to further isolate the USSR.

Although both communist states, China and the USSR were at the best of times rivals, and at the worst of times adversaries, with tensions going back to the 1950s. Over the decades, the animosity and mistrust between the two giants continued to escalate, as each competed for worldwide influence, and the title of the one true voice of world socialism.

By the late 1960s Sino-Soviet relations had hit bottom, and the two nuclear powers faced off over a border dispute that nearly resulted in an all-out war.

All superpowers compete for influence, and for years the Soviets sought to bring India—one of the world's most populous nations into their column. China and the US worked together to block this, and had cooperated on other ventures where similar alliances would subvert Soviet expansionism.

Reagan was loathe to do anything that helped a communist regime, but he also understood the strategic value of pitting Beijing against Moscow. It was also an extension of a policy that went back to President Richard Nixon, that other ardent anti-communist, who shocked the world in 1972 with his bold steps to normalize relations between the US and the PRC.

It was a risky move politically, especially for a politician who had already alienated much of his conservative base by pursuing a negotiated peace, rather than a military victory in Vietnam. But Nixon was nothing if not a pragmatist, and the soundness of his decision to engage China had been affirmed with each passing year.

As with every administration, US-China relations during Reagan's first two terms had their ups and downs. These were most notably due to differences on issues such as the Israeli-PLO conflict and the Falkland War, where the two nations were publicly on opposite sides. In contrast, the US and China were very much aligned against the Soviet invasion of Afghanistan—with China joining US efforts in support of the Mujahideen guerrillas.

Lastly, China placed a lot of value on personal relations, and so the fact that Vice President Bush had once served as the US Ambassador to China added special depth to relations with the Reagan Administration that carried over to the third term.

Under Gorbachev, efforts were made to improve Sino-Soviet relations, and substantive progress was made in a number of areas—as had been the case with Soviet and American relations. For the Chinese, this all changed with the coup headed by Sergey Sokolov—the man they denounced for his role commanding the invasion of Afghanistan.

Much to Beijing's ire, promises made by Gorbachev to withdraw from Afghanistan had not been observed by the new regime. Instead, reports of Soviet aggression and barbarism constituting war crimes had increased, committed by furious Russians seemingly bent on revenge.

The Chinese despised and distrusted Sokolov, certainly as much as the Americans, and possibly more. Fears of a Soviet invasion of Chinese territory had been a consistent concern, which now gained even more credibility given the USSR's revived interest in expansionism. Fueling concerns was an uptick in relations between the Soviets and the North Koreans, one of Moscow's puppets which shared a border with China.

The Chinese felt surrounded.

While it seemed unlikely that the Soviets would take on two superpowers at once, in war, reason seldom prevails. Nazi Germany had opened that same can of worms, when it attacked Russia while already battling the US and its allies. Was Sokolov as crazy and ego-driven as Hitler? No one knew for sure, but the Chinese weren't about to take any chances.

Inexplicably, and much to the frustration of the White House, Beijing refused to publicly criticize the USSR. The Chinese abstained from all anti-Soviet votes in the UN, and, at least on the surface, assumed a position of neutrality.

Still, when the United States asked for a loan, China did not hesitate. While it was obvious why the US needed money, the Chinese preferred not to ask — or even hear — the details. For Beijing, mixing business and politics was just not how things were done.

Besides, according to the Chinese calendar, this was the year of the Snake. In observation of this, the Chinese were advised to keep calm and not jump into situations. Snakes were reputed to guard their partners, but if spurned, would not rest until they had their revenge.

50

Piper at the Gate

In April of 1989, 61-year-old James Roderick Lilley became America's new ambassador to the Peoples Republic of China, taking over from Winston Lord, who had held the position for nearly four years.

Born in pre-communist China to American ex-pat parents, Lilley grew up speaking fluent Mandarin, but returned to the United States at the start of World War II — which began early in Asia when the (then) Empire of Japan attacked and invaded the (then) Republic of China in the summer of 1937.

Fearing that foreigners would be killed or taken as hostages, the Lilley family was forced to return to the safety of the United States. However, in less than four years after attacking its giant neighbor to the west, Japan turned its gaze east, across the great expanse of the Pacific, and to Pearl Harbor, Hawaii.

The attack on Pearl Harbor ended US isolationism in what had now become a global conflict, and prompted James Lilley to enlist in the US army. When his service ended in 1946, the young veteran set off for college, first to Yale, then on to George Washington University where he earned a master's degree in International Relations.

Many expected that Lilley would enter civil service in the diplomatic corps, but instead he pursued a career in the CIA, with an emphasis on Asia. After nearly 30 years at the agency, he was returning to the country of his birth as America's top diplomat.

Preceding the ambassadorship to China, Lilley had served on the National Security Council. Prior to that, as America's ambassador to South Korea. During his tenure in Seoul, Lilley had played an important role in advancing a range of US-backed democratic reforms, including those leading to the nation's first legitimate presidential elections since the 1960s.

Lilley had also served as America's unofficial ambassador to Taiwan, and was known to have managed US spies in the PRC (during his time as the CIA station chief in Beijing).

Despite his record, the Chinese were willing to welcome him back home; much to the surprise, and delight, of the White House.

Historically, Lilley's appointment came at a critical time in relations between Washington and Beijing. To finance the war effort, the United States was now deeply indebted to China, a situation that Washington hoped would lead to a new era of cooperation—and influence—across a range of areas. In time, business partners would become friends, or at least not do anything that would hurt areas of common interest.

China also saw the strategic value in developing this relationship. Funding the war would cause problems for its Soviet adversaries, while giving it greater influence over the US as its creditor. Just as the Soviets were attempting to buy friends in Europe with economic initiatives, the Chinese saw their loans as a way to first influence, then control America.

He who pays the piper calls the tune.

In support of the argument that each side would increase influence, Red China had steadily been modernizing since Nixon first opened the door to improving relations. The fact that the PRC now had money to loan was a testament to its embrace, and the triumph, of Western capitalism.

But while the People's Republic of China was open to economic change, political reforms were not a subject for discussion. The country's record on human rights was among the world's worst, maintained by a huge internal security force and a network of secret prisons where torture and execution were commonplace.

What Reagan understood—but which the Chinese Party Leaders did not, was that economic and political freedoms are intrinsically linked. As the Chinese people developed greater economic power and autonomy, they began to demand more personal liberties, including those of speech, assembly, religion, and the right to petition their government for change.

As money flowed in from the outside world, so did ideas, and by the spring of 1989 things seemed destined for a collision.

The White House had been carefully following these developments, and was anxious to support the people's quest for both economic and political reform.

Not only was America the world's voice for freedom, but it was also the leading supporter of democratic movements around the world.

From Russian dissidents to the Contras, America stood with the oppressed yearning to breathe free; and this commitment was never more evident than during the presidency of Ronald Reagan.

But now, with a genuine revolutionary peoples' movement building in China, the question of what America should do — or could do — became much more complicated.

Supporting the pro-democracy movement would undeniably drive a wedge between the countries — a point the Chinese had been quick to make. While a certain amount of agitation was to be expected (and tolerated), any significant meddling in China's internal affairs would result in an immediate severance of relations between Beijing and Washington.

The message was clear and the ramifications undeniable. If China felt under siege by the United States, this might very well open the door to an alignment with the Soviets. At the very least, the funding needed for the war effort would be cut off, which would all but guarantee victory for the USSR.

Group consensus suggested that the US should continue to speak out for liberty as it had in the past, but without directly referencing the Chinese.

Meanwhile, the White House would pursue a program of intensified quiet diplomacy directly with their counterparts in Beijing. The US would make the case for the association between economic progress and political freedoms, warning that governments not open to reforms only encourage violent revolutions — as had been the case in Russia, the United States, and even China itself just four decades earlier.

Before committing to a specific policy, Reagan wanted to hear from those on all sides of the issue, including not just those in his administration, but from those who had dealt with China in the past, so as to gain a larger historical perspective.

Both former President Nixon and his Secretary of State Henry Kissinger recommended caution, and advised against mixing business and politics.

"Continue to play China against the USSR," Kissinger advised. "The protestors are pawns, and some pawns are lost in every game."

Nixon discounted any possibility of a democratic China in the near future, believing the principles were completely foreign with tradition.

"Look at Mao—essentially just another emperor—and the people are still peasants, living under feudalism. Maybe in 100 years, but China is ancient, and change comes slowly, especially if the path is blocked with rifles."

The former president, on speaker phone from his home, La Casa Pacifica (The House of Peace) in San Clemente, California, continued with his assessment, while the current president, his hand upon his chin, his brow furrowed, listened intently.

"China has a large population of young people—and they're learning fast. But I'm not sure that this is the time ... their time, anyway.

"Carter pushed human rights too hard, and we're still paying for that. With China, it's all about the long game; small steps.

"Both sides need to understand what's at stake. The future is about freedom and democracy, but I think it's too soon for us to push it.

"A small amount of idealism is no match for a lot of tanks and guns.

"In the end, everyone will lose."

To date, democratic opposition had been small and sporadic, representing no serious threat to the state security forces. Many "crimes" were isolated incidents, involving only a few people, typified by some old man who distributed a half-dozen copies of a handwritten manifesto criticizing one-party elections.

Again, no big deal.

But then, one day in spring, things begin to change in a city square in downtown Beijing that had over many centuries been the cradle of large-scale protest and rebellion.

Initially neither the number of protestors (acting as mourners) nor their actions was worrisome to the authorities; although their choice of location seemed somewhat suspicious.

At the entrance to the Forbidden City—once home to China's emperors, was an ornate portal, built in the 15th century, and known as the Gate of Heavenly Peace—or by its Chinese name, Tiananmen Gate.

Through the Gate of Heavenly Peace is Tiananmen Square, a shrine to the heroes and symbols of the last revolution, including the Great Hall of the People, and the embalmed corpse of Chairman Mao.

At first, there was no real cause for alarm when a small number of persons began to congregate and mourn the death of Hu Yaobang, a

Communist Party General Secretary who had advocated for economic *and* political reforms—before being deposed by party hardliners.

But then slowly and steadily, like the transformation from night to morning, mourners morphed into protestors. At some point things became clear; a new day was beginning.

The sun was rising in the East.

Caught off guard, the Chinese authorities squinted and blinked. They ordered security forces not to intervene, believing the protest would soon subside on its own accord.

Conscious of the world's eyes being upon them, China hoped to avoid escalation or the type of crackdown that might create martyrdom, or affect their image and stance in the community of the world's civilized nations.

But things did not settle down. In fact, each day they grew exponentially worse, spreading beyond Tiananmen Square then across China itself.

On the twentieth of May, ten days after the US invasion to liberate Panama, China imposed martial law and sent 300,000 armed troops into Beijing.

Lilley, who had been monitoring the situation closely as both a diplomat and intelligence officer, was terrified by what he saw. "The guns are loaded, and both sides are digging in. I don't think the protestors understand what they're up against. This is going to be a bloodbath—and I think we'll likely get the blame from both sides."

The showdown was eerily familiar, echoing the uprising in Prague's Wenceslas Square roughly a year prior. Things had not gone well in Czechoslovakia for those seeking freedom, and so it was with a terrible sense of déjà vu that the world watched as things slid, like a car wreck in slow motion, to what promised to be an even greater slaughter of innocents.

51

Tiananmen Square Off

Once again, world events demanded an emergency Sunday morning meeting at the White House.

After reviews and updates, the floor was opened to discussion on how the US should respond. As expected, there were strong differences of opinion between the factions present. But in the end, the decision of which course to take would be the President's responsibility.

Reagan listened attentively to each argument, occasionally asking questions, but not signifying a tilt in any particular direction.

One contingent advocated supporting the revolution; arming protestors, adding covert US assistance and a range of other actions that would make it unequivocally clear to the world which side America was on. A revolution in China would create worldwide ripples, and present a major setback for the Soviets.

It would be the shot heard round the world.

Having a giant (and adversarial) democratic superpower on its border was not something Moscow was prepared for, and it would almost certainly stall plans for expansion into Western Europe.

Furthermore, a people's revolution in the world's most populous communist nation might just be the spark needed to set off a similar uprising in the USSR. If the Soviet Union could be brought down internally, this would spare the need for a major military confrontation led by the United States.

Others representing the intelligence services did not believe a revolution had sufficient popular support to succeed — even if all available US resources were applied.

They argued that if America acted now it would likely backfire, and set back any chance of even modest reforms for years to come. Pushing for regime change would derail Sino-US relations, making it harder for the US to maintain a presence in the country, which often flourished under the cover of the diplomatic service.

Those representing military interests were worried about the prospect of getting caught up in a long Chinese civil war. "We tried this on a smaller scale in Vietnam, and I would hope that we have learned something from that," said Admiral William Crowe, Chairman of the Joint Chiefs of Staff.

"Besides, where would we pull the troops from? We're understaffed as is ... We can't cover all the hotspots we're already committed to, much less take on something as large as China.

"If the war erupts in Europe we're going to need everyone we can muster to take on the armies of the Warsaw Pact. We're ramping up as quickly as possible, but we are not prepared to fight two major wars on two different fronts.

"Don't forget, China has a large nuclear arsenal, spread out across a huge area that would be vulnerable. This is not something we would be able to easily reach, much less secure promptly.

"Keep in mind they share a border with North Korea — another Soviet client state. Do we really want the North Koreans getting their hands on nukes? That's the kind of scenario that keeps me awake at night."

Another perspective argued that if simultaneously threatened from within by revolution, and externally by the US, Beijing would likely do anything — including partner with the Soviets — rather than lose control and face the people's wrath.

"Totalitarian governments are only concerned with holding on to power. They are willing to support the US not because they like us, but because they are using us to achieve this end; this control," warned a representative from the NSA.

The meeting went on like this for most of the day, with no clear consensus.

It seemed the US was damned if it did, damned if it didn't. There was no easy way out. Deciding what to do would be the President's responsibility; it was a difficult and unenviable position to be in given the stakes involved.

Reagan made sure that everyone had the opportunity to speak. But now people were getting tired, and beginning to repeat themselves. The same basic arguments and rebuttals were getting sharper, although no more convincing, as civility was giving way to exasperation tinged with irritability.

During the marathon session, the President only asked a few questions. Some were broad and open-ended, while others concerned specifics relating to resources and timetables. But for the most part he just listened, nodding respectfully, but not providing any real clues as to what he was thinking.

The President looked at his watch; he'd heard enough. It was nearly 5 o'clock; time to wrap things up for the day.

Given the urgency of the situation, Reagan would not have time to sleep on the matter. Besides, he knew what he needed to do.

President Reagan adjourned the meeting, and called forth two members of his support staff.

The first was Dave Fischer, his longtime personal assistant, who was generally at the President's side from morning to night. Reagan asked Fischer to let Nancy know he'd be running late, but that there was nothing to worry about.

The second assistant was tasked with arranging a direct personal call to Chairman Deng Xiaoping, the leader of China.

The President then took a moment of silent prayer at his desk, as he waited for the call to be placed.

Reagan had first met Xiaoping five years earlier on a trip to China that mixed business and pleasure. The two disagreed over a number of issues — notably Reagan's support for Taiwan — but ultimately the two world leaders parted on cordial terms; respectful of one another's position and authority.

Xiaoping and the Chinese had been generous hosts, and the Reagans were quick to express their appreciation, along with an invitation to come visit them in America.

The Chairman had last visited the US during the final year of the Carter administration, prompting Reagan to joke that "Our country is so much better now — you'll hardly recognize the place." Deng appeared confused at first, until he realized that the President had been making a joke about his predecessor.

The two laughed heartily. Xiaoping had not taken to Carter, having found him preachy and condescending. But Reagan was something different. This was someone he could trust, someone he could work with.

These were the kinds of personal, one-to-one relationships that were very important to the Chinese, and something that Reagan excelled at cultivating.

With most world leaders, President Reagan tried to remove the formalities of office and engage with his peers on a first name basis. Therefore, Ron was delighted that Deng was available to take a personal call from America.

As it turned out, Reagan called at just the right time; it was morning in Beijing, and the Chairman welcomed the opportunity to speak directly (albeit through translators) with the American president.

Chairman Xiaoping knew why Reagan was calling. As the two leaders conversed, they discovered that they had much in common, and also much at stake. Although they spoke for just under an hour, the exact text of the conversation was never made public.

The next morning, the full team was assembled and waiting for the President's decision on how to address the situation in China.

As always, Reagan seemed well-rested, upbeat, and ready to take on the day. All eyes were on him, and like an actor taking his cue, Reagan broke the silence to speak in only the most general terms of his conversation with the Chinese leader.

"We had a good talk; I can't say I always agree with his politics, but I think we found some common ground. He's committed to reform, and he needs us as much as we need him.

"Anyway, he seems a decent fellow, and I got him to promise me there'd be no violence," Reagan said, smiling.

And there wasn't.

The protests continued to build. Then started to decline as rapidly as they had begun, and were completely over before the month ended. The people seemed happy with their first steps towards democracy, as represented by freedom of speech and assembly.

This was the start of a long process, which would unfold on its own timetable, for a society and culture that prides itself—regardless of politics—by thinking about, and seeking long-term solutions.

By exhibiting restraint and tolerance, the government discovered the true meaning of the ancient Chinese proverb, which stated "If a man is patient in one moment of anger, he will escape one hundred days of sorrow."

52

Iceland

Iceland is a small island nation, tucked away at the top of the world where the icy waters of the Atlantic and Arctic Oceans converge. Officially considered a part of Europe from the first days of colonization, Iceland was ruled by other nations for more than a thousand years until it finally became an independent republic during World War II.

Despite independence, Iceland continued to be occupied by allied forces until 1946. In 1949, it joined the United States as a founding member of NATO—along with its former masters Norway and Denmark. Two years later, Iceland ceded responsibility for its defenses to the United States, which is how things stayed until the late spring of 1988.

For years, public support for the American military presence had been in decline, so when the Soviets began making overtures to Iceland shortly after the Valentine's Day coup, it warmly accepted. Iceland's participation in NATO was to be reevaluated, and the American troops serving as the Iceland Defense Force were given orders to stand down or get out.

On paper, the arrangement sought by Iceland was to provide a neutral space where the two superpowers might coexist peacefully.

Both sides would be welcome, so long as each behaved non-aggressively, respected the other's rights and territories—and above all, Iceland's sovereignty and independence. It was to be a model of what was possible; an inspiration to the entire world.

Neither side seemed entirely happy with the arrangement, but for Moscow, it was at least a foot in the door. Washington had no choice but to remain as a counterbalance, obligated to defending what was—at least on paper—still a NATO member state.

Isolated from much of the world, and perhaps reality, Icelanders viewed their country as a magical place where peace might blossom.

It had, after all, just recently hosted an important summit between Gorbachev and Reagan, and had generally avoided international conflicts for most of its history. Tiny Iceland also secretly enjoyed playing the role of dominatrix to the two most powerful empires on the planet.

If the Americans or the Soviets refused to get down on their hands and knees and crawl they would be spanked and sent home. Their missiles were no match for Reykjavik's whip.

With the American presence already long established, the Soviets were forced to take less strategic locations, while still observing a small demilitarized buffer zone to avoid any accidental incursions.

Given the country's small size, American and Soviet forces frequently overlapped (at least on a personal level). Interactions — never good — had become especially tense after the US shot down a Soviet transport plane *en route* to Iceland as retaliation for the Alaska incident last July.

Much to the despair of the Icelanders, the streets of the capital had not become some serene Shangri-La, but rather something more akin to the Wild West, in which opposing gangs circled each other and tried hard not to blink.

In charge of the US mission in Iceland was Scott Alan Doohan, a four-star General. Ginger-haired and with sparkling blue eyes, Doohan was proud of the fact that he still had, at 55 years of age, *perfect* 20-20 vision and "most" of his hair.

Married, but with no children, the still boyish-looking Doohan was the end of the line for a family whose ties to military service could be traced all the way back to George Washington's Continental Army and the Revolutionary War.

Most recently, his father Robert had served in the navy; much of his time spent stationed in Hawaii, where both his children had been born.

Scott had come first, followed three years later by his sister, Cathrine. Although born during the Great Depression, it was still a time of peace, and Doohan recalled his early years as "idyllic ... bordering on magical," with days spent at the beach watching the waves and palm trees gently swaying in the breeze.

Unbeknownst to the boy, that paradise would soon be lost.

On the morning of December 7, 1941, seven-year-old "Scotty" was up early, listening to the newspaper "funnies" being read over the radio.

It was a typically serene Sunday morning, until just before 8am when the roar of planes began, soon followed by gunfire, explosions, screams, and sirens. World War II was starting, and young Mr Doohan was watching it unfold live from his front porch.

Most people think of America's 50th state as a tranquil utopia, a land of hula dancers, luaus, coconuts, Elvis with a ukulele, and good times. But in reality, few states harbor as many ghosts of war as Hawaii, or as many reminders of its horrors.

Growing up on the island of Oahu, Doohan saw war's effects on a daily basis. Men with badly burned faces passed him on the way to school; amputees struggled to make change at the grocery store; hulks of ships lay partially sunken in the harbor. For Doohan, the lessons of unpreparedness had shaped his life and outlook.

After graduating high school, Doohan received a commission to West Point, and upon completion, was sent as an officer to Vietnam where he served several tours. Highly decorated, and well respected, he rose through the ranks and was given one important assignment after another.

His command assignment in Iceland was generally expected to be his last; a nice finish to a career that, in Doohan's words, "began on a warm little island in the Pacific, and ended on a big, cold one in the Atlantic."

The last Sunday in May was typical for Iceland. Skies were overcast, rain was likely. Here, at this latitude, morning was something of a misnomer; the darkness of night only lasted for a few hours.

At 7:57am a Soviet aircraft entered US airspace. Given the proximity of the two camps, this was not, in and of itself unusual, nor a cause for major concern. Still, there were protocols to be observed, and US forces assumed alert status.

The plane was coming in at a very low altitude and at a very slow speed, and soon it was visible from the ground as it lazily moved closer on an unsteady path. Something was definitely not right, and attempts to contact the craft were unsuccessful.

Two more Soviet aircraft appeared. Unlike the first plane, these were moving quickly to close the gap. Quickly towards the US base.

Perhaps now that he had a visual of the ground below him, the pilot adjusted course, and as he banked eastward, dropped a single bomb onto the tarmac at the US base at Keflavik.

The bomb did not explode, but its impact would be felt around the world.

Before the plane could turn back around towards the Americans for a second time, General Doohan gave a direct order to have it brought down.

As the fragments of man and machine entered the dark waters of the North Atlantic, they took with them the reason for the pilot's actions, along with any hope for a peaceful resolution to the standoff between the US and the USSR.

The Soviet response was immediate, and expected: both sides engaged fully, and both suffered debilitating losses that went right up the chain of command to include General Doohan, who died a warrior's death alongside the brave troops under his command.

Such is the nature of war.

The battle was quick, but indecisive, given that forces on both sides had been utterly wiped out within hours.

Reykjavik was in ruins, a casualty of its good intentions. There would be no rush by either the Soviets or NATO to reestablish a presence here, and assistance to the civilian population would be left largely to the Red Cross, the UN, and a patchwork of charitable organizations.

Instead of providing an oasis of peace, Iceland had provided the flashpoint by which the Cold War had turned hot.

53

Europe Prepares for War

Before Iceland, it had been almost a year since the last big showdown between US and Soviet forces. In response to an incursion into US airspace near Alaska, the Americans had responded forcefully by hitting a number of Soviet targets around the world. Most understood this for just what it was: an exercise to test America's resolve, and to position Reagan as either a trigger-happy warmonger or a paper tiger, and then spin the outcome as propaganda.

Following the incident, the Soviets sought to play up their innocence and martyrdom, and downplay the saber rattling. Instead they pursued an all-out charm offensive to win the hearts and minds of Europe, relying on surrogates such as Libya to militarily engage the Americans or its NATO allies.

The battle in Iceland marked a turning point in the conflict. The Soviets responded to the downing of a single plane with a rapaciousness that drove them to kill everything in sight, whether the target was the civilian population, NATO forces, or one of their own pilots who was shot in the back as he tried to flee the base with upraised hands indicating a desire to surrender.

What happened over the course of a few hours on a remote island in the North Atlantic changed everything, and there was no turning back now. All involved understood the ramifications of the Soviet actions: An attack on the defensive forces of any NATO member nation was an attack on all.

NATO had been formed from the ashes of World War II specifically to protect small countries like Iceland. While the alliance could not reverse Soviet acquisitions in Europe, it had managed to stop the Iron Curtain at the border of a divided Germany in 1945.

As part of the deal cut between the three western allies and the Soviets, Berlin had also been quartered, despite the fact that the former capital was located deep within territory surrendered to Moscow, now called the German Democratic Republic (GDR).

Having lost the war, the German people had no say in how their land was being carved up and given away. Trouble began almost immediately.

Years before the Hungarians and Czechs revolted against their communist oppressors, a similar uprising in the GDR in 1953 had been violently crushed by a coalition of Soviet and German forces. The message was clear: No one was coming to help. East Germany was now property of the Soviets. (On paper, the Soviet Union was still technically at war with Germany. Peace would not be officially declared until 1955.)

The border that partitioned Germany became one of the most fortified, and dangerous divides on the planet. It was here that the line had been drawn, reinforced by nuclear-armed superpowers. This was Ground Zero in the Cold War.

If there was to be another world war, it was assumed that it would begin here, where the last one had ended.

In response to the coup, and to a lesser degree, concerns about the reliability of its European NATO partners, the US had greatly increased its presence along the German border. The Soviets had responded similarly, although not quite to the same degree.

The USSR had other obligations and interests around the continent, and the leaders were also still hoping to roll westward by invitation, once the Americans had been evicted. Massing too many troops on the border would only serve to induce public paranoia and reinforce Washington's warnings of an imminent invasion.

Thus, the Soviet plan was simple: Play nice, don't scare — *seduce*. Smile. Use propaganda to win hearts and minds. Convince the Europeans to dissolve NATO and send the Americans back home. Once gone, take the nukes and tighten the noose.

This strategy would save on resources needed elsewhere, and avoid the costs of once again rebuilding a war-torn continent.

After years of buildup, the forces of the Warsaw Pact were formidable, and this was no more evident than with those already positioned in East Germany.

As the fortified barrier between east and west, the GDR held special significance as the first line of defense for the Soviet Union. Any army attacking from the west would have to fight through several other countries first — all of which were expendable — before reaching Russian soil.

By every matrix, the best of these forces was said to be the East Germans. As a people long-steeped in Prussian military traditions, they were well trained and highly disciplined. And, as Moscow was quick to remind them, they were beholden to the Russians, who had fought to rescue them first from Hitler, and then from the Americans.

While their treatment of the German people both during and following the war had been vicious and inhuman, in recent decades it had improved to being only brutally oppressive, thus serving as a testament to Soviet goodwill and forgiveness.

As the Russians were quick to point out, the Germans owed them more than could ever be repaid—although laying down their lives at Moscow's command would be seen as modest down payment.

While West Germany made reparations for the Holocaust, East Germany's reparations went directly to Moscow. In exchange for cash and anything of value that couldn't be hidden or nailed down (such as works of art), the Russians generously reciprocated by shipping eastward monolithic statues of Lenin.

Russian hatred for Germans was deeply ingrained, and despite the promises of a Socialist Utopian Brotherhood, this execration was evident in nearly every exchange. From the rapes committed by the Red Army, to the endless reparations demanded by Moscow, the East Germans were prisoners in their own country, a nation that, unlike any other in Europe, had been split in a manner that divided families, communities, and destinies.

Despite attempts to impose a unified and homogenous Soviet culture, strong nationalist identities persisted in the GDR and among the other nations of the Eastern Bloc. Whether the result of genuine cultural differences or intransigent opposition to Moscow, assimilation had not succeeded as planned.

Like caged lions, the Germans were a star attraction in the Soviet circus. Smart, fit, and ferocious—not something to turn one's back on. But with adequate controls: a gun, a chair, a whip, they were reliable performers.

The Soviets were their victors, and the Germans did as they were told. As a people, they were assumed to be incapable of thinking for themselves. They were a nation of followers, who fell in line and fell in battle when ordered, whether for Hitler or Sokolov.

Under Soviet domination, even Germans privately at odds with their government's directives stoically followed orders—just as Moscow had assumed. Soon the GDR's troops were among the most polished and trustworthy in the Warsaw Pact.

As had been the case under the Nazis, German forces were spread out among various entities that blurred the lines between policing and military classifications. These were complemented by an array of personnel with clear military objectives, including an army (Landstreitkräfte), an air force (Luftstreitkräfte/Luftverteidigung), a navy (Volksmarine), and border troops.

Conquered, compliant, competent, *and* communist—East Germany was given the special honor of defending the frontier. It was also expected to lead the charge westward when Moscow called with marching orders.

Their allegiance and discipline were beyond question. The Germans were Dobermans: docile until given the signal by their master, at which point they would attack with vicious fury.

Whether to lead the people's struggle into Western Europe, or just take some revenge on old adversaries like the French and British, the East Germans would be the Kremlin's front line in the battle to unite Europe.

But, with every shift in the wind, Moscow's plans had to be changed and updated. Because the Soviets had played their hand as aggressors in Iceland, the credibility of their proposal to play nicely and peacefully unify Europe was now in question.

Despite efforts to spin what happened as "heroic Soviet self-defense" against "another instance of unprovoked American aggression," the Kremlin privately acknowledged the dream of taking Western Europe without firing a shot was now pretty much a fantasy.

Instead, it was time to look at what had nearly succeeded in the past; to learn from the mistakes of Napoleon, Hitler, Stalin—and then try again.

Talks of "liberation" were shelved, and plans to take the continent by force were revived. This was something Commander Sokolov understood, and what he had been waiting for.

Peace had been given a chance, and it had failed. Surrounded by his pack in a deep underground bunker, Sokolov pored over maps and strategies, questioning his generals and commenting on even the most minor of details.

Time was of the essence, and the Soviets needed to hit hard, and hit fast. There was no margin for error or delays.

The attack on the West would involve three fronts — one against Norway led primarily by Russian troops, one in the south through Austria led by Warsaw Pact troops (mostly Czechoslovakians and Hungarians), and finally, the major offensive that would flow westward from the GDR, first into West Germany, then straight through into the heart of Europe.

Rebellions, sabotage, and proxy wars would divert the Americans and rattle the Europeans. Generals fantasized about attacks on Europe, and even suicide missions by the Cubans to attack points on the US mainland.

Europeans would capitulate rather than risk nuclear war. Reagan would not dare attack Russia if he knew that it would be matched by a retaliatory strike against the United States. He was a warmonger, but he'd sooner throw the ungrateful Europeans overboard than risk having his own country reduced to smoldering, radioactive waste.

It was time to call his bluff.

Sokolov was ecstatic. Although a major military offensive wasn't possible for at least ten days, the thought of trading in the tailored suit for his old commander's uniform was something he had been hoping for since the coup forced him to adopt the sheep's clothing.

In the meantime, the Soviets braced for American revenge over Iceland. Again, with tepid NATO support, they would likely behave unilaterally, and attempt to emphasize their strength as a global force by hitting a string of small targets.

Syria? Likely.

As were Soviet outposts in the Mediterranean and Africa. Possibly Cuba, definitely a few ships harbored elsewhere or in the vast expanses of the open seas.

Meanwhile, the KGB set about plans to create mayhem and terror within the United States.

Blow up some bridges, knock out a power grid, perhaps assassinate or kidnap a member of the administration. The Soviets already had hundreds of operatives placed in the United States, and the ability to deliver more across America's long and open borders.

If America was fighting a war at home it would forget all about Europe.

"Yes," Sokolov thought to himself, "now I'm back in familiar territory. I am ready to lead my nation to victory in the next Great War!"

He looked at his calendar, noting that an important date in Soviet history was just about two weeks away.

On June 16, 1944, a contingent of Soviet forces led by a 32-year-old Brigade Commander named Sergey Sokolov had scored an important victory against rapidly retreating Nazi troops. Although the Russians believed the Germans were running in terror from the Red Army, they were in actuality rushing westward to repulse a major allied assault that had begun ten days earlier on the shores of Normandy. Known as the D-Day invasion, allied troops had opened up the continent, and were now advancing towards Nazi Germany. In response, German troops were forced to retreat from the east and assume defensive positioning.

For his courage, dedication, bravery, heroism, leadership, and so forth, Sokolov would receive a special citation upon his return to Russia.

Yes, June 16th had been an important day in history, thought Sokolov, allowing himself to bask in a moment of nostalgia and pride.

The 45th anniversary of that great day—*his great day*—deserved to be commemorated. And what better way to do this, than to show that the same Soviet spirit of heroism was still alive, and on the march to another great victory?

Sokolov gave the order: Let the liberation of Europe begin on June 16th, 1989!

54

Liberation

Like Sokolov, Reagan was also a student of history.

As one who had grown up in a century defined by seemingly endless war and conflict, the President subscribed to the philosophy that those who ignored history's lessons were doomed to repeat its mistakes.

Living through two world wars had profoundly influenced Reagan's worldview, and it was no secret that he did not believe in appeasement, *détente*, non-verifiable treaties, or peace at any cost.

Which is not to say that he wasn't a man of peace — because he was. But Reagan believed in peace through strength, peace through victory.

As Commander-in-Chief he knew there was never a perfect time to start a war, and that every conflict had its consequences.

But Reagan, the realist, also knew that there were windows of opportunity.

Before the smoke had even lifted from the rubble in Iceland, the US saw the beginnings of big changes in Eastern Europe, as the Soviets set about repositioning their forces into western-facing aggressive formations. Progress was slow, at times chaotic, but undeniable.

The US had long been prepared for such a move with more than 300,000 troops in Europe — most stationed in West Germany.

Still, in the days following the attack in Iceland there was much debate within the administration as to how, where, and when the United States should respond.

Of particular concern was the level of commitment the US could expect from its NATO partners. Without solid support by traditional forces, the US might need to rely upon its nuclear arsenal, which was not something anyone wanted to see happen — especially President Reagan.

No option looked good or enjoyed unanimous support.

Meanwhile, with every hour the Soviets were growing stronger. Military and intelligence services estimated the buildup would be complete in less than two weeks, and even if the US could muster all available NATO support, the Western forces would still not match what the

East could pull together.

The odds assessment was that holding back an invasion from the East was possible, but it would come with a heavy price.

Reagan nodded, tilted his head, sighed, and began to speak.

"I am not a military strategist, so I will concede that trying to stop the Soviet advance will be costly, perhaps even impossible."

The President paused, knowing that what he was about to say next would be extremely controversial.

"Once put on the battlefield soldiers will do what is expected of them; they will fight until they are killed or are victorious. Therefore, we cannot allow this war to start—at least not on these terms.

"I don't believe we are dealing with troops that *want* to fight. So instead of waiting for them to attack us, I suggest that we move first, not to conquer, but to free them.

"Germany, Hungary, Czechoslovakia: they are all nations held prisoner by Moscow's tyranny. Regimes planted by bayonets do not take root, and so we must make it clear that we are on the side of the people; here to correct an historic injustice.

"We will come in friendship, not as an occupying army, but as partners to help them tear down the Iron Curtain.

"This is something that we should have done long ago, but instead, out of fear or convenience we were willing to sacrifice the nations of Eastern Europe rather than challenge the Russians—but now they have challenged us—and we no longer have an excuse for inaction.

"We cannot escape our destiny, nor should we try to do so. This is our window of opportunity.

"No matter which course we take there will be consequences and casualties. We did not choose this war, but if we are forced to fight, then let it be for something we believe in; something worth dying for; something noble; and that which is the responsibility given to us by God.

"If not us, who? And if not now, when?"

It was a Wednesday, the last day of May, and only four days after the battle in Iceland.

Reagan turned to his military team.

"Unless there is some really compelling reason that I'm not aware of, I want the liberation of East Germany to begin next Tuesday."

Being Right

Reagan was right about Germany.

He was right in every sense of the word; from strategic timing to the moral obligation of freeing a people who had been held prisoner by a succession of totalitarian governments for more than half a century.

He was right about the short-term and long-term ramifications of his actions, and, as the world teetered on the edge of darkness, he was on the right side of history.

Reagan was right because he wasn't afraid to follow his conscience, and to do what leaders are supposed to: lead with courage and conviction.

Blitzkrieg

As ordered by President Reagan, the first wave of US and NATO troops hit the East German border in the early hours of Tuesday morning, June 6.

At first, resistance was relatively light, sporadic, and chaotic, but in short order it collapsed entirely as the GDR's forces either quickly surrendered or retreated.

The fiercest battles occurred in the north, along the Baltic coastline, and around the city of Rostock. But even these skirmishes resulted in relatively few casualties.

Many military outposts were found to be abandoned, or only staffed by a skeleton crew that quickly surrendered without resistance.

Advancing eastward, it appeared that many of the biggest battles were occurring before the American and other NATO troops arrived, as warring factions within the GDR's forces fought it out amongst themselves. In nearly every case, those loyal to the communist regime were either put down, absent, or provided no significant threat to the fast moving allied armies.

Most towns appeared vacant as well—at least initially—as civilians took cover indoors. However, as soon as each district was secured, the German people left their homes to—just as Reagan had predicted— welcome their liberators.

As the allied troops pushed north and east towards Berlin, exchanges dropped off dramatically, then increased ever so slightly as the borders of Poland and Czechoslovakia became visible on the horizon. Despite their incredible successes, Western troops were given orders not to cross into Polish or Czechoslovakian territory, and so this is where they came to rest after less than three days.

The rapid collapse and swift victory came as a surprise to nearly everyone (except perhaps the American president).

Reagan's bold initiative had changed the face of Europe in less than 72 hours since the campaign began, on the 45th anniversary of the D-Day invasion that had also redrawn the map, and put momentum on the side of an allied victory over Nazi Germany.

Invading the GDR changed the momentum of this new war; derailing Soviet plans for an invasion of Western Europe, scheduled by Sokolov personally for mid-month.

While the Russians always knew that such an attack from the west was possible, the suddenness of it had caught them completely off guard. But even more disconcerting was the manner in which the East Germans had not just capitulated, but had actually flipped sides. (Including reports of forces still wearing GDR uniforms joining with units from West Germany to attack other Warsaw Pact troops.)

Those loyal to the Soviets, such as the GDR's dictatorial leader Erich Honecker quickly fled east, and were already safe in Moscow before the first allied troops arrived on the outskirts of Berlin. When it became clear that the German people were not willing to sacrifice their lives defending their communist leader, he had caught the first plane out of town — leaving many in his despised regime to flee on foot, or by whatever means was available on such short notice.

General Secretary Honecker, 77, knew that his own life was just too valuable to risk dying a martyr in what appeared an unwinnable battle. He still had so much to give to the cause of socialism!

After filling a medical evacuation plane with art, antiquities, and gold, the Secretary and his third wife Margot (Minister of People's Education), abandoned the Fatherland for the safety of Mother Russia.

Few in government knew of the couple's plans in advance. After a brief Wednesday morning meeting dominated by bad news, Honecker, who also held the title of Chairman of the National Defense Council, directly ordered his people — including members of his administration — to stay in place and fight to the death defending the capital.

A few did, and died battling the citizens they once ruled. The majority scattered like rats, and were either caught or opted for suicide.

Leader of the GDR since 1971, Honecker was neither a loved or respected figure. He was right to fear the wrath of his own people, but more significantly, to fear justice itself, for the German people love a good trial.

Although a bit dusty after sitting unused since the Nuremberg trials, the high-quality, German-made gallows were likely in perfectly good working order, and waiting for him. Wisely, Honecker decided not to wait around to defend his legacy by claiming that he was only "following orders" sent from Moscow.

This particular excuse hadn't worked in the past, and Erich Honecker was a man with plenty of blood on his hands. Rather than take his chances in neighboring Czechoslovakia or Poland, he went straight to Russia, where he knew he would be protected and celebrated as a hero.

Or so he thought.

The loss of East Germany sent shockwaves through the Soviet regime.

The GDR was supposed to be Moscow's first—and reputedly best—line of defense. This was the nation that was being prepped to lead the charge into the West—not surrender to it. This was the nation that had been given the honor to die in battle protecting the Motherland.

Instead, this was the nation that was, in typically and orderly Teutonic fashion, already fast at work removing all public symbols and reminders of its association with the USSR. No looting, no smashing, no anarchy—but just a methodical and organized effort to purge all reminders of their long nightmare under communism.

German citizens sealed off government buildings and stood guard over institutions like STASI headquarters. Once the home of the feared secret police, the sprawling compound was now being treated as a crime scene, cordoned off, secured, awaiting the arrival of investigators.

Those at the KGB could not help but wonder if a similar fate might befall them someday as well, prompting a few to begin planning for a future that had once seemed unimaginable.

If the GDR could not be trusted, what about the other nations of the Warsaw Pact? Would the Poles or Czechs behave similarly? Although no one would express it publicly, or at least in Sokolov's presence, how firm was support even among the Russian people themselves?

General Secretary Honecker did not receive the hero's welcome he was expecting in Moscow. Instead, he received a speedy trial for his responsibility in the loss of the GDR to the West.

After his verdict was read, Honecker was instructed to turn and face the wall. Sokolov walked up behind him, raised his pistol, and shot him in the back of the head.

It was June 16, 1989—and the 45th anniversary of Sokolov's citation for heroism in battle against the retreating Germans.

57

The Lifeguard

"They counted on America to be passive.
They counted wrong."

— Ronald Wilson Reagan

There was disarray in the Soviet high command in light of what happened with Germany. Plans for a grand European invasion were immediately put on hold — then scaled back to only include Norway.

Norway was a small country. According to the generals, a land invasion could be staged using primarily Russian troops via the tiny shared border in the north, and across the sparsely-populated expanses of northern Finland and Sweden. Most of this region was a frozen wasteland, and at least initially, not worth the bother.

Instead, the main thrust of a Soviet ground invasion would need to come through Sweden. Most of the Norwegian population was concentrated in the south, and the capital of Oslo was just miles from the border.

The major thrust of the attack however, would need to come by air and sea.

As a coastal nation, Norway held tremendous strategic value. Capturing the Nordic state would demonstrate Soviet military might and provide an important morale boost to counterbalance the loss of the GDR.

Still, the generals acknowledged that this was a well-fortified NATO member nation, and so it would take some time to work out a plan.

What the Soviets did not know is that President Reagan had given his word to the Norwegian Prime Minister that he would not let her country fall. He had made it clear that he was prepared to go to the wall defending Norway, even if America was forced to act alone. If the Soviets had known this, they likely would have abandoned their goal, as it was now becoming clear who, and what, they were up against when they decided to take on Ronald Reagan.

Meanwhile, Germans united to return order to their nation and discuss plans for a full political reunification.

Symbols of the communist regime such as the Berlin Wall were attacked with ferocity, and cities like Karl-Marx-Stadt (southwest of Dresden) resumed its former pre-communist name of Chemnitz.

Most of those who had once held power in the GDR (and had not escaped) soon gave up the game and surrendered without resistance. Many just waited peacefully at home until the authorities came to arrest them, then release them under their own recognizance.

Among those that stayed and surrendered to "atone for his sins" was Markus Wolf, a former STASI agent who had once headed East Germany's foreign intelligence service.

Although officially retired from government service, the 66-year-old Wolf had maintained many of his former connections, and still worked in service to the state when called upon. As a founding member of the GDR's spy agency, the Russians valued Wolf's perspectives, and he was a frequent consultant to the KGB.

Wolf had last been in Moscow in late May, returning to East Berlin just days before the incident in Iceland.

During his visit, Wolf told the Russians he had deep concerns about the continued allegiance of his fellow East Germans. The people were restless, and he felt it was only a matter of time until they began to engage in widespread protests—similar to what happened last year in Wenceslas Square. "Oh, and no one believes the official story of the Prague Massacre," added Wolf. "They have become immune to state propaganda.

"Things are unraveling at an ever-increasing rate."

Wolf felt that the seeds planted by Gorbachev had taken root, and that he remained a more popular figure than "Honecker, Lenin, Marx, or even ..."

Wolf realized he was going too far and caught himself just in time. Adding Sokolov's name to this list would accomplish nothing, so he quickly substituted in "Beethoven" which brought laughter to the room, and smiles to the faces of the Russians who had been staring incredulously at him.

Comrade Wolf had been very useful in the past, but now his insights and observations were suspect. Whether due to dementia or ignorance, he was simply wrong about the loyalty of the German people.

Maybe it was Wolf's allegiance that was in question?

Alexander Bukin, the 60-something KGB officer who was directing the meeting made a quick note to increase surveillance on Wolf. Still, what the former intelligence officer had to say about popular support for Gorbachev corresponded with the KGB's own findings.

"Because of our plan to peacefully unite Europe we obviously could not execute him—even if we had a trial first," Bukin said, laughing, as he made a comically casual gesture with his left hand.

"Nor could we have him out in public, sowing dissent. He is still worshipped, regarded by many as the true leader. He could be a free man tomorrow if he would just accept reality and support us, but instead he chooses to oppose us. He is defiant.

"So, for now, Gorbachev is back home, under house arrest at his residence in Crimea. And there he will stay until the public has forgotten him, or until keeping him alive is no longer in the greater interests of the state."

Wolf looked puzzled.

"If we go to war," said Bukin. "If we have to liberate the West by force, then he is of no value. But neither is he a priority."

Wolf nodded.

At his debriefing by the victorious Western allies, news of Gorbachev's whereabouts was an important revelation, now underscored by urgency. The war had indeed gone hot, which put Gorbachev's life in immediate danger.

Given the recent turn of events, it was unlikely that the Soviets would waste time on a trial. No, Gorbachev would need to be executed privately, but still in a way that did not implicate the state.

The Soviets could not risk turning him into a martyr.

Apparently, what the Soviets had not given consideration to was Gorbachev's value leading the opposition—as head of a government-in-exile.

Reagan grasped this immediately. "We need to get him out of there. *Now.*"

Those in attendance at the President's briefing expected this response, and knew that this order was to be given the highest possible priority.

They looked at Reagan, waiting for him to continue.

"In the old days, out west, we'd just ride a horse up to the side of the jail, rope up the bars and yell 'giddy up' and the prisoner would be free," said the man who had certainly seen, and performed in more than a few westerns.

Reagan pursed his lips, nodded his head; he was brainstorming. Let somebody else figure out how to spring him—delegate. The President was already on to the big picture.

"Yes, the legitimate government of the USSR, operating in exile … But where? Not Britain. Not here—that would make him look like a puppet. Can Switzerland be secured?

"How about we just never say for sure?" mused the President. "He could be anywhere …"

Leaning back in his chair, the President looked upwards towards the ceiling, his expression clouding over. "What about other members of his team? Can we get the Foreign Minister … Eduard Shevardnadze?"

Reagan was thinking out loud now, his comments not directed to anyone in particular, although all listened with rapt attention, hanging on every word.

"Crimea, eh? Well, that's doable … Just across the water to Turkey and then he's free.

"If he falls in the Black Sea I'll jump in and rescue him myself," Reagan said, a smile spreading across his face, his blue eyes twinkling. "As you know, I used to be a lifeguard—and I never lost a single soul."

The President and his team laughed at the mental picture suggested by Reagan in swim trunks dragging Gorbachev to shore. Laughable, but as a lifeguard, Reagan had indeed saved nearly 80 people from drowning.

"Okay boys, go read some Tom Clancy novels, and let's get the show on the road. But for God's sake, let's take note of how Carter screwed things up trying to free the hostages."

Reagan's team was indeed familiar with Operation Eagle Claw, a horribly failed operation designed to rescue 52 American hostages being held by Iran. Many regarded the debacle as a major factor contributing to Carter's loss of the presidency, and a painful symbol of how far he'd let the military's preparedness decline under his tenure as Commander-in-Chief.

Operation Eagle Claw. Eight Americans killed, four injured. Not a single hostage rescued.

The moment turned somber, in remembrance of those lost, and in recognition of the challenges ahead.

The President summed it up.

"We need to do this. We can't leave Gorbachev there, because that's abandoning hope, and we never give up hope. We're the United States of America. Time to call in the cavalry."

The odds were high—but so were the stakes. Once again, the President had taken a complicated situation and presented it simply, establishing what was right, and thus what America was morally compelled to do.

The United States was back with a vengeance.

58

Norway

As anticipated, the Soviets attacked, and attempted to invade and conquer Norway.

The US and its NATO allies had been prepared for the assault, which began on a Monday evening and was over with by midweek. Despite varying levels of public support for NATO, its European troops fought with gallantry and heroism to repulse an assault on a fellow member state.

If there was ever any question as to NATO's competency and resolve, it was put to rest by the performance of so many men and women working together to stop a small ally from being crushed by an aggressive superpower.

Playing a major supporting role in Norway's defense was Great Britain, which lost several ships and planes in the battle. Despite their deployment's small size, the Danes fought with ferocity and contributed greatly, as did the Swedes — much to the surprise of nearly everyone — especially the Soviets.

The Russians had a sizable presence in Sweden, and had expected its defense forces and population to remain passive and neutral. But when the Swedes saw their country being used as a launching pad for aggression towards their peaceful Scandinavian neighbor they decided to take action.

While direct military confrontation was minimal and not officially sanctioned, Swedish civilians engaged in a number of guerilla activities such as blocking roads to hinder Soviet ground forces.

For the most part, the government (at least on a national level) remained publicly neutral until the vanquished Soviets retreated. Once the conflict was over, Stockholm ordered the Russians to leave their country, backed by a well-intentioned, but mostly toothless UN resolution.

Assaults of such magnitude as the attack on Norway are rarely a complete surprise, given logistical issues and the technological advances of modern warfare. So, in addition to ramping up Norway's defenses, the US used its advance notice to take up plans for rescuing Gorbachev.

Not only was time running out, but the Soviet move on Norway would provide the perfect diversion. All eyes would be looking to the great conquest of the west, and not to securing a single prisoner under house arrest far away in the presumably safe, and therefore largely undefended, east.

Thanks to information provided by ex-STASI agent Markus Wolf and other former East Germans, (supplemented by operatives working covertly in the Soviet Union), the US was able to learn the whereabouts of several members of Gorbachev's administration (known as the Council of Ministers), along with other key officials.

Unfortunately, only a few were good candidates for rescuing.

Some individuals were now backing Sokolov; others were simply missing. Given the limited time frame, attempting to track down lesser administration figures also held the danger of tipping off the Soviets to the grander plan, and so their rescues would have to wait until conditions improved.

Such was also the case for those known to be in Moscow or held at secure military or KGB locations. The effort required to free them and then get them out of the country was deemed just too risky for now.

Incredibly, Gorbachev, the biggest prize of all, appeared to be the easiest to grab. Under house arrest at his summer home (or *dacha*) in Crimea (Ukraine), the former world leader was now guarded by only a minor security detail.

Located far from Moscow, Gorbachev's residence was right on the water—adding the option of a marine assault. As the crow flies, Gorbachev was less than 200 miles from Turkey—and freedom.

Even closer was Georgia, or by its official name, the Georgian Soviet Socialist Republic, which shared a land border with Turkey as well as a western coastline on the Black Sea. And it was here, in western Georgia, that Gorbachev's Foreign Minister, Eduard Shevardnadze was being held under similar conditions. Making him also, as they say, "ripe for the picking."

And so the plan (code name Operation Rock 'n' Roll) was devised, then put on standby until the Soviets were sufficiently distracted.

The Soviet attack on Norway used textbook military strategy and began at just after 8pm local time in Oslo. By 5am the next morning, Gorbachev and Shevardnadze were reunited at a US base in Germany.

In order to avoid Soviet air space, the two had first been flown separately into Turkey, then west across the Mediterranean, before heading north up into Italy and Switzerland, eventually landing in Wiesbaden, Germany.

There, they would receive services such as medical care, although both men appeared in good physical shape. But for now, it was time for a joyous reunion between the two old friends and their families (who had also been rescued by the Americans).

The group was enjoying their new-found freedom — along with a hearty breakfast when Gorbachev was informed that he had a phone call.

It was President Reagan, elated to hear of the mission's success, and to learn that his old friend and partner was now safely in the West.

"How are you?" asked Reagan.

"Fine, thank you."

"Well, I hope so. But I guess we'll just have to see what the doctors say ... You know me, Mikhail: *Doveryai, no proveryai* (Trust, but verify)!"

At this the two men laughed, just like old times. Spoken in Russian, the line had become a running joke between them.

Yes, there was nothing like freedom. And if things went as planned, it wouldn't end with just Gorbachev.

59

The Mask Falls

With the arrival of summer, the Soviets were really starting to feel the heat.

Failing to take Norway had dealt them a humiliating blow, with widespread reverberations. Simultaneously, it had exposed both the incompetency of the Soviet forces while casting aside any doubts about the commitment and superiority of the NATO forces.

The unprovoked and aggressive military action against a small country like Norway also affirmed the true nature of the USSR as an empire set on expansion by any means. The promise of a continent united peacefully, respectful of individual differences was now clearly seen as just a ploy to remove the Americans from the equation, and with it, the only real obstacle to Russian conquest and domination of Western Europe.

With the mask having fallen, the Europeans awoke to the fact that Sokolov was not their friend and savior, nor was he even a man of peace and tolerance. He was a false prophet, a ruthless dictator in the tradition of his old friend and mentor Joseph Stalin.

Conversely, Reagan was now seen as a brilliant strategist who displayed restraint, and a willingness to risk American lives in defense of a small European ally. A man of his word.

Overnight, the washed-up, B-movie actor had been reborn as a classic American hero: standing tall, riding high, and willing to take on the bad guys who were intent on taking over the town.

Norway was the breaking point for Sweden, whose relations with the USSR were already cracking following the incident in Iceland. Discontent was also seeping over the border into occupied Finland, and, most amazingly, across the narrow gulf to the shores of Estonia, otherwise known as the Estonian Soviet Socialist Republic.

Freedom was in the air, and the winds were now blowing in from the west and right through the tattered Iron Curtain.

Only a few hundred miles across the North Sea from Norway was Great Britain, whose population had been bitterly divided on how to deal with the Soviets. Protests against the government had at times turned violent, as had the response from Prime Minister Thatcher, who had been forced to resort to extreme means in order to retain power and maintain social stability.

The Soviet assault on Norway changed all of that.

Here, just as Thatcher had warned, were Soviet forces in the air and seas off the British coast, intent on conquering a sovereign nation. Would Britain be next? Not as long as the Iron Lady was residing at 10 Downing Street!

As part of NATO, the United Kingdom had participated in the fight to keep Norway free, but had a paid a high price in British lives.

But what Britain lost in battle, it gained in the perspective that when it comes to war and aggression, one cannot sit passively by and watch the waters rise around it. In a nation so rich in history, so defined by conflict, the lessons couldn't be more obvious.

When Nazi Germany began its conquest of Europe, Britain, under Prime Minister Neville Chamberlain looked the other way and pursued a policy of appeasement. This only emboldened and strengthened Adolf Hitler, creating a larger problem for Chamberlain's successor, Winston Churchill. Unlike Chamberlain, Churchill opted to stand and fight— actions which not only saved the UK, but which also changed the course of the war.

With Churchill in charge, Britain waged a come-from-behind fight for its very survival. Cities were bombed relentlessly, children evacuated to the countryside, while adults huddled in underground tunnels for survival.

But the British did not surrender. They found the strength and courage to fight back; first in the defense of their island nation, then to cross the channel and take on Hitler's occupying armies on the continent. But the fight didn't end in Europe. Under Churchill, the British effort to stop Axis aggression spanned the globe, confronting the enemy wherever it had taken root.

The United Kingdom paid an immense toll for its part in World War II. When the guns finally fell silent, Britain lost roughly 700,000 soldiers, and more than 60,000 civilians. It was a huge price to pay for freedom, especially for such a small nation. (By comparison, the US total for military casualties was 416,000 troops.)

As Churchill reminded his people, "The price of greatness is responsibility."

Ironically, just as the war was ending, a liberal Labour Party government headed by Clement Atlee deposed Churchill and his conservatives.

Over the course of two meetings held in Potsdam following Germany's surrender, Atlee, and his similarly inexperienced American counterpart, Harry S Truman, gave Stalin exactly what he wanted; complete Soviet control of Eastern Europe.

Stalin, who had been in power since the early 1920s, couldn't believe his good fortune. The Soviet empire would now extend all the way west so as to include a sizable chunk of Germany.

But now, 44 years after the end of World War II, the Russians had been deposed, and the once divided Germans were working in unison to formally reunite as a free and democratic state.

Thanks to Ronald Reagan, the Iron Curtain had been pushed back; changing not just physical borders, but the very idea of the invincibility and permanence of the Soviet empire.

A free and unified Germany quickly became a magnet for Polish and Czechoslovakian neighbors seeking freedom. Because all three nations had been members of the Eastern Bloc, border controls were neither developed nor very sophisticated, and as a result, a large number of refugees began to stream westward into the former GDR.

Many were just average persons, seeking to escape totalitarianism. But also included with the influx were military personnel, and those who were abandoning positions in the government and intelligence services.

These "defectors" were of special interest, and what they revealed was stunning news: namely, that the USSR was already collapsing from within.

Poles and Czechs affirmed widespread public unrest within their own countries, and a lack of support for another war in Europe. The populations were already exhausted by the long war in Afghanistan (now in its tenth year), and had no interest in taking on their "brothers" in the West.

Attempts to demonize President Reagan had only backfired, who was now regarded by many as an almost a mystical figure sent to save them.

Most were angry about the coup that took out Gorbachev. They had been supportive of his policies, whether towards liberalization, or for better relations with the West and a peaceful resolution to the Cold War.

In short, they hated Sokolov, hated Russian domination, and would not follow orders to fight as part of the Warsaw Pact.

Russia's eastern satellites were wobbling out of orbit.

According to those who travelled frequently to Moscow, similar sentiments were present even in the Russian people themselves. As with South Africa, there was a sense of the ground shifting and crumbling, as the ruling minority became increasingly dependent on brute force in order to maintain its hold on power.

Perhaps the biggest revelation concerned the leadership of the USSR, which was described as fragmented and disorganized. Sokolov was said to be presiding over a fractured administration, and had himself been subject to at least one violent coup attempt.

No, things were not going well in the Soviet Union; but this was not necessarily a good thing. When a nation is disintegrating it can create a very dangerous situation, especially if it is large and powerful and filled with ruthless opportunists.

Just something else for Reagan to contend with; the USSR collapsing into civil war, if not all-out anarchy, leaving an opening for some despot who would likely be even more dangerous than Sokolov.

But as one administration was collapsing, another was rising to take its place.

With encouragement and backing from President Reagan and the Americans, Gorbachev and his fellow Soviet expats were actively working towards establishing a government-in-exile, based in Switzerland. Once in place, news of its formation and claim to legitimacy would be transmitted into the nations of the Eastern Bloc—and even Russia itself.

Hope was on the horizon.

The liberation of East Germany, and revitalized connections with the neighboring nations of Poland and Czechoslovakia had created many fresh opportunities for carrying the news back across the Iron Curtain.

Similarly, Moscow was frustrated by a lack of resolve by the Poles and Czechs to stem the flow of their citizens to the West. News and information was now flowing both ways across the border.

But what angered them the most was Gorbachev.

Naturally, the US denied any role in the rescue operation, which had gone off without a hitch.

As planned, the Americans had zipped in, and zipped out, rescuing Gorbachev, Shevardnadze, and their families, then getting them to safety before Moscow even knew they were gone. The elite American teams had practiced for missions like this in the past, and were careful to avoid leaving any telltale traces behind that would provide the Soviets with definitive proof of US involvement.

In despite of these precautions, the Soviets knew who was responsible, and they didn't require any physical proof in order to justify their revenge.

It was time to teach America a lesson.

60

Alaska

The Soviets were furious about Gorbachev. Furious they hadn't executed him when they had the chance, furious that the Americans had penetrated their security parameters, furious about what he, as a free man, might now say or do.

The rescue mission had resulted in the loss of 19 Soviet lives. Some casualties were to be expected, but also something the Americans had taken great pains to avoid.

The persons assigned to guarding Gorbachev and Shevardnadze weren't really the enemy; they were just low-level personnel, likely conscripted and then assigned this duty with no say or interest in the matter whatsoever.

But such is the nature of warfare, and with it a cost that can only be measured in lost lives and sorrow. Every death has ripples.

It made no difference to Reagan that these were Soviets who were killed; when he heard of the news that eleven people had died for simply doing their duty the President said a small prayer for their souls. This was Reagan's way. While he might not understand the motivations of his opponents, he was above all a man of deep faith who tried hard to follow God's commandment for empathy, compassion, and forgiveness.

In fact, Reagan even prayed on behalf of his would-be assassin, John Hinckley, Jr.

Following a speech at the Washington Hilton, Hinckley opened fire on the President hitting him and severely wounding his friend and Press Secretary Jim Brady. Also injured in the hail of "Devastator" bullets were a District Patrolman and a member of the Secret Service detail.

While waiting in the Emergency Room, the President was deeply troubled at the sight of Brady, who was wheeled past him, still bleeding profusely from a head wound. Realizing the seriousness of the situation, Reagan immediately said a prayer for Brady, and for all the others who had also been injured or affected by the attack.

But then, as he sat suffering in pain and waiting for medical care,

Reagan experienced a truly Christ-inspired epiphany; "I couldn't ask God to heal Jim and the others at the same time as feeling hatred for the man who shot us." And so the President said a second prayer, in which he asked God to help heal the mind of the man so troubled and ill as to be driven to commit such heinous acts.

For Ronald Reagan, all lives were sacred.

Also upsetting was the likelihood that those Soviets died without ever coming to know God. As an officially atheistic nation, religion was not welcome in the Soviet Union, and no doubt those selected for service would have been tightly screened to avoid persons of faith. Reagan asked for the Lord to show mercy for these innocent victims who died without ever experiencing His love and the promise of salvation.

Sadly, the 19 lives lost during the rescue attempt were just the beginning, as the Kremlin itself set out upon a retaliatory rampage. Nearly three-dozen others were promptly executed for charges ranging from incompetency to cowardice and treason. Scores more received harsh prison sentences, or were dealt with in other ways, despite no direct evidence of involvement or failure on their part.

The Soviets decided the Americans should also pay a price, and set out to exact revenge. Some targets were small (an embassy bombing in Mexico), while others displayed an ugliness and contempt for all life, including nature.

Once again, the Russians decided to strike at Alaska. But unlike their previous incursion, this would only involve a small commando team that could slip in and slip out, undetected. Such an attack, mirroring the covert approach used by the Americans to free Gorbachev and Shevardnadze, was designed to show the US that two could play this game. But whereas the US would use the cover of the Black Sea to stage their operation, the Soviets would seek to cover the sea in black, as their target was an unprotected oil-laden supertanker.

After filling up with crude oil at Alaska's Prudhoe Bay, the nearly thousand foot ship set sail south towards the refineries in Long Beach, California. Shortly after midnight on the 24th of July, while plying its way through the quiet channels of Prince William Sound, the hull of the Exxon *Valdez* was ripped open by a massive explosion which caused it to begin spilling millions of gallons of oil into the pristine waters of Alaska.

Local efforts to contain the damage were quickly overwhelmed by the magnitude of the crisis. Almost immediately, a huge dark slick began to spread outwards from the ship, which was now resting partially on its side after having run aground on a reef.

Reagan, briefed on the situation the next morning was outraged. He cursed, then threw his reading glasses down hard, breaking them instantly.

"Damn it!"

He paused for just a moment, eyes closed to regain his composure.

In addition to the horrific waste at a time when America needed every last drop of oil it could secure, the assault on the environment represented a new and despicable low.

Reagan saw nature as God's creation, to be used and protected by Man. In fact, Reagan saw God's presence in nature itself, and a desecration of such a pristine wilderness area sickened him.

Pushing aside all other items on his plate, the President made the unfolding environmental disaster his top priority. This was a race against time, and something needed to be done. Something major. Something only a President could authorize and implement. But what?

"Options?" demanded the President of his cabinet.

Most, including EPA Director Lee Thomas advocated a salvage and cleanup operation. Thomas noted that it was not a perfect solution, and that the spreading oil would cause damage lasting decades.

"And who pays for that?" asked the President. "Exxon?"

"Unlikely," said Thomas.

Attorney General Bork confirmed this, explaining that Exxon would be liable for some costs, but given the nature of the attack—as an act of terrorism—the federal government would be responsible for most of the costs of cleanup, and for other damages to the affected communities and businesses.

"As a ballpark figure, we could be looking at something in the range of … at least a billion dollars," said Thomas.

Reagan's face was red, his lips pursed.

Defense Secretary Powell spoke up.

"Granted, I'm not a scientist or an economist, but it seems to me that we're paying for this oil one way or the other—and the cost of cleaning it up will be many times greater than the actual dollar value of the oil itself."

Almost in unison, the Secretaries of Energy, Commerce, Treasury, and the Environment nodded in agreement of Powell's assessment.

"It has also been my experience that oil floats on water, and unlike water, it's highly flammable ..."

Reagan immediately sensed where this was going, and took Powell's lead, "So why can't we just light it up?"

Powell smiled, and Reagan nodded approvingly in his direction.

"Granted, there would still be damage to the environment, but it would stop the oil from spreading ... from covering the rocks and beaches. I think it would save a lot of wildlife; and it would be quick. But we'd also lose the ship and any oil still in the hull," Powell added.

"The ship already looks to be heavily damaged by the blast," stated Navy Secretary William Ball. "I don't think there's much left to salvage. I agree with Secretary Powell. This is something we could do in short order—something we're trained to do. We have people in Alaska ready to go."

The group paused to consider this option. Reagan assigned a quick— *emphasis on quick*—feasibility study and plan for implementation.

"This thing is leaking at a horrific rate, and we need to do something sooner than later," the President said firmly. "I want the calculations to-day—by one o'clock."

When the group returned from lunch the President was presented with their findings. The plan seemed promising, but there was no consensus on whether it would succeed.

While the group had sought answers in chemistry and calculations, Reagan had turned to prayer, asking God for guidance.

"Let's do this," and with that note of approval, the fuse was lit.

The resulting explosion was seen and felt for miles, but when it was over nearly all the oil had been burned away.

This had been a major gamble, but once again the President had trusted his gut and acted decisively. While it was not a perfect solution, it did turn out to be the best possible one given the circumstances.

Sometimes life is like that: no good choices, and doing nothing is the worst option of all.

61

Won't You Please
Come to Chicago?

The situation with the Exxon *Valdez* had upset the President more than he thought it would. When he returned to his quarters for the night he felt unusually tired and restless.

His daily ritual of a concentrated workout, followed by showering and supper with Mrs Reagan did little to relax him. Still feeling tense and somewhat anxious, he decided to put aside his after-hours official duties that usually kept him busy until bedtime.

His heart just wasn't in it. Nor was any of this critical. It was just what he did.

The President sat at his desk and surveyed the well-organized stacks of papers that had been left for him. He removed his "readers" and rubbed his face and eyes.

The room was quiet, save for the ticking of a nearby clock.

He was now past the six-month point in his third term, and by all measures—given the circumstances—things were going reasonably well. Still, he had never imagined serving a third term, much less under these conditions.

Reagan had always envisioned himself as a revolutionary; not a war president. But destiny had dealt him a different set of cards, and so he had played his hand to the best of his ability.

There was no guidebook. Instead, he was forced to make it up as he went along, trusting his instincts. He was doing the best he could, but he was also feeling the strain of being pulled in a million different directions. Although supported by family, friends, and a first-rate dream team, ultimately everything was his responsibility.

He accepted this burden willingly. The war, and all the reverberations caused by a situation of such enormity had taken precedent over everything else. Reagan understood that. Keeping America safe would always be his top priority.

But what of the other promises he had made? The pledges to transform America and restore conservative values to government? Was he doing all that he could?

No.

The President realized the people had put their faith in him, and that there were certain things that only he could do. Issues, that if they were to succeed, would require his personal involvement.

Some were financial: the need for a balanced budget, and with it, an end to deficits that mortgaged the nation's future. Taking on the irresponsible spenders would not be easy, but he had promised to lead the fight.

Other issues centered on returning the nation to its Judeo-Christian moral roots, so that America might truly live up to its promise as a shining city on a hill, worthy of God's blessings. In support of this were constitutional amendments to ban abortion and return voluntary prayer to the nation's schools.

The school prayer proposal he had personally drafted and submitted to Congress last November was … ? Hmmm … Bogged down in some committee? But which committee? Even the President himself wasn't sure of its status.

He did know that the amendment had its critics. Well-funded lobbyists and special interest groups determined to either directly kill the amendment, or let it wither away by attrition.

So far the opposition was winning. Without his personal attention, the issue had dropped completely off the radar, with both lawmakers and the media.

But what about the people? This was something they had supported by an overwhelming majority. Something they had *hired* him to do. So far they were being patient. They were trusting him.

Now was the time to reward that trust and patience with action.

The office clock began to chime, signifying the start of a new hour. The President glanced at his watch, affirming it was in sync. It was.

Ronald Reagan understood the preciousness of time. He accepted the underlying truth of the popular adage postulating that how one chooses to spend one's days ultimately adds up to how one spends one's life. Or in his case, one's presidency.

So, at that moment, as the clock finished striking eight, the President decided he must recommit himself to the domestic agenda. Push some lesser matters to the side and re-prioritize. First thing tomorrow morning he would make his wishes known to the staff that worked on his schedule.

He would make it clear that the nation's defense would stay his number one priority, and that as Commander-in-Chief he would retain responsibility for all key decisions. But, feeling comfortable with how Secretary Powell and the Joint Chiefs were handling things, he would begin delegating more authority to them for managing day-to-day operations.

Other items, such as entertaining minor heads of state, photo ops passed off as meetings and other non-essential busywork, would need to be scaled back. Vice President Meese could take up more of the slack, as well.

Looking at his schedule, the President noted that he was slated to record a video message for an upcoming event in Chicago. But as he read through the details, he decided then and there, that this was something he wanted to attend personally.

The event was a non-denominational celebration of the power and importance of prayer. Featured speakers included exiles from the Soviet Union who would talk about the role that prayer had played in their own lives, and the lack of religious freedom in the USSR.

Christians, Jews, Muslims—all under one roof, united in body and spirit.

The event was scheduled for a Sunday, and the travel time would not be that great. His ten-minute speech for the video message was already written, but it could easily be expanded by rolling in some of the material he had already used previously at the National Prayer Breakfast back in February.

Reagan's mind was racing, as he mapped out what needed to be done.

"Yep," thought the President, "I'm going to do this, even though I'm sure Nancy won't like it."

He was correct: *Nancy did not like it.*

Not because she didn't support the cause, but because she worried about his safety—especially if it involved a road trip.

Every day the President received threats, although most were not credible. Rather than argue against leaving Washington (due to security issues), Nancy tried to use reverse psychology, making a case for sending along a video that could be reshown again and again — as had been the original plan.

Reagan was ready for this argument, noting that if he were there in person, they could film his appearance and reshow that instead.

Nancy pretended to pout, then she reminded him that it being a Sunday, he'd miss one of his favorite TV shows, *Murder, She Wrote*.

To which her husband pointed out that the show was in re-runs for the summer, so he wouldn't be missing anything. Score one for Ronnie.

And so it went, back and forth — but Nancy knew her husband, and knew that once he put his mind to something there was no stopping him. He could be incredibly stubborn *and* charming — and that was an unbeatable combination that could wear down anyone — and eventually it did.

The next day the President met with his schedulers and provided them with the grand overview of the changes he wanted to make. Then, he turned from the macro to the micro.

"And tell the folks in Chicago that I will be honored to attend."

And so it was to be.

The trip out to Chicago was as expected: quick and uneventful. The President's speech went well, and he felt he was once again back on track in regards to bringing the issue of prayer back into the national dialogue.

It was a rare public appearance, and all the major media were present. Despite the topic — not one popular with the liberal media — Reagan was optimistic that his appearance would be well covered, thereby spotlighting the issue, and hopefully reviving momentum for his amendment.

After meeting with other participants and organizers, the President was still on schedule to be back home, and in bed at the White House before midnight.

On that evening of Sunday, August 6, the weather in Chicago was typically warm and humid — although DC would not be much better. Thankfully the President's limousine and Air Force One both had excellent air conditioning.

As the motorcade rounded the corner *en route* to the airport it was hit by a spray of bullets that seemed to come from every direction, which were then followed by a series of explosions.

62

Waking Up

The President was aware of someone holding his hand, and when he opened his eyes he saw it was Nancy. As his eyes slowly focused, he saw a circle of other familiar faces gathered around his bedside.

There was Vice President Meese, Chief of Staff Baker, Deputy Chief of Staff Deaver, Secretary of State Schultz, NSA Director McFarlane, Defense Secretary Powell, and his personal physician Dr Hutton.

Reagan struggled to speak ... "There's no place like home," he said. And then he repeated it again, two more times.

"There's no place like home, there's no place like home ..."

Nancy gasped, and the faces around him looked shocked, then deeply troubled. The President seemed utterly disconnected from reality. Confused. Dreamily repeating the same phrase over and over.

Reagan smiled broadly, his eyes twinkling with mirth, "Oh come on, now! I thought everyone had seen *The Wizard of Oz!*"

Glancing at Secretary Schultz, Reagan asked, "Seriously George, hasn't anyone ever told you that you're a dead ringer for the Cowardly Lion? You know, I actually worked with Burt Lahr once ... He was a real nice fella ..."

Once again, the President's sense of humor had broken the tension, and the hospital room erupted with laughter.

Reagan touched his bandaged head and winced. "This is why I don't drink; I can't imagine what it's like to wake up with this kind of headache, or worse yet, not remembering what I did the night before ... So tell me, did I embarrass myself at the party?"

Nancy was overcome by emotion and her eyes were filled with tears. For a time, she thought she would never have another moment like this again. But now she had her husband back.

"Welcome back, my love," she whispered, squeezing his hand tightly.

"It's good to be back. But where was I?"

The President had no recollection of recent events. The last thing he could remember was getting into the limousine after his speech and asking his driver about the result of that day's baseball game between the San Francisco Giants and Houston Astros.

The Giants had lost that game 3-2—almost ten days ago.

The attempt on the President's life had resulted in a traumatic brain injury, requiring that he be placed in a chemically-induced coma to facilitate the healing process. Luckily he had not required brain surgery, but how soon he would be able to return to his duties was yet to be determined. At this point, no one could be sure of his exact condition and fitness, and thereby his ability to take on the demands of being president.

Immediately following news of the attack, and in accordance with the Constitution, Vice President Meese had assumed the presidency, and was then promptly tested by a series of small exchanges with the Soviets.

Meese had served well as the President's "understudy," but now Reagan was anxious to get back to work. Worn down by his persistence and impressed by his vitality, the medical team soon signed off on his limited return to duty, with certain qualifiers relating to workload and rest periods.

The road back wasn't as easy as Reagan had hoped, nor as difficult as others thought it might be.

But somehow he rose to the occasion, and was delighted to receive a phone call from actor Arnold Schwarzenegger who called Reagan "the real Terminator!" Reagan laughed at the compliment, noting that being an indestructible fighting machine represented a major upgrade from simply being just the "Teflon President."

The two men laughed, and Reagan asked Schwarzenegger if had ever considered a career in politics. "Or would going from Mr Universe to just Governor of California seem like too much of a drop in status?"

Schwarzenegger said he wanted to keep all his options open. "Right now, I'm still enjoying Hollywood. But if my career ever gets to the point of playing opposite a chimp named Bonzo, I might just consider running for office."

Again, the two men laughed as the good-natured banter continued.

But not every day offered such light moments, as the President both struggled hard against his disabilities, and to keep the depth of his injuries private. He wanted no sympathy or special considerations. All he wanted was a chance to continue serving in the role that God had chosen for him.

The assassination attempt had slowed him, but it hadn't stopped him. It was time to continue the fight.

Perhaps in recognition of his heroic struggle, Congress passed the Americans With Disabilities Act by a huge majority, and Reagan immediately signed it into law.

✳ 63 ✳

The Soviet Disunion

A government-in-exile headed by Mikhail Gorbachev was officially launched on Sunday, September 9, 1990. Based at a secret location in the Swiss Alps, Gorbachev used the opportunity to make a passionate speech condemning the illegality of the Sokolov regime, and to denounce its aggressive actions.

This was not a message Moscow wanted shared, but Gorbachev's speech quickly made it into the USSR via direct live broadcast, copies smuggled in on cassette tapes, and printed transcripts. As expected, it had an immediate and jarring effect.

News of Gorbachev's escape had been kept a secret, so proof that he was alive and safe was a cause for great celebration by the people.

In short order, nations around the world (led by the United States), officially recognized the new government as the legitimate political representation of the USSR, and Gorbachev as its official and legal head of state.

Politically, the move had tremendous ramifications in the Eastern Bloc, where nations like Poland and Czechoslovakia had themselves both operated governments-in-exile during the period of Nazi occupation. Likewise, Georgia and Ukraine had also formed similar political bodies to resist the original wave of Soviet subjugations in the 1920s.

Most recently, in 1953, the Estonians had formed a government-in-exile based in Sweden to counter that nation's annexation into the USSR.

Things were definitely not going well for the Russians.

Still dazed from a string of defeats, the leadership in Moscow was said to be in a state of stunned disbelief. Not only had they been unable to conquer a small neighboring nation like Norway, but now they were in retreat all across the continent, from Sweden to Greece. Perhaps most humiliating of all was East Germany, which was not just lost, but was now formally aligned with the enemy.

Doubts about both Russian military competency and the commitment of the Warsaw Pact forces meant that any further conquests were put on hold. And now, Gorbachev was spreading dissent by offering a genuine alternative to what was viewed by most people — including the citizens of the USSR — as Sokolov's illegal government.

For the Soviet people, and the world community, Gorbachev represented hope: an experienced leader who was ready to step in and provide a stable transition.

Here was a way to make things right again. To put the USSR back on the path to peace and progress, and to remove the threat of an all-out war between the superpowers that threatened all life on Earth.

As things continued to crumble internally, a few additional former members of Gorbachev's administration managed to escape and reunite with him in Switzerland — but only after careful vetting by a coalition of American and European forces entrusted with his security.

These precautions were necessary and the fears well-founded, as at least one member was discovered to be a double agent sent to kill Gorbachev and the others.

With the conquest of the continent now on ice, Sokolov turned his attention to crushing dissent within his administration, and to the protests spreading across the entire Soviet Union. News of purges and attempted coups indicated a government with deep problems at home and abroad.

The attempt to assassinate Reagan in Chicago had backfired horribly. Not only had the 78-year-old President survived, but he now seemed invincible — almost super-human. He became both a martyr and a hero, and even those in Sokolov's regime were in awe of a man who now seemed unstoppable.

But, as head of the official Soviet opposition, Gorbachev now replaced Reagan as the number one target for assassination in the world.

Killing Gorbachev would no doubt make him a martyr, but it would also end the political challenge he represented, as there was no one else ready to step in and fill his shoes.

As the hot war chilled, the Soviets turned to other battlefields. They were now fighting a war for the hearts and minds of their own people.

To counter domestic dissent, the KGB recommended initiating a series of actions designed to inspire patriotism in the Soviet people, which it believed would translate into support for the government.

What about an attack on someone even more beloved than Gorbachev?

Especially, if it could be "proven" to be the work of the Americans?

A short list of prominent Soviet citizens was drawn up. All were actual heroes; cosmonauts and Olympians—generally regarded as non-political symbols of national pride. Most were apolitical, although each had regularly been used by the state for propaganda purposes.

Near the top of everyone's list was Vladimir Shatalov, the cosmonaut who in 1969 commanded the first successful space docking—beating the Americans (and Apollo 9) by two months. A bona fide national hero across the USSR, the 62-year-old Shatalov was currently serving as Director of the Cosmonaut Training Center—and was deemed expendable.

Another figure under consideration was Boris Lagutin, who won medals—including two golds—for boxing in three separate Olympics.

Dispensable—and easier to hit than Shatalov. The list grew, along with the desperation.

A military victory by a reliable ally would also serve to humiliate the US, and show that America was not invincible. This would also help to affirm global Soviet solidarity.

In the Philippines, it wouldn't take much for an already powerful Marxist guerilla army to cause some real problems for one of America's leading regional allies. The US maintained a considerable military presence on the island nation, now ruled by the political novice and self-proclaimed "plain housewife" Corazon Acquino.

Acquino, in power for just three years, lacked the ruthlessness of her predecessor Ferdinand Marcos. Although a huge recipient of US military aide, the Soviets sensed an opportunity, relishing the idea of luring the Americans into another long war in Southeast Asia.

Also in the neighborhood was longtime ally North Korea.

In many ways, the Soviet Union gave birth to North Korea, having occupied the northern portion of the Korean peninsula from the end of World War II until 1950—the period during which the Democratic People's Republic of Korea was founded.

As a result of the peninsula's division, a civil war—the Korean War—began, with more than 25,000 Russians fighting in support of their North Korean allies.

In the decades since armistice was declared, North Korea had developed an impressive military, with the ability (and stated intent) of causing some real damage. They had already done much in support of Sokolov, and were anxious to do more, especially if it involved inflicting pain on the United States.

Latin America?

Granted, Cuba had failed on Panama, but maybe Castro would really step up the effort—especially if he knew there was something in it for him.

Sokolov had difficulty grasping how killing off a cosmonaut would do much to unite the nation. And even if it did, who wanted a nation of martyrs?

If the Americans could slip into Russia and assassinate a national hero, then no one would feel safe.

"*Nyet!*" screamed Sokolov, waving his pistol. "Why show our vulnerability? We need to show that it is the Americans who are weak and vulnerable—not us!"

"Idiots" Sokolov thought to himself as he looked around the table. Many of the faces were new, unfamiliar replacements for those who had been purged or who had already disappeared for one reason or another.

Secretary Sokolov felt like a school teacher addressing a room full of children and he wasn't amused by their childlike behaviors; the fidgeting, the looking at the clock, the little giggles, whispers and gestures they didn't think he noticed.

He just shook his head, and spoke with the voice of experience.

"We need a bold move to show everyone how weak America is. This will unify the Soviet people, fill their hearts with courage and pride, and break the Americans once and for all!

"We must hit them hard. Hard! Where it hurts. They are cowards, and it is time … for them to *burn!* BURN!"

The General Secretary's rant was met with blank stares and awkward glances, but no one dared contradict him. As fortunes soured, Sokolov began to engage in such rants with increasing frequency, but luckily nothing ever came from them.

Still, this time he seemed especially delusional and agitated. Faces were frozen, no one was quite sure what to do.

Burn? Was Sokolov suggesting a nuclear strike?

The old military commander dismissed his lackeys, cursing them as they exited the room.

Once out of his sight, the group went into overdrive. Launching missiles meant Mutually Assured Destruction. Something needed to be done, and soon.

Alone, Sokolov just shook his head and reached for the phone.

It was just after 4PM in Moscow, which would make it ... ? Sokolov wasn't sure what time it would be in Havana. Who cares? The Cubans worked for him, and were expected to be on call 24/7.

64

Red Dawn

Although it was morning in the New World, Castro sounded tired as he answered the phone. It was Secretary Sokolov calling to personally share his plan for the next Great Leap in the worldwide People's Revolution.

In a nutshell, the plan entailed the attack, invasion, and occupation of the United States using traditional military forces.

Castro's eyebrows shot up in surprise, but he held his silence as Sokolov laid in the broad strokes of a plan to hit America from three sides at once in a massive surprise attack.

Soviet forces would invade the northeast, taking everything from Maine to Virginia—including Washington DC.

Meanwhile, the North Koreans would attack the west coast—all the way from the border with Canada in the north to the border with Mexico in the south—and then push inland to the Rockies.

Castro couldn't believe what he was hearing: The west coast was a huge area with numerous military bases and tens of millions of well-armed citizens. The Koreans have no real navy or air force to speak of—how could they possibly …?

"But …" began Castro, only to be interrupted by Sokolov, anxious to continue detailing his plan to crush, then rebuild a liberated America.

Cubans would spearhead an attack up from the Gulf Coast, stretching from Florida to Texas, then fanning out as they advanced to the north and west, up into the heartland and the across southwest.

The Cuban troops would be reinforced by Nicaraguans. "I will trust *you* to manage the Sandinistas," said Sokolov, chuckling. "They are fierce fighters, ready to die for the cause—but not as disciplined as yours, nor do they speak good Russian."

Following closely behind the Latin contingent would be Jamaicans and Angolans, entrusted with launching a race war in the Old South, then pushing north towards the upper Midwest and states such as Illinois, Ohio and Michigan, where they would rally their black brothers and sisters to rise up and shake off the chains of their white oppressors and the inherent racism of the capitalist system.

Castro's brow furrowed as he brought to mind an image of the United States, and the vast amount of territory being discussed. Was Secretary Sokolov joking with him? Was he drunk? Or was this some kind of loyalty test?

Once the upper Midwest was brought under submission, Soviets would take over the factories and other assets, freeing the Jamaicans, Angolans and "liberated" American blacks to return to the warmer climes of the south, where they might enjoy the simple life as peasant farmers.

The Russians would "take back" Alaska, and wanted Hawaii, along with most of the coastal west—leaving the arid interior—up to the mountains—for the Koreans to manage, supported by "some Syrians and Libyans" who were already adapted to living in barren deserts.

"What to do about Canada, a role for the Vietnamese and others … these are minor concerns for now. All options remain open!" exclaimed Sokolov.

Castro said nothing, and the conversation paused awkwardly, prompting the old Russian to personally offer him the prize of Florida, along with most of Spanish-speaking parts of the southwest—except for Texas. As a fan of the TV show *Dallas*—and in particular its star character, JR Ewing—Sokolov wanted the Lone Star state for himself.

Rather than reference the difficulties currently being experienced with the status of the Worldwide People's Revolution in El Salvador and Nicaragua—just two small countries in Central America—Castro listened politely, but decided not to ask any questions.

As one quite familiar with US geography and its strengths, the plan, at least in its present incarnation, didn't stand a chance. Still, Castro thought it best if Sokolov heard this from his generals, rather than from him.

The Panamanian fiasco was still fresh in Castro's mind. But what really drew his ire was the fact that most of the work of attacking the United States was being assigned to Moscow's "partners," with the spoils going to the Soviets.

Sokolov had no set date for the attack, as he would still need to work out the logistics. Details aside, he was glad to have Castro on board, confiding that many within his own administration seem to lack both courage and vision.

President Castro placed the phone back in its cradle and exhaled a thick cloud of cigar smoke, watching with amusement at how quickly it dissipated in the breeze.

Turning and turning in the widening gyre
The falcon cannot hear the falconer;
Things fall apart; the centre cannot hold;
Mere anarchy is loosed upon the world,
The blood-dimmed tide is loosed, and everywhere
The ceremony of innocence is drowned;
The best lack all conviction, while the worst
Are full of passionate intensity.

— WB Yeats
The Second Coming
1919

65

Victory Parades
from Moscow to Managua

As October faded into November, a fragile peace was holding.

The great conquest of the United States by the combined forces of the USSR, Cuba, Jamaica, North Korea, and select invited guests was apparently on hold.

Meanwhile, the Soviets were attempting to stir up patriotic fervor at home for the official state holiday commemorating the Great October Socialist Revolution, held each year on the seventh of November.

Yes, November.

When the day came to publicly celebrate the holiday, turnout and participation was virtually nonexistent by the common people, who stayed home, too "ill" to attend.

Those who did turn out were mostly persons with connections to the state: party officials, members of the armed forces, pickpockets, and so forth. In several instances, parades were cancelled when not enough people showed up to march. In others (as in those featuring long columns of tightly choreographed troops), the participants frequently outnumbered the spectators.

In accordance with tradition, the government insisted that the show must go on. Crowds in Red Square were down significantly, but reinforced by prisoners brought in to shore things up for those watching around the world on television. In smaller cities, attendance was way off, and in Leningrad, more than half the audience seemed to be comprised of pensioners too old to care, and children too young to know better.

Later that week in the US, President Reagan addressed the largest crowd ever gathered for a Veterans Day event in the nation's capital. Then, much to everyone's surprise, he welcomed Secretary Gorbachev to the stage, who thanked the American military for its ongoing efforts to liberate the Soviet people.

But the celebratory feeling would be short-lived. Exactly a week later on Saturday, November 18, the President received a 5am call summoning him to yet another early-morning emergency meeting.

After a quick breakfast with real coffee (in lieu of his usual Sanka decaf), President Reagan met with his core cabinet, along with representatives from the military and intelligence services.

The reason for the meeting was concern over a buildup of Nicaraguan troops on the border with Honduras, suggesting an impending invasion.

Southwestern Honduras had long been a hot spot for incursions by both the Nicaraguan Sandinistas and by Marxist guerillas from El Salvador. It was an area with a long history of conflict, amplified by contrasting political systems and agendas in addition to the usual territorial disputes.

Honduras had also fought an actual border war with El Salvador just 20 years earlier, but for now, at least on official governmental levels, the two neighboring states were at peace, and united in confronting their own Marxist rebellions—both of which were largely funded from abroad.

Because of its relatively small size and limited defensive capabilities, the Hondurans (like the Salvadorans) had turned to the United States for help, and the Americans provided limited support with both troops and training. While never completely eradicating the rebels, American assistance provided a critical lifeline for the democratically-elected government of the Honduras.

But now, it looked as if the country was in danger of being overrun by a large, well-organized, professional fighting force from abroad.

Under Daniel Ortega's Sandinistas, the Nicaraguan military had been scaling up for some time, with a significant boost occurring in anticipation of Panama's conversion to socialism under Noriega. Presumably, with Marxist states on both sides, Nicaraguan forces would expand southward into Costa Rica, where they would meet up with their socialist brothers from Panama to form a chain of three contiguous communist states.

But when the Panama plan imploded with Comrade Noriega's demise, Nicaragua's Sandinistas needed someone else to liberate, and their relatively defenseless neighbor, independent from Spain since 1821, appeared to fit the bill.

Slightly smaller in size, but with a marginally larger population,

Honduras would seem to represent a bit too much for the Nicaraguans to bite off—if it hadn't been for Managua's overwhelming military superiority. By that matrix they had the Hondurans beaten on every count, and they now seemed intent upon proving it.

With no warning, the Nicaraguans had begun mobilizing everything they had starting sometime Friday morning and moving it towards the border with Honduras. The Hondurans panicked, and responded accordingly, scrambling to reinforce the border with everything they had—which was not much. The best weapon in their arsenal was the telephone, which they used to make an emergency call for US assistance.

But why now?

If Nicaragua were to conquer Honduras it would put the Sandinistas in a better position to support neighboring El Salvador's Marxist guerillas. While the expansion of communism in Europe might temporarily be on hold, it wouldn't take much to topple the fragile new Salvadoran government led by President Alfredo Cristiani.

Was there a connection to Moscow? Possibly, although most signs pointed to Cuba.

While the Soviets had once looked to their surrogates to distract the US while they advanced on the Old World, Castro was now using the American preoccupation with the USSR to advance his own expansionist dreams in the New World.

Reagan sat listening to his advisors. Slowly he began to speak, leaning forward towards the desk, his right thumb pressed against his temple, his fingers on his forehead at the hairline.

The look in his eyes suggested he was elsewhere. Someplace where he could see the big picture forming as pieces were added and removed from the puzzle set out for him to solve.

"Taking out the Nicaraguan military would be a setback for the Sandinistas—and a boost for the Contras.

"It would help our relations with Honduras, and underscore US support for democracy in Latin America. It would also curtail Nicaragua's efforts supporting the rebels in El Salvador. That border region with Honduras is already a problem … full of holes. With Nicaragua occupying the region, the border would become non-existent, giving the guerillas safe haven in Honduras … El Salvador wouldn't have a chance."

The President scowled as he mulled over the consequences.

"The Hondurans can't do this on their own; it'll be like when Hitler took Poland ... Horses against tanks. Mexico won't get involved; diplomacy will be too late ... sanctions would be useless. No, it's up to us.

"Now the downside is that any action we take is going to tick off the Cubans and the Russians—but I'm not really too worried about that at this point. If my memory serves me correctly, I don't think we received a Christmas card from either Moscow or Havana last year, and so they're off my list for now."

"Actually we did get one from Moscow," noted Chief of Staff Baker, "but because it was ticking we just forwarded it along to the bomb disposal guys."

Reagan laughed.

"Yes—how could I forget? Well, let's maybe treat them to a surprise of our own. Gentlemen, might this be a good opportunity to introduce the B-2?"

The military contingent quickly exchanged glances, then all eyes turned to the head of the air force, for his take on the matter. The B-2, also known as the Stealth bomber, had only recently made its maiden flight a few months earlier. Although it had performed admirably, it was untried in actual combat.

Reagan believed that a bombing mission to Nicaragua would be a great opportunity to field test it, especially given the relatively close distance and the fact that it would only be traveling through friendly skies.

"Plus, I want the news to get back to Moscow ... That we have this incredible new invisible plane. Granted, they probably already know all about it, but this will give them a demonstration of what it can do. Of course, if they want a personal demonstration, they know what they need to do in order to get one."

And with that, the plan was launched.

The B-2 Spirit squadron took off from Edwards Air Force Base in California at sunset. It was joined in flight by a contingent of support craft, and shadowed by other US forces including those from the navy which were positioned off the shared Pacific coastline that linked El Salvador, Honduras, and Nicaragua.

The B-2 performed with stunning precision and force, utterly decimating the would-be invaders from Nicaragua. The speed of the attack left few units able to escape. The once feared and mighty military of the Sandinistas was history.

As expected, news traveled fast. When the B-2s turned back towards home, it was now early morning in Moscow, and no one thought it would be a good idea to wake up Sokolov.

They were right.

66

Thanksgiving at Heaven's Ranch

In the face of growing internal problems, the Soviets were forced to make a number of deep changes to the positioning of their armed forces. Troops once configured offensively were now being deployed elsewhere, indicating a defensive strategy against both an invasion from (or coming through) their Warsaw Pact neighbors, and internally as a safeguard against a domestic uprising.

Dreams of a united Europe ruled by Moscow had long been scrapped. As for now, the USSR was focused on just keeping its own socialist union intact.

We have met the enemy, and it is us.

As the Russian bear hibernated, the free world began to breathe a little easier. Economic growth, resulting from the President's reforms had been modest, but solid. The US economy was now benefitting from both the compounding effect of Reagan's economic policies and greater global stability.

In fact, things were looking quiet enough so as to permit the Reagans a short trip out to their ranch in California for Thanksgiving. The trip would serve as a belated 40th anniversary celebration of sorts, commemorating the date when Ron and Nancy first met on November 15, 1949.

Located in the Santa Ynez Mountains near Santa Barbara, Rancho del Cielo (Heaven's Ranch) had been Reagan's home away from home since the 1970s, and his days as governor. Sometimes referred to as "the Western White House," the President never embraced that term, although there was no contesting that this was his version of Jefferson's Monticello, or Washington's Mount Vernon.

"From the first day we saw it, Rancho del Cielo cast a spell over us. No place before or since has ever given Nancy and me the joy and serenity it does.

"If not Heaven itself, it probably has the same ZIP code," said Reagan.

It was here where he did his deep thinking and soul searching. It was at "the Ranch" where Reagan went to contemplate running for the presidency in 1976. Over the course of his first two terms, Reagan spent more than a tenth of his days at the Ranch, which he believed restored him physically, emotionally, philosophically, and spiritually.

But all of that had changed following the coup in the Soviet Union, as the President chose to stay close to Washington and his team. So, while there had been a few weekend excursions to Camp David in nearby Maryland, Reagan's beloved California ranch remained out of bounds.

Now with events favoring a trip west after so long, Reagan looked forward to making the most of his Thanksgiving getaway to the Golden State.

Beyond its connections to Reagan's personal and political history, the Ranch's origins went back to the early days of California statehood, when it was first settled by Mexican immigrants who received the title to the land in accordance with Lincoln's Homestead Act of 1862.

The symbolic connection between two Republican presidents was not lost on Reagan, nor was the do-it-yourself work ethic of the property's first resident.

In 1871, José Pico used adobe and his own two hands to build the first house on the property. Although the Reagans added on to it and made many improvements, it remained a modest ranch home of roughly 1500 square feet, true to its humble and unpretentious roots.

Hardly something one might think of when envisioning a presidential retreat or a vacation home of former movie stars, Rancho del Cielo was rustic and homey, with worn 1970s décor and furnishings, and standard home-grade GE appliances (including an old, occasionally noisy cocoa brown refrigerator).

The compound featured a few other vintage buildings including a working tack barn. The only truly recent construction had been to add a helicopter port and a place for the President's Secret Service detail, which kept watch over Reagan day and night, including from a hilltop ominously named "Sniper's Point."

Just steps from the front door was Lucky Lake, where the President and Mrs Reagan moored a canoe they had named *Tru Luv*. Weather permitting—almost a certainty given this was California—the couple would enjoy some private time on the water.

A true westerner at heart, Reagan's preferred method for traveling around the 688-acre ranch was by horseback. Long before the nation came to regard him figuratively as the hero who rode in on the white horse to save the day, Reagan did in fact ride a white Arabian horse when he stayed at the Ranch.

The President loved his horses, and personally tended to many of the other animals he kept there. When "El Alamein" finally galloped off into the sunset, he was buried at the Ranch, alongside other treasured members of Reagan's four-legged family in a makeshift cemetery he had dubbed "Boot Hill." Each grave was marked with a personalized headstone, which Reagan lovingly carved by hand in his shop.

At the Ranch, the President could get his hands dirty doing real physical work like clearing brush, chopping wood, building fences, and repairing buildings — in addition to having a bit of fun riding, shooting guns, and hanging with his posse of Secret Service agents.

It was also here in the untamed wilderness of the property that Reagan went to recharge, to reconnect, and experience a different dimension of his faith. As one who saw God's hand in all of creation, the Ranch was a place for spiritual celebration and renewal.

In accordance with this mission, he had named a favorite outlook on the property after the 121st Psalm.

"I look to the hills from whence cometh my strength? My help cometh from the Lord — the Maker of heaven and earth."

Although this trip would also be a working holiday, news of it would not be made public. For one thing, security was an obvious and major concern. Unfortunately, so was public perception, which Reagan's critics would attempt to manipulate in order to make the President appear to be lazy or delinquent in the demands of his office; shirking his duties and leaving Washington to run on autopilot.

But in reality, nothing could be further from the truth. Yes, the President did delegate — as all leaders must do. Yes, he sought input from others — wisely respectful of those who knew more about a particular subject than he did. Although Reagan was able to quickly see the "big picture," he did rely on his staff and other expert opinions to supply him with the details he needed to make informed decisions. (As was the case with deploying the B-2 against Nicaragua.)

But when there was work to be done, Reagan rolled up his sleeves and did it.

As president, and especially since the coup, he had toiled tirelessly, even when Congress was in recess, good-naturedly acknowledging that "Nancy was right; presidents don't have vacations—they just have a change of scenery."

The difference was that Reagan did not seem to show the strain, the wear, and the tear. Instead, he always appeared robust, energized, and fit. Ready to take on whatever was thrown at him, whether it be a Soviet missile or a horse shoe.

Although now late in his 78th year, he was in excellent physical shape, save for a few lingering issues related to the most recent assassination attempt. The President was a fitness buff and had legendary stamina. One thing he especially loved about visiting the Ranch was that it afforded him the opportunity to participate in hard physical labor that was as productive as it was a pleasurable way of getting some good exercise.

Having something to show for his efforts made him happy, whether it was a cord of wood chopped and stacked, or a bill sent to Congress.

While Reagan viewed the trip west as an opportunity to work with fewer distractions, he was savvy enough to know how his opponents would spin it.

Never mind the lengthy and frequent breaks taken by Congress and others in government; as the Top Dog, he was always in the crosshairs— and expected to be working. And for the most part he was.

But different environments are conducive to different types of work. The solitude of Heaven's Ranch allowed the President the quiet time he needed to think deeply on big issues.

Gone were the constant interruptions and diversions of the nation's capital, replaced by undisturbed moments of personal reflection watching the sun setting over the Pacific, and nights spent reading by the hearth.

It had been a productive and rejuvenating break. But now, almost as soon as it began, it was time to say goodbye to the Ranch and return to Washington.

As the helicopter lifted off and headed towards its rendezvous with Air Force One, the President looked out the window, and down across the rugged terrain of the Ranch, and the magnificence of the California landscape.

Here was a landscape that mirrored Reagan himself, the natural, and the manmade, the hills and the highways, the ocean and the swimming pools, the trees and the buildings. The timeless and the contemporary, and where the past and present align in a way that reveals the hand of God.

The trips home to California always helped to ground him and to remind him of who he was, and why he was here.

And now was time to get back to Washington and do what needed to be done.

67

Prayer

Following the Thanksgiving visit to the Ranch, the Reagans returned to Washington revitalized; their spirits lifted, their hearts now full with the holiday spirit.

As per tradition—and out of appreciation for staff and other administration members—the Reagans always spent Christmas at the White House, and now Nancy was back at work pulling together all the last-minute details to ensure some seasonal cheer for their worn and weary extended family.

Meanwhile, the President attended to the daily demands of office, as well as trying to make progress on what he had been working on over the Thanksgiving break in California.

Taking advantage of a lull in hostilities with the Soviets, and the general feelings of goodwill inherent in the Christmas season, the President sought meetings (sometimes thinly disguised as holiday parties), with members of Congress to lobby on behalf of constitutional amendments permitting school prayer and banning abortion.

Both had been campaign promises, supported by voters who had given him a mandate to implement these social components of America's conservative revival.

Even with a Republican majority in Congress, support was tepid. Many in the GOP would have preferred that the President focus his time on less controversial matters, like fundraising or opening new post offices.

But Ronald Reagan was a man of his word. He had made campaign promises to the people, and they had come through on their part of the deal by electing him and a Republican majority to Congress.

It had been more than a year since the election, yet both initiatives were going nowhere. Channeling his frustration into action, Reagan went to work.

Strategically, the school prayer amendment had the best chance of succeeding. He would continue to press for a ban on abortion, but knew his chances would be better after the midterm elections, which would likely give Republicans a supermajority in Congress.

School prayer it would be. And he would personally lead the fight.

While some might disagree with his positions, rarely did anyone question Reagan's sincerity, courage, or tenacity. Those who did almost always lost.

Still, amending the Constitution for any reason is not an easy task. The last successful change (in 1971) had been to lower the voting age to 18, and was a delayed response to FDR's dropping the age for military conscription in 1942.

Many critics regarded Reagan's initiatives as driven by his own religious beliefs and were thereby flatly opposed on principle, noting the lack of other such faith-centered amendments — save for the First Amendment, which both prohibited the government's establishment of any particular official state religion, while restricting government's power to prohibit the practicing of one's beliefs.

No one loved or respected the US Constitution more than the President, who was in full support of provisions assuring the separation of church and state. Nor did he believe in any official or state-imposed religion. Reagan had many close, and life-long friends of different faiths, and he never sought to evangelize, except by the example of how he lived his life.

In particular was the issue of prayer. Reagan prayed several times a day, and never made a major decision without it. He openly acknowledged the important role it played in his life, and in the nation's history.

"The public expression through prayer of our faith in God is a fundamental part of our American heritage, and a privilege which should not be excluded by law from any American school, public or private," stated the President.

Reagan also supported the rights of non-believers to dissent — even though he secretly prayed they might one day come to see the light! As one who fought to get government out of people's lives, the President was fine with non-believers using school prayer time as each person determined appropriate — and not the state.

Such a compromising stance was also a matter of personal practice, as exemplified by how Reagan had responded when his own son, Ron Jr, declared himself an atheist at the age of 12. Although naturally disappointed, Reagan did not use his power as a parent to force compliance.

Instead, he used the situation as an opportunity to teach the lessons of tolerance, mutual respect, and the right of dissent.

The senior Reagan did not demand his son attend church, read the Bible, or participate in any religious activities—including prayers offered at the dinner table, which he continued to lead. Instead, there was an open acceptance of those with differing viewpoints—even if that person was a child.

When the time came to present a proposal for amending the US Constitution, these core values of tolerance and respect for the rights of *all* individuals helped guide Reagan's framing of the issue, evident in the clearly defined caveat that "No person shall be required by the United States or by any state to participate in prayer."

What could be clearer?

The President hoped this opt-out clause would satisfy his critics, even though a similar measure had been attempted during his first term in office. While the President had the support of the public with his first try, he did not have the votes in Congress to pass it, and his proposal to return prayer to the nation's schools failed.

Given the long history of the issue, opponents had a well-established strategy for fighting it. Supporters in Congress were threatened with political consequences should they back a "scheme to impose Christianity on impressionable young minds."

Reagan disputed this narrow and biased interpretation, stating that reserving a few moments for personal reflection need not be narrowly defined as only having a religious connection. Rather, this was time for the young mind to calm itself, to meditate, or dream.

Yes, most people would likely use the time for praying; but there would be no official or sanctioned prayers. "Prayer" was a non-denominational term to describe a period of reflective thought. "Prayer" was simply a term that most people were familiar with. How one used the time was completely up to each individual.

Nor was this something new and radical.

For most of America's history, actual organized prayer had been a standard component of public school life, until the Supreme Court outlawed it in 1962, citing concerns about the separation of church and state. In other words, if a child's private thoughts turned to God while in the classroom, the separations clause was being breached and the nation was in danger of becoming a theocracy.

Reagan disagreed. He knew that persons of faith thought about God all the time — it was natural. The vast majority of Americans were, and always had been, believers in God; noting "the public expression through prayer of our faith in God is a fundamental part of our American heritage."

In support of this argument, Reagan was quick to reference America's Founding Fathers, including President George Washington, who stated in his farewell address, "Of all the dispositions and habits which lead to political prosperity, religion and morality are indispensable supports."

For the President, this was a clear-cut, black and white issue. The right to pray needed to be restored and protected. Congress alone had the power to override the court, and in doing such, reflect the wishes of the American people who had deliberately elected candidates from the President on down that would act in accordance with their wishes.

But, because this activity would occur in the classroom, the President once again found himself butting heads with the Teachers Union, an organization that had been growing increasingly more vocal and con-frontational across a range of issues. Much of the union's leadership was shaped by the radicalized sixties, which advocated using public schools as a means of indoctrinating the nation's youth in leftist and anti-American ideologies.

In other words, they believed that it was okay to use schools to promote ideologies only if it reflected their particular set of leftist liberal biases. That wasn't brainwashing — *that was education!* But a few moments of personal, unstructured quiet time? Never — that was "mind control" by the Religious Right!

The union regarded Reagan as public enemy number one, and had campaigned heavily against him in the last election.

Naturally, conservatives saw the union's position on prayer as inconsistent and politically motivated. How could they accept children acknowledging "One nation under God" during the morning's flag salute, but take issue with a few moments of silence? How could a rally by neo-Nazis be protected as "free speech," without affording the same rights of free expression to those engaging in a few moments of silent contemplation?

Well-funded by a member base forced by law to provide for its financial support with their dues, the nation's largest union was a commanding force with the power to sway elections, and make, or break, political careers.

Although most Americans — including the rank and file membership of actual classroom teachers — supported the President's position, the union leadership signaled its intent to fight Reagan personally and to go after his supporters in Congress.

To the President, the Teachers Union was just another wealthy special interest group that had no right to impose its minority viewpoint on the entire nation. An offer to speak directly to the union was rebuffed, so Reagan turned to personally meeting with lawmakers to make his case. Slowly, but steadily, he won over nearly all holdouts in his own party, and even several Democrats. In the end, the President was promised legislation would be on his desk by the spring.

Still, Reagan the politician knew that promises from other politicians sometimes had a way of gathering dust instead of momentum. In the spirit of the season, the President accepted their pledges on faith, but knew he would likely need to continue playing Border Collie to the easily-sidetracked flock if anything was to be accomplished.

The issue of prayer (both in the religious sense and in relation to the amendment) would also be central to Reagan's holiday message, which he intended to broadcast live to the world on Christmas Day. This was a speech that Reagan had personally worked on over Thanksgiving at the Ranch, and as a result, it had very little input from staff.

While not generally acknowledged, Reagan was an excellent writer. He drafted many of his own speeches, and had a genuine knack for connecting when using words and phrases that were his own. Those who worked for him respected this talent, and sought to incorporate as much input from the President as was possible into their own work. In most instances he was happy, and honored, to comply.

Christmas Day 1989 fell on a Monday, and it was one of the coldest on record. As Reagan prepared to deliver his speech, he got a call from Secretary Schultz wishing him a Merry Christmas.

"Oh, and in addition to the other gifts, I have one more for you," Schultz said, a note of excitement in his voice.

"Last night, in Warsaw, more than 200,000 people turned out to celebrate Christmas and to listen to a message from the Pope.

"The mood was peaceful, but the tone was revolutionary ... We have reports of people carrying Solidarity signs, and making demands not just for full democratic rights—of religion and free expression—but also calling for the end to single party rule ... to the communist state itself."

Reagan was taken aback by the news

"What about General Jaruzelski?" asked the President, referring to Poland's military dictator.

"Treading water ... Just trying to keep his head above the rising tide. He probably doesn't have the power to put it down at this point, and likely doesn't have any guarantees of backup from the Kremlin. They're busy with their own internal problems."

Reagan just whistled, then smiled broadly. "Well, George, you're right, that's an incredible Christmas present."

"But wait," interrupted Schultz, "don't you want to hear about your stocking stuffers from Czechoslovakia, Hungary, and Romania? Each has experienced its own version of a Christmas Uprising."

The President could not believe what he was hearing.

"And no violence? No big crackdowns?"

"Nothing major. Things just seem to be steadily crumbling."

"You know, George, this is what I've been praying for. This is just the beginning."

With that, Reagan looked at the clock, and then to his assistants standing by with anxious expressions. It was time to leave: Reagan's speech was to be broadcast live, and time was running out.

The President, never one to miss a cue, nodded to his assistants, thanked Schultz and headed off to deliver his Christmas broadcast—which, in light of world events, would take on a new significance.

In response to Schultz's revelations, Reagan decided to set aside his prepared remarks and speak from the heart. Using his text only as an outline, the President spoke passionately about the struggle for freedom now unfolding behind the Iron Curtain.

In his speech, Reagan spoke of the promise of Christmas, and how people of faith had changed the world. He spoke of how throughout history, religious conviction had given the common man the strength needed to take on empires, and how that same spirit was alive and stirring change in the Soviet Union.

Citing Poland in particular, the President asked people of all faiths to join him in prayer, and to stand in solidarity with the people pushing back the darkness of tyranny by the light of faith.

Yes, God was listening to the prayers of those yearning to be free. A thin sliver of light had appeared on the horizon, and with it, the promise of a new day.

68

A New Year, A New World

Anticipation for the big battle had been building for weeks. Both sides were driven by the dream of a winner-take-all victory, and it was simply a matter of time until they confronted one another head on.

In a contest of this nature, only one side would emerge victorious. The other, broken and defeated, would retreat, intent on revenge.

And so began the New Year of 1990, and with it a stunning victory for the President, as his beloved twelfth-ranked USC Trojans defeated the third-ranked Michigan Wolverines 17-10 to win the Rose Bowl.

For the President, the game offered a short, but welcome diversion from world affairs. Reagan loved football in every sense. He had played the game, announced it on radio, and starred in a movie about a famous player (as George "the Gipper" Gipp, in 1940's *Knute Rockne, All American*).

He watched it whenever he could, which was not as often as he would have liked. Also restricted, due to security concerns, was the freedom to watch a game played live in a public stadium.

Despite being the most powerful person on the planet, the President was also a prisoner. The types of everyday activities enjoyed by most people — such as attending a football game — would be denied him for the rest of his life.

His movements were even restricted at the White House. Many outside areas were permanently off limits, as were several locations within the building itself for fear of sharpshooters, should he stray too close to a particular window.

But Ronald Reagan was not one to complain. He soldiered on, ever the optimist, happy to watch the game from the comfort of his favorite chair, with a bowl of popcorn and his faithful dog Rex at his side.

By most measures, the New Year seemed off to a promising start.

External direct threats by the Soviets remained low, as the Kremlin was now preoccupied with maintaining control internally in the wake of domestic uprisings, most recently expressed in the Christmas uprisings.

Forces and resources previously allocated for an attack on the West, were now bogged down trying to quell the rising tide of domestic turmoil, from the Balkans to Siberia.

Militarily, the empire was still reeling following the loss of Norway and East Germany. Having Gorbachev snatched from within the USSR itself had been terribly humiliating. To save face, the failed attempt to assassinate Reagan in Chicago was not attributed to Soviet incompetency, but instead to Reagan's incredible luck.

Perhaps they were right.

Outposts in Scandinavia, Austria and Greece had been abandoned. Relationships with countries like Turkey and Iceland were beyond repair.

Challenges to the legitimacy of Sokolov's regime were compounding, as a growing number of countries recognized Gorbachev, and his government-in-exile, as the legal representatives of the Soviet Union.

Only a handful of pro-western nations still maintained embassies in Moscow. Those that did described life in the capital as being increasingly chaotic, with some districts now under the control of criminal gangs.

Tales of power struggles within the Sokolov administration were rampant, and columns of heavily-armed troops now guarded most government buildings. Overhead, helicopters buzzed night and day.

In addition, the Soviet military was now forced to consider the addition of the B-2 Stealth bomber to the American arsenal.

As predicted, the B-2 was a game-changer, and Reagan's use of it to shut down the Sandinistas sent shockwaves through the Russian defense establishment. Even worse were the rumors concerning breakthroughs in SDI, suggesting that Reagan's directive to fast-track work on the program was already delivering results.

If successful, the threat of a nuclear holocaust—the last big card held by the Soviets—would be useless. Game over. Reagan wins.

With no official notice made, Soviet forces began to make a hasty retreat from Afghanistan. After more than a decade of fighting, this had been the USSR's longest war and most humiliating defeat. The pullout must have been especially hard for Sokolov, who had once led the Soviet conquest with a sense of invincibility.

Abandoning Afghanistan spoke volumes. Not only did it signify a huge blow to the dream of an expansionist empire, it also suggested that every available troop was now needed back home to defend the Motherland.

The USSR was bleeding out.

In contrast, things were going quite well in the West—and particularly in the United States.

As the President had predicted, Americans were feeling better with more money in their pockets resulting from his across-the-board tax cuts. This change created a domino effect, reducing unemployment and spurring gains across most sectors. Growth was modest, but at least people had a sense that things were moving in the right direction.

A basic tenet of the administration's policies was quickly borne out by irrefutable hard data that showed the average person did indeed spend faster, more directly, and across a broader range of segments than the government did. Nor did the infusion of extra cash contribute to inflation. Instead, the rate of inflation remained stable, contrary to what usually happens when more money enters an economy.

Earlier problems with inflation were not the result of normal factors, such as a currency devaluation, but stemmed directly from the most basic of all economic principles; that of supply and demand.

Lack of global stability caused by the war created shortages.

Making matters worse was how markets and individuals reacted. Some people panicked and stockpiled goods. Prices rose as speculators took advantage of these fears, with those living on fixed-incomes hit especially hard by the surging cost of even basic goods.

But now, things were returning to normal, and those who had hoarded resources like plywood and drums of gasoline sought ways to use up their stockpiles, if only to get their cars back in the garages again.

It had been a rough slog, but most Americans never lost faith in their president. Things were not yet perfect by any account, but there was a sense that the worst had passed. America had weathered the storm.

At its darkest hour, Ronald Reagan had offered hope, and now he had delivered on it.

The improving morale also had an effect on drug usage and crime. As spirits lifted, the despondency that led to substance abuse declined, as did crimes committed by those who engaged in illegal activity to support their habits. Many more found honest employment as the economy grew and created new jobs.

Encouraged by the effects of Reagan's reforms, the White House looked to further reduce and simplify taxes, but ran into some unexpected resistance from Congress. The hesitancy was attributed to a variety of reasons, none of which seemed to make much sense or could be explained in layman's terms.

Reagan, however, suspected other motives might be at play, owing to the fact that many—including members of his own party, were personally benefitting from the current (and overly complicated) tax code.

Cutting taxes would not add to the deficit if government spending was also scaled back—something that many politicians weren't willing to do.

The President was not happy about this, but for now he'd have to pick his battles. Plans for a Balanced Budget Amendment would need to wait, and at least for the immediate future the deficit would continue to grow. So instead, Reagan stayed focused on the School Prayer Amendment, which was now on track to become law in April—just in time for Easter.

As January gave way to February, Ronald Reagan turned 79 on the sixth of that month, breaking his own record to once more become the oldest sitting president in US history. Hale, and in fine fettle—Reagan certainly did not look, act, or feel his age—a perspective affirmed by his medical team, led by Dr Hutton.

"I still feel the same as I did when I was in my 30s," Reagan said. "Unfortunately, when I adjust my current pay for inflation, I don't think I'm making anywhere near the same amount of money," he noted, shaking his head in mock embarrassment and disappointment.

Because his actual birthday would fall on a weekday, Nancy held a small party for him at the White House on the previous Sunday, allowing the President to celebrate the "40th anniversary of his 39th birthday" without detracting from his normal weekday work schedule.

Among those in attendance were the President's older brother Moon, and his wife Bess, who were visiting from California.

As the two brothers stood together joking and reminiscing, Moon seemed so much more than just three years older than Dutch. Granted, Moon had been ill (including a bout with cancer), but the contrast between the two brothers was quite striking. While the strain of the presidency always seemed to age men beyond their years, it appeared to have had the opposite effect on Reagan, who seemed to have found the fountain of youth in a life dedicated to serving his country.

The gathering marked a rare afternoon of unguarded levity for the President, who had quite the time sharing anecdotes and telling jokes — including a few that most had already heard more than once. Or twice. Or three times. Or …

But in truth, no one minded. Being *his* birthday, Reagan was given the audience he relished entertaining, and allowed to set aside his troubles for a few short hours.

His was an awful burden for one man to shoulder. For those close to him, simply seeing the President laughing and smiling was grounds for celebration.

There was a real sense of joy and magic in the air that afternoon, and a poignant reminder of what Reagan had given up in order to serve another four-year term as president during one of the century's darkest and most dangerous periods.

For Nancy, who stood at a distance as she watched her husband playfully reach out and tug Ron Jr's earlobe, it was indeed a bittersweet moment.

Just as the afternoon's festivities were wrapping up, the President received word of a call from Gorbachev. Nancy froze, fearing the worst, watching as her husband left the gathering to go take the call.

It was already evening in Switzerland, and Gorbachev (whose English was good and always improving), announced that he was calling with "some good news, some bad news."

"Good is that I am declaring February 6 to be President Reagan Day in the USSR. The bad news is that I don't imagine there will be much in the way of public celebrations."

Both men laughed.

"Well, maybe next year Mikhail. Thank you. Oh, and I see you have a birthday coming up next month as well. Now, as you know, I'm running up a real deficit here, but I will call, and I promise it won't be collect!"

Again, the two men laughed.

Reagan genuinely liked Gorbachev, and had been privy to the incredible changes the Soviet leader was secretly planning to bring to the USSR once he was restored to power. These included a full transformation of how the nation did business from the ground up; from substantive arms reductions, to a market-based economy, on through deep democratic reforms that would likely end the USSR in its present form.

If Gorbachev succeeded, this would be the end of the Cold War.

But what if it was all a trick? What if Gorbachev was just using the Americans to get back in power?

Reagan's gut told him otherwise. And so he had personally intervened to have the US bankroll Gorbachev's government-in-exile and to provide security for it and its operations — much to the ire of some Americans, including many on the fringes of his own party.

Changing the world takes bold initiatives by true visionaries.

Reagan and Gorbachev were men of courage and initiative, and together as partners they would work in unison to make their shared vision a reality. They weren't just changing the world; they were building a new and better one.

69

North Korea

This year the President's birthday fell on a Tuesday, and so, for the most part, it would be treated as just another "day at the office."

In acknowledgement of this reality, the President got up at the usual time of half-past seven, ate breakfast, and read the papers. Nancy had the TV on, tuned to *Good Morning America*, anchored by the team of Charlie Gibson and Joan Lunden.

Reagan liked Gibson, a fellow Illinoisan. Although the ABC show required jovial neutrality, Reagan suspected Gibson to be a fellow conservative, and someone he might have considered as Press Secretary if Rush Limbaugh, his first choice, had not taken the job.

Tuesday morning. Time to put on a crisp blue suit and head down to work.

As usual, Reagan tried to begin his daily meetings with a bit of humor. Being his birthday, he offered up a few one-liners about birthdays and getting older, before settling down to business.

But the morning's levity was to be short-lived, as the President was confronted with news of a situation developing in North Korea.

A longtime ally of the Soviet Union, the "Democratic Republic" of North Korea (DPRK) had been a problem for every US president since its formation more than 40 years prior, growing from the ashes and opportunism of World War II.

For most of the early 20th century the entire Korean peninsula had been under Japanese control. During the war, Imperial Japan used its forces to savagely conquer and occupy much of Asia, including what is now Vietnam, Cambodia, Laos, Thailand, Malaysia, Burma, Singapore, Guam, New Guinea, Indonesia, the Philippines, large chunks of China—and more.

Some of the war's bloodiest battles had been fought in Asia, as allied troops often battled the Japanese one island at a time in direct hand-to-hand combat. A number of people on Reagan's White House team had served in the Pacific Theatre, including Secretary of State Schultz.

Because of Japan's role in the Axis alliance, the US was committed to fighting major wars in both Asia and Europe. After defeating Nazi Germany in May of 1945, the Americans were now able to turn their full attention to the war in the East.

The Japanese refused to surrender; vowing to defeat America or to continue the fight until the last man fell. They dug in, resolved to resist invasion, even if it meant using human shields and suicide attacks.

Fighting a conventional war would mean huge casualties on both sides.

How long might they last? No one knew for sure. So President Harry Truman made the difficult decision to use the one weapon in America's arsenal that he knew would end the war. Something the Japanese had no defense against, something the world had never encountered.

Under Truman's orders, on August 6, 1945, the United States dropped an atomic bomb on the Japanese city of Hiroshima.

The reverberations of what the Americans had unleashed sent shockwaves throughout the world. Japan was given the ultimatum: Surrender, or more bombs would follow.

The war must end, and it will—one way or another. The choice is yours.

But before a second bomb could be dropped three days later—which did indeed result in Japan's surrender—the Soviets, (a bit late to the party), decided to finally declare war on Japan on August 8, 1945.

Because of this official declaration of war, the Russians now felt they had the right to invade and occupy Japanese territory—including the Korean peninsula. The Red Army met little resistance by the war-ravaged Koreans, and was soon in control of Pyongyang, which Moscow declared as the provisional capital of a new socialist state. The portion of the country under Soviet occupation officially became the Democratic People's Republic of Korea in 1948, and in less than two years (with encouragement from the Russians) attacked the South, now known as the Republic of Korea. Despite lacking the inclusion of "Democratic" as part of its official name—having forfeited this term to the North—from the outset there was no confusion as to which side was a true democracy, and which was another totalitarian Soviet puppet.

Although all-out formal hostilities officially ended in 1953 by the signing of an armistice, North and South Korea remained officially at war. The border became one of the most heavily militarized in the world, reinforced by the protective presence of American troops stationed in the South, in the event that the North decided to act on its recurring threat to invade, conquer, and unify.

The president at the time of the armistice was still Harry Truman — a Democrat that Reagan generally liked and respected for a range of reasons. One major disagreement however, concerned Korea, and Truman's decision to not back General Douglas MacArthur's plan to push on and win the war to free the north.

Because of this lapse, Korea, like Germany, had been divided for decades. The South became open and independent, while the North fell under Soviet domination. As had been the case with its other client states, the relationship between Moscow and Pyongyang had cooled under Gorbachev, then revived under Sokolov.

Although Sokolov was new, he got on well with Kim Il-sung, the dictator who had ruled North Korea with an iron fist since 1948. Like Sokolov, Kim had also served in the Soviet Red Army, rising to Major, before his leadership gifts were officially acknowledged by his being awarded a lifetime presidency of the DPRK by his Russian sponsors.

It was a role he was made for.

Modestly referred to as the "Supreme Leader," Kim seemed to enjoy acts of provocation, which, owing to Soviet backing, had the power to inflict some real damage if he decided to act out his fantasies.

As Kim grew older (he was just a year younger than Sokolov), concerns developed about how the man who liked to compare himself to the sun, might choose to commemorate his legacy. Although officially "eternal," Kim was an obese old man, in failing health, and with nothing much to lose by packing it in on his own terms.

If "the sun" decided to call it a day and supernova, the damage would be extensive.

Going out in a blaze of glory, martyred as a hero for the ages, holds a sick allure to some, and Kim was near the top of the CIA's list as those most likely to wrap up his tenure by taking as many innocents with him as possible.

In a land where the state heavily subsidized a cult of personality, to die serving the Great Leader was officially promoted as an exceptional honor. While few in the officially atheistic state believed in an afterlife, the thrill of perishing as part of world liberation had an appeal at least on par with what lemmings must feel as they free-fall over the cliff and into the sea.

Despite the adulation of his own people, Kim also craved the affection and respect of the Russians, which resulted in at times desperate attempts to gain their attention. Following the Sokolov's coup, Kim, via his threats, had been instrumental in getting the 1988 Summer Olympics scheduled for Seoul (South Korea) cancelled.

The status of the games was already shaky, and a move was underway to ban the USSR from participating. Whether just a case of sour grapes, or an opportunity for Kim to grab center stage and get a thumbs up from Comrade Sokolov, the elderly Korean announced that he would personally "open the gates of Hell" if the games (minus the Soviets) were to be held in Seoul.

At the last minute, the summer Olympics were scaled back, and rescheduled for Los Angeles, where they had last been held in 1984. A parallel set of games was staged in Pyongyang, which honored every Soviet and Korean participant with their own hastily derived knockoff version of an Olympic gold medal featuring the likenesses of Kim and Sokolov in profile.

There was no denying that the North Koreans had a genuine gift for improvisation. Having banned all religious observations, they created their own non-secular holidays as substitutes, including one commemorating the Great Leader's birthday. The honor of just living at the same time as Kim was more than many could bear, and the sight of his image (which was everywhere) brought forth tears of joy.

Grown men were known to collapse weeping on city streets, their faces wet with tears, from simply being exposed to a glimpse of the benevolence radiating from a portrait of Kim.

Celebrated at every level, many believed that Kim held incredible mystical powers; among them that he had created the world, and controlled the weather. At the very least, he had created a powerful and disciplined military, willing to follow the Great Leader's orders without hesitation.

Yes, North Korea was a special place indeed.

Largely isolated (by their own choosing) from the rest of the international community, the North Koreans placed a high degree of emphasis on self-sufficiency. As a result, and due to their special sheltering (courtesy of the USSR), the outside world had very little influence on the Hermit Kingdom.

This became especially apparent when, following Sokolov's coup, the North Koreans began an ambitious program of building several new "defensive" missile bases (with direct assistance from Moscow). In response, sanctions were levied against Pyongyang, but these had little or no impact.

Now came word that the bases were nearing completion, and would be used to deploy a very dangerous class of Russian-made missiles.

The addition of Soviet missiles would completely change the balance of power in the region. Now, North Korea would be able to hit targets not just in South Korea, but all across Asia, including Japan, and even deep within their old adversary, China. In time, perhaps even Alaska and the west coast of the United States.

Even more disturbing was the fact that these missiles could be outfitted with nuclear warheads.

Welcome to your Tuesday morning briefing; happy birthday Mr President.

President Reagan grimaced, visibly dismayed by this latest provocation. For what seemed a very long time he stared at the gallery of enlarged satellite photos and maps with brightly highlighted missile sites and potential lines of trajectory and targets. He then turned to the room of faces looking to him for leadership.

Reagan paused, and surveyed the group which included leading representatives of the military and intelligence services, along with those from the state department.

Out of left field came a question that no one was anticipating.

"What happens to North Korea when the USSR collapses?" asked the President.

The group looked puzzled, so he elaborated. "When Sokolov is gone, when Russia comes back into the civilized world?"

A lively discussion ensued, with most agreeing that it was unlikely that Pyongyang would follow Moscow's lead. Likely some famine, but no major unrest.

They'd tough it out, and soldier on.

North Korea was very different from other communist nations.

Certainly it was much more self-sufficient, but in time it was presumed that the Koreans would cozy up to the Chinese. As a small country, it needed the protection of a larger state to replace what it would lose without Russia.

"It will take a while, but the Chinese will also benefit. For one thing, they don't want US troops moving up the peninsula and camping out on their backdoor," noted a representative from the military.

A representative from the National Security Council pointed out that the relationship of the North Korean people to Kim was different than in other communist nations, where the enslaved citizens were generally dismissive of their masters.

"Think of how much Texans love you, Mr President," said NSA Director McFarlane, "now multiply that by a million."

McFarlane's joke brought a small laugh. But it was true: Kim was regarded as something akin to a god, worthy of a fanatical devotion on par with what the Tibetans felt towards the Dalai Lama, or the reverence the Japanese held for Emperor Hirohito during the Second World War.

Economic and intelligence advisors addressed the North Korean economy.

"As we know, they can't really feed their own people. Instead of producing food, the economy is largely focused on manufacturing, specifically on items with military applications. Most of these are sold to the USSR; the Eastern Bloc.

"Right now, they are going at full capacity just to meet the demands of the Soviets. If that dried up, there would be a huge influx of high-quality weaponry suddenly available to some very unstable regimes, rogue states that can't buy it elsewhere.

"Guerrilla armies, terrorists ... those who seek revolution by force. Even some criminal organizations."

The advisors nodded affirming this assessment, while the President shook his head, horrified by the prospect.

McFarlane continued.

"One of the first things they'd do is back-engineer and then start reproducing the Russian missiles.

"We'd have our hands full fighting them on many different fronts. Proliferation is a real and major concern. Sanctions won't stop them:

the missiles would be everywhere … going to whoever is willing to pay their asking price."

CIA Director Webster continued. "Pakistan is on track to a nuclear bomb in less than 10 years. Now imagine a situation where they and the North Koreans become trading partners … Both with nuclear-armed missiles."

"Nuts with nukes," muttered Reagan, shaking his head.

"For now, Pakistan is relatively stable, but there is a developing threat of Islamic extremism, both internally, and spilling across the border from Afghanistan.

"The Soviet pullout has left a real mess, as different factions of the Mujahideens fight for control and to establish a fundamentalist Islamic state. In no time, they'll be using the profits from making heroin to go shopping for weapons, which will stir up more problems — and which likely will extend beyond their borders.

"Then of course there's Qaddafi, and Iran …"

The prospect of a post-USSR North Korea presented one horrifying scenario after another. The US, its allies, the UN — every sane player on the world stage had already exerted every last ounce of influence to persuade Pyongyang to suspend development on the missile sites, but so far nothing had worked.

In fact, the North Koreans had responded with even greater belligerence, stating that as soon as the missiles were in place they would use them to destroy America, Japan, and any other nation that opposed their plans to unite the Korean people.

Big talk, but something that had to be taken seriously. A raving lunatic is just that — a raving lunatic. But a raving lunatic with a gun is a different matter altogether. That is an urgent, life-or-death situation, which cannot be ignored.

North Korea and the US were on a collision course, and Kim was pushing down on the throttle with all his might.

Grim-faced, the President exhaled forcefully, and then addressed the group. "Alright. How long do we have?"

Guesses ranged from a month or two just to complete work on the bases. Missile deployment was likely some time off. "We imagine they'll work day and night to please the Great Leader by having everything ready to honor him on his birthday, which is April 15th," said McFarlane.

"Tax day," noted the President ominously. "I never thought I'd see anything worse for April 15th, but I think this tops it."

The President shook his head firmly. He took a deep a breath, then began to speak.

"We cannot allow these missiles to be installed; that will be a turning point from which there will be no return—regardless of what happens with the Soviet Union.

"They've been warned, but they have opted to play this game of brinkmanship.

"They're counting on appeasement, or the fact that we're distracted by events in Europe—which is exactly what happened 45 years ago."

It was clear what the President felt needed to be done. Reagan paused, carefully weighing his words, while the room braced for what was coming next.

"Their allies, the Soviets are not likely to be of much use, but still, taking them on will be a bloody mess. I have no doubt that these folks will fight with ferocity while Kim safely cheers them on from some reinforced rat hole deep beneath the ground.

"We will be victorious, but it will come with a heavy price.

"But that price is only going to get higher over time if we do nothing. One way or another, eventually it will come to this, and we need to do it now, while we have this window of opportunity ... Before they have the power to knock out Seoul, Tokyo, then Seattle ... Just out of some crazy, scorched-earth policy.

The President paused.

"How much time do we need?" he asked.

The Joint Chiefs of Staff conferred briefly, then suggested two weeks at the most. Defense Secretary Powell nodded in support of this assessment.

"We're already on high-alert, with plenty of personnel and systems in place. We are regularly performing maneuvers, but I think they might suspect something—given the issue of the missiles."

Reagan wanted to make sure his orders were clear.

"I want every last missile base taken out.

"I also want all the factories making armaments hit as well. I want their entire war-based economy destroyed ... reduced to ruins, like what we did against the Nazis. Nothing left standing when the smoke clears.

"Do we know where these targets are?"

"Most," said CIA Director Webster. "Some appear to serve dual purposes, but we have detailed intelligence on all the major ones."

"Good. As the North Koreans like to remind us, we are still in a state of war. Let's show them what war is about."

Although no fan of the North Koreans, Secretary of State Schultz still wanted to give diplomacy one more try.

"Nope," said the President firmly. "That'll only give them more of a warning and result in more casualties of the wrong kind—innocents dying while allowing their high command to burrow deeper underground."

Schultz nodded, knowing that the President was right. He had also known Reagan long enough to know that once the President set his mind to something there would be no waffling or turning back.

And so a date was selected: February 22, 1990.

70

Shock & Awe

The buck stops here.

The President did not like the position that he had been pushed into, but he had no alternative. If he did not deal with the North Koreans now, somebody would have to do it eventually, and this delay would most certainly result in even greater carnage.

If only SDI was ready.

While there had been many promising trials, the missile defense system was not yet a reality, and waiting for something that might never happen was not an option given the circumstances.

With the installation of the Soviet missiles likely in less than two months, the clock was ticking down, and time was on the side of the North Koreans.

The activation of a sophisticated new missile system would, at the very least, significantly complicate any future military action against North Korea. Even without nuclear warheads, long-range missiles that could be launched at a moment's notice offered a serious deterrent.

How could America, entrusted to protect its allies in the region, inform them that it had allowed Pyongyang to target their nations with nuclear weapons? How would the citizens of Seoul, Tokyo, Anchorage, or even Beijing live, knowing their cities could be reduced to radioactive ash at any time if it suited the whims of a madman in Pyongyang?

As much as it troubled President Reagan to authorize the surprise attack, he knew it was necessary. The North Koreans had to be stopped.

This President would not kick the can down the road. He would not be party to permitting a dangerous shift in regional power. He would not surrender or endanger America's allies. He would not allow North Korea to become a major arms supplier to other outlaw nations, terrorists, and criminals. He would not allow the free world to be blackmailed and bullied by a nuclear-armed tyrant like Kim Il-sung.

Due to North Korea's paranoid mindset, the country was in a perpetual state of alert. Because an attack was expected at any moment, the nation was always prepared to launch a full-stage counter offensive with only a moment's notice.

Therefore, this would have to be a different kind of war. North Korea would need to be hit with everything America had—and all at once. This would not be a slow war, a traditional war. This would not be the same type of long bloody war that played out over three decades ago; battling it out to the last man standing for control of fields, hillsides, and tiny villages.

No, there would be no ground invasion this time. That would only increase civilian casualties, as every man, woman and child took up arms to defend the reign of the Supreme Leader.

Plus, a ground invasion led by the US would be a concern for China, which would not welcome the presence of American troops on its eastern border. China was not on good terms with North Korea, and would likely welcome—albeit it unofficially—any action that reduced Pyongyang's ability to cause it problems. Beijing would be happy to see this threat neutralized, so long as it was not replaced by something even greater.

As an added benefit, the *modus operandi* of the American assault would create huge ripples internationally, especially with the Soviets. As with the introduction of the B-2 against the Nicaraguan invaders, the assault on North Korea would offer a jaw-dropping example of American force and resolve.

Reagan was determined that this would not be another Vietnam. This would be more akin to a first round knockout punch. Something fast, furious, and utterly overwhelming that would come to be nicknamed "shock and awe" for its speed and devastative power.

The attack began right on schedule, and, as expected, the North Koreans fought back with incredible ferocity.

As feared, Kim's troops were more than willing to commit suicide in defense of the Eternal Leader. Many died unnecessarily; hoping to the end that their sacrifice might at least cause their enemies some pain, and delay the conquest of their homeland.

Within 48 hours, all the key targets had been hit and destroyed.

As the first bombs began to fall, the North Koreans set about shelling targets in the South and setting forth on a counter-offensive to invade by land and sea.

Although most were repulsed, North Korean forces did make some incursions and succeeded in causing significant damage due to their willingness to attack defenseless civilian targets, including fishing boats, schools, and even hospitals.

US and South Korean forces suffered many casualties, and each lost a fair number of ships, planes and other equipment.

Although it was a lopsided victory, the South Koreans and the Americans also paid a heavy toll. But in the end, North Korea's ability to wage war had been decimated, and the country lay in ruins.

While no official total was ever released, it was estimated that upwards of 200,000 North Koreans had died; as contrasted with fewer than 2000 American/South Korean troops. Instead, most casualties came from South Korea's civilian population, which was attacked mercilessly, resulting in charging those responsible with war crimes.

President Kim Il-sung had not been officially targeted, and had waited out the conflict deep underground in a secret reinforced bunker. When he finally emerged, Kim remained defiant and bellicose. While not publicly blaming his military, his first official actions were devoted to publicly executing those, who in his opinion, had "failed" the North Korean people.

Kim, in his view, was in no way responsible for what had happened. In fact, it would have been many times worse had he not been directly leading the battle, fighting back the Americans in one hand-to-hand skirmish after another.

Not one to boast, Kim modestly noted that he had personally killed more than a thousand Americans defending the capital against the invaders. Naturally, his heroism was celebrated at a number of glorious state events, where he was awarded various medals and commendations for his service to the people — some of whom remained stacked like kindling, rotting, and awaiting disposal in huge funeral pyres to discourage cannibalism.

Despite all that had happened, the citizens remained loyal to their Great Leader. While many had died unintentionally as a consequence of war, Reagan's decision to avoid a ground invasion had spared millions.

Those who had attempted to flee the North, first out of self-preservation during the conflict, then as refugees, were usually stopped, and murdered, by their own people. Survivors, if lucky enough to receive a show trial were shipped off to prison camps. There they faced a life sentence of forced labor, torture, rape, starvation, and death.

Assistance from their great and powerful ally, the USSR, was not a significant factor in either the war, or in addressing its aftermath. The Soviets had provided limited air support, but even this was withdrawn after some of their craft veered off course, and signaled a desire to surrender and defect to the Americans.

Offers to provide emergency assistance from even neutral parties (such as the UN) were rebuffed; and so the Hermit Kingdom turned inward to lick its wounds. North Korea would remain closed.

Normally, the Soviets would have used the attack for propaganda purposes, and indeed some efforts were made to exploit the tragedy, and as a warning of what the Americans had in store for the USSR.

Such attempts were limited though, as depicting what had happened to North Korea would only serve to reinforce the popularly-held image of the incredible power and resolve of the Americans, and specifically of their leader, President Reagan.

While satisfied that the North Korean threat had been neutralized, the nature and scope of what had happened still troubled the President.

It was, like so many things, a compromise. Reagan understood that some needed to die, so that the majority might live.

After the initial combative rhetoric from Kim tapered off, Pyongyang secretly began to accept assistance from the outside world. A charity, specifically devoted to helping war orphans was established, seeded by a generous donation from an anonymous donor residing in Washington DC.

Yearly contributions would continue, although in time they would come to bear a California postmark.

71

Race & Culture Wars

Ronald Reagan's personal commitment to matters of equality and civil rights was a deep and defining characteristic of who he was.

Evidence of these beliefs went back to a time before such was fashionable, or even the norm; the roots of which can be traced to his family, his faith, and the founding political principle that declared all men are created equal.

Certainly, these values began with his religious upbringing, and the influence of his mother Nelle, who made studying the scriptures and attending church staples of her son's life. From an early age, the Reagan boys were taught that all persons were made in God's image, that the Lord loved equally, and that we must love and respect all others without prejudice or bias.

These were family values not just in name, but also in everyday practice in the Reagan household. There was no greater sin than a racial slur or evidence of intolerance — a stance that often put the family at odds with their own community. Although Illinois was not as racially segregated as certain states, there were divisions. So, for instance, when Moon went to the movies with his best friend (who was black), the two were forced to sit in the balcony—the only area in the theater open to persons of color.

When DW Griffith's blockbuster *Birth Of A Nation* played town, Jack Reagan forbade his sons from seeing it. He blasted the movie for its overt racism, and specifically for depicting the Ku Klux Klan as heroic.

For Jack Reagan, Klansmen were not heroes — but "bums in sheets."

The family patriarch's stance sent an important message. Just because something is popular doesn't make it right. *Racism is never right.* It is not something to be supported or even just ignored. It is something that must be directly challenged whenever, and wherever, it appears.

Although devoutly Christian, the Reagan family also emphasized respect for different faiths.

When Ronnie was just a boy, Jack, a Catholic, nearly died sleeping in his car one cold winter's night rather than stay in a hotel that proudly boasted that Jews were not welcome there. Unfortunately, it was the only shelter in town, and Jack's refusal to patronize a bigot led to a life-threatening bout of pneumonia. This was followed by his first heart attack—which seems to have contributed to his premature death at just 57 years of age.

The elder Reagan's stance had both positive and negative consequences. Although his sacrifice had affected his health and lifespan, its lesson of leading by example had a profound and lasting effect on his sons.

Years later, at a different Illinois hotel, Ron confronted similar bigotry directed at fellow members of his college football team. When two African-American players were denied lodging after a game, Reagan brought his teammates back to the family home to spend the night, where they were welcomed with open arms by Jack and Nelle.

In a time in which blacks and whites lived in separate worlds this was unthinkable. Blacks rarely set foot in white households, except as servants. The idea that two strangers would be welcomed in, offered beds, and seats at the table as welcome guests — as equals — was revolutionary.

The Reagan Family believed that words must be backed by deeds.

"Yea, a man may say, Thou hast faith, and I have works: shew me thy faith without thy works, and I will shew thee my faith by my works." (James 2:18)

In the 1930s, American society was still bitterly, and racially, divided.

At the time, there were still many Illinoisans who had been alive during the years in which Lincoln had been president. But so was Pleasant Riggs Crump, a Confederate veteran of the Civil War. Crump, who had personally witnessed General Robert E Lee's surrender to Ulysses S Grant at the Appomattox Court House, would live roughly another 20 years, passing on the cusp of the Civil Rights movement.

Seeing her son take a stand against racism was one of Nelle's proudest moments. It had not been an easy thing to do, and there would be a price to pay.

But for Ron, there had been no other option. By 20, his character was already established; his commitment to equality, fairness, and moral courage were at the core of who he was as a person.

After graduating, Reagan's love of sports led him to a career in broadcasting. While working as an announcer for a radio station in Iowa, he took a public stand against segregation in Major League Baseball. It was a bold move for someone just beginning one's career, as even criticizing discrimination in the 1930s could be legal grounds for termination.

The color barrier would not be broken until 1947, when the Brooklyn Dodgers added Jackie Robinson to their roster.

Working in Hollywood as a performer and later as the head of a union, Reagan developed a reputation for fairness. Even in those days, Southern California was a rich melting pot—which Reagan celebrated as part of America's great cultural heritage. Open, tolerant, and with a genuinely easygoing, live-and-let-live libertarian spirit, Reagan embraced the Golden Rule in all his dealings.

When he did encounter bigotry (as with a Los Angeles country club that wouldn't admit Jews), he spoke out and cancelled his membership. In a town that was all about networking, there is no doubt his stance hurt his career.

So be it.

During his time as the Republican Governor of California, Reagan had more persons with minority backgrounds on his staff than all previous administrations *combined*. In addition, the Governor made a regular practice of traveling into communities of color for direct, one-to-one dialogues with the residents as a means of getting unfiltered feedback on issues of concern.

While some denounced his belief in self-reliance as a cover for bigotry, Reagan contested this, citing his constancy in all matters dedicated to personal independence and responsibility, and advocacy for a society in which all were provided with equal opportunity.

For Reagan, issues of equality and fairness weren't the domain of any political party or movement, but central to what it meant to be an American.

He had, after all, been an early and vocal supporter of the Civil Rights Act of 1964. Initially proposed by Kennedy, signed into law by Johnson, this landmark piece of legislation outlawed discrimination based on race, skin color, religion, gender, or nationality. In many ways, this was a fulfillment of the 14th Amendment (passed in 1868), which sought to provide equal protection under the law for all Americans.

The law put an end to unequal voter registration requirements and racial segregation in schools, the workplace, and places that served the general public. Being a federal law, the legislation became the law of the land, overriding a patchwork of restrictive state laws.

Although generally an advocate of states' rights, Reagan viewed this as a defining national issue, going so far as to say that the new law should be enforced at "gunpoint" if necessary. There would be no turning back in the march towards equality, fairness, and justice.

Reagan's tough stand against discrimination of any sort also led him to oppose Affirmative Action. Again, he was consistent in his belief that any bias based on race, ethnicity, gender, or any other similar criteria was totally unacceptable.

Call it bias or call it preference — two wrongs never make a right.

Reagan advocated that persons be judged by the content of their character, and not by the color of their skin. And it was Reagan who, during his first term as president, signed into law a national holiday commemorating the life and contributions of Martin Luther King Jr.

Initially opposed for financial reasons related to the costs of adding a new federal holiday, the President came around when he saw that his reticence was being misconstrued and used as a catalyst for bigotry. In the end, he weighed the financial costs against the societal costs, and compromised in support of what he regarded as the long term, best interests of the nation.

By supporting the holiday, Ronald Reagan took a courageous stand against a small, but vocal minority of his fellow Republicans. Much had changed in the 15 years since King's assassination, but not everyone was comfortable with, or accepting of where society — much less the GOP — seemed to be moving.

Reagan's one-time mentor Barry Goldwater opposed it — as did his successor, Arizona Senator John McCain. Meanwhile, fellow Republican Senator Strom Thurmond of South Carolina aligned with the President and the majority of Republicans in both houses.

Thurmond's defection was an important symbol of how far his party had grown. For most of his career, Thurmond had been denounced as a racist and seen as openly hostile to the concerns of African-Americans. In fact, like many southerners, he had even abandoned the Democratic Party over its support of the 1964 Civil Rights Act.

But Thurmond was a complicated man. As one who had earned the Purple Heart for valor in combat, Thurmond knew something about bravery. He knew when to advance, and when to retreat. He was a survivor.

Leading Congressional opposition was Senator Jesse Helms. As one still strongly associated with the segregationist movement, many assumed the North Carolina Republican's opposition to King was racially-motivated; a charge that Helms vehemently denied.

Instead, Helms focused on character issues, citing King's opposition to the Vietnam War, along with allegations of communist sympathies, and "philandering."

Nor did Helms believe that King, (a Nobel laureate who had led America's Civil Rights Movement), was historically significant enough to warrant a dedicated national holiday.

Directly challenging Senator Helms was another well-known southern Republican, Senate majority leader, Howard Baker of Tennessee. Nicknamed the "Great Conciliator," Baker had been the first Republican senator elected by his state (1966) since Reconstruction.

Baker had a reputation as a nice guy who knew how to get things done. As the bill was debated, most in the Senate, including the majority of Republicans, supported Baker and Reagan. But Helms, a notorious obstructionist who delighted in his nickname of "Senator No" thrived on controversy and the limelight. He would not go without a fight.

Backed into a corner, Helms made a last-ditch appeal to fiscal conservatives; claiming the holiday would cost taxpayers $12 billion dollars a year. The accuracy of the Senator's estimate was contested by the (non-partisan) Congressional Budget Office, which placed the actual total closer to $18 million.

But by then, everyone knew the game was over. After 16 days of filibustering, "Senator No" abandoned his crusade in exchange for support on a pro-tobacco bill.

The MLK holiday bill easily passed on a vote of 78-22, denounced by Helms as a "tyranny of the minority."

Albeit a minor insurrection, some states such as Alabama, Arkansas, and Mississippi combined the King holiday with one honoring the Confederate General Robert E Lee. In Virginia, King was flanked by two Confederate generals, Lee, and Stonewall Jackson.

Those on both extremes of society's fringes had a stake in portraying Reagan as a racist, and his every word and action were analyzed for clues, then spun to fit a particular agenda. For liberals, exposing him as a bigot would provide them the "proof" they needed to denounce policies they asserted were motivated by hate and prejudice. For actual bona fide racists, officially adding Reagan to their ranks would be seen as an incredible trophy, lending legitimacy to their views and serving as an important recruiting tool. But once again, Reagan stayed true to his own path, doing what he felt was right, and best for the nation he was sworn to serve with honor.

America had a complicated history. Some traditions strengthened the country, while others hindered it. Reagan was both a pragmatist and an optimist: his focus was always on the future, and it was this mindset that served as his guiding light.

Embrace the good and stand up for what you believe in. As he liked to say, "If they try to run you out of town, smile, wave, and act like you're leading the parade."

Whenever possible, Reagan used his power to correct historical wrongs, facilitate healing, and build national unity.

President Reagan was also committed to publicly celebrating the lives of those who had given so much back to the country, often at times when they had been unwelcome and shunned for who they were as individuals. He did this in a variety of ways, including his frequent presentations of the Presidential Medal of Freedom to women, persons of color, non-Christians, and even homosexuals.

In just his first two terms, Reagan saluted more persons with this prestigious award than any other administration in history—and more than the previous three presidents combined. Reagan used the awards to acknowledge contributions made by a wide range of Americans, across many different disciplines. Those who contributed to the arts, and the nation's culture were also among his favorite recipients, including homosexuals such as Lincoln Kirstien, and African-Americans such as Pearl Bailey, Eubie Blake and James E Cheek.

A significant portion of the recipients were persons with whom he disagreed with politically, including Teddy Kennedy's sister, Eunice Kennedy Shriver, who was honored for her charitable work.

As always, the President was tolerant and gracious, trying hard to never lose sight of the bigger picture, and the role he could play to help heal and unify the nation.

But despite such overtures, Reagan was a frequent target of many in the left-leaning arts community. Sensing an opening to embarrass and challenge the President, some sought to see how far things might be pushed, firing the first shots in what would come to be known as the Culture Wars.

As an artist, entertainer, and defender of the constitutional guarantees of free expression, Reagan generally did not support censorship. Simply because something was "not his cup of tea" did not mean that it was necessarily his business or concern. He did, however, take issue when it was taxpayer money being used to support the exhibition of objectionable, intentionally provocative pornographic material being passed off as art by a small minority of cultural elitists anxious to impose their tastes on the general public.

Wisely, Reagan refused to be personally baited into a discussion of what constituted art. The President knew that even critics couldn't agree on how to define it, so therefore he prudently stayed above the fray when it pertained to publicly criticizing individual artists and works. In such instances, Reagan was quick to quote Lincoln, who had so wisely noted that it was "better to remain silent and be thought a fool than to speak out and remove all doubt." With this in mind, Reagan deliberately avoided criticizing particular artists or works.

In his stead, others in the administration picked up the torch, working with Congress to restore accountability to the government's spending on the arts.

For many cultural and social conservatives, the breaking point had come with an exhibition of works by Robert Mapplethorpe, which opened at the Cincinnati Contemporary Arts Center in early April. A native of New York City, Mapplethorpe had died the previous year at the age of 42 from AIDS.

Titled "The Perfect Moment," the exhibition featured nude photographs of a graphic nature, often depicting acts of homosexuality and sadomasochistic practices. Much to the administration's embarrassment, the exhibition had been at least partially sponsored by the National Endowment for the Arts.

The President found himself caught in the crossfire. Critics on both sides demanded that he drop everything and jump into the debate. Reagan kept his cool. Shutting out the noise of the crowd, he steadied himself, and walked out on to the tightrope.

President Reagan was a longtime supporter of the arts and the NEA.

He saw such support not only as adding to the nation's cultural legacy, but also valued it for its pure economic impact, in that every dollar seeded to the arts produced many more in return.

In other words, arts spending made good economic sense. Despite a reputation for frugality, budgeting for the arts had grown higher each year under Reagan and a fiscally conservative Congress dominated by Republicans.

But the Mapplethorpe show was the straw that broke the camel's back. Even if each dollar spent generated a million in return, this was a losing proposition. Some things were more important than money.

Disgusted and embarrassed, Reagan, did not finish reviewing the portfolio of "adults only" black and white photos placed on his desk. Instead, he closed the folder and looked away, wondering how long such images would haunt him.

Once again, but in a different sense, Reagan would now separate what, for the sake of description, is termed "art" and "artist."

After years in show business, the Reagans had many gay and lesbian friends. While he might personally find the behaviors objectionable, he did not see it as being his place to judge. God had created them; God would judge them.

Reagan shocked many fellow conservatives when he opposed a law in California that would have barred homosexuals from teaching in public schools, and once, when vacationing, the Reagans had left their children in the care of a well-known lesbian couple.

The ability to separate actions from individuals was not about the embrace of moral permissiveness, but rather religious teachings that stated it was not his place to question or condemn what God had created.

In accordance with this, he would not make issue of Mapplethorpe's sexuality. But the President would, however, make clear that taxpayer money should never be used to fund things like this again.

Never.

Sometimes, compromise means that both sides win. But in this instance, both sides lost, and Reagan was not happy about having been forced into this position.

Frustrated, repulsed, feeling betrayed, the President tossed Mapplethorpe's portfolio into the trash and decided to call it a day.

72

History Lessons

As promised, Congress passed a constitutional amendment permitting school prayer, and President Reagan signed it into law on Good Friday at a special ceremony in the Rose Garden at the White House.

As expected, the Teachers Union reacted immediately — and negatively.

Despite their best efforts to intimidate Congress into backing down, the union had been no match for the President, who had lobbied hard for its passage. The issue of school prayer had long been important to Reagan, who had been unsuccessful in previous bids to turn it into law during his first two terms in office. This time, Reagan had made the issue a campaign promise, which he pledged to fulfill if voters supported him by electing like-minded representatives to Congress.

Although voters did their part, the bill (which Reagan, in frustration personally outlined) had been bogged down in Congress; stalled by Democrats who used procedural delays to coordinate opposition efforts and solicit campaign contributions.

When the bill finally became law — ominously on Friday the 13th of April — the opposition, led by the national Teachers Union was fully prepared with a plan of attack.

Although the union began as a non-partisan organization with wide public support, its positions on issues — many of which had nothing to do with education — had been steadily sliding towards the far left side of the political scale since the 1970s. While membership was generally on the liberal side of most issues, the current leadership headed by Dr Caryn Freilauder embraced the extreme and radical fringe.

As a result, the union's "official" positions were frequently at odds not just with the American public, but also with its own rank-and-file dues-paying membership.

The chasm between the union bosses and teachers varied by issue. Most teachers wanted those who were incompetent removed from their ranks, while the union supported tenure regardless of job performance, and resisted even peer-based performance reviews. But it was on the issue of school prayer where the biggest split occurred. Union leadership, specifically President Freilauder, vehemently opposed it, while the majority of classroom educators supported it in percentages reflective of the American public.

Despite this divergence, the union brass decided to come out swinging against the amendment, with or without the support of its members.

In Freilauder's opinion, the amendment violated the separation of church and state, and so she believed her union had not just the right—*but the responsibility*—to fight it. Of the mindset that the proposition was both illegal and dangerous, she vowed to stop it by whatever means necessary, regardless of the havoc that ensued or the legality of the opposition's tactics.

Although the union immediately filed a lawsuit to stop implementation of the 27th Amendment, it would likely take years for the case to move through the courts, before eventually being heard by the US Supreme Court, which already had a conservative majority.

Three of the justices currently serving on the court were Reagan appointees: Kennedy, O'Connor, and Scalia. If the President had the opportunity to make another appointment—which seemed likely, he would be able to choose a true and unapologetic conservative, given the GOP's control of Congress—and thereby the Senate Judiciary Committee—the body entrusted with confirming new justices to the court.

A conservative appointment by Reagan would tilt the court even further to the right, which in the opinion of Freilauder, meant her challenge was, well, literally without a prayer.

Worse yet, if implemented, and school prayer did not result in the immediate downfall of Western Civilization, whatever momentum that existed based on the fear of the unknown would dissipate as the practice of prayer became the new norm.

Owing to this sense of urgency, Freilauder felt that any legal challenge must be preceded by immediate, defiant action to stop the first prayer from taking place.

The flag hoisted, Freilauder called her minions to battle.

First, to draw attention to this "emergency," the union would call upon members to participate in wildcat strikes, sit-ins, sick outs, and other orchestrated acts of civil disobedience. By making the public aware of what was at stake, the union hoped to pressure Congress into rescinding the amendment before it could be implemented at the start of the next school year.

The Teachers Union was the largest union in America, and possessed sizable cash reserves, which it threatened to exhaust in the fight.

This money would not just fund an army of high-paid attorneys, but also pay for a slick advertising campaign to "educate" voters about the dire consequences of their uniformed choices. The union also declared war on Republicans (and turncoat Democrats), vowing to use its resources to defeat any candidate at the next election who supported school prayer.

While this sort of political retaliation was nothing new, the union had money to burn and could scale things up to a level never before seen. But the matter that generated the most concern was the threat to shut down the schools; thereby using the tactic of collective punishment to force submission.

Closures would begin starting in May. If the measure was not promptly repealed by Congress, school would not resume in September. Under no condition would the union permit the return of prayer into the nation's classrooms.

Freilauder readily acknowledged that the impact of shutting down the schools on families and society would be "unfortunate," but this was a matter of principle, and there could be no backing down. And when it concerns schools, the principle has the final word.

If the children missed some school, well, so what? How parents would cover childcare needs (and costs) was not the union's concern. This was a lesson in activism and the power of the people to bring down a government, even if it had to use children as hostages.

A diminutive white woman with closely-cropped salt-and-pepper hair, Freilauder raised her fist in the air, evoking the gesture made popular by the Black Power movement during the late 1960s.

"This is history in the making!" proclaimed Freilauder, her little eyes flashing behind tiny round plastic-framed glasses.

Although the union did not have the power to directly fire members, it did have the authority to revoke individual memberships, and would do so, for any teacher that sided with the law instead of the union. Because it had complete control of the nation's school system, loss of union membership would effectively end one's career working in public education.

Freilauder had drawn a line in the sand, and there was no room for dissent.

While the White House had anticipated both a legal challenge and the usual threats to target politicians, other elements of the union's strategy came as a shock, if only for the reason that many of the threatened actions were flat-out illegal.

As a former six-term head of a union and lifetime member of the AFL-CIO, Reagan was personally taken aback.

He had always publicly supported unions in his comments and actions, although relations with organized labor had taken a dip after he had fired striking air traffic controllers during his first year in office.

Despite "representing" management in the dispute, the President appeared conciliatory and generally sympathetic to the demands of the union members. Reagan felt he had a good rapport with PATCO (the air traffic controllers union), which had endorsed him when he ran for office. Certainly something could be worked out.

But how giving would the President be? To test his resolve, union leadership rejected the administration's offers and pleas, and ordered its members to the picket line.

There was no disputing that the PATCO strike was illegal — and that it threatened public safety. Reagan responded by setting a deadline for the strikers to return to work; promising to continue with good faith negotiations.

Despite an escalating war of words with union leaders, the President remained optimistic: Every member had personally signed a binding pledge not to strike, plus, he had given them a couple of days to cool down and think things over. Most importantly, with Ronald Reagan, they were dealing with a fellow union brother — a man who had himself once led a strike. He gave his word to be fair and asked for their trust.

But Reagan also made it clear that he would not back down from his deadline. Some members accepted the President's call, broke rank, and returned to duty, while those who followed the union's orders were indeed fired.

The action had huge political consequences, but it also cemented the President's reputation as someone who wouldn't be bluffed or give in to extortion.

But now the teachers wanted to test him again.

Weeks before the amendment's signing, Press Secretary Limbaugh—who always had his ear to the ground, warned the President of trouble brewing, and the possibility that things might turn ugly. For years, Limbaugh had been aware of the fissures within the union, and the increasingly radicalized positions taken by the organization's out-of-touch president and top officials. Still, the union's threats to flagrantly break the law caught everyone by surprise.

Rather than add fuel to the fire with a public rebuttal, the President first sent Education Secretary William Bennett to meet privately with the group. Reagan hoped establishing a personal dialogue would at least remove some vitriol from the debate, and show his commitment to resolving differences in a civil manner. "We might never agree on the issue, but I hope that we can at least agree on the importance of civility, mutual respect, and finding areas of commonality."

One area where Reagan sought common ground concerned respect for the law, and the need to have the legal system—not mob rule—determine the legitimacy of the amendment. He understood their impatience, but was adamant that in America no one was above the law.

As the President was quick to point out, although he had disagreed with the 1962 Supreme Court decision ending school prayer, one does not pick and choose which laws they will obey. Instead, one must work within the system to enact change—even if, in the case of returning prayer to the classroom, it had taken more than a quarter century.

Nor should one abuse a position of leadership by encouraging lawlessness. While Reagan had personally disagreed with the court's ban on prayer, he did not, as governor, or president, call upon people to break laws based on philosophical differences. This onus to lead by example was a special responsibility for those entrusted to serve as society's role models: politicians, police officers, and especially school teachers—because of their direct involvement with children.

So, Secretary Bennett was sent off with an olive branch. While the White House could not undo the amendment at this point, Reagan hoped that both sides could at least agree to disagree in a manner that was respectful, and observant of the law.

The union president did not share this perspective. Freilauder felt that it was the citizen's responsibility to stand up and oppose laws that were unjust, and compared herself to Nelson Mandela and the struggle to topple Apartheid in South Africa.

As a student at NYU during the sixties, Freilauder had participated in a number of strikes, protests, and various illegal activities she felt were justified as serving the greater good.

Seeking to cast her union in a similar light, Freilauder made it clear that there would be no backing down. The hierarchy of her organization was behind her 100%, and would not be intimidated. They were ready to "do the right thing," no matter the consequences.

Reagan just rolled his eyes, shook his head, and tried not to laugh. "I remember when protestors used to quote Marx to me, but now we're down to just movie titles."

Bennett cracked a smile, acknowledging the reference to the recent film by Spike Lee.

The President removed his glasses, and looked directly at Bennett.

"Would it help if I met with them personally? Spoke with Freilauder one-to-one?"

"No, boss," said Bennett, shaking his head. "They're hardened. We need Plan B. Now."

The President was neither happy nor surprised. Unlike the air traffic controllers, the leaders of the Teachers Union were not federal employees he could directly fire. Still, they were breaking the law, and threatening to break more until the government capitulated to their demands.

Although one of the few politicians in Washington who was not an attorney, Reagan nonetheless had a solid understanding of the law. To him, a number of the union's actions seemed to suggest illegal practices such as extortion and conspiracy, of the manner usually practiced by organized crime bosses.

This opinion was confirmed by the White House legal staff, led by Attorney General Bork who had been monitoring the union's words and actions.

Reagan felt as if he had given the group the chance to take a different approach, but now there was no going back. They had made their choice — and so had the President.

"Like it or not, we live in a nation of laws, and no one is above the law — even the President, whether it be of the nation, or some renegade union.

"If the teachers were thinking we'd just give in, well, then they just failed history.

"Book 'em Danno," said Reagan, quoting the line made famous on the long-running TV show *Hawaii 5-0*.

With that, Bork, along with help from his team at the Justice Department and the FBI began assembling their case.

Ever respectful of putting the interests of the school children first, no moves would be taken until the bell rang for the start of summer recess.

When it did, action was quick and firm: union president Freilauder, and six other top officials were arrested. Complicating matters further was the discovery of certain financial improprieties, resulting in additional criminal charges.

If a report card was to be issued instead of arrest warrants, the teachers would have flunked not just history, but civics, and accounting as well.

With Freilauder and her cronies under indictment, elections were promptly held to select replacements, who were (at least on the surface) somewhat more reasonable, and accountable to their members. A full house cleaning was long overdue, and would proceed accordingly.

The union's lawsuit challenging the legality of the prayer amendment would proceed, and the organization would continue to support Democrats.

While the union continued to be an annoyance, the leadership toned down its antagonistic rhetoric, distanced itself from any further (overt) criminal activity, and signaled its intent to comply with an amendment that permitted, but would never require, children a moment of prayer.

73

Taking a Stand

Even though an illegal revolt against the school prayer amendment had been avoided, the Teachers Union was still intent on challenging the law in court, and was aggressively working to defeat any candidate who supported it at the November midterm elections. Thanks to its massive financial reserves, the union became the single largest contributor to the Democratic Party.

As the head of his party, Ronald Reagan was expected — and anxious — to campaign on behalf of fellow Republicans. According to the polls, the GOP would likely add several new seats in both houses, further increasing its majority status in Congress.

Among those up for grabs was a block in the Senate that had been a consequence of Teddy Kennedy's failed attempt at a *coup d'état*. Rather than face prosecution and public humiliation, Kennedy's co-conspirators had resigned *en masse*, unceremoniously ending political careers that went back decades.

Following the wave of resignations in March of the previous year, the vacant Senate seats had been filled in various ways in accordance with each state's protocols. From appointments to special rushed partisan elections, all were presently occupied by Democrats. Many of these new Democratic Senators were political novices, party hacks and ideologues that now appeared to be in serious trouble.

The fact that Democrats held all eight seats was not so much a reflection of public sentiment, as it was an example of how entrenched partisanship rigs the system to ensure the continuity of party representation. In other words, the public never had a choice to vote for a Republican candidate to fill any of these vacancies. But all of that was destined to change as soon as the voters were given their say in the November elections.

While having a Republican majority in both houses had greatly reduced gridlock and allowed the President to make progress on many campaign promises, he had also encountered resistance even from within his own party on certain issues. Some had genuine philosophical differences, whereas as others were simply too afraid of alienating well-funded special interest groups.

The President understood, and accepted, compromise as a part of politics. But he also firmly believed in honesty, and the need to take a stand on issues that mattered. Reagan held a special contempt for RINOS — *Republicans In Name Only* — who were in many cases no better than a conservative Democrat.

In accordance with these values, Reagan limited his campaigning (including endorsements) to those that were genuinely willing to support him in doing what Americans — by an overwhelming major-ity — had returned him to Washington to do.

The people wanted the Reagan Revolution to continue, and to provide their leader with the support troops he needed to succeed.

For the most part, these decisions were pretty simple. The GOP majority was never threatened, so now the President could be a bit more selective — and he was: going as far as endorsing a few Independents and even one renegade Democrat over a less-committed Republican running for a seat in the House of Representatives.

In advance of the elections, the President announced that he wanted Congress to support him on two more major initiatives: line-item veto power, and an overhaul of the welfare system. If a candidate was not willing to do this, please step aside for one that would.

Emphasizing these two goals — both campaign promises from 1988 — was the essence of the Reagan Revolution as a movement that combined fiscal and socially conservative values. As initiatives, line-item veto power and welfare reform merged objectives, although in different ratios.

Welfare reform certainly had a financial component, but it was also driven by the opinion that some recipients needed an incentive to become contributing members to society, rather than life-long depend-ents. No one would be forced to work, but those who did, would not be forced to permanently support those able-bodied adults who chose not to.

As Reagan was quick to note, "Most people don't like to work — that's why they pay you. Taking money from those who work to subsidize someone else's endless vacation is unfair and indefensible."

Meanwhile line-item veto power would help the President to rein in spending by trimming "pork" from the budget. Without such authority, the Chief Executive of the United States had little recourse but to sign off on whatever Congress threw at him. Tax, borrow, spend was an anathema to the principle of reducing the size of government.

Most politicians want to be loved, and they regard showering voters with gifts as one way to achieve this. The current system was all about short-term gratification and denial of the long-term consequences.

As governor, Reagan had used his veto power nearly a thousand times to put the brakes on irresponsible state spending. The line-item veto was a standard tool available to most governors—although not to the President.

Yes, there would be grumbling and even protests. But enough was enough. It was time to spend some of his accrued political capital to do what was best for America.

Striking a defiant tone, Reagan let it be known that he was willing to personally take the heat for doing what the pleasers in Congress either couldn't — or wouldn't.

"The buck stops here. I'll take the criticism, so long as I also get the credit for doing what everyone knows needs to be done.

"With this authority, members of Congress can continue the practice of submitting wasteful proposals to satisfy the special interest groups that fund their campaigns, while sparing taxpayers the cost of such superfluous spending."

Line-item veto power was central to producing a balanced budget.

Balancing the budget was already law for most state governments, and was also something that Reagan intended to seek—as a constitutional amendment—once the war was over and the economy had a chance to stabilize. But for now the federal government had extraordinary responsibilities different from the states, and such a proposal just wasn't practical at this time.

For now, the line-item veto was a fair and reasonable compromise.

While the measure stood a good chance of passing, any proposal to overhaul the current welfare system was likely to meet with much broader opposition. While those on both sides of the issue acknowledged that the system was broken, until Reagan, no one had the will or courage necessary to take on such a divisive and explosive issue at the national level.

The President attributed much of the opposition to an irrational fear of the unknown. To address these concerns, he would present a comprehensive proposal detailing how reforms were not just necessary, but how they would actually benefit all concerned — from taxpayers to recipients.

The ultimate goal was to preserve and expand benefits for the truly needy by ensuring the solvency of the program, eliminating waste and fraud, and providing a pathway for able-bodied adults to become self-sufficient.

Acknowledging the immensity, and inherent controversy of the issue, the White House saw the overhaul as a transition that would take place in stages over a period of years, emphasizing that no one would be cut off immediately, or without sufficient notice.

Paralleling the tightening of eligibility requirements would be new employment opportunities created by worker training programs, assisted by the President's economic policies, which were, despite the on-going effects of the war, producing results in the area of new job creation and hiring.

Still, any suggestion of change provided the Democrats with an issue to rally their base of frightened and uninformed constituents. Liberal activists seized the opportunity to denounce the proposals as racist, and more specifically, as an assault on the black community — which constituted the largest non-white block in the Democrat's coalition.

In debates fueled by emotion, facts are irrelevant. While liberals sought to attack reform as a war on persons of color, in terms of sheer numbers, the overwhelming majority of those on public assistance were actually white and able-bodied.

In desperation, liberals again tried to play the race card. Reforming welfare was racist, as was every aspect of Reagan's economic policy, now referred to as "Racist-nomics."

Not surprisingly, this particular smear campaign had little credibility, given the mounting body of evidence illustrating how the black community had benefited from Reagan's economic policies. In fact, African-Americans had gained significantly more than any other group — including whites — under President Reagan.

After inheriting an economy in tatters, Reagan's economic recovery program began to gain traction within a year, and between 1982 and the end of his second term, black employment was up by almost 30%, while the number of black families in the highest income bracket (over $50,000 at the time) soared by a whopping 86%. More than 2.6 million African-Americans were added to the nation's workforce—resulting in their unemployment rate being cut by more than half.

Under the previous "black friendly" Democratic administration of Jimmy Carter, per capita income for blacks was up by barely 1%—and 2.4% for whites. Under Reagan (82-88), per-capita earning by blacks actually outperformed whites (18% to 14%).

In contrast, incomes for those on public assistance barely rose at all. Those who stayed on welfare were stagnating in poverty, while those who took advantage of the opportunities being created by Reagan were succeeding as never before.

While the President always intended his programs to be colorblind and not favor any group over another, there was no denying the data that the black population had—despite public perception—benefitted significantly, and had outperformed all other races, including whites.

The President expected similar gains under welfare reform, and hoped that in time African-Americans would once again identify with the GOP—and not the Democrats, as the party that had their long-term best interests at heart.

This was, as Reagan liked to remind those who would listen, the party of Lincoln. With emancipation, the Republicans offered freedom with uncertainty, as contrasted with the Democratic alternative of slavery, but stability.

More than a 150 years later not much had changed, except that most had forgotten that Abraham Lincoln was a Republican, and that Jefferson Davis, the President of the Confederacy, had been a Democrat.

Tackling entrenched perceptions and stereotypes would be difficult, but Reagan felt it was not just possible—but necessary. As he saw it, the current welfare system created despondency and dependency rather than optimism and opportunity.

Like patients hooked on pain pills, the Democrats exploited the fears of getting off the meds and healing oneself with physical therapy. If people actually gained strength and cleared their perceptions, they might see themselves, and the opportunities before them in a different light.

As governor, Reagan had at least partially succeeded in reforming the welfare system in California — despite a left-leaning legislature. Now, with a conservative majority in Congress, he hoped to go even further in his dream of making America truly a land of opportunity for all.

74

A House Divided Cannot Stand

Now is the *spring* of our discontent …

As temperatures rose across Europe, opposition to Soviet rule began to heat up from all corners of their empire.

With expansionist plans cast aside, the Kremlin made a feeble attempt to resume "normal" relations with the West, including an overture regarding arms control talks with Washington. Refusing to acknowledge the legitimacy of the Sokolov regime, Reagan made it clear that negotiations were already under way between the United States and the Soviet government-in-exile, headed by Secretary General Mikhail Gorbachev.

Similar rebuffs came from other Western nations, most of which no longer maintained a diplomatic relationship with what was being passed off as the USSR these days. In sharp contrast to the initial wave of goodwill and trust that had followed the coup, these days the Russians found themselves shunned and despised by most of the world they once dreamed would be theirs by now.

It had been a hard fall on the international stage, but the USSR's problems went much, much deeper, and were only getting worse by the day.

Internally, Moscow was bracing for what promised to be widespread public protests against its rule, organized under the auspices of International Workers' Day, also known as May Day—May first.

When May Day came, the demonstrations were worse than the KGB had predicted. There was a uneasy feeling that the foundation was cracking, but how things would split, and where they would fall was unknown. With great ambiguity comes great danger.

Attempts to put down the May Day protests were unevenly enforced. In some places (such as the Ukraine), the crackdown was harsh, as armed government forces brutally turned on their own people. In contrast was Czechoslovakia, where protests led by Vaclav Havel, a well-known dissident and playwright, were largely ignored. Such was also the case in Poland, where demonstrators, headed by Solidarity founder Lech Walesa, demanded more religious freedom and rights for workers.

While different republics prioritized different issues, all were united in calling for an end to Moscow's rule, and demanding that elections be open to non-socialist candidates. In short, an end to the USSR, and to imposed socialism.

Most protests were large public affairs, but also short-lived, and seemed more intended to test the waters than to actually initiate revolutions. Demonstrators kept things peaceful, employing tactics of non-violent resistance popularized in the United States by Dr Martin Luther King Jr and the Civil Rights movement.

While the US attempted to assist in any way it could, the inspiration and implementation had mostly been homegrown, which no doubt caused the Kremlin even greater cause for alarm. Worse yet, was the fear of what might happen if the forces called upon to crush the protestors revolted, and turned their weapons back towards their Soviet masters.

Still, pro-democracy support had come from America, Western Europe, and perhaps most notably, from the now liberated, eastern section of Germany.

Many in the former GDR still had connections with the neighboring states of Poland and Czechoslovakia, especially in the regions with large concentrations of German speakers, which had longstanding cultural and historical ties to Germany.

East Germany's freedom added new hope to those still imprisoned behind the Iron Curtain. The fact that change—liberation and freedom—had all happened so quickly, with so little bloodshed, and without Russian retaliation suggested that anything was now possible.

With spring came hope.

Thanks to broadcast towers erected near the newly revised borders, the Voice of America, the BBC, and other entities were now able to reach much further into the Eastern Bloc than ever before, providing an important alternative to the officially-sanctioned state propaganda.

The physical borders between East and West were also increasingly porous. Given that East Germany, Czechoslovakia, and Poland had all, until just recently, been on the same side, border reinforcements had never been as pronounced—or as necessary—as those that had partitioned East and West Germany. While the Poles under direct orders from General Wojciech Jaruzelski continued to station troops along the German border and issue threats, Milos Jakes, the communist leader of Czechoslovakia seemed much less concerned; seemingly resigned to the shifting sands of history.

Things were slowly imploding across the USSR, but how matters would eventually play out was still a mystery. For now, there were just too many open variables.

The West, and for its part, the entire world had a vested interest in making sure that the transition was orderly. The idea of one government collapsing, only to be replaced by mobocracy or something far worse, remained a distinct possibility — especially in Russia.

According to intelligence sources, Sokolov was now wobbling, and being circled by packs of wolves intent on wresting control. Whether Sokolov was playing one group against the other to maintain authority was unknown, but as the clock ran down on his regime, so did the need to have actionable plans for whatever threat, or opportunity, arose next.

75

The Bully of Baghdad

As the internal crisis in the USSR deepened, America and its allies prepared for invasion—and occupation. If the Soviet empire began to fragment, it would be necessary to have a strong stabilizing presence to guard against anarchy, and to ensure that the vast stockpiles of weapons—notably the nukes—were secured, and protected from falling into the wrong hands—be they domestic or foreign.

Perhaps in acknowledgement of this uncertain future, Moscow expedited the repatriation of the last of its "advisors" and troops positioned around the world; a process that had begun with the withdrawal from Afghanistan, but which was now expanding to include forces in Africa, Latin America, and to a lesser degree, the Middle East.

The Soviet withdrawal from Afghanistan created a power vacuum, as several factions were now embroiled in a bloody civil war to gain control. It was a horrific mess, but not something the United States could afford to be dragged into. Instead, the US needed to stay focused on making sure a similar situation didn't occur within the borders of the USSR itself.

Watching world events carefully was Iraqi President Saddam Hussein.

Saddam had ruled Iraq since the 1970s—although he was not officially recognized as president until 1979, just as neighboring Iran was beginning its Islamic Revolution. While the relationship between Iran and Iraq was never great, things were relatively stable until the revolution, when Iran became a theocracy ruled by the Ayatollah Ruhollah Khomeini.

Saddam personally despised the Ayatollah. He also believed, and rightfully so, that Khomeini would attempt to export, and incite, Islamic religious fanaticism in order to destabilize Iraq and topple Saddam's rule.

Therefore, when Iraq attacked Iran in September of 1980, it came as little surprise. Evenly matched, the two nations slugged it out for eight years, earning it the unwelcome distinction of being the 20th century's longest conventional war.

For the most part, the United States — under Carter, then Reagan — remained essentially neutral in the dispute, although given the region's reputation as a source of oil and terrorism, Washington maintained a watchful eye.

In spite of the war's heavy toll, it now seemed that Iraq was gearing up for another fight, although this time it was moving in on a much smaller and weaker neighbor: Kuwait.

Despite its tiny size, Kuwait was a major supplier of oil, and therefore any threat to the stability of this resource was a cause for concern by the West — and especially the Europeans.

As the issue was brought before the UN Security Council, a parallel review took place at the White House. As standard protocol for situations of this nature, the President assembled a team representing military, intelligence, diplomatic, and other related interests he needed to determine how the United States should best respond.

The President's briefing began with an overview of Iraq's origins — from the definition of its borders in 1920 — up through its colonial period (under the British) on up to the rise of Saddam Hussein and the Ba'ath Party.

Due to how the borders were drawn, Iraq was not a homogeneous nation. Within its boundaries existed several different religious groups that were generally at odds with one another, each vying for power, each a desire to become a separate nation.

Of particular concern was a large segment of the population that identified as Shia, the branch of Islam popular in Iran. Opposing the Shia were the majority Sunnis, the group to which Saddam belonged. But even within these two main divisions there were deeply divided factions, each convinced that because it held the truth, it should also hold the power.

Maintaining order over such a diverse and divisive population required an iron fist, and this was something Saddam excelled at, as any disloyalty or threats to his rule were quickly, and violently dealt with.

President Hussein didn't believe in taking chances. He was determined not to be brought down either like the Shah of Iran by a religious uprising, or by rogue elements within his own military — as had been the case in Egypt and Libya.

Like Colonel Qaddafi, Saddam was descended from a family of

shepherds, and was resolved to not lose control of his flock.

Although oil rich, the long war with Iran had taken a measurable toll on Iraq and its economy. Rather than seek a rematch, or take on the well-armed Syrians to the east (who had resources of little value), Saddam set his sights on his wealthy southern neighbor, a constitutional monarchy with roughly one-tenth Iraq's population.

The formal reasons provided for Iraq's dispute with Kuwait came down to two main grievances. First, Saddam contested the legitimacy of borders created by the British. Secondly, he claimed that Kuwait was using an illegal process known as slant-drilling to siphon away Iraqi oil. Although both claims had some legitimacy, efforts to resolve them peacefully, using established protocols had gone nowhere.

Unofficially, Saddam had other reasons to attack. To fund his war against Iran, he had borrowed roughly $10 billion from the Kuwaitis, which they now wanted repaid—with interest. But perhaps more importantly, Saddam fancied himself as a warrior who found his mojo by leading his nation in battle.

So, within two years of wrapping up the war with Iran, the bad boy of Baghdad was now positioning himself to take Kuwait—unless someone stepped in to stop it.

Acknowledging the stakes and complexities of the situation, President Reagan needed a tremendous amount of information—and contrasting perspectives—in order to make the right decision. He also needed to act quickly, given the speed at which the situation was escalating.

The "Carter Doctrine" (established by Jimmy Carter in 1980, then modified by the Reagan administration a year later), was frequently cited as justification for the use of military force by the United States to protect its national interests in the Persian Gulf. For many, this seemed to provide a clear-cut directive for Kuwait's defense.

Leading the case for US action against Iraq was Energy Secretary Schlesinger, who had also served as Carter's first Energy Secretary.

In support of this position, Schlesinger read from a personal letter sent to him by his former boss, reflecting a consensus opinion of the former administration, including both Secretaries of State (Edmund Muskie and Cyrus Vance), Secretary of Defense Harold Brown, UN Representative Andrew Young, and NSA Advisor Zbignew Brzezinski.

Former Vice President Bush also weighed in to express support for military intervention to "send a message."

Bush, who had very close personal ties with the Saudi royal family, relayed shared concerns that Saddam would not stop with Kuwait, but instead wanted to control all of the region's oil fields.

The marathon White House briefings lasted for the better part of two days, veering from impassioned calls to action, to page after page of calculations concerning oil production figures.

Reagan listened attentively, occasionally asking questions, sometimes making notes, but usually just maintaining his typical reserve.

As a former actor, Reagan knew how to maintain his composure as the presenters made their cases. Some passionately shook and pounded their fists, while others, contrasted in both policy and body language adopted a grim and foreboding tone, their voices so overwhelmed by the dire seriousness of it all as to be barely audible. The only unifying element was the attention that each paid to Reagan, searching for some sign that he was supportive of their position.

By not tipping his hand to indicate a preference one way or the other, the President felt he had a better chance of hearing all sides of the issue—which is what he wanted and needed. Being surrounded by a team of yes men (and women)—only saying what they thought he wanted to hear—was a character flaw driven by ego and the need to be flattered.

It was probably what Saddam was subjected to—Reagan would be different.

By early Friday afternoon the President announced that he had heard enough, and asked that the meeting be adjourned until Monday, at which time he would reveal his decision.

Within two hours, the Reagans were on their way to Camp David.

News of the trip was immediately leaked, and Reagan was attacked by many even within his own party for what they regarded as a dereliction of duty. Former Vice President Bush was said to be furious, wondering if Reagan was "still right in the head."

Most of those in the current administration remained loyal to the President and understood the magnitude of the decision he was being forced to make. The President was always available in the event of an emergency, but deciding what to do about Iraq required he put aside all but the most urgent item before him.

Two days away would not have any significant effect on the Iraqis, but it would provide the time the President needed in order to fully consider options and consequences without distractions.

Reagan needed the solitude of "Aspen," and in particular, the opportunity to go horseback riding, as he found this activity especially conducive to making major decisions. As the President rode the trails, he envisioned the road ahead. This path led here, that one there.

All the while he was aware of sand running through the hourglass.

After a lengthy ride early Sunday morning, Reagan returned for lunch, and then, before heading back to Washington, went for a swim.

For more than an hour the President swam laps by himself. It was one of his favorite activities, something he found both therapeutic and meditative.

Rising from the water, Reagan knew what needed to be done, and knew it wouldn't be easy.

76

Reagan's Decision

Reinvigorated by his weekend at Camp David, the President met with his team bright and early Monday morning to address the situation with Iraq's impending invasion of Kuwait.

President Reagan realized there was no perfect solution to the problem, and this would be another case of damned if you do, damned if you don't.

The President began his comments noting that by the time the US could deploy forces to the region it would not be to reinforce Kuwait, but to do battle with the Iraqis.

"How far are we prepared to go with such a war? he asked, looking around the room.

"Do we just drive them out of Kuwait, and stop there, or do we push on up into Iraq? Once there, do we occupy Iraq and initiate regime change?

"Do we have clear objectives? Do we have the support of the American people?

"What are our interests?"

The President paused, as the group reflected on this point.

"Certainly, we are opposed to some tyrannical dictator attacking a defenseless neighbor. But this is an ongoing problem, all over the world. We can't stop every single incidence of aggression.

"Our interests in this conflict are limited … and are mostly about oil. While Kuwait is important, it is not on par with Saudi Arabia. If it was, it would make my decision much easier."

Reagan then spoke of his contempt for Iraq's president, Saddam Hussein, whom he regarded as a thug, a bully, and a criminal—but also typical of that which passed for "leadership" in the Middle East.

"If we take out Saddam, who, or what, fills the void? Do the Syrians, heavily armed and backed by the Soviets, spill in from the east? Or do the Iranians invade from the west? Do borders begin to dissolve, giving rise to pan-national fundamentalist religious states?

"As we know, our dear friend Colonel Qaddafi has been seeking to unite the Islamic world into a socialist theocracy. For years he's been using Libya's oil wealth, Russian arms, and terrorism in pursuit of a radical Islamic state … a *caliphate*. He's also pals with both the Iranians and the Syrians—so who better to take over from Saddam?

"Do we really want a state like this, ruled by a madman, on the border with moderate Arab nations like Turkey and Jordan? Within striking distance of the Saudi oil fields?

"Right now, Iraq's neighbors—Syria and Iran—have reason to fear it and keep their distance. Iraq is well armed, backed by a large and disciplined fighting force.

"The Joint Chiefs of Staff tell me Iraq has the fourth largest army in the world—more than a million men … thousands of tanks, artillery pieces … sophisticated aircraft and weapons systems.

"If the Iraqis attack Kuwait, they'll overtake it pretty quickly … Kuwait hasn't spent its oil riches on defense; instead it is relying on others to defend it—so as to protect the flow of oil. It's too small to do anything on its own—it needs us.

"But do we need it? And what are we prepared to do to preserve it?" asked the President.

"Pushing Iraq out of Kuwait will require at least 100,000 troops—and that still gives them a ten-to-one-man advantage over us. Now, I guess we could divide things up a bit, and build some kind of a coalition with other countries, so that the commitment—troops, costs, and so forth might be shared—as Secretary Schultz has suggested.

"I think this is a good idea, and under normal circumstances, I'd support it. But where will we pull these troops from? If the Soviet Union implodes, we're going to need all hands on deck to prevent a nuclear situation.

"Let's be clear: Saddam wants Kuwait for financial reasons—he's after the oil revenue. As I said, he's typical of that region—just another pompous criminal. Ruthless, a despot—but I don't think he's completely crazy like Qaddafi. But, like Qaddafi, he'll sell the oil to whoever is willing to pay his price—as he needs that money to maintain his grip on power.

"I don't like him, and I'd prefer to see him gone ASAP—but I also need to be realistic about what America's interests are globally.

"My cabinet secretaries tell me that Kuwait is not critical to the world's supply of oil. Kuwait is not a democracy. Kuwait has not been especially supportive of the United States, and *our* interests. They regard us as *customers* ... We have a business relationship with them, and that's the extent of it."

Reagan let the truth of this assessment sink in. He was right, and they knew it.

"I think the US should continue to use whatever diplomatic pressure is at our disposal to convince the Iraqis that invading Kuwait is not in their best interest, even if that means suggesting that we are prepared to take military action against them.

"That said, Saddam is no idiot, and he'll likely call our bluff. He knows that if we were to do anything—even a small response—we'd be pulling troops from elsewhere. Do we abandon Europe? Israel? Do we leave Qaddafi with a box of matches and no babysitter?

"No, and the Iraqis know that.

"Next, I think we should put pressure on the Saudis to form a coalition of like-minded states to prepare for their own defense.

"We've given them untold billions in oil revenue, and they need to pony up more of that for their own defense.

"I don't think Saddam will try to take them on; I think he'll stop at the border. If he does start to move on Saudi Arabia, we'll address that. If he starts in soon—before things play out with Russia—well, we won't have the conventional forces to stop him, and so I think he knows what that would mean."

Was the President suggesting he'd use nuclear weapons against Iraq? The same president who had spent the better part of his political life campaigning for the end of such weapons?

Reagan sensed the discomfort.

"This is not an action I would take lightly, but not one I would walk away from if I had no other choice.

"Saddam knows this, and I don't think he'll push it. He wants money and power, and for now, we need to let him have it."

Looking somber, Reagan stated what everyone was thinking.

"I wish we could save everyone, but we can't, and so we need to prioritize.

"The Soviet Union—with its nuclear arsenal—is our top concern.

If that goes, everything goes, and that includes us.

"I'm sorry for the Kuwaitis and for the Saudis. But maybe it's time for them to cooperate on more than just fixing oil prices and complaining about Israel."

It was true, heads nodded in agreement, as all eyes stayed on the Commander-in-Chief.

It was clear that his mind was made up. When the President spoke, it was with a tone of firmness and resolve.

"So that's it: We apply diplomatic pressure, we support the Kuwaitis and Saudis in any way we can—with intelligence data and so forth, but we don't get involved in a major ground war in Iraq. Not now, preferably not ever."

The meeting adjourned, and events began to unfold as forecast.

Diplomatic pressure had no effect. Iraq invaded and occupied Kuwait with little resistance, but did not cross into Saudi Arabia.

Iraq's actions were widely criticized and denounced, but given the world's dependency on a steady supply of oil, no one took action of any consequence that threatened either Saddam's rule or the West's addiction to black gold.

Boycotting Iraq (which now occupied Kuwait's oilfields), would only help fellow oil producers Libya and Iran. Saudi Arabia was already pumping at full capacity and was in no position to increase production, at least anytime in the near future.

Iraq's invasion created some temporary anxiety on world markets, and the price of oil fluctuated wildly for a few weeks. But soon the amount of crude entering the market actually began to increase, resulting in lower prices.

A hero to his people, Saddam set about remodeling his palaces and raising monuments to himself in different parts of the country. Fearful of their emboldened neighbor, Iran was forced to scale back its support of international terrorism in order to shore up defenses at home.

With the price of oil falling fast, the economies of Iran and Libya went into shock, as both experienced turbulence caused by inflation and shortages. Accompanying the economic turmoil were signs of social unrest. Small at first, but the seeds had been planted and were beginning to grow.

It was truly a crude awakening.

As suggested, the Saudis began to assemble a coalition of moderate Arab states and enhance their defenses. Mercenary troops, (primarily from Sub-Saharan Africa and including many non-Muslims) were brought in and stationed appropriately, away from the cities and at a distance from the general public.

Attempts by the Saudi-led Arab coalition member states to purchase sophisticated military equipment were somewhat less successful. Not only did the US need nearly everything at its disposal for whatever happened next with the USSR, but Israel was also able to exert significant influence on the US Congress to restrict the sale of anything it thought might one day be used against it.

Despite assurances that the US would continue to make Israel's defense a priority, Prime Minister Yitzhak Shamir was naturally worried about the rise of a wealthier, larger, and more powerful Iraq, as well as a new defense-based coalition of Arab states.

Reagan understood completely.

Saddam had frequently threatened the Jewish state, and when it looked as if his words might be backed up with action (by developing atomic weapons), Israel responded in 1981, using a squadron of US supplied F-16s to knock out Iraq's only nuclear reactor.

The battle over proposed weapon sales to Arab countries had a familiar ring to it. Under a deal made during the Carter administration — and honored by President Reagan, the US had supplied the Saudis with AWACs — an airborne early warning and control aircraft manufactured by Boeing. So far, the Saudis had used the aircraft responsibly and not against Israel, or to support any of the other more radicalized Arab states in the region.

Reagan believed encouraging moderate Arab nations was the key to peace in the Middle East, but given the long history of broken promises, Israel had reason for concern.

All the old rules were changing, and Israel was now in the difficult and dangerous position of being forced to choose between the lesser of two evils: either trust and support a buildup led by the Saudis, or risk having Iraq take control of the world's oil.

The world was rapidly changing, and no one knew what the future held. But at least Shamir knew he could trust Reagan and depend on the United States to stand with Israel no matter what lay ahead.

Which was good, because just as it seemed that forces were aligning for peace, new threats were forming in the shadows. But for now, Israel could rest assured knowing it had a true friend and ally in the American president.

77

An Opening at the Supreme Court

In July, the President was informed that Supreme Court Justice William Brennan wanted to retire as soon as a replacement could be found.

The news was not entirely unexpected; Brennan was 84, had been a jurist since the 1950s, and was the court's longest serving member.

Although he had been appointed by President Eisenhower — a Republican — Brennan soon revealed himself to be a liberal on most issues. In 1962 he voted to outlaw school prayer, then eleven years later, in favor of Roe v Wade — the landmark case that legalized abortion. Brennan was a bane to conservatives, who despite charges of judicial activism had few options for his removal beyond the slow passage of time.

The son of Irish immigrants, the New Jersey native (and Roman Catholic) was a veteran of World War II, which he entered as a Major, and exited as a Colonel. Prior to becoming Ike's recess appointment, Brennan had served on the Supreme Court of New Jersey — having been appointed by the state's Republican governor, Alfred E Driscoll.

Although Brennan was a fellow Irishman, Reagan regarded the opportunity to pick his successor as something akin to finding a four-leaf clover. Because Supreme Court justices serve for life, the appointment (Reagan's fourth) would extend his legacy decades beyond his term in the Oval Office.

Granted, there were certain protocols that needed to be observed regarding the selection process, culminating with senatorial approval of the nominee. Still, given the current conservative make-up and the absence of perennial partisan obstructionists like Teddy Kennedy, even an ultra-conservative was likely to receive a quick confirmation.

The freedom available this time around was quite different than what had been in the case with his previous selection, Anthony Kennedy; a moderate that Reagan had been forced to pick in order to secure approval by a Senate then controlled by the Democrats.

That aside, Reagan seemed happy with his choice, a fellow Californian, who just so happened to be Catholic, (as was Antonin Scalia — Reagan's second appointment). His first appointment, Sandra Day O'Connor, who many assumed was Catholic, was in fact Protestant; an Episcopalian.

Believing that Reagan was intending to stack the court with those whose fundamental religious beliefs were pro-life in preparation for a challenge to Roe v Wade, or a constitutional amendment banning abortion, many were surprised when the President made it clear that he wanted politics kept out of the initial search.

Yes, he *preferred* a conservative — but he didn't want another ideologue like Brennan. Instead, the President made it clear that he wanted a judge that would "interpret, not override" the Constitution.

For Reagan, intellect and respect for the Constitution would top his list of qualifiers. For such an important decision, the President did not want even a taint of impropriety to shadow one of his appointments. Above all, he sought someone whose personal and professional qualifications made it clear that this individual, irrespective of politics, was the best choice available to serve on the nation's highest court.

This stance was consistent with that which Reagan had taken as Governor of California, relying on a blind selection process for appointing judges that began with recommendations from members of the legal community — and not politicians, businessmen, or the clergy.

Only once a candidate had the support of her/his peers, would Reagan then make his selection, opting for a conservative from the candidates presented for his review.

With this expressed caveat, Reagan was asked to consider David Souter, whom he had recently nominated just two months earlier to the US Court of Appeals for the Fifth Circuit.

Like Brennan, Souter hailed from New England and was a graduate of the prestigious Harvard law school. Although a Christian, Souter was not a staunchly pro-life Catholic, but an Episcopalian.

Prior to attending Harvard, Souter had studied in England in the swinging sixties as a Rhodes scholar. Before his appointment to a spot on the First Circuit, he had been serving on the Supreme Court of New Hampshire — the state he now called home. His ascent within the state legal system had been impressive, rising from prosecutor to Attorney General to judge in less than fifteen years.

Despite Reagan's plea that politics be kept out of the decision making process, Transportation Secretary (and fellow New Hampshirite) John Sununu assured the President that Souter would be a "home run for conservatism." Souter also had strong backing from New Hampshire Republican Senator Warren Rudman, who had been elected as part of Reagan's 1980 landslide. Like Souter, Rudman had also been Attorney General for the Granite State, where he had earned high marks for fairness.

Needing to make a selection quickly, Reagan scheduled a meeting with Souter at the White House in July. Although it was decided in advance that they should avoid discussing politics, Souter was known to have had many friends in the GOP—including former Vice President Bush, who called to lobby for his selection on the morning of the candidate's scheduled interview.

The President was impressed by the applicant's intellect and personality, and found common ground in a shared love of nature and do-it-yourself home repairs. Souter, a bachelor, was also an ideal age—just months shy of turning 52.

As he prepared to leave, Reagan shook his hand and thanked him. Souter left feeling things had gone well, and began thinking ahead to the confirmation process.

The President, however, had other thoughts. That night he discussed the matter with Nancy, and although he was unable to cite anything specific, felt that he still wanted to review other candidates.

Reagan knew this decision would offend those who recommended Souter as the perfect choice, but so be it. Maybe Souter *would* be the one, but for now the President decided to follow his gut and review the other candidates on his short list.

Although not on the list, Reagan would have liked to renominate Robert Bork, who he felt had been denied a fair shot due to partisan grandstanding by the Democrats on the Senate Judiciary Committee.

But Bork was needed as Attorney General. Also, the circus that had surrounded Bork's confirmation hearings was still fresh in people's minds—having only been played out three years earlier. Lastly, although the Senate was solidly Republican, there remained a contingent of Democrats that would delight in one last skirmish before the November elections.

Bork would have to wait.

Instead, on the list was another selection that caught his eye: Edith Jones.

A decade younger than Souter, and with a somewhat less prestigious background, Jones was also a recent Reagan appointee (to the Fifth Circuit Court), where she had been serving for more than five years.

Although born and raised in the east, Jones had attended law school in Texas and, like the President, identified as a Westerner now.

Jones was invited to Washington, and Reagan enjoyed the visit, finding her outgoing, articulate, and clearly conservative. As expected, the conversation turned to the court, and its present make-up. Naturally, Jones was quite familiar with the records of the other justices, and was anxious to offer her opinions on each. Reagan encouraged this, as he felt that any new appointment would also need to be a good cultural fit with the existing court, so as to avoid the kind of extreme ideological polarization that might undermine its ability to function effectively.

Reagan sat back and listened while Jones spoke.

Judge Jones shared the President's disdain for how Brennan had politicized and divided the court, agreeing that these actions undermined its legitimacy and functionality. But in her opinion, even worse than Brennan, was Justice Thurgood Marshall—an unapologetic liberal who had been placed by LBJ.

Thanks to his outspoken views and love of the limelight, Marshall, the court's first African-American justice, had made his share of enemies since his appointment in 1967. Jones noted in particular Marshall's espoused legal philosophy that suggested ideological activism, citing his inflammatory pronouncement that "You do what you think is right and let the law catch up."

As with Souter, Jones was a good age, healthy, and very interested in joining the court. She also came highly recommended by many in the conservative wing of the GOP, especially from those in Texas, Louisiana, and Mississippi—states she currently presided over as a judge.

But again, something just didn't set right with the President, and so he decided to continue the search.

Yes, he could hold off on making his nomination until after the upcoming election, and yes, he certainly had lots of other items on his plate. But he also viewed the selection of court justices as part of his constitutional duty that was above day-to-day political issues, and thereby something that he needed to pursue in a timely manner.

Next on his list for consideration was Cynthia Holcomb Hall, a native Californian, and Stanford graduate.

Reagan knew Hall and liked her quite a bit. He had appointed her to fill other spots — first in 1981 to the US District Court (for Central California), then after three years, to the Court of Appeals for the Ninth Circuit.

Hall seemed perfect in nearly every way, and came with a long record reflecting fairness and consistency. Brilliant, but not flashy, getting her confirmed would be a slam-dunk.

Regrettably, at 61, Hall was much older than the other candidates on his list.

Reagan had no worries about her age based on competency. He himself was nearing 80, and there were no concerns about his state of mind, stamina, or dedication to duty. He still had the photographic memory he had used as an actor, and the body of an athlete who enjoyed marathons of lap swimming and hard physical labor.

The President was, however, cognizant of the fact that this would be a lifetime appointment to the court.

Hall appeared to be in good health, and was a reputed workaholic — but she was also unmarried. What if she found someone, and decided she needed to retire early in order to catch up on a personal life that had been put on hold while she served the public?

Could he blame her? No. But neither could he afford to take the chance — not when he had a list of so many other qualified candidates.

Nearly twenty years Hall's junior was another Westerner on the short list: Emilio M Garza.

As with the others, Reagan was familiar with Garza, having most recently appointed him to the US District Court for Western Texas.

Reagan recalled Garza as having made a strong personal impression: smart, modest, and principled. Soft-spoken, and, *dignified* beyond his years.

Garza had grown up poor in San Antonio, Texas, before going on to attend Notre Dame — "home of the Gipper," Reagan noted with a smile as he reviewed the candidate's file.

Like his father, who became a corporate chief financial officer despite having only a sixth-grade formal education, Emilio Garza had been a determined, hardworking, and very much self-made man.

After graduating with a master's degree in 1970, Garza, then already in his early 20s, enlisted in the Marine Corps, where he rose to the rank of Captain.

Garza's enlistment seemed to many an odd — if not suicidal decision, coming at the height of the Vietnam War, and a time when most men were scrambling just to avoid being drafted. Enlisting was practically unheard of, except for those trying to avoid the draft by signing up for a cushy assignment to keep them off the front lines.

But enlisting in the Marine Corps was hardly what anyone would consider cushy. Not in 1970, not when the war was raging, and not when having black or brown skin pretty much guaranteed a trip to the front line.

But for Garza, enlistment was just a way to give back to a country that he felt had given so much to him.

This sensibility had also shaped the arc of his professional career. After a decade establishing his credentials as a popular, up-and-coming attorney, the ambitious young Texan left a lucrative private practice in order to serve the public interest.

While the President deeply objected to the concept of quotas and advocated for a color-blind society, he also believed in making the Supreme Court more inclusive, and reflective of the nation it served. When he ran for President in 1980, he had promised to add a woman to the court — which he did as soon as a vacancy became available with his nomination of Sandra Day O'Connor.

During the run for his third term, Reagan had made many promises, but had not specifically addressed the issue of court appointments in regards to gender or race. His last two nominations had been white men, but now, he once again looked at expanding his legacy by reaching out to others that he believed were past due for consideration.

As a longtime resident of Southern California, Reagan had many Hispanic friends, and he respected the often unrecognized role Latinos had played in the nation's history. The idea of taking a stand against a rising tide of anti-immigration bigotry and prejudice appealed to Reagan on a personal level. He viewed the opportunity of appointing a minority to the court as another way to provide leadership by example to some fellow conservatives who hadn't been as quick to fulfill America's promise as a land of opportunity for all of its citizens.

Nominating a Hispanic who just so happened to be a brilliant legal mind, a committed public servant, a bona fide patriot—and genuine conservative—satisfied all of the President's criteria.

Plus, although an experienced judge, Garza was still just 43 years old. If he lasted as long as Brennan, he could continue to influence the court into the 2030s.

He was, in short, perfect.

Judge Garza was summoned to meet with the President to discuss the position, and although he was not thrilled about relocating to Washington for life, he stated that he would be "honored to serve" if selected.

And so he would be.

Garza received a unanimous confirmation vote, and Brennan was at last free to go enjoy life with his former secretary (and now wife), Mary.

78

Taking on Welfare

As the summer of 1990 drew to a close, most of the world remained relatively calm and stable, as the USSR was too preoccupied with internal struggles to be a problem to others. Congress was in recess, and things were so quiet that the First Couple was able to slip away for a short trip out west to the Ranch.

This would, however, be a typical working vacation for the President. In addition to the incessant demands of office, Reagan used his time at the Ranch to take on projects of a more physical nature; clearing trails, chopping wood, repairing buildings and fences. In truth, he loved this kind of work, as much for the exercise as for the sense of accomplishment that resulted from activity that produced clearly visible and beneficial results.

Time spent at Rancho del Cielo also afforded Reagan the seclusion he needed to think deeply; to plan and strategize about major problems and defining issues. This was often accomplished as he rode El Alamein, his prized Arabian horse around the bucolic and untamed estate.

It was only here, as he navigated the rustic and twisting trails that he was truly free. Free from meetings, phones, staffers. Free from people seeking favors and advice. Free from the dozens of other minor distractions that fill the day by sake of volume, not substance.

At the top of the President's schedule was finalizing a plan for overhauling the welfare system. Campaigning for his third term, he had made reforming welfare part of his platform. The current system was not working, and voters wanted him to fix it.

The issue had been on the President's to-do list since his first term, but partisan obstructionists consistently blocked all previous efforts. Time after time, even the most basic attempts had been shut down before ever reaching the floor for a vote — but things were changing now.

Democrats — especially the wild-eyed uncompromising variety — were a small minority now, and their numbers would likely be reduced even further after the upcoming November elections.

So, the President's plan was to develop the proposal, pass it on to his team to flesh out specifics, then formally submit it in January once the new (Republican supermajority) Congress had been sworn in.

Sensing what Reagan was planning, Democrats sounded the alarm. Grandstanding on this issue would be the last big hurrah for those being booted at the midterm elections, and they intended to milk it for all it was worth.

Worse yet, Reagan's proposals had yet to be formally presented. Attacks were based solely on speculation and worst-case scenarios.

Kicking and punching as they were being shown the door, much of the opposition was lacking civility and laced with vitriol. Rather than propose solutions, liberal kamikazes went after Reagan as a person: At best he was oblivious to the needs of the underprivileged, at worst, a cruel racist. Welfare reform was nothing more than a cover for genocide and a diabolical scheme to starve defenseless black children.

The President refused to dignify such comments with a response. He understood that reform was a complicated and emotional topic, which lent itself to distortion and misrepresentation by those who had a vested interest in maintaining the status quo.

That's politics.

Still, it sickened him to see the American public manipulated in this way.

The world remained a dangerous place, and ratcheting up further anxiety was inexcusable. Under FDR and JFK the Democrats had radiated hope and optimism, and a willingness to take on difficult problems. But in the years since, they had become the party that had traded big dreams for petty criticisms, relying on negativity and cynicism, because it was all they had left.

"I didn't leave the Democratic Party," Reagan once famously stated, "the Democratic Party left me."

As someone who had himself grown up in poverty, Reagan understood the mindset of fear and want. Hardship defined most of his early years, and the Great Depression itself did not end until he was nearly 30 years old, only to be replaced by war and rationing.

Roosevelt's programs had helped the country get through some very difficult days. Reagan had supported them then, and continued to support the idea that the government needed to provide assistance to the truly disadvantaged and needy. But over the course of decades, the safety nets of FDR had evolved into hammocks, providing lifelong coverage for able-bodied adults who used welfare as a no-strings alternative to working.

Democratic opposition to any reform had an early lead and was gaining traction with voters, forcing the President to play defense — which is not where he wanted to be until all the details of his plan could be worked out. As desperation grew on the left, many saw this as a signature issue that could help to mitigate Democratic losses at the midterm elections.

No matter what happened, Republicans would be the majority party in both houses after the 1990 midterms; still there was no 100% guarantee they would back his reforms. Every entitlement group has its supporters and lobbyists, and too often politicians — even some Republicans — will follow the money rather than their consciences.

As with the school prayer amendment, welfare reform would demand lots of direct engagement and lobbying by the President. But after previous failed attempts, chances for passage looked considerably better this time around.

Still, it was a highly controversial issue, and Reagan knew that if he didn't take it on, no one else would. This would be his last shot, and so he was bound and determined to make it happen, as both a legacy issue, and to fulfill another of his promises to the people who had elected him.

On issues he believed in, Ronald Reagan could be extremely stubborn, and was not one to be lectured to about "political ramifications" if it meant avoiding doing what he believed was right.

"If you're afraid of hard work and just want to be adored, then get out of politics and go get a job at the mall playing Santa," Reagan told a herd of RINOs who asked him to tone down his rhetoric leading up to the midterm elections.

Yes, there were financial imperatives to addressing welfare, but that was only part of what was driving him on this issue. A bigger waste than that measured in dollars lost to fraud and abuse was what Reagan regarded as the loss of human potential: a form of slow death that robbed able-bodied individuals of dignity, and the opportunity to discover their potential as fully-engaged working members of society.

Reagan was of the school that believed everyone should pull their own weight, to the best of their ability.

Work benefitted the society, and the individual. It was the natural order of things, but so was the fact that some people could not fend for themselves through no fault of their own. Therefore, it was the responsibility of society to step in and provide compassionate assistance to those individuals.

But persons genuinely in need represented only a small fraction of those who drew benefits. The vast majority was made up of healthy, able-bodied adults, many from families, in which across generations, no member had ever held a job. Ever.

As Reagan saw it, guaranteed-no-questions-asked welfare had created a permanently segregated underclass; individuals whose dependency left them just barely getting by, denying them their rightful place in the American Dream. Big government was not helping these people — it was hurting them.

The President believed their country owed them more. Change would not be easy, but it was necessary. The cycle must be broken.

Democrats had exploited them for decades, kept them in a prison of fear, on a starvation diet of lies and broken promises.

But now Reagan was here with a key to unlock the cell door.

Acknowledging the complexity of the situation, the President's proposal would be structured as a transition plan spread out over years, geared towards replacing dependency with opportunity.

As always, Reagan's focus was on the future: a brighter, more prosperous future that accentuated personal liberty and freedom.

It was this personal optimism, this lust for life that would in the end be essential to helping people understand that the opportunities of the future could not be realized until one was willing to let go of the past.

And now, once again, it was up to the President to convince the American people that he had their best interests at heart.

79

Gorbachev's Plan

For Gorbachev, the solitude he needed for deep thought was to be found in the Swiss Alps.

Like Reagan, Gorbachev had also been mapping out a plan to overhaul a failed system that denied opportunity to those it pretended to serve. But Gorbachev's goal was much more ambitious, as it was nothing less than a proposal to dissolve the USSR and to replace Kremlin-controlled communist states with non-aligned free-market democracies.

Under Gorbachev's proposal, the existing 15-nation Union of Soviet Socialist Republics, held together by force, would be replaced by a new voluntary alliance of independent nations. Each country would have the right to adopt whatever form of political leadership its citizens wanted, as determined by free and open multi-party elections.

Although mostly drafted by Gorbachev himself, the proposal reflected the official stance of the USSR government-in-exile, now residing roughly 1,700 miles southwest of Moscow.

Following the coup, many nations — including the United States — had broken off relations with the Kremlin, refusing to acknowledge the legitimacy of the Sokolov regime. But, just as America was among the first to sever ties with Moscow, it had also led the movement to help establish, then recognize, Gorbachev's government-in-exile as the true representative of the USSR and its citizens.

This was now the position of most countries.

Granted, some nations (such as client states like Syria and Cuba) continued formal relations with Moscow, while a few others (most notably China) remained officially neutral (having broken off relations with Moscow following the coup, but then failing to recognize the government-in-exile).

With Gorbachev's proposal, a clear line would be drawn. By offering a genuine alternative, each country would have to decide which version of the USSR it would choose to back in the coming showdown.

And the differences between the two couldn't have been more extreme.

Sokolov wanted to rebuild the empire; Gorbachev to dissolve it.

According to Gorbachev's plan, the existing political structure of the USSR would remain in place for a short transition period—although all those who had been directly involved in the *coup d'état* would be immediately removed from power. Rulers of other Eastern Bloc nations (such as Hungary's Miklós Németh, a moderate who had been in office only a few years) would be allowed to continue on until open elections could be held.

Each member state of the Soviet Union would be required to hold open multi-party monitored elections within 90 days. Existing communist heads of state would be barred from running—even if they formally rejected communism.

In his official proposal, Gorbachev would make no mention of his personal support for purging *all* vestiges of communism from the former USSR—in a program similar to the denazification that the victorious allies (including the Soviets) had applied to post-war Germany. Understanding the delicate political realities of the situation, and not wanting to push Sokolov into a fight-or-die contest, Gorbachev thought it best to avoid such provocations for now.

Still, the message was clear: The days of single-party rule were over. Communism as a form of governance would be banned, and the party itself would be barred from running any candidates for a period of five years. While Gorbachev conceded this banishment was contrary to the spirit of free and open elections, he felt that some time, unburdened by the long shadow of communist domination, was necessary in order for populations to make the transition.

Gorbachev himself signaled a preference for a parliamentary system similar to that of other Western European democracies (such as Germany), and expressed a personal interest in running for Prime Minister of Russia.

As independent nations, former Soviet states would be free to continue on as members of the Warsaw Pact, to seek membership in NATO, or to declare neutrality.

Gorbachev supported German unification, and although opposed to the breakup of individual nations (such as Czechoslovakia), accepted that it was likely inevitable.

He did express concern for Yugoslavia, a country that (like Iraq) had required a high degree of force to hold it together, and worried that fragmentation might not be as civil as that which would likely end the marriage of the Czechs and Slovaks. In recognition of this, Gorbachev advocated maintaining the Warsaw Pact, so that troops already familiar with the region might be called up to provide stability, should individual divisions descend into violence and civil war if Yugoslavia splintered into smaller states along ethnic and religious lines.

Gorbachev's greatest concern was reserved for the less-developed republics of the south and east: Kazakhstan, Kyrgyzstan, Tajikistan, Turkmenistan, and Uzbekistan. He spoke of a different mindset, both in the populations, and in those who sought to rule these nations at the empire's fringes.

These were also Russia's buffers between potential adversaries like Iran, Afghanistan, and China. Once released from Moscow's control, these nations would be caught in a tug of war between allying with a changing and progressive Europe, or increasingly fundamentalist and authoritarian neighbors.

At the very least, Gorbachev thought it best that any advanced weapon systems deployed in these nations be brought back to Russia for safekeeping — and, when agreed upon by treaties, destroyed.

Gorbachev's fears were supported by a consensus that spanned representatives of the US state department, as well as those from intelligence and defense. On the plus side, the Soviets had long been aware of potential problems in the "lands of the 'stans," that covered everything from matters such as renegade frontier status, to rising tides of Islamic fundamentalism. In response to these concerns, Moscow had supposedly taken precautions to safeguard military establishments, but as far as anyone knew, all the dangerous stockpiles were still in place.

Removing nuclear missiles it had deployed in unstable nations wasn't exactly the type of story that made the front page of *Pravda*.

Secretary Gorbachev's proposal was a sprawling document, addressing in detail matters across every conceivable topic pertinent to the task at hand. Although Gorbachev was the primary architect of the proposal, representatives of several Western governments (most notably Secretary Schultz), had been working with the government-in-exile on the various components. President Reagan had been watching the progress from a distance, checking in periodically to offer his thoughts and, in a moment of humor, warning Gorbachev how difficult it would be to get anything done if, once in office, he was stuck with an opposition party like the Democrats.

Gorbachev just laughed, reminding Reagan that he still had to be elected first.

For now, the issue of most concern to Gorbachev was how to introduce his proposal.

After some discussion, it was decided that the proposal should first be submitted privately to the Kremlin. It was hoped that they would see the inevitability of the situation, and agree to a peaceful transition of power.

To sweeten the deal, Secretary Gorbachev was willing to offer amnesty—providing that those who had participated in the coup were willing to leave the USSR and never return. If they chose to stay, they would be formally charged and prosecuted for their crimes.

The Soviet leader-in-exile pointed out that a number of countries—including Finland—would welcome them and provide for their security. (Finland was one of the few non-client states that still maintained relations with Moscow. Although it had long since purged itself of the occupying Soviets, the relationship had remained cordial. Finland also provided a valuable link for relaying communications between the Russians and other nations such as the US.)

Other nations, notably client states such as Cuba would likely follow suit with similar offers; although none had yet been approached, given the need to maintain secrecy during the negotiations.

The proposal also presented a plan for the transfer of power. It would begin by restoring the pre-coup Politburo, then placing, or reinstating, Gorbachev supporters into key positions of governance, the military, and state affairs (such as heading the KGB). Many supporters were still being held in detention, although a few had been able to escape— including a handful currently serving as part of the government in Switzerland.

Granted, there would be much in the way of preparatory work that would need to be done first over the next few months, but the proposal did come with a timetable based on actionable steps: Implementation of the plan would begin on December first, and needed to be wrapped up by the end of the year.

Once Sokolov and his administration were out of the country, and his safety guaranteed, Gorbachev would return to Russia. The ninety-day countdown for democratic elections would begin on January 1, 1991.

To accompany the proposal, Gorbachev included a long and persuasive handwritten letter in which he addressed the unsustainability of the current situation. In it, he also made a personal appeal, emphasizing a shared love for Mother Russia, and a plea to avoid imposing any further bloodshed and suffering upon the Soviet people.

In his heart, Gorbachev acknowledged that Sokolov was almost certainly a lost cause. This was a despotic old man who had shown no respect for law, much less even the pretense of civility.

Secretary Gorbachev had personally fired this "Hero" of the Soviet Union once before, and it seemed improbable that he would go willingly a second time.

But, Sokolov also displayed a history of incompetency and overplaying his hand. While he no doubt was surrounded and supported by loyalists, there were also those in key positions who were realists, such as career military officers who might, if the opportunity presented itself, turn on him for the sake of the nation.

Therefore, Gorbachev would address his proposal, dated October 1, to the acting government, with copies going to two-dozen key officials.

The Finns, sworn to secrecy would serve as couriers. However, the proposal also came with a caveat and a threat: Gorbachev expected a formal response by the end of the month. He was not interested in negotiating the core points of the proposal, and if rejected by the Kremlin, the call to revolution would be taken directly to the people.

Gorbachev's finger was now on the button to blow up the Soviet Union. He hit start, and Moscow had 30 days to respond.

80

Nyet & Da

Rooster today, feather duster tomorrow.

— Russian proverb

General Secretary Sokolov replied directly to "citizen Gorbachev" within two weeks. His response was cold and curt: He rejected the proposal in its entirety, and demanded that Gorbachev, as a fugitive from justice, return to the Soviet Union to face criminal charges.

The response was disheartening, but not entirely unexpected. In recent months, Western intelligence had been increasingly successful at collecting information on even the most secretive and uppermost levels of Sokolov's regime. Reports presented a picture of a government ever more in disarray, as realists, loyalists, and power-hungry successors fought for control of the wheel.

While officially rejected by Sokolov, he was not the only recipient of the proposal, which soon began circulating beyond the original core of two-dozen government and military officials — despite threats that any caught sharing such information would be immediately executed for treason.

Official responses to Gorbachev's proposition were uniformly negative, while Sokolov sat nodding in agreement. Privately, however, most acknowledged that the game was up, and began making plans for how best to deal with the inevitable change Gorbachev was set to unleash.

Gorbachev's threat to present the proposal directly to the people was a tremendous motivator, as those at the top had a well-justified fear of the citizens they held as captives. Many legitimately worried that when called to fight, those pledged to protect them would instead turn and join ranks with the "enemy," as had been the case with the East Germans.

Because Sokolov had spurned the offer of amnesty, those who had backed him would be subject to legal prosecution — *if* they survived a peoples' uprising. Many began packing their bags immediately, planning their exodus before the last exits could be sealed.

The situation soon came to parallel the final days of Nazi Germany. Sokolov, evermore detached from reality, cheered on by a dwindling contingent of delusional loyalists, while others, sick of conflict, braced for what promised to be a bloody and horrific end.

Faced with this prospect, many in key positions began secretly conspiring for Sokolov's overthrow. Competing plans for coups were drawn up, some which involved his assassination. Meanwhile, military leaders, developed surrender plans, protocols to avoid entering a hot war with the West, and to responsibly secure the USSR's nuclear arsenal.

Alexander Yefimov, the Commander-in-Chief of the Soviet Air Force took the lead advocating that Sokolov had to be removed from power, as soon as possible, by any means necessary. In addition, he issued a similar edict for Defense Minister Dmitry Yazov. Yefimov's boss had been an early supporter of the coup and remained loyal to Sokolov.

Whoever controlled the military would control the nation. If something were to happen to Yazov, Yefimov would take his place, with or without Sokolov's blessing.

At great personal risk, Yefimov began to circulate his transition plan among his peers in the Soviet defense forces.

First, Gorbachev's proposal must be officially adopted before he followed up on his threat to take his case to the people. If this happened, Yefimov believed the country would descend into civil war, and likely end up under Western occupation.

"Not exactly Secretary Sokolov's version of a unified Europe," he noted. "I can work with the Americans, but I cannot take orders from them. Face the facts, one way or another, our days are numbered. My old friend Sokolov is done.

"Change is coming. It can be orderly and from the top down, or it can be a bloodbath if brought about by a peoples' revolution. We must act now so that this does not happen."

Yefimov, a World War II veteran and Double Hero of the Soviet Union, then took the initiative of responding directly to Gorbachev. When rumors of Yefimov's treasonous activities began to leak, he was approached by the KGB for questioning.

White haired and rosy-cheeked, the 67-year-old former fighter pilot laughed off the agent's threats.

"Using a pistol to threaten a man who commands fighter jets will result in a lopsided battle," he said, as he broke into laughter.

Much to his surprise, the KGB agent also began to laugh, acknowledging he was only following orders to investigate rumors of dissent within the military.

"You are correct, but as I am sure you realize, you will find dissent is everywhere. The world is different, and the future belongs to those who are prepared to meet it," cautioned the man who had personally flown more than 200 sorties, and wore a chest full of medals documenting his courage, patriotism, and service to his nation.

It was a surreal moment, one that neither of the two Russians who had made careers in serving the state, ever thought they'd share.

Meanwhile, the KGB continued to supply official reports slanted to Sokolov's liking, which were now mostly fabricated fables, providing the old man with the jolt of optimism he needed each morning to begin his day under ever-darkening October skies.

81

Waves of Change

Outside the Soviet Union, things were not going well for Sokolov either.

In the US, President Reagan's popularity, already at record highs, had translated directly into solid gains for the GOP at the midterm elections held November 6, 1990. Six of the eight senatorial seats that had temporarily been filled by Democrats (following the Teddy Kennedy-led coup and conspiracy resignations), were won by Republicans, further widening their majority status in Congress' upper chamber.

The Democrats also lost heavily in the House of Representatives, including many seats once considered untouchable.

When the final tolls were tallied, Republicans now held 438 seats in Congress. This gave them a majority that exceeded 80% — topping the previous record set by the 75th Congress (1937-1939), which was then dominated by FDR and the New Deal Democrats.

The losses — even in traditionally Blue districts — were so staggering that many pundits began to wonder if this might be the end of the Democratic Party, at least in terms of having a significant national presence.

Later that month, Prime Minister Margaret Thatcher won re-election as head of the Conservative Party in Britain. In Germany, Helmut Kohl appeared poised to win his third term, with elections scheduled for December.

But the biggest shocker came in Central America, as Nicaraguan voters rejected socialism, and the use of their country by the Soviets to extend their empire into the New World.

Since the violent overthrow of dictator Anastasio Somoza in 1979, Nicaragua had been under the control of the Sandinistas (Sandinista National Liberation Front), who not only turned the country into another Marxist state, but with Soviet encouragement, had aggressively pursued imposing communism on its neighbors.

Like the Cubans, the Sandinistas had been backed by Moscow, which provided them the training, equipment, and financial resources needed to pursue an expansionist agenda, along with whatever else was needed to suppress their own democratic rebels, the US-backed Contras.

Buoyed by the change in leadership following the Soviet coup, and gambling that the US was preoccupied by events elsewhere, the Nicaraguans had attempted to invade their neighbor, Honduras, roughly a year previously.

After years of buildup, the Nicaraguan forces had a considerable edge over the Hondurans, and in a real show of force, put nearly every troop and piece of equipment at their disposal on the border, waiting for President Daniel Ortega to wave them on to victory.

But before the invasion could begin, Reagan stepped in and shut it down.

The President's prompt and decisive action not only derailed Nicaragua's plans for conquest, but also wiped out nearly every item in the Sandinista's arsenal. At the time, it was expected that these items would be promptly replaced, whether for use in some future conquest, or to meet the more pressing need of suppressing the domestic, pro-democracy movement.

When Managua's wish list went unanswered, it hinted at growing problems within the USSR, and provided an opening for those Nicaraguans advocating on behalf of peaceful democratic reform.

Finding themselves painted into a corner, the Sandinistas had two options: Peaceful elections or trying to suppress a violent revolution with skittish, hollow-eyed troops and empty armories. Believing its own propaganda, the government arrogantly assumed victory would be theirs — and they would be returned to power with a landslide, an unquestionable mandate to rule by grateful and obedient citizens.

But when Election Day came, the Sandinistas were solidly defeated. Heading the opposition party (the Democratic Union of Opposition), was Violeta Chamorro, a 51-year-old former newspaper publisher who had been educated in the United States, and had a long association with democratic political initiatives.

No one was more surprised than Ortega himself: unseated by a former ally who had also opposed the Somoza regime, before then turning on the Sandinistas once they took control, and began to employ similar tactics to hold on to power.

Perhaps most humiliating in a macho, male-dominated, youth-centric culture, was that *El Presidente* Ortega, strutting about in army fatigues and combat boots, had just been beaten by a smartly-dressed, middle-aged woman.

The absence of Moscow's support sent a chill through other Soviet client states, as letting Nicaragua slip free from communism was directly at odds with the Breznev Doctrine, which stated:

"When forces that are hostile to Socialism try to turn the development of some socialist country towards Capitalism, it becomes not only a problem of the country concerned, but a common problem and concern of all Socialist countries."

And yet, no one came to save Nicaragua's socialists.

Although the transfer of power in Managua had been peaceful, by ballot—not bullet, many other communist leaders wondered if their citizens would behave with similar restraint. Very few were willing to take the chance, and thus set about developing escape plans.

Even in Russia there was a growing sense of doom, as word of Gorbachev's proposal—and Sokolov's rejection of it—rapidly spread beyond the original recipients, then on to the upper echelons of societal and party elites.

Soon, actual physical copies of the proposal were everywhere, circulating freely, downwards to the dissidents and unwashed masses; bringing a great sense of anxiety and foreboding to those at the top.

Reasonable voices called for compromise while there was still time to respond before Gorbachev acted on his threat to open the jar and shake its contents into the wind.

The writing was on the wall: it was time to cut a deal. Now, or risk losing everything.

But Sokolov would not budge. Nor would he tolerate dissent; demanding that the KGB investigate and charge any person whose loyalty was suspect—whether they be a top-ranking government official or a street sweeper.

Scores of people began to disappear without a trace. Some were no doubt anti-government conspirators who had been arrested, while others were likely just trying to beat the mass exodus and bloodletting that was certain to follow a peoples' uprising.

What Sokolov did not realize though, was that many of these arrests were actually just elaborate covers to facilitate the safe escape of key people who would be needed to rebuild post-Soviet Russia. Such "catch and release" arrests relocated dozens of government officials, including a fair number of Sokolov's top aides. In response, the Soviet leader grew even more reclusive and paranoid, disappearing completely from public view altogether by the end of November.

During the two months since submitting his proposal, Gorbachev had engaged in meaningful and substantive dialogues with supporters within Sokolov's government and the military, including Alexander Yefimov, head of the air force. But ultimately, none had any significant influence over their leader, who made it clear he was prepared to fight until the bitter end.

In a society so steeped in distrust and secrecy, conspiring for Sokolov's overthrow was extremely dangerous. Alliances shifted frequently, and people were played like pawns in power struggles that pitted one faction against another.

Like most parts of the Soviet government, the KGB seemed split between extremes. On the surface, it was often impossible to tell who was aligned with which camp.

In a long dark hall, one door might open to freedom, another into a prison cell.

Many had heard rumors that the KGB was helping people to escape—but for a price. Others worried that this was just one more trick by the much-despised, and much-feared state security agency, still headed by Vladimir Kryuchkov, Sokolov's personal friend and a key architect of the coup that brought him to power.

No one felt safe.

By the first of December it became clear to all that nothing would happen (with regard to implementing Gorbachev's proposal), so long as Sokolov remained in control.

Without acceptance from within the regime, the push for change would now have to come externally, forcing Gorbachev to move forward with his plan to rally the Soviet people to overthrow their government.

It would be dangerous, and there would no doubt be lives lost in the struggle for freedom. But at its heart, Gorbachev envisioned a peaceful revolution, embracing nonviolent protest and civil disobedience.

Such movements had worked in the past, and the numbers were certainly on the side of the people.

Gorbachev also had reason to believe, that as the tides of protestors grew, many entrusted to push them back would simply not follow orders. From key figures in the Kremlin, to disillusioned troops, the will to fight their own people was not there.

Still, there remained many uncertainties. But Gorbachev understood that every great leap forward involved risk, and that history provided windows of opportunity that were only open for brief periods of time.

The evening of Sunday, December 2, was cold and clear, lit by a full moon.

Gorbachev's plan for taking his case directly to the people had been ready for some time now, but given the secrecy necessary during the negotiations period, it would still require some time to launch.

It would in fact take two weeks, coinciding with the last new moon of 1990.

Gorbachev Calls Upon His People

"The Soviet people want full-blooded and unconditional democracy."

— Mikhail Gorbachev

A government-in-exile usually has few, if any, resources.

The Soviet version, headed by Mikhail Gorbachev, was different however, as it had the full support of President Reagan and the United States of America.

By helping to establish and sponsor a parallel Soviet government based in Switzerland, the Americans had given it legitimacy and the recognition it deserved as a counterpoint to Sokolov's illegal regime headquartered in Moscow.

But unlike Sokolov, Gorbachev had no state treasury, no military, and no communication platform that allowed him to push his message into nearly every household in the USSR.

But Gorbachev had something Sokolov never would: the support of the people.

Reaching the people—especially with a call to revolution—would not be easy. Even more difficult would be directing and supporting the uprising from afar, but Gorbachev and Reagan were determined to try.

Both leaders recognized their place at a rare moment in history, and the need to take decisive action on behalf of not just liberating the Soviet people, but in turn, ending the Cold War, and with it, the prospect of nuclear conflict between the world's two great superpowers.

Following the *coup d'état*, there had been no significant mention of Gorbachev in the official Soviet state media. Despite attempts at a news blackout, word of Gorbachev's rescue by the Americans, and his establishment of a government challenging the Kremlin, had circulated throughout the empire, and by now most knew the real story.

Since the loss of East Germany to the West, broadcast facilities had been greatly enhanced along the borders with Poland and Czechoslovakia. Towers, together with other land and marine-based facilities were brought online so as to provide deeper penetration into Russia itself, as well as into other states that shared borders and waterways with the West.

Still, given the limited reach coupled with the ability to jam most foreign electronic communications, Gorbachev's call to action would have to rely heavily on word of mouth, phone trees, and through the distribution of physical objects such as pamphlets, cassette tapes and even vinyl record albums.

Fortunately, these kinds of low-tech items could be easily produced "behind enemy lines," at already established safe facilities such as a converted warehouse in Kiev that could dub 1000 cassette tapes a day, or at a print shop in Warsaw that could turn out 20,000 pamphlets a week without anyone raising an eyebrow.

Production costs would be covered primarily by the Americans, who already had a large and well-funded covert network in place throughout the USSR. In addition to facilitating the distribution of Gorbachev's revolutionary message, the network was also ready to provide other forms of support needed by a civilian populace attempting to overthrow an entrenched and well-armed government.

By the end of the first week of December, Gorbachev had recorded video and audio versions of his speech, and signed off on the print editions. Rather than attempt to smuggle in large quantities of such objects, or rely on a few large facilities, copies would be mass-produced at various smaller locations throughout the USSR. Setting up multiple production facilities would help with distribution to different regions, and also make state efforts to locate, and shut down, operations considerably more difficult.

The speech would also be broadcast on a regular basis, commencing on Sunday, December 16. There would be a new moon that night, and from this point of absolute darkness would come a ray of hope.

After years heading the USSR, Gorbachev's voice was instantly recognizable to the Soviet people. His broadcast message began by asserting his claim to being the legitimate leader of the USSR, followed by news of a Soviet government-in-exile. Gorbachev stated his government was the official representation of the Soviet people, and the one recognized by most nations of the world.

As proof, he called for Russian people to look upon the now vacant embassies. "Where are the French? The Canadians? The Chinese? The Brazilians? The Indians? The Nigerians? The Mexicans? The Moroccans?

"All gone. The only ones remaining are those who are paid to stay and put on a show, to perpetuate the lie."

He denounced the illegal coup that had driven him from power, and called upon Sokolov and his regime to resign peacefully.

"They have no claim, no legitimacy."

Gorbachev accused Sokolov of endangering the Soviet people by starting World War III, and for pushing the planet to the brink of nuclear annihilation.

Then he changed direction and began to talk about his vision of the future—and the dissolution of the Soviet Union. Gorbachev spoke of ending Moscow's rule, and the terminus of totalitarian oppression. In conclusion, people would be free to do as they chose, in thoughts, words, actions. In politics, in economics, and in religious practice.

The message concluded with a plan to bring about these changes peacefully, starting with non-violent protests and civil disobedience to begin on New Year's Day, 1991, and continue on until the heads of government agreed to support open and free elections within 90 days.

Given that most Soviets were familiar with Gandhi and Martin Luther King Jr, Gorbachev cited them as examples of how non-violent protests could change the course of nations. Again, he emphasized the need to keep things peaceful, and avoid the type of provocation that would lead to bloodshed.

He followed this with some words of caution. To the people, he warned them that state security services would likely infiltrate their ranks and attempt to incite violence so as to justify retaliatory gestures. "Do not let them bait you in this way. Be calm and steady; do not resort to violence or destruction."

To his "brothers and sisters" in the military, in government, and in the state security services, Gorbachev told them they were on the wrong side of history, and asked that they join him before it was too late. "The people have the numbers and time on their side, and they will be victorious. If you cannot find the will to join us, at the very least, do nothing to obstruct our march to freedom."

Lastly, Gorbachev presented the conditions by which he would return to Russia, and hinted at his intent to run for office—if supported by a free vote of the people.

Word began to spread even more quickly than had been anticipated, and efforts to stop distribution of Gorbachev's message were disorganized and sporadic.

As planned, the speech was officially broadcast for the first time on December 16, but by then, copies were already commonplace in most large cities throughout Russia and the Eastern Bloc. In many ways, the authorities—outnumbered and without clear guidance—were playing a game of Whac-A-Mole against the dissidents. As soon as one printing plant was discovered and shut down, two more would pop up to take its place.

Just as one student was arrested for playing a tape of Gorbachev's speech on the streets of Belgrade, a trusted member of the Estonian Communist Party "mistakenly" played it over state radio during the dinner hour on December 19.

In Leningrad, visual references incorporating the letter "G" (for Gorbachev) began to appear everywhere; from traced in the snow on the sidewalk in front of the communist party headquarters, to defaced copies of *Pravda* left in cafes.

Even in the far-flung fringes of the empire—such as the "'stans—word was spreading, although often accompanied by violence.

Transition would not be easy here.

As Gorbachev's call for revolution spread, so did panic among the sequestered elite.

Moscow took some comfort in recalling the words of Lenin, who once extolled that one man with a gun can control one hundred others.

But what happens when the man runs out of bullets?

Or worse yet, what if he refuses to shoot? After all, years before Lenin,

Karl Marx himself had prophesized that peaceful revolution was a possibility—if the people were supported by the military.

Unfortunately for Commander Sokolov, it now appeared that even his military was marching to the beat of a different drummer.

83

Peace Like a River

No one was sure exactly when the protests actually began, but as the sun was rising on New Year's Day, protestors suddenly seemed to be everywhere, and their numbers were growing by the hour.

The morning was typical for winter in January: cold, dark, and miserable. But despite the frigid temperatures, the people had heeded Gorbachev's call to make a stand in support of a new beginning.

Riga. Warsaw. Budapest. Kiev. Sofia. Leningrad.

All across the Soviet Union it was the same story: a rising sea of humanity fed by streams, then rivers of people from all directions, all walks of life, all ages, genders, backgrounds — united in a shared quest for freedom.

By noon, authorities estimated the crowd in Moscow's Red Square alone had surpassed 400,000 demonstrators.

As protests continued on into the workweek, the numbers grew, as did their disruption to society. Traffic was being blocked, and rolling strikes were having an impact on the flow of goods and services.

Officials from the various republics turned to Moscow for leadership, and guidance, and most importantly, for a pledge of military support should things begin to boil over.

The Kremlin was in disarray. Sokolov had not been seen publicly for some time, and it was rumored that he was either dead, or was, for one reason or another, no longer in charge. If so, this might explain the indecisiveness coming from a government now seemingly managed by committee.

But still, those tasked with maintaining Soviet rule across the empire demanded to know: *If we open fire, and we run out of bullets, will you send more?*

As the protests entered a second week, things stayed mostly peaceful. There had been a few isolated incidents, with provocations starting on both sides. But for the most part the people stood their ground. Some held signs, some chanted or sang, but most just bore silent witness in support of peaceful revolution.

During this period, Gorbachev continued to make daily radio broadcasts, and issue new *communiqués*. Many were simply messages of solidarity and of encouragement, always accompanied by a request to keep demonstrations civil and non-violent.

The people's movement was dubbed "The River," in acknowledgement of its rising volumes and power. Unlike a hammer that smashes, or a sickle that slashes, a river will wear down whatever blocks its path; relentless, forceful, and unstoppable.

As the scales of power tipped, demonstrators began to broadcast their exiled leader's words publicly over sophisticated PA systems, and at times on what was supposed to be tightly-regulated state media. Lengthy pamphlets explaining other options for governmental structures became popular reading material circulating among the protestors. Also popular, were the proposals that guaranteed human rights as the foundation for the new free societies possible with the dissolution of the USSR.

Locations for protests were varied, but most were in close proximity to government offices. As the crowds grew, the organizational structures evolved and expanded. Many became like cities within cities, with medical facilities, restrooms, food preparation areas, lending libraries, daycares, and even areas were protestors could go to warm up, take a nap, or strategize.

One area of particular concern for authorities was the effect being caused by the strikes. In short order food supplies would begin to run low in some areas, and no one could be sure how the protestors would respond.

Would the hunger weaken them into giving up? Or would it turn them into voracious animals willing to attack their keepers?

Will there be enough bullets?

Foreign news broadcasts were making it into the USSR at an ever-increasing rate, and protestors were comforted knowing the outside world was watching, and supportive of their struggle.

One important communications link with the outside world was provided by flotillas of "pirate radio" ships stationed just off the mainland in the Baltic and Black Seas. Charging the ships with foreign interference, the military was given orders for their destruction, which it promptly ignored.

After three weeks of protests, neither side seemed willing to blink. Although state propaganda was at this point useless, President Reagan was careful to keep a low profile in regards to overt American support for the insurrection. He was, however, actively engaged in every possible way, from authorizing the transfer and stockpiling of food and supplies as an emergency response for the post-Soviet era, to developing plans to occupy and stabilize regions in danger of slipping into mobocracy, civil war, or even total anarchy.

Also in the works was a comprehensive plan to help the newly independent nations of the former USSR rebuild and transition to market-based economies. The plan, which brought together representatives from across the President's team, would be similar to the Marshall Plan, which America had implemented to help Western Europe get back on its feet in the aftermath of World War II.

The Soviet plan, first conceived by Secretary Schultz, would receive some financial support by the Western allies, the IMF, and the World Bank, although the bulk of the costs—estimated to be well into the billions—would be carried by the US.

When Reagan heard this total he just shook his head and laughed, and put a new spin on an old adage, "They say God won't stick you with any deficit so large that you can't pay off somehow. I just wish he didn't trust us so much."

Reagan knew that costs would be spread out across time, while the benefits of expanding trade and establishing new economies and markets would begin compounding almost immediately. In addition, the military savings would be considerable.

While still too early to discuss such matters, everyone knew that the end of the Cold War would have a significant impact on defense spending. But for now, nothing would change.

Slow and steady wins the game.

84

Transitions

It is a hard winter when one wolf devours another.

— Russian proverb

Throughout January, the people and governments of the USSR remained in a tense standoff, each waiting for the other side to give in.

Meanwhile, the US and its Western allies continued to prepare for whatever might come next. The fact that things had remained relatively free of violence was a good omen, but as the stalemate dragged on, patience on both sides seemed to be thinning.

One matter of particular concern was the complete disappearance of Sokolov, and ambiguity concerning who was now in control. According to intelligence sources, Sokolov was still alive, but his authority had been challenged and compromised. Rule was now, as suspected, by committee.

The exodus from the top had continued, with many important persons suddenly turning up in the West. Defection rates for troops had become such a problem that most had been grounded and not allowed to leave Russian territory.

The final straw had come when a Soviet warship, sent to intercept a pirate radio broadcaster in the Baltic Sea surrendered, despite the fact that the navy ship was armed, and with a crew outnumbering the unarmed British "pirates" by more than 100 to 1!

A photo of the grinning Russian captain surrendering ran on the front pages of most papers the next day, along with the headline "We want peace, and to hear more Beatles!"

But, for every reassuring gesture, there seemed one that raised eyebrows, if not anxieties, as when a squadron of nuclear-armed submarines began converging in the waters off Greenland.

The submarines neither engaged in aggressive behaviors, nor did they respond to Western attempts at communications. Instead, they just seemed to be waiting things out in the dark and cold neutral northern waters of the North Atlantic.

With no clear sense of what might happen next, US and NATO forces had no choice but to remain on high alert and stay positioned for whatever scenario might unfold, whether it be by intent or accident.

The best-case scenario for the dismantling of the USSR involved governments surrendering in orderly succession to the demands of the protestors, and adopting a timetable for a transition to democracy. But even a peaceful resolution would require a massive involvement by the US, both in the short and long terms.

Naturally, the top priority would be to work with the Soviet authorities to secure weapon systems and arsenals. Depending on how things collapsed, the US might need to take over food distribution, utilities, and even policing. No one knew for sure, so the Americans once again prepared for the worst, but hoped for the best.

The expense of reconstruction would be considerable, and once again, would mostly be borne by the United States, as had been most of the costs of the war itself. Still, things could have been much, much worse.

Considering this had been a war between two nuclear superpowers, the loss of life had been incredibly low. And, unlike previous wars, major cities were nearly unscathed — and none were radioactive wastelands. Yes, there had been considerable devastation in places such as North Korea, Nicaragua, and Iceland, but this was nothing compared to the last world war.

When, and to what degree, the US might experience a peace dividend remained to be seen. President Reagan would never concede to leaving America vulnerable, but neither was he likely to waste taxpayer money if there was no justifiable threat.

Only time would tell.

The very fact that the US had been prepared to meet the challenge of the war was a testament to the buildup that Reagan had initiated beginning with his first term, and which he had accelerated during his third.

Funding had gone across a range of areas, from high-tech and classified R & D on the Strategic Defense Initiative, to pay raises for the lowest-ranking recruits.

Reagan's military spending had also resulted in many new civilian jobs and other forms of stimulus that had rippled through the economy, and it wouldn't be possible to just simply flip the switch to the off position. Gearing down would take time.

Anxiety in wartime is natural. It was something Reagan's opponents—whether they were KGB propagandists, or domestic liberal sensationalists—had worked to incite and exploit.

With anxiety comes economic volatility, which begets social instability, which begets further uncertainty, as the cycle feeds upon itself. But fortunately, these never really materialized in America under Reagan.

As a wartime president, Ronald Reagan stood calm and resolved, displaying great reserve. In a time of crisis he had radiated strength and stability, which gave the people the confidence they needed to override their fears and trust in the future.

Reagan first helped people feel safe and secure, then he primed the pump economically so the sense of psychological well-being was reinforced by measurable material gains.

As someone who had lived through wars and the Great Depression, Reagan understood about the need for a little escapism. Making sure the American people had a few extra dollars in their pockets to have a meal out, to go see a movie, or put gas in the car for a Sunday drive is what gave them the strength they needed to make it through the darkest days.

He had, after all, not just studied Economics in college, but also Sociology, and understood how the two were intertwined.

As the Cold War was drawing to a close, everything that had been assumed of Reagan by his critics was turning out to be wrong. He was not a suicidal hawk that would destroy the planet in a flash of light, or a clueless ideologue that would crash the economy.

"Reaganomics" (a term coined by radio entertainer Paul Harvey), had taken root under difficult conditions and borne fruit, with growth solid across most sectors and income levels. Inflation was in check, down to less than 2%—helped in large part by stable oil prices, with much of the credit going to Reagan's avoidance of a ground war in the Middle East.

By every matrix, the US economy was finding its way: Job creation was up, wages were up, consumer confidence was up.

The people had put their faith in the President, and now they were seeing their investment pay dividends. Things were good, and getting better all the time.

But the story was far from over: The President's economic agenda had many other components, but like ingredients in a recipe, were to be added in only when the time was right.

And the time was now right for welfare reform. When the 102nd US Congress was seated on Thursday, January 3, 1991, President Reagan's welfare overhaul proposal was on the table waiting for them.

"After all," Reagan joked, "if even those Democrats who got voted out last fall can find work, it seems like employers are willing to give pretty much anybody a shot."

While colloquially referred to as just "Welfare Reform," the actual title of Reagan's proposal was the Personal Responsibility and Work Opportunity Act (PRWOA). Among its key provisions was ending welfare as an entitlement program for able-bodied adults, placing a two-year lifetime limit on benefits, adjustment of payments to discourage out-of-wedlock births and single-parent households, new rules covering enforcement of child support payments, tightening limits on applicant assets, and the prohibition of paying benefits to those not in the country legally.

Related to this would be a statute restricting the use of publicly funded legal services by persons in the country illegally. In other words, if one was not in the country legally, that person was not entitled to a legal defense paid for by US taxpayers. While any individual had a right to challenge something in court—such as a denial of welfare benefits based on citizenship status—the plaintiff, not the taxpayer—would be responsible for the cost of her/his own legal expenses.

PRWOA also included a number of provisions concerning personal accountability and the law. For instance, anyone convicted of a felony would be banned from collecting benefits for life. There was, however, a clause exempting those being released from prison, and who would naturally require extra assistance to reenter the workforce.

Reagan was surprised to find this was a sticking point for many conservatives bent on retribution.

But in accordance with his Christian beliefs, Reagan believed that the man being released from jail had paid his debt to society and now deserved a second chance.

The President was also a realist. Citing data showing how hard it was for an ex-con to find immediate employment, a short period of public assistance reduced the likelihood that this individual, with no other means of making an honest living, would be lured back into criminal activity.

Welfare was not only preferable to incarceration, but considerably cheaper. It also offered the best approach to breaking the cycle of recidivism.

Acknowledging the lack of job training programs available in prison, those being paroled would also be eligible for worker retraining classes and apprenticeships while receiving public assistance. These were costly additions that Reagan personally fought for, reflecting a pragmatism not obsessed by the need to punish, or blinded to the reality that long-term problems need long-term solutions.

Eligibility for those using illegal drugs would also be affected. To monitor compliance, all recipients over the age of 18 would be subject to periodic and random drug testing. Recipients refusing to participate in testing would have their benefits suspended until they complied. Those testing positive for drugs would be subject to an automatic one-year suspension of benefits. A second offense would result in a five-year suspension. If the recipient tested positive again, they would be banned for life. Three strikes and you're out.

Parental responsibility and accountability would be increased as well, specifically when dependent minors were involved in drug use and/or other criminal activity.

As the President saw it, parents needed to step up and take more responsibility for the actions of their own children. Those who didn't would suffer consequences.

One of the more controversial components of the proposal included provisions intended to discourage illegitimacy and teen pregnancies by cutting back on direct cash payments to those under the age of 18. This was coupled with a plan to eliminate the automatic financial incentive for having additional children while receiving public assistance. As an attempt to stabilize families, there were specific financial incentives linked to keeping fathers part of the household — reversing the decades old practice of encouraging single-parent households.

The Act also included regulations and penalties for states that might attempt to subvert the core policies and spirit of the law. Reagan knew from firsthand experience, that recipients would shop the different states for where they thought they might get the best deal, and then gravitate there. As governor, Reagan had dealt with the generosity of California's assistance programs serving as a national magnet for benefit seekers who brazenly joked, "Come for the weather, stay for the welfare!"

If people were willing to pull up stakes and move across country, it should be for a job — not a bigger welfare check. Nor was it fair to burden one state's taxpayers with supporting those who only migrated there solely to take advantage of their generosity.

PRWOA addressed this scheme by capping benefits at the new location to those matching the newcomer's previous allocation, or with those of the new state, whichever was lower, for a period of one year.

With regional qualifiers, the President was adamant about not just pushing the problem elsewhere. In a free country, the government can't stop people from moving, but it can remove the financial incentive for those being subsidized by the taxpayer.

In general, it costs more to live in New York than it does in Alabama. But there are parts of New York where one can live that are comparable. Yes, one might wish to see the bright lights of Broadway — but it was not fair to the taxpayers of the Empire State to subsidize this. For those who claimed they had no choice but to move from Nebraska to Hawaii in order to "be closer to family," then it should be their families, and not the state of Hawaii that should be on the hook if they opt to trade the snow of Omaha for the sunshine of Oahu.

PRWOA did not specifically address somewhat-related issues such as food stamps, unemployment, and job training, as these would be dealt with in separate, supplementary proposals and targeted legislation. A companion set of reforms tackling fraud in programs for the disabled would be taken up later.

But for now, the President had kept another of his campaign promises, and it was up to Congress to do its part.

Dominoes

By early February, the struggle for freedom had reached the tipping point. Across the Union of Soviet Socialist Republics, governments were under siege and paralyzed; and without support from Moscow, were buckling, crumpling, and collapsing.

The first to give in to the protestors was Czechoslovakia, following the abrupt resignation of General Secretary Miloš Jakeš, who ceded control to Karel Urbánek.

Although himself a communist, Urbánek's first official action in office was to cancel the constitutional clause that provided the Communist Party with a monopoly on fielding political candidates. His second action was to ban the party, his third, to set a date for free and open multi-party elections in May.

Urbánek, a former railway station manager, agreed to stay on during the transition period. He was, however, quite clear that he intended only to serve as a manager — not the leader.

The Urbánek administration — Czechoslovakia's first non-communist government since 1948 — would rule by a committee comprised of dissidents including playwright Václav Havel, and Alexander Dubček, who had been forced out of office for his support of the Prague Spring uprisings of 1968. The youngest member of the committee was 20 year-old Josef Diviš, one of the key organizers, and few remaining survivors, of the Wenceslas Square protests and massacre.

The fact that Czechoslovakia flipped first came as no great surprise, as the nation had a long history of challenging communist rule. But the speed at which it had happened was a shot heard round the world.

Havel, Dubček, and Diviš were all considered national heroes by the people, and their ascendency to power was viewed as an irrefutable sign that not only was the Iron Curtain rusted and falling apart, but that no one was coming to stop its demolition.

The peaceful transformation was saluted by Gorbachev, Reagan, and other world leaders who held it up as an example of non-violent revolution. Within hours, Czechoslovakia's borders with the West were opened, and the plug was pulled on all Soviet-slanted state programming. Radio stations began carrying Voice of America, the BBC, and the types of decadent Western programming previously banned and jammed, including American jazz and the BBC World Service.

Teams from the United Nations, the World Bank, and other Western agencies soon arrived on the scene to assist with daily affairs (including matters relating to banking and finance), and to provide temporary support services. Given the expanse of the transformations taking place, help was especially needed in the financial sector.

This was an area where the US had special expertise, and due to the foresight of Reagan and Schultz, programs were already in place and ready for immediate implementation.

Without the US, there would have likely been a degree of chaos if one system had been allowed to fold without something else ready to take its place.

Inspired by the Czechoslovakian "miracle," other Eastern European states began to overthrow their own communist governments and slip free from Moscow's control.

Next to break loose was Hungary. Like Czechoslovakia, the Hungarians also had a long and contentious relationship with Soviet-rule. The last major attempt to depose the Russians had come in 1956, which resulted in thousands of deaths, and nearly 15,000 Hungarians injured in a lopsided battle for independence.

Following the Czechoslovakian model, a transitional ruling council was put in place until elections could be held. The council included several communists, most notably Miklós Németh, who, like Jakeš, had only been in office a short time before being swept away by the changing tides of history.

As a communist, neither Németh, nor his party would be allowed to participate in the upcoming election. The communists were now on the run, as the Hungarian people resoundingly turned on any visible reminders of their nation's totalitarian past.

Statues of Lenin were pulled down, government buildings vandalized, currency defaced. The communist emblem was cut from flags, and the Budapest headquarters of the secret police was set on fire after being left abandoned, its once feared agents scrambling like cockroaches exposed to the light.

The long struggle for freedom had perhaps been no more obvious than in Poland. Here, the battle had been raging on two fronts—religious and political—for more than a decade, while the country went through various convulsive cycles of reform and repression.

The first major challenge in modern times had come in 1978, with the election of Karol Wojtlya, as Pope John Paul II. A deeply Catholic nation, the new Polish pope had used his position to advocate on behalf of a number of human rights issues, in addition to greater religious freedom.

On the political side, the Solidarity Union (headed by electrician Lech Walesa) had been involved in organizing strikes against the government, one of which had resulted in the 1981 imposition of martial law.

The leader of Poland's government then, and now, was Wojciech Jaruzelski, a pompous 67-year-old career military officer who usually presented himself in a heavily decorated uniform. In response to permanent eye damage caused by snow blindness, he often wore sunglasses—even indoors—as part of his trademark look.

During his tenure as the country's Defense Minister, Jaruzelski had commanded the Polish forces sent in (as part of the Warsaw Pact) to crush the 1968 uprising in neighboring Czechoslovakia. Two years later, he called up 27,000 military troops to violently put down a revolt by unarmed Polish strikers.

Jaruzelski was a man who believed in using force to maintain compliance and social order. Although a previous request for Soviet troops in 1981 had been denied, Jaruzelski didn't think Moscow would let him down this time. Unlike the uprisings of a decade earlier, these threatened a complete revolution and an end to socialist rule. Poland's western and southern neighbors had already fallen; Polonia, "land of fields," must not be ploughed under.

Secretary Jaruzelski was willing to fire the first shot, but he was also enough of a military strategist to acknowledge the battle would be lost without reinforcements from Mother Russia.

Time was running out. Rebels already controlled most of Zakopane, Gdansk, and complete regions along the borders with Czechoslovakia and Germany. Even Krakow had gone down without much of a fight, as government forces broke ranks and joined with protestors.

Lodz would soon be lost, and Warsaw was wobbling. The situation was dire, but with reinforcements from abroad, Jaruzelski felt he could turn things around. But if no help arrived soon, Poland would fall, and rebel forces would be on Russia's doorstep.

Unthinkable!

Jaruzelski declared a state of emergency and prepared for battle, but demands to speak directly to Sokolov as "one military commander to another" were ignored.

After waiting on hold once for nearly an hour he slammed the phone down hard enough to break it. For a moment, he thought of flying directly to Moscow to personally make his case, before acknowledging the country would likely fall as soon as he left Polish airspace.

Feeling as if he had been backed against the wall, Jaruzelski went on the offensive. He doubled down on his threats to both Moscow and his own people, issuing a series of warnings and ultimatums that grew ever more surreal and ludicrous while he stalled for time.

Hiding behind his dark glasses, Jaruzelski was playing a game of poker, relying on bluffs.

When it became obvious no help was coming to prop him up, and the people were not backing down, Jaruzelski folded, and caught a military jet to Moscow on Saturday morning, February 23.

General Jaruzelski's weekend departure surprised everyone, as publicly he had vowed to fight on until the end. Joining the weekend exodus were many top government and military officials, whose sudden disappearance resulted in immediate and widespread chaos.

Fortunately, leaders such as Walesa and the Pope stepped in with calls for calm and order until a temporary emergency ruling authority could be established.

The situation in Poland was much more complicated than had been the case in Hungary and Czechoslovakia. In addition, it appeared that the departures had been in the works for some time, as reflected by a series of financial withdrawals made against state treasuries, and the widespread destruction of public records.

Many other key components of government and the nation's infrastructure were intentionally sabotaged in accordance with Jaruzelski's scorched-earth policy against his own people. In response, one of the first actions taken by Poland's transitional government was the issuance of arrest warrants for Jaruzelski and the former members of his administration.

The loss of Poland was a huge shock, but the message was no unmistakably clear: Moscow is not coming to save you. Good luck.

Emboldened, other Soviet states began to fall in rapid succession, with little violence, and most in an orderly and civil fashion. Following Poland were its neighbors to the north, the Baltic States of Estonia, Latvia, and Lithuania. Each quickly formed transitional governments, and welcomed the arrival of foreign assistance.

Throughout March, pro-democracy movements continued to grow, spreading to Albania, Bulgaria, Belarus, and Ukraine.

For other states the transitions were slower and stickier.

In Romania, Nicolae Ceaușescu held on throughout most of March owing to an early—and brutal—use of troops, and reliance on state security forces to smash the opposition and maintain order. Executions were broadcast live on state TV.

As gruesome as the practice was, the broadcasts drew huge ratings. This was, after all, the same nation that gave the world Vlad the Impaler. Ceaușescu was only giving the people what they wanted, which in this instance aligned with what he wanted.

With no signs of a visible dissent, life in paradise would continue on as usual. At least for those who stayed on his good side.

On Friday evening, March 29, a grand party (organized by Mrs Ceaușescu), was held at the Presidential Palace in celebration of her husband being named Romania's First President on March 28, 1965.

This was the type of affair that President Ceaușescu reveled in, as for years he had worked hard to develop and nurture a cult of personality. Despite the nation's dire economic conditions, the Ceaușescu's *soirée* was quite the event; overflowing with gourmet delicacies, and even French champagne.

As the first couple took turns raising toasts to themselves, President Ceaușescu sensed the people wanted to hear more from him, so he obliged them by launching into a rambling speech about his vision of Romania's socialist utopian future, his words somewhat slurred by the alcohol. Grumbling began almost immediately, and from the periphery there began to rise rude noises, along with mumbled comments that were, at least initially, indecipherable.

Soon the chatter and heckling grew louder, and Ceaușescu, infuriated, demanded to know who had dared to interrupt him.

"It is I," answered the head of the dictator's personal security detail, much to the astonishment of all.

"Then you have given me no choice but to publicly slap your face. On your knees, you dirty drunken baboon!"

As Ceaușescu walked over to confront his servant, he was struck in the head by a large silver serving bowl someone lobbed from the edge of the crowd. Caught off balance, he fell to the ground, where the crashing sound of his impact was immediately followed by the sound of gunshots. Realizing what was happening, Mrs Ceaușescu turned and ran, but like her husband, was quickly brought down in a hail of bullets, still holding her glass of Dom Perignon, vintage 1969.

A quick trial was held the next day, and the Ceaușescus (although dead) were found guilty of a range of offenses all punishable by death. Those who had participated in the assassination were now exempt from prosecution, and would instead be honored as Heroes of the Second People's Revolution.

Communism, like the Ceaușescus, was dead in Romania. The military would take over, and in time, form a coalition government that would eventually revert to civilian rule.

Similar military-dominated governments would spring up in other nations as well; namely in the republics of Kazakhstan, Kyrgyzstan, Tajikistan, Turkmenistan and Uzbekistan. Here, the transition to democracy would be more nuanced. All would adopt economic reforms, and while officially rejecting communism, totalitarianism would remain the only item on the political menu.

In contrast to the waves of democracy lapping against its shores, Russia remained an island of communist rule. As had been the case elsewhere, protests were large and ongoing, and yet somehow the Kremlin had managed to cobble together the resources it needed to continue functioning.

Functioning, but not necessarily thriving. Disorder was apparent everywhere, from uncollected garbage piling up on the streets to rolling electrical blackouts. Although there had been no major violent crackdowns, the country was, for the most part, under a state of martial law. Few dared to venture out after dark.

The lack of democratic progress was both puzzling and frustrating. Although its empire was collapsing, Russia seemed caught between worlds. There was no clear sense of who was in charge, or of any particular direction.

It was, however, understood that things could not continue on like this indefinitely. Something needed to give, and soon.

By the start of April, most of Eastern and Central Europe were now under independent democratic rule and looking forward to elections that would officially signify the death knell of communism. During the transition period, many of the old institutions had remained, most notably the Warsaw Pact, now under civilian control.

Although most member states seemed to favor eventual integration into a larger entity (such as NATO) that included states from across all of Europe, the Warsaw Pact was seen as a temporary deterrent for any move by Russia to re-exert domination over the breakaway republics.

While relationships and cooperation between former regional communist states continued to develop, Russia remained cloistered. Official government-to-government relations were largely nonexistent.

Although travel into Russia was now deemed risky, the flow of people attempting to leave the nation was accelerating as the country continued its slow motion implosion.

As Russia's endgame dragged on, Vaclav Havel, the presumed next leader of a non-communist Czechoslovakia proposed a novel solution, suggesting that it might be time for history to reverse itself … and that soon it would be time for the members of the Warsaw Pact to "invade and liberate Russia."

Giddy with the newfound freedoms of speech, Havel's remark had been intended as a joke; just a bit of political satire that first spread among the liberated, then on to their former oppressors at the Kremlin. Sokolov failed to see the humor in this remark, only the horror.

Here he was, a true national hero, a man who had commanded the invasion of other nations and had ruled over an empire, being threatened by a smug, chain-smoking poet who reminded him of a French pimp.

Frustrated by the lack of resolve from those around him, and determined not to see Mother Russia subjected to such humiliation, the old man decided to put a stop to things then and there.

Born before the advent of the USSR, he would not sit

passively and preside over its demise. Before his personal power could be compromised any further, Sokolov decided to take strong and decisive action, by putting a pistol in his mouth and pulling the trigger.

86

A New Day in Russia

President Reagan was awakened shortly after four o'clock in the morning on Friday, April 5, by a call from National Security Director Bud McFarlane: Sokolov was dead.

Details were sketchy: No cause of death had been provided, and the suddenness of the announcement was reason for concern.

Had this been an assassination? Was it part of another coup? If so, who was now in charge?

Russian state media continued to report the story throughout the day, but offered little in the way of new information. Still, what is missing can often be as revealing as what is included. Notably absent from the official broadcasts were tributes from other current or former communist leaders, or Soviet allies such as Castro and Qaddafi.

The US, which had never really relaxed its guard, remained on high alert. Early Sunday evening, Gorbachev phoned Reagan directly with an update.

The conversation would be short, but dramatic: Sokolov had largely been removed from most official decision-making some time ago. Most decisions were being made by a council that had been steadily consolidating power and removing hardliners from any positions of authority.

Gorbachev's proposal, which was known to have the backing of the Americans, had been the catalyst needed. At that point, the government was already severely fragmented, as different factions tussled for control. As the inevitability of change set in, moderates had gained more authority, keeping Sokolov as a figurehead and using the military (now headed by Alexander Yefimov), as a counterforce against the conservative wing of the KGB.

Most of those who had participated in the original coup were already long gone, as were most of the old guard communists and hardliners. While the council did not incorporate any political dissidents, it did feature a number of Gorbachev supporters who had sided with him on behalf of reforms, such as *glasnost* and *perestroika*.

The council had behaved conservatively, but responsibly, noting that it had acted proactively to secure the USSR's arsenals, and establish new systems and protocols to maintain order—which would extend to a transfer of power to civilian authority, as determined by democratic elections.

Moscow was surrendering.

Reagan was stunned; tears forming in his eyes.

This was it; this was the end. The end of Soviet Communism. The end of the Cold War. The end of the nuclear nightmare. Here, at last, the promise of peace was now becoming reality.

The battle he had spent his lifetime fighting was over, and he had won.

The Evil Empire was history.

Reagan smiled and shook his head in disbelief. In the next room, Nancy had the TV on, and the President heard the familiar clock-ticking introduction that signaled the start of *60 Minutes*.

There was a slight lull in the conversation while the two leaders took a moment to reflect on what happened, and what lay ahead. There was much to be done, and both men knew it. But the worst was over now.

On Monday, the Russian council would appoint a new leader; Boris Yeltsin, a 60-year-old former member of the Politburo who had also served as something equivalent to being the mayor of Moscow. Although he was a lifelong communist, he had no military ties and was known for being something of a populist and rebel. Unfortunately, Gorbachev knew him to also be something of a drunk and a buffoon.

Not perfect, but a step in the right direction.

Whether Yeltsin and the others would be open to outside assistance to help make the transition to democracy was unknown; as were details concerning the merger of the government-in-exile headed by Gorbachev, with the one now under Yeltsin's control.

It was a new day, and for the first time in many years, a sense of genuine hope had come to Russia, and the world.

87

Economic Matters

As things continued to stabilize politically around the world, so did individual economies.

This was nowhere more apparent than in the United States, which had benefitted not just from the relatively smooth and peaceful end to the Cold War, but also from the President's economic policies.

With the validity of Reaganomics now irrefutable even to its harshest critics, the President continued to push ahead by introducing the Tax Reduction Act of 1991 (TRA).

Inspired by the successes resulting from earlier tax cuts directed at lower income brackets, the TRA would target the other end of the scale, providing a mix of relief and incentives for both individuals and businesses.

Included in the act was a provision to cut capital gains taxes by the largest margins in history. Under the President's proposal, the dollar amount for exempted profits from the sale of one's personal residence would double—thus putting them more in line with the actual real estate market.

The TRA also included provisions reducing, and in some cases, eliminating, inheritance taxes. Reagan had been especially troubled by stories of family farms that could not be passed from one generation to the next due to excessive "death taxes."

To illustrate by example, the President shared the story of a family in Wisconsin that had tended the same plot of land since homesteading it in the early 19th century. The farm had provided a home and livelihood for generations of the Brandt family through wars, depressions, recessions, and changing markets. But now the old family farm was being lost due to what Reagan denounced as a "heartless and short-sighted tax system that was decimating rural America."

In response to the President's citation, donations flooded in from all across America and the Brandt family farm was saved at the last minute. However, this did nothing to address the underlying conditions of a tax system that was essentially doing the same thing to dozens of other less fortunate families every single day.

Besides farms, the TRA would also help secure the inheritance of other similar assets, such small family businesses, which Reagan regarded as not just a key component of job creation and the economy, but also as an important societal stabilizer.

To stimulate investing, taxes on earned profits would be reduced percentage wise, and actual dollar levels increased.

While low-wage earners tended to quickly stimulate the economy with increased spending on basic goods and services, it was typically those in the upper income brackets who funded the kinds of large capital investments needed to facilitate growing consumer demand. Only this class had the resources to take on the big projects, and so the TRA provided an incentive to pump their profits right back into starting, and expanding businesses.

This was the one-two punch the economy needed, which the President illustrated with a very simple example:

For the part-time worker at McDonald's, the original set of tax cuts instantly translated into a larger weekly paycheck. This meant the employee's personal spending power was increased, but not in a way that negatively affected his employer's profitability (as would be the case with a salary increase).

By providing millions of Americans in a similar tax bracket with a "raise," new money flowed into the economy. Being a federal tax reduction, the benefits were dispersed all across the nation.

While the individual dollar amounts might be modest, cumulatively they added up to quite a wave. To meet the growing consumer demand, businesses responded by purchasing additional goods and services, and increased spending on staff.

This led to job creation, more full-time employees, and higher wages. No longer living paycheck-to-paycheck, workers purchased new clothes, ate more meals out, spent on entertainment, and took longer vacations.

Those still living at home now had the resources to move out. For others, extra money meant moving up. A new place that needed furniture, housewares, appliances. A stereo, a TV. If not a new car, some long overdue repairs on the old one.

The stability to get married, and start a family.

Growth creates demand, demands stimulates growth.

However, if businesses cannot keep up with consumer demand, shortages occur, and prices increase. Inflation stifles growth, which can lead to recession.

Inflation also leads to higher interest rates, which makes it more costly for businesses to borrow the money they need, whether it be for expansion (to meet demand), or to weather a downturn.

Soon, the cycle is moving in the opposite direction. The economy is contracting, and the first to take the hit will be the workers. Hiring will grind to a standstill. Hours will be cut to match the reduction in demand for goods and services. Wages will decline, and many businesses will close.

Laid-off workers will look to the government for assistance. Skilled workers will become rusty, frustrated, and despondent. Forced to live on meager benefits, consumer spending continues its decline, leading to more layoffs and closures.

This kind of downward spiral takes a huge toll that goes way beyond just economics. It ruins lives and destabilizes nations.

When a major economy like the United States goes down, the contagion spreads across the globe.

Before the problem could take root, Reagan wanted businesses to have the tools they needed to keep the economy healthy and growing. The TRA supported this goal by freeing up capital and presenting a broad range of incentives for its investment back into the US economy.

Policies such as the TRA were at the core of Reaganomics. Rather than punitively tax and redistribute wealth from a small and already overburdened segment, Reagan sought to grow the entire economy as a whole.

As Reagan saw it, the "little guy" had done his part. He had taken things as far as he could with the kind of direct stimulus needed to get the ball rolling. Now, it was up to the investor class to do its part.

What began as "bubble up" would now meet in the middle by "trickle down."

By providing new opportunities across the board, each segment can grow accordingly, and proportionately, expanding naturally.

It couldn't be simpler.

And, as the President had explained so many times before, even though actual percentage rates would decline, the sheer number of those paying in would increase. In tandem with welfare reforms, tens of millions of new employees would enter the workforce and begin paying taxes, rather than drawing out of the system.

As the President presented it, this wasn't just a win-win deal. It was win, win, win, win, and win again. *And again.*

But, Reagan understood human nature, and knew there would be a natural temptation to tamper with success. He worried that at some future date, politicians would be persuaded to start skimming off the system, taking a piece here, a bit from over there, until the whole thing collapsed.

Therefore, the TRA would contain a "poison pill" provision to ensure its protection, by instituting a requirement that a two-thirds congressional majority approve any future tax increases.

Before Congress adjourned for the summer recess, it approved the President's longstanding request for a line-item veto, and promised to have a version of his Welfare To Work bill ready for him to sign in the fall.

Although certain details still needed to be ironed out, the TRA proposal was well received in principle by Congress, economists, and especially by the public who saw the logic — and direct benefit of the provisions.

As the President noted with a smile, "Very few refuse having extra dollars to spend — especially if it was their money to begin with."

One initiative noticeably absent from legislative proposals being advanced by the White House, was a call for a Balanced Budget Amendment. It was no secret that Reagan favored such, and had consistently campaigned on it.

In the past, Democrats had blocked his efforts in Congress. But now, the massive financial obligations resulting from the war meant this idea would just have to wait a little longer.

The military buildup had been unlike anything else in history, and some costs would continue on for an indefinite period of time. One major obligation concerned troop size, which would need to be decreased gradually so as to avoid flooding the job market with too many discharged vets.

Without jobs waiting for them, many would be forced to draw

unemployment. Not only would the government be financially obligated, but Reagan was also concerned with the psychological ramifications of such actions, and the underlying message that those who had risked all were now worthless; society's detritus, requiring pity and charity.

No, these were America's *heroes* who deserved respect and opportunity. And their Commander-in-Chief was determined to see that they got it.

88

"Just Say No"

As the world continued to heal from global conflict, the President turned renewed attention to a different war; a war that had been raging for decades. It was one that took thousands of lives each year, and one that had turned cities into battlegrounds.

It was the war on drugs.

The war, or at least the term "War On Drugs" went back to the Nixon administration, which pioneered a coordinated national effort to address the burgeoning use of illegal drugs in America.

In the decades that followed, drug abuse and the associated criminal activity had grown progressively worse. Subsequent administrations took up the fight with varying degrees of zeal and success, hindered by a naive public permissiveness still rooted in the counterculture of the 1960s.

The Reagan Administration made the war an early priority. Eager to do her part, First Lady Nancy Reagan launched the "Just Say No" campaign in 1982. This was a revolutionary approach, in that for the first time it placed emphasis on elements of personal choice and individual responsibility.

"Just Say No" was not a complicated six-month regimen or 12-step program. It did not cost thousands of dollars to personally implement, or require third-party supervision.

Instead, it was a start: Three little words of encouragement, a message and strategy that would be successfully mimicked years later with Nike's "Just Do It" campaign, which also put the onus of positive change on the individual.

Although ridiculed by liberals and lampooned in the media, the "Just Say No" program provided a simple, single-action solution that stopped the problem before it could get a foothold. By empowering the individual, "Just Say No" confronted the sense of powerlessness that often leads to substance abuse.

It was, in every sense, quintessentially Reaganesque, in that it underscored the First Couple's unshakable belief, and trust, in the common person.

Undaunted by her detractors, Mrs Reagan traveled the country in support of her message, stating, "If you can save just one child, it's worth it."

And it was.

The campaign attracted widespread celebrity support, as well as endorsements from former users who credited the simplicity of the "Just Say No" directive to their own personal victory over drugs.

Meanwhile, the White House took on a complimentary set of initiatives related to interdiction, and to stemming the flow of hard drugs such as cocaine and heroin that had been pouring into the country on palettes and in container ships. These actions were supported by other policies and programs targeting domestic activities, including manufacturing, distribution, sales, and a web of other, often violent, related criminal activities.

Although the President was engaged on a personal level, direct command of this war was the bailiwick of Ed Meese, just as it been the responsibility of George Bush, when he was Vice President. Colonel Meese hit the ground hard, with a "take no prisoners" style that quickly garnered the praise of law enforcement, and resulted in the offer of a cameo role (playing himself) on the hit NBC TV drama *L.A. Law*. Meese declined the invitation.

Reagan found the invite amusing; and while it offered the opportunity to help spread the administration's message, he reminded his VP that it would be a step backwards, noting his path had been "acting first, *then* politics."

Still, the White House was happy to see a growing awareness, and a change in stance by Hollywood, an industry that had a well-founded reputation for permissiveness and acceptance of the drug culture.

After the loss of so much life and potential, the entertainment industry was once again embracing heroes, not villains.

Seeing things turning around was more than just a political or policy victory for the Reagans. Over the years they had been personally touched more than once by drug and alcohol-related problems affecting people they knew from the entertainment industry.

This was not a new problem, and it would not be solved overnight.

It was a complicated issue with tentacles that extended into many different areas. It affected users, their friends and family, communities, and the nation.

Under President Reagan, America's approach to fighting the scourge of drugs was multi-faceted and constantly evolving, with a key component to the President's proposal for welfare reform being a provision requiring that recipients be randomly tested for drugs, backed by penalties for those who tested positive.

Reagan was quick to defend this provision, noting that a similar statute was already in place for many workers in both the public and private sectors. "Why should those on public assistance be less accountable than those who are employed?" he demanded to know.

"If people are found to be using drugs we will provide two options: medical treatment or jail. We cannot ask the public to subsidize their self-destruction and the related harm it causes to the society."

Drug abuse was, as the President saw it, "a repudiation of everything America is."

While President Reagan did not agree with the Reverend Jesse Jackson on many things, he did support his adage that people needed "hope, not dope." Like Jackson, Reagan believed that religious faith provided a path for personal redemption (as affirmed by numerous academic studies, and the most successful 12-step programs).

In recognition of this, the President also looked to the faith-based community for help. Despite its proven effectiveness, economic assistance had been derailed by political partisanship, forcing the President to rely on volunteers and those who felt the calling to serve God, simply for the sake of doing good and helping others.

Many faiths worked together to address the problem, either directly or through financial sponsorship. The President was especially encouraged by stories such as one involving a collaboration between Jews and Christians in Miami.

While drug abuse was not a significant problem within Miami's Jewish community, members pooled resources to assist efforts by some Christian neighbors that were on the verge of collapsing due to a lack of funding. Meanwhile, the Hindu community in Detroit developed a similar program to assist Muslims.

As Reagan was pleased to note, "In times of crisis, even big differences like religion are set aside, as we are reminded of that which connects us, rather than divides us. We are all Americans; we are all our brother's keepers."

Reagan's presidency had also scored victories in the War On Drugs in ways that no one had predicted. Case in point being the military buildup that had provided a range of opportunities for millions of young men and women (as a side benefit to serving their country).

For starters, enlistment offered immediate, steady employment — even to those without a high school diploma. While in the service, enlist-ees could learn valuable vocational skills, attend college, and earn col-lege benefits to be used following their discharge. The service provided a ticket out of troubled communities, which often had few financial alternatives to the illegal drug trade. Joining the US military offered a respectable and stable lifestyle that paid a lifetime of dividends.

In the 1980s, violent criminal gangs became a rising problem in many American cities. Too many young people, growing up in broken homes and fractured communities, with that basic human need simply to "belong" were being targeted and exploited by gangs. The military offered an alternative; an invitation to become part of a community that cared for, and looked out for one another, whether times were good or bad.

As they say, "Once a Marine, *always* a Marine."

Service also offered a way to put down roots and embrace the American Dream. For those who had lived for generations in squalid public housing, a home of one's own was now possible with a VA loan.

Above all, those who served had the respect and gratitude of their country. They had been reborn and empowered. There would be no turning back now.

The combined economic impact of Reaganomics and the military build-up was transforming America.

89

"Dirty Ronnie"

With the expanding job market came new opportunities for legal employment, and with it, a sense of personal worth and value that replaced feelings of worthlessness and dependency. Whereas drugs usually offered a downward spiral of addiction, jail, disability, and/or death, employment offered a path to prosperity and upward social mobility.

Even the most hard-hit inner city neighborhoods began to undergo amazing transformations thanks to Reagan. Small businesses began to spring up everywhere, and streets became safe to walk again—even at night.

The pride was back.

But not everyone was happy with these changes, especially those who profited from the illegal drug trade, whether it be financially, or in the perverted idolatry that came from heading a criminal operation.

These were evil and ruthless individuals who thrived on power and violence. Drug lords who targeted ever younger and more defenseless members of their communities—and even their own families—to serve as disposable pawns in illicit empires.

But try as they might, their operations were collapsing as people turned away from drugs. By every measurable marker, from seizures, to arrests, to overdoses—the numbers were down dramatically. The good guys were winning the war.

Dealers were understandably angry, and as their influence and territory shrank they viciously turned on each other in desperate fights over ever diminishing markets. As the demand for drugs fell, so did all the other crimes associated with it, including robbery, prostitution, and murder. Suicide, vandalism, and homelessness were also in decline.

Just as the dealers had turned on their own communities, using crime and addiction to gain control, communities were now turning the tables and fighting back. Gangs and drugs were not welcome.

Like most major American cities, Washington DC had endured its own struggle against these problems.

The city was, in many ways typical; home to an underclass no one seemed to care about or even acknowledge. Here was the capital of the world's richest nation, held in poverty and despair by failed social programs that offered no hope or accountability. It was the perfect environment for the drug culture to flourish.

Drug abuse, however, was not limited to just the poor and powerless, but extended right up to the office of Marion Barry, the city's veteran mayor, who had been busted the previous year at the Ramada Inn for freebasing cocaine and having sex with a lady friend who was not his wife.

My, how far the former Eagle Scout from Mississippi had fallen! If only he had been able to just say "no" instead of "blow." Boldly defiant, Barry refused to accept personal responsibility for his choices, blaming his downfall on a targeted sting orchestrated by the FBI.

The mayor's demise was a sad ending for a man who had been idolized and celebrated by the Democratic Party as a role model for the minority community—both in DC and nationally. But just as the three-term Democratic mayor had been spiraling downward, those far less privileged were pulling themselves up around him.

By taking advantage of the opportunities that had come under President Reagan, the capital district was undergoing a renaissance.

But as was the case with the drug lords, politicians who benefitted from a status quo based on exploiting pain sought to push back.

Being unable to refute the economic benefits of Reaganomics, liberals instead decided to take aim on the President's War On Drugs and the policies included in the Welfare To Work proposal. Both initiatives were branded as inherently racist, and as such, reflected the bigotry of the conservative movement that, emboldened by economic success and power, was finally playing its hand.

As absurd as it was, the administration worried that such lies might undermine faith in the programs, and thereby impact their effectiveness. In response to these concerns, the President's team began searching for ways to counter these assertions with real world success stories, all the while careful to avoid any appearance of tokenism.

Whether termed damage control or spin, PR is a part of politics, and the President, as the face of the administration had no choice but to step into the fray to defend his initiatives.

Exactly how, was a topic for debate.

Then, one Monday morning Deputy Chief of Staff Mike Deaver approached him with an idea.Over the weekend, Deaver had read a story in the *Washington Post* about the incredible transformation of a former crack house located less than a mile from the White House. A local church had purchased the property at auction, and then converted it into a daycare for women who were now working in the area.

Just two years prior, many of the women now associated with the facility had been drug users. Some had even been former residents of the house when it been a drug den ruled by squatters and gang members. But that was then. This was now.

The turnaround had been miraculous, and would serve as a testimony of how the President's various policies had intertwined to create hope and opportunity, where before there had only been desperation and poverty.

At the time, the population of DC was approximately two-thirds African-American, and from what Deaver could gather, the daycare served mostly members of the black community. Before bringing up the matter with the President, Deaver undertook his own investigation, confirming what had been reported in the news article. In addition, he learned that the daycare had been central to revitalizing an entire neighborhood, now home to many new small businesses, safe streets, and parks where children could play.

Intrigued, Deaver decided to make a personal visit and was delighted by what he found. The atmosphere was warm and friendly, the facility clean and professional. He was welcomed with open arms and enjoyed a delicious healthy lunch prepared by a woman who would soon begin a new job at a prestigious downtown restaurant.

Not the tallest man in the world, Deaver ate lunch at a community table opposite a young boy who reminded him to "eat his vegetables and drink his milk," as this would "help him to grow." Smiling in acknowledgement, the 53-year-old air force veteran wisely followed the advice.

Afterwards, Deaver and his new friend helped bus dishes.

Being a co-operative daycare, those who used the facility were also required to volunteer some of their own time at the center. This served a variety of purposes, including enhancing a sense of community and providing opportunities for professional networking.

But most amazing of all, Deaver found that he was not the only man there that day. Due to a provision in the volunteer contract, fathers could also serve as volunteers. This allowed the women greater vocational flexibility, while creating stronger family units by having the dads more directly involved in the responsibilities of parenting.

Satisfied, Deaver floated the idea of a presidential visit to the site, and Reagan was intrigued. He especially liked the idea of fathers being involved, noting with some sadness how he had missed so much of his own children growing up due to being away at work.

The issue of race was never brought up, but Deaver decided to move on what he felt might be a good "photo op" to counter the smear campaign targeting welfare reform. In his view, the daycare was an example of good old-fashioned self-reliance, and an uplifting story of how hard work and discipline had transformed lives. The staff seemed apolitical, and welcomed the opportunity to showcase, and inspire others, with their achievements.

The visit started out well, and the President (now a grandfather) really appeared to be enjoying himself. He was a natural with children, and at his playful best posing for photos and expressing a genuine interest in the activities.

At one point, a little girl asked Reagan if he thought she might grow up to be President, to which Reagan answered yes. "After all, when I was your age, I lived thousands of miles away—whereas you can see the White House from your window. Now just stay focused, and try not to waste any time going off to California to make movies with monkeys," said the President with a wink.

"Never forget, you can do whatever you put your mind to doing."

It was a moment—and message—that she would indeed remember always.

Like Deaver, the President was impressed by the number of young fathers at the daycare. But as one approached him carrying a baby and some diapers Reagan raised his hands, smiled and quipped, "Sorry, I can't help you with that. It's been so long since I've changed a diaper that I don't think I'd remember where to start!"

As the crowd laughed, the man dropped the baby and the diapers, revealing a gun, which he drew and aimed at the President.

Time seemed to freeze.

The Secret Service detail entrusted with protecting the President swung into action, but before they could respond, Reagan himself pulled a revolver from a holster inside his coat and fired twice hitting his assailant and knocking him to ground.

The man lay on the ground screaming and convulsing. Blood was everywhere, and the room erupted into panic as some people hit the ground, while others ran for the doors.

Secret Service agents jumped on the shooter and restrained him, while others rushed to surround and defend the President who still stood holding his gun, ready.

Although right-handed, Reagan shot left—and with deadly accuracy. Having once been nearly killed by a gun-wielding assassin, the President had been determined to never let down his guard again, and was rarely without a concealed weapon. Although he trusted his security detail, packing his own protection provided the President with genuine peace of mind.

While the Secret Service was not supportive of his choice to carry a firearm, they would never again raise the issue after that day, as it was obvious that if Reagan had not drawn and fired first, he probably would have been killed.

Following the incident, the President was immediately whisked away in accordance with security protocols, and the facility—now a crime scene—was sealed off.

Badly shaken, the President sought solace from Mrs Reagan. While his actions had been completely justified, having to shoot someone in front of a group of children caused him tremendous anguish—even if it had been in self-defense. Granted, many of these children had already experienced violence first hand, and the attacker, although severely wounded, was expected to make a full recovery.

Worst of all, what had started out as a very positive visit had instead gone in just the opposite direction. Footage of Reagan drawing and shooting was looped endlessly on the evening news, and blurry stills of the President, gun in hand were featured on the front pages of every paper in America. Whether intended as satire or a tribute, Reagan was being compared to Dirty Harry, the rogue San Francisco cop portrayed by Clint Eastwood.

The President was now "Dirty Ronnie," and audio of him previously uttering the line "Go ahead, make my day" (as made famous by the Dirty Harry character) was repeated endlessly.

The incident, for better or worse, reinforced Reagan's image as a gunslinging cowboy, and would stick in the public's mind as one of the signature events of his presidency.

Deaver offered to resign, but Reagan wouldn't have it. "There's nothing we can do about it now, except to be glad that no one died."

No one blamed Deaver, but Nancy saw to it that heads rolled at the Secret Service. Not only had they been slow to respond, they had failed to adequately secure the facility.

The President's would-be assassin, William "Ghost Justice" Benson was not a parent or regular member of the daycare, but an acquaintance of a woman who was in the process of being ejected due to relapsed drug usage. Although unaware of the man's true intentions, she had brought him in that day and had allowed him to hold her baby.

Benson, 26, had an extensive criminal record, mostly related to activities committed as the leader of a local gang. As had been the case with so many others of his ilk, Ghost Justice's criminal enterprise had been in severe decline, and he decided it was time to give the President some "payback."

When the final score was tallied no one was a winner that day.

But as Benson lay in his hospital bed a sense of calm came over him. While his personal transformation was still a ways off, he did have one tremendous thing going for him: the daily prayers of the man he had tried to kill.

90

Another Supreme Court Vacancy

Within a week of the incident at the daycare center, the President received a call from Thurgood Marshall, the first, and only black justice currently serving on the US Supreme Court.

Reagan and Marshall were frequently at odds politically, but neither questioned the other's patriotism and commitment to public service. The two had clashed a few times previously, most recently in 1987 when during a television interview, Marshall implied that Reagan was a racist — the "worst" in the White House since Herbert Hoover.

At Reagan's request, the two met to discuss Marshall's comments. During a meeting held in the private family living quarters of the White House, the President shared his life story, relating how his personal experiences confronting bigotry and racism had shaped a lifelong commitment to the principles of fairness and equal opportunity.

It was an honest and revealing conversation, and afterwards, Reagan felt that he had made a personal friend, despite their political differences. In the years since, the relationship had been cordial, although not necessarily close. When Marshall called out of the blue that evening, Reagan assumed that the justice wanted to discuss the recent allegations of racism stemming from his welfare proposals, and the fallout from having shot a black man at the daycare.

While Marshall, the grandson of a slave, did not accuse Reagan of being personally racist, he did call upon him to be more vocal in going after those elements in his party who were. Marshall believed the lack of activism by the President was being read as tacit acceptance of bigotry, and that Reagan needed to do more to take on racists who Marshall believed were infiltrating the Republican Party. Reagan disagreed with this assessment, but now aware of this perspective, would make his stance clearer: Racists were not, and never were, welcome in the GOP. Bigotry and prejudice were the antithesis of the party's core values of equality and opportunity for all.

Marshall thanked the President for his pledge, and commended him on his selection of Emilio Garza, as a person of color, to the bench. Although the two justices had ideological differences, Marshall respected the younger justice's intellect and work ethic.

Then, for a moment, there was an awkward pause. When Marshall continued, he sounded weary.

"I can only hope that you will work as hard to find someone equally worthy to be my successor."

Reagan hesitated from interrupting; he knew where the conversation was going.

"As perhaps you've heard, Mr President, I haven't been well of late … I just turned 83, and I've been on the bench since 1967. I'm tired."

Marshall let out a long sigh, then cleared his throat.

"To tell you the truth, Ron, I thought I could outlast you; to hang on long enough to have a nice liberal Democrat like Dukakis or Kennedy pick my successor—but I don't think that's going to happen now."

Marshall chuckled, coughed slightly, and then continued.

"I really can't see myself making it another couple of years, so I'm calling today to tender my resignation, effective as soon as my replacement can take over."

The two spoke for a few minutes longer, and then wrapped things up on a positive, personal note.

Reagan sat at his desk and considered the magnitude of what had just transpired. Replacing Marshall would mean that five of the court's nine justices would now be his appointees, which in turn would further expand the conservative majority.

If Reagan could place another young justice like his last pick (the 43-year-old Garza), he could likely extend his legacy on to the court for many decades to come.

But instead, the President decided on a different course. He knew what he needed to do, and his decision was quick and clear.

His choice would reflect a personal commitment to righting a past wrong, picking someone who would have been perfect for the court, but who had been unfairly savaged for the spectacle of a partisan sideshow.

Before notice of Marshall's retirement and the lobbying for his replacement could begin, Reagan would announce his decision: he would nominate Robert Heron Bork to the United States Supreme Court.

Bork, 64, was currently serving as Attorney General in the Reagan

White House. His selection as AG had been a bold move to restore his reputation, which had been severely tarnished during his previous bid for a seat on the court.

As Attorney General during the third term, Bork had been serving admirably and had earned the respect of the American people.

He deserved a second chance.

Four years earlier, Reagan had nominated Bork to replace Lewis Powell, a centrist who had been placed on the court by Richard Nixon. At the time, Bork, a former Marine and Yale Law School professor, had been serving on the Court of Appeals for the District of Columbia Circuit. At his confirmation hearings in 1982, Bork had received *unanimous* bipartisan support from the US Senate.

But the climate in Washington had changed considerably between 1982 and 1987. Partisan Democrats had gained control of the Senate, and were increasingly using their power to strike back at and belittle the President.

In many ways, the period surrounding Bork's original nomination in 1987 had been a low point personally, and professionally, for Reagan, as he found himself fighting battles on multiple fronts. The Stock Market had crashed, fallout from Iran-Contra was a recurring distraction, and Nancy had just been diagnosed with breast cancer.

Smelling blood, Democrats conspired to take down whomever Reagan nominated, and decided to use the confirmation hearings as an opportunity to play to their liberal base in advance of the upcoming elections.

The mission to rout Bork and humiliate Reagan was led by Teddy Kennedy, with backup from a number of other Senators with similar presidential ambitions, including Delaware's Joe Biden, then Chair of the Senate Judiciary Committee.

No one, least of all Bork, was prepared for the sneak attack, which hit him from all sides. Still, he tried to keep his cool and play along with the witch trial.

Robert Bork was honest and upfront about his conservative personal values, but maintained that such would not affect his performance on the bench. Instead, the nominee believed judges should exercise restraint and impartiality in deciding cases. He was not an ideologue, and he had the record to back it up.

Like the President, Bork shared the opinion that judges should adjudicate—not legislate, from the bench, staying true to the framer's original understanding of the Constitution.

In the end it made no difference: Bork's fate had been sealed before the hearings even began. The game had been rigged from the get-go, and the Democrats in charge of tallying the score won: Bork's application was rejected.

But things had changed.

The Democrats were now the minority party in the Senate, their numbers reduced further by each of the past two elections.

Massachusetts' Teddy Kennedy, who had led the original attack on Judge Bork was long gone, and wouldn't even be available for comment; shielded from any further public embarrassment while he underwent psychiatric counseling.

Through the prism of history, one wondered if the seeds of Kennedy's paranoid delusions were already present at the time of his ranting denunciation of Bork?

"Robert Bork's America is a land in which women would be forced into back-alley abortions, blacks would sit at segregated lunch counters, rogue police could break down citizens' doors in midnight raids, schoolchildren could not be taught about evolution, writers and artists could be censored at the whim of the Government, and the doors of the Federal courts would be shut on the fingers of millions of citizens for whom the judiciary is—and is often the only—protector of the individual rights that are the heart of our democracy."

Although the vote had mostly been divided along party lines, Kennedy had received the support of a few Republicans, including Pennsylvania's Arlen Specter, whose party-loyalty could best be described as shifting and opportunistic.

Specter and Kennedy were known to be good pals, and although "Benedict Arlen" had been investigated as part of Kennedy's would-be coup, the FBI did not have sufficient evidence to formally charge him with any wrongdoing.

If so, it would have been an interesting historical twist in terms of conspiracies. Decades earlier, while still a Democrat, Specter, at the recommendation of (then Michigan Congressman) Gerald Ford, served on the Warren Commission, the body charged with investigating the assassination of President John Kennedy, where Specter had co-authored the "single bullet" theory.

In 1980, Specter jumped on board the Reagan Revolution, and won his first seat in the US Senate. Riding Reagan's coattails, he was re-elected in 1986.

Up for re-election next year, Specter knew he was on thin ice with voters and the administration, and would likely not cause any further problems for Bork. In fact, if Specter stayed true to character, this time he would likely be leading the charge of support for Bork's confirmation.

Ah, politics!

In opposition to his second bid for a seat on the court, most of the objections centered on Bork's ethnicity, as some felt that a seat being vacated by a black justice should only be filled by another person of color. While Reagan acknowledged the passion of this argument, he believed the selection process should be guided by logic, and not emotion. In his view, Bork was simply the best person for what was a critically important job.

As hoped for, the confirmation hearings proceeded in an orderly fashion: The Senate performed its constitutional duty without regard to what made for titillating TV, or to provide sound bites for liberal fundraisers.

This time Bork received a thorough and fair hearing, and was unanimously approved to serve on the Supreme Court of the United States beginning in the fall.

91

A Rising Starr

The confirmation of Robert Bork to the United States Supreme Court filled one opening, but created another, as the President would now need to find a new Attorney General.

Reagan was sorry to see Bork go, as he had done a stellar job as AG. But Ronald Reagan was never one to stand in the way of someone's quest for advancement, or to not make good on setting right a past wrong.

Over the past few years, Reagan had come to know and like Bork on a personal level; discovering a genuine warmth and wit in his personality that helped others feel at ease when in the presence of what was clearly a towering intellect.

Like Reagan, Bork enjoyed movies—especially comedies. During his tenure as AG, he had been a regular guest at White House movie nights, reveling in classic slapstick comedies such as *A Day At The Races* (starring the Marx Brothers), as well as more contemporary titles like *City Slickers*. A highlight for all was the running of Alfred Hitchcock's *The Man Who Knew Too Much*, which was attended by a special surprise guest, Reagan's old friend, and star of the film, Jimmy Stewart.

Reagan made it clear that Bork would be welcome to continue attending the screenings, but reminded him that even though he might sit as a justice on the nation's highest court, this did not necessarily qualify him to pass judgment on any of the movies Reagan himself had starred in. The new Supreme Court justice acquiesced—so long as an endless supply of free popcorn would be included in the deal.

Bork's departure had been the only significant loss to the White House team to date. Normally, in any administration, there would be a certain number of turnovers, whether due to personal conflicts, exhaustion, or the desire to pursue other opportunities. While some lesser figures had indeed departed, they tended to be persons like the special assistant to the executive assistant of the acting under secretary.

Losing a member of the core team was like losing a family member, and adding anyone new to the mix would certainly affect the dynamics of what was a remarkably cohesive and highly functioning administration. In recognition of this reality, Reagan first looked at candidates he was already familiar with for who might be the best fit.

At the top of his list was Kenneth Starr, currently serving as Solicitor General. Prior to this position — and like Bork — Starr had been appointed by Reagan to the Court of Appeals for the District of Columbia. He had also been on the President's list of candidates to replace Justice Brennan, the position that eventually went to Emilio Garza.

At just 45, Starr was young and energetic. The son of a minister, and himself devoutly Christian, Starr had married young and quickly started a family. He had attended the prestigious law school at Duke University, which led to an assignment clerking for Warren Burger, the former Chief Justice of the Supreme Court; an impressive honor for one so young.

As with David Souter, Starr came heavily recommended by former Vice President Bush — which was almost enough for Reagan to reconsider his candidacy. But other voices supported him, namely his fellow Texans and current cabinet members James Baker and William Bennett.

As was Reagan's way, the pair first met privately so he could get a feel for Starr as a person. Things got off to a somewhat rough start, until the conversation turned to football — a subject that both men were passionate about.

With the ice having been broken, the conversation quickly flowed, and the President found the chemistry he was looking for in what would be a critical new addition to his inner circle. Satisfied, Reagan offered him the job (contingent on passing the ratification process), and Starr accepted on the spot with a broad boyish smile and firm handshake.

Reagan liked his decisiveness and the addition of another young conservative to the team. He felt good about his choice, and Starr was quickly confirmed; smoothly transitioning into the top spot at the Justice Department as Bork moved on to the Supreme Court.

As anticipated, Starr clicked well with other members of the President's team. While his sense of humor wasn't as raucous as that of Press Secretary Limbaugh, the two also bonded over a shared love of football — despite favoring rival teams. When HUD Secretary (and former NFL star) Jack Kemp joined in on the discussion it was hard for

Reagan to get a word in, visibly delighted by the camaraderie, and the playful, competitive banter of his White House team members.

Bork had left some pretty big shoes to fill, but all in all, Kenneth Winston Starr seemed to be a pretty good fit.

92

Jack Kemp

As 1991 entered its final quarter, there was a feeling of it being the start of a new golden age for America.

The bond between the people and their government was strong. At the top was a President who had kept them safe, kept his word, and remained committed to fulfilling his campaign promises.

Acknowledging the importance of teamwork, the President was quick to credit the roles played by the members of his administration, from his VP on down to the members of his cabinet. Things almost seemed too good to be true, and as is usually the case, they were.

Within weeks of Bork's departure, Housing and Urban Development Secretary Jack Kemp announced his intention to resign—so as to pursue a run for the presidency. This had been his life's dream, and many in the conservative movement regarded the affable former Congressman and sports legend as Reagan's natural heir.

Both were Presbyterians, aligned on social issues, foreign policy, defense. Kemp also supported the President's economic policies, and had been a key architect of the 1981 Economic Recovery Act.

They had their differences, but ideologically, and physically, (both being 6´1) the two men saw things very much eye-to-eye.

Like Reagan, Kemp also had life experience beyond politics. He had lived and worked outside of Washington, and was able to connect with, and understand, the concerns of the common man.

Kemp, now 56, had been steadfast in his core conservative views for most of his life. Politics hadn't changed him; he had changed politics.

Before entering public service, Jack Kemp had enjoyed a successful career as a quarterback in the NFL. Joking about how this experience had prepared him for the political life, Kemp stated "Pro football gave me a good perspective. When I entered the political arena, I had already been booed, cheered, cut, sold, traded, and hung in effigy."

But Kemp was no newcomer to the world of politics. While still in his 20s, he had worked on presidential campaigns for Richard Nixon

(1960) and Barry Goldwater—as well as Reagan's 1966 gubernatorial run, before going on to serve on the governor's staff.

Kemp had been a Reagan man all his life, and now the President looked forward to returning the favor.

Besides, Vice President Meese would not be running—so there would be no conflict between his two close friends.

Usually a sitting Vice President is seen as the natural choice, but Ed Meese was ready to move on; expressing no interest in the Presidency. A native Californian, the soon-to-be 60 year-old VP was looking forward to moving back home to the Golden State with his wife Ursula. Meese had been by Reagan's side since the 1960s, and it was hard to imagine serving in government without his old friend and mentor. The two had come to Washington together, and would leave together when their work was done.

For months, Reagan had made it clear that he had no intention, much less interest, in running for a fourth term—even though Congress' repeal of the 22nd Amendment had left this door open. He had accomplished most of what he had set out to do, and, as those around him were fond of noting, "saving the world would be a tough act to follow."

The comment was usually made tongue-in-cheek, but Reagan did deserve high praise for how he steered the nation—and the world—through one of the most difficult periods in human history.

But it was time to move on; to quit while you're ahead.

Reagan was now 80 years old, and ready to enjoy retired life back in California—and in particular, at the Ranch. Mentally sharp, in great physical shape, still passionate about issues and serving the public interest—but ready to hang up his hat. Yes, he still had a few things he wanted to finish up as the President, but he also had a full year ahead of him, a unified Congress, and a supportive public.

The story of America's conservative revival was bigger than any one man, even if that man was a giant like Ronald Reagan. In order for the revolution to continue, it would need a worthy successor; and it was no secret that he saw Jack Kemp as that person.

Still, Reagan knew that his departure would leave an open door at the White House, and that Kemp would not be the only one running for the Republican nomination. He would, however, have significant built-in advantages, given that no one else from the current administration had expressed an interest in running.

As always, rumors were already circulating about potential GOP candidates; the usual cadre of senators and governors.

Reagan would do what he could to help his former HUD secretary, but his options were limited. As a matter of etiquette and tradition, a sitting President was restricted from displaying any public preference until all the primaries were over, and the choice made official by the party convention.

In order to be competitive, Kemp would need to leave his official duties soon in order to focus on the grueling job of running for the presidency. As a veteran of such contests, Reagan knew what lay ahead, and was glad his days of campaigning were over.

"I can still coach," he told Nancy, "but it's time for a young man like Jack to move the ball downfield now."

If Kemp succeeded in winning the primaries and becoming the Republican candidate, he would still have a long battle ahead. To date, he'd only run for a seat in the House, which is very different from the pressures surrounding a national campaign.

Despite his savvy as an economist, Kemp was known to despise fundraising. He would definitely need help in this area, as Reagan knew it would take more than just a dream to run for president these days.

Until another candidate officially entered the race, the President was technically free to help his protégée. Knowing that others would inevitably jump in, Reagan would need to act quickly, and discretely. Even his own staff would be kept in the dark as to his preference and assistance.

Reagan's first major act on Kemp's behalf was to connect him with Stuart Spencer, a California-based political consultant. Spencer was a trusted friend who had worked on both of Reagan's gubernatorial runs, in addition to his last three bids for the White House.

Spencer was delighted at the invitation, and Kemp welcomed the addition of a seasoned veteran with such a winning record. Little did Kemp know that Spencer had been already been contacted by another candidate — a fellow Republican — who had yet to publicly announce his candidacy. Spencer had turned this person down, and made no mention of the request when Reagan called.

If — or when — this person entered the race things would change dramatically; but for now, Kemp was the first to formally declare his intentions on the Republican side.

Seeking to capitalize on this lead, Spencer went right to work, lining up donors, adding staff, and reaching out to those who had supported Reagan and the GOP in the past.

With the Democrats it was a different story. The party had several battle-tested prospects anxious to run — as well as many fresh new faces. And, although way down in the polls, the party still had a base of wealthy donors and special interest groups that would be willing to spend whatever was necessary to buy back the White House.

No, it would not be easy, especially if the Republican field — now without Reagan — became cluttered. Even worse if things turned nasty, as candidates jettisoned the "Eleventh Commandment" and turned on one another, desperate to distinguish themselves from the crowd.

Granted, there was always an element of this: It was natural, and to be expected.

Reagan had personally experienced it running against George HW Bush in 1980 primaries. While the two opponents buried the hatchet for the sake of party unity and formed a united Republican front, Bush had returned to his old self during his failed 1988 bid by once again criticizing Reagan.

While Bush's campaign had failed for a number of reasons, there was no disputing that his negativity — especially in regards to Reagan — had been a factor. But Bush was retired now; dividing his time between Maine and Texas, supposedly working on his memoirs. Whether or not he'd even weigh in to endorse a candidate was a big unknown. By all accounts, Bush was a bitter and broken man; and finished with politics.

Therefore it came as a huge surprise when, just days after Kemp's announcement, that Chief of Staff Baker informed Reagan that Bush was intending to run again.

In the big deck of cards where name recognition was critical, Bush trumped Kemp by a wide margin. He would be a tough, well-financed competitor, and according to Baker, would expect Reagan to tilt his way during the primaries, then fully endorse him once he secured the party's nomination.

Noting that Kemp had already announced, Reagan reminded Baker that he was obligated to stay neutral.

Checkmate.

Baker pursed his lips and nodded. This is what he expected, but not what he wanted. Carefully choosing his words so as to not sound disrespectful, Baker reminded his boss that Kemp was a long-shot, and that any dithering by the President would only serve to help the Democrats.

But the President stuck to his guns: There could be no public endorsement until the party convention officially picked a nominee.

He would, however, call Bush directly and wish him luck.

Reagan and Bush hadn't spoken much in the past few years, and his announcement—relayed via Baker rather than made personally—caught the President off guard, and put him in a difficult position. Reagan simply didn't see his former VP as either a worthy successor, or for that matter, as someone capable of winning the general election.

But if it came down to Bush or a Democrat, Reagan would have no choice: He would endorse his former VP.

But in his heart (and prayers) Reagan hoped the GOP nominee for 1992 would be Jack Kemp, to spare him, and the nation, from what he feared would be a disastrous Bush presidency.

Whereas Kemp suggested ideological continuity, Reagan and Bush had been worlds apart on a range of issues. These divisions were kept private during his tenure as Vice President, but surged to the forefront whenever he ran for office. Simply put, the two men had fundamentally different views of what it meant to be a Republican, and where the party needed to—and should—go.

After leaving Washington, Bush had frequently commented on matters, much to the chagrin of the White House. Lately, his appearances had increased; which everyone assumed was intended to drum up pre-publication interest in his memoirs. But now, in retrospect, it appears that Bush was instead trying to stay in the public eye in advance of announcing another bid for the presidency.

Unbeknownst to the public, at various points during Reagan's third term, Bush had also contacted the President with advice—most of which had turned out to be wrong. Whereas Reagan chose to increase spending and cut taxes to stimulate growth, Bush supported higher taxes and austerity. After the fall of East Germany, Bush endorsed using US troops to push into Eastern Europe, and if possible, take Russia.

But the biggest break in foreign policy occurred over Iraq's invasion of Kuwait. While Reagan kept his focus on the showdown with the USSR (and imminent collapse of a nuclear superpower), Bush had advocated on behalf of a ground war against Saddam Hussein.

This would be Bush's third attempt, and likely his last chance. He believed it was his turn now. "Third time's the charm," he quipped to Reagan, chuckling. "Yes, sir. Gonna do it this time, really feeling the wind beneath my wings now. Gonna soar — fly like an eagle!"

Reagan was glad that the conversation was taking place by phone, alleviating him from having to fake an enthusiastic smile while Bush rambled on. Instead, he just closed his eyes hard for a moment and shook his head.

With George HW Bush in the race, there would be no clear frontrunner. While Kemp had "conservative cred," Bush had name recognition, unparalleled experience, and a presumed closeness to President Reagan. And so, as a result of this ambiguity, the gates opened, and Republicans of all stripes began to publicly announce their plans to run, most of which had likely been in the works for some time.

Next to jump in was Senator Bob Dole.

The Kansan was a moderate, and while neither a soldier in the Reagan Revolution or a man of any major ideas, he was nonetheless a well-known national figure, and able to quickly raise the money needed to mount a serious challenge. Dole's decision also meant that his wife Elizabeth, currently serving as Reagan's Labor Secretary, would likely resign her post to help with her husband's campaign.

At 68, Dole was also getting on years; essentially the same age as Bush, and like "Poppy," did not seem to have much support from young conservatives or Evangelicals.

Fellow sexagenarian Senator Paul Laxalt was also considering a run. Not a bad choice, and a person Reagan liked — and trusted. He was also a competent administrator, and someone the President had seriously considered for a cabinet position as Secretary of the Interior.

Like Reagan, Laxalt was a Westerner (from Nevada) and had also served as a governor. In fact, Laxalt's first term had overlapped with Reagan's second, and the two had enjoyed a productive relationship as governors with bordering states. Most notable was their cooperation to preserve and protect the scenic beauty and wilderness around Lake Tahoe, which included territory in both California and Nevada.

Laxalt was also a genuine fiscal and social conservative. Old school, hands on type of guy — and a close personal friend of the President. Supporting a Laxalt candidacy would not be difficult.

Still, Reagan hoped the nominee would be Jack Kemp.

A Kemp-Laxalt ticket? Perhaps, so long as Kemp was at the top of the ticket. Nearing 70, Laxalt would best be positioned as the elder statesman with solid administrative experience — and not Reagan's successor.

The President's focus was on the future: to a new generation, with new ideas. Kemp was the bridge.

Whether attributable to good genes or a lifelong commitment to fitness, Reagan was in excellent shape, and he knew how physically demanding the presidency could be. Kemp was young, a former athlete, fit and ready to fight. With any luck, he could serve multiple terms.

Like Reagan, Kemp was someone who wanted to grow the party, and who sought to build a coalition of voters who had not traditionally been pursued by, or in some cases, even welcomed by the GOP establishment.

The election was still a year away. So for now, Reagan would need to focus on the task at hand: finding new secretaries for Labor and HUD, and hoping that no one else would decide to quit the team.

As the President sat down to take lunch at his desk, Press Secretary Limbaugh popped his head in the door.

Caught off-guard, Reagan wondered what bad news might prompt such an interruption.

"Have you heard? Arlen Specter just announced he's running," said Limbaugh.

"As a Republican or a Democrat?" asked Reagan, trying hard to suppress a smile.

Limbaugh just raised his eyebrows and made and made an open-handed gesture synonymous with, "Who knows."

The two men laughed.

"So, Rush, are you here to tell me that you're leaving to go help manage his campaign?"

"Only if you agree to be on the ticket as his VP," returned Limbaugh — a master of giving it as good he took it.

Again, the two men laughed heartily.

While Limbaugh had certainly entertained his share of serious offers to leave the White House, the former radio talk show host had never wavered in his support for the President, or in answering the call of his country.

He had sacrificed much, jumping into public service right as he had been poised to reach huge new commercial audiences—along with untold wealth and fame—from national syndication.

But instead, Limbaugh had taken a different path, and Reagan was thankful that he had.

Limbaugh had put service to country over to service to self, and in his heart, was happy to have done such, if only for the reason that this is how things are supposed to be.

93

The Keystone State

November did not begin well. Much of the nation was still digging out from the Halloween Blizzard, and cool temperatures suggested the country might be in for an unusually hard winter.

Although it had been scheduled some time in advance, Friday, November first, was also the day that former Vice President Bush chose to publicly announce his intention to run for president. The announcement barely made the national news; overshadowed by the ongoing coverage of the storm, which had even extended down to the candidate's adopted home state of Texas.

Although he divided his time between residences in Maine and Texas, the Lone Star state made for a better backdrop, as Bush sought to shake off the long-standing wimp image, and position himself as America's kindly new sheriff.

In his pitch, Bush presented himself as Reagan's natural heir, with the experience and vision needed to keep the good times rolling. Lifting one of Reagan's signature lines, Bush assured the nation that "the best was yet to come."

Watching the announcement on live TV, the President just winced, while Mrs Reagan made a face; tilting her head, and sticking out her tongue. The silliness of her response caused the President to laugh, as Bush made his pitch.

Here was the "new" George HW Bush: talking tough, but, also "kinder and gentler"; promising something for everyone. A little bit of Ron, a little bit of George. A little bit of conservatism, a little bit of liberalism. A firm handshake, but with lips soft enough to kiss a baby.

Weather was cool that day in Houston, and so was the reception.

The event had been heavily promoted, and the Bush team anticipated record-breaking crowds. When these failed to materialize, it was written off to the fact that Bush had been out of the public eye for some time. This was spun internally as mostly being a good thing, as it would allow the campaign staff more leeway in revising, and updating his image for voters.

Party officials were a bit more concerned, as the former VP was the GOP's presumptive candidate for the White House. Bush's polling numbers were also worrisome, but there was still plenty of time—and money—to turn things around. Bush had the resources and the experience needed to win.

What really sent a chill down the spine of conservatives took place four days later in Pennsylvania, when a Democrat won the special election to fill a vacancy created by the sudden death of Republican Senator John Heinz.

Heinz had been a party stalwart for decades; winning his first Senate seat in 1976—the same year that Jimmy Carter and the Democrats swept the country, riding a wave of fallout from Watergate and Vietnam. It had been a tough time to run as a Republican, but Heinz beat the long odds. Prior to entering the Senate, he had served in the lower house representing Pennsylvania's 18th District since 1971.

By all estimations, the native Pennsylvanian seemed to have a promising future in politics. He was articulate, good-looking, and fantastically wealthy, given his position as an heir to the Heinz food company fortune.

A graduate of both Harvard and Yale, Heinz had taught business at Carnegie Mellon University and had served in the US Air Force Reserve. Politically, the Roman Catholic's views were on the moderate to liberal side of the conservative scale, although he had supported President Reagan on most key issues, especially during the third term.

Well-known and well-liked, Heinz had helped redefine the Grand Old Party in the Keystone State, providing a path forward from the declines of heavy industry and a collapsing steel industry. Heinz was optimistic, energetic, and able to woo Democratic voters due to his stance on issues related to race, Social Security, and trade.

Many saw him as a potential presidential candidate.

Senator Heinz would be tough to replace, but after a period of mourning, GOP state party leaders presented a list of recommendations to Governor Bob Casey.

Given that Heinz had been a Republican, protocol demanded that Casey select someone from the same party to serve until voters could pick a permanent replacement in the November special election.

But in an outrageous example of partisan politics, Pennsylvania's first-term Democratic governor ignored the list of GOP recommendations, and selected a fellow Democrat, 65-year-old Harris Wofford to fill Heinz's seat.

Although the NYC-born Wofford came with no working political experience, Casey must have thought there wasn't all that much to the position of being a US Senator, and that his dear friend could quickly learn what he needed on the job—just as one might apprentice at one of those 30-minute oil and lube shops.

At the time of Casey's lavish bequest, Wofford had been serving as the state's Secretary of Labor and Industry—a position to which he had also been appointed by Governor Casey. Preceding this appointment, Wofford had served a six-month stint as Chairman of the state's Democratic Party—which, coincidentally just happened to span the period in which Casey was running for governor.

Incestuous? Perhaps. Legal? Certainly.

Casey, a New York-born attorney, could not resist adding some fine print to his offer: 1) Wofford *must* agree to run for re-election, and 2) He *must* agree to bring in James Carville, a political consultant from Louisiana to run his campaign.

Deal.

Despite never having been elected to political office, Wofford's insider connections to the Democratic machine went back decades. He had first met John F Kennedy in 1947, and had contributed to his 1960 run for the White House. As part of the campaign staff, the 30-something Wofford worked in tandem with the candidate's brother-in-law Sargent Shriver, where he, a fellow white man, had been tasked with securing the black vote.

Raised Episcopalian, Wofford had recently converted to Catholicism, and was a self-described Gandhi scholar. In the special November election, Wofford's Republican challenger would be Dick Thornburgh, Pennsylvania's popular ex-governor.

As the person who had heroically guided his state through the nuclear crisis at Three Mile Island, Thornburgh was expected to win easily. The native Pennsylvanian had the experience, the qualifications, and was on the right side politically for a state, and a nation, that had been moving evermore to embrace conservatism.

It seemed that Thornburgh had things in the bag.

The former governor made no major gaffes, and his campaign had been well-funded, and encouraged by polls showing him with a solid lead—at one point by more than 40 points over his inexperienced and relatively unknown Democratic rival.

But things did not pan out as the bookies predicted, and Thornburgh hit the canvas hard and the referee counted to ten.

How Dick Thornburgh could lose to *any* Democrat, especially one like Harris Wofford—by more than ten points, was a real shot across the bow, and a cause for deep concern within the GOP establishment.

Were things changing in America?

Pennsylvania was a large and important state, but it was also a swing state. If it went to the left, what did this say about the future of the GOP—especially with national elections just a year away?

Was this a party that couldn't stay in power without Ronald Reagan? Or was this the start of a referendum against Reagan himself?

The President remained optimistic, and saw Pennsylvania as a fluke.

Still, there did seem to be some echoes of how that other great 20th century hero Winston Churchill had been treated when he and his conservative party were turned out of office just months after winning the war in Europe by defeating Hitler and Nazi Germany.

Although so much had been achieved, would American voters lose sight of what still needed to be done? Would they be seduced away by the fantastic promises of liberals like Wofford?

Was Thornburgh's loss a referendum on conservatism?

Reagan didn't think so. In fact, he felt just the opposite. The President believed that the party must stay true to its conservative roots, and not move to the left. Internally, a schism was opening in the GOP between the conservative and liberal wings. Even the chair of the Republican National Committee was quoted as saying his party needed to "evolve, or die."

Reagan disagreed, believing that the GOP needed to present a clear alternative to the Democrats. But there was no denying reality: Without Reagan as a unifier, the party was splitting apart.

How far Bush might "evolve" remained to be seen. But at least Reagan felt confident that Kemp would offer Republicans a genuinely conservative option. Kemp was an independent thinker. Progressive in his own way, but true to the essence and spirit of conservatism.

The President could do little now to support Kemp directly, and by all accounts, the serious money was already flowing in Bush's direction. Having twice run with Reagan, Bush still had the Rolodex with the names and numbers of all the old donors, which his team worked relentlessly.

Directing the fundraising effort was Don Regan, who had served alongside Bush during Reagan's first two terms; first as Treasury Secretary, then as Chief of Staff. A former Wall Street executive, Regan seamlessly bridged the worlds of politics and finance.

While there was no disputing his talents, Regan had been a highly controversial figure at the White House. Forced out as part of the Iran-Contra scandal, few (including the President), had been sad to see him leave.

Apparently unconcerned about burning his bridges, Regan penned a nasty tell-all memoir rife with personal attacks on the President and Mrs Reagan. In the book, Bush faired much better. The Vice President had done little to challenge Regan, and therefore been spared his wrath.

The two had remained in contact during Bush's years of exile. Neither could remember who first came up with the idea of joining forces for the 92 campaign, but so far things were working out — at least as far as Regan was concerned. And if Don Regan was happy, everybody was happy.

The partnership was going so well that Regan expressed an interest in being part of a future Bush administration, where he could once again have a hand in shaping economic policy. This made the big donors happy, as Regan was a known quantity; someone who could be trusted to look out for their best interests.

Besides, Bush's grasp of economics was limited, which left him open to the wrong kinds of influence. Having someone with Regan's record, values, and domineering personality on the team insured that Bush would be steered in the right direction.

In addition to his work raising money, Regan (for an additional fee) was also serving as an adviser, and the primary architect of Bush's pro-business, pro-Wall Street, economic policy.

Money talks, and the message was clear: George Bush for president.

Both parties like stability, and the GOP is especially loyal. It is slow to embrace an upstart, whether it be Governor Reagan taking on

President Ford in 1976, or Secretary Kemp challenging Vice President Bush in 1992. There was a hierarchy in place: Protocols that needed to be observed. Jack Kemp just needed to go sit on the bench and wait his turn.

When it came to playing the game, whether it was sports or politics, Reagan and Kemp knew that the best defense is a good offense.

There was no denying that Bush's entry had changed the race and Kemp's odds. The first out of the gate was now the dark horse. But this was not the time to surrender, much less retreat. It was time to dig in and fight even harder.

Quoting the revolutionary war hero John Paul Jones, Kemp assured his backers that "I have not yet begun to fight." Despite the candidate's optimism, the impact on fundraising was immediate.

Although most conservative donors were loath to jump on the Bush bandwagon, many were now taking a wait-and-see stance. Fortunately, Spencer's involvement suggested Reagan's personal support for Kemp. If it had not been for this connection, someone of Kemp's stature and limited means would have likely been crushed by the Bush juggernaut.

Reagan had provided Kemp a critical lifeline. But for now he had no choice but step back and let history take its course. Still, it was early in the game, and much would change between now and November third.

Kemp had been a loyal supporter of the President, and although he had tendered his resignation in order to run for the White House, he refused to abandon his position as HUD Secretary until Reagan could locate a replacement.

Fortunately, Kemp's need to commit full time to his campaign coincided with Thornburgh's loss, enabling Reagan to offer him the job at HUD. Although Thornburgh's tenure and ability to affect policy at the agency would be limited, he had proven himself to be a competent administrator and a person with a genuine commitment to helping the less fortunate.

There was no disputing that Kemp would leave behind some very big shoes to fill. He had redefined the agency, and for many, the GOP itself. Under Kemp's direction, HUD became not just a symbol of government compassion and handouts, but of a political party that provided action-able plans for helping America's disadvantaged to escape dependency and poverty.

With Kemp at the helm, HUD had changed direction, changed lives, and changed perceptions. Many low income and minority voters now saw Republicans in a new light. Like most Americans, all they wanted was a hand up—not a hand out—and this administration had delivered on that promise. Through his innovative policies and leadership, Kemp had turned Reagan's vision of HUD into a reality.

And now, Jack Kemp was embarking on a journey to help all Americans.

Reagan would also miss Kemp personally. Even when the two had differed, the exchanges had always been civil and informative. Kemp was always on top of the facts, and more than once he had helped the President see things in a new way.

Yep. He would be tough to replace.

Privately, Reagan felt that Thornburgh, a former prosecutor would have also made a fine Attorney General, but that ship had sailed, and now Kenneth Starr was the captain.

To the President's delight, Thornburgh accepted the invitation to join his cabinet, freeing up Kemp to go play the game of his life.

94

The Road Forward

A promise is a debt that must be paid.

— Irish Proverb

As 1991 was drawing to a close, normalcy was returning to the private lives of the Reagans; allowing them to enjoy another Thanksgiving at the Ranch, to be followed by a traditional Christmas at the White House.

For New Year's, Ron and Nancy were back in California, spending time in Palm Springs with their old friend Walter Annenberg. Visits with the Annenbergs were a tradition, as was the President playing—and losing badly—at golf.

As comedian Bob Hope reminded him, this was one of the few things he couldn't blame on the Democrats.

Reagan quickly contested this, noting that he had learned to play back in the days when he was still a Democrat.

Hope, unused to being played for the straight man, had no choice but to laugh at the President's clever comeback.

It had been a good day on the greens, under magnificent clear blue skies and temperatures in the low 80s. Not bad for January, no sir, not bad at all.

As the President stood smiling in the afternoon sun, he was warmed both physically and by the realization that in just over a year, he'd be back home in California for good.

While repealing the 22nd Amendment permitted him to run for office indefinitely, Reagan was adamant that he had no interest in a fourth term, despite pleas and calls that he consider otherwise. Some were driven by fears that the party and country couldn't get on without him, while others were just expressing gratitude and respect.

The President merely smiled, shook his head no, and thanked his supporters. America was in a much better place than it had been in 1988, and he now felt comfortable stepping aside to make way for someone else.

"Besides," he joked, "I want kids growing up to remember me as President Reagan, and not King Ronnie … who held the office for life."

Ronald Reagan remained incredibly popular with the American people. Had he run again, he would have won by another landslide. But the third term had not been easy. He had stepped in during a time of unprecedented crisis, and had for the most part, worked long hours, seven days a week. It was an amazing burden to be put on any one person's shoulders, especially for a man who was in his late 70s when he agreed to serve another four years doing the hardest job in the world.

Next month he would turn 81. Healthy in mind, body, and spirit— Reagan wanted to leave while he was still at the top of his game. This would be his last year.

Time to roll the credits.

Naturally, he would leave office with mixed feelings. There was still so much to be done, and time was no longer on his side.

Privately, Reagan was also concerned about what seemed to be a drift by voters to the left. This would affect candidates running for office, as well as congressional support for legislation he wanted to see passed before leaving office—items he considered to be part of his legacy.

This would be his last year, so it was now or never.

Many of these proposals had been on the backburner for some time, pushed aside by the more pressing needs of the war. A fair number were also very controversial social issues, which the President had been forced to downplay in order to secure broader support for less polarizing initiatives such as rebuilding the economies and political institutions of the former USSR.

As they say, you gotta pick your battles if your goal is to win the war.

The President's list would be a start, but one that he hoped would grow, added to by the true heirs to the conservative revolution he had inspired. *Reagan's* GOP was the party of big ideas and bold initiatives; epitomized by proposals such as Jack Kemp's plan for inner-city enterprise zones.

But Kemp was just one option on a rapidly burgeoning buffet.

Reagan's decision not to run again opened the field, and in response, challengers from all sides were now rushing in, jockeying for position, and pitching new visions for the country, usually accompanied by grand, and at times, ridiculous promises.

At last count, more than nine different challengers were running as Republicans. Most had no chance whatsoever, and were running either for ego, or to prime the pump for some future race.

Things were in a state of flux. Pundits and readers of tea leaves were all given their due, at least until they were contradicted by the latest poll.

On one point however, the polls were consistent: Many found it hard to imagine a future without Ronald Reagan. He had been the face of government for nearly a dozen years; a familiar face. Trusted. Stable. Many were uncertain how it would be possible for his ideas to continue on if he was no longer personally involved.

While a solid majority of Americans felt the country was "on the right track," a roughly equal number was open to "change."

Much of this confusion and discontent was being fanned and exploited by blindfolded liberals who regarded the defense budget as some kind of piñata. With the Cold War over, it was time to free up the "peace dividend" and throw a victory party. Those who suggested that the world was still a dangerous place were living in the past, and using fear to maintain control.

In the real world, problems and solutions are more complicated than that which lends itself to a bumper sticker or sound bite.

As the ancient Greek playwright Aeschylus once wrote, "In war, truth is the first casualty," and make no mistake: politics is war.

Sensing vulnerability, Democrats made the budget an issue, forcing the President to play defense.

Yes, he conceded, some cuts were justified, and some resources needed to be redirected towards emerging threats. The world remained a dangerous place, and one does not disband the fire department just because one fire appears to be extinguished. Instead, Reagan would advocate for measured steps, both militarily, and with regard to fiscal policy.

The Commander-in-Chief was also quick to point out that the biggest item in the defense budget was not "the $600 toilet seats we inherited from Jimmy Carter," but personnel.

"Discharging that many people into the work force will not create a dividend; it will create massive unemployment, which will bring about a recession.

"The economy must be expanded, and workers added in as needed. This will ensure growth, lead to higher wages, and increased tax revenues to pay down the deficit."

"The deficit *you* created!" came the reply.

Democrats argued that a huge US military presence made the world uncomfortable. As the only remaining superpower, it was time for America to take the lead in disarmament and make a stand for peace.

Many liberals envisioned a new America based on the socialist ideal of a cradle-to-grave welfare state. Democrats conceded that cutting troop size would swell the ranks of the unemployed. However, money saved on defense could be used to expand welfare, public housing, and so forth, while the US transitioned away from an economy dependent on the military industrial complex.

Basing the economy on war would only make future conflicts more likely.

The Cold War was over; in 1992 America stood at the crossroads.

It was time for change.

Regrettably, this kind of pandering was also creeping into the talking points of some "new" Republicans. Although Reagan held such candidates in contempt, he was bound to observe the GOP's commandment of not saying anything negative about a fellow Republican. So instead, he would remain true to his principles, and behave accordingly. He would stand as a true and unapologetic conservative, and continue to speak out as a voice of experience and reason.

Some stances, such as those on defense, would be expressed both as opinion, and in the budget he would submit to Congress in February. And yes, the defense budget Reagan proposed did include a number of cuts, along with provisions to have the European allies cover more of their share.

But the budget was all about prudence; slowly letting out the clutch as one presses down on the gas pedal. It was not about turning off the engine on the freeway and then hoping for the best.

Other Reagan-inspired proposals for legislation were dusted off and introduced in rapid succession, led by constitutional amendments banning abortion and requiring a balanced budget.

While initially opposed to the idea (based on early projections), the economy had rebounded beyond expectations. Unemployment was down to around 2%, tax revenues were way up, and expenditures were down, led by declines in those drawing public assistance and healthcare spending.

Thus, a balanced budget now seemed possible if Congress was willing to do some belt-tightening.

As a proposal, the balanced budget amendment could be set to take effect at some point in the future, while still including a provision for emergency overrides.

As he had stated many times, Reagan didn't believe that deficits were caused by too little taxation — but by unchecked spending. Government, just like any typical American household, needed to live within its means — as eventually the bill — along with plenty of interest, would come due.

Not behaving in a fiscally responsible manner only postponed the inevitable: sticking some future generation with the tab for the predecessor's recklessness and irresponsibility.

Cutting spending also trimmed the size of government — killing two birds with one stone.

Granted, there might be a time in the future when some crisis (such as another war) might require running a deficit. If so, the President included a provision authorizing an override of the balanced budget if supported by a super majority of sixty percent in Congress.

Protecting the unborn had also been an issue central to Reagan's heart since he first ran for office. He was not shy about admitting that he was on Earth to serve God's will, and the Creator had been very specific in tasking him to fight on behalf of the unborn.

Now, in his final year, the President was prepared to resume the battle, and push for a constitutional ban on abortion, thus making it the law of the land from coast to coast.

Abortion was a tremendously divisive issue, and he understood the inability of politicians — especially at the state level — to stop it. During his first year as governor, Reagan himself had been forced to sign a law that liberalized abortion in California years before Roe v Wade legalized it nationally. As a consequence of his signing, abortions in the state increased dramatically, while rates just over the border in Nevada, (home to "Sin City") remained low — and stable.

Much to his chagrin, California became a destination for abortion seekers from other states. Whether this helped to contribute to the state's open and permissive attitude regarding sexual behavior is unknown — but it certainly didn't help.

Soon, America became a confusing patchwork of yes and no zones, a system that prevailed to this day. While the President was a strong supporter of states' rights, he knew that stopping abortion in one area only pushed the problem elsewhere. Dealing with a national problem required a national solution.

During his third term, Reagan had made tremendous progress on the issue by placing five pro-life justices on the Supreme Court. If a challenge to Roe v Wade were to be presented to the court anytime soon, it would most certainly be struck down by the conservative majority. As such, abortion would no longer be legal.

But justices come and go, and no one could predict how future courts might respond.

Even though a constitutional amendment could itself be overturned, it would still provide a significant hurdle for any future congress. In the meantime, untold numbers of innocent lives would be saved. Refusing to fight simply because something might one day flip back the other way was not a reason to give up without trying, especially when dealing with something as significant as the sanctity of human life.

Besides, if the nation had a breather from this barbarous process, the abortion-on-demand culture might be seen for what it is: unnecessary and wrong. Unwanted babies could now go to families seeking to adopt, anxious to provide a loving home to an innocent angel — as Reagan himself had done, adopting a baby boy which he would christen Michael Edward Reagan, to be loved and raised as his own.

In support of the ban on abortion, the White House pushed for tax incentives assisting adoptions, including those specifically targeting hard-to-place children born with special needs. This initiative would be complemented by new proposals benefiting families willing to open their homes to foster children.

Although education was a significant chunk of the federal budget, the President did not think that taxpayers were receiving a very good return on their investment. The ratio of administrators and other personnel to actual classroom teachers was at a record high. Schools were becoming top heavy with managers and administrators, and children were paying the price.

It was time for the schools to focus on their core mission: providing children with a quality education.

In response, the President proposed steep cuts, and the introduction of a voucher program to provide tax credits for students wishing to attend private schools.

While the entire US school system needed an overhaul, allowing parents more options was one way to immediately address the problem of dangerous and under-performing public schools, and stop the victimization of children who were being used as pawns to prop up a failing system.

Reagan also took on the issue of tax loopholes, denouncing so-called special "friend/campaign contributor" exemptions, while pushing for greater simplification to the overall code by reducing the number of brackets.

Restrictions on the power of the IRS would also be revived. Reagan felt that the agency had too much power, and repeatedly abused its authority. This was an issue he had brought up in his inaugural address, and despite previous legislative attempts, it was something that had languished for years in one committee after another.

Meanwhile, the President wanted the Office of Budget and Management to be given new authority to monitor Congress itself for fraud, waste and abuse. To underscore the fairness of the initiative, White House's own spending would be included in the deal.

Reagan did not believe in an "Imperial Presidency" or that anyone or branch of government was above the law. Those serving the public had a responsibility to those who put them in office, and must be held accountable for their actions.

It would be hard to get Congress on board for this, but the President was up for making a stand on behalf of fairness and accountability.

Transparency was essential to creating trust in government.

Another bold initiative would focus on the threat to public safety stemming from inconsistencies in gun laws.

The President was a gun owner and strong supporter of Second Amendment rights. He was also a big believer in law and order, and the need to keep guns out of the hands of criminals, terrorists, and the mentally ill. In response to conflicting state standards, he would propose a comprehensive national system of background checks.

As with the issue of abortion, Reagan's gun proposal would establish a single, federal system to bring consistency and close loopholes.

On the subject of loopholes, the President would propose making it a requirement that all laws passed by Congress also apply to the Congress. Related to this, would be a ban on proxy votes in committee.

Though not an official proposal, Reagan made it known that he opposed setting term limits on elected officials. This movement seemed to be catching on with both fringes of the political spectrum, but the President was totally against it, as he saw term limits as restricting the freedom of voters to pick whomever they wanted.

While term limits might have national consequences, Reagan did not regard their imposition as an issue needing to be addressed at the federal level.

"Voters have a right to make mistakes, and the means to correct them."

If asked, the President would offer an opinion on pretty much any topic. However, he would not devote time and energy to issues that he felt were better addressed at the state level. Reagan was a firm supporter of states' rights, and generally opposed to anything that shifted more authority to Washington, or that increased the size of the federal government.

Many hoped that in his final year Reagan would take on the issue of capital punishment. He was known to support the death penalty, and had been publicly dismayed at its having been declared illegal in California the very year that he became governor.

The majority of Americans supported capital punishment, and proponents felt federal legislation was needed to stop, and roll back these kinds of state bans. Reagan was sympathetic to their arguments, but for now his focus would be on saving lives; by ending abortion and curtailing the spread, and threat, of nuclear weapons.

Regarding defense, the President continued to support SDI; quick to note that it was not just the nations of the former USSR that had access to missiles and nuclear weapons. If anything, the collapse of the Soviet Union had made the world more dangerous, as scientists and materials moved across borders and fell under the control of rogue states like Libya and Iran.

Taking on the unions was a real long shot, but America's Chief Executive was willing to wade into the controversy. And, as with abortion and guns, he saw this as a national problem that needed to be addressed by federal, not state law.

Despite being a former union president and lifetime member of the AFL-CIO, Reagan believed the period of organized labor's usefulness had largely come and gone. Although once generally regarded as helping the average person, he felt unions had replaced management in terms of tyrannical control, and believed that legislation was now needed to restore some balance by reining in their powers.

Although not specifically targeting the Teachers Union, Reagan wanted to see a national right-to-work policy that would block union membership as a requirement for employment. In other words, joining should be optional — not mandatory.

Employers would be free to hire the best candidate for the job, whether that person was a union member or not.

He also sought to limit a union's ability to deduct dues from the paychecks of non-members. This was a simple black and white issue for Reagan, who regarded taking someone's money without her or his consent as just another form of robbery. If backed by a threat of employment termination, it was now extortion. Time to end it.

But, in a truly libertarian twist, Reagan also supported the right of employers to provide union and non-union workers with different employment contracts. This meant that those who chose not to join the union would not be guaranteed the same compensation packages as provided due to collective bargaining by the unions. They could be fired at will, exempted from lower, negotiated rates for health plans, and so forth.

Reagan conceded that any attempt to reign in the power of the unions was a real stretch, but felt it was a subject worthy of discussion.

Another "third rail" topic was Affirmative Action, which the President wanted to end. His opposition was nothing new, nor was the malicious and dishonest campaign to link his views to racism.

Affirmative Action was a deeply polarizing topic even within the GOP, and one many Republicans wanted him to drop — at least in terms of speaking about it publicly during an election year. But the President would not be silenced, and made clear these were his opinions, and not necessarily reflective of the party as a whole.

Simply put, Reagan believed that America must become a completely color blind society with absolutely no preferences based on race, ethnicity, or gender, or any other surface qualifier.

All discrimination is wrong—however, in Reagan's opinion, you don't correct it with more discrimination. Noting, "Only in the mind of a liberal can two wrongs make a right."

Acknowledging the good intentions, but failed outcomes of his 1986 Immigration bill, the President felt it was time to revisit the subject. At the top of his list was a provision to significantly expand the number of persons legally applying for citizenship—while getting tougher on illegal immigrants and those who profited from them.

Those found to be in the country illegally would be given the choice of being deported, or paying a fine and then getting in line and applying like everyone else. Those opting for deportation would not be allowed to reenter and reapply for a period of three years. Any immigrant who had been convicted of a serious crime, either in the US or in their country of origin, would be deemed ineligible for citizenship, and promptly deported.

Illegal aliens currently in the US would not be allowed to access benefits created for citizens and legal migrants, such as driver's licenses, or any government financial aid (such as scholarships or housing assistance). The bottom line: If you have no right to be here, you have no right to the benefits paid for by taxpayers.

Foreign-born children brought into the US illegally would be allowed to continue attending public school while their parents worked their way through the process of becoming citizens. Meanwhile, the citizenship status of children born in the US of illegal immigrants would remain unchanged, as such was already protected and guaranteed by the Constitution.

Some proposals, such as those dealing with immigration were bound to antagonize the fringes on both sides of the issue. On the left, many were demanding complete amnesty and an opening of the borders. Conversely, some on the far right were pushing for building a wall along the border with Mexico and authorizing a "shoot to kill" policy for anyone attempting to enter the US illegally.

Compromise is never easy, and both sides were hardening their stances. Reagan regarded his proposals as driven by pragmatism, not emotion. He also feared that the positions held by some in his own party would push Hispanics towards the Democrats.

Hispanics were a larger, and faster growing demographic than African-Americans, a group the GOP had already lost to the Democrats. But even more importantly, Reagan believed the GOP was the natural fit for Latinos; a family-oriented, often religious people who believed in hard work and sacrifice in pursuit of a better future.

As Reagan reviewed his proposals, he was the first to acknowledge that each would generate controversy. Levels would vary, as would the sources of opposition.

Taking a stand on issues is what defines a leader. Perhaps better than anyone, Reagan understood about the difference between doing what was popular and doing what was right.

This principle had been the star which guided Ronald Reagan's political life, and it would remain his beacon to the end.

95

Bush for President

It had been George Herbert Walker Bush's lifelong aspiration to be the President of the United States.

He had come close twice before, only to be pushed to the side by Ronald Reagan. But Reagan would not be a factor this time. If he was, it would only be to stand in the background applauding, while Bush accepted his party's nomination.

While proud to have served as Vice President, Bush still harbored deep feelings of jealously and bitterness. He had been the odds-on favorite entering the 1980 primaries, as Reagan was dismissed as too ideological, too uncompromising, too polarizing.

Although he had served two terms as governor of a large and prosperous state, many wrote off the campaign, and the man, as a joke. For many outside of California, Reagan was nothing more than a former actor who had once played second banana to a chimp named Bonzo.

Bush, in contrast, was a younger, well-connected centrist. He was a graduate of a prestigious university (Yale), a war hero, a former diplomat and the son of a Senator. Someone who was deeply integrated into the mainstream Republican establishment.

The 1980 race got off to a promising start, as Bush bested Reagan in two very different contests (Iowa, followed by Puerto Rico.). But then came New Hampshire, where Reagan landed a roundhouse punch, beating him 50% to 23%. A week later, Bush, still wobbling from the blow, barely managed a two-point victory in his birth state of Massachusetts.

Soon, the Gipper seemed invincible, racking up impressive wins in match after match. In Alabama, he beat Bush 70-26; in Georgia, 73-13; in Louisiana, 74-19; in Kansas 63-13; in Indiana, 74-16, and in Nebraska 76-15.

Over the course of the campaign, Bush had offered a spirited—at times mean-spirited fight. But by the time he lost his adopted home state of Texas by nearly double-digits it was obvious that America had made its choice—and it was not George HW Bush. There would be no

Texas-turnaround, no May miracle.

On May 27, the day after suspending his bid, he lost Idaho (83-4) along with Kentucky and Nevada by similar margins. The money and the enthusiasm were gone: Bush had hit bottom.

Despite the rancor of the campaign trail, Reagan graciously offered him the VP spot on the ticket in a bid to unite the party. Willing to let bygones be bygones, Reagan then extended the hand of friendship.

Without Reagan, Bush knew he had no future. At least as the VP he would remain visible and be first in line to move up when Reagan moved on. That's how things worked.

Lacking personal chemistry, theirs was a marriage of convenience. It was a difficult eight years for a man who saw himself superior in every way, but who had no choice other than to wait in the wings until Reagan left the stage.

Despite his frustrations, Bush observed the punctilio of his station, rarely challenging the President, and when he did, mostly restricting it to respectful comments made during their private Thursday afternoon lunches.

The man code-named "Timberwolf" by the Secret Service was always on good behavior, careful not to bite the hand that fed him.

During the first two terms, Bush had served as acting president during periods when Reagan had been unable to perform the duties of office due to medical reasons. By most accounts Bush had performed as a competent, albeit lackluster superintendent, unchallenged by any significant threats or crises.

After years passably playing second fiddle, Bush felt that he had maintained his part of the deal, and in accordance with tradition, was now entitled to be president. By law, Reagan was limited to two terms, and as VP, Bush was his natural successor.

Timberwolf made no attempt to hide his ambitions, and the groundwork for the Bush 88 campaign was up and running early in Reagan's second term. Money and endorsements were being actively solicited, and Bush had the full support of the Republican National Committee.

There was, after all, no one else. Of the last two Republican vice presidents, one (Nelson Rockefeller) was dead; the other (Spiro Agnew) had resigned in disgrace after being charged with extortion, bribery, tax fraud and conspiracy.

Legally, Reagan could not serve a third term. While he was on record as opposing term limits (including the 22nd Amendment), he hadn't made either a strong push for its repeal or expressed an interest in running again.

Plagued by the Iran-Contra scandal and stymied by a congress controlled by antagonistic Democrats, "morning in America" had passed. It was a new day, and time for a new president.

As expected, Bush 88 started out with a sense of inevitability, but then came the coup in the Soviet Union, which put everything into unfamiliar territory. Desperate to be seen as his own man, candidate Bush again distanced himself from Reagan, and quickly dug his own grave with a series of missteps, flip-flops, and gaffes, likely ensuring the Democrats would take the White House, only to surrender to Soviet blackmail.

In acknowledgement of the seriousness of the situation, Reagan was forced to saddle up and ride back in to save the day. Bush, severely disillusioned and publicly estranged by his criticisms, chose not to continue on as Vice President.

Instead, he returned home and secretly plotted his return — or revenge — depending on one's perspective.

The first year away was largely one of exile and self-reflection. He did, however, maintain connections, and as time went by, began to assemble a team to back another run for the White House should the clouds part and the road ahead shimmer and beckon.

Privately, Bush worried that Reagan might pursue a fourth run — attributing the decision to a mix of party pressure and vanity.

Although Reagan had repeatedly dismissed such invitations, Bush regarded this as part of his "act." He knew that Reagan was a showman who loved the limelight, and wouldn't pass up the opportunity for an encore. But first he was waiting for the crowd to call him back with a standing ovation.

REAGAN! REAGAN! REAGAN!

"Well, okay, if you insist ... A fourth term it is!"

Just the thought of this tired shtick made Bush feel queasy. He'd seen a very different side of Reagan, and was genuinely perplexed why no one else seemed capable of seeing through his ridiculous chicanery.

Even his wife Barbara was enchanted by President Reagan, teasing George that perhaps his contempt was nothing more than a sign that he was a "latent Democrat."

Funny.

Serving a fourth term would allow Reagan to match — and top FDR's record, making him the longest-serving president in US history. In addition wearing the crown of America's Most Popular President, Bush suspected that Reagan believed he was "owed" this time to bask in four years of tributes and good times after an especially trying third term.

Four goddamn years of Ron receiving awards, having things dedicated to him, acting — yes, *acting* — like a goddamn king.

If Reagan ran again there would be no point in Bush challenging him. The party establishment always backed the incumbent, and the money just wouldn't be there for a serious fight.

No, if Reagan ran again he'd *win* again — Bush was sure of that. He was also sure that a fourth term would be disastrous for all, and especially him personally.

It would not only push him further out of the public eye, but likely ruin the GOP "brand" as wrinkly old Reagan, just to satisfy his ego, coasted along making cornball jokes, winking and nodding while the country ran on autopilot or was hijacked by a cabal of rightwing extremists.

Without a war to preoccupy him, Reagan would waste valuable political capital on controversial social issues. Four more years of Reagan would not only destroy the country, but with it, the chance of any Republican being elected for many years to come.

Worse than Nixon.

Yes, a fourth term for Reagan would be the end of George HW Bush. So, when it became certain that the President would not run for re-election in 1992, the Bush campaign organization went into overdrive.

As a bonus, Ed Meese, who had replaced him as Vice President during Reagan's third term, announced his retirement from politics as well. Not that Meese was ever regarded as a major threat. Still, it cleared the way for Bush by removing a challenge from Reagan's "other" VP.

This was the moment Bush had been waiting for, but he knew that others had also likely been on standby until Reagan's decision became official. With Reagan bowing out, Bush realized he would soon have plenty of competition — from Democrats as well as those from within his own party — and he was right.

On the Republican side, several former and current Senators announced their intentions, including Bob Dole of Kansas, Arlen Specter of Pennsylvania, and John Danforth of Missouri.

Reagan mentor, (and previous presidential contender) Barry Goldwater formed an exploratory committee, but at 83, the former Senator was forced to acknowledge that his time had come and gone.

Senator Paul Laxalt passed on efforts to be drafted, as did Indiana's Richard Lugar, who many suspected was hoping to position himself as a potential VP pick by staying above the fray.

Newly elected California Governor (and former Senator) Pete Wilson was supposedly interested, as was Governor Mike Castle of Delaware.

Long shots include included Al Haig and the "two Pats" (Buchanan and Robertson).

Haig, or *General* Haig had briefly served as Secretary of State during the first Reagan/Bush White House, where he quickly wore out his welcome and managed to alienate almost everyone — including the President. Despite a long career in the military and in government (going back to the Nixon administration), Haig had few friends — and even fewer with the resources necessary to fund a serious national campaign. Haig was doomed right out of the gate.

Bush personally disliked Haig, and regarded him as a hothead and a frother, whose image of declaring himself "in control" following the 1981 assassination attempt on President Reagan was indelibly, and negatively, etched in the public mind. Besides, the chain of command clearly stated that if something happened to the President, it was the Vice President — not the Secretary of State — who assumed control.

Haig did, however, have the endorsement of his old boss, Richard Nixon, who had written an Op-Ed piece for the *Wall Street Journal* supporting his candidacy.

Haig made frequent reference to his ties with the former president, either unaware or indifferent to the fact that most voters did not view this as a positive association. Although it had been many years since Nixon had been forced to resign, his role in the Watergate scandal remained an open wound.

Pardoned, exiled, ostracized: Nixon was a pariah even within his own party; his name still treated as a swear word; his endorsement the kiss of death.

But Haig was fearless, once more marching into a tunnel with no light at the end.

Bush just laughed at the prospect of a run by Haig, slipping into an impression of comedian Dana Carvey doing an impression of him, "Not a problem; not gonna happen ..."

Bush also discounted any serious threat by Pat Robertson, an evangelist who had recently attempted to cure someone's hemorrhoids on live TV. Robertson would likely push the debate to the far right (especially on social issues), but the Rev had *no* money, *no* experience, and *no* organization.

Let the shepherd gather his flock. When November came and Bush was the nominee, these sheep would have nowhere else to go. Even if Bush only got a percentage, he had no fears about them breaking ranks and going over to the Democrats.

They were sheep, and sheep don't jump fences.

Pat Buchanan? His chances were about as good as those of comedian Pat Paulsen. Buchanan might a sell a few books, while Paulsen hustled t-shirts in comedy clubs. Same difference.

The Senators offered more genuine competition, but Bush had no real worries there either. Dole was old news; no one cared. Specter was an even bigger flip-flopper than Bush, and Danforth? Big dreams, no bucks. All his likely contributors were already behind Bush, and you can't finance a presidential campaign off the proceeds from a community chili feed at the Jefferson City farmer's co-op.

Governor Pete Wilson could be a bigger problem. But would he really walk out after less than a year on the job? Not likely.

Bush's biggest concern—and rightfully so—was Jack Kemp. The "Golden Boy" of the right. *Reagan's boy.*

While Kemp had not exactly been in the international spotlight as HUD Secretary, he had served admirably in Congress (for New York state), and enjoyed national name recognition, at least partially owing to his years playing in the NFL.

Whereas Reagan had gained fame from playing a football player in the movies, Kemp had played it for real.

It was also no secret that Reagan liked Kemp, and credited him with introducing him to supply-side economics, which the President had adopted and rebranded as Reaganomics.

Apparently, Reagan regarded Kemp as such a kindred spirit that he personally pushed to have him be his running mate in 1980 instead of Bush, before party bosses prevailed.

In the years since, Kemp's star had continued to rise. He became a hero to the conservative wing of the party, and was generally regarded as natural heir to the Reagan Revolution.

Like his mentor, he was confident and charismatic, and knew how to build a team. As a politician, Kemp, like Reagan, had that rare ability to connect with groups and individuals beyond the party's traditional (and shrinking) base.

Nicknamed the "bleeding-heart conservative," Kemp had a long reputation for reaching out to African-Americans and other minority groups. He was "one of those" that regarded the GOP as the party of Lincoln, and therefore the natural home for blacks long taken for granted, and exploited for political gain by the Democrats. If Kemp could succeed in building a multi-racial coalition he would be hard to beat, especially for someone like Bush.

Whether in sports, or in politics, Kemp had a reputation as someone who played fair, but hard. He would be in it to win.

Yes, Jack Kemp was dangerous. Very dangerous.

Fortunately, Bush knew that Reagan would not publicly endorse a successor until the party convention in August—and by then, Kemp would be long gone, and Reagan would have no choice but to back him.

The Bush 92 campaign began to map out its playbook.

Sacking the quarterback and seeing that he left the game on a stretcher early in the first quarter would be the game plan.

Kemp needed to be gone by St Patrick's Day at the latest. If he made it as far as the Michigan primary on March 17, he might pick up momentum and have a shot at delegate-rich New York, where he had played football (for the Buffalo Bills until 1970), only to be elected to Congress the following year.

But before Kemp could get to New York, there were four other states, including Illinois and Michigan.

Like New York, Kemp had also played pro football in Michigan—for the Detroit Lions. The Wolverine State had a fair number of minority voters—along with a decent number of delegates. This was Kemp territory. He had the home field advantage.

As Bush's strategists put it, if Kemp succeeded on Super Tuesday, the quarterback would get a first down and it would be a new game. He mustn't be allowed to get that close to the end zone.

Bush needed to tackle him before then and get control of the ball. Hit him hard, but don't take any penalties for unnecessary roughness. Let the DT — the Defensive Tackle — handle the rush.

Bush grimaced, as much for the prospect of Kemp's success, as how his advisors had phrased it.

Although he had lived for many years in Texas where football was almost a religion, Bush still hated the sport. He was a baseball fan: He'd played first base in college, and his son, George Jr, was now part owner of the Texas Rangers franchise.

Baseball was the thinking man's sport, and Bush preferred the cerebral qualities of America's national pastime to football any day.

Still, his campaign team persisted with football metaphors and expressions. Bush just nodded, and then rephrased the mission:

"Okay, then. *Got it*. We can't let Kemp make it to first. If he gets on base, he could steal his way to home. Can't risk walking him, no sir. We need a quick strike out — shut 'em down, a slider right down Broadway. Don't give the fence buster a chance."

Bush smiled and cackled at his own cleverness. Never let it be said that he couldn't throw it right back across home plate for a strike.

Sitting around a large wood table on real leather chairs, the candidate and his staff scrutinized a wall-sized color-coded map of the Super Tuesday contests.

The Bush 92 team felt confident about Texas, but worried that if Kemp could rally the black vote in other southern states like Tennessee, Louisiana and Mississippi he would pick up momentum — and funding. Therefore, Bush would need to utilize a different "southern strategy"... a more *traditional* approach that had worked so well in the past. One that would rally the white vote around him — and against Kemp.

Bush sighed, realizing how this would be a perfect assignment for his dear friend Lee Atwater, whose knack for delivering votes in difficult contests was the stuff of legends. While Atwater's success often relied upon negative campaigning, dirty tricks, and exploiting racism, there was no denying the fact that the man produced results.

Most recently, the Dark Prince of politics had served as Bush's 1988 campaign director, where his talents were put to early use, and great effect.

As Reagan's presumed successor, Bush had few serious challengers for his party's nomination in the 1988 primaries, thus enabling him to get a jump on attacking Governor Michael Dukakis, his presumed Democratic opponent.

Sensing vulnerability on the issue of race, Atwater moved in and started working his magic, performing a succession of tricks, culminating in his *pièce de résistance*, the infamous Willie Horton "Revolving Door" commercial.

Bush squirmed as he watched the ad roll for the first time. It was good, but … well, um. Too much?

"I'm just getting started," stated Atwater, boasting that "by the time we're finished, they're going to wonder whether Willie Horton is Dukakis' running mate."

Bush signed off on the spot, and almost immediately white voters either lost enthusiasm for Dukakis, or began migrating in his direction.

Atwater had done it again!

While denounced as blatantly racist, there was no disputing that Atwater had dealt the Dukakis campaign a serious, if not fatal blow. At least until Bush did himself in.

When Bush withdrew from the race, Atwater attempted to jump on board the Reagan 88 campaign—offering up an exceptionally nasty ad attacking Dukakis' successor, Teddy Kennedy. When Reagan's team opted to pass on the commercial and keep the tone of the campaign positive, Atwater slithered away.

After a short period in exile spent soul searching, Bush began to think about running again as early as the fall of 1989. Deciding it best to keep his intentions secret, he began to covertly assemble a team, and Lee Atwater was among the first to be brought onboard.

Although it was assumed that he would direct the campaign, it wasn't long until Atwater was diagnosed with terminal brain cancer. As his illness progressed (leaving him partially paralyzed and in a wheelchair), Atwater continued to give his all to the campaign, lining up donors, and even recruiting a successor, "Sunny" Jim Crockett, to take over some of the less savory aspects of the campaign.

Crockett, a 31-year-old former TV weatherman from Raleigh, North

Carolina, claimed to be a direct descendent of Davy Crockett, the legendary 19th century frontiersman. Whether it was true or not was irrelevant. What mattered was that Crockett, like Atwater, "understood" the south, and was willing to do what was needed to deliver it for Bush.

Atwater died in the last week of March 1991, roughly six months before Bush publicly announced his candidacy. He had just turned 40.

The Bush family sent condolences, but did not attend the funeral.

96

The Republican Primaries Begin

The 1992 Republican race for the White House got off to an uneven and inconclusive start.

With the largest war chest and most experienced organization, Bush 92 hit hard right out of the gate, with a sophisticated ground game and heavy media saturation. The centerpiece of the campaign was a slickly produced television spot designed to reintroduce Bush to voters after largely being out of the public eye during Reagan's third term.

Using Bush's life story as the organizing structure, the ad presented the candidate as a war hero, statesman, and visionary who had the ability to unite the nation and deliver a new golden age. The ad affirmed Bush's vision of himself as all things to all people, and was overwhelmingly positive in tone.

The spots employed the same familiar narrator who had provided the voiceover work for Reagan's "Morning In America" commercial, set against a backdrop of still images and video clips. Despite the resonances to the legendary campaign spot, Reagan himself was barely shown in the commercial. Consultants felt the ad needed to spotlight Bush, and the candidate agreed.

In addition to the professional narration calling for a "kinder, gentler" America, Bush himself opted to throw a bone to fiscal conservatives with a bold pledge promising "no new taxes," a pitch recycled from his 1988 campaign. But, for the most part, the Bush ad was typical in that it was big on image and brand, while leaving specific policy positions to be rolled out during interviews and stump speeches.

Though very much a traditional kind of campaign commercial, it was quite different than the simple and direct ads Reagan had featured in his run for a third term, which were focused on policy specifics. Although the Bush campaign had been at work for some time, consultants recommended against ads that were too issue heavy, especially given the inconclusive views garnered from recent opinion polls of likely voters. Alienating this group or that group at the outset of the race could create negative momentum, and the stakes were too high this time around to risk it.

Game on!

Republican caucuses began in January and flowed into early February, and most were non-binding.

The Bush campaign spent heavily from the beginning, but only managed a narrow win over Dole in Hawaii, the first contest of the season.

Next up was Iowa, a state Bush had won in both 1980 and 1988. His team, feeling good about back-to-back victories was stunned when their man was beaten by televangelist Pat Robertson.

In retrospect they should have seen it coming, given the importance of the evangelical Christian vote. At the bottom with less than one percent of the take was Arlen Specter, Pennsylvania's moderate two-term Senator. Specter's dismal showing was not especially surprising, given that he had not campaigned in Iowa and apparently had no real ground operation in the Hawkeye State.

Following "the Preacher" in the number two slot was Missouri Senator Danforth; which Bush 92 attributed to regional familiarity, given the shared border. A similar, albeit less-convincing, argument could be made for Dole's third place finish. Although Kansas did not actually border Iowa, the states were in the same general part of the country, and both were predominantly rural. Dole had campaigned there hard in the past, and well … who cares? At least Bush had still beaten Kemp, even if it was only by two points. A win was a win, and it was time to focus on New Hampshire—the first "real" primary.

If there was a regional bump to be gained in New England, it seemed likely to go in Bush's favor. He had been born in Massachusetts, grown up in Connecticut, and was known to spend much of the year at his home in Kennebunkport, Maine.

Another big assist for New Hampshire came in the form of personal appearances by its former governor, John Sununu, currently serving as Reagan's Transportation Secretary. Sununu genuinely liked Bush, and looked forward to a spot in his cabinet once "New England's native son" became America's 41st president.

On the campaign trail through the northeast, Bush proudly played up his "Yankee" roots and unveiled a proposal to ban flag burning.

Still, New Hampshire was not to be taken for granted. This was the state where momentum shifted towards Reagan in 1980, and so this time around he wouldn't be taking any chances; for every dollar the campaign spent on promoting Bush in New Hampshire, an equal amount would be spent taking down his rivals.

Specter was hit first in an ad that featured his cartoonish profile flipping back and forth, while the narrator reminded viewers of how many times he had switched positions on issues, and even with his party affiliation. Specter was branded as a smarmy opportunist.

Not only were the charges essentially true, but Specter had no money to rebut them. If he had, he could have essentially reworked the same ad and used it against Bush. But whether it was economics, or a sense of how mean things had turned, Specter would call it quits after New Hampshire and endorse his rival.

Meanwhile, the Bush campaign sought to position Kemp and Danforth as in over their heads when contrasted with the much more experienced two-term former Vice President. Although the campaign had a special Plan B waiting for Kemp, lampooning him as a young lightweight would be a good first step in a staid, and reliably conservative state like New Hampshire.

In the first attack ad, Kemp, the big sweaty dumb jock, was pictured in his football uniform, a dopey exhausted grin on his face, while a sympathetic fatherly voice warned voters "Quarterback Jack is just not ready for the big game."

Bush's anti-Danforth ads took aim at a rudderless career and lack of vision. It also noted that he had attended Divinity School, which unlike Iowa, was not viewed as a plus with New Hampshire's more secular electorate. Likewise for Robertson, whose reputation preceded him. He would take the hardcore evangelical vote, but nothing more.

In New Hampshire, the *700 Club* translated into less than 700 votes.

Pat Buchanan, the man who had coined the phrase "The Silent Majority" (while working as a speechwriter for Nixon), never officially entered the race. Although disappointing to the Bush campaign (which believed he would draw support away from Kemp), the former White House Communications Director instead embarked on a book tour to promote his 1988 memoir *Right from the Beginning*.

Comedian Pat Paulsen (a perennial candidate since 1968) continued to work the club scene, deadpanning that "If elected, I will win." After his shows, Paulsen posed for pictures, signed autographs, and sold "Made In The USA (for profit)" campaign memorabilia, such as t-shirts and buttons.

In the end, it was hard to tell which of the three Pats fared the best, although most suspected it was probably Paulsen.

Going into New Hampshire, Bush's biggest concern was Bob Dole. The veteran Senator was a seasoned campaigner, had high name recognition, and as a moderate, had done well there during previous bids. In an attempt to counter the Sununu factor, Dole's wife Elizabeth, currently serving as Labor Secretary, hit the trail to stump for her husband.

Mrs Dole (aka "Sugar Lips") was a popular and likeable figure, and successful at attracting the female vote in support of her husband. She spoke of his four decades of government experience, and a life spent dedicated to helping everyday Americans.

Dole first entered politics in 1950 as a member of the Kansas House of Representatives. His had been an amazing resurrection, as just eight years earlier, the 21-year-old had been written off for dead, after being severely injured by machine gun fire while fighting to liberate Italy from the Nazis.

For his service, Dole had been awarded two Purple Hearts and a Bronze star. Even though his injuries left him permanently disabled, Dole was of that "Greatest Generation" that took such sacrifices in stride. He rarely spoke of what happened all those years ago, while continuing to fight on in Congress on behalf of his fellow vets.

Given the length of Dole's career in government, there were numerous areas in which he might be vulnerable to attack ads. For instance, his association with liberal Democratic Senator George McGovern on expanding the food stamps program.

But instead, Bush 92's ambush on Dole came from a direction that no one had anticipated, targeting character issues; specifically questioning his honesty and courage as relating to his service during World War II. The strategy also sought to spin his support for fellow disabled veterans as nothing more than disingenuous political showmanship. Position Dole as a liar, a coward, and a turncoat—someone unfit to lead.

Anticipating Dole's inevitable run, Atwater had crafted a campaign to discredit any challenge to Bush as the only "true war hero" in the race. While military service was not at the top of the list of qualifications for New Hampshire voters, Atwater believed it was important to plant the seeds early, so as to leave Dole hemorrhaging by the time his campaign reached Super Tuesday, and states such as South Carolina, Texas, and Tennessee, where one's military record was a bigger issue for voters.

The first shot against Dole was a TV commercial presenting testimonies by other veterans from Dole's World War II unit (the Army's 10th Mountain Division). In it, three different men questioned the Senator's version of events, as well as his heroism, which was dismissed as "recklessness," and "hot dogging" that had endangered others.

Dole did not recognize any of the men in the commercial, whose version of events were quickly contested in a *New York Times* story featuring new interviews (and previously published accounts) with veterans whose claims of having served with Dole had already been established as true. But one article, even in a major newspaper, can do little against commercials that seem to run endlessly.

A second ad featured vignettes of handicapped children, infirm seniors, and "disabled veterans" (actually paid actors in rented wheel-chairs), warning that if elected, "heartless Bob Dole" would destroy safety nets for the disabled.

Lastly, in a radio commercial that seemed to run constantly on every station in the state, listeners were warned that Dole had a plan to raise taxes "by the highest margins in history" if elected president.

Nearly every accusation was false, but the ads were effective; Atwater was worth every cent he had been paid. If smiling was permitted in Hell, Lee was grinning from ear to ear as he fanned the flames higher.

When the votes were tallied, Dole came in near the bottom, just barely above Robertson and Specter who had barely registered. Danforth did slightly better, while the big dumb jock came within two points of toppling the former Vice President of the United States.

In New Hampshire, Bush's opponents (including Dole) had all run traditional and predictable campaigns, which is to say they focused on the positive aspects of what each candidate stood for, and what each wanted to do for the country.

Dole's poor finish was a jolt, given that he had spent large amounts of both time and money in the state. The loss had an immediate impact on fundraising, and within the organization, the call went out to "go nuclear" on Bush as revenge.

Even Dole himself had been angered and surprised by how odious things had gotten, as he had long considered Bush a friend and colleague.

Yes, politics was a nasty business. Yes, Bush was known to be a tough campaigner. But the *viciousness* of this assault ... So early in the campaign, against a Republican brother *and* fellow combat veteran.

Dole felt as if he had been stabbed in the back. He wanted an explanation, a retraction, and an apology. In fact, he demanded it.

When the two spoke, Bush calmly explained that he was only doing what he had to do: Dole could simply not win, and it was better that he exit now, rather than lose later and let a Democrat take the White House. Then, in an effort to pass the peace pipe, Bush offered Dole a spot in his cabinet—*possibly* Secretary of Defense, or even the VP slot, if he would agree to drop out now and endorse Bush.

Dole just hung up the phone, a scowl across his face.

Reagan, disgusted by the way things were going, conveyed his dissatisfaction to Sununu, who promised to relay the message on to Bush.

There had been a number of recent changes in the Bush campaign, in both staffing and tactics since the loss in Iowa, and his staff now included several former and current members of the Reagan White House.

How many? Nobody knew.

This only added to the President's disappointment and distrust, suggesting parallels to the Iran-Contra affair.

The scandal that had nearly destroyed his presidency, also involved administration figures operating nefariously and in contempt for the ethical standards set by Reagan, who had welcomed them into his White House and had trusted them with the keys.

As with Bush's campaign operatives, the Iran-Contra conspirators claimed they were doing what was best for the country, and the less Reagan knew, the better.

Sununu was expressionless. He nodded to the President's request, turned, and walked off down the hall.

A week later, Bush easily won South Dakota, with Kemp a close second. The strategy of the hard offense, hard defense was working, so the same was to be applied for the next set of primaries, scheduled for Colorado, Maryland, and Georgia.

Still reeling from the attack ads, the Dole campaign hit back with one of its own, by bringing together some of those who had served with Bush during the war, and questioning *his* official account of what had happened in the skies over the South Pacific in 1944.

Even more damaging, was the assertion that Bush's decision to bail out and save himself had cost the lives of his crewmates.

Take that, Lieutenant.

Bush was furious, but Dole's campaign was essentially finished. Still, the old combat vet from Kansas had fired off one last shot, vowing to remain a rock in Bush's shoe for as long as possible.

General Haig's campaign had failed to catch, never approaching even one percent. When word came that Haig would suspend operations "effective immediately" it came as no surprise — as most people weren't aware that he was even in the race. Upon exiting, Bush called to congratulate him, then asked for his endorsement which Haig promised would happen if — and when — Bush got the nomination.

At least for the time being, Haig was in control here.

Robertson had largely disappeared from the campaign trail, save for a few fundraising events in suburban Atlanta churches. Danforth pinned his hopes on Colorado, emphasizing his legislative efforts on behalf of farmers, ranchers, and other rural concerns. He didn't fare as well in the big cities, drawing less than 100 people to a venue in Denver that seated 1200.

Kemp meanwhile, was everywhere; anxious to talk to anyone who was willing to listen to his upbeat and enthusiastic message. His appearances were often low-frill events, and unlike Danforth, Kemp did extremely well in the cities. Brimming with energy and optimism, Kemp's campaign events began to attract ever-larger crowds.

In contrast to the other candidates, Kemp rallies were also drawing significant numbers of minority voters, especially in Georgia where he was now, for the first time, polling slightly ahead of Bush. Thanks to Baltimore, Kemp was neck and neck in the race with Bush for Maryland.

As someone who had grown up in a major American city, Kemp understood the concerns of urban voters. His speeches focused on ways to encourage economic growth, and featured "big idea" proposals (such as urban enterprise zones). In accordance with the Eleventh Commandment, he avoided any personal attacks on his opponents. As Kemp was quick to remind himself, "With so much that's positive, why waste time on the negative?"

Reagan hoped the success of this approach would get through to Bush, whose campaign thus far seemed rather thin on ideas and big on venom.

Instead, the candidate stuck to less controversial topics, and vague promises to "restore greatness to America's schools," and vowing to "get tough on those who threaten us."

As his advisors were quick to caution, this was "his race to lose." Bush was told to act presidential and focus on his resume. Don't deviate from the script, and avoid controversy.

Kemp did the opposite. He wanted to talk about the future, and was upfront about embracing many of Reagan's so-called "legacy issues" (such as the ban on abortion).

In cases where there was a genuine difference of opinion (as with Reagan's right-to-work proposal), he defended his position without personally referencing the President. With Kemp, it was always about the message — not the messenger.

As a candidate, he was difficult to manage. Running for president is a costly endeavor, and the candidate loathed fundraising — especially if it seemed like the donor expected something in return. Kemp was prone to making quick decisions, and had burned more than a few bridges along the way.

But this was nothing new, and his staff adjusted accordingly. If Kemp chose to be late to a fundraising event because he was signing footballs for kids, well, so be it. This is who he was.

March came in like a lion — a Detroit Lion, as Kemp won Maryland by a solid margin and nearly tied Bush in Georgia. In the battle for the Peach State, Kemp did well in the cities, although turnout was light.

In addition to his exhausting schedule of personal campaign stops, Kemp had also benefitted by help from Georgian Newt Gingrich, who had served with Kemp in Congress, and regarded him as not just a good personal friend—but as the future of the Republican Party.

The 49-year-old Gingrich, now House Majority Leader, shared Kemp's passion for supply-side economics, as well as the same core conservative principles. Like Kemp, he believed that the GOP needed to become more inclusive, and live up its legacy as a party for all people, and for all times.

What saved Bush in Georgia was strong support from suburbs, rural districts—and predominantly white areas that were traditional stalwarts of the GOP. Although many were former Democrats, most had abandoned the Donkey Party long ago.

Not surprisingly, Bush ("your neighbor from Texas") won Colorado by a respectable margin. Kemp had performed well in Denver and Boulder, but the rest of the state was definitely Bush country.

Still, there was a sense that the momentum was shifting. Kemp was now receiving positive national news coverage, and with it, greater name recognition and funding.

Kemp knew that Super Tuesday would be critical, so even though Bush was ahead on the delegate count, his old grid iron instincts kicked in: when you're down on points, keep your eyes on the game, not the score board.

97

Super Tuesday

Like any good military campaign, Bush's strategy for Super Tuesday would involve fighting on multiple fronts.

When campaigning in northern states, such as Massachusetts, Bush was a Yankee, the native son. This claim actually had some legitimacy, in that he had been born in Milton—an affluent suburb of Boston.

But Super Tuesday was mostly about the South, so Bush adapted as necessary. His new home state (delegate-rich Texas) was solidly in his pocket; Oklahoma would likely follow, more apt to trend with Texas than to support Dole, who, if only to spite Bush, was likely making his final stand in the Sooner State. Oklahoma would probably be Danforth's last hurrah as well, given that he was now polling nationally at less than two percent.

Kemp wasn't willing to concede either Oklahoma or Texas, and decided to take on Bush on his home turf, as well as fight him for the other big prize—Florida.

One of Bush's sons, the 39-year-old John, (aka Jeb, an acronym for John Ellis Bush) not only resided in Florida, but had previously served as the Sunshine State's Secretary of Commerce. He was his father's son: well-connected to the GOP establishment and its deep-pocketed donors.

In Florida, whatever bump Kemp received from being perceived as tougher on Fidel Castro than Bush, was lost when he suggested the Miami Dolphins would likely "do better" than they had during the 1991 season, and "probably make the playoffs," but that he did not foresee them going it to the super bowl that year under quarterback Dan Marino.

Seeing an opening, Team Bush scrambled to arrange a photo op of their man flanked by Marino and Head Coach Don Shula.

In Mississippi, the Kemp campaign was helped by the support of Senator Trent Lott. While Lott did not enjoy the same ease at connecting with prospective minority voters, it was hoped that he could shore up support with white conservatives who were beginning to abandon Kemp in droves.

If the polls were correct, Mississippi would be a real struggle, with Dole and even "Done for" Danforth now mysteriously besting Kemp in the standings.

Mississippi was not, however, unique. Although many African-Americans were turning out to hear Kemp speak, most were not registered to vote in the Republican primaries. Still, Kemp's team felt good about the long game, looking towards November, and being able to, as Reagan had, reach groups that had not traditionally supported the Republican ticket.

The likelihood of a Kemp insurgency had been something the Bush campaign had long anticipated, and was already addressing.

Acknowledging the importance of winning big on Super Tuesday — and hopefully finishing off the competition — the Bush campaign flooded the airwaves with ads. In addition to his standard generic TV spot, campaigns were individualized and tailored to different regions. In southern Florida, Dolphins fan Bush was ready to "finish off Castro"; in Oklahoma, he was all about less regulation of the oil and gas industries; in Louisiana, Mississippi, and Tennessee he spoke of welfare fraud, gun rights, school choice, and his own deep Christian faith.

After direct personal pleas from the President, Bush and Dole both agreed to drop the ads questioning each other's military service. Bush did, however, follow up with another series of negative ads, exaggerating and distorting Dole's voting record on tax increases.

Dole had no money to fight back with any new ads to rebut the charges. Instead, all resources were being dedicated to just keeping the lights on at campaign headquarters.

Danforth was in a tailspin, and Robertson was completely missing in action. Neither warranted the time of day.

Instead, all guns were trained on Kemp.

One attack ad was based on twisting Kemp's own definition of himself as "a different kind of Republican" who envisioned a broader, more inclusive party. To illustrate this, the ad used a series of photos of Kemp with *blacks*. Here he was shaking hands with one, here he was surrounded by them. Here he was speaking to a crowd of them, presumably telling them what *his* Republican party wanted to do for them.

The imagery was backed by a distorted explanation of Kemp's advocacy of inner-city enterprise zones, and a fallacious spin on his plan to "give away" public housing to the residents. These were valuable properties, "paid for by taxpayers." As in white taxpayers—black recipients. Was this the start of some secret "bleeding-heart" plan for "reparations?" No thanks!

The attack ads ended with a goofy, grinning shot of Kemp from his football days, arms around his black teammates, while a stern voice encouraged voters to "send Jack back to the bench," while strains of "Hit The Road Jack" played in the background.

The song's originator, Ray Charles, was a lifelong Republican who had even played at the 1984 convention in support of the Reagan/Bush ticket. Whether Charles was indeed a Bush friend and supporter, or had merely licensed the rights was never disclosed.

Were the ads racist? Kemp was proud of his efforts to connect with, and attract voters beyond the GOP's traditional white base, but he also saw through what Bush was trying to do. Rather than bring people together, the Bush campaign was seeking to divide and stir up fear.

Rebutting the ads would force Kemp into a positioning of distancing himself from friends and supporters.

Was he willing to do that?

No.

And the Bush campaign knew this.

Kemp was proud of these associations. No explanations, no apologies were needed, nor would they be given.

But many others didn't see it this way. Instead, they saw someone who was intent on taking the party in a direction that was, well, *different* … and breaking with "traditional" values. As such, they began to have doubts about Kemp as a leader, and where he might be wanting to take the country. All in all, it was just too much, too soon.

The ads were tremendously successful, and a real legacy to what Atwater had been able to bring to the campaign. Just far enough to make people uncomfortable, but not enough to create significant blowback.

Stick to the playbook: Sack the quarterback, but don't draw any penalties.

Given the importance of Super Tuesday, a second covert front had also been opened by Atwater's protégé —"Sunny" Jim Crockett.

For weeks, Crockett had been circulating rumors about Kemp, which grew and became ever more exaggerated as they traveled from mouth to ear, with nothing ever set down in writing on official campaign letterhead.

For instance, many people were surprised to learn that Kemp was a card-carrying lifetime member of the NAACP. It made sense, given all the TV spots showing him hanging out with blacks.

Didn't it?

Crockett continued his whispers. While Kemp was presented as a tough ex-football player, it seemed odd that he had been so adamant about wanting to always *sleep* in the same room as his black teammates. In fact, Kemp had threatened to quit if he wasn't allowed to share accommodations with them while on the road.

How odd was that?

Although married and a father, Kemp had reportedly joked about having showered with more blacks than most Republicans had ever met. Just the image of this made many people uncomfortable, and for a variety of reasons.

Working a similar muddy patch, was the revival of an old story going back to the days when Kemp had been a volunteer for (then) Governor Reagan.

In 1967, a newspaper columnist wrote a story about the firing of a "homosexual ring" that was operating out of the governor's communications office. Although Kemp was not personally named in the story, the group supposedly included a well-known sports figure — a description that would seem to apply to Kemp, who was interning for Reagan during his offseason as quarterback for the Buffalo Bills.

Allegations linking Kemp to the scandal had been investigated and debunked numerous times. Kemp was neither gay, nor had he been part of the "ring" which had been fired.

But the allegations continued to circulate, the story grew and mutated, and in 1992 — thanks to Crockett — it became super-charged to now include tales of interracial homosexual orgies at the governor's mansion.

Suddenly it all made sense, didn't it?

Kemp simply did not have the quality of character needed to be America's next President, and Bush swept Super Tuesday.

Acknowledging the inevitable, Danforth and Dole suspended their campaigns. Dole had hoped to hang on at least for another month, believing that if he could win his home state of Kansas he could start to turn things around, or at least end his quest, dying with honor on home turf.

With Dole, the money to fight on simply wasn't there. The cost of defending himself against Bush's attack ads had been an unforeseen expense, which had been accompanied by a sharp drop-off in campaign contributions.

Unlike Haig, Dole decided not to wait until the convention to offer his endorsement. With Illinois and Michigan scheduled for the following week, Dole heartily endorsed Kemp.

Buoyed by this support, Kemp headed north to the Land of Lincoln, intent to win, no matter how far down he was at this point in the game.

He'd seen worse in the past, and besides, winners never quit.

98

The Bumpy Road to Space City

Following Super Tuesday, it was now a two-man race on the Republican side.

Bush, the establishment candidate, held the lead by a solid margin. He had the funding, the delegates, and all the trappings that come with being the frontrunner.

The former Vice President flew first class, stayed in the best hotels, and met with the most important people. When his rival flew, it was often in a single-engine plane or with a discount carrier. Mostly, Kemp travelled by bus or by car.

With the backing of the Republican National Committee, dinners for Bush were glitzy, $1000-a-plate fundraisers, while Kemp shared a bucket of Kentucky Fried Chicken with his staff.

Nearly every scheduled appearance resulted in a wave of new donations to the Bush campaign. For Kemp, the cash flow was usually in the opposite direction.

Bush had the best-paid staffers available. Kemp, meanwhile, was forced to rely on volunteers that ran the gamut from the passionately competent to frustratingly unreliable.

Because of its dependence on volunteers, the Kemp campaign was relatively easy for Bush supporters to infiltrate. While most simply relayed information back to headquarters, a select few committed minor acts of sabotage.

In politics, as in life, you get what you pay for. Bush paid the money; Kemp paid the price.

From the outset — and out of sheer necessity — frugality had defined Kemp's rag-tag campaign. But as the race wore on, this lack of funding began to undermine the basics needed to mount a serious challenge. Even the *Wall Street Journal* turned on Kemp; referring to him as a "zombie," a dead man who kept walking, someone who needed to be put out of his misery, so as to end a doomed campaign of carnage and destruction.

Most of the old guard was solidly behind Bush, including former President Ford, who became an unofficial advisor to the campaign. Ford's insights in how to beat an idealistic upstart were especially valuable, based on his defeat of Ronald Reagan in the 1976 GOP primary race.

The bad blood between Ford and the man who he had once referred to as a "son of a bitch" went way back, and went way beyond just political differences. Like Bush, Ford blamed Reagan for derailing his political career. While neither could do anything to hit Reagan directly, they could work together to torpedo his heir.

It seemed only a matter of time.

But Kemp was determined to hang on. Not that he was delusional: He openly acknowledged that the odds were against him, and that he had alienated much of the party's top brass.

So what?

He believed voters deserved a genuine choice. That they had the right to hear from a true conservative, and to be reminded that the revolution started by Reagan was neither dead, nor dependent on just one man. It was a peoples' revolution, and it must continue.

If nothing else, Kemp would use the campaign to introduce, and debate, big ideas. He would work hard to grow the party, especially in regards to communities not traditionally courted by the GOP.

In his heart, Kemp believed that he was fighting for something much bigger than himself. He was fighting for the very future of his party. If the GOP was to survive, it must continue to be a party of ideas and inclusion. It needed to take clear stands on issues, and have the courage to defend them.

Watching Kemp struggle pained Reagan deeply, especially given how Bush had resorted to playing dirty pool to knock his fellow Republicans out of the race. Bush's antics evoked associations to Richard Nixon's dirty tricks, which eventually contributed to not only to his personal downfall, but which continued to haunt the party.

In contrast, Reagan admired Kemp for sticking to the high road, and never stooping to attack Bush personally. He also appreciated Kemp's advocacy of conservative principles, even when they (respectfully) differed on certain key issues that might cost him votes.

Likewise for Barry Goldwater, who endorsed Kemp four days

after Super Tuesday. A week later, Henry Kissinger announced his support for Bush, hinting that he might be interested in serving again as Secretary of State.

Reagan believed that many Washington insiders and party leaders — including those in charge of the Bush campaign — operated in a bubble. They might control the capitol, but the people were with Kemp.

Technically, Kemp could still win the nomination. But because the Bush campaign was so flush with money, it could outspend Kemp at every turn, which usually left him with just crumbs; a mix of the genuinely conservative and the "anyone but Bush" contingent.

Kemp's greatest challenge was simply getting his message out. When he did, he won converts. But every day was a struggle just to be heard.

Given his commanding lead, and recognition that the "Uptight Reagan Right" was a lost cause, Bush began to move further and further to the left, or as he described it, to the GOP's "new frontier," which was sounding evermore like what was coming from the Democratic candidates.

Illinois and Michigan would vote on March 17, with Connecticut to follow a week later. Vermont caucuses, scheduled for March 31, would round out the month. Needing to conserve resources, Kemp focused his efforts on the Midwest.

Feeling the need to land a knockout punch, the Bush campaign spent heavily on Illinois and Michigan. Both were viewed as moderate, and likely to go his way.

At a rally in Lansing, former president Gerald Ford officially endorsed Bush. The event was followed by a black tie fundraiser, attended by many prominent captains of industry, including leading executives from the auto industry anxious to hear how a Bush presidency would directly benefit them.

Ford's support turned out to be a mixed blessing; dogged by protestors wearing Nixon masks. Meanwhile, the inspiration for the masks, remained silent, knowing that a public endorsement of Bush would do more harm than good. It certainly hadn't helped Haig.

A centrist, Bush was clearly the lesser of the two evils.

So why not endorse Jack Kemp? Nixon smiled at the deviousness of such a stunt, but chose not to act on it.

After all, he had no dog in this fight. He had already done Bush plenty of favors over the years, and had not received anything in return. Nada.

Bush would use him in private, and then quickly close the door before stepping out in public.

Nixon frowned, concluding that "Timberwolf" had played him the same way he had done with Jennifer Fitzgerald, his "executive assistant."

Maybe he *should* endorse Bush? Nope. Let it go. Stay focused on numero uno. Screw them both. Screw them all. Bush will do himself in.

Bastard.

Hard hit by the loss of manufacturing jobs, Kemp's economic message resonated in Michigan, even attracting crossover interest from blue collar Democrats. Meanwhile, Illinois, the land of Lincoln and birthplace of Reagan, also appeared to be sliding into the Kemp column, abetted by a strong endorsement from the *Chicago Tribune*.

When the votes were tallied, Kemp managed dual wins in Illinois and Michigan, only to lose to Bush in Vermont, and then again in Connecticut — as expected. Despite hopes that his wins in the two large Midwestern states would translate into a big influx of contributions, this never really materialized, or at least not to the degree that would permit Kemp to seriously challenge Bush in the next wave of primaries: Kansas, Wisconsin, and Minnesota, and even Kemp's home state of New York, where Bush was already outspending him by 25 to 1.

The Kemp campaign was sputtering, and what had once been viewed as heroic — a David versus Goliath battle for the soul and future of the GOP — was now being dismissed as divisive, egocentric, and delusional.

The Chair of the Republican National Committee warned Kemp that his ongoing campaign was affecting party unity. Yes, the two candidates had their differences, but it was now time that Kemp bow out, throw his support behind Bush, and be a team player. It was time to work together in order to stop the Democrats.

Capiche?

But what did the spiritual head of the Republicans think? The man who had single-handedly rebuilt the party from scratch after Nixon and Ford had run it into the ditch?

All throughout the campaign, Reagan had been in Kemp's corner, privately mentoring his protégé. The two spoke by phone several times a week, with Reagan offering insights and encouragement. Like Kemp, he had been disturbed by the ruthlessness of the Bush campaign, acknowledging that he himself had been the victim of it when he ran against him in 1980.

Bush was much more desperate now, and desperate men do desperate things.

When Kemp called late on Tuesday night, March 31, Reagan knew what the conversation would be about. Kemp had just lost Vermont, and the drumbeat of calls for him to throw in the towel had reached a crescendo. Time to get in line, they said.

But Kemp did not want to get in line. True, he was down, but he was determined to fight on to the bitter end. He still had a chance.

Was he making the right choice?

The President could see both sides of the issue. He certainly understood about the long odds and the need to unify, but he also worried that Bush might be unelectable.

"He has moved so far to the left that he isn't offering voters a true conservative option," said Reagan. "When did standing up and fighting for what you believe in become a bad thing?"

Reagan then related the story of his own run against Gerald Ford in 1976.

Ford, a sitting president running for re-election seemed a shoo-in for his party's nomination. Like Bush, Ford was a moderate who had never won a national election.

Reagan disagreed with Ford on a host of issues, and felt the voters had a right to hear from a bona fide *conservative* Republican. If need be, he'd take it right down to the convention floor.

Given the advantage of his incumbency, Ford raised a lot of money and used it to win a string of early victories. Reagan ran a much leaner campaign, but what he lacked in money, he made up for in passion.

Meanwhile, Reagan was being hit from all sides. "Good cops" were suggesting that if he dropped out and endorsed Ford now he might have a spot in the new administration — maybe even on the ticket as Ford's VP. Applying pressure from the other side, "bad cops" hinted that if Reagan continued to hurt the party, it would not support him in the future.

The chorus of "Run! Ron! Run!" was being replaced by "Fold, Ron, Fold!"

Then suddenly, with the help of Senator Jesse Helms, Reagan finally won a state—North Carolina, and from there his fortunes began to change.

The victory had come just in time, as the campaign was nearly broke. But with the win came donations; small at first, then larger, followed by endorsements that allowed him to fight on—which he did—trading wins right up to the August convention, held in Kansas City, Missouri.

When the final delegate count took place, Ford had barely edged past Reagan to get the party's nomination.

Three months later, Ford the moderate, lost to Democrat Jimmy Carter.

"As they say, 'those condemned to repeat history often forget it,'" joked Reagan, as both men laughed in unison at his intentional malapropism, and the parallels to the 1992 race.

"Thank you, Mr President."

"No, thank you Jack. I know it's difficult, but your country needs you. Now get in there … and win one for the Gipper!"

Energized by the pep talk, Kemp did just that, and went on to rack up wins across all regions of the country—including his home state of New York, where he trounced Bush by double digits.

Anticipating Kemp's withdrawal by mid-April at the latest, the Bush campaign had scaled back spending for the next group of Republican primary contests. Donations for Bush were dropping off, and it was decided resources needed to be conserved for use in the November general election. Following his back-to-back wins in Connecticut and Vermont, Bush had turned his attention to fundraising, cancelling most campaign appearances.

This proved to be the break Kemp needed. Money that had once been going towards Bush was now moving Kemp's way. "Big Mo" had turned 180 degrees, and Bush was furious.

"Goddamn it, goddamn it, goddamn it!"

Fueled by irrational rage, the Bush 92 campaign went through a bloodletting, laying off more than half the staff—further hobbling the organization's effectiveness. Things seemed to be in a nosedive, as Bush and his campaign director fought for control over whom to blame—and what to do about it.

With Danforth's endorsement, Kemp handily won Missouri. Specter campaigned vigorously on behalf of Bush in Pennsylvania, who took the delegate-rich state by less three points. Kemp did well in traditionally conservative contests like Utah and Indiana, but as the season wound down, all eyes were on California.

Bush still had a slight lead, and believed that he would take the Golden State.

He was, after all, a Westerner (now officially 100% Texan), and "progressively moderate."

What Bush failed to realize was that Californians were not necessarily enamored by Texans, nor were California's Republicans necessarily all that moderate. This was the state that had produced Reagan and Herbert Hoover, but most importantly, it was where the first shot had been fired in the war against big government and taxes.

California's Proposition 13—officially titled the "People's Initiative To Limit Property Taxation—had passed with nearly a 65% majority, and was credited not just with the national revolt against taxes, but as providing rocket fuel for Reagan's 1980 run for the White House.

Kemp had been born and raised in California. His political team included many from then Governor Reagan's Kitchen Cabinet, and was being advised by Stuart Spencer, another native Californian and Reagan veteran.

Leading his team as Campaign Director was Ed Rollins. Although born back east, Rollins had grown up in California and had been friends with Reagan since the early 1970s. The two had also worked together on numerous occasions, including Reagan's last two presidential runs.

While not disclosed at the time, Rollins had also turned down an early, and lucrative, invitation to work on the Bush 92 campaign. Having spurned a similar offer in 1988, Rollins thought it odd that Bush would contact him again.

Bush was already known to have a campaign director in mind, leaving Rollins to speculate the invite was nothing more than an effort to buy him off; an insurance policy to keep his talents from going to work for someone else.

Despite being advised by some very savvy individuals, the Bush campaign had seriously miscalculated by attempting to put a price on someone like Rollins. Although a former Democrat, when Rollins switched teams it was for ideology, not personal gain—and he was now coaching Team Kemp.

Kemp, Reagan, and Rollins knew California. They understood the complexity and importance of the state. This was a different kind of game entirely, and Bush was out of his league.

Quarterback Jack had home field advantage, and he was playing to win.

On June 2, Bush won the Alabama primary by a sizable margin — one of the largest in the state's history. Meanwhile, Kemp took New Jersey, New Mexico, Ohio, and the biggest prize of all: California.

Thanks to the Golden State, Kemp now had the delegate count he needed to be the Republican nominee. No one could have been happier than Reagan, who called to congratulate him even before Bush had formally conceded.

In a break with protocol, Reagan decided to publicly congratulate and endorse Kemp immediately, even though he would not technically be the GOP's candidate until officially nominated two months later at the party convention set for August.

Perhaps in anticipation of a Bush candidacy, the 1992 GOP convention had been scheduled for Houston, Texas. It was here that Bush had started his political career, and it was here that it would end in the dust and heat of the Lone Star state.

Bush expected that, for the "sake of party unity," his young victor would offer him the VP spot. But it was not something he envisioned for himself, not at this stage in life. No sir.

For the "sake of party unity" Bush would endorse Kemp, but he would not suffer the humiliation of being his Vice President, or anyone's Vice President, ever again.

So, before such an offer could be made, Bush's campaign chair called Kemp's chair to convey Bush's lack of interest in the number two spot. By acting preemptively, Bush was able to save face and retire with some semblance of dignity, because as it turned out, he was not even on Kemp's list for consideration.

With this matter behind him, Kemp called to congratulate Bush on waging a good campaign, and for bringing up many important issues.

Kemp did not ask Bush to actively campaign on his behalf, but did say that he was looking forward to standing with him on stage in Houston, and for his support against the Democrats in November.

"Certainly. Right. Absolutely," muttered Bush. He was a team player, even if that team had a new quarterback.

99

The Democratic Primaries

The primary battles on the Democratic side had been even more cluttered and contentious than what had played out among the Republicans.

For the GOP nomination, Bush, as a former VP had been the established frontrunner from the moment his intentions became public. For the Democrats, there was no one of a similar stature. Most of those running were new faces, at least in regards to the national scene. It was a crowded free-for-all; a clown car overflowing with a motley crew of starry-eyed dreamers, each jockeying to grab the brass ring.

Not all would be young, fresh fellows, but the word was out to avoid running those who names might be familiar—but for all the wrong reasons.

Prominent Democrats like Carter and Mondale who had been pummeled in the past knew better than to try again—even if it wouldn't be against Reagan this time around. Dukakis, who had called in sick at the last minute in 1988 was now a political exile, a *persona non grata*.

Teddy Kennedy's career was over. While he could, based on the family name, still be forgiven for his past losses, his part in the conspiracy against the President, followed by a complete mental breakdown meant that he would likely never hold public office—or any position of real authority—ever again. For one whose name was so entrenched in party history and folklore, Teddy had reached the end of the road—barred from even attending the Democratic convention.

Ironically, the convention scheduled for New York City in July, would be taking place just 250 miles from Hyannis Port, MA, where the former Senator now spent his days napping and undergoing therapy.

Instead, the Irish Catholic left-wing of the party would be represented in the primaries by New York Senator Daniel Patrick Moynihan. He was a longtime Kennedy family associate, and although a bit ripe on the vine at 65 for a party seeking a new face, many thought he could absorb the Camelot mojo by some sort of magic osmosis.

All that mattered was that he was younger than Bush, albeit by only three years.

A sociologist and author of the seminal work *The Negro Family: The Case For National Action*, Moynihan, a true man of the world, had been ambassador to India, and a consistent critic of Reagan's Cold War policies—that is, until Reagan *won* the Cold War—and did it without launching a single nuke.

Moynihan's dream of snoozing in the Oval Office became just that— a dream that awoke to the reality that it was over almost as soon as it began. Outside of Moynihan's own family, enthusiasm was nil—as was funding. Like a soggy cocktail napkin, Danny Boy's campaign just couldn't catch fire.

Challenging Moynihan most directly for the Big Apple benefactors had been fellow New Yorker, Governor Mario Cuomo.

Like Moynihan, the "Hamlet On The Hudson" had the admiration of the left for his fiery attacks on Reagan, the most famous of which had been at the 1984 Democratic National Convention in San Francisco—the same convention which had nominated—or sacrificed— Walter Mondale as its candidate.

A baseball player at heart, Cuomo relied on his instincts to tell him when to run, and had wisely avoided challenging Reagan in 1988. But with the Gipper out of the game, Cuomo made his move in 1992, only to be tagged out by his inability to connect with voters outside of a few eastern states.

Former pro-basketball player and Arizona Congressman Mo Udall fared even worse. A Mormon who had actually run to the left of Carter in 1976, his inability to register above a single percentage point in the first four contests ended his run—meaning the first four became the final four, for the 6'5" former Denver Nugget.

No Mo for America.

The last of the easterners to make a run was former Massachusetts Senator Paul Tsongas.

Although relatively young and energetic at just 51, Tsongas had taken a break from Congress to battle cancer. He had recovered, and now with a clean bill of health he was ready to employ radical new therapies to cure America from its case of Reaganitis.

While his enthusiasm had been catchy, his vocal style, which reminded many of the old cartoon character Elmer Fudd, undermined his message, as voters decided there was no way they could stand listening to his voice — much less his screwy ideas — for the next four years.

Maimed in New Hampshire, the campaign never really recovered, and Tsongas was gone.

The voters had spoken, and it sounded like "Th-th-th-that's all, folks!" when it came to the prospect of a President Tsongas.

From the beginning, the candidate with the best odds-on average was 54-year-old Jerry Brown. He had, after all, succeeded Reagan as governor of California in 1975, so who better to replace him as president?

Adding to the musical chairs aspect of the equation was the fact that Reagan himself had succeeded Brown's father as governor in 1966. If only Reagan's son, Ron Jr, had replaced Brown as governor in 1983, the cycle would have been complete.

But such was not to be, as Ron Jr, at 25, was too busy dancing his life away, having long ago traded his father's big shoes for ballet slippers.

Nicknamed "Governor Moonbeam" by *Doonesbury* cartoonist Garry Trudeau, Brown, an ambitious and restless young man had made his first run for the White House in 1976 — after serving only a year of his six-year term as governor.

Although he lost the nomination to Carter, he was up for a rematch, and ran again at the next possible opportunity in 1980, but wisely chose to hang on to his day job at the state house while traveling across the nation campaigning.

When his term as governor ended, Brown decided the next logical step in life should be to study Buddhism in Japan. When he was certain that at that he knew the sound of one hand clapping, Moonbeam returned to politics, presumably bringing this insight to his tenure as Chair of the California Democratic Party.

And it was here that he stayed until the opportunity to slide into yet another seat warmed up by Reagan presented itself. Most surprisingly, Brown appeared to be adopting some of Reagan's views on fiscal conservatism, going so far as to having his tax plan developed by Arthur Laffer, originator of the Laffer Curve, and a key contributor to the field of supply-side economic theory.

Talk about karma! The one hand is really clapping now.

Given that this would be Brown's third run for the White House, funding was difficult to line up this time, even from the usual cadre of the politically liberal Hollywood elite. The Brown name no longer seemed so golden, forcing the former Jesuit to once again look to his Buddhist teachings for guidance.

And there it was! In the Buddha's own teachings, a message so plain and direct as to fit into a fortune cookie:

"He who travels the lightest travels the farthest."

Inspired by this piece of ancient wisdom, Brown threw his suitcase in the car and hit the road. Out of necessity he ran a fairly low budget campaign, largely funded by soliciting donations via a gimmicky, toll-free 800 number that he breathlessly promoted at every venue.

The gimmick began to pay off, and was spun as proof that Moonbeam was "the only candidate capable of providing innovative solutions to old problems."

As Brown began to win or place highly in the primaries and caucuses, the mainstream money tap turned on, and soon the happy face governor was able to park his old Plymouth Satellite sedan at the airport and start flying first class.

Across America, a bubbling Brown tide was rising—until a complete nobody stepped in and pulled the plug.

For Jerry the spiritual pilgrim, there was little solace in the Buddha's teaching that it was all about the journey, not the destination. Stuck in a ditch in the middle of nowhere, he had been run off the road by a saxophone-playing governor of Arkansas.

100

Hope

"Hope is a waking dream. Hope in reality is the worst of all evils because it prolongs the torments of man."

— Friedrich Nietzsche

At 46 years of age, Bill Clinton was the youngest candidate in the race on the Democratic side. Born William Jefferson Blythe III in the small town of Hope, Arkansas, he was the son of a traveling salesman who died before his son was born. At age four, Bill's mother Virginia married Roger Clinton, an alcoholic car dealer with a penchant for gambling, who agreed to raise the boy as his own.

It was while attending school in Hot Springs that young Clinton's gifts at oratory and persuasion began to gain notice. In a mock trial, the adolescent's skills were showcased in his rousing defense of Catiline, a first century BC Roman Senator accused of adultery.

Making his first run for public office while still in his twenties, Clinton's political rise was rapid, and by 32 he was the youngest governor in the nation. Those who knew him were not surprised: he was a natural politician in the worst possible sense — propelled by insatiable ambition, and ethically untethered.

He had the touch.

If not yet the world, then at least the state of Arkansas became his oyster, along with its legendary properties as an aphrodisiac. Few could resist his charms.

Clinton understood human weakness, and there was no greater weakness than hope. Mixing fantasy and reality, he campaigned as "the man from Hope."

Clinton campaigned using a secret family recipe, learned first-hand from his abusive car dealer stepfather: Smile incessantly, and tell the people exactly what they wanted to hear, even if they knew it was complete nonsense.

Above all, be complimentary. Acknowledge how smart the people are who support you. Those who say "flattery will get you nowhere" have obviously never sold a car with a bad transmission, or been elected to office.

If votes were measured as commissioned earnings, Clinton would rank as Salesman of the Year.

For most of his gubernatorial tenure, Clinton stayed under the radar in the "Natural State" while he perfected his act and fattened his résumé. Mostly he fraternized with other governors. His first step into the national spotlight came when he was tapped to give the official Democratic rebuttal to Reagan's 1985 State of the Union speech.

Encouraged by the pats on the back he received from shaking his finger at the President, Clinton (then nicknamed "The Boy Governor") briefly flirted with running for the White House in 1988. But instead he stayed in Little Rock and pursued flirtations of a different nature.

As governor he accomplished much, and it was during his reign that milk was officially recognized as Arkansas' official beverage. Now, nearly through his second term as governor of the state that invented the cheese dog (1956), Clinton decided the entire nation was ready for him.

If nothing else, running for president would provide him with the opportunity to get out of the house, and away from the nagging of his wife Hillary, a woman who was said to have political aspirations of her own.

The governor looked forward to life on the road: meeting new people, and checking into nice motels in cities far from home. But Mrs Clinton, a lawyer (and former pupil of Robert Bork at Yale), made a strong case for not just staying home and baking cookies, and soon became the governor's governor.

If not as a wife, then at least for adult supervision, the Boy Governor depended on her. She knew when to look away and when to give the evil eye.

Most importantly, Mrs Clinton made sure her husband didn't get caught with his pants down. This was not easy, but the Chicago-born fishwife was ready to ditch the phony southern accent and take the Clinton show to a new audience.

Although in a different sense from her husband, Hillary had also gone about as far as one could go in Arkansas. She'd been a lawyer, had a baby, and served on one board after another, from Wal-Mart, to TCBY (The Country's Best Yogurt). Then, the self-proclaimed former "Goldwater Girl" moved on to the New World Foundation; a New York-based organization that funded a mixed bag of "New Left" political interest groups.

From the beginning, it was clear that the First Couple of Arkansas had appetites bigger than what Little Rock could sate, and so, after honing their skills playing in the farm league, the Clintons were ready to give it to America as a whole.

After losing the season opener in Iowa, Bill Clinton refined his pitch and headed on to New Hampshire — the home turf of eastern rivals Moynihan, Cuomo, and Tsongas. Surprisingly, the Boy Governor was holding his own, until stories broke involving an adulterous affair with Gennifer Flowers, an actress perhaps best remembered for her role in the seminal 1986 Australian film *Frenchman's Farm.*

Clinton's hopes for a victory in the Granite State dropped like a stone, and it appeared that he was doomed to a fate similar to that which had befallen that other great Democratic party hopeful, Gary Hart, whose presidential dreams had also been shipwrecked by allegations of rocking the Captain's cabin while the missus was back on shore.

As a disgusted President Reagan had quipped at the time of the scandal, "Boys will be boys. But boys do not deserve to be president."

Needing to do damage control in advance of Super Tuesday, Mr and Mrs Clinton went on *60 Minutes* and presented a united front. While not a political speech per se, the Clintons treated it as such; gaining free national exposure on the nation's top-rated television show.

For many Americans, this would be their first exposure to the man who eventually came to be known as "Slick Willy." Experienced at having been called a bad boy in the past, Clinton offered up a well-rehearsed mix of contrition and defiance. In doing so, he affirmed the wisdom of the great Irish playwright Oscar Wilde, who so aptly noted that once one learns how to fake sincerity, everything else is easy.

Reagan, a regular viewer of the show was watching that night. As a former actor, he was incredibly savvy at seeing through this kind of theater, and immediately called Bush, then the front-runner, to warn him.

"This guy is a real showman; be careful."

Bush just laughed it off. His staff was already quite familiar with these allegations, and they did not regard Clinton's candidacy—even before the scandal—as a serious threat.

As Bush's team saw it, "Hill-Billy" was a long shot: the governor of a small "backward" southern state. He had no chance against either Brown or Cuomo; popular governors from large, wealthy states like California and New York.

Besides, after the Gennifer Flowers scandal—and how it had torpedoed his chances in New Hampshire, the Clinton flotilla was dead in the water.

The President disagreed. "Normally a sex scandal would be the end, but after what I saw in that piece on *60 Minutes*, it's clear that this fellow can turn lemons into lemonade. Watch out, George."

Reagan then called Kemp, who took the warning more seriously. Although Kemp always tried to always see the best in others, he knew enough to trust Reagan's instincts when it came to reading people. He also knew, from playing sports, the danger of being overly confident. More than once he had seen an upset resulting from arrogance and a sense of invincibility.

As it turned out Reagan was indeed right: Bill Clinton was welcomed back with open arms, and with no additional questions about the lipstick on his collar.

Less than two weeks after being counted out for dead in the wake of New Hampshire, Clinton rose from the ashes, winning Georgia and placing near the top in several other Super Tuesday states, earning him the new nickname of the "Comeback Kid."

At least the Bush camp had been right about Brown, who would be Clinton's main rival as the crowd of other Democratic hopefuls dropped off one by one.

The nature of the primary season is different than the regular campaign, in that those running typically waste little time or money on who might potentially win the nomination for the other side. Instead, Democrats attacked one another, and whenever possible, Reagan.

With the Republicans, there were no direct attacks on Reagan, although some, especially Bush, sought to find balance between capitalizing on the positive aspects of continuity while striving to establish his own twinkling vision for America's future.

But, for the most part, Bush was uncharacteristically tight-lipped; careful to avoid the same kinds of blunders which had come back to bite him in 1988. Any public comments on Reagan were now carefully scripted to suggest just the right balance of reverence and independence.

By late May it was clear that Clinton had the nomination sewn up, beating Brown in each subsequent contest. Adding insult to injury, Clinton even robbed him of California, taking the former governor's home state on June 2 by more than seven points.

At the DNC convention in July, the Man from Hope won his party's nomination on the first ballot.

What was a surprise was that the VP slot would not be offered to Brown, leading to speculation that it might go to Mrs Clinton.

Was nominating one's wife even legal?

It was, but it would not have been the kind of mistake that the Clintons would make. They were much too clever than to have kept the show going this long, only to have the audience boo and walk out when the star's wife joined him onstage, shaking a tambourine and singing off-key like some kind of amateur act at the Little Rock Rotary Club. The run for the White House was serious business, not a vanity project.

Sorry Hillary, your time will just have to wait. Don't give up *hope*.

Instead, the Clintons decided to pick someone who had both the correct credentials and a clean (as in unknown) national reputation.

The person they chose was John Forbes Kerry, a recently divorced, 48-year-old first-term Senator from Massachusetts.

The selection was indeed a surprise, as it rejected the traditional strategy of choosing a primary rival like Jerry Brown. Not only had he finished a decent second, but he brought with him the riches that only a large state like California can deliver.

But the Clintons and Brown lived in different worlds, and Governor Moonbeam was not welcome on *their* planet.

Fair enough.

Meanwhile the Democratic Party establishment had been pushing for Super Mario: Governor of the Empire State, and someone, who at age 60, was on the cusp of reaching his sell-by date. Mario had paid into the system for decades, and was now entitled to collect.

Party bosses lobbied hard, noting that Cuomo would have balanced the ticket regionally—just like Kennedy and Johnson.

Hmmm ... Clinton liked the Kennedy comparison, even if the geography was reversed.

But wait—there's more! Super Mario would bring bags of money. Lots and lots of money. *Wall Street money.*

But the Clintons worried about a power struggle with the old party silverback. Besides, Senator Kerry would bring his own pluses.

First, Kerry was—like Clinton—a relatively fresh face, albeit one that bore more than a passing resemblance to actor Fred Gwynne in the roll of TV's Herman Munster.

Clinton & Kerry: Two new faces with a new vision for a new America. New, new, new!

As a Senator, Kerry had experience dealing with national affairs and matters of international importance—which Clinton did not. Kerry had also succeeded in first winning his Senate seat in 1984—the same year that Reagan won re-election by a landslide, even taking Massachusetts.

Best of all, the Colorado-born Kerry was well connected to the liberal gravy train which welcomed him with open checkbooks, acknowledging that they had, at least temporarily, run out of Kennedys.

Although he did not have an actual drop of Irish blood in him, his Austrian grandfather's decision to change the family name from Kohn to Kerry, and trade Judaism for Catholicism served well the political career of the faux Celt in a place like Beantown, where one's connection to the Emerald Isle was celebrated as a lucky charm more valuable than a dyed green rabbit's foot.

Kerry, not O'Kerry, or McKerry, did his part. Sporting the colors, he piously marched in every St Paddy's Day parade holding a shamrock, and like Hillary, had adopted the accent of his newfound home state.

He was as clean, and as authentic as a bar of Irish Spring.

John Kerry's entry to the US Senate was prompted when incumbent Paul Tsongas announced he would not seek re-election due to health issues. Despite lacking the full backing of the Massachusetts Democratic Machine (notably kingmaker Tip O'Neill), Kerry, then the state Attorney General, managed to win the party primary. Within the Commonwealth, Kerry the chameleon had high name recognition, and the support of his current boss, Governor Michael Dukakis.

With a little help from some very powerful friends, Kerry was elected as the new Senator from Massachusetts. As Teddy Kennedy's junior apprentice, unseen doors would open for the former altar boy.

Then, in the type of partisan game playing that gives voters reason to be cynical, Tsongas opted to resign one day before his senate term officially ended. This allowed Dukakis to appoint Kerry to fill the vacancy, giving him a leg up in seniority. Granted, it was only by 24 hours, and although devious, it was completely legal. The little game of Democratic senatorial switcheroo allowed Kerry to cut to the front of the line of all the other incoming senators, most of whom were Republicans.

"May the road rise up to meet you" say the Irish; and certainly it did for Mr Kerry, thanks to a couple of Greeks.

Once seated, Kerry soon set about making a name for himself as an irritant to President Reagan, and within three months was in Nicaragua shaking hands and posing for photos with Daniel Ortega. From this fortuitous start, Kerry jumped into the jungle, first investigating a contras-cocaine connection, the results of which were published in the Kerry Committee report. When the Iran-Contra scandal began to unfold, Kerry was already in uniform and ready for active duty.

At the time, many Americans were concerned that Nicaragua might become "another Vietnam." Capitalizing on these fears, Kerry, a veteran of Vietnam, brokered a good-faith, cease-fire agreement with Managua in exchange for the US dropping its support for the Contras.

Much to the frustration of President Reagan, the Democratically-controlled House backed Kerry's plan, and rejected the administration's $14 million dollar aid package for the Contras.

With support for the democratic resistance gutted, President Ortega hopped on a plane for Moscow the very next day, where the Gromyko regime wrote him a check for $200 million—presumably to further facilitate the spirit of peace and goodwill pioneered by Senator Kerry.

Or maybe not.

Kerry, warrior turned peacemaker, became a hero to the "peace at any price" crowd, saluted for his efforts to save America from another Vietnam.

Unlike Kerry, Bill Clinton had worn a different kind of uniform during the Vietnam War.

His was the uniform of the anti-war protestor: ragged jeans and scruffy thrift store sweaters. Thanks to a series of student deferments, the wooly-headed Arkansan was able to courageously command peace brigades from such dangerous international hotspots as the campuses of Oxford and Yale.

Still, Clinton was careful to avoid any activity that might affect his taxpayer-subsidized scholarships. He might be full of hot air, but vehemently denied ever inhaling marijuana smoke. Nixon's War on Drugs was raging, and the man from Hope needed to pick his battles. Hope, not dope, indeed.

When Clinton finally left Yale in 1973 with a law degree, the war in Vietnam was winding down. He was in his late 20s, and through a mix of luck and cunning, had triumphed over the US military.

John Kerry, also managed to avoid conscription thanks to a student deferment, but after graduating from Yale the lacrosse-playing frat boy realized his number was coming up fast and his options were dropping. Rather than wait to be drafted, he decided to enlist in the Naval Reserve, which had seemed like a fairly safe bet—especially for a former Skull and Bones member from a good family. Ultimately, Kerry still ended up in Vietnam, the result of having applied to command a Fast Patrol Craft (also known as a "Swift Boat").

Not surprisingly, Vietnam didn't deliver the same kind of fun-in-the-sun high jinks celebrated in songs like "Sea Cruise" (as made famous by Huey Smith & The Clowns). For one thing, there was a major war going on, and people were dying.

Twenty years later, Senator Kerry reflected on the matter. "I didn't really want to get involved in the war. When I signed up for the swift boats, they had very little to do with the war. They were engaged in coastal patrolling and that's what I thought I was going to be doing."

Kerry soon discovered the downside of coastal cruising during wartime, and was twice hit by shrapnel. Within three years he was back in the states, mad as a wet hen, and heavily involved in the anti-war movement.

Although he relished the wild life of an unkempt revolutionary decked out in military fatigues, Kerry, who had a degree in political science, soon came to the realization that while foot soldiers can win battles, the wars are won or lost by politicians.

Therefore, he would need to run for congress. After a campaign tainted by scandal, the fightin' Irishman won the primary, only to lose the main election, in a nasty contest that would earn the dubious distinction of being the most expensive congressional race in the country.

In one of those rare instances in American politics, Kerry was unable to buy the election. So instead he returned to school, became a talk radio host, and deepened his connections to moneyed-elite. A decade after his failed run for congress, Kerry was elected Lieutenant Governor of the Commonwealth of Massachusetts.

Halfway through his first term as Dukakis' Number Two Man, Kerry thanked the people and unexpectedly made a dash for the US Senate. Now, just two years into his second term as a Senator, he was again looking to conquer new ground.

Ah, the luck o' the Irish!

Like most politicians, Senator Kerry was a man of grand aspirations; he hoped that serving as VP would provide a steppingstone to the presidency.

Hope.

While Lieutenant Kerry dreamed of one day saluting the Marine band as it played "Hail To Chief," the Boy Governor was focused on the immediate future, and how his choice of a running mate could be used most effectively as a veteran and an ATM.

Kerry would bring bags of gold, as well as medals of bronze and silver. Let's rock!

At the time of Kerry's selection, Jack Kemp's VP choice was a mystery, as the Republican convention was still a month away. Even though Kemp was not a combat veteran, he had served in the reserves, and his support for the military was never a matter of question.

Clinton saw Kerry as a way to neutralize this, and prayed that Kemp would not reinforce the Republican ticket with his own combat veteran … someone like Arizona Senator John McCain who had just taken over for Barry Goldwater.

Like Kerry, McCain had served in Vietnam. But unlike Kerry,

McCain never turned on his country or the military. Although badly broken and permanently disabled by his war injuries (compounded by a lack of medical attention during his years held as a POW), McCain spoke proudly of his service, and avoided engaging in activities that would embarrass the United States, or lend comfort to its enemies.

The Clintons did not necessarily regard Kerry's anti-war activism as a problem—in fact, it actually helped with their base. Still, whenever possible, the plan would be to present an image of a clean cut young Kerry in his Navy whites, having a medal pinned on his chest—and not that of the raging protestor throwing the same medals away on the steps of the Capitol just a few years later.

Besides, who better to dispute the need for a big defense budget than an actual veteran? A Senator who knew the *real* story?

War was over; whether it had been World War III or the Cold War. Without the USSR there would probably never be another war. Never. Ever. We won. It was time for a victory party. Uniforms were costumes, relics of the past.

Clinton smiled.

101

Kemp Chooses a Running Mate

After four consecutive losses of the White House, the Democratic Party was in shambles.

In the 1980 presidential contest, Ronald Reagan beat Jimmy Carter, the Democratic incumbent, with nearly 91% of the vote in the Electoral College. Four years later, Reagan returned to beat Walter Mondale, Carter's Vice President, upping the margin to nearly 97%.

In 1988, running for his third term against Teddy Kennedy, Reagan triumphed by the largest popular vote landslide in US history, leaving the Senator with nothing more to claim than a dubious victory in his home state of Massachusetts.

While the win in Massachusetts had been open to challenge, Reagan decided not to pursue it, so as to spare Kennedy the humiliation of being the first major party candidate in history to actually lose all 50 states. The President had the mandate he needed. It was time to unify the nation and deal with more important issues.

Campaigning for a third term, Reagan had run on a platform that emphasized specific policies needed to advance America's conservative revolution. If voters supported this agenda, and were committed to its implementation, they were asked to provide the President with a Congress not bogged down by partisan gridlock.

Heeding the President's request was difficult for some voters, as it would mean voting out Democratic incumbents who had been relied upon to bring home the bacon—even if it meant charging it on Uncle Sam's credit card.

Democrats had been comfortable—and successful—with a divided government under Reagan's second term. As the opposition party, it alleviated them of the responsibility of actually doing anything, while allowing them to gain notoriety (and funding) by serving as vocal irritants.

With no ideas of their own, the donkeys in Congress seemed content to play the role of spoilers—and as a result, nothing was getting done.

It was an untenable situation; voters were frustrated, and for most of his second term Reagan was essentially powerless.

The coup in the Soviet Union changed everything. It was time to get serious and support a president and a party that offered strong and clear leadership—and which was ready to take action. It was time to back a party that ran on actual issues, and not just fear and fluff. It was time to elect politicians willing to do what they were entrusted to do, and who stood up for the traditional American values of hard work, courage, liberty, fairness, and faith.

Voters responded to Reagan's call for unity and progress, and awarded Republicans control of Congress in 1988. Happy with the changes being made, this margin was increased even further by the midterm elections of 1990, when the GOP majority rose to roughly 80%—beating the previous record set by Democrats in the 1930s under FDR.

But now, with Reagan set to retire, the Democrats had *hope* for the first time in many years.

Consultants reminded the party faithful that America had always gone through political cycles. Unable to understand the appeal of conservatism, many liberals wrote it off as nothing more than a personality cult based on Ronald Reagan himself.

But now he was leaving town.

Liberals felt confident that without Reagan to sell it, conservative ideology would fail. Better yet, if his successor was someone not worthy of the job. Someone like George HW Bush.

Democratic strategists smelled blood.

Bush had never been all that popular, and was now (after 1980 and 1988) a two-time loser; damaged goods. Focus groups used a range of negatives to describe him, including arrogant, elitist, out-of-touch, condescending, old news, wrinkly, a flip-flopper, dishonest—and a wimp. Of course, these terms were completely at odds with what Bush's own consultants were hearing from likely voters on the right, but with politics, as in life, you get what you pay for. Consultants will always tell you exactly what they think you want to hear, but unlike politicians, they will do it using a thesaurus.

From the beginning, it seemed obvious that Bush would be the Republican nominee. He had the cash and the connections, and with Reagan unable (or unwilling) to publicly anoint a preferred successor until the convention, Bush would gain the title by assumption.

Yes, Bush was the establishment candidate—and the Democratic machine was thankful for this, as here was a well-established playbook for taking on, and taking down a cranky old loser by offering a vibrant young upstart.

1992 would be a repeat of 1960, when the Democrats successfully beat a tired and detached former VP by offering up a charismatic young visionary.

If Jack Kemp were to win the Republican nomination it would be a different story, but the Democrats presumed he had no chance—and were thankful for it.

Although confident that the GOP would do their work for them, too much was at stake to not have a contingency plan. Therefore, should Kemp start to catch fire during the primaries, the Democrats were prepared to use some of their money to help out the Bush campaign.

Funneling Democratic dollars to a Republican candidate is not exactly what some 77-year-old widow, a lifelong Democrat from Ohio (worried about Social Security), thought would happen with her $5 monthly donations, but that's how the game is played when your entire focus is on winning.

Bush had the resources needed to win. Forcing him to spend his own money fighting off Kemp would only leave him weaker for the general election.

The longer Kemp hung on the better, prompting some to suggest diverting funds to *his* campaign instead. But in the end, gridlock within the Democratic Party itself prevailed, and the decision was made to "hold the powder" for November.

Until then, let the two slug it out. Let them hurt each other, and their party. Eventually, Bush, bloodied and weakened by the ordeal would stagger into the ring, only to be knocked out by a single quick punch from his Democratic challenger.

The view of Kemp as dangerous was one of the few things the Democratic and pro-Bush faction of the Republican establishment agreed upon. Despite Bush's mudslinging, Kemp had managed to hold his head high and keep the tone positive. He had ideas, not just slogans. He also had a plan to grow the party, move the country forward; and soon, the most popular president in US history would be out campaigning on his behalf.

The Democratic establishment knew that it would have to deal with him eventually, but trusted it wouldn't be until 1996 at the soonest. But as the fight dragged on a sense of panic began to grip the party. When Kemp emerged victorious after California they were genuinely stunned.

Bush would not be the Republican candidate. All the money and the connections and traditions hadn't helped. The polls were wrong.

He was done.

No one really expected Bush to serve as VP again. The old line about unifying the party no longer applied. The playbook had gone out the window, and the maverick young quarterback was holding the ball now.

It was a new game.

Speculation, from Democratic strategists to Republican pundits was rampant. Lists were drawn up, and predictions made. But Kemp would keep his list of possibilities private—and that was the only roster that really mattered.

Who would it be?

Phil Gramm, a solidly fiscal conservative Senator who could help with Texas? Perhaps.

Prior to being elected to the Senate in 1984, the Georgia-born former Democrat had served in the US House, and was well respected by his colleagues on both sides of the aisle. At 50, he reflected generational change without compromising traditional party values. He had a minority wife (of Korean and Hawaiian ancestry) and together they had two children.

Dr Gramm was also a former (Texas A & M) Economics professor who understood and supported Reaganomics, including the Kemp-Roth tax cuts.

He would be an obvious choice for everyone's short list—including Kemp's. When asked, Kemp just grinned, but refused to confirm or deny Gramm as being under consideration for the Number Two spot.

What about Lamar Alexander?

Like Gramm, the former Eagle Scout was now in the Senate, having been elected as part of the GOP wave that accompanied Reagan's 1988 third term landslide.

Prior to the Senate, Alexander had served two terms as governor of Tennessee, but had been prevented from making it three in a row due to state term limits. A competent administrator, Alexander certainly had his strengths and had many friends advocating on his behalf— including his former roommate, and Kemp's close pal, Trent Lott.

Alexander might also help with the South, an area where support for Kemp was building, but still weak.

John McCain was out.

Too much of a renegade, too much of a hothead, and too used to being in charge for himself. A good man, but too close to the S & L scandal and the collapse of Lincoln Savings and Loan. Certainly not the kind of Lincoln association Kemp was looking for in a running mate.

Next.

Near the bottom of everyone's list was Bob Dole. While most in the GOP establishment had come to see the light on the need to bring in new faces, the Old Boy coterie wanted one of their own to add depth to the ticket.

Kemp/Dole 92?

Many influential party leaders regarded Kemp as a bit of an *enfant terrible*, and wanted a seasoned veteran like the old Kansan as a babysitter in case Jack got too big for his britches. Dole, a moderate, also added political balance, making the ticket more palatable to swing voters.

Although there hadn't been any real bad blood between the two during the primaries, Dole was widely known to be dismissive of Kemp, whom he referred to as "the quarterback."

Senator Dole could bring decades of experience, this was not necessarily a good thing. With experience comes baggage, and Kemp did not envision himself becoming a bellhop.

No, there would be no Kemp/Dole ticket. Dole would return to Kansas, and start trying to line up donors for yet another run in four years.

After Bill Clinton passed on teaming up with Zen master Jerry Brown, some wondered if Kemp wouldn't look to Illinois-born Pete Wilson, currently serving as the Republican governor of California.

At 59, he was a well-connected and seasoned political veteran. Prior to winning the state house, Wilson, a former marine, had been mayor of San Diego, and then served in the US Senate. Reagan knew Wilson; going so far as to have campaigned on his behalf when he ran for the Senate in 1983 against, yes, Jerry Brown.

At the request of party matchmakers, a meeting with Wilson was arranged, but Kemp decided not to make an offer. While the two were in step on many issues, Kemp felt a hesitancy from this potential running mate when it came to where the GOP needed to go in order to grow and become more inclusive.

One major division concerned the issue of immigration. Kemp was more aligned with Reagan's position on the matter, whereas Wilson reflected a harder line being taken by some in his adopted state.

Wilson was doing fine as is, and had the record to prove it. Kemp, however, had bigger dreams. They shook hands and parted.

Kemp, born and raised in California had won the state by a solid margin; adding Wilson provided no measurable bump. The governor would support the ticket, working his connections, while Kemp worked his. In some cases the two factions paralleled one another, but in other areas they diverged.

Hasta la vista, Mr Wilson.

Central to Kemp's Golden State network was Dan Lungren, a close friend and former colleague from his days in Congress; now serving as the state's attorney general.

A native Californian and Roman Catholic, Lungren was happy to do whatever was needed, but had no interest in being considered for the ticket. For Lungren, this was only about helping an old friend, who just so happened to be the best candidate running.

Whether Trent Lott, another former member of Kemp's congressional backfield, was personally interested in the "veep slot" was unknown.

Senator Lott had solid regional support, but was deemed simply too divisive for a national ticket, and in many ways, he and Kemp had grown apart. Having failed to even deliver his home state of Mississippi during the primaries, it was clear that Lott added little, if anything.

Georgia Congressman Newt Gingrich ranked considerably higher. Like Lott, he was a colleague and friend from Congress, and someone who would bring a sense of generational change and intellect to the ticket. But Gingrich was himself a leader, and in Kemp's view, the team only needed one quarterback.

Like Gramm, the 49-year-old Gingrich also held a PhD — although his area of study had been history. Exceptionally bright, well-rounded, and passionate, Kemp envisioned "the professor" playing an important role in his administration.

Another old friend and kindred spirit from Kemp's days in the House, and now serving in the Senate, was Florida's Connie Mack III.

Born Cornelius Alexander McGillicuddy III, "Mack" (along with Gingrich and Lott), had been an important member of Kemp's crew in Congress. Mack and Kemp had both been members of the House's Chowder and Marching Club, as well as the "Conservative Opportunity Society."

The two shared a common sense of humor, and their families enjoyed socializing together. Unfortunately, Mack was also a genuinely nice person. Normally, this would be a good thing, but in politics, the Vice President is often relegated to the role of being the president's attack dog, engaging in the type of nasty street battles that are deemed inappropriate for the Chief Executive.

Like Kemp, Mack had been branded a "bleeding heart" conservative, owing to his advocacy on behalf of women's issues and healthcare. Both men viewed themselves as bridge-builders; and Mack, as a "proudly different kind of Republican," enjoyed strong support from a diverse population of the state's elderly, blacks, Latinos, and non-Christians, including the Jewish community—as well as the traditional conservative Republican base.

Originally from Philadelphia, Mack, 51, came from a line of office holders; although the most famous member of the family had made his name in sports—not politics. Mack's paternal grandfather (the original Connie Mack) was a member of the Baseball Hall of Fame.

Kemp stared at the closed manila folder that held Mack's dossier and sighed, acknowledging the many strikes against his suitability for Vice President: The worst (understandable given his heritage), that Mack preferred baseball over football!

"Nobody's perfect," Kemp thought to himself smiling, and effective politics usually involves compromise—even Reagan had said that.

With this in mind, Kemp picked up the phone, and invited the first-term Senator from Florida to be his running mate.

Reagan approved, and would have no problem supporting the ticket. What Mack lacked in experience, he made up for in character. But most important, Kemp and Mack were friends, not rivals, who would work effectively as a team.

Still, Kemp's choice of Mack was not a cause for celebration by the party bosses. Although Florida brought strategic value as a large state—the biggest prize in the South—the establishment was still pushing hard for Wilson. Before any decision could be made publicly, they wanted to lobby on behalf of the Governor—who also just so happened to be a graduate of Yale, and an attorney with a degree from Cal Berkeley's prestigious Boalt Hall.

Kemp was once again called in to the principal's office (RNC headquarters), and if not exactly read the Riot Act, was still forced to look at spread sheets, stacks of surveys, and special White Papers prepared by consultants and brand managers.

Like Clinton, Wilson had experience governing a state, but on a much grander scale. As a Californian, it was also believed Wilson would also attract the Reagan/Washington-outsider vote. Mack was just too inexperienced, too nice, too close in age, too … lacking of what was needed to balance the ticket.

While the Democratic ticket would feature two "Yalies," Mack, with only a Bachelor's degree in Business Administration would be a target for critics seeking to write him off an intellectual lightweight.

But wait Jack, there's more. Please pay attention!

Mack was pretty much an unknown, which would make fundraising difficult. In addition, if he were to leave the Senate, Lawton Chiles, Florida's Democratic governor would get to pick his replacement.

What about a moderate like … Arlen Spector?

But the bosses were talking to the wrong man. What they failed to grasp was that Kemp, by winning the nomination, was now their boss, and he'd do what he thought was best.

Fiercely independent, and prone to doing just the opposite of what others tried to tell him to do, Kemp had long relied on his instincts to guide him. He could be extremely impulsive, and did not shy away from taking risks. This drove the GOP establishment nuts—and was a major reason why his run for the presidency had been initially written off in favor of more conventional options like Bush and Dole.

Much to their surprise, Kemp's independence turned out to be his secret weapon, as his gambles on the campaign trail turned into victories. The harder the Old Guard tried, the more Kemp dug in, until exhausted, they threw their hands up and took out the checkbooks.

He had won.

On Thursday, August 20, on the final night of the GOP convention, Reagan made an appearance to announce his support for the Kemp/ Mack ticket.

Greeted by a standing ovation, the President's speech was met with frequent cheers, applause, and calls of "Four More Years! Four More Years! Four More Years!"

Reagan just smiled, and then returned to his heartfelt endorsement of Jack Kemp. The President made it clear that he felt he was passing the torch to a worthy successor, a great man, who, with their support, would take over and lead America's conservative revolution.

The President spoke not just of Kemp's character and leadership abilities, but also of his stand on the issues, and how this would extend America's claim as a "shining city on the hill." The reference was especially poignant, in that it was one Reagan had first used when announcing his candidacy for the presidency in 1979.

Standing beside Kemp and Mack at the podium, President Reagan rallied the crowd — and the millions watching at home with his soaring endorsement of the ticket, and why the 1992 election was so important to the future of conservatism.

"When we talk about Jack Kemp one word comes to mind: The *cause*. As president, he will work for that cause; *he will fight for that cause!* And what unites every person here tonight is our commitment to that cause.

"Jack Kemp has already fought, and won, more battles than most men ever dream of, and we are all better for it. But now he faces his biggest battle, to become president, and to assume his rightful place as the leader of that revolution that came to Washington twelve years ago.

"Jack likes to say that I gave America back its future. But if I can return the compliment, I would like to say that it was his ideas and his courage that helped us to go further into the future than any of us — except perhaps Jack — that eternal optimist — ever dreamed possible.

"But now, as I saddle up and prepare to ride off into the sunset, I know that the future will not just be secure, but something truly magnificent under President Jack Kemp!"

Reagan's words brought down the house, and many had tears in their eyes. Tears of sadness in recognition that the man who had given so much, for so long, was leaving, forever.

This was to be it.

But there were also tears brought by genuine hope and optimism, as Americans of all stripes opened their hearts to President Reagan's signature pledge that the "best was yet to come."

It was now time to unite around Kemp/Mack, and prepare for the election set for Tuesday, November 3, 1992.

The selection of Mack gave the GOP ticket a slight boost, but as August gave way to September, the two sides were essentially polling neck and neck with voters. A few polls even had the Democrats ahead by a slight margin.

The clock was running down and it was now up to the quarterback to step up, save the day; throw a Hail Mary pass, and win the White House.

As a professional football player, Kemp had actually thrown more interceptions than touchdowns. On the surface he projected confidence, but deep down he understood the responsibility placed upon him, and the consequences, should he let the Reagan Revolution end with him, and allow Bill Clinton to win the presidency of the United States of America.

102

No Man Can Serve Two Masters

It was Friday afternoon, February 14, 1992—*another* Valentine's Day, and so far all was quiet on the western front, and pretty much everywhere else for that matter.

Things were going well for President Reagan. Despite the fact that he had turned 81 on the sixth, there was a growing movement calling for him to run for a fourth term.

The President was flattered; but adamant about moving on, despite being at the peak of his popularity.

After a dozen years in DC, it was time to hitch up the wagon and head home to California. Although he did not feel his age, he knew that no man could stop the march of time. What years he had left would be devoted to Nancy, the woman who had already sacrificed so much of her life in support of his. What the days ahead might lack in quantity, he would try to make up for in quality.

Ronald Reagan had transformed America in a way unlike any other president in history, and would depart knowing he had left the nation strong, prosperous, and at peace. The future had never seemed brighter.

Never one to rest on his laurels, the President would use his remaining days in Washington to focus on legacy issues and fulfilling his remaining promises to the American people. He would go out on his feet, fighting the good fight right down to his last day.

While he might be able to apply some of his own personal popularity in pushing forward conservatism's new frontiers, the President knew much of this would be left to whoever followed him in the White House. Therefore it was critical that the next president was not just a Republican, but also the right kind of Republican.

And that meant Jack Kemp.

But nearly as soon as Kemp made his intentions known the previous fall, Bush followed by publicly announcing *his* candidacy. Although it was a surprise to many, Bush had apparently been planning a comeback for some time, lining up his campaign staff and financial backers.

No one was more surprised, or dismayed, by Bush's decision than Reagan.

When he left under a cloud it was assumed that he was done with political life; banished to the Home for Retired Vice Presidents, along with Agnew and Mondale. Bush was seemingly resigned to a stress-free life watching baseball and working on his memoirs.

If he had any political ambitions, these were rumored to be focused on his son, George, Jr. Although his namesake's only previous run for office had failed, Bush senior envisioned greater things for his boy than simply being a managing partner of a baseball team.

Bush the Elder apparently liked the idea of a political dynasty to rival the Kennedys, but also saw it as a way to one-up his old boss, whose son Ron Jr had no interest in public office.

Then came the October surprise. Although his return to political life was unexpected, donors quickly rallied behind him as the party's best hope to hold on to the White House.

Reagan's former VP reflected continuity *and* change — something for everybody. The primaries were deemed nothing more than a formality; an opportunity to reintroduce George Herbert Walker Bush to the nation.

It was a strategy so simple it could fit on a post-it note: Sweep the primaries, then, with Reagan's support, take the White House. After that? Who knows? Re-election? A third term? Fourth term? Hand things off to Junior?

And what about Jeb? Maybe George's younger brother could become Attorney General — just like Bobby Kennedy had done for JFK?

President Jeb Bush? Sure, why not?

Bush saw himself — and his family — as the future of the Republican Party.

But this was not the future of the Republican Party that Reagan envisioned. If only he had picked Kemp in 1980 instead of Bush; or in 1988 instead of Meese. Or what if Meese had resigned after the 1990 midterms to make room for Kemp?

"Oh well, what's done is done," thought Reagan, never one to dwell on the past or be hindered by regret.

The President would do what he could to help Kemp, but acknowledged that party allegiance, at least at the outset, would be with the former Vice President.

But for how long?

Even though the Republican primaries were just beginning, Reagan didn't think much of Bush's chances. He hoped that his former VP would get the message sooner than later, then bow out gracefully in order to clear a path for Kemp.

Bush had barely won the caucus in Hawaii. Then, despite spending heavily on Iowa, had come in near the bottom. Still, he had done marginally better than Kemp—which was a surprise, given that Kemp was far more socially conservative.

Maybe Kemp as Bush's Vice President?

Reagan laughed at such a possibility. As he gathered up his papers with thoughts of a Presidents' Day weekend getaway to Camp David there was a tentative knock at the door. Reagan looked up to see James Baker, his Chief of Staff, hovering in the doorway.

After some quick pleasantries, Baker revealed the reason for his visit: He was resigning so that he might commit himself fulltime as Bush's campaign director.

The President knew that Baker had been involved in the campaign, but never discussed the issue with him directly. Reagan did not want to be pressured into pledging his support, and the campaign did not want to affirm what it already knew regarding Reagan's preferred successor. So instead, the situation became one of the few instances in which the President embraced any form of diplomatic *détente.*

Don't ask, don't tell.

As head of the Republican Party, Reagan would need to stay publicly neutral, even though divisions were already established within his cabinet and staff. Some like Transportation Secretary Sununu, and Defense Secretary Powell were outspoken Bush supporters, whereas Commerce Secretary Simon, Education Secretary Bennett, and Health and Human Services Secretary Schweiker were backing Kemp.

Bush, taking a cue from his old days as spymaster, had strategized his comeback in absolute secrecy. In fact, he never even bothered to personally inform Reagan, relying instead on Baker to deliver the news for him shortly after Kemp announced his intentions.

And now, here was Baker again, showing up late on a Friday afternoon with another bombshell. While it was not uncommon for an administration to lose staff during its final year—the lack of any advance notice caught the President off guard.

"Going to work for George, eh? Well, at least I won't have to worry about writing you a letter of recommendation."

Reagan smiled and winked, while his soon-to-be ex-Chief of Staff chuckled nervously.

The President's nonchalant attitude and comment rattled him. After all their years together, Baker still couldn't read Reagan.

Rather than allow the awkwardness to linger, Baker forced a smile, steering the conversation back to the matter at hand, while the President continued to tidy the items on his desk and pack up for the day.

Filling in the gaps, Baker explained that although negotiations had been in the works for some time, he had decided it best to keep the degree of his commitment to the campaign limited, and private, until the last possible minute. But after Bush's less than stellar performance in January's primaries and caucuses, the candidate needed him to fully commit.

Baker stared at the President, sure that he would understand.

"Just as you needed the support of an old friend like Ed, George needs me now," he said.

Reagan nodded, wondering if Bush had already floated the possibility of choosing Baker as his VP. Or maybe Secretary of State?

Like Reagan and Meese, Bush and Baker went way back, their personal lives and careers deeply intertwined since the 1950s.

Longtime tennis partners, Baker had managed Bush's first Texas congressional campaign in 1966. Despite being self-professed moderates, Bush's campaign had focused on opposing the nation's growing civil rights movement, which he denounced as a threat to states' rights.

Whether or not Bush truly believed this was open to speculation. It was, however, a winning strategy for that particular race, and he was elected to the US House representing the 7th District of Texas. Predominantly white, the district included parts of suburban Houston, and was one of the wealthiest in the state.

Meanwhile, that same year, a political novice named Ronald Reagan unseated California's popular two-term Democratic incumbent governor.

Despite being an unapologetic conservative, Reagan won by a solid margin. It was a startling upset.

But while Reagan stayed true to his conservative roots, Bush, reflecting the rising tide of liberalism, broke with his party on a range of issues, from support for birth control to abolishing the draft.

After only two years in office, Reagan's name was already being bandied about as a possible presidential contender. But for now, he was content to serve as governor of the nation's largest, and perhaps most divided state. He had taken on a big job, and was determined to see it through.

The late 1960s were a difficult time for America. The Vietnam War was escalating, and the country was roiled in lawlessness. A feeling of revolution was in the air, and the nation was deeply divided by not just the issues, but also along lines defined by race, gender, and generations.

The 1968 Republican presidential ticket, headed by Richard Nixon, promised a return to order along with a "secret plan" to end the Vietnam War. With the help of the so-called Silent Majority, Nixon won the election, beating Democrat Hubert Humphrey by less than a single percentage point of the popular vote.

As a strong supporter of an increasingly unpopular war, Congressman Bush caught Nixon's attention, who convinced him to resign his position in the House and run for the Senate—which he did, only to be beaten by Democrat Lloyd Bentsen.

It was a humiliating loss for a man whose father, Prescott Sheldon Bush, had twice been elected to the US Senate representing Connecticut. Now 75 and in poor health, the elder Bush would go to his grave without ever seeing his son reach any elected office higher than that of Congressman.

But perhaps it should have been expected. Before setting his sights on the House, Bush had run for the Texas Senate two years earlier, losing to liberal Democrat Ralph Yarborough by nearly 13 points.

Out of a job and with a family to support, desperation began to set in. It seemed that with less than four years of serving in office, George HW Bush's political career was over.

At the time, the top song in the country was "One Bad Apple" by The Osmonds. Despite its catchy message of hope, Bush found himself under a dark cloud.

But then, true to the song's message on hope, someone reached out to stop the hurt.

Richard Nixon, the man who had led him down the path of disaster was back with a consolation prize: US Ambassador to the United Nations. Bush enjoyed his tenure at the UN, but within two years jumped at the chance to replace Bob Dole as Chair of the Republican National Committee.

This would better position him to network and coordinate a political comeback, and also offered a safe place to hunker down and wait out the worst of Watergate. A month after Nixon's resignation, President Ford rewarded Bush for his loyalty by choosing him as America's new ambassador to China.

After less than a year and a half on the job, Ford offered him the top spot at the CIA. Although Bush had no experience in the area of intelligence, he delighted in being the nation's spymaster, going so far as to sign his memos "Head Spook."

Being a political appointment, Bush's year at the CIA abruptly ended with the election of Jimmy Carter, who immediately replaced him with Rhodes Scholar (and career military man), Stansfield Turner.

Once again, the former this, former that, 52-year-old transplanted Texan was out pounding the pavement, resentful of how his fate was so dependent on the generosity of "superiors." It was this realization, tainted with indignation, which provided the push he needed to turn the tables on his patrons, and run for the highest office in the land—at the next possible opportunity.

Destiny seemed to favor Bush's decision. With no former Republican Vice President in the race, the line of ascendency to the White House was hazy, and soon the field was crowded with a thundering herd of active (and former) congressmen, senators, governors, and lunatics.

For a while, there was even speculation that an actual spaceman might enter the race, owing to efforts to draft Gemini/Apollo astronaut Frank Borman, the man who had wished us a merry Christmas while orbiting the moon in 1968.

But Borman, recently retired from Eastern Airlines, failed to initiate launch sequence, leaving politics to John Glenn, a Democrat.

As is always the case, many of those running had little or no chance, usually because they had little or no money.

As the race began, the Bush 80 campaign ranked their man's

likely opponents. At the top of the list were Senators Bob Dole and Howard Baker. Congressman John Anderson of Illinois, now running as an independent, was of little concern. Instead, the campaign was most worried about a formerly Democratic ex-governor of a large and powerful western state: John Connolly of Texas.

But in the end, it would be a different former governor that would beat him 44-7 in the race for his party's nomination.

Ronald Wilson Reagan.

The Bush people never saw it saw coming until it was too late. Entering the race well-lubed with oil money, Bush dismissed Reagan as a long-shot—if not a joke. The 69-year-old B-movie actor had already run once before in 1976, and was deemed too much of an extremist to win in 1980.

Reagan's time had come and gone. It was time for George HW Bush.

In tune with the zeitgeist, Bush had assembled a posse of experienced hired guns, led by his old pal James Baker.

As the Bush 80 campaign director, Baker was hoping to rebound after two significant back-to-back failures: First, directing Gerald Ford's unsuccessful re-election campaign in 1976; then losing out two years later on his own bid to become the Attorney General of Texas. (Despite having lost the 1978 election by more than 11 points, Baker bore no hard feelings towards *his* campaign director—George HW Bush.)

The Bush 80 campaign started out solidly, but when the chairs were put on the tables and the floors mopped, Bush was left standing at the stage door, hat in hand.

When he formally suspended his campaign on the last Monday in May, the number one song on the charts was "Call Me," by Blondie. A lively little dance number (which had been featured in the film *American Gigolo*), the tune would soon be bumped down by "Funky Town" from Lipps Inc.

Although Bush had the backing of the GOP establishment he had little else, and once again, his political future hinged on the charity of others. But this time, it was dependent on someone he had fought tooth and nail, someone he deemed inferior in every sense.

Goddamn it.

If you can't change the music, then you need to learn a new dance, especially if you want to go to Funkytown.

Like the song says, gotta move on. Indeed.

Bush had two options: eat humble pie or starve. Almost overnight, he began to backpedal and retract, hoping that Reagan was the type to forgive and forget.

And he was.

As Reagan's VP, this would be Bush's longest job in public office.

While not the top dog, Timberwolf was a heartbeat away from America's oldest president.

Bush began marking his territory. As VP, he had the power of making (and influencing) appointments, and soon set about bringing aboard as many of his pack as possible, starting with James Baker, placing him as the President's first Chief of Staff.

Never one to hold grudges, Reagan welcomed his two-time former adversary's defection to his team. Baker rewarded Reagan's trust by becoming a reliable team player and trusted advisor.

By most measures, the former Marine Captain had served the President well over the years. But now, as Bush's 1992 campaign was taking on water and in danger of capsizing, it was time for all hands to get on deck.

So, on a cold Friday afternoon in mid-February, Reagan accepted Baker's resignation with typical grace and encouragement. As his successor, Baker was offering — and endorsing — his assistant, 47-year-old Kenneth Duberstein.

Reagan was familiar with the Brooklyn native and liked him. Their connection went back to Reagan's first term, and Duberstein's role as Baker's Number Two man had grown considerably in recent months — for reasons that were now obvious.

Monday was the Presidents' Day holiday; Duberstein would take over on Tuesday, allowing Baker to take his position in the wheelhouse of the *Titanic* by Wednesday.

"Just a matter of pushing through the paperwork," said Reagan, smiling.

"Already done, and awaiting your signature, Mr President," said Baker.
Yup.

"Well, happy trails," said the President, with a smile and a nod.

" *... until we meet again,*" sang Baker, completing the line from the song made famous by Roy Rogers and Dale Evans. "Hopefully it'll be before the convention in August, in Houston … Anyway, thank you Mr President, and Vice President Bush thanks you as well."

As Baker spoke, Reagan's thoughts were already elsewhere.

Standing alone the Oval Office, the President slowly looked around the room; to the clock on the wall, to the bronze sculpture of a bent man riding an old horse, then to sign on his desk, which read "It Can Be Done."

Time to call it a day, and go home.

But first, there was one last thing he needed to do. Taking out his personal checkbook, he wrote a check—the maximum allowable by law—to the Kemp for President campaign.

103

Reagan's Final Battles

"If not us, who? And if not now, when?"

— Ronald Reagan

As the contest for who would succeed him in the White House was being played out in the party primaries, the President was busy fighting his own political battles back in Washington.

When Reagan had run for his third term four years ago, he had made a series of promises to the voters that he felt could be accomplished if backed by a solid Republican majority in Congress. Voters gave Reagan a GOP majority Congress in 1988, then provided him with a super majority at the 1990 midterm elections.

With partisan gridlock removed from the equation, it seemed that the President would at last be able to make good on the agenda he had been elected to implement.

On his list of campaign promises were some old issues (such as the line-item veto, which went back to his first term), along with many new proposals, spanning everything from tax policy to social issues. Then, in the sunset of his third term, Reagan presented an ambitious new set of goals and objectives. Some would pass Congress easily, while others would serve to inspire those wishing to continue the revolution once he had left office.

Thanks to the amazing success of Reaganomics, most proposals of a fiscal nature passed quickly, with few, if any changes. Congress agreed to further reduce taxes and regulations, make substantive adjustments to the code itself to close loopholes, support families, and generally simplify things.

While giving the President line-item veto had passed with little opposition, the chances of a Balanced Budget amendment did not appear good—especially during an election year.

With the line-item veto, the President is the "bad guy" who is empowered to go through Congress' budget and remove items usually inserted to benefit special interest groups—while sticking the country with the tab. Requiring a Balanced Budget however, shifts responsibility *back* to Congress, and therein lay the problem. Instead of passing the buck (or the allocation of it) to the President to red-pen, Congress would need to make its own hard choices—and then be subject to the consequences.

Reagan had been pushing for this amendment for years, and was especially disappointed by the lack of support from those in his own party who, although claiming to be fiscal conservatives, were unable to get their own house in order.

Not only was the economy healing at a record rate, but Reagan's proposal offered options for delayed implementation and for overrides. But even with these compromises, passage of the Balanced Budget amendment was stalled, and most certainly doomed if the Democrats gained power.

On a more encouraging front, significant welfare reform had passed with only minor tampering. With the economy booming, and unemployment hovering around 2%, the argument for indefinitely supporting those who simply refused to work became indefensible. Reagan's reforms maintained protections for those who were unable to work, while providing a timetable for able-bodied individuals to transition into the workforce. Programs supporting job training and assistance with childcare had been expanded, as were caveats related to penalties for illegal behavior while receiving public assistance.

Most importantly, Reagan's reforms returned accountability and solvency to the program.

Support for defense—or rather, defense *spending* was declining. With the end of the Cold War, and the demise of the USSR, many voters were beginning to question the military's tab, which accounted for a sizable chunk of the total US budget. Backing for SDI was especially unpopular, given the program's cost and no perceptible sign of results.

The President remained committed to the program. Reagan's support for SDI was based on highly classified information, that for reasons of national security, he was prohibited from making public. Unable to cite specifics, the President was forced to speak in broad terms, limited to phrases such as, "impressive breakthroughs," and "developing threats."

While no one dared contradict the President directly, many on the left implied that his advisers, and those with a stake in "Star Wars," were misleading him.

Those who disagreed with the program were free to reference "unnamed sources" and just blatantly lie, whereas "The Great Communicator" was left with a script so heavily censored as to be nearly useless. All he could do was ask that the American people continue to trust him, and have faith that he was only doing what needed to be done in order to keep America safe. No more, and no less.

Reagan stated that he would trim Pentagon spending as appropriate, and then followed through on his pledge with the budget he sent to Congress in February. Reductions were generally modest, and spread across a range of areas. But for the first time in years, actual defense spending would slightly decrease.

Although the President's cautious approach was backed by a consensus that spanned everyone from military analysts to economists, it was an increasingly unpopular position among the electorate, which felt that deeper and more immediate cuts were justified.

The President's request for a comprehensive system of national background checks for gun buyers had been rolled into a larger crime bill, and had passed both houses easily with support from law enforcement and the gun lobby. Despite a challenge from some critics, the measure did not restrict purchases by qualified buyers; instead it simply closed loopholes that were permitting criminals (including terrorists) and the mentally ill, to in some cases, travel five feet across state lines to make their purchases.

The bill was signed with much fanfare at a ceremony that included James Brady, Reagan's friend and Press Secretary who had been permanently disabled during the same 1981 assassination attempt that had almost killed the President. In the years since the attack (by a mentally ill drifter), the Bradys had become active in the anti-gun movement, and had hoped for stronger action by the President.

The bill was a compromise. It did not ban guns; only tightened access to those who should never have had them in the first place.

Reagan's proposed union reforms were not faring as well, given organized labor's considerable economic clout and lobbying power. Still, he had drafted a conservative template that if unsuccessful at the federal level, could be applied by the states.

Similarly doomed were any substantive reforms to Affirmative Action. Most GOP candidates were afraid to commit one way or another. In a pronounced break with the President, Kemp stated that he felt many provisions were still useful and needed for the immediate future.

Immigration reform was also stalled. Some saw it as too generous, others as too punitive.

Reagan agreed; noting that this was the nature of compromise — and this is how things worked if one expected to make progress. Bush, likely under pressure from donors in border states would not comment on the issue, but instead offered to present his own plan once elected. Dole and Danforth, representing states dependent on foreign workers supported Reagan's proposal, as did Kemp.

The biggest legislative failure concerned a constitutional amendment banning abortion.

While the American people were still polling as solidly pro-life, political support for "legislating morality" at the national level was steadily declining. Fearful of taking a stand that might cost them votes, Congress was choosing to punt; justifying the status quo in the name of states' rights.

Besides, if someone contested the law, it would eventually be decided by the Supreme Court, which Reagan had succeeded in reshaping into a solidly conservative, pro-life court.

Instead of picking up the fight and making it a defining issue (as Reagan had done), the party establishment, now "informed" by consultants and led by moderates (in anticipation of a Bush presidency), was backing away. In their view, it was better to have those justices (with lifetime appointments) take the heat for striking down Roe v Wade, than to have some Republican Congressman lose his seat in a swing district because he supported a complete constitutional ban.

Reagan was furious — and and heartbroken. Disgusted by the coward-ice of those who spoke about the sanctity of life, but when it came down to choosing to defend the lives of the unborn or to protect their own political lives, they chose self-preservation.

Determined, Reagan prayed for guidance and strength — and he received it. He would continue to advocate on behalf of this issue until his own dying day.

★ 104 ★

Something From Nothing

With the respective Democratic and Republican tickets officially established by the party conventions, the contest for the White House could now begin in earnest.

The Democrats had an early advantage going into the race, in that their convention had taken place in mid-July—nearly a month ahead of the Republicans. While it had been clear for some time that it would be Bill Clinton vs Jack Kemp, choices for their running mates—John Kerry and Connie Mack—had been genuine surprises.

The first Democratic attack ads began airing on August 22—the day after the GOP convention ended. In spots airing in swing states like Ohio and Pennsylvania, Kemp was criticized for embracing an "extremist right-wing ideology" that was "out of step with American values."

In other commercials, especially those targeting conservative districts and the Deep South, Kemp was presented as a flaming closet liberal, rehashing many of the themes Atwater and Crockett had developed for Bush.

Clinton's strategists appreciated that the Bush campaign had already succeeded to a certain degree in defining Kemp, and, with some tweaking, just ran with the script that had been provided for them.

While messages were tailored to different markets, the connecting theme was to discredit Kemp as an intellectual lightweight lacking the experience to lead.

Whereas Clinton was a graduate of Yale (as was his running mate John Kerry), Kemp had attended Occidental College—a small college in southern California that most people had never even heard of.

Like Reagan, Kemp was not the polished product of some posh Ivy League university; nor had he majored in law or political science—details that would be twisted by academic elitists to imply that his politics were informed more by ideology than education.

Never mind that Kemp was a voracious reader and a lifelong learner who had gone on to a post-graduate study of economics. For individuals with curiosity and discipline, self-education is not just possible, but a catalyst for independent thought.

Those who knew Jack Kemp regarded him as an original thinker and a genuine intellectual. But like the Scarecrow from *The Wizard of Oz*, he just didn't have the paper diploma to prove it.

As anxious as the Democrats were to dismiss him as having a head full of straw, they were wary of how such tactics might backfire as an attack on all those who still believed in an America where the common man, through hard work and discipline, might still rise to the top.

Kemp had grown up with few breaks, but he made the best of what he had been given. His was a classic American success story.

One of four boys, Jack French Kemp had been born and raised in Los Angeles. His mother Frances was fluent in Spanish, and had a Masters Degree from UC Berkeley, which she put to good use as a social worker and school administrator. Paul, the patriarch of the family, was a quiet man and a Navy veteran. An entrepreneur at heart, he had grown his one-person motorcycle messenger service into a small trucking company that now provided reliable living wage jobs for many in the community.

Committed to the principles of fairness and equality, Kemp hired, and worked alongside persons of many different races and backgrounds.

Realizing early the importance of education, the Kemp family had deliberately settled in the Melrose neighborhood — LA's predominantly Jewish section, where the public schools were ranked among the city's best. Although personally a Christian, 95% of Kemp's classmates were Jewish, including musician Herb Alpert, who would later go on to fame heading the chart-topping Latin music group The Tijuana Brass.

All through high school, the Kemp boys worked for their father and saved for college. In his spare time, Jack devoured books on history and philosophy — unusual choices for an adolescent, but early indicators of genuine intellectual curiosity and a commitment to self-education.

But any ribbing that the "four-eyed egghead" received from classmates was quickly overshadowed by his athletic prowess.

Gifted with natural talent, Kemp decided to focus on football, and soon became the star player of his high school team. The team mascot for Fairfax High School was the Lion, and Jack Kemp was the head of the pride.

While eligible to attend a more prominent regional school (such as USC or UCLA), Kemp's modest physical stature, (in addition to being near-sighted) would have likely restricted his playing for either the Trojans or the Bruins.

So instead, he looked to an arena where his odds were better, and found it at Occidental College, located in the nearby Los Angeles neighborhood of Eagle Rock.

His course of study would be Physical Education; a back up plan in case a pro career never materialized, or was cut short by injury; as this would allow him the option of teaching (and coaching) after his playing days had ended.

Being a private school, tuition was considerably higher than that of other public institutions, forcing him to make a number of sacrifices. On the plus side, Occidental was a founding member of the NCAA Division III Southern California Intercollegiate Athletic Conference, and used professional-style formations and plays.

This would be a major gamble, but Kemp was confident. He believed in his abilities and was willing to do whatever was needed to follow his dream of playing professional football.

"Oxy" it would be.

While there, he set a record for javelin throwing and led the nation's small colleges in passing, including one year in which he threw for more than a thousand yards.

Kemp had indeed made the right choice, and was drafted to play professionally right out of college.

Like Kemp, Reagan had also dreamed of playing professional football, and hoped his years at Eureka College might be the launch pad for a career in the big league—but the world had other plans. Similarly near-sighted, but not of the same athletic caliber, as one ended another began. Reagan set aside the football, picked up the microphone, and moved towards a career in broadcasting.

But, even as Kemp's professional sports career was unfolding (starting with the Pittsburgh Steelers), he still made time to serve in the Army reserve and continue on with his education. He also married his college sweetheart Joanne, and started a family.

As planned, playing pro football turned out to be his golden ticket. It paid well, and catapulted him into the national spotlight.

Sports also taught him invaluable lessons about teamwork and leadership. Most of Kemp's teammates came from similar lower and working class backgrounds, and many became lifetime friends.

Just as Reagan, (in the role of Screen Actors Guild president) had battled the big Hollywood studio heads on behalf of his fellow actors, Kemp took on the responsibility of representing his fellow players against the team owners and management. Many of the issues were discriminatory and race-based, with Kemp taking the side of minority players in opposition to established, and prevalent, segregationist policies that were common at the time.

Likeable, but tough, Kemp earned a reputation as a firm defender of the underdog, and one personally willing to stand and take a hit for doing what he believed was right.

When he left sports for politics, Kemp was able to take his advocacy on behalf of the less advantaged to a different arena—namely one where he could help shape policy on everything from education to civil rights and programs focused on empowerment.

As a conservative, he believed in creating opportunity—not dependency. In short, establish a society that provides the means for every citizen to rise to the best of her/his abilities and desires.

Or, as the Democrats spun it, throw everyone into a pit and let them fight it out. Survival of the fittest.Reliant on stereotypes, the Democrats would seek to brand Kemp as just another wealthy, out-of-touch Republican, unconcerned about the poor and the need for safety nets. In hopes of stirring up class warfare (a standard tactic), Kemp would be positioned as living a life of wealth and privilege, only seeking office in order to advance the interests of the super-rich.

On matters of race, the Democrats would be forced to tread a bit more lightly. They regarded the minority vote as something they *owned*, but if caught engaging in racist fear mongering, things could really blow up in their faces. Still, they were tempted, and would eventually (out of desperation) take the plunge in an attempt to alienate the more race-conscious and frightened fringe.

But at least initially, Democrats emphasized equally dishonest, albeit less dangerous themes, shrouded in language that would resonate with persons susceptible to the stereotype that all conservatives were greedy and uncaring. Voters were urged to look beyond his smile and the calls for unity: Kemp was just another heartless zealot intent on destroying the last protections for the nation's most defenseless citizens.

Heartless? A man who had fought cuts to Social Security, Medicare, food stamps, WIC, and Head Start? Who spoke of enterprise zones and defended welfare?

Hardly. As Kemp saw it, life was a lot like football. If you were injured or unable to play, there was still a place for you — and you'd be taken care of. But if you were up to it, you were expected to take the field, catch the ball that is thrown to you, and then go as far as you can.

The quarterback can help provide some opportunities, but the running back must also do his part — and that's called teamwork. People in different positions with different skills working together towards a common goal.

Although he had been warned, Kemp was still caught off guard by the lies and vitriol being hurled at him. Watching a commercial at campaign headquarters, the candidate turned to his wife Joanne and laughed it off, joking that they must be confusing him with "some other Jack Kemp — maybe the serial killer who was on the run after setting fire to an orphanage."

"*Shhhh* ..." she whispered, "don't give them any more ideas."

GOP strategists were not surprised.

Not since JFK's run in 1960, had the Democrats run on anything even remotely resembling a positive message. Kennedy's campaign radiated optimism and offered bold ideas.

It had also inspired another, younger, JFK — *Jack French Kemp* — to begin thinking about a career in politics once his football days ended. Rather than open a sports bar or become a real estate investor (as so many others did after retiring), Kemp decided that he would do something to give back. (Coincidentally, one of his first big campaign promises was to push for a tax cut matching what Kennedy had presented.)

The early 1960s were a different time for the Democrats, but that era ended with Kennedy himself. By the time Lyndon Johnson ran, it was back to the sewer, as exemplified by the infamous "Daisy" commercial.

The ad, which was used against Republican presidential candidate Barry Goldwater in the 1964 campaign, depicted a little girl counting down the petals on a daisy. When she reaches zero the screen goes black, only to be replaced by a shot of a nuclear bomb exploding, followed by a message urging voters to support Johnson because "The stakes are too high."

Johnson went on to beat Goldwater, and ever since, the Democrats had relied on exploiting fear and division. Although it hadn't worked against Reagan, it was pretty much all they had.

Hippocrates, the ancient Greek physician credited as the founder of modern medicine noted that, "Extreme remedies are appropriate for extreme diseases," or, in the translation preferred by the Democrats, "Desperate times call for desperate measures."

The campaign of 1992 would show just how desperate the Democrats had become.

105

Pennies From Heaven

Democrats and Republicans approach economics from different perspectives. Broadly speaking, Republicans are optimists, Democrats … well, not so much.

Republicans believe in tearing down barriers and empowering the individual, and view lower taxes and fewer regulations as the primary catalysts for growing the economy and creating opportunity. Republicans put their trust in the people, and in the basic laws of economics.

In contrast, Democrats favor high tax rates and lots of regulatory authority, backed by the wisdom and power of Big Government. When excessive taxes and regulations begin to smother the economy, they rely on the redistribution of wealth (via taxation) to pay for government assistance programs established to support the victims of their policies. If tax revenues are insufficient, they will turn to borrowing money and deficit spending.

Many liberals are genuinely compassionate people motivated by a desire to do good. All they ask in return is that one vote the Democratic ticket, and when times are tough, many will.

Unfortunately for the Democrats, in 1992 the American economy was booming—thanks in no small part to Kemp's theories and Reagan's championing of them into policy. The number of persons relying on government programs was in steep decline, and all economic indicators—including consumer confidence—were pointing up going into the election.

Making the argument that Reagan and the Republicans had ruined the economy, and that people needed government assistance would be a tough sell. So instead of relying upon facts to make their case, the Democrats would use emotional appeals.

Strategists recommended they begin with fear and uncertainty. If things sound too good to be true, they usually are.

A central component to this approach would be to disassociate Kemp from Reagan, and brand his policies as "Kempanomics," to imply something new, untested, irresponsible, dangerous—and cruel; as nothing more than a scheme to reward the rich and inflate the deficit—thus forcing draconian cuts in social programs.

"Jack Kemp is no Ronald Reagan. Kempanomics will bankrupt America ... and when the next Great Depression hits, you'll be on your own—all the social safety nets shredded to fund tax cuts for the super rich!"

Language controls thought.

Whenever possible, use words and hot-button terms like "extremist," "radical" and "out of touch" to describe Kemp and his fellow Republicans. Demand "a return to fairness," to insinuate that the rich were not paying their share in taxes.

After all, who could possibly be opposed to fairness? That's easy: *Extremist Jack Kemp, and his super rich Wall Street masters!*

While this "fairness" proposition did stir up some feelings of jealousy, the Democrats were grasping at straws. The great class war they were banking on never developed, and nearly every poll showed them trailing when voters were asked who they trusted to best manage the economy.

For most of the primary season, Democrats campaigned on familiar and tried-and-true party themes, drawing inspiration from the Seven Deadly Sins. They promised a restoration of programs for those not inclined to work (sloth), paid for by the rich (envy), and a pledge to go after those fat cats who were robbing the poor (wrath).

But Bill Clinton was a different type of Democrat. While he may have personally been driven by the sins of lust and pride, elections are about what the *people* wanted, and he was willing to bet that what they wanted was more.

Too much is never enough.

Of all the deadly sins, the only one written off was greed. To appeal to voter greed was something Republicans did—something denounced by self-righteous card-carrying Democrats. It was not to be embraced under any conditions.

The movie *Wall Street* was still fresh in the public's mind, with its signature line about greed being good, as delivered by the fictional villain Gordon Geckko, played by actor Michael Douglas.

The Democratic establishment was adamant: Greed was bad; it was a Republican trait. Using greed to attract voters was as wrong as baiting bears with donuts—and one must never stoop so low.

Denounce the Republicans as greedy, and for trying to exploit greed in voters with promises of lower taxes and so forth. It was wrong. We are Democrats—and we're better than that.

We are the party of Robin Hood! We will take and take and take from the rich, and give to the poor, until there aren't any more rich.

Then we'll …. Well, we'll cross that bridge when we come to it.

Privately, their candidate for president disagreed with this well-worn, and losing theme. He was, after all, a "New Democrat," and did not feel bound by the party's reliance on sacrifice and martyrdom—at least not if he wanted to win the election—which he did. Very much so.

Governor Clinton knew he had an uphill battle, and that would require some innovative thinking. Then one day he had an epiphany, in of all places, at the Presidential Suite of the Four Seasons Hotel in Seattle, Washington.

It was a balmy day in late July, and the candidate was in town for a morning rally and evening fundraiser. In the interim, he was able to meet with a young campaign supporter, eager to personally thank him for his progressive positions on women's reproductive issues.

The meeting went well, albeit rather quickly. After showering, Clinton, wrapped in a plush white robe and sandals looked out his tenth story window, enjoying the sweeping view of Puget Sound.

He turned on the radio, delighted to hear "Pennies From Heaven," one of his favorites by Stan Getz. Clinton, a player himself, loved good sax, and Getz was a true jazz master.

But before another song began, the announcer came on to remind listeners that no one else was playing music like this—and that if people wanted this kind of programming to continue, they needed to call and make a donation.

"It's time to show your support for your NPR station … Please call in and pledge now … We need to hear from you, otherwise, the programming you love—and depend on—might just go away. Volunteers are standing by, so please pledge whatever you can …" The voice was somewhat nasal; the overall tone pathetic and depressing.

The begging went on for several minutes, rehashing the same themes, until Clinton decided he'd heard enough. In just a few hours he'd be in a similar position, working a room full of donors for campaign contributions.

He hit the button for the next station, coming in on the tail end of one of the year's biggest hits, "Baby Got Back," by Sir Mix-A-Lot.

He loved that song, knew it well. Gyrating slowly, he sang along and thought about the video. The song ended with the unmistakable sound of a slot machine making a payout, the clatter of coins rapidly dropping to fill a metal tray. This lasted for just a moment though; interrupted by a high-energy deejay informing listeners that they were tuned in to Seattle's top-rated music station … The station that was giving away a thousand dollars an hour—every hour.

"Call now and win!"

Clinton looked for the phone, but in a rare moment of restraint he was able to resist temptation.

As the song "I'm Too Sexy" by Right Said Fred played out, the deejay cut to the phones and awarded a cool grand to some woman named Paula who couldn't stop crying and screaming, "Oh my God! Oh my God! Oh my God!"

Clinton thought she sounded like she was having an orgasm. Maybe she was.

This was Paula's favorite radio station. She listened to it all day, and would listen to it forever.

"Oh my God! Thank you, thank you, thank you."

No Paula, thank *you*. A smile spread across Clinton's face.

As the man who would be president watched the sun breaking through the clouds it all became clear. If Clinton wanted to be Number One, he needed to start giving away things—even if they weren't his to give.

But what? Kemp was already promising additional tax cuts.

The Man from Hope grabbed a sheet of hotel stationery and wrote down two words that would become the foundation of his campaign.

"Peace Dividend." Then, he drew a happy little cartoon face.

106

Shoot For the Moon

As a term, "Peace Dividend" was nothing new. In fact, it was originally conceived by the Sokolov regime as an incentive for Western nations to resign from NATO, and join Moscow's proposed European Union.

Why waste money preparing to fight your fellow Europeans? asked the Soviets, who then went on to answer their own question.

As the Cold War concluded, the term took on new relevance in Europe, and then spread to the United States.

During the Reagan years, a sizable portion of the US budget had been devoted to building up the military, and history had confirmed the wisdom of this policy.

But now, the old adversary was no more. The USSR had dissolved, and former member states were now committed to peaceful engagement and cooperation. Most of the old Soviet allies and client states were either gone, or in the process of collapsing.

In recognition of this reality, both sides of the American political spectrum began to talk about scaling down the defense budget.

President Reagan supported the idea, but urged prudence, preferring a graduated approach. The world remained a dangerous place, and defenses should be adjusted accordingly.

Kemp agreed. The President and his would-be successor were also in agreement about the economic ramifications, given that the bulk of the defense budget was used for personnel.

The GOP candidate's response was frank. "It took us a while to get to this point, and it will take us a while to get back. There will be a peace dividend, and it will be significant — but it will be gradual."

If you work hard, and you're a good boy ... *blah, blah, blah.* Maybe some day you'll get a little something ... *blah, blah, blah.*

This was Kemp's Achilles Heel.

Americans wanted instant gratification, and Clinton was just the man who would give it to them. This was his show. He was in it to win it.

Was it the deejay's concern as to where the money came from and how it would be paid out? Hell no — that was somebody else's problem.

The deejay was a performer, and this was a show. He did what he did best: he got some woman so worked up that she probably wet her pants. The reason this radio station was Number One was because it gave away something people understood and wanted, and it did it in the present tense.

Thank you Seattle!

It was truly Christmas in July, and from that moment forward, Clinton would position himself as Santa Claus.

But, as every child knows, Santa will only come if you have been good — and being good means voting for Bill Clinton and the Democrats.

The candidate began to brainstorm. In the past, Democrats had done well with big promises, from Kennedy's vision of a New Frontier to Johnson's Great Society.

Kennedy literally offered Americans the moon and they went for it; while LBJ convinced them a great society needed government programs to prove its greatness.

Santa turned the sheet of hotel stationery over and began to make a list. This would not be a list of who was naughty, and who was nice, but rather the presents he would promise to deliver.

Take that defense budget and dole it out. The wilder the better.

Topping the list was "CASH BACK." Model the program after what Alaska had done with refunding oil revenues, and send every adult ... *a thousand dollars!*

While Kemp talked tax cuts, these were expressed in percentages, forcing people to do math in their heads, to calculate a total with missing variables.

A thousand bucks was a clear round figure; sent as a direct check. This was something everybody understood.

ONE THOUSAND DOLLARS!!!

Oh my God! Oh my God! Oh my God!

Free college. Healthcare. Dental and optical.

Subsidized — no, FREE home repairs for seniors.

Increase their Social Security — they earned it. Plus, they actually turn out and vote.

Reparations for slavery? Too controversial. The black vote was a given.

Kemp was making inroads, but trying to get rid of the legacy of people like Jesse Helms would take time.

Reparations for housewives? Clinton smiled like the cat that had just eaten the canary. Why not? Housewives had been very good to him in the past.

Parks, green spaces, museums, libraries. No brainer.

Pay hikes for government employees. Ditto. This was a huge unionized workforce, and a raise would seal the deal. Would it be seen as a bribe? Trying to buy the vote?

Who cares?

Infrastructure — roads, bridges, mass transit. All good.

Schools — whatever they want. The Teachers Union was huge — and loaded with money. Time to tap that bank.

Free "healthy" school lunches? Hmmm … Get Hillary on this one.

Free bikes as an "investment" in healthy communities? Sounds legit.

What about a national buy-back plan to get older, gas-guzzling cars off the road by providing generous cash incentives and zero-percent loans? (The auto union will love this one.) Even though car sales were at their highest levels in decades thanks to the thriving economy, who didn't want a new car? Especially if Uncle Sam would help pay for it.

Clinton started to add "Increase Food Stamp/Welfare Payments" but then caught himself. These folks were already in his pocket, and advocating on their behalf offered no benefit; instead it only acknowledged the problem and aligned him too closely with the tired old Democratic Party of the past.

Although he would not admit it publicly, he actually supported many of Reagan's welfare reforms — and probably would have signed off on it himself if it had come about during his administration.

As governor he had dealt with similar frustrations over people who felt the world owed them a living; most of which were too lazy to even get off their asses and vote.

These people weren't worth the time of day.

It was getting late, and Clinton needed to get going — time to go beg. He would continue to add to the list, but felt he needed one more item while he was on a hot streak. Something dramatic … something *Kennedyesque*.

Why not restore some glory to the space program? No one cared

about the shuttle or the space station. It was time to revisit the moon …
To send a woman to the moon!

Promising to put a woman on the moon would be huge — bigger than
what Reagan had done with putting that hag on the Supreme Court.

Clinton smiled broadly. What if that woman was Hillary? That would
kill two birds with one stone.

While the cat's away, the mice will play.

Closing his eyes for just a moment, he inhaled the smell of his own
cologne and allowed an image of Mariah Carey wearing a Santa cap to
enter his mind.

Morning in America now meant Christmas in July.

As planned, the list was added to and adjusted regionally. Soon, the
Clinton/Kerry campaign was surging in the polls, and encouraging
everyday Americans to write in with their suggestions as to how they
wanted the dividend to be spent. (Or as Clinton pitched it, "invested in
America's future.")

Much of the candidate's rhetoric on the topic was inspired by nontra-
ditional sources, such as that of the credit card industry and others that
used flattery and deception to encourage irresponsible borrowing and
impulse spending.

*"You're smart — and you've earned it! You deserve it — now come claim
your share!!!"*

Almost immediately, the soundness and ethics of Clinton's plan was
called into question; criticized as dangerous, economically unfeasible,
and as nothing more than a cheap ploy to buy votes.

Clinton just laughed off the naysayers, whom he referred to as
"Chicken Littles," as his poll numbers continued to climb. He was
definitely on to something.

Come a certain age, most children figure out that Santa isn't real,
but they go along with the story out of fear that if they questioned it,
Christmas would be cancelled.

A similar sentiment was affecting voters; knowing that Clinton was
probably just some fat guy in a suit, but *hoping* he would deliver if they
played along and sat on his lap.

Ho, ho, ho. *Hope, hope, hope.*

In some ways, the people had already been primed for a miracle.

Thanks to President Reagan, the threat of nuclear Armageddon was gone. Most people had never lived a day without this horrible specter hanging over them, and the sense of relief and optimism was incalculable. Things seemed right in the world, for the first time in a long time.

American confidence was at record levels; it now seemed as if anything was possible.

At first the Democratic establishment was hesitant to jump on board Santa's sleigh. Amazingly, Clinton's grand giveaway was not denounced for being impractical, but for exploiting human weakness, specifically greed.

Shame on you Bill! Voters are like children, and you're abusing their trust and vulnerability. You're encouraging them to be bad and selfish!

Clinton appeared incredulous, then slowly shook his head. It was obvious that this criticism had hurt him deeply. He stuck his lower lip out, and it looked as if he might start to cry. Hillary gently patted his arm, and somehow, from deep within his soul, he found the strength to speak.

He understood the confusion, but the party bosses had it all wrong.

The Governor went on to eloquently explain that his was no radical break with protocol; instead, it was only building on the party's established tradition of solving society's problems with innovative government programs!

Nothing more than moving money from one account to another, borrowing a bit if needed.

This was not about greed, but *meeting the need*. Not everyone could afford a bike — much less send a woman to the moon.

And this, my friends, is what bold Democratic leadership looks like. It was time to build a bridge towards the 21st century.

The money bundlers and elders of the DNC nodded in unison. Bathed in moon glow, they had seen the light. With enough funding, any social problem could be fixed. Clinton was right.

With his troops behind him, it was time to conquer America.

The candidate smiled and returned to his campaign bus, now nicknamed "The Prize Patrol." It was time to take the show on the road.

107

The High Road

"Our goals for this nation must be nothing less than to double the size of our economy and bring prosperity and jobs, ownership and equality of opportunity to all Americans, especially those living in our nation's pockets of poverty."

— Jack Kemp

The Kemp/Mack campaign would be directed by veteran strategist Ed Rollins, and assisted by Stuart Spencer — the same team which had been with Kemp during his grueling, but ultimately victorious, primary run.

Both were well-established leaders in the field who had worked extensively with Ronald Reagan as well.

Born in Boston, Rollins was an Irish Catholic ex-boxer who had given up the ring for the rough-and-tumble game of politics. Originally a Democrat, he formally switched to the GOP after getting to know Reagan while working on Richard Nixon's 1972 re-election campaign.

The two remained friends, and Reagan had tapped Rollins to manage his last two presidential runs. Like Reagan, Rollins had been an early Kemp supporter, first working behind the scenes, then officially as his campaign director. During the primaries, Rollins had helped Kemp come from behind to win his party's nomination. Now he was tasked with helping him to win the White House. And once again, the polls were not in Kemp's favor.

Kemp made it clear that he wanted a clean fight, based on contrasting views of where each wanted to take the country as president.

As with Reagan's 1988 run, this campaign would be uplifting and focused on ideas. The candidate himself set the tone; stating, "Bill Clinton is my opponent—not my enemy." In particular, Kemp sought to avoid the "low hanging fruit" of personal attacks against Clinton's character and ethics.

"People already get that stuff from the supermarket tabloids," said Kemp. "Why waste time in the gutter when there are skyscrapers to build?"

While some in the party establishment questioned "the quarter-back's naiveté," there was no contesting that he had the moral integrity Americans expect of their president. Kemp believed in the rules of good conduct, of sportsmanship, and that character mattered.

When the Democrats punched below the belt Kemp simply ignored it. Each blow, each slash, each splash of mud only seemed to energize him and make him more determined.

Allegations ran from lurid to the ludicrous. After years of being booed and jeered on the football field by fans of the opposing team, Kemp had mastered the ability to tune it out and stay focused on what really mattered.

Despite their lack of success at luring him into the mud, the Democrats persisted with their attempts at character assassination. Having been spurned by the Kemp/Mack campaign, it was rumored that Bush's new pal "Sunny" Jim Crockett had flipped sides, and was now working on behalf of the Donkey Party.

Who else but a protégé of Atwater would launch a whisper campaign claiming that Kemp, during his days playing football, had fathered several children out of wedlock with African-American women?

The candidate just laughed off such allegations. "If this was true, how come none of these kids have turned pro?"

Kemp certainly had a point. Where there was no question concerning paternity, two of Kemp's sons were following in their father's footsteps. Son Jimmy was a starter at Wake Forest University, and was already being pursued by the scouts. Meanwhile, older brother Jeff was an established star in the NFL, having played for the Rams, the 49ers, the Seahawks and the Eagles.

Frustrated by Kemp's refusal to engage, some on the GOP's dark periphery couldn't resist cooking up some plans to help their boy should things start to go south. But with someone like Clinton, where do you even begin?

The Democrats were desperate to win, and Clinton had a reputation for ruthlessness. He was an aggressive, well-financed candidate, and his party's best hope in years to take back the White House as indicated by how the race had tightened.

For better or for worse, the party was 100% behind him. Many big name Democrats campaigned on Clinton's behalf, including all the usual suspects from the entertainment industry.

Things had been somewhat more difficult for Kemp. Once he became the official party nominee, Republicans rallied around him, but with varying degrees of intensity. Members of Kemp's backfield—the new generation of conservatives like Newt Gingrich, Trent Lott, Vin Weber, and Dan Lungren talked themselves hoarse stumping for him. Other, older moderates like Ford, Bush, and Dole were somewhat less enthusiastic.

Bush, in particular, had been a letdown, but perhaps that was to be expected given what happened in the primaries, and to his dreams of being America's 41st president. Bush officially endorsed Kemp, but made no personal appearances on his behalf. Instead, Kemp relied on other Texans, including Phil Gramm and Dick Armey, to help lasso the Lone Star state.

The real star power endorsement came from Ronald Reagan, who along with Mrs Reagan, campaigned fervently for the Kemp/Mack ticket whenever and wherever they could. The Reagans drew huge crowds at every stop, even in districts where Clinton was far ahead in the polls, and in large swing states like Ohio and Pennsylvania.

Although Reagan once had nightmares of appearing on stage with Pennsylvania Senator Arlen Specter as the nominee, the circumstances had changed, and the President actually seemed to enjoy himself at a rally in Philadelphia, teasing Specter about whom he was supporting.

"Kemp and Mack," shouted Specter, beaming, his fist raised high above his head.

Reagan turned to the audience. "Well, that's a relief! Every vote counts, and I was worried he might be backing that slick salesman from Arkansas!"

The crowd went wild. Reagan smiled, and Specter had no choice but to stand there grinning. He knew which side his bread was buttered on, and at this point, the only thing that mattered was being seen next to Reagan smiling, so as to get plenty of photos he could use in support of his own next political campaign.

At every event, the Great Communicator made an impassioned argument on behalf of his "conservative heir" Jack Kemp. He cited Kemp's work on the economy, his moral character, and his firm commitment to a defense strategy that had resulted in peace through strength.

"A man of his word, who fought with courage and dignity, who believes in the American people, and that like me, believes the best is yet to come."

As Kemp campaigned across America, the rallies were getting larger, and the audiences more diverse. Like Reagan before him, he was building a coalition of groups that had formerly backed the Democratic ticket. A coalition that was as rich as the nation itself, reflective of Kemp's vision to unify Americans and grow the GOP.

Building on the momentum he had created during the primaries, Kemp was attracting ever-larger numbers of minority voters anxious to check out his message. Most had never been to a rally for a Republican, and were surprised at how Kemp shattered the stereotypes being fed to them by the Democrats and their left-leaning friends in the media and entertainment industry.

For one thing, Kemp was not calling for the end to welfare and food stamps—a standard scare tactic used by Democrats. Instead, the Republican candidate factored these expenditures into the equation, as a "cost of doing business" during a period of transition. Kemp believed that as the economy grew, dependence upon these programs would decline naturally.

As Kemp was quick to point out, "Economic growth doesn't mean anything if it leaves people out. We must create opportunity—equal opportunity—for all Americans."

He did, however, support all the key provisions of Reagan's welfare reforms, including a time cap on benefits for able-bodied adults, when supported by job training programs. Rather than flood the economy with unskilled workers, Kemp preferred introducing them in waves, and across different segments of the economy.

Many turning out to hear Kemp's economic message had already benefitted considerably thanks to growth-oriented, Republican economic policies, as contrasted with years of just barely scraping by on the charity of Democrats.

But what really moved the ball was the man himself. Kemp spoke with passion about inclusiveness and his dream of having the GOP grow to reflect a changing America in both appearance and objectives.

In less formal gatherings (after speeches or in town hall meetings), he listened, and treated people with respect.

At every event, he ended by asking people to believe in themselves, concluding with a quote from one of his heroes, Abraham Lincoln — one of America's great *Republican* presidents:

"It is with your aid, as the people, that I think we shall be able to preserve — not the country, for the country will preserve itself, but the institutions of the country—those institutions which have made us free, intelligent and happy—the most free, the most intelligent, and the happiest people on the globe."

Then, as the applause died down, with a tone of genuine humility and respect, Kemp would ask for their votes. The events often went long into the night; and owing to the candidate's propensity to mingle and jump into crowds, were an absolute nightmare for his Secret Service detail.

Kemp had no worries, no fears. These were his people; he was their servant. He trusted them; they trusted him.

"We the People ..." meant everyone. Everyone was welcome — and needed — in the ongoing quest to form a more perfect union.

Like his mentor, Jack Kemp had become a Great Communicator in his own right, connecting with people of all kinds in a way that made them feel he was a friend who had their best interests at heart.

Because he did.

108

The Debates

Clinton and Kemp would debate twice, and in between, their running mates would brawl just once. The first of the two presidential debates was scheduled for October 11, in St Louis, sponsored by the Commission on Presidential Debates—a private organization that had taken over from the League of Women Voters.

Coming roughly six weeks after the GOP convention, most national polls showed the two candidates in a dead heat, with the trend favoring Clinton, especially among undecided voters.

The Democratic establishment had done a good job of positioning Kemp, and were looking to the "Rumble in Saint Louie" to reinforce their messaging.

Clinton was known to be an excellent debater; Kemp, much less so.

Vegas odds makers lined up behind the Yale-educated lawyer. At best, it was hoped that Kemp would be able to hold his own and not do anything disastrous.

On the night of the event, a new poll showed Kemp now trailing Clinton by four points. It was a tough spot to be in. On one side, no one expected him to do very well. On the other, there was even more pressure to win now that he was falling behind.

Given that there had been no debates in 1988, and voters were being asked to choose Reagan's successor, anticipation and viewership was at record levels for the Sunday evening broadcast.

At first glance, Clinton presented better. Down to "fighting weight," with a head of dark hair and a face yet to be lined by responsibility, the Boy Governor projected youth and vitality. Kemp was 11 years older, his hair mostly gray. Clinton knew how to smile with his eyes, while Kemp's were obscured by the bright studio lights reflecting off his glasses.

Clinton felt at home on the stage and radiated confidence. He used the event to enhance his image as Santa, and treated what was supposed to be a serious forum addressing the nation's future like a TV game show.

And the people loved it!

Emboldened, Clinton played to the audience, going so far as to encourage applause and even take a bow.

Santa was on a roll, but moderator Jim Lehrer was not amused. Clinton ignored questions that didn't interest him, repeatedly interrupted, and talked past his allotted time. Increasingly frustrated, Lehrer could do little to contain the exuberant "bad boy."

To be fair, the Arkansas governor gave an amazing performance, never once breaking character. He was an "outsider" who had "listened to everyday Americans" and was ready to restore "fairness" to government.

Then, as his *pièce de résistance,* Clinton offered Americans the moon — literally. Channeling a mix of JFK and the opening monologue from *STAR TREK*, he spoke of returning to the moon, and beyond. It was time to lead the world again! It was time to recapture America's pioneering spirit, and send a woman to the moon within five years!

But wait, *there's more* ...

Oozing southern charm, Clinton was all smiles, nods, and winks: the fun uncle who was willing to give you the toys your parents wouldn't.

Kemp's genuine enthusiasm and optimism seemed pale when pitted against the jolly "man from Hope."

While Clinton focused on winning hearts, Kemp had been directed by his advisers to win minds: Shake off the image of being a dumb jock, and show that you understand math and can read a pie chart. Wear glasses — not contact lenses. Glasses make you look smarter. Try to appear less effervescent, and more "presidential."

Do this, but don't do that. Oh, and don't forget to bring up ...

So the Quarterback diligently followed the committee-approved game plan. He stuck to facts and figures, making a solid case for the continuation and expansion of responsible, and proven, economic policies. Like Reagan, he supported a strong defense (including SDI), but also backed the idea of responsibly downsizing the budget as the US transitioned away from wartime and a post-Soviet world.

He provided exact numbers and concise explanations. Details, equations, facts.

After one especially dry monologue Clinton just mugged the camera and smiled. Rather than refute the math, he decided to play the exchange for laughs.

"They say the Devil is in the details — and apparently so is Jack Kemp.

Better be careful when doing a deal with the Devil."

The audience roared with laughter, while Kemp stood stiffly holding the sides of the podium waiting for it to abate. As Lehrer attempted to restore order, Kemp stared straight ahead, his flushed red face suggesting a mixture of anger and embarrassment. This would be the shot that most newspapers would run the next day, while Clinton was depicted as looking friendly, approachable, and with just a slight, welcoming smile.

Technically Kemp won the debate, but lost in the public opinion polls, which awarded the supercharged Clinton top marks for "energy, enthusiasm, boldness of vision, and likability."

Clinton had told the people exactly what they wanted to hear, and the Democrats got an immediate boost in the polls, especially with younger voters and women.

All eyes next turned to the vice presidential debate, scheduled for just two nights later in Atlanta. Would Connie Mack be able to hit the reset button, or would he stumble down the same path as Kemp?

Again, the odds were not in his favor. Although he had been practicing, the University of Florida Business School graduate was deemed no match for the former star of the Yale debate team.

Supporters braced for the worst.

Much to everyone's surprise, Mack came out swinging, and quickly turned the tables on the Democrats by directly addressing what the GOP had already delivered on, while Kerry grimly continued to hammer on a "bloated" defense budget that continued to "enrich über-wealthy Republican donors."

The contest was seen as a draw, and did not attract anywhere near the audience that the Clinton-Kemp debate had garnered. It was, however, an opportunity for most Americans to view the vice presidential choices in action. For viewers, Mack won points for sincerity and passion, while Kerry was dinged for lacking Clinton's smooth salesmanship. Mack also did much better with two other critical voter blocks: women and veterans.

Women, because the debate allowed a forum for Mack to address his work on behalf of healthcare issues, and specifically those in support of children.

And veterans? Although Mack hadn't served in uniform like Kerry, at least he never threw his medals on the ground in disgust — and apparently that still meant something to a lot of people in America.

Adding to this, was a zinger from Mack, who asked why, if Kerry was indeed so opposed to the war and "bloated military budgets," had he continued to draw a commission for being in the navy reserves until 1978 — eight years after he left active duty, and three years after the war had ended.

The rubber-faced Kerry, obviously not expecting this, stared ahead like a deer in the headlights, then sputtered off something about "deserving it," before attempting to move the subject on to Iran-Contra, and what his committee had uncovered all those years ago.

Paraded as a warrior who had seen the light, Kerry's image as a war hero was now under suspicion. Although he had been honorably discharged, many felt his post-service activist behavior was dishonor-able, if not treasonous.

The second, and final presidential debate was scheduled for Monday, October 19 in East Lansing, Michigan.

Michigan was a state where Kemp had played football for the Detroit Lions, and where his primary campaign had really turned around. With the election just two weeks away, this would be his last chance to change public perception and save his faltering campaign.

Pressure was on Kemp to go negative and hit hard. He was urged to confront Clinton's character issues, and challenge his budget proposals as dangerous, dishonest fantasies. It was time to out Clinton for what he was: a smooth-talking con man who could not be trusted.

If you couldn't trust Bill Clinton with your teenaged daughter, how could you trust him as your President?

All the party heavyweights were calling with advice on how to "save" the campaign. Nixon congratulated Kemp on the first debate, and for shaking off the dumb jock image, but said it was now time to take off the gloves and "go for the jugular." Ford reminded him, "nice guys finish last." Even Bob Dole checked in, demanding "the quarterback to get off the bench and into the game."

The problem with Kemp was that he was stubborn, and often tended to do the exact opposite of what others told him to do.

The President understood his protégé's independent streak, and how important it was to stay true to one's own self. All during his political career Reagan had also been told "do this" or "don't do that," and in some cases he took the advice—but in others he did not. Reagan, like Kemp, would respectfully listen, but in the end, always made his own decisions.

One classic example of Reagan's independence involved his 1986 visit to Germany. For the occasion, Reagan had personally written a speech that included a line designed to provoke the Soviets. Disregarding the warnings, the President stood in the shadow of the Berlin Wall, and courageously called upon Gorbachev to "Tear down this wall!"

Reagan's defiant cry for freedom became one of the defining moments of his presidency—and of the 20th century.

Like Kemp, Reagan made snap decisions, and could be unpredictable in other ways when it came to speaking his mind.

Nor was Reagan afraid to use humor to cut through a challenging situation. When confronted about matters of age and competency in his second debate with Walter Mondale, Reagan turned the tables by joking that he would not make an issue of Mondale's youth and inexperience.

No one expected it. But it worked.

That is the difference between leaders and followers, and Kemp was not a follower. Never was, and wasn't about to start.

No one knew what the Democrats were planning for round two, so Kemp would just have to trust his instincts and respond accordingly. Jack be nimble, Jack be quick.

The debate began with Clinton getting to speak first. Sensing weakness from their first encounter, this would be his chance to finish Kemp off. He was ready.

But unlike the jolly ol' St Nick of the first debate, viewers now saw another side of Clinton; one intended to showcase his fiery passion and toughness.

For the rematch, the Governor came out punching. Intense and aggressive, Clinton launched into a vicious personal attack on Kemp as cold and uncaring, willing to throw America's most defenseless—women, children, seniors, and minorities—under the bus.

Kemp paused, his hands affixed to the podium, his eyes looking at his notes. The Republican candidate slowly shook his head, then began to speak.

"If that's who you think I am, then Governor, you don't know Jack."

There was a moment of silence, then a gasp, then laughter that gave way to a wave of applause and cheering that went beyond the auditorium and out across America.

Kemp then began to speak, rebutting Clinton's falsehoods with facts. Intertwining his own rags-to-riches story, the candidate offered a vision of America based on fairness, opportunity, and unity. He spoke of liberty, equality, and compassion.

It was a rousing speech, and a quick cut to the audience showed many in the auditorium wiping their eyes, visibly moved by the power of Kemp's words and passion.

He had just thrown an incredible 90-yard pass and won the game.

This was the Jack Kemp that America had been waiting for—and he delivered beyond anyone's expectations.

Clinton never recovered. He had been critically wounded; shot by his own gun. Whatever goodwill and trust he had developed was gone.

Even diehard supporters were rattled by his Jekyll to Hyde transformation. Mr Sunshine had gone behind a dark cloud, and was now denounced as phony, dishonest, and dangerously unpredictable.

The word on everyone's lips was "untrustworthy."

Clinton scrambled to reboot, but the damage was done. As his poll numbers dropped, he pulled his party down with him.

Jack jumped over the candlestick, and on November 3, 1992, went on to win the election taking 44 states, plus the District of Columbia.

While it was not the landslide Reagan had enjoyed in his last run, it was a clear mandate from the American people. They were sold on Kemp's ideas, and on Kemp as a person worthy of becoming president.

Before Clinton called to concede, Reagan himself phoned to congratulate his successor, noting that in his first run in 1980, he had also won by "just" 44 states—and that Carter had taken DC.

The difference this time around was DC's black vote; 75% of which went for Kemp.

109

Libya

"Whatever I wear becomes a fad. I wear a certain shirt and suddenly everyone is wearing it."

— Muammar Qaddafi

Libya, or more specifically, its criminal leader Muammar Qaddafi, had been a thorn in Reagan's side since Day One of his presidency. Although things had definitely escalated under Reagan, Qaddafi had been an irritant for every administration since he first seized power during a military coup in 1969.

Although Reagan had accomplished so much in office, passing down the Qaddafi problem to the next president was a source of frustration, but he had few legal options available.

Unlike other Soviet satellite states like Cuba and North Korea, oil-rich Libya had never been financially dependent on Moscow for child support. It had, however, relied on the Soviets for weapons, training, and intelligence — which it had put to good use; attacking its neighbors, sponsoring terrorism, and engaging in a range of provocations from minor, to all-out military confrontations with the United States.

Over the years, the majority Muslim state had spent huge sums on building up its military, and turning it into a force to be reckoned with. Libya's self-proclaimed Brotherly Leader and Guide of the Revolution regarded the nation's forces as an extension of himself; a tool to advance twisted personal fantasies of power and conquest.

Qaddafi relished the international spotlight: parades and grandiose displays of power were a regular occurrence. Decked out in full uniform, the Colonel used the military to affirm his vision of self as a great and powerful leader for the ages.

He also understood that without such force, his regime was doomed.

Although unsure whether his end would come from the outside, or be administered by his own people, Qaddafi knew it would not be pleasant. Attempting to maintain power with nothing more than a few bands of whip-wielding loyalists on camels was not a solid backup plan. No, he must not let it get to that point. If the end was indeed coming, he would choose to go out in a blaze of glory, a hero, a martyr for the struggle — and not someone like that naive narcissist Ceaușescu.

So, as the USSR was collapsing, the Colonel set out on a shopping spree to stock his war pantry. He recruited (or possibly kidnapped) a number of Soviet scientists and others loyal to the Sokolov regime, and soon amassed an impressive stockpile of weapons from the black market.

The world around him was changing, and Qaddafi was feeling the need to double down on his dream. He believed that history had chosen him to lead the start of a new world order. He must fire the first shot; the shot that would be heard around the world.

His would be the spark that would ignite a new golden age: The Age of Qaddafi! Just as Libya's oil fueled the world, Qaddafi's ideas would fuel humanity for all time.

Suddenly it all became clear. He was a modern prophet. He had seen the future, and it would begin with a holy war.

He would be suppressed no longer! Yes. He had seen the light! The dawn of a new day; the flash of the bomb.

Soon, all of the Islamic world would celebrate the Prophet Muammar Qaddafi! His birthplace near Sirte would become a holy shrine; Tripoli a destination for pilgrims and scholars!

According to US intelligence, the Colonel was starting to experience a serious "in the bunker" meltdown. Delusional, highly agitated, and paranoid. Not a good mix.

Libya was capable of causing some real damage, and Reagan sensed that Qaddafi would rather die a martyr by making one last lunge for infamy, than slowly wind down to his place alongside Idi Amin in the old despot's hall of fame.

"Prophet Muammar" was a ticking time bomb.

By mid-September things really started to unravel. It began with Qaddafi denouncing Iraq's occupation of Kuwait, which he blamed as undercutting the price Libya had been receiving for oil.

In retaliation, he issued a formal threat against Iraq, and his intention to topple Saddam's regime by force, and make the nation the first addition in a pan-Islamic state — that he would lead.

In a call for global jihad, the world's newest prophet summoned his Muslim brothers to rise up and heed God's will. The invitation failed to catch beyond the Colonel's immediate circle, which saluted its boldness, brilliance, and modesty for at least partially crediting God with the plan.

Whatever friends Qaddafi once had were now abandoning him in droves. Thanks to his flamboyant generosity, he still had a few supporters on the continent. However, most Muslims were deeply offended by his self-declaration of prophethood, which they regarded as blasphemous and an insult to Muhammad.

While the Saudis were not happy with Iraq's occupation of Kuwait, Saddam had indeed stopped at the border and had made no further menacing gestures. In fact, relations had warmed between the two nations. Iraq's president was a gangster, but one the Saudis could do business with. Stability was good. And besides, they appreciated the fact that Saddam was sticking it to both home-grown extremists *and* the Iranians.

As they say, "My enemy's enemy is my friend," and in the Mid East, that's often as good as it gets. When the Saudis politely declined the mad Libyan's overtures to join him in toppling Iraq, Qaddafi turned on them. The Saudi royal family was denounced as "America's dogs," who must be slaughtered so that Mecca might be liberated for "true" Muslims.

With his worldwide Islamic revolution temporarily on hold, Colonel Cuckoo next turned his attention to neighboring Egypt. He vilified the Mubarak regime as Zionist puppets, and called for the destruction of the Suez Canal.

When word began to circulate about plans to rebuild the Great Sphinx of Giza adorned with a likeness of Qaddafi, it seemed absurd enough to be true.

Privately, the nations of the region began meeting to draw up their own set of plans, although these would be focused on more practical and pressing matters, beginning with regime change in Libya. Things seemed to be imploding at an accelerating rate, as Libyan pilots defected (taking their planes with them), and insiders described mass executions of those the former goat herder-turned-prophet suspected of plotting against him.

As September gave way to October, Qaddafi continued to issue bellicose new threats, but seemed to be doing little militarily, until one day when it became clear that the Libyans were positioning missiles in preparation for a strike.

Despite his recent tirades of anti-Arab rhetoric, it was always understood that Qaddafi's number one target was Israel. He hated Jews, and he hated the Jewish state. He also hated Reagan, whom he referred to as "the King Jew" or "the Jew's slave" depending on time of day and/or temperament.

Publicly, Reagan laughed off the madman's words, reminding him that there had only been one "King of the Jews," and that was the Lord Jesus Christ.

Qaddafi was furious with Reagan, and with US support for Israel. Nothing would make him happier than to destroy the Jewish state while Reagan was president. But time was running out.

Yes, there would likely be consequences, possibly fatal. But here was his chance to go out with a bang, not a whimper. A hero for the Islamic world! His name would live for ten thousand years — at least. Maybe more.

The US had long prepared for such an attack, and when it was clear that Qaddafi was serious this time, things went into overdrive. Working collaboratively, the Americans and the Israelis coordinated defenses, including the activation of a sophisticated new missile defense system.

The Libyan missiles were SCUDS, a category of tactical ballistic missiles that had been supplied by the Soviet Union. Especially ironic was the fact that the design of the SCUD was derived from the V-2 rockets developed by Nazi Germany. When the war ended, the Soviets, with the forced assistance of German scientists, created the SCUD, which the Russians recklessly distributed all over the world without thought to how they might one day be used.

According to a high-ranking Libyan defector, that day would be October sixth — the start of Yom Kippur. On the sacred Day of Atonement, Qaddafi planned to wipe Israel off the map with Nazi missiles.

With all defenses in place, Reagan made a point of displaying

American power by increasing the US military presence in the area. Analysts were puzzled by certain aspects of the buildup however, and throughout the impending crisis Reagan seemed cool and collected, dividing his time between many high-level meetings with representatives of the military and the state department.

What did Reagan know that others didn't?

In accordance with the warnings, Libya launched a barrage of missiles towards Israel just as the sun was setting and Yom Kippur was beginning in the Holy Land.

Although it was late evening in Washington, the President had insisted on staying up late to monitor events in real time. From the White House Situation Room, Reagan watched calmly as the fireworks show over Libya began. Surprisingly, while on high-alert, no US planes were dispatched to hit any of the launch sites.

The skies over Israel remained calm, with no missiles ever leaving Libyan air space. Instead, every last SCUD failed at some point fairly soon after launching, exploding into fiery chunks that dropped back to Earth.

Qaddafi's dream of destroying Israel had literally come falling down upon his own head.

But how had this happened? The failure of the Libyan missiles seemed incredibly suspicious. Had there been mass sabotage, or had this been a test of SDI?

The White House declined to comment.

Despite it having been a late night, the President was awake at the usual time the next morning, and looking forward to updates on Libya—but unprepared for the news he was about to receive.

Although it was yet to be confirmed, the US had received reports that Qaddafi was dead. Details were sketchy and contradictory: some said he had died in an explosion related to a coup, others said a missile had malfunctioned.

By midday it was confirmed that Qaddafi had been killed at a launch site by falling missile debris. Ironically, the Colonel who had been at the site to personally initiate the death of Israel had been among the first to perish.

News of the Brotherly Leader's death spread quickly, and true to his vision of immortality, there was no succession plan in place. This created an immediate power vacuum, as three major factions battled for control, one of which was being led by the head of the army. The second was fronted by one of Qaddafi's young sons, now dressed in one of his father's old uniforms. Rounding things out was "God's Army," led by a crazed one-eyed cleric seeking to establish a fundamentalist Islamic state based on Sharia Law.

While it was good news that Colonel Qaddafi was history, none of his would-be successors seemed much better, and the Libyan people were paying the price for it as their country promptly descended into a bloody civil war.

All three leaders were adamant that the other two must be destroyed. In the turmoil that ensued, rebel factions fought for control of cities and government buildings, and it was often difficult, if not impossible, to know who was in charge. Oftentimes it was no one.

Schools and hospitals were gutted and shuttered, as were most commercial businesses. Traffic, other than military convoys, disappeared almost immediately. Everything seemed to be shot full of holes, burning, collapsing.

With no police, fire fighters, and only limited government services in place, looting, arson, rape, and murder became widespread. Despite its incredible energy reserves, the power grid had been destroyed, plunging most of the nation into darkness. Even municipal water plants were being targeted and destroyed with irrational fury.

The Libyan people had no recourse but to stay locked up in their homes, and pray for deliverance.

International calls for a cease-fire fell on deaf ears, and after two weeks, President Reagan was forced to give the order authorizing US forces to occupy and stabilize the country. While the Americans did receive some assistance and support from its allies (namely the British), the urgency of the situation had not provided enough time to create a genuine coalition.

Reagan had no choice: this was a rescue operation. The carnage and destruction had to be stopped.

Fortunately, the large US presence in the area provided the force that was needed to take control of the situation. American planes made quick work of what had once been an impressive military, now fractured and focused on attacking competing divisions in a mad struggle for control. Under direct orders from the President, US forces were given the authority to neutralize as much of Libya's arsenal as possible — whether in use by rebel forces or sitting forgotten at some abandoned base in the desert.

Some of the fiercest battles took place in urban settings, where US troops were often forced to confront everything from well-armed criminal gangs, to suicidal religious fanatics hell-bent on jihad.

Under Reagan's defense buildup, US troops had been highly trained for these kinds of scenarios, and in the end, the Americans prevailed.

Hit with overwhelming force and tactical superiority, the country was quickly brought under control and stabilized. Basic services were restored, and the streets were once again safe to walk thanks to the Americans. The Libyan people welcomed their liberators, and begged the troops to remain.

But the Reagan administration was intent on making the US stay a short one — and had made this clear from the outset. The Americans were there to respond to an emergency, and had no plans to take on the responsibility of occupying the nation until it could stand on its own.

Like the President, both the military and state department had been cautious about entering into a situation in Libya without a clear exit strategy, and so before the first US marines hit the shores of Tripoli, a plan was in place for their departure.

The plan would unfold in stages: First, the US would turn over responsibility for the occupation to NATO, with operations to be headed by the British and the Italians. For most of the century, Libya had either been an Italian colony or occupied by the British, and with the end of fighting and tensions in Europe, both nations now had adequate resources that could be deployed to North Africa. A small number of Americans would stay on as well, although these would be in support of the NATO mission only — and not in a direct, supervisory capacity.

Meanwhile, plans were in development for NATO to begin transferring authority to the Arab League, which would then be responsible for helping to establish a new government, and oversee Libya's return to the community of peaceful nations.

Founded towards the end of the Second World War, the Arab League was a political organization headquartered in Cairo, Egypt. It represented all the major Arabic states across the Middle East and North

Africa, and although it had no direct military power, it would be able to influence the governments of its member states to provide support for an emergency mission like Libya.

With the end of the Qaddafi regime, Libya needed outside help first to establish social stability, then to assist with a political transformation. Secretary Schultz and the state department believed that this was a task best left to other Arab nations, given common interests, traditions, culture, and basic issues of identity. Attempting to impose a western-style democracy was simply not viewed as practical. Instead, a better solution — and one most likely to be embraced by the Libyan people — should come from a fellow moderate state like Jordan.

The current head of the Arab League was Ahmed Asmat Abdel-Meguid, who also served as Egypt's Foreign Minister. He supported the US plan, and took the lead (initially with Egyptian troops), relieving NATO forces of the day-to-day responsibility of managing Libya. Egypt was a good choice in that it had a large military, a shared border, and above all, was a fellow Arabic nation with an interest in seeing a non-aggressive Libya as its neighbor. To the west, the nations of Tunisia and Algeria also had vested interests in Libya's transition from bully to peaceful ally.

The transformation would take some time to complete, and not be fully resolved until almost two years after Reagan left office. But as his term wound to a close, the President was relieved to know that Qaddafi was gone, and Libya was no longer a threat.

Politically, Libya would become a constitutional monarchy (similar to Jordan), welcoming back a descendent of King Idris, whom Qaddafi had ousted during the 1969 coup. The Libyan military would be purged of Qaddafi loyalists, and scaled back to a defensive force only, in line with levels that no longer posed either a regional threat, or cause for international concern.

Members of the former regime and agents of the state security forces were tried, and many were executed — including Qaddafi's son Mutassim, along with other members of the Colonel's large and extended family.

Considerable amounts of money found hidden in foreign banks was uncovered and returned to the state treasury. A plan for making reparations to nations and individuals harmed by the Qaddafi regime was quickly and unanimously approved by the new Libyan parliament.

The new King formally apologized to the world for the harm his nation had caused and asked for forgiveness. He also personally apologized to the Jewish people, announcing that Libya would recognize Israel's right to exist, and that Tripoli would pursue full diplomatic relations with its former adversary.

Constitutionally rejecting Qaddafi's imposed socialism, Libya became a free-market economy, applying its oil wealth to the benefit of its people, and existing once more as a peaceful and law-abiding member in the world community of nations.

110

A New Spirit

"A people free to choose will always choose peace."

— Ronald Reagan

The world was at peace.

The Cold War was over, and the Soviet Union was no more. Just as Reagan had prophesized a decade earlier, all across the globe freedom and democracy were leaving Marxism and Leninism to the ash heap of history.

Gorbachev was now the elected Prime Minister of Russia, and personally overseeing his nation's transformation into a vibrant, free-market based democracy. Russia's transition from communism to capitalism had, with western help, gone relatively smoothly, and the resource-rich nation was fast on its way to becoming an economic powerhouse.

Similar success stories were the norm all across the former nations of the USSR, as each, now free from totalitarianism, underwent a renaissance few ever dreamed possible. The fact that the collapse had happened so quickly, and with so little bloodshed, created a sense of euphoria felt around the world.

Owing to a series of tough treaties, the two former adversaries had walked the world back from the precipice of a nuclear holocaust. The future was now about genuine peace and cooperation, with plans under development to integrate Warsaw Pact members into an expanded version of NATO.

East and West Germany had officially reunited in January, and were able to send a unified national team to the Olympics for the first time in decades. This year's winter games were held in France, which in March had elected a conservative center-right government—its first in many years.

All across Europe, borders between east and west had come down, allowing for people, ideas, and goods to move freely across frontiers once blockaded by troops and tanks. Even the Berlin Wall had been reduced to rubble, sold off in chunks as souvenirs, until authorities stepped in to preserve portions as a reminder of what totalitarianism was about.

Without backing by the Soviets, threats to Israel had dropped precipitously. The Jewish state was at peace; enjoying new levels of security and prosperity.

Proxy wars were now a thing of the past, and the region was relatively stable. Iran remained a concern, but in response to a revitalized Iraq, it was now focused on defense—and self-preservation.

Inspired by democratic uprisings elsewhere, the Iranian people were growing increasingly rebellious, and once again there was talk of revolution in the air. In particular, the nation's burgeoning youth population was pushing for the return of a secular state that respected individual rights, treated women with equality, and was not constantly mired in conflict.

Iran had few friends, and lots of enemies. With threats foreign and domestic, Tehran simply did not have the resources to export terrorism and instability. Most experts gave the Islamic Republic three to five years at best.

The fuse had been lit and was burning down quickly.

Peace had also come to El Salvador in January, when, perhaps acknowledging the inevitable, Marxist rebels gave up the fight and accepted the government's terms of surrender. The Chapultepec Peace Accords, signed in Mexico City, brought a formal end to the country's bloody 12-year civil war that had resulted in at least 75,000 deaths.

The cutoff of money from Moscow left Cuba reeling on the ropes. Unable to even feed itself, Cubans were risking all for the promise of freedom and a better life elsewhere. Many found refuge in the United States, their journey assisted by everyone from the US Coast Guard and Navy, to sport fishermen.

President Castro was rarely seen in public. Insulated from the failures of socialism, he had been giving a speech celebrating Cuban independence when the mood of the crowd began to turn ugly. Castro tried to shout down the protestors, but this only increased their agitation. As the angry mob pushed closer to the stage, Castro calculated his odds, and decided it was time to flee with his life.

When there was a public appearance, no one was sure if it was really Castro or one of his many body doubles. In any event, throngs of well-armed security personnel always surrounded the individual in question. Crowds were kept small, and at a safe distance.

Apparently, this was the best plan Castro had at his disposal.

Fearing anarchy (and a mass exodus) if the government collapsed, the US was prepared to intervene and provide stability until the island nation was able to restore order and provide for its roughly ten million citizens.

Although much less volatile than Libya, any collapse at the national level would be problematic. Castro, like Qaddafi, remained stubborn and defiant; willing to take the nation down with him rather than admit failure.

It wouldn't take much more than a mild tropical storm to topple the red banners in Havana, and hurricane season was only a few months away.

Since gaining independence from Portugal in 1975, Angola had been ruled by the MPLA (People's Movement for the Liberation of Angola). But without aid from Cuba, the Marxist regime collapsed in upon itself, only to reemerge as a capitalist social democracy.

North Korea, a similar basket case without its Soviet sugar daddy was already cozying up to China. Although decimated by war and famine, Pyongyang clung to its ideal of being a socialist paradise, but acknowledged the need for some temporary assistance from Beijing.

In time, the PRC would attempt to wean the Koreans from their dependency. But for now it made more sense to prop up the broken regime, than to risk having millions of refugees spill into China, or to have it reunite with the prosperous south, which would position another US ally on its backdoor.

Ironically, even the Chinese had edged closer to free-market capitalism, when in October, the Communist Party went so far as to promote several outspoken reformers to the Politburo Standing Committee. Although politically China remained an authoritarian state, the economic transformation led to greater cooperation with other countries, and in particular, the United States.

As trade increased between the two nations, so did cooperation in other areas, and with it a reduction in tensions and the likelihood of a military confrontation. China still had a long way to go, but for now, it was at least marching in the right direction.

Yes, there were still many problem spots, but none to the degree that threatened global security or seemed a candidate to spark another world war.

Instead, the grand trend was arcing to a path of peaceful coexistence; to democracy and freedom, to justice, to liberty, and prosperity — all thanks to the courage of one man.

Following the Soviet coup the world worried that this man, a renowned anti-communist, would destroy all life on the planet rather than accept the triumph of socialism.

But instead, the three-term American president did just the opposite. He did not start a hot war, but by standing firm, ended a cold one. His vision of a new world had come true, and for this, Ronald Wilson Reagan was awarded the 1992 Nobel Peace Prize.

111

The Season of Miracles

It came upon the midnight clear,
That glorious song of old,
From angels bending near the earth,
To touch their harps of gold:
Peace on the earth, goodwill to men.

While Christmas was much more relaxed than it had been in recent years, there was also a sense of melancholy and nostalgia, as this would be the last spent by the Reagans as residents of 1600 Pennsylvania Avenue.

This year's festivities had been especially poignant, as they had been joined by many dear friends and family, including their daughter Patti. Now 40 and recently divorced, old differences had been put aside, replaced by a familial love that remains ever hopeful, ever forgiving. Patti's return to the fold had been an answered prayer.

Before retiring upstairs on Christmas Eve, the First Couple stood and looked at the decorated tree for a few moments, the twinkling lights reflecting in Nancy's eyes now moist with tears. She had always put so much into the holidays, and it was hard to imagine saying goodbye to this place after all these years.

But in less than a month, this would be home to the Kemps, and the Reagans would be back in California, starting a new chapter in their lives together.

So much still needed to be done.

The remaining weeks in Washington would be busy ones, with many official events scheduled in commemoration of Reagan's presidency. There would also be a slew of activities of a more personal nature, as close friends stopped by for one last visit at the White House.

One visit that Reagan was especially looking forward to was with the Gorbachevs—Mikhail, now Prime Minister of Russia, and his wife

Raisa. The couple would be joining the Reagans for dinner at the White House on December 27, the first Sunday after Christmas. Prior to the evening meal (which included more than 50 other guests), Gorbachev would meet privately with Reagan, so that the two former adversaries might enjoy one last personal chat as friends in front of the fireplace.

Gorbachev arrived shortly after lunch, bearing gifts — including some with Christmas wrapping. These were reciprocated by presents from the Reagans, celebrating a friendship that had grown and flourished over the years, even during very difficult and trying times.

Liberated from the rigid protocols of heading the USSR, Gorbachev was now free to smile, and share a warm Russian bear hug with his American friends.

There did, however, seem to be an undercurrent of sadness about him on this day. Although Russia's transformation under his leadership had been nothing short of miraculous, Reagan knew that it had not been easy, and the toll it had taken was physically obvious. Gorbachev looked tired, and Reagan wondered if perhaps he hadn't been ill.

During official communications Gorbachev preferred to speak through a translator. His command of the English language had always been good, but during his period in exile he had made mastering English a priority, and was now able to converse one-to-one with the ease and fluency of a native. For the visit today the two men would speak directly, with no translators joining them, no lag times in their exchanges.

From the time of their first meeting, Reagan had regarded Gorbachev as a different kind of Soviet leader — and he had been correct. As respective heads of their governments, the two rivals had taken bold steps to decrease tensions and work collaboratively on a range of issues, from arms control to human rights. For his efforts, Gorbachev had been toppled from power and imprisoned by hardliners within his own government.

Thanks to a personal commitment by Reagan, Gorbachev had been rescued and provided with a safe haven. Following the demise of the USSR, he had returned to his homeland a hero; the leader of a new democratic government.

He had much to thank the American president for, and was anxious to express his gratitude.

As the two discussed history, Gorbachev spoke of the dark days, when all had seemed lost. He marveled at Reagan's courage, and asked if his friend had also experienced similar periods of doubt and hopelessness.

Reagan paused, and nodded in empathy, explaining that for him, such periods were nothing more than passing moments, quickly displaced by a faith that gave him strength no matter how dire things seemed.

"It's said that God will never give us more than we can handle; I just wish he hadn't trusted me so much," quipped Reagan, his eyes sparkling.

The two heads of state shared a smile.

"But how can you be so sure that God exists?" asked the Russian.

"Well, you're an atheist, yes?" asked Reagan.

Gorbachev paused, then nodded tentatively.

"Such certainty—that there is no God—also requires a leap of faith," said Reagan. "So, I guess it's just a matter of perspective, of whether you want to see the glass half-full, or half-empty. Being an optimist, I see it half-full. I see evidence of Him, and His plan, in all things.

"He guides me, and I am His servant. I know that he hears my prayers, and that He will never abandon me.

"And *that*, is the source of my strength."

Gorbachev nodded, then revealed that he had been studying world religions, and in particular Christianity. One of his first acts as prime minister had been to restore the freedom of worship in Russia.

He told Reagan that his grandmother had been a Christian, and that she used to read the Bible to him when he was a child.

"I look at Christianity as a deaf man might watch a musical performance. I see many happy people, each behaving individually, but finding unity. I cannot hear the melody, but I can see the rhythm."

Reagan paused, then tended to the fire. He took a Bible off the book-shelf and sat back down. He sensed a spiritual hunger, and felt God calling upon him to once again help his friend.

Continuing with Gorbachev's metaphor, Reagan questioned if it was not deafness, but distance? A barrier that one *chooses* to accept? "As in a recording studio, where the performers are behind a wall of soundproof glass."

Gorbachev laughed. "Okay, so I suppose your advice is 'Mr Gorbachev, tear down this wall'?"

The two laughed heartily at the historical reference.

"No, in this case Mikhail, all you have to do is open the door."

As Gorbachev listened attentively, Reagan began, in his own simple, and heartfelt way, to explain how one might transcend a manmade partition, and by stepping across the threshold, transform one's life.

"It is never too late to experience His love. God loves unconditionally, He accepts, and forgives. We are all His children, and He cares for us all equally. He understands our troubles, our pain, our doubts, our fears, and our weaknesses.

"In the Bible, in the book of Psalms, there's a line, a teaching that brings me great comfort: '*The Lord is with me. I will not be afraid.*'"

Gorbachev was familiar with this scripture, and nodded in recognition. Reagan, smiling slightly, continued.

"We have a popular saying, that 'Christians aren't perfect, just forgiven'—and it's true. We're all works in progress, and every day we make mistakes. We give in to fear, anger, and suspicion. All the darkness that humanity is capable of … None of us are innocent, nor better than any other.

"But we are *forgiven*, because our sins were paid for by Jesus' death on the cross."

The President opened his Bible to John 3:16 and read, "*For God so loved the world, that He gave his only begotten Son, that whosoever believeth in Him should not perish, but have everlasting life.*"

"It sounds so simple …"

"The best things usually are," said Reagan. "Becoming a Christian means believing in Jesus as the Son of God, and acknowledging the sacrifice He made for you."

Gorbachev sighed heavily. "I'm so tired, so frightened. I've done so many things I am not proud of …"

"We all have. But if you open that door—open your heart, the Lord will enter to bring peace and comfort. He will heal you, and give you the strength you need."

"Yes, I want this," said Gorbachev.

The two men continued to talk, and to Reagan's surprise, Gorbachev was familiar with what he needed to do. He had not, however, made that personal connection, until his friend extended his hand.

Just a few years previous, Reagan had saved Gorbachev's life, and now he would save his soul by leading him to God.

The two men bowed their heads in prayer, and Gorbachev confessed his sins. He proclaimed his belief in a living God, and faith in God's gift, His son, the Lord Jesus Christ. He asked for God's forgiveness, help and guidance, and that he be accepted as God's servant.

When he looked up, his face was wet with tears of joy.

Reagan felt the emotion as well. Mikhail Gorbachev: partner, friend, and now, brother in Christ.

The wall had come down, and Gorbachev's heart was at last full with God's love.

Somewhere down the hall music was playing, a familiar Christmas carol—"O Little Town of Bethlehem," the meaning of which Gorbachev now understood for the first time, on the first day of his new life.

How silently, how silently
The wondrous gift is given!
So God imparts to human hearts
The blessings of His heaven.
No ear may hear His coming,
But in this world of sin,
Where meek souls will receive him still,
The dear Christ enters in.

Epilogue

The helicopter lifted off, deviating from what was the expected course and back towards the Capitol. As it did, a spectacular panorama unfolded: here was the stately Washington Monument, over there the memorials to Jefferson and Lincoln, shimmering in the sunlight.

The streets below were teeming with people, the floats and bands of the inaugural parades. And somewhere down there was Jack French Kemp, America's 41st President.

In what seemed a familiar ritual, the copter began to descend as it approached the White House, but it would not land. This time it was just to hover briefly, then slowly circle so as to provide the Reagans with one last look at the place that had been their home during good times, and during bad times, for the last twelve years.

It was Monday, January 20, 1993, and the time had come to say goodbye.

The copter landed at Andrews Air Force base in Maryland, where the Reagans boarded the plane they had once known as Air Force One.

As President, Reagan had flown on this plane so many times he'd lost count. Across the world, and all across America. But this would be his last flight on this magnificent aircraft; a one-way trip west, and home to California.

It was a strange feeling; dreamlike. Many things seemed so familiar, others recast in a new context.

Joining them for the journey was Dr John Hutton, who had been the President's personal physician, and who would now continue on in a similar capacity for *former* President Reagan.

Another former White House staff member making the transition to Reagan's post presidential staff was Chief of Staff Kenneth Duberstein, who had stepped in — and up — when James Baker left to work on the Bush campaign just over a year ago.

Although he would return to the private sector to resume his career in broadcasting, now *former* Press Secretary Limbaugh was here as well, but only to share one last trip with a man he came to know as both a mentor and friend. (And perhaps talk a little football on the long flight home.)

Limbaugh had sacrificed much to join Reagan's team, as the call had come just as he was embarking on nationally syndicating his radio show. But what he had lost in earnings and fame, he had gained in so many other ways, as the years spent serving in the Reagan White House would always be among his most treasured.

The two would stay close, with Reagan (a true radio junkie) appearing as a frequent guest on Limbaugh's show.

Old friends like Ed Meese and Mike Deaver who had worked with Reagan since his days as governor, would also leave the political realm. Both would remain close to the man they revered as a friend, and true to the conservative revolution he brought to America.

Their service had been as much about Reagan the man as it had been about service to the country.

But every administration has similar figures: Those who share a political vision, and provide the personal support so important to that one lonely figure at the top that carries the weight of the world upon his shoulders.

True friends, loyal to the core.

Others, like US Trade Representative Charles Koch, had been recruited by Reagan into public service to perform a specific task for a set period of time; now that time had passed and the adventure was over. Leaving Oz, Koch would return home to the black and white world of Kansas, to literally run the family business with his younger brother David.

Transportation Secretary (and Bush supporter) John Sununu would leave government service altogether, and move towards a career in broadcasting, becoming host of the popular cable TV show *Crossfire*.

Some departures had been more awkward. It was obvious from the beginning that OMB Director Richard Darman would have no place in the Kemp administration, freeing him to pursue a lucrative career on Wall Street.

A select few, such as CIA Director Webster and Education Secretary William Bennett would continue on in the same capacity with the Kemp administration. NSA Director McFarlane was up for Secretary of Defense, replacing General Powell.

Looking around the plane, noticeably absent was the ever-present military aide entrusted with the ominous duty of facilitating the presidential orders required to launch a nuclear strike. For a millisecond Reagan panicked, as such a presence had been a constant in his life every day since had assumed power exactly a dozen years ago to the day.

But then he caught his breath, jolted back to the reality that despite all that seemed so familiar, he was no longer Commander-in-Chief. Reagan closed his eyes and sighed; honored to have served, thankful he never had to unleash that horrible power.

As he opened his eyes he saw the face of his wife Nancy, the woman who had loved him, supported him, and made him what he was.

She smiled, and placed her hand gently on his.

Through thick and thin she had been by his side for what had been an incredible journey, and now as they watched the sun setting in the west, they were chasing it home, back to the Golden State, back to their beloved Ranch of the Sky.

Yes, the world was in a good place, and in his heart, Ronald Wilson Reagan knew the best was yet to come.

END